"Chiaverini's many fans and every
historical fiction reader who enjoys strong
female characters, will find much to love in this
revealing WWII novel." —*Booklist*

SHE WAS AN AMERICAN WOMAN
FROM WISCONSIN WITH NO TRAINING
AS A SPY OR A SOLDIER.

BUT SHE AND HER FRIENDS
WOULD SACRIFICE ALL TO WAGE
A CLANDESTINE BATTLE AGAINST
HITLER IN NAZI BERLIN.

Based on the extraordinary true story of
Mildred Fish Harnack, *Resistance Women* is an
unforgettable tale of the triumph of love over
despair, of courage over fear, and of dignity
and compassion over evil.

THE ODDS WERE AGAINST HER. . . . .

Resistance Women

Also by Jennifer Chiaverini

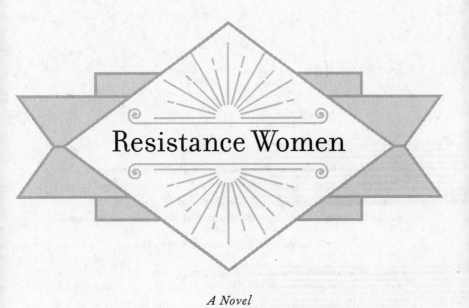

Resistance Women

A Novel

JENNIFER CHIAVERINI

wm

WILLIAM MORROW
An Imprint of HarperCollins*Publishers*

P.S.™ is a trademark of HarperCollins Publishers.

RESISTANCE WOMEN. Copyright © 2019 by Jennifer Chiaverini. Excerpt from MRS. LINCOLN'S SISTERS © 2020 by Jennifer Chiaverini. All rights reserved. Printed in the United States of America. No part of this book may be used or reproduced in any manner whatsoever without written permission except in the case of brief quotations embodied in critical articles and reviews. For information, address HarperCollins Publishers, 195 Broadway, New York, NY 10007.

HarperCollins books may be purchased for educational, business, or sales promotional use. For information, please email the Special Markets Department at SPsales@harpercollins.com.

A hardcover edition of this book was published in 2019 by William Morrow, an imprint of HarperCollins Publishers.

FIRST WILLIAM MORROW PAPERBACK EDITION PUBLISHED 2020.

Designed by Leah Carlson-Stanisic

Library of Congress Cataloging-in-Publication Data has been applied for.

ISBN 978-0-06-284112-4

20 21 22 23 24   LSC   10 9 8 7 6 5 4 3 2 1

To the resistance women, past and present

Resistance Women

November 1942

Mildred

The heavy iron doors open and for a moment Mildred stands motion-less and blinking in the sunlight, breathless from the sudden rush of cool, fresh air caressing her face and lifting her hair. The guard pro-pels her forward into the prison yard, his grip painful and unyielding around her upper arm. Other women clad in identical drab, shape-less garments walk slowly in pairs around the perimeter of the gravel square. Their cells within the *Hausgefängnis* of the Gestapo's Prinz-Albrecht-Strasse headquarters are so cramped that they can scarcely move, and now the prisoners spread their arms and lift their faces to the sky, like dancers, like dry autumn leaves scattered in a gust of wind.

How many of them would never again know more freedom than this?

"No talking," the guard reminds her, shoving her into the open yard. Stumbling, she regains her footing and begins treading a diago-nal path between two corners of the high encircling walls, forbidden to walk with the others. She has done this ten precious minutes each day since her arrest two months before, and her stiff, aching limbs fall into the routine before she is conscious of it.

Deliberately, she holds her head up and takes long, steady strides in a false show of strength that costs her dearly. She has lost weight, and from the strands she finds on her bunk each morning, she knows that her once luxuriant blond hair has gone brittle and white. Coughs rack her almost constantly. Earlier that day she brought her hand away from her mouth and nose to find her palm spotted with blood. There is no medicine to spare for people like her, traitors to the Third Reich—although is it correct to call her a traitor, since she is American?

It does not matter, not to her jailers and not to the law, to whom she is American by birth, a dual citizen by marriage. To Adolf Hitler it matters very much that she is an American, or so she has been warned. And yet Germany is her adopted home, the birthplace of her beloved husband. It was because she could not bear to be parted from him that she had remained in Berlin even after the United States government warned its citizens to leave the country.

Arvid. Her heart aches as she imagines him languishing in a cramped, cold, dimly lit cell like her own, somewhere not far away, but impossibly beyond her reach. Their trial is pending. Perhaps they will be reunited in the courtroom, they and all of their brave, unfortunate friends in the resistance cell the Nazis call Rote Kapelle, Red Orchestra, for the illicit "music" they had broadcast to enemies of the Reich. How strange it is that the Gestapo considered them so formidable an enemy that they merited a sinister name, like something plucked from a spy novel—and yet among their diffuse network of writers, teachers, economists, bureaucrats, office workers, and laborers, they count not one professional spy.

They are ordinary people from every walk of life. Her dear friend Greta Kuckhoff grew up poor, earned her education, and is determined to provide her young son with a better life. Sara Weitz enjoyed wealth and privilege until the Nazis declared the Jews undesirable and robbed them of every civil and human right. Mildred's heart aches as she thinks of Sara and the other students in their circle—brave, determined, idealistic, with their whole lives ahead of them, risking more than they can fully understand. Where are they now? Scattered, some imprisoned elsewhere, some in hiding, others fled to distant lands. If only Mildred could seek help from Martha Dodd one last time, but Martha returned to the United States after her father was relieved of his duties as ambassador. Even if Mildred could somehow get word to her impulsive, outspoken friend, what could Martha do?

A fit of coughing seizes her. She doubles over, clutching her shoulders to brace herself until the hoarse racking stops. When she can, she straightens, inhales deeply, ignores the foreboding rattle in her lungs, and resumes her diagonal path across the yard—

And almost stops short from astonishment. Another prisoner holds her gaze as she treads along the edge of the prison yard, her stricken sympathy plain for Mildred to see. The woman is too pale and thin to be new to the prison; surely she is aware of the grim consequences she will face if the guards see her regarding Mildred with such concern, after she has been set apart as a warning to others. The woman must know, for she quickly looks away. Mildred's heart sinks, only to rise again when the woman glances back and offers her the barest trace of an encouraging smile.

Mildred feels new strength flow through her. It is just a glance, but it nourishes her starved soul. Her heart pounds as she works out the timing of her diagonal strides and the woman's slow circuit of the yard. She quickens her pace, not enough to draw the guards' attention, but sufficiently that eventually her path and the woman's will intersect in the far corner of the yard. All the while they steal glances at each other, silent messages that they are not alone, that there is always hope, that when one least expects it a shaft of light might pierce the darkest sky.

And then they intersect, though they cannot pause long enough even to touch fingertips.

"Take care of yourself," Mildred murmurs as they shuffle toward each other and away. "I am in cell 25. Don't forget me when you get out. My name is Mildred Harnack."

I am Mildred Harnack, she repeats silently to herself as she turns to cross the yard again. Mildred Fish Harnack. Wife, sister, aunt. Author, scholar, teacher. Resistance fighter. Spy.

Don't forget me.

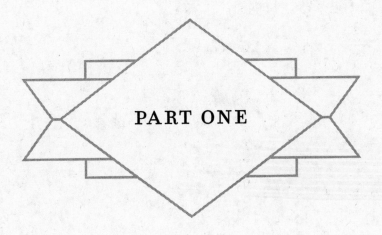

PART ONE

CHAPTER ONE

June–October 1929

Mildred

The sharp wind off the water where the North Sea met the Weser River whipped locks of hair from Mildred's braid and brought tears to her eyes, but nothing could compel her away from the railing of the upper deck of the SS *Berlin* as it approached Bremerhaven. Ten days earlier the ship had set out from Manhattan for Germany—ten long days after nine lonely months apart from her beloved husband—but the last few hours had passed with excruciating slowness. As the ship came into harbor, she scanned the crowd gathered on the pier for the man she loved, knowing that he stood somewhere among them, waiting to welcome her to his homeland.

The ship's horn bellowed overhead, two long blasts; sailors and dockworkers tossed ropes and deftly secured knots. The passengers shifted in anticipation as the ramps were made ready for their descent. Where the pier met the shore, a brass band played a merry tune in welcome; men clad in traditional lederhosen, embroidered vests, and feathered caps; women in pink-and-green dirndls and white blouses with wreaths of ribbons and flowers in their hair.

Hearing her name aloft on the wind above the music, Mildred searched the crowd, her grip tightening on the rail—and then she saw him, her beloved Arvid, his fair hair neatly combed back from his wide brow, his blue eyes kind and intelligent behind wire-rimmed glasses. He waved his hat in slow arcs above his head, calling her name, radiant with joy.

"Arvid," she cried, and he waved back, and soon she was ashore and darting through the crowd into his embrace. Tears of joy spilled over as she kissed him, heedless of the sidelong glances of the more reserved passengers and families all around them.

"My darling wife," Arvid murmured, his lips nuzzling her ear. "It's wonderful to hold you again. You're even lovelier than I remember."

She smiled and held him close, her happiness too great for words. If absence had made her lovelier in his eyes, he was even more handsome in hers.

How immeasurably beloved he had become to her since the day they met three years before. In March 1926, soon after Arvid came to the University of Wisconsin on a prestigious Rockefeller Fellowship, he had wandered into her Bascom Hall classroom expecting a lecture by the renowned economist John R. Commons, only to discover Mildred leading a discussion on Walt Whitman. Enchanted, he took a seat in the back row, and afterward he stayed behind to apologize for the interruption, explaining in endearingly imperfect English that he had meant to go to Sterling Hall but had apparently lost his way. Charmed, Mildred had offered to escort him to the correct building. They enjoyed a chat along the way, and in parting agreed to meet again to study together. She would help Arvid master English, and he would help her improve her German, which she had allowed to lapse after learning the rudiments as a child in Milwaukee, that most German of American cities.

Arvid arrived for their study session bearing a lovely bouquet of fragrant white gardenias. Their language lesson over coffee at a diner on the corner of State and Lake streets turned into a long walk along the forested path on the shore of Lake Mendota. As they conversed in a mix of English and German, Mildred discovered that Arvid had earned his doctorate of law degree in 1924 and was pursuing a second doctorate in economics. He had come to the United States to study the American labor movement, and like herself he was deeply concerned about the rights of workers, women, children, and the poor. They shared a passion for education and aspired to become university professors, although Mildred also yearned to write, not only academic essays and reviews, but also novels and poetry.

One date led to another, and soon Mildred realized she had fallen in love with him—inevitably, utterly. And in return, she found herself beloved, admired, and respected by the finest man she had ever known.

On Saturday, August 7, 1926, two days after Mildred passed her master's degree exams, she and Arvid married in an outdoor ceremony on her brother Bob's 180-acre farm about twenty miles south of the university. For two years the couple worked, studied, and enjoyed newlywed bliss in Madison, but when Arvid's Rockefeller Fellowship ended in the spring of 1928, they realized that they could not afford for her to accompany him back to Germany.

"Let's check the numbers again," Mildred had said, studying the neat columns of notes and calculations written in Arvid's precise hand on a yellow notepad, calculations of his income and estimates of their expenses, adjusted for Germany's excessive inflation. When Arvid smiled wryly and handed her his pencil, she laughed and added, "Although I suppose a doctoral student in economics can work out a simple family budget."

Arvid removed his glasses and rubbed his tired eyes. "The facts distress me too, *Liebling*, but they're still facts. I can't support you as a graduate student, and given the state of the German economy, we can't assume you'll be able to find work there."

Mildred reached across the table and clasped his hand. "Then I'll find a faculty position here in the States and we'll pinch pennies until we can afford to be together."

Until then, they would have to live apart.

When Arvid returned to Germany to continue his studies at the University of Jena, Mildred had moved to Baltimore to teach at Goucher College. The months had slowly passed in loneliness and longing, but in the spring Mildred won a fellowship for postgraduate study at a German university of her choice. With her stipend added to the money they had saved, they could finally afford for her to join Arvid in Jena.

Now, with her overseas journey behind her, they were reunited at last—and if it were up to her, they would never be parted again.

They gathered her luggage and boarded the port train to Bremen, where Arvid suggested a walking tour to stretch her legs. Mildred could hardly take her eyes from the dear face she had missed and dreamt of all those long months apart, yet the charming city stole her gaze away time and again. She admired the tall peaked, half-timbered buildings lining the cobblestone streets and the sun-splashed, manicured squares, the window boxes bursting with red alpine geraniums, white peonies, and green trailing ivy. Bicycles were everywhere, their handlebar bells chiming out a ceaseless melody, but the occasional motorcar also drove sedately past, and now and then a horse-drawn wagon.

"How picturesque it is," Mildred exclaimed, briefly resting her head on Arvid's shoulder as they strolled arm in arm. "And to think how Greta tried to lower my expectations."

Arvid's eyebrows rose. "Greta Lorke disparaged her own homeland?"

"Not exactly," said Mildred, amused by his instinct to assume the worst of his former academic rival. Mildred was loyal to Arvid, of course, but she had become very fond of Greta after they met through the Friday Niters, Professor Collins's renowned group of graduate students and faculty who studied social welfare, economic, and labor policies and helped the Wisconsin state legislators draft progressive laws. Where Mildred was tall, slender, and blond, Greta was petite, curvy, and dark-eyed, and she wore her dark brown hair cropped in a wavy bob. She had high cheekbones and a full mouth fashioned for warm, beckoning smiles, but a certain wariness in her manner suggested that she was not unaccustomed to strife.

"Greta once told me that she feared my understanding of Germany comes from your poetry, novels, and fairy tales," Mildred explained. "She warned me that my perspective is romantic and idealized, and that I ought to read German newspapers to learn about the real Germany, for my own good."

"How foreboding."

"And yet it was good advice. Why shouldn't I learn all I could about your home?"

Mildred knew that Germany was not perfect, that like the United

States it grappled with various economic, political, and social problems, but now, exploring Bremen with Arvid, she felt a keen sense of relief. Greta—dear, smart, serious, skeptical Greta—had painted a far too ominous picture of her country.

Mildred and Arvid left Bremen just as the bells of St. Peter's Cathedral rang out the noon hour. The sun shone brightly in a perfect blue sky as they set out in a gleaming cream-colored Mercedes convertible that Arvid had borrowed from a cousin, passing through forests and farmland, rolling hills and charming villages. For hours the beautiful scenery captivated Mildred's attention, but after they stopped for lunch in Hanover and continued southeast through Lower Saxony, she felt waves of trepidation rising and receding with increasing frequency. Although Arvid never boasted, she knew that his distinguished family was admired and respected throughout Germany, especially in academic, political, and religious circles. They were, as Greta put it, intellectual royalty. Mildred had far humbler origins. Her father, a handsome, unfaithful, irresponsible dilettante who had habitually squandered his pay at the racetrack, had been temperamentally incapable of holding on to any job for long. Mildred's mother, an intelligent, self-reliant Christian Scientist, had supported the family with domestic work and by taking in boarders, but despite her best efforts the family had moved every year one step ahead of landlords demanding overdue rent.

Mildred wondered how much of this Arvid had revealed to his family. Although they had been unfailingly warm and gracious to her in their letters, Greta had warned that the Harnacks and their extended clan of Bonhoeffers and Dohnányis might receive her with cold disdain.

It was early evening by the time their borrowed Mercedes crossed the Harz Mountains and descended into the hills of eastern Thuringia. When they reached Jena, Arvid pointed out the university, the city square, and other significant landmarks they passed on the way to his childhood home. Eventually he pulled up to a tall white half-timbered residence with black shutters, balconies on the first and second floors connecting the two perpendicular wings. Arvid's mother had moved with her children into this house when Arvid was fourteen, after his father's suicide. Mildred took a deep, steadying breath as Arvid parked the car and turned off the ignition. "They're going to love you," he said, taking her hand and raising it to his lips. She managed a smile.

As he escorted her up the cobblestone path to the front door, her heart thumped as several men and women and two eager young boys hurried outside to welcome them. Her nervousness faded as they embraced her, smiling, greeting her warmly in German and English. As Arvid proudly made introductions, Mildred felt a curious sense of recognition when she learned that the handsome young man with Arvid's warm smile was his seventeen-year-old brother Falk. The two lovely women with familiar blue eyes and bobbed blond hair were his sisters, Inge and Angela, and the two cheerful boys were Inge's sons, Wulf and Claus. Mildred also met several cousins, including one Arvid had often mentioned when reminiscing about home—Dietrich Bonhoeffer, a Lutheran minister, a round-cheeked, bespectacled fellow with a strong chin.

Next Arvid escorted Mildred inside to meet his mother. "My dear child," Mutti Clara said warmly in flawless English, clasping Mildred's hands and kissing her on both cheeks. She had strong features and a keen, intelligent gaze, and she wore her graying light brown hair in a soft chignon. "You are even more beautiful than Arvid described. Welcome to Germany. Welcome home."

She summoned the family to gather around the supper table, where Dietrich led them in prayer. The meal of bratwurst in a vinegar and caper sauce, potato dumplings, and cabbage rolls, with poppyseed cake for dessert, was delicious and satisfying after a long day of travel. Everything was seasoned with warm smiles and laughter as the family teased and praised one another, joking in Greek and Latin, quoting Goethe, quizzing Falk and the younger boys on their schoolwork. Mildred marveled at how delightful it was, and how very different from the family dinners of her childhood, marked by tension between her parents, worries about money, and her father's frequent absences.

At the end of a perfect evening, Arvid took her home—at long last, a home they would share, a suite of rented rooms in a house on the Landgrafenstieg, small but cleverly arranged to make the most of the limited space. The front windows offered wonderful views of the mountains, and plenty of room remained on the bookshelves for the new volumes they hoped to acquire in the years to come. After a few days in Jena, Mildred and Arvid embarked on a second honeymoon to the Black Forest, where the loneliness of their long separation soon faded to a distant memory.

In autumn, Mildred began her doctoral studies at the University of Jena. Once again her life was satisfyingly full, her days devoted to study, her nights to her beloved Arvid. She missed her family in America, but the Harnacks made her feel so welcome that she could not complain of homesickness.

Then, on a beautifully clear, vividly hued autumn day at the end of October, Arvid found her in the garden studying in the afternoon sunshine. "I'm sorry, *Liebling*," he said grimly, handing her a newspaper. "Bad news from America."

As she scanned the headlines, her heart plummeted. The stock market had crashed, losing more than three billion dollars over the span of two days.

She steeled herself. "Arvid?" With his academic training and expertise, he would know as well as anyone on Wall Street what this meant for her country.

He held her gaze and shook his head. She knew then that much worse was yet to come.

CHAPTER TWO

October 1929–July 1930

Greta

In her last letter from Wisconsin, Greta had told her family not to meet her ship in Hamburg, but when she disembarked and took her first few unsteady paces along the pier, she felt a pang of profound loneliness and wished they had ignored her instructions. All around her, couples embraced and families greeted long-absent loved ones, while she walked alone, a suitcase in each hand.

From the station office, she telegraphed her parents to let them know when to expect her and hurried to catch the train to Frankfurt an der Oder. As the train carried her nearly four hundred kilometers south and east, she watched the scenery speeding past the window of her second-class carriage, curiously moved, marveling how her homeland had changed so little during the two years she had been studying abroad though she had changed so much.

Hours later, the train jerked to a halt at a station near the Polish border. "Frankfurt an der Oder," the conductor announced, sending a thrill of expectation up her spine. She gathered her belongings and descended to the platform, where she was immediately swept up in a strong embrace. Startled, she dropped her suitcases. "Hans," she exclaimed. She kissed her brother on the cheek, breathless. How well he looked, tall and sturdy, his blue eyes bright and cheerful, his hair darker and curlier than she remembered.

"Welcome home, little sister," he said, seizing the handles of her suitcases and heading to the exit from the platform. "You've gotten thin. Couldn't you find any good German food in Wisconsin? Mutti will want to fatten you up."

Greta's stomach rumbled in anticipation. "She's welcome to try."

"She's planning a dinner party for tomorrow night," Hans said as he led her through the crowd to the street. "Just the family and a few neighbors, and all your favorite dishes."

"I hope she won't go to too much expense."

"You know Mutti. She'll haggle with the butcher and trade mending work for bread with the baker and Papa will boast about her shrewdness until she blushes."

Greta laughed and agreed, tears of happiness pricking her eyes. She had missed joking with her brother about the endearing quirks of the people they loved, which included their mother's frugality. Mutti had a gift for making something nourishing and delicious from meager ingredients, a skill her family extolled as a moral virtue while tactfully overlooking that it was born of necessity.

Throughout the wretched, tumultuous years of the Great War, Greta's parents had kept poverty at bay through relentless effort and sheer force of will. Greta's father was a metalworker in a musical instrument factory, and her most vivid childhood memories involved watching him roll out gleaming sheets of brass, placing patterns upon them, and meticulously cutting out intricate pieces from which he shaped cornets, flügelhorns, and tubas. Her mother was a seamstress who took in piecework, mostly clothing and blankets for an upscale department store in Berlin.

As soon as Greta had been old enough, she had helped earn her keep by polishing shoes, but her parents had emphasized that education came before everything but the church. They had scrimped and sacrificed to afford their children's tuition at the *Oberschule*, and when Greta was older they had nearly burst with pride when she had been accepted into the University of Berlin. Determined to pay her own way, she had taken a work-study job looking after two dozen boys at an orphanage in Neukölln, a rough industrial neighborhood favored by Communists and laborers and the indigent. Her time at the orphanage had taught her that although her own family had struggled, others had suffered far greater hardships. She learned gratitude for what she had and compassion for the vast multitude of people who had far less. She acquired indignation for the suffering of the innocent and resolve to make their lot better, however she could, whenever she could.

Through it all, her parents had encouraged her and had taken great pride in her achievements. What would they think now that she had returned from her grand and glorious adventure in America with wonderful memories but no doctorate to show for all her hard work and all their sacrifice?

Greta's apprehensions surged at the sight of her childhood home, three narrow stories of stone and plaster, modest but meticulously kept, reassuringly solid and enduring after Madison, where even the oldest buildings seemed startlingly new. But when she crossed the familiar threshold, her parents met her with warm embraces and tears of joy. She choked back sobs as she hugged them as hard as she dared, mindful of their new wrinkles, more silver in their hair, a slight stoop to her father's back, and yet the same love and pride shining in their eyes.

At the dinner party the following evening, friends and family cheerfully proclaimed their certainty that she had represented Frankfurt an der Oder with honor and distinction. They were all so kind and proud that Greta briefly feared she had forgotten to tell them that she had not earned her degree.

The next morning, as she helped her mother tidy the kitchen after breakfast, she stoked her courage, took a deep breath, and said, "Mutti, I'm sorry I failed you and Papa."

Her mother's soft, round face creased in puzzlement. "What nonsense is this?"

"To travel so far and to be gone so long, when I could have been here helping the family, only to return empty-handed—"

"My dear child." Her mother guided her into a seat at the kitchen table and sat down beside her. "You haven't achieved your goal yet. That doesn't mean you never will."

"But I have no doctorate, no work—"

"So you'll earn one and find the other." Her mother regarded her with loving sympathy. "I know from your last letter that you're exhausted and discouraged. Take some time off before you go back to school."

"Mutti—" Greta chose her words carefully. "I don't think my problems will be solved by a holiday."

"Time off will do you good nonetheless. You couldn't resume your studies in the middle of the term anyway."

Her mother's expression was so full of pride and confidence that Greta did not have the heart to confess her doubts. "I'll have to find something to do in the meantime," she said instead. "I thought I might look for a job in Berlin. I hate to leave you so soon after coming home—"

"Don't worry about us. Of course you must go, unless you want to stay here and help me sew piecework."

Greta suspected she would have more success in Berlin. After a few restful days with her family, she took the morning train to the capital, and by nightfall she had rented a furnished room in a boardinghouse, smaller and plainer than what she could have had for the same price in Madison, but clean and fairly quiet. The threadbare rug and faded curtains gave the room an air of weary futility, one she could all too well imagine steadily leaching into its occupant. She hoped it would not be long until she could afford a better place.

She had barely settled in when the devastating stock market crash in America rocked Europe. Thanks to her economics training, she understood the alarming implications for Germany even before the failing American banks desperately called in their foreign loans. The fragile German economy, already suffering from staggering inflation and unemployment, could not withstand the blow. Without foreign investment, factories closed, construction projects halted, and thousand of workers lost their jobs.

As the financial disaster unfolded, Greta struggled to secure an elusive university scholarship, to convince a professor to take her on, to find a job as a lecturer or a researcher or even a lowly assistant. There were no vacancies anywhere, of any kind. Professors clung to their tenure, postponing retirement out of fear that their pensions would disappear overnight. Students stayed enrolled, hoping that one more advanced degree would give them an edge over their peers when they were finally forced to graduate and join the wretched millions of unemployed.

Greta willingly accepted the only work she could find—tutoring, freelance editing, some copywriting. It reminded her of her mother's piecework, but with pen and ink and words instead of needle and thread. With almost nothing to spend on entertainment, she rediscovered her lifelong love of literature and drama, disappearing into the pages of a novel or a play, scraping together enough marks for cheap seats at the Staatstheater or the Deutsches Theater. On long winter evenings, she would huddle under blankets in her room's lone armchair and lose herself in dramas and comedies, the greatest masterpieces ever written in German, French, and English.

As winter turned to spring, she toyed with the idea of finding a new career in theater. Perhaps she could translate English and French works for the German stage. She could become a playwright or dramaturge.

"You should attend the Internationaler Theaterkongresse," urged her friend Ursula, an actress. "Nine glorious June days in Hamburg devoted to all things theater—performances, seminars, lectures."

"It sounds wonderful," said Greta. "Wonderful, and very expensive."

"Yes, but theater companies and professionals from around the world attend. What better occasion to make contacts that might lead to a job?"

Greta could not dispute that, so she quickly pulled together the necessary funds, skipping meals and forgoing sleep to finish two lengthy editing projects ahead of schedule. She took on three new English language students and requested a month's payment in advance. Just in time she saved enough to cover her registration fees, train fare, and lodgings, but as she packed her suitcase, she felt a pang of worry. She could be squandering her money on nine days of revelry that would ultimately leave her significantly poorer but no closer to finding a job.

On her first full day in Hamburg, she fell in with a jovial group of French authors and performers staying at her hotel. Her French was fluent enough to win their approval, their conversation clever enough to win hers. When they invited her to consider herself one of the company, she gladly did.

On the third day, Greta and her new friends attended a special lecture by Leopold Jessner, renowned producer and director of German Expressionist theater, honorary president of the Theaterkongresse, head of the Preussisches Staatstheater at Gendarmenmarkt, and one of the most important figures in Berlin theater. In the lecture hall, a delegation of artists from the Staatstheater accompanied Jessner onto the stage. When Jessner introduced Dr. Adam Kuckhoff, his head dramaturge, a square, solid man in his early forties with a full mouth and a brooding look strode to the podium.

Greta settled back in her seat, resigned to a dry lecture about the logistics of theater administration, but instead Kuckhoff delivered a fiery, passionate speech about the nature of theater and film in the modern era. Riveted, Greta absorbed every word in wonder, never taking her eyes from his face. Suddenly she realized that he was the author of a powerful essay she had read earlier that winter, "Arbeiter und Film," a denunciation of the "sentimental lies of the typical society film" and the "outmoded spirit and patriotic hurrah of nationalist cinema." She listened, enthralled, as he developed those concepts into a bold, astonishing vision for the future of German theater.

Her fervent attention did not escape Kuckhoff's notice. From time to time as his gaze swept over the crowd, it rested upon hers, curious and searching.

After the program, Greta and her companions were debating which session to attend next when Kuckhoff approached her. "You seemed very intent upon my remarks," he said in French. "Was that a sign of agreement or dissent?"

She regarded him for a moment, bewildered—but of course he assumed she was French, given her companions. She decided to play along. "Agreement, for whatever that's worth. I'm rather new to the theater," she said in French, extending her hand. "Greta Lorke, a mere aspiring playwright, or dramaturge, or whatever role might find me."

His gaze held hers as he shook her hand. "I doubt the word 'mere' ever suits you, mademoiselle." When he invited her to discuss his lecture in more detail on a boat tour of the Hamburg harbor, she hesitated only a moment before agreeing.

The Theaterkongresse was forgotten as the hours passed swiftly and wonderfully in sightseeing and engrossing conversation. The excursion led to a romantic dinner at one of the city's finest hotels, at a table overlooking the Elbe. After the most delicious meal Greta had ever tasted and a magnificent bottle of wine, their talk drifted pleasurably into lingering glances and subtle touches, his hand resting upon hers on the table, her leg pressed against his beneath it.

When, with almost formal politeness, he invited her upstairs to his room, she nodded and gave him her hand.

In the morning she woke in Adam's arms and knew from the sunlight streaming through the windows that the morning conference sessions were already well under way. She had not intended to stay the night, or to make love with him, but Adam's touch and his words had evoked desires she had not known she possessed. At the last moment, when prudence had shouted warnings that she must tear herself from his arms or risk losing everything—her future, her reputation—all for a moment of passion, Adam had produced a small packet that she needed a moment to recognize as a condom. Of course she was not his first, as he was hers; of course a worldly man would have come prepared. And she had been profoundly glad for it.

When Adam stirred, she snuggled closer and rested her head on his shoulder. Drowsily he kissed her forehead, inhaled deeply, and sighed. "*Ah, ma chère mam'selle*," he lamented, smiling. "You are too young and lovely for an old man like me."

"How old are you?"

"I confess that I'm forty-three."

"How ancient," she teased, but then she hesitated. "I have a confession of my own. I'm not French. I was born in Frankfurt an der Oder and I live in Berlin."

For a moment he only gaped at her, but then he laughed. "Why didn't you tell me?" he demanded in German, propping himself up on one elbow. "I assumed—"

"Yes, you did assume." She smiled wickedly. "It amused me to play along."

He ran his hand down her side from her shoulder to her hip and gave her buttocks a light slap. "What a naughty girl you are, deceiving me like that."

"I'm sure you have many secrets of your own."

"Not me. My life's an open book." He shifted onto his back, one arm holding her close, the other tucked beneath his head. "Go ahead. Ask me anything."

"I suppose the most important question is—" She paused, thought better of the questions that immediately sprang to mind, and asked instead, "How are we going to spend the day?"

"First, breakfast. Then you should spend the day however you please. I could recommend a few programs for you, but I have hours of appointments and lectures ahead of me and I won't be able to keep you company."

"Of course not," she said quickly, crushed. "I didn't mean—"

"But I hope you'll have dinner with me this evening."

"Dinner?"

"And more after, if you're willing."

He spoke nonchalantly, but his voice carried a thrilling undercurrent of promise. "I may be," she replied, cupping his chin with her hand and turning his face toward hers for a kiss.

For the rest of the Theaterkongresse, Greta spent her days with the French delegation and her nights with Adam. Sometimes a few of his colleagues joined them for dinner, and she marveled at her good fortune when they gave her their cards and encouraged her to contact them about jobs in various Berlin theaters—unglamorous, low-paying work that would help her get her foot in the door and could lead to something better. Yet somehow her all-important job search had faded in the shadow of her burgeoning romance with Adam. She had never fallen so swiftly or so hard, and it was as frightening as it was intoxicating.

On the last day of the conference, she packed her suitcase with a heavy heart. She wished she and Adam were taking the same train back to Berlin, but he was staying on an extra day to teach a master class at the Universität Hamburg.

Adam saw her off at the station. They had already exchanged cards, but after he kissed her goodbye and she began to board the train, she hesitated on the stairs. "Will we see each other again?" she asked, ashamed of the forlorn tone in her voice.

"Of course, darling," he said, his brow furrowing in puzzlement. "Why wouldn't we? As soon as I sort through all the work that's piled up at the Staatstheater in my absence, I'll call you."

"Promise you will."

He placed a hand on his heart. "I promise."

Greta smiled briefly and turned away to board the train before he saw the doubt in her eyes and mistook it for regret.

Once home again, she threw open the windows to the balmy summer breeze and plunged into her work, tutoring, editing, and following up on contacts from the Theaterkongresse in search of a more lucrative and fulfilling job. The memory of Adam's touch, his voice, and his keen gaze fixed admiringly upon hers as they discussed drama and politics haunted her day and night.

Three days passed with no word from him, but she resisted the temptation to stroll past the Staatstheater in the hope of a chance encounter. Then, on the fourth day, when she returned home from delivering an edited manuscript to the publisher, her landlady met her in the foyer, a slip of paper in her hand. "A Dr. Kuckhoff phoned for you twice this morning," she said, handing Greta the note. "He wants you to call him back at your earliest convenience. Are you ill?"

"No, I'm fine, thank you," said Greta over her shoulder as she hurried off to return his call.

Adam's voice was warm and enticing, and when he asked her to meet him for dinner that evening, she immediately agreed. Conscious of Frau Kellerman's watchful eye and reluctant to make her private life grist for her housemates' gossip mill, Greta did not invite Adam to her room when he brought her home long after midnight, though both of them were slightly drunk and full of desire. On their next date, two nights later, they abandoned caution and crept upstairs, suppressing laughter, falling into each other's arms as soon as she closed the door behind them. He left long before dawn while the rest of the house slept, carrying his shoes as he stole down the staircase.

For Greta, July passed in glorious, sensuous pleasure and soaring hopes. She and Adam spent so many evenings together that in order to avoid offending Frau Kellerman's sense of propriety, she occasionally suggested that they go to his place instead. He always found a reason to decline. Her place was closer, he might say, or his cleaning woman had not been in and the mess embarrassed him. Greta would have been suspicious except that Adam readily introduced her to his friends whenever they crossed paths at a restaurant or in the Tiergarten, the former royal hunting preserve that was now a lovely public park, 630 acres of walking paths and riding trails winding through forest groves, cultivated flower gardens, fountains, and statuary. One of Adam's colleagues even hired her to organize his theater's chaotic script library, a job that would pay fairly decent wages for as long as the project lasted. His acquaintances were unfailingly friendly and courteous, with not the faintest trace of disapproval behind their smiles. So she ordered herself not to spoil things with pointless worry.

Then, one day in early August, they had just taken a table at a café popular with theater folk when Adam spotted a director with whom he urgently needed to speak. "I'll be right back, darling," he said, bending to kiss her on the cheek. "Order something good for us."

She did as he suggested, but when the waiter departed, Ursula slipped into Adam's vacant chair. "So," she said, drawing out the word, raising her eyebrows. "You and Kuckhoff?"

Greta shrugged noncommittally, but she could not suppress a smile.

"I see." Ursula sat back in her chair and eyed her appraisingly. "Well, if you're sleeping with him to advance your career, I'd be the last person to judge you, but I certainly hope you don't fall in love with him."

"Why is that?"

"Because I don't think his wife would like it."

For a moment Greta could only stare at her. "His wife?"

"You didn't know?"

Greta shook her head.

"I suppose he also didn't mention that he has a son with his first wife?"

First wife? So there were two? And a son? Feeling faint, Greta shook her head again.

"He really should have told you. A few years ago his first wife left him for Hans Otto—yes, *that* Hans Otto, the actor—and a year or two later, Kuckhoff married her sister. Somehow they've all managed to stay friends."

Suddenly Greta was certain that she was about to be violently ill. "Will you excuse me?" she murmured as she stood, blood rushing in her ears. Ursula called after her as she fled the café, but Greta did not look back. As she walked home alone, she could only wonder if Adam had seen her go.

The next morning, he was waiting for her on the corner just down the block from the theater where, she thought bitterly, she had a job thanks to him. Her employer, one of his friends, was either oblivious to the nature of her relationship with Adam, or, she realized with horror, he and every other acquaintance to whom Adam had introduced her assumed that she knew she was the other woman.

At the sight of Adam, she pursed her mouth and continued briskly straight ahead, but he quickly moved to intercept. "Greta—"

"Don't speak to me."

He caught her by the elbow. "I said you could ask me anything. You never asked if I was married."

She yanked her arm free. "That's the sort of detail people of integrity usually volunteer."

"My wife and I have an open relationship." His gaze was earnest and pleading. "I've told Gertrud about you. She wants to meet you."

"That will never happen. I'd be too ashamed to look her in the eye."

"Greta, please. What we have is unique, powerful, inexorable. We both know it. Do you think this happens every day?"

"We've had two months," she retorted shakily. "You'll forget me in another two."

"You know I never will. Greta, I love you."

The words she had so longed to hear rang hollow. "Then call me when you're single."

Heart aching, she pushed past him and strode off to the theater, blinking away tears of anger and disappointment. He did not follow.

CHAPTER THREE

October 1930

Sara

After her last class of the day, Sara Weitz hurried off to meet her brother and sister for lunch to celebrate Natan's promotion to associate news editor of the *Berliner Tageblatt*. Glancing at her watch, she decided to walk from the University of Berlin to the Palast-Café rather than take the Untergrundbahn. Why descend into stifling underground darkness on such a beautiful autumn day when cool, refreshing breezes swept the streets and sunlight streamed down from cloudless blue skies? Winter would be upon them soon enough.

From campus she strolled west on Unter den Linden, her satchel slung over her shoulder, heavy with books and papers. With the first few days of the term, American literature had become her favorite course and Frau Harnack her favorite teacher. Like Sara, Frau Harnack was new to the university, a graduate student in American literature who had recently transferred to the University of Berlin. At first Sara and her classmates had not quite known what to make of their lively, warmhearted teacher, who treated her students as equals and sometimes broke into song to illuminate a particular literary point, but Frau Harnack soon won them over with her kindness and genuine concern for their well-being. Her stories about life in America so vividly illuminated the texts the class analyzed that Sara had recently begun to think that perhaps she ought to pursue a doctorate in the States after graduation.

She shook her head to clear away the daydream. It was tempting to lose herself in fond imaginings in such uncertain times. Her father's job as a manager at the Jacquier and Securius Bank was secure, Natan's career was on the rise, Amalie was happily married to a wealthy baron, and so the family did not struggle to make ends meet, unlike so many unfortunate others. Yet they could not ignore the political turmoil that stalked the borders of their comfortable home in the Grunewald. They tried to ignore the surge of antisemitism in Germany, concealing their apprehension and living exemplary lives, taking care not to provoke spite and fear from their Christian neighbors. That had always been enough to shield them in a modern, cosmopolitan city like Berlin. Their Jewish elders assured them it would suffice this time too.

Sara cut through the Tiergarten to avoid the Reichstagsgebäude and whatever crowd might have gathered to observe the opening of the new Reichstag that afternoon. The results of the September 14 election had stunned everyone—except perhaps the leader of the Nationalsozialistische Deutsche Arbeiterpartei, an Austrian named Adolf Hitler. Although the National Socialists had existed as a fringe party for years, this time they had won six and a half million votes, increasing their representation from 12 seats to 107.

"How could anyone vote for the party of Adolf Hitler?" Sara's mother had wondered aloud, aghast, after the results had come in. "He served nine months in prison for treason."

"People are struggling," Sara replied, thinking of her fellow students, their weary faces, their threadbare clothes, their grim prospects, their anger and hopelessness. "They can't find work and they're afraid of what the future holds."

"Then along comes this loud, angry man," Natan said, "promising to take them back to a mythical golden age of prosperity, swearing to punish Germany's enemies for wronging them. Some people respond to that—in this case, vast numbers of people."

As Sara approached the Palast-Café, it occurred to her that it might have been more appropriate to celebrate Natan's promotion with a picnic in the Tiergarten near the Reichstagsgebäude. He probably would have preferred to munch a sandwich while observing the size and temper of the crowd awaiting the arrival of the new deputies.

She spotted Amalie standing alone outside the Palast-Café and hurried across the street to meet her. Although only a few days had passed since Sara had seen her sister for Shabbat at their parents' home, Amalie greeted her with a fond embrace as if they had been apart for weeks.

Amalie was breathtakingly beautiful, willowy and tall, with dark, expressive eyes and ebony hair that shone like silk whether it cascaded down her back or was put up in a carelessly elegant chignon, as it was then. Some kind people generously said that Sara resembled her, but Sara was dubious, and not only because she was several inches shorter, her hair was a lighter brown, and her eyes were hazel. Amalie was the beauty of the family, and everyone knew it.

Amalie's hands were smooth, her fingers long and graceful, and even when resting on her lap they seemed poised to move to music she alone heard. She was a wonderfully gifted pianist, but a few years before she had given up the professional concert circuit for marriage and motherhood. She rarely played in public anymore, restricting herself to a few benefit concerts a year and informal performances at the numerous parties they hosted at their luxurious home on Tiergartenstrasse or her husband's ancestral estate in Minden-Lübbecke. Her husband, the Baron Wilhelm von Riechmann, was an officer in the Wehrmacht and as handsome as she was beautiful. Their daughters, three years old and ten months, were dark-haired and lovely like their mother and cheerfully exuberant like their father.

Sara had never seen a couple more devoted to each other or more perfectly suited, despite the difference of religion. She sometimes wished that Dieter looked at her the way Wilhelm looked at Amalie, but she knew that wasn't quite fair. She and Dieter had been together only a few months, and surely true love needed more time to take deep root and flourish.

Unlike Wilhelm, Dieter had not grown up surrounded by comfort and luxury. After his father died in a muddy trench in France in the Great War, his mother had raised him on a housekeeper's wages. He had gone to work in a carpet shop when he was only twelve, continuing his education on his own as well as he could with borrowed books. Eventually one of the shopkeeper's suppliers, a successful importer, had recognized his latent abilities and had taken him on as an apprentice. Since then Dieter had risen steadily in the business, determined to become a partner one day. He was pragmatic and sensible, and he expressed his affection by bringing Sara American and English books he collected on his business travels, and by encouraging her to pursue her education, even though hers already far surpassed his. Unlike many other men Sara knew, Dieter did not need her to be helpless and ignorant so that he might feel strong and wise.

"I suppose we could have chosen a better day to celebrate Natan's promotion," Amalie mused after they had chatted for a bit and their brother had still not appeared.

"He's probably at the Reichstag as we speak, cornering delegates and pressing them for exclusives."

"But he's an editor now. Shouldn't he assign that to a reporter?"

Sara laughed. "Can you imagine Natan content to sit behind a desk managing things instead of chasing down an exciting lead?"

They waited a while longer, joking about how to punish Natan for his tardiness when he finally appeared, but eventually hunger drove them inside the café.

"Shall we talk politics?" Amalie teased as they were seated at a small round table covered in a white damask tablecloth.

"Please, no, anything but that." Sara kept her voice low and glanced about, suppressing a smile. "I wouldn't want to start a brawl. They might not let us come back. How are my darling nieces?"

Amalie's face glowed as she described her daughters' latest antics, from the baby's attempts to walk to her elder sister's amusing observations and turns of phrase. The conversation shifted from family matters to Sara's studies and back to the children, diverting now and then, as the waiter took their orders and brought them their savory soup and delicate sandwiches, to wondering aloud about how Natan might be spending his afternoon.

After lunch, the sisters decided to stroll through the Tiergarten, but they had only just put on their coats and were heading for the door when a loud crash of shattering glass startled them. "Sara," Amalie cried, pulling her out of the way as a second brick tore through what remained of the front plate-glass window.

"Heil Hitler!" a man shouted outside. Boots pounded on pavement and other voices took up the cry.

The door swung open and a couple darted inside, breathless and wide-eyed. "Don't go out there," the man warned shakily, ushering his companion farther into the room. "They're rioting, from the Reichstagsgebäude to the Potsdamer Platz and God knows where else."

Heart thudding, Sara stole to the broken window, stepping carefully over fragments of glass and staying close to the wall. Peering through the frame, she glimpsed a throng of men—dozens, hundreds of men—storming down the street, breaking shop windows and shouting: "*Heil Hitler! Deutschland erwache! Juda verrecke!*" One man paused and raised his hand in the air, holding something that gleamed in the sunlight. There was a puff of smoke, and Sara flinched while others in the café shrieked at the sound of a gunshot. Other pistols fired in reply, some distant, others frighteningly near.

"Madam, please step back from the window," a man called out. Glancing over her shoulder, Sara spotted the maître d' waving guests toward the back of the café.

Sara obeyed, and when she returned to Amalie's side, her sister clutched her arm. "I have to get home," she said, as the sounds of shouting and breaking glass rose just beyond the window. "Sylvie and Leah—"

"They'll be perfectly safe indoors."

Amalie shook her head, frantic. "The nurse always takes them to play in the park at this time of day."

Sara's heart plummeted. "All right." She glanced through the window, enough to see that the riot seemed to be escalating. "Let's stay together and keep our heads down."

"Ladies, please, don't go!" a waiter shouted as Sara inched the door open and peered outside. Up and down the street, men in suits or workmen's clothing marched, shouted, and broke windows, their eyes lit up with a strange, fierce glow. Others—men and women, some clutching children by the hand—fled before them. The sound of swift hooves heralded the arrival of the Prussian police on horseback, but their attempts to disperse the mob with rubber truncheons only heightened the frenzy.

A lull in the chaos beckoned. Sara seized Amalie's hand and led her outside, instinctively fleeing perpendicular to the path of the mob, although it was opposite to the direction of home. Pulling Amalie after her, she darted down a quiet alley, around a corner, and onto a wide boulevard, where some citizens hurried in one direction—men grasping attaché cases as they ran, women clutching purses to their sides and hobbling as quickly as they could in their high-heeled pumps. Others, mostly younger men, grinned eagerly as they raced off to watch the fray, or to join it.

A taxicab sped past. Frantically, Sara waved, but the driver ignored her though he carried no passengers. "Frau Gruen would have taken the girls home by now," she assured Amalie, scanning the street for another cab. "I'm sure they're safe—"

Suddenly a red-faced young man rushed around a corner and nearly plowed into them. "Heil Hitler!" he shouted, his face inches from Amalie's. He snapped out a one-armed, flat-palmed salute so sharply that Sara felt the rush of air from the movement. "*Juda verrecke!*"

Amalie gasped, hand to her throat, but Sara pulled her aside and the man bolted away.

Another taxi approached; Sara released Amalie's hand, put two fingertips in her mouth, and let out a loud, shrill whistle just as Natan had taught her. The driver slammed on the brakes, and before his reason overcame instinct, Sara flung the door open, pushed Amalie inside, and scrambled in after her. She gave him Amalie's address, adding, "Take the long way around, if it's safer."

He nodded and sped off again.

"What is happening?" asked Amalie, her face pale, her voice trembling. "This is Berlin. This sort of thing doesn't happen here."

Peering through the windshield, Sara took in the thinning crowds before them, then turned in her seat to study the madness they were leaving behind. "It must have something to do with the opening of the Reichstag."

The rioters were fascists. That much was evident from their shouts and salutes, even though they were not clad in Brownshirt attire.

The drive home took more than twice as long as it would have on an ordinary day. Sara and Amalie found the children safe indoors with their anxious, wide-eyed nanny, distracted by toys. As Amalie tearfully embraced her bemused daughters, Sara quietly told Frau Gruen what they had witnessed.

"Fascist beasts," the nurse said flatly.

Sara nodded agreement. And where was Natan in all the madness? When her eyes met Amalie's, she knew her sister wondered too.

Eventually Wilhelm rushed in, shaken and outraged, to embrace his wife and kiss his darling girls. "Why do they hate us so much?" lamented Amalie, clinging to her husband, her luminous eyes brimming with unshed tears. "Women and Jews—what threat do we pose to those men, that they call for our deaths?"

"Don't let those cowards frighten you," said Wilhelm. "I would never let anyone harm you or the girls. Never."

Amalie nodded and rested her head on his chest, but when she closed her eyes, two tears slipped down her cheeks. Sara said nothing. Wilhelm meant well—Sara knew he did—but his wealth, rank, and even his Christianity could not have protected his family earlier that day if they had taken a wrong turn into the thick of the riot.

Wilhelm placed some calls, and when he was satisfied it was safe, he had his driver take Sara home to the gracious residence in the Grunewald where she had lived nearly all her life. Her parents met her at the door, her mother pale and trembling, her father grimly quiet. Behind them stood Natan, hands in his jacket pockets, frowning pensively.

"Where have you been?" Sara cried, breaking free of her mother's embrace to fling her arms around her brother.

"Covering the opening of the Reichstag, of course," he replied. "And then the riot. One led to another. Listen to this: When the new session opened, the National Socialists marched in wearing their brown uniforms, despite strict rules against party regalia in the Reichstagsgebäude. They snapped to attention, gave that Hitler salute, and—" Suddenly understanding dawned. "Oh, Sara. I'm sorry. Lunch."

"Yes, lunch." She thumped him lightly on the chest. "Amalie and I were worried sick. At least tell me you got a good story. In that case I'll forgive you."

"There is no good story to tell about what happened today," their mother declared. "But at least we're all safe. I don't want to hear another word about this tonight or I'll never be able to sleep."

Her children exchanged a look behind her back, but when their father raised his eyebrows at them in warning, they obediently murmured consent.

As the days passed, Sara followed the story in the press, looking for Natan's name in the byline and, despite the harrowing events, feeling a stir of pride at his new title. She was shocked to learn that none of the roughly three hundred protesters had been arrested, less surprised to read that most of the windows broken belonged to businesses owned by Jews.

And though there was not a word of truth to it, the National Socialist press spread the rumor that the Communists had started the riot. They proclaimed the lie so often and so emphatically that those who had not seen the riot for themselves could not distinguish truth from falsehood.

CHAPTER FOUR

October 1930–August 1931

Mildred

When Mildred transferred to the University of Berlin in the autumn of 1930, she went alone.

Earlier that summer, Arvid had received his PhD in economics, summa cum laude, and had applied to the University of Berlin to complete his *Habilitationsarbeit*, the postdoctorate research and publishing essential for acquiring a professorship. When he was assured that the position was all but certain, Mildred arranged to accompany him, but just as her transfer to the university was complete, Arvid's application was declined due to budget cuts and faculty reductions. The only offer he received was from the University of Marburg, about five hundred kilometers southwest of Berlin.

"To think I've crossed an ocean to be with you, only to part from you again," Mildred had lamented after her frantic last-minute attempts to find a position at Marburg failed.

"It will only be for a little while," he had assured her, cupping her face in his hands and gently raising it to meet his kiss. "I'll see you almost every weekend, and you won't be lonely with Inge and the boys. She'll be glad for your company too."

In the aftermath of Inge's recent divorce from the sculptor Johannes Auerbach, she had moved with their two sons from their home in Paris to an apartment in Berlin. "Stay with me until Arvid can join you here," she had offered when she learned of Arvid and Mildred's impending separation. "I have the space, and we'll be less lonely if we're together."

Mildred had accepted gratefully. She adored Inge and the boys, and she and Arvid could barely afford one monthly rent payment, much less two leases in separate cities. But even knowing that she would have Inge for company, she had dreaded parting from Arvid. They had promised to write daily, letters so rich in detail and expression that they would feel as if they had spent every moment together. They were each other's most devoted advocate and most insightful critic, partners in all things, colleagues as well as lovers. A mere five hundred kilometers could not change that.

Once in Berlin, Mildred had settled into Inge's spare room, and, almost as easily, into her roles as graduate student and lecturer. She filled her hours with both duties and pleasures—studying, teaching, attending concerts and theater performances—and playing with her young nephews. Arvid visited when he could. One morning a few days after the October 13 riot, he and Mildred took his nephews to the zoo in the Tiergarten. Mildred marveled at how quickly the broken glass had been swept up, the scrawled graffiti painted over. One could almost pretend the new Reichstag had opened to utter tranquility.

Wulf and Claus seemed to have forgotten the uproar entirely, if they had ever been aware of it. Mildred and Arvid shared smiles as the boys darted from one exhibit to the next, imitating a family of baboons, marveling at the enormity of the elephants. Someday, Mildred hoped, she and Arvid would bring their own children there.

Even when Arvid could not be with her in Berlin, Mildred found much to love about the city—the museums, the opera, the parks, the theaters, and above all, the renowned university. Some of her new colleagues expressed surprise that a woman from Wisconsin would come to Germany to study for a doctorate in American literature, but she explained that studying American literature from a European perspective helped her to see it more objectively, to better understand her country's place in the world.

Berlin also provided some respite from the steadily increasing popularity of the Nazis in Jena and Giessen where she had previously taught. While teaching at the latter, Mildred had been shocked and dismayed when, in response to a university newspaper poll about political preferences, nearly half of the students said they supported the National Socialists. On several unsettling occasions she had witnessed hostile students openly confronting faculty members they suspected of being socialists or pacifists. At the University of Berlin, although increasing numbers of Mildred's students wore Brownshirt uniforms or Nazi lapel pins to class, they kept their outrage at a simmer rather than a full boil, which was less than ideal but still better than elsewhere.

On weekends when Arvid could not visit her in Berlin, Mildred went to him in Marburg if she could. She found the city's Gothic character enchanting, especially after she learned that the Brothers Grimm had collected many of their fairy tales there. Throughout the autumn and into the winter, she and Arvid strolled through the narrow, twisting streets of the medieval district, occasionally accompanied by Arvid's new friend Egmont Zechlin, a history lecturer at the university. Until the first heavy snowfalls made the trek too difficult, the three enjoyed hiking along the Lahn River or making strenuous climbs up Frauenberg to see the castle ruins, debating politics, the economic crisis, and whether the Soviets were on to something with their Five-Year Plan. Capitalism certainly seemed to have failed both the United States and Germany. Perhaps another economic system entirely would be required to pull them out of the Great Depression.

Mildred and Arvid spent the Christmas holidays with the extended Harnack clan in Jena, nearly inseparable for a blissful fortnight filled with love and laughter, family and friends. When they parted early in the New Year to return to their separate campuses in far-flung cities, Mildred's heart ached with loneliness despite the comfort of Inge's friendship and the distraction of work. And yet as the new term got under way, she glimpsed promising signs that better days were just ahead. In February, quite unexpectedly, the university invited her to present a special lecture on American literature to faculty and students. She chose as her topic "Romantic and Married Love in the Works of Hawthorne," and she was gratified—and relieved—by the audience's overwhelmingly positive response.

More lecture requests followed. "Don't they know I'm only a graduate student?" she asked Inge over breakfast the morning after her third lecture, still glowing from the unusual honor. "Some people wait their entire careers to lecture at Berlin University, and many more never get the chance."

"Who better to lecture on American literature than an American?" said Inge, eyes dancing with their shared happiness.

To Mildred, both her university and Arvid's were islands of peace and rationality compared to the roiling sea of unrest surrounding them. Germany seemed more volatile by the day, with street fights between Communist Reds and Nazi Browns erupting frequently.

"I'm almost not surprised anymore when I read about these brawls in the papers," she told Arvid one Saturday afternoon in early spring as they strolled down a cobblestone street in Marburg.

Arvid stopped short and touched her cheek with the backs of his fingers. "Darling, you must never become accustomed to the extraordinary and the outrageous. If you do, little by little, you'll learn to accept anything."

She took his advice to heart, and as spring passed and summer came, and as Nazi belligerence toward women, Communists, and Jews became a daily occurrence, she refused to pretend it was not happening, to let it become background noise like so much passing traffic.

On August 7, Mildred and Arvid celebrated their fifth anniversary with a two-day excursion to the Black Forest. They hiked through lovely pine and beech forests to a mountain cabin, where they celebrated with flowers and a cake that had survived the journey rather well considering that it had been packed in Arvid's knapsack. When they discovered two narrow cots where they had expected a bed for two, they laughed, spread blankets on the floor, and made love to the sounds of nightbirds and wind in the trees.

Afterward, as they lay close together, contented and deliciously fatigued, Arvid took her hand and laced his fingers through hers. "These have been the most wonderful five years of my life."

"Mine too," said Mildred, resting her head on his shoulder, thoroughly content.

"I have an anniversary gift for you—for us both, really." He stroked her hair, his fingertips brushing her cheek. "I've found a temporary job doing legal work in Berlin beginning in late September. We'll be together again."

She gasped, delighted. "But what about your *Habilitationsarbeit?*"

"I'm mostly working on my own at this stage. I can do that in Berlin as easily as in Marburg. I'll ply my trade by day, write in the evenings, and return to the university once a month to consult with my professors." He kissed her tenderly. "Are you happy?"

"I'm beyond happy! I'm overjoyed."

"Only one more wish remains to be granted."

She smiled wistfully. "We've been trying."

"Yes, and enjoying every attempt."

She laughed lightly to conceal a pang of worry. "I'll be twenty-nine next month. I can't help feeling that we're running out of time."

"You mustn't worry, darling." Arvid brushed a long strand of golden hair out of her eyes. "We're still young. Once we're together for good, it will happen. You'll see."

Mildred nodded, hoping he was right. She had seen her doctor, who confirmed that she was in excellent health. Every morning she did twenty minutes of stomach exercises meant to make conception and childbirth easier. And yet every month her period came, their dream of a baby eluding them yet again.

"Perhaps I should see another doctor," Mildred said. "A specialist."

Arvid agreed that it could do no harm. "I should see a specialist too," he added, "but I truly believe if we were together more, these things would sort themselves out."

Inge recommended her own gynecologist to Mildred, but before she could arrange an appointment, she learned that a well-known authority on women's reproductive health would be giving a public lecture in Marburg in the middle of August. Dr. Else Kienle, an outspoken opponent of laws banning abortion and discouraging birth control, had been jailed earlier that year for performing abortions, but she had won her release after a hunger strike. Mildred expected the lecture to be fascinating even if Dr. Kienle did not address her own specific concerns. If no question-and-answer session followed, she could try to speak with the doctor privately afterward.

Arvid had a prior engagement with Egmont Zechlin and a few other men with whom he hoped to form a new economic study group, so Mildred attended the lecture alone. Although she arrived early, the hall was already quite full, but she found a seat near the back and prepared to take notes. She had expected the audience to be mostly women, so she was surprised to discover many men scattered throughout the rows in groups of three or four. Most of them were clad in Nazi brown.

Her heart sank. Why else would they be there except to make trouble?

She checked her watch; the lecture was scheduled to begin at any moment. She glanced over her shoulder at the door, where a few women waiting to enter looked askance at several Brownshirts who sauntered past the queue and looked about imperiously for empty seats. Mildred turned back to face the empty stage and checked her watch again. Surely someone had informed Dr. Kienle that she would face a hostile audience; perhaps she would decline to take the stage. But just as she was wondering if she ought to leave, a white-bearded, stoop-shouldered professor approached the podium and introduced Dr. Kienle.

The doctor took the stage to resounding applause, but when she shook the professor's hand and approached the podium, a chorus of piercing whistles went up from the Brownshirts. She regarded them steadily over the rims of her glasses as she arranged her papers, as if she thought they might settle down if she showed no fear. The professor raised his hands for silence, and briefly the unruliness subsided, but as soon as Dr. Kienle began to speak, the men shouted her down, hurling profanities, demanding the closure of birth control clinics, and chanting, "*Kinder, Kirche, Küche!*" Children, church, kitchen—the alliterative phrase Nazis employed to describe a woman's proper priorities.

Dr. Kienle grasped the podium with both hands and spoke in a loud, clear, energetic voice, though nearly every sentence was punctuated with catcalls and jeers from the audience. Mildred listened attentively, determined to learn as much as she could. The doctor persisted, but when she finished her lecture and boldly offered to take questions, the professor shook his head and replaced her at the podium. His concluding remarks were drowned out by another blast of shrill whistles and profane jeers as a younger man swiftly escorted the doctor offstage.

Mildred joined in when the rest of the audience applauded thunderously, hoping that Dr. Kienle could hear it and would know she had supporters there. Meanwhile, the Brownshirts strode from the room with military crispness, smug and smiling, well satisfied with having put the doctor in her place.

Mildred knew then that outspoken, independent women made up one more class of undesirables that must be suppressed if the Nazis were to remake Germany in their own image.

CHAPTER FIVE

September 1931–January 1932

Greta

For months after their furious parting, Adam sent Greta pained, apologetic letters begging forgiveness for not immediately revealing the truth about his complicated relationship with the sisters Marie and Gertrud Viehmeyer, his first wife and second. "I swear I would have told you before we became lovers if our relationship had proceeded at a normal pace," he wrote, "but our passion overwhelmed us both. I fell for you so quickly, and afterward, I was desperate not to lose you."

His letters provoked arousing memories of their passionate months together, but she forcibly pushed them aside. "There's no point in explaining your domestic entanglements now," she wrote back. "I have no interest in joining your ménage à trois."

It occurred to her after she posted her letter that she might have made her point more emphatically by not responding at all, but she was angry and wanted to rebuke him.

"It isn't a ménage à trois," he protested in his reply. "Marie and I are divorced. I married Gertrud later. Marie is my former wife, the mother of my only child, and my sister-in-law, but we are absolutely not romantically involved. We've remained friends because it's in our professional interest to do so, but more importantly, because it's in our son's best interest."

Greta fired back, "None of this makes you any less married to Gertrud."

His reply confounded her. "Darling, you're right to say that my marriage, albeit unconventional, is indeed a marriage." Then, as if that would resolve everything to any reasonable person's satisfaction, he changed the subject, describing at length a new project he hoped to begin soon with Günther Weisenborn, the brilliant author of the antiwar play *U-Boot S4*, which the National Socialists had denounced as pacifist propaganda when it premiered in 1928.

Adam concluded on a regretful note: "Unfortunately, I think our collaboration will be deferred until Weisenborn finishes adapting Gorky's *Die Mutter* for Piscator. Brecht is set to direct and Helene Weigel to star. If you forgive me by then, I would love to escort you to the premiere. If you're still angry, come anyway, and take pleasure in my suffering as I burn with jealousy that I had no part in the production."

Very much annoyed, Greta wanted to fling the letter aside, but she could not resist devouring every word. Weisenborn was one of the most promising playwrights in Germany, Erwin Piscator one of the most skilled, radical, and influential producers and directors. Bertolt Brecht—playwright, dramaturge, winner of the prestigious Kleist Prize for drama, and the man Adam considered his chief rival—had been lauded by critics for transforming German literature, giving their postwar era "a new tone, a new melody, a new vision." Helene Weigel was his astonishingly talented Austrian Jewish wife, a rising star and unapologetic Communist.

How could Greta not be enthralled by a letter that tossed their names about with such casual familiarity? Adam knew everyone Greta longed to meet, thrived in the world she yearned to make her own. She imagined him holding the stage door open and beckoning her across the threshold. She could join him there, but at what price?

She tried to lose herself in her own work instead of dwelling starry-eyed upon his, but curiosity won out every time her landlady slipped a new envelope beneath her door. Finally, after months of sending deliberately abrupt replies to his increasingly detailed and compelling letters, Greta agreed to meet him for coffee.

More than a year had passed since their two-month affair, and she hoped that the intense attraction she had once felt for him would have faded with time. But the moment she entered the café and spotted him seated at a table near the window, all the old feelings surged through her anew. She had to pause to compose herself before she could cross the room to join him. She wondered how long he had been waiting for her. Then she wondered whether he had kissed his wife goodbye that morning and told her whom he was meeting later, and her heart hardened.

He rose quickly as she approached, and although she had intended to treat this as a strictly professional meeting, before she knew it he had taken her hands and pulled her close to kiss her cheek. For a moment she froze, overcome by wistful longing, but then she pulled her hands free, murmured a greeting, and sat down. He managed a smile as he seated himself, but she could tell her coldness disappointed him.

"How have you been?" he asked, leaning forward and searching her face.

She remembered the intensity of his gaze, how it had once warmed every inch of her. "Well enough," she said, scanning the menu. If she held his gaze too long, her resolve would evaporate like mist in sunlight. "Are you as busy as your letters suggest?"

"Busier. Have you been working on your novel?"

She was so surprised she laughed. "No. What novel?"

"The one you said you hope to write someday."

"Well, *someday*." She shook her head slightly and turned her wrist, a gesture signifying the folly of attempting to predict the future.

"But you have been writing, I hope."

"Well—" She hesitated. "I jot down my thoughts and observations whenever inspiration strikes. Then I'm struck by the realization that one must actually accomplish something to merit a memoir, and that I'm a twenty-eight-year-old former prodigy with very little to show for all my early promise, and I fling down my pen and shove my papers away in disgust."

His brow furrowed. "You're much too hard on yourself. Keep it up, and whatever you do, don't destroy whatever it is you've already written. There are always gems in the dross, waiting to be found and polished."

She shrugged, eyes downcast, making no promises.

He craned his neck to catch her eye. "But you are working?"

"A bit of copywriting, some editing, tutoring university students in English. Enough to pay my bills and send a bit home to my parents each month. But it's never enough."

She glanced up as the waiter approached, grateful that her complaint had been cut off. After he left with their orders, she inquired about Adam's current productions at the Staatstheater, determined to say nothing more about her diminishing prospects.

Soon she almost forgot that they were estranged. His tales of the theater were so fascinating, his obvious interest in her perspective so flattering, that her icy reserve melted, and once again she felt as exhilarated in his company as she had in Hamburg, as if they had been friends for ages but could always look forward to discovering something new, unexpected, and delightful in the other.

The afternoon passed too swiftly. Greta had stayed hours longer than she had intended and had drunk more coffee than was good for her, but when she glanced a third time at her wristwatch, Adam took her hand across the table. "Greta, darling," he said, his hand warm and firm around hers. "My feelings for you haven't changed. I love you."

"Adam, please." She glanced around, but to her relief, saw no one she knew. "Let's not have this conversation here."

"Agreed. Let me come home with you."

"Don't be ridiculous."

"Are you afraid we won't talk?"

Afraid was not the word for it, not when she wanted more than anything to taste his mouth and feels his hands on her skin. "It wouldn't be wise."

"Perhaps not, but it would be wonderful."

"Adam, you're a married man. We could never be more than friends and colleagues."

"Tell me you don't love me and I'll never again suggest we be more."

She inhaled deeply and sat back in her chair, unwilling to lie.

"I knew it," he said quietly, but with so much elation that he might as well have shouted.

"My feelings change nothing," she said sharply. "You're married. That's the end of it."

"Greta, I'm offering you my heart and asking for nothing in return but your love. What more do you want?"

What did she want? What she *didn't* want was to be his mistress, his young bit on the side, a cliché. She wanted a true partnership fueled by intellect and creativity, respect and desire. She wanted steadfast integrity, enduring faithfulness, love. She wanted what her friend Mildred had with Arvid, something true and real and lasting, not a stage prop, something that only served for the moment in the proper lighting if one did not examine it too closely.

"If you really want to be with me," she said, "get a divorce."

His expression clouded over. "So you want a husband, is that it?"

"Is that too bourgeois? It's more that I *don't* want someone else's husband."

"That's not possible," he said, shaking his head. "It would crush her. It would destroy the friendship we four have built so carefully— Gertrud, Marie, Otto, and I. Do you think Marie would continue to let me be a part of my son's life if I hurt her sister?"

"I couldn't say. I've never met Marie. As for hurting Gertrud, aren't you doing that already?" Abruptly she shouldered her purse and rose, unable to bear another moment. "Goodbye, Adam. I can't see you anymore."

He called after her as she fled the café, but she did not look back.

Weeks passed before she heard from him again. In late autumn he sent her a brief letter—an apology for the heartache he had caused her, a wistful hope that she might reconsider, and then, in a postscript, the name and phone number of an editor at *Rote Fahne*, the largest Communist newspaper in Germany, who, Adam said, was seeking an assistant and was expecting her call.

Greta did not write back, nor did she contact the editor. She was not a Communist and had never worked for a newspaper, so she was fairly confident her only real qualification for the job was that Adam had recommended her. She did not want to feel any more indebted to him than she already was, even though she was always one paycheck away from eviction. Somehow good freelance opportunities continued to come her way, as one satisfied client recommended her to another. By the first snowfall of the season, she had begun to suspect that Adam was behind most of the unsolicited job offers, but she did not ask. She could not afford to turn down any more work out of pride, so it was better not to know.

She spent the Christmas holidays with her family in Frankfurt an der Oder, but she returned to Berlin in time to attend a New Year's Eve party at the Charlottenburg town house of an old college friend. At first she had declined the invitation because she dreaded the thought of admitting to former classmates, in response to the inevitable question, that she teetered on the brink of unemployment. Kerstin had refused to accept that excuse. "Everyone else is struggling too," she had said one evening when Greta came for dinner. "We're all poor these days."

"You're not," Greta said pointedly, gesturing left and right to indicate Kerstin's lovely home.

"I'm a civil servant," Kerstin replied airily. "I pay for my comfort by enduring endless tedium in a stifling office. Anyway, who knows how much longer I'll hold on to my job with the Brownshirts marching around demanding that women stay home to cook dinner and make babies. Let's celebrate while we can. What's the alternative?"

Greta had no good answer for that, so she accepted the invitation.

When she arrived at ten o'clock on the last night of the year, the party was well under way. Jazz played on the phonograph, bursts of laughter punctuated lively conversations, and scents of perfume and cigarettes intertwined with woodsmoke from the hearth. She had scarcely removed her hat and coat when several acquaintances she had not seen in ages called out greetings or crossed the room to embrace her. Her dread swiftly vanished as one friend poured her a beer and another dragged her off to introduce her to a group of aspiring artists. Kerstin had not exaggerated; several of her old friends were gainfully employed, but more ruefully admitted that they too were barely making ends meet. They cracked wry jokes about taking in waistlines and patching the patches on worn-out shoes, and they shared advice about the best shops to find cheap but edible cuts of meat and day-old bread for mere pennies. And yet Greta sensed—and suspected they did not—that they perceived their similar straitened circumstances very differently. She was a metalworker's daughter, accustomed to poverty; these children of architects and dentists considered it a bemusing novelty. They took for granted that their situation was only temporary, and that the money would flow their way again when the economy improved. Greta knew that anyone could be one illness, one estrangement, one job loss away from utter ruin.

Sometime later, Kerstin found Greta in the crowd and steered her into the dining room, where her mouth watered at the sight of the wonderful spread and she grew dizzy taking in the savory aromas of lentil soup, roast pork with apples, and sauerkraut—finely chopped, the first mouthful revealed, mildly flavored, and thickened with barley. She polished off her first serving, had just finished her beer, and was unabashedly loading up her plate a second time when Kerstin sailed past with a tray of *Pfannkuchen*. "Felix is at the fireplace making *Feuerzangenbowle* if you need something to wash that down with," she called over the din.

"Don't mind if I do," Greta replied, but then the name registered. "Felix Henrich from university?"

Kerstin laughed. "Who else?"

Immediately Greta set off to find him, nibbling from her carefully balanced plate as she worked her way through the crowd. She found him at the fireside attending a black kettle suspended over the flames by an iron hook. Steam rose as Felix stirred the mixture with a long wooden spoon, the delicious aromas of red wine, the spicy notes of cinnamon, allspice, cardamom, and the sweet, fruity fragrances of lemon and orange wafting on the air. He was almost comically homely, small of stature, with jug ears and an enormous Adam's apple, but he was a brilliant scholar, one of the best in their class, and one of the kindest, most generous people Greta had ever met. From university he had gone on to law school and immediately thereafter had been hired at the most prestigious law firm in Berlin. Greta had heard that he had married the beautiful daughter of one of the founding partners and had two delightful young children. No one deserved such happiness more than Felix.

She set down her plate, drew closer to the hearth, and spoke his name in an undertone. His face lit up at the sight of her. "Greta!" he shouted, dropping the spoon into the kettle, seizing her hand, and pumping it vigorously. "I had heard you were back in Berlin. How good it is to see you! How did you like America?"

"I liked it very much," she said, pulling up a chair near his.

"Felix, the punch!" someone exclaimed.

"Oh, yes, yes." Rolling up his sleeve, Felix carefully reached into the kettle and grasped the end of the spoon, careful not to touch the sides of the pot or the simmering liquid. "You must tell me all about it. You were in Wisconsin, yes?"

"That's right," said Greta, pleased that he remembered. As he tended the punch, she gave him the brief, cheerful version of her Madison story, taking care not to sound too wistful or homesick, mindful of the other guests standing nearby, eagerly anticipating a taste of the hot drink.

Soon Felix traded the long-handled spoon for a sturdy pair of tongs, grasped a sugar cone in the pincers, and held it above the kettle. With his free hand, he slowly poured rum over the *Zuckerhut* and waited for the liquor to soak into the fine, compressed sugar. "Greta," he said, tilting his head to indicate a basket of wooden skewers on the floor nearby, "would you do the honors?"

Greta took a skewer from the basket, held the tip into the flames, and raised the burning end to the *Zuckerhut*, setting it afire. The people nearby murmured appreciation as the bluish flame danced across the sugar cone and caramelized the sugar, which dripped into the steaming punch below. When the flame threatened to flicker out, Felix poured more rum over the *Zuckerhut* until the bottle was empty and the sugar melted away. With a sigh of anticipated pleasure, the guests pressed forward with cups as Felix picked up the ladle and began to serve.

Cradling her mug in her hands, glowing from the warmth of the fire and the wine and rum, Greta listened as her companions shared hopes and plans for the New Year. She raised her cup and chimed in fervently whenever someone offered a toast to a better, more prosperous, and more peaceful year ahead.

Eventually Felix relinquished his duties as master of the punch, passed the ladle on, and drew Greta aside into a quieter room. "How have things been for you since you returned from Germany?"

The usual bland assurances sprang to mind, but before she could speak, his expression told her that he already suspected the truth. "Not well," she confessed. "I tried to get into a university, any university, either as teacher or student, but I failed. I've been patching together some work, teaching and editing, mostly." She forced a laugh. "Maybe I should have gone to law school instead, like you."

"Kerstin told me that you worked at a theater, organizing a script library."

"Yes. I quite enjoyed that job too, while it lasted."

"I have a proposition for you, but promise me you won't decline until you think it over."

Greta shrugged and drained the last of her punch. "I promise."

"In spring, I'm being transferred to our firm's offices in Zurich. Julia loves Switzerland and we're both very pleased, but—" He shook his head. "Setting up a new household is daunting, and I'll be busy with my cases."

"Of course," said Greta, curious how she fit in.

"I wondered if you would consider coming along. I have a large private library that will need to be unpacked and organized, and I'd also like the girls to learn English. You'll have a salary, of course, and a large private suite where you can write undisturbed, and we'll insist that you consider yourself a member of the family."

"It's—that's very generous, but I—I don't know."

"The house is lovely," he added earnestly, "and my daughters are sweet and good. I know all parents think their children are wonderful, but in our case, it's true. You'd adore them."

Greta smiled. "I'm sure I would."

"Please tell me you'll think about it. We desperately need the help, and I can't think of anyone who would be better company than you."

Flattered, Greta agreed, more hopeful than she had been since the ill-fated Internationaler Theaterkongresse. She loved to travel, she needed steady work, she was tired of her cramped rented room, and she longed for the peace of mind that came from knowing where her next meal was coming from. A change of scene would give her a new perspective, help her choose a new direction for her aimless life. And it would also be a relief to put a few hundred kilometers between herself and Adam.

As the New Year unfolded, cold, grim, and blustery, Greta mulled over Felix's offer. Her list of the job's advantages grew as the weeks passed, but she worried that if she went abroad without first establishing herself solidly in the Berlin theater, upon her return she would have to start all over again, making contacts, establishing her credentials, proving herself anew. Perhaps she would not be gone long enough to be forgotten and it would not matter. Perhaps the economy would improve while she was away, and she would return to an abundance of opportunities. She feared it was far more likely that the situation would worsen and she would find herself at the back of the queue for the scarce few jobs that remained. Perhaps she would be wise to stay and hold on to the little she had.

In late January, Greta was walking down Weydingerstrasse, avoiding piles of dirty slush on the sidewalks and shivering in her threadbare wool coat, when she came upon a workers' protest in front of the Karl-Liebknecht-Haus, home to the Central Committee of the Communist Party. As she tried to pass, a crowd of Nazi Brownshirts swarmed upon the scene, shouting slogans and swinging fists. Instinctively she shrank back against a building, watching with increasing alarm as a terrible confrontation erupted. As the Reds and Browns fought, the police arrived and promptly took the side of the fascists, beating back the protesting workers with rubber truncheons and erecting a cordon around the square, detaining the Communists while allowing the Brownshirts through. Around the perimeter of the police cordon, the protestors—workers and the unemployed, Communists and Social Democrats—strode up and down the street in small groups, watchful and glaring, until Greta could almost feel the bitterly cold air crackle with animosity.

Ducking her head against the relentless wind, burying her chin in her scarf, she continued on her way, only to encounter another protest near the Alexanderplatz. Desperate unemployed workers marched around the square, demanding food and jobs from the government, calling out to skeptical onlookers for support.

"Our families are starving!" one man shouted, shaking his fist in the air.

"Join the Communists, and together we'll fight for bread and for work!" another man cried out to passersby. Most hardened their expressions and hurried on their way.

"Don't shoot!" an older man beseeched a pair of police officers on horseback impassively observing the protest. "You should be standing with us, not with the fascists!"

Everything about the scene warned that violence would erupt at any moment, so Greta quickened her pace and did not stop until she crossed the Spree. It was outrageous that the police should take sides in a political struggle instead of reserving their loyalty for the rule of law. They should remain impartial public servants, not lackeys of Hitler's Sturmabteilung.

She was exhausted, worn out from hunger and worry and the ceaseless conflict that made a simple walk through the city an ordeal. She needed a respite from loneliness and dread. If going abroad meant that she would have to rebuild her fragile career from square one upon her return, so be it. Perhaps she would not come back to Berlin at all.

That evening she called Felix and told him she would take the job. Now that she had made up her mind, her only regret was that they would not depart for Switzerland until spring.

CHAPTER SIX

January–June 1932

Mildred

Mildred had high hopes for the New Year, inspired by her immeasurable happiness that she and Arvid were together again.

In autumn, they had moved into a small home in suburban Zehlendorf near the Grunewald. Their modest flat belonged to a new woodland housing development that mixed three- and four-story apartment buildings with terraced single-family homes, all with flat roofs and angular lines in the Bauhaus style. Mildred adored the bright colors chosen for the exteriors of the buildings, which had earned their neighborhood the nickname *Papageiensiedlung*, "parrot estate." Even after the brilliant autumn leaves had faded and winter's snow had begun to fall, she and Arvid enjoyed walking in the lovely adjacent woods before breakfast or after supper. They often remarked that their new home felt like a country retreat, a peaceful oasis far from the increasing unrest of the cities.

Mildred's commute to the University of Berlin was longer from Zehlendorf, but she loved their new home and her work and studies so much that she did not mind. Her students were clever and interesting, and they never used hunger or hardship as an excuse to be unprepared for class. Students enrolled in her courses in steadily rising numbers, a promising development since as a junior faculty member she was paid not by the section or the number of hours she taught, but by the number of students who attended her lectures.

If only Arvid's search for a faculty position had been as successful. A series of promising interviews in Marburg had abruptly ceased when the university declined to hire him as an assistant professor because, as one distinguished professor had bluntly put it, his research proved that he was not Nazi enough.

"Imagine how more vehemently they would have rejected me if they knew about ARPLAN," said Arvid wearily, referring to the research organization he had founded for prominent economists to study the Soviet Union's planned economy and adapt its strategies to improve Germany's steadily worsening financial situation. Although sometimes Mildred worried that Arvid's outspokenness on the merits of Marxism might draw the ire of the Brownshirts, she told herself that if ARPLAN developed a plan that saved Germany, all would be forgiven. The trick was to avoid trouble with the Nazis until then.

Unfortunately, trouble seemed more likely by the day.

When spring arrived, the *Papageiensiedlung* felt more like a country retreat than ever as pale green leaves unfurled on the trees and birdsong returned to the skies. The conflicts of the city receded to a faint echo as Mildred and Arvid strolled through the awakening forest, but one morning they returned from their daily walk to discover a red, black, and white swastika flag hanging from a neighbor's window. The next week, two more hung from poles newly installed outside other front doors. A man who lived around the corner, a low-level civil servant in the transportation ministry, began engaging Arvid in conversation on the train platform each morning, praising the National Socialists, condemning the Communists, and promising that soon Herr Hitler would make Germany great again, as it had been before the war.

"It's as if he's trying to provoke me into an argument," Arvid told Mildred one evening over supper. "I refuse to give him the pleasure. When I try to speak with him rationally, he dismisses what I say if it doesn't confirm what he already believes."

"I know exactly what you mean. Frau Schmidt does the same."

"The sweet woman from down the block who brought us *Apfelkuchen* when we moved in?"

"That sweet woman now displays swastika flags in every window. She's become so fervently Nazi that whenever I see her, I just smile, wave, and hurry on my way."

"Eventually the Frau Schmidts of the world will recognize Hitler for the blustering clown he is and he'll fall out of favor," said Arvid. "The National Socialists will diminish to the fringe party it used to be, and progressive factions will work together to make policies that will finally get Germany out of this financial mess."

Mildred wanted to believe him, but as the days grew longer and warmer, more swastika flags cropped up in their neighborhood like prickly weeds among the spring flowers. In central Berlin, Mildred encountered the swastika as well as strutting Brownshirts and photos of Adolf Hitler glowering from every newsstand, but the university remained a refuge from the madness of politics, an oasis of sanity where reason and art and science still reigned.

In May, as she was preparing for final exams and working extra hours to help her students with their term papers, Mildred learned that Friedrich Schönemann, one of her former professors from Giessen, had joined their faculty. According to chatter she overheard in the halls, he had recently returned from an extended leave in the United States and had been appointed director of the American section of the English Department. Mildred meant to stop by to congratulate him and renew their acquaintance, but before she found the time, she received a summons to his office.

He greeted her formally, meeting her at the door and showing her to a chair in front of his desk. "Frau Harnack-Fish," he mused, returning to his own more imposing seat and studying her over his steepled fingers. "When I took over as director here, I was surprised to see your name on the faculty list."

"Perhaps you left on your American tour before I transferred from Giessen," she suggested, a bit taken aback by his cool, distant tone. Had he forgotten their many long talks about literature and society at his favorite *Bierpalast* not so many years before? "Did you learn more about Americans and our culture during your trip? I still agree with your assertion that studying our literature is a wonderful way to learn about us, but travel teaches lessons one won't find in any book."

He gave her a thin smile and rested his hands on the desk. When he leaned forward, a pin on his lapel caught the light; her heart sank when she saw the swastika. "Frau Harnack, you are perhaps aware that the university is suffering financial difficulties, like so many other institutions these days."

"Yes, of course. These are challenging times."

"Then you will understand why we cannot renew your appointment for the next term. Many excellent German men with qualifications equal or surpassing your own are out of work. I cannot justify appointing a woman, and an American, instead of someone more deserving."

"I'm an American, teaching American literature," she said, stunned. "I have a unique perspective that not even the best of my German male colleagues can provide."

"Tell me, Frau Harnack," Schönemann said, leafing through some papers on his desktop. "Do you still encourage your students to study Marxism as 'a practical solution to the evils of the present,' as you wrote a few months ago?"

Mildred hesitated. "I do."

"How unfortunate. Perhaps the department tolerated such deviant pedagogy under previous directors, but no longer." Abruptly he rose, but although she understood the interview was over, she remained seated, numb. "Keep that in mind as you continue your studies. Although you are dismissed from the faculty, you have not been expelled from the university."

"Herr Schönemann, I would ask you to reconsider. Please look over my file. You'll find that my teaching evaluations have been excellent and I've received several commendations—"

"Then I trust you will continue to fill your days with productive work." He gestured to the door. "Since it would be difficult to find a replacement instructor so close to the end of the school year, you may finish out the term. Good day, Frau Harnack."

She nodded and left before he changed his mind and expelled her from the graduate school too.

Later, when she told her Modern American Literature class she would not be teaching in the fall, the students' voices rose so loudly in outrage and indignation that she feared professors from nearby classrooms would complain. In the days that followed, her student Sara Weitz circulated a petition demanding that she be reinstated. Sara and her friends collected more than one hundred signatures, but although the students' loyalty heartened Mildred, their efforts failed.

On the last day of the term, after she proctored her last final exam, a group of students appeared at her office as she was cleaning out her desk. "We all wish you the very best," Sara said as she presented Mildred with a beautiful bouquet of flowers.

"Schönemann is making a terrible mistake," declared another student, Paul Thomas, an army veteran who had lost an arm in the Great War.

"I agree," said Mildred lightly, forcing a smile, "but please don't take out your anger on your new teacher."

Sara, Paul, and a dozen other students insisted upon escorting her home all the way to Zehlendorf, carrying her boxes of books and files. Frau Schmidt glared suspiciously from her front window as Mildred ushered the boisterous group of young people into her flat, but Mildred merely smiled, tugged on the brim of her hat in a chipper salute, and shut the door.

Inside, she set out bread, cheese, and slices of smoked sausages, and she passed around a bottle of schnapps. Later Arvid arrived with groceries, interrupting a heated debate about the relative merits of socialism versus communism. He eagerly joined in the conversation while Mildred set out more food for their guests until it felt like a proper party.

They stayed up until midnight discussing politics and literature, and some of the more imaginative students wove elaborate schemes for how they might get Mildred her job back. It was not until the last half hour that the mood turned melancholy.

"You'll still see me on campus," Mildred reminded them as they said their goodbyes. "We can form our own study group. Herr Schönemann can dismiss me from the faculty, but no one can prevent us from gathering on our own to discuss whatever we like."

"Not yet, anyway," muttered Paul.

"Not ever," said Mildred firmly, but although her students nodded, their expressions were clouded over with anger and doubt.

The loss of Mildred's income meant that she and Arvid could no longer afford their home in the *Papageiensiedlung*. As much as Mildred regretted leaving the woodland retreat where she and Arvid had been so happy, she would not miss the suspicious glares of their National Socialist neighbors. After a brief search and a recommendation from a friend in ARPLAN, they sublet three rooms in a flat on the fifth floor of Hasenheide 61, about a kilometer north of the Tempelhof airfield near St. Johannes-Basilica and the Volkspark Hasenheide. Their building was on the northwest edge of Neukölln, a working-class neighborhood popular with Communists.

"If I have to choose between living among Browns or Reds, I'll choose Reds every time," said Arvid after they signed the lease.

They moved out of their old flat quietly under the cover of night and left no forwarding address, reminding Mildred uncomfortably of her childhood in Milwaukee and the many times her father, unemployed and months behind on the rent, had moved the family from one home to another to flee a disgruntled landlord.

As she and Arvid unpacked and settled in, Mildred resolved to focus on everything she loved about the new place and not dwell upon what she missed about the old. The rooms were beautifully decorated in appealing modern colors—warm yellows, dove tans, soft blues and greens—and the cupola in the front room offered plenty of sunshine, cooling breezes, and lovely views of the broad tree-lined avenues below. Mildred had a small, sunny room of her own for her desk, her bookshelves, and her favorite lamp, and although neither she nor Arvid said so aloud, someday it would make a perfect nursery, should the need arise. Arvid set up his own desk in the front room, near two tall vases where Mildred arranged bouquets of lavender cosmos. Throughout the day, but especially early in the morning, sweet, enticing aromas wafted into the flat from the patisserie on the ground floor.

"This is the perfect place for two scholars like us," she told Arvid when they finished unpacking. "The light, the air, and the pleasantness of the rooms will encourage excellent work, I'm sure of it."

Her first task was to find a new teaching position for the fall term.

She updated her résumé, collected letters of recommendation, and made dozens of inquiries, steeling herself to meet with indifference or even hostility. She would persist as long as it took. All she had to do was find one school where being an antifascist American woman was an asset, not a liability.

CHAPTER SEVEN

July 1932

Sara

Dieter had been traveling on business to Budapest and Belgrade for more than a fortnight, but when Sara's mother suggested they celebrate his homecoming with a family supper at the Weitz residence, Sara was so surprised that she hesitated before accepting. Her parents sometimes chatted briefly with Dieter when he picked her up for dates, and one afternoon after he escorted her home he had been asked in for *Kaffee und Kuchen*, but an invitation to dinner was something different altogether. Sara could only hope that this marked a shift in her parents' feelings for Dieter, a thawing of the polite reserve that she feared concealed dismay and disappointment.

From the beginning Sara had suspected that her parents did not wholeheartedly approve of her relationship with Dieter, even if they did not object to him personally. She and Dieter had met through Wilhelm and Dieter's employer, whom Wilhelm had hired to supply rare Italian marble to refurbish a crumbling fireplace in the east wing of Schloss Federle. Sara happened to be visiting her sister when Dieter had come to the estate to work out some details about payment and delivery, and she had been immediately struck by his good looks, confidence, and courteous manner. Amalie had invited him to join the family for lunch before making the long trip back to Berlin, and he and

Sara had become so engrossed in conversation that Amalie laughingly declared that she felt quite forgotten. In parting, he asked if he and Sara could meet again in Berlin to continue their conversation, and she feigned a moment's prudent reflection before agreeing. Amalie and Wilhelm teased her for swooning over Dieter's dreamy blue eyes and dazzling smile, but what she admired most about him was his calm confidence, his stories of travel abroad to remote provinces and re-nowned capitals she had only read about in books, and his astonishing perseverance, which had enabled him to build a successful career from almost nothing. He had worked for everything he had, and Sara had never heard him utter a word of bitterness or envy for other men who enjoyed the benefits of family connections and fortunes.

Sara's parents had not objected to their first date, but they had raised their eyebrows and exchanged significant looks when she had told them about their second. She and Dieter had been dating for two months when Sara overheard her mother lamenting to a friend about her daugh-ters' unfortunate penchant for gentiles. Wilhelm was wonderful, she had hastened to add, and she did not for a moment regret that Amalie had married him and had given her two beautiful granddaughters, but to see Sara follow a similar path was heartbreaking. To have one child marry a gentile was unfortunate. Two would be a tragedy.

Sara's cheeks had burned as she silently withdrew. She had not been thinking about marriage, not with Dieter or anyone else, certainly not anytime soon. She had resolved long before to earn her doctorate, travel abroad, and establish a career before she married and started a family. But as she and Dieter continued to see each other, she began almost unwillingly to mull it over. She wanted to keep things as they were, but Dieter was a few years older and might want to settle down soon. Sometimes they discussed their religious beliefs and traditions, but never the daunting challenges faced by Jews and Christians who intermarried. And although Amalie and Wilhelm had proven that it could be done with understanding and grace, Sara knew from her sis-ter's shared confidences that their happiness had not been easily won.

For now, she just wanted to enjoy her time with Dieter without worrying about their future. In the years to come, though, if their feelings deepened and they remained as happy together as they were now—that would be a different matter. When it became impossible to imagine living without him, she would marry him, if he asked.

For weeks, the predominant topic of discussion in cafés and in the press had been the upcoming elections. President Hindenburg, eighty-four years old and in poor health, had been persuaded to run for reelection because his party, the Social Democrats, considered him the only man who could defeat Adolf Hitler and persuade rival factions to cooperate for the greater good. On the streets of Berlin, fascists and Communists seemed perpetually embattled, an attack of one group upon the other leading to a retaliatory strike in an escalating spiral of violence. Frau Harnack had once told their study group that the back-and-forth shootings reminded her of Mafia gangs fighting over territory in Chicago.

On the day before the dinner, the National Socialists held a massive campaign rally in the Lustgarten, the vast plaza in front of the palace of the kaiser. Thousands of Communist workers and intellectuals marched upon the Lustgarten to stage a protest, but they found the plaza already packed with ardent National Socialists, most clad in full Nazi regalia. Natan covered the event for the *Berliner Tageblatt*, and afterward he told the family that judging by the slogans on lofted banners, the triumphant songs, the wild flutter of miniature swastika flags like a vast swarm of furious red, black, and white moths, the Nazis had outnumbered the Communists at least four to one.

Sara listened in disbelief as her brother described the scene. How could so many people have crowded into the Lustgarten to cheer on the Nazis? Did they not understand what fascists believed? The Nazis had always been a fringe party. Where had these enormous crowds of supporters come from?

"The rally is over, but there's more to come." Natan caught Sara's eye, and she knew to brace herself for an apology. "I'm sorry, Sara, but I won't be able to come to dinner tomorrow."

"But I want you to meet Dieter," she protested.

"I've met him."

"I want you to get to know him better. Amalie and Wilhelm already declined. What will Dieter think if you do too?"

Natan shrugged. "He'll think that important events sometimes occur at inconvenient times and I have to get the story before the competition does. He's a businessman. Give him my apologies and he'll understand."

Of course Dieter would understand, but that wasn't the point. Sara had been counting on her brother to help with the conversation in case it caught an errant current and drifted into treacherous waters. Natan could talk to anyone, lead them deftly from topic to topic, draw information from them with such amiable ease that they did not realize how much they had divulged until it was too late.

Then again, maybe it would be better if Natan didn't come.

The following evening, Sara put on her best floral summer dress, helped her mother and the cook with last-minute preparations, and paced in the foyer until the doorbell rang. Her parents were right behind her when she opened the door and welcomed Dieter inside, which, to Sara's chagrin, meant that their long-awaited reunion was regrettably stilted, a swift clasp of hands and a chaste kiss on the cheek, their eyes promising more if they could find a moment alone.

Dieter had come bearing gifts, a bottle of Tokaji wine for her parents, a fine piece of traditional embroidered lace for her, so lovely that she cried out with delight when she unwrapped the tissue paper. What she could not say aloud was that Dieter himself was the far more pleasing sight. He wore his best suit, which showed off his broad shoulders and slim waist; his honey-blond hair was neatly parted and combed to the side, where it would stay until she had the opportunity to tousle it; and when he smiled, the dimple in his left cheek made her feel slightly giddy. He chatted with her parents over roast duck and potatoes, describing his travels—the sights he had seen, the business he had successfully conducted. Sara tried to contribute intelligently to the conversation, but she probably spent the entire meal gazing at him adoringly, like a silly girl dazzled in the company of a film star.

The spell broke over dessert when Dieter mentioned that he had read Natan's report on the Lustgarten rally in the morning paper. "He described it so vividly I felt as if I had seen it myself," Dieter remarked. "I'm sorry to have missed it."

From the corner of her eye, Sara saw her parents exchange a significant glance. "Not that Dieter would have attended, even if he could have," she quickly said, forcing a smile. "Dieter isn't a National Socialist or a Communist."

"Neither is Natan, and he was there," said Dieter.

"In a professional capacity," Sara replied, with a warning look.

He seemed not to notice it. "If I hadn't been at work, I might have wandered over for a look."

"A sightseer rather than a participant, of course?" prompted Sara's father.

Dieter smiled. "I prefer the term objective observer. I think it's important to listen to both sides, don't you?"

Sara desperately wanted to change the subject, but the longer his question hung in the air unanswered, the more urgently it demanded a response. "Yes, listen to both sides," she said brightly. "Then, if you discover that one side is irrational and utterly wrong in every way, you know you're free to ignore them."

Dieter laughed and her parents smiled, and Sara quickly changed the subject.

After supper, declining her parents' invitation to join them in the living room, Sara took Dieter's hand and led him outside to the garden, behind a stand of linden trees where she knew they could not be seen from the house. "Welcome home, Dieter," she said, interlacing her fingers behind his neck and rising up on her toes to kiss him.

"My pretty Sara," he murmured, cupping her face in his hands and kissing her back. "I missed you."

She pulled him down to sit beside her on a hidden bench. "We can't stay out here alone too long or my father will invent some excuse to examine the flower beds."

He gave a wry snort. "So, did I pass?"

"What do you mean?"

"You know what I mean. Did I pass your parents' inspection?"

"Of course you passed. There was no inspection."

He laughed. "Well, which is it?"

She feigned indignation and gave him a little shove. He grinned, wrapped his arms around her, and kissed her again, sending her heart pounding with joy and desire. Soon he seemed to forget that she had not really answered his question, which was just as well because she didn't know what to say.

Two weeks later, Natan's byline led with a harrowing report of rumors that roughly seven thousand Nazi SA and SS in Prussia had taunted their political enemies by marching through Altona, a strongly Communist suburb of Hamburg, only to be fired upon by rooftop snipers. In the next day's edition, the city's correspondents confirmed that seventeen people had died of gunshot wounds and several hundred more had been wounded. Three days after that, Chancellor Papen declared that the events of *Altonær Blutsonntag*—Altona Bloody Sunday—required him to dissolve the center-left coalition government of Prussia, as well as its formidable police force, and place both under federal control.

"This is a coup," Sara's father declared, shaking his head in disbelief as he set one newspaper aside and picked up another, searching in vain for some good news. "This is nothing short of an overthrow of the Free State of Prussia."

The national elections of July 31 leveled another blow. The National Socialists won more than fourteen million votes, or 37 percent of the electorate. Even more dismaying to Sara, university students voted for Adolf Hitler in overwhelmingly disproportionate numbers. How could her peers be so enthralled by Hitler's rhetoric, his obvious pandering to people's worst fears and prejudices?

"What does the younger generation see in the Nazis?" Sara's mother asked her.

"I have no idea," said Sara, sick at heart. "None of my friends are getting swept up in all of this."

"I'll tell you what the young people see," said her father. "Something different. Something disruptive. For as long as they can remember, their government has failed them. They have no jobs, no hope, only anger, and they have no reason to believe the political parties they've trusted in the past will stave off further decline. To them, change must equal improvement."

"And what about the rest of the electorate?" said Sara. "Your generation should know better, shouldn't they?"

"Older generations still resent how the rest of the world punished them after the Great War. I'm sure Hitler's promise to restore the country to some mythical golden age appeals to them."

"This is dreadful, dreadful," said her mother, voice shaking. "Perhaps we should get out of the city. We could stay at Wilhelm and Amalie's estate for the rest of the summer, until the violence subsides."

Sara's father shook his head. "I know things look bleak, but Hitler isn't president, nor chancellor, and he never will be. The German people would never accept someone like him as their leader. He's utterly unqualified for the role."

"How can you be so sure?" Sara's mother countered. "Those thousands of German people who rallied for the Nazis at the Lustgarten seemed quite prepared to crown him king."

"Their enthusiasm will burn itself out," her father said firmly. "Within a year, Hitler's star will fade, and with it the influence of the National Socialists. They can sow hatred and violence, but they cannot rule."

Sara's mother nodded, mollified, but Sara's own doubts lingered. She wanted to believe her father, but she could not forget Natan's description of the wild fervor in the eyes of the masses at the rally. Some fires burned themselves out only after consuming everything within reach of the flames.

CHAPTER EIGHT

April–November 1932

Greta

Zurich was everything Felix had promised and more. The gracious Henrich residence was an oasis of serene prosperity, and since Felix and Julia treated her as a member of the family, Greta enjoyed luxuries that she had never before known—Périgord truffles, Russian caviar, the finest champagne. Her suite, comprised of a large bedroom, a sitting room, and an en suite bath, was larger than any apartment she had ever called home, and her windows boasted lovely views of snowcapped mountains and meadow valleys awash in violet asters and yellow chamois ragwort. Felix and Julia included her on their outings to the theaters, operas, and concert halls, and she had as much time as she wished to explore Zurich and the environs on her own.

Her work was interesting and enjoyable, and never so arduous as to invite complaint. Felix's library was a bibliophile's dream, vast in quantity and scope, but packed so arbitrarily that when she first opened the cartons, Greta laughed aloud in astonishment at the disorder. The Henrich daughters were clever and delightful, generous with hugs and kisses and sweet compliments, so quick to master their simple English lessons that Julia declared herself amazed and envious of their gifts. For all this, Felix paid Greta a generous salary in addition to her room and board. She was able to provide for her necessities, save for less bountiful times, and send a considerable amount home to her parents, thankful to be able to repay at long last a small portion of all that they had sacrificed for her.

As if all this did not suffice, her job in Zurich also put more than eight hundred kilometers between her and Adam, whose letters, when she neglected to reply, became infrequent, and then rare, and then ceased coming altogether.

Greta had always known that the work would not last forever, but she felt a pang of regret when she placed the last of Felix's books in its proper place on the shelves and realized her Swiss idyll was nearing its end. Felix and Julia assured her that she was welcome to stay on as the girls' English tutor as long as she liked, but their lessons occupied only a few hours each week, and she found herself restless, impatient for a new challenge.

For quite some time, she had watched students passing between classes and lectures at the Universität Zürich or poring over books at the library or in the courtyards, scenes reminiscent of her days at the University of Wisconsin. She thought wistfully of her incomplete dissertation, her unfulfilled plans, and began to wonder if perhaps she should finish what she started. As much as she had enjoyed her diversion into theater, it was difficult to see how she could continue along that path without eventually colliding with Adam. Time and distance had eased her heartache, but her wounds were too newly healed to risk tearing them open again.

During the long afternoons that followed the girls' English lessons, Greta wrote letters of inquiry to universities throughout Germany, beginning with her former professors at the University of Berlin. She sent other inquiries to the University of Jena, wondering if Arvid and Mildred Harnack were on the faculty there, thinking how wonderful it would be to reunite with them—with Mildred, at least. Other letters followed, to universities in Giessen, Frankfurt, and Hamburg—which reminded her painfully of the Internationaler Theaterkongresse—and to a few places in Austria and Switzerland for good measure.

In early September, she received a reply from Karl Mannheim, a professor of sociology at Universität Frankfurt am Main. "He says he finds my credentials impressive," Greta told Felix and Julia after supper that evening, "but he insists upon an interview before officially taking me on."

"You must go to the interview, of course," said Felix. "We won't find the girls a new tutor until you decide to take the position."

"It might not be offered to me."

"I'm certain it will."

"The only question is whether you will accept," said Julia. "If you don't think you'll like the work or Professor Mannheim, you must come home to us."

Touched that Julia thought of their home as her own, Greta thanked them and promised to keep their kind offer in mind. And yet when the time came, she purchased a one-way train ticket and packed all of her belongings. Even if Professor Mannheim did not hire her, she knew her future did not lie in Zurich.

After an early morning farewell with the Henrich family, where her young pupils shed a few tears and sweetly begged her to come back soon, Greta traveled four hundred kilometers north to Frankfurt am Main, a thriving city spanning the Main River in Hesse. Dr. Mannheim was not quite forty, with dark, receding hair and a keen, intelligent gaze, his voice warmed by a charming Hungarian accent. He greeted her cordially, smoked a pipe throughout the interview, and seemed especially curious about Greta's research at the University of Wisconsin and her work with Professor John Commons and the Friday Niters. He explained that his own intellectual focus was the sociology of knowledge, and he hoped she could tell him more about academic developments in the United States.

"I have sufficient funds in my budget to take on a graduate student who will also serve as my assistant and secretary," he told her. "One of that student's first duties would be to put my library in order."

"As it happens," said Greta, "I have considerable experience organizing libraries."

When she left his office twenty minutes later, she had the job, as well as his signature on precious documents admitting her to the university as a doctoral student.

Once again her days were full. She took a room in a boardinghouse within a short walk of campus, settled in, and familiarized herself with the sociology section of the university library. Another library demanded most of her attention: Dr. Mannheim's massive personal collection of books, haphazardly crammed onto bowing bookshelves and piled in precarious heaps on the floor of his office. When Greta was not sorting volumes, she was typing letters, organizing papers, grading undergraduate essays, and handling every other sort of dull but essential task Dr. Mannheim entrusted to her. Along the way, she met several other graduate students in the department, all as overworked and as relieved to be employed as she was.

Once, on a particularly exhausting day, she ran into another doctoral student grabbing a quick lunch at a cheap café within a short sprint of the Sociology Department. When she paused between gulps of coffee to bemoan the impossibility of putting together two consecutive hours to work on her dissertation, he nodded knowingly. "This is what we get for choosing such professors," he remarked. "Next time we'll know better than to consent to work for Jews, won't we?"

"I have no idea what you mean," said Greta, recoiling. She had become very fond of Dr. Mannheim and it irked her to hear him insulted, especially with the sort of cheap, nasty antisemitic slur that required no truth to sustain it or any particular wit to speak it.

"Surely you do," the student protested, grinning. "You know what Jews are like."

"Which Jews do you mean?" Greta shot back. "All of them? Surely not. No serious aspiring sociologist would be so unscientific as to imagine he could describe millions of people who happen to share the same religion with a handful of convenient adjectives and ludicrous stereotypes."

"You don't understand. All I meant—"

"The Jews I know are hardworking people, brilliant scholars, generous friends—and, granted, some of them are less so, but even the worst of those would be better company than you." She gathered up her plate and cup and books and moved to another table.

He never spoke to her again and avoided her gaze if they passed in the halls, but Greta did not miss him. Scapegoating Jews—or Communists, Poles, women, immigrants—was the refuge of the lazy, envious, and unimaginative. It made the world an ugly, hostile place to live in and did nothing to solve any actual problems. She would rather be solitary than count bigots among her friends.

Fortunately, she met many more congenial students in the department, and several soon became good friends. She also organized a graduate student study group, in part because studying with companions always helped motivate her, but also because she longed to replicate the camaraderie of the Friday Niters. The group was quite small at first, just Greta and a few amiable classmates she had invited out for coffee one afternoon, but when they decided to expand, flyers she posted throughout the department drew a crowd nearly four times as large. It was impossible to choose one day and time that worked well for so many students, so Greta decided to schedule their meetings on different weekdays and at varying hours, so that members could attend whenever they were available. They varied their meeting sites too, but they always chose cafés and common rooms on Zeppelinallee, just west of campus. Since they flew from one important topic to another as often as they changed meeting times and locations, Greta called the seminar their *Fliegergruppe*, in an amusing nod to their habits as well as their favorite street.

On other occasions, usually late at night after she dragged herself wearily from Dr. Mannheim's office, shoulders aching from carrying heavy tomes and reaching overhead to sort them on high shelves, Greta would meet up with students from other departments, friends who shared her interest in politics and her loathing for fascism. Throughout that tense autumn, they could not tune out the cacophony of campaigning as Nazis and Communists fought to win over voters from other parties before the upcoming elections. In the previous round of voting in July, while Greta had been in Zurich contemplating her future, neither Hindenburg nor Hitler had gained enough seats in the Reichstag to have a ruling majority, so another round of elections had been scheduled for early November. Most of Greta's new friends argued that the Social Democrats had governed the country into near ruin, but all agreed that the National Socialists had no real solutions, only outrage, vague promises to make Germany great again, and loud voices.

A few days before the German people cast their ballots, the voters of the United States would choose their next president. This election too Greta followed with great interest. She knew that with the Great Depression grinding on and unemployment soaring over 20 percent, President Herbert Hoover would have a hard time convincing anyone that he deserved four more years. She favored his Democratic challenger, New York governor Franklin D. Roosevelt. Roosevelt's proposed New Deal, with its progressive policies to help the impoverished and revive the economy, could very well save that country, while Hoover offered nothing but prolonged stagnation.

Wednesday, November 2, was already well under way in Berlin when Greta learned that Roosevelt had won in a landslide. "Seven million votes," she exclaimed in wonder as the radio at the *Bierpalast* announced the news, as "Happy Days Are Here Again" played in the background.

"That's fine for the Americans," grumbled one friend, "but what does that mean for us here in Germany?"

"Perhaps it's a sign that the world is turning in a new, progressive direction," said Greta.

Josef regarded her in disbelief. "Did you pick up this habit of unwarranted optimism in the States?"

Greta almost laughed. "You're the first person I've ever met who considers me an optimist."

"It's all relative. Go ask Professor Einstein."

Another friend raised his hands, a plea for peace. "If Mr. Roosevelt can turn the American economy around, perhaps their banks will resume issuing foreign loans. That would help us here."

"Eventually, perhaps," said Josef, "but not for years."

"Then happy days aren't here quite yet," Greta conceded, "but perhaps they're coming."

Her hopes seemed prescient a few days later when the National Socialists were dealt an unexpected blow at the German polls—the loss of two million votes and thirty-four seats in the Reichstag. The Social Democrats fared better, losing only twelve seats, but that still put them in second place behind the Nazis. The Communists finished third, but they boasted a gain of eleven seats in the Reichstag, while all the other parties shifted negligibly for better or worse.

It was about as good an outcome as Greta could have hoped for, and she smiled as she went about her work that day, more lighthearted and hopeful than she had been since those sunny, peaceful days in Zurich. Even Professor Mannheim noticed. "You're fairly dancing as you shelve those books," he remarked, looking up from his paper-strewn desk to study her over the rims of his glasses. "To what do we owe your good spirits?"

"The election, of course," said Greta, resting a stack of books on her hip. "Aren't you pleased?"

He shrugged. "It could have been much worse."

"Yes, and how very happy I am that it wasn't! Until now, the Nazis have gained seats with every election. Finally their streak is broken. Germany has rejected fascism at last."

"Let's not open the champagne just yet," Professor Mannheim cautioned. "The National Socialists may have lost seats, but they still carried a third of the electorate. More than eleven million seven hundred thousand Germans believe that Adolf Hitler is fit to govern."

"But perhaps this marks a turning point. As more people finally understand what the Nazis represent, more people will reject them."

"I fear that people do indeed know what Hitler wants, and what he intends, and that is precisely why they vote for him. Not because they misunderstand him, but because they understand him very well, and approve."

"I hope you're wrong, Professor."

"I hope so too," he replied. "But you're right that we must celebrate victories, however small. The Nazis may hold the most seats in the Reichstag, but they don't have a majority. Unless they form a coalition with another party, they will not be able to govern unimpeded. It's likely that President Hindenburg and Chancellor von Papen will continue to rule by decree."

Greta shrugged, unwilling to relinquish hope on such a day. "Better their decrees than Hitler's."

Professor Mannheim nodded grimly. "On that point, Miss Lorke, I wholeheartedly agree."

CHAPTER NINE

December 1932–February 1933

Mildred

In August, Mildred received a job offer to teach night classes at the Berlin Abendgymnasium, a new school founded by the Social Democrats where working-class adults could complete their secondary education and qualify for university. Although the new position paid less and lacked the prestige of the University of Berlin, Mildred admired the school's mission and was relieved to have beaten the odds by finding work at all.

Most of her students were around her age, experienced in office or factory work but unfamiliar with the classroom. Unemployed or barely hanging on to jobs they feared soon would disappear, they had enrolled in night school hoping that study would help them rise in society. Tuition was nominal, textbooks were provided free of charge, and needy students were offered subsidized meals at a nearby restaurant before classes. When Mildred observed her students from the front of the classroom, she saw determined, hopeful men and women, neatly attired in dark suits and dresses, shoes shined, hair carefully groomed, expressions revealing a sincere willingness to learn.

The only woman and the only American on the faculty, Mildred had also been appointed supervisor of the English Club, which sponsored lectures on academic and cultural topics and occasionally put on

Shakespeare plays. Many of her own students had signed up, and as she got to know them better through club activities, she learned that several shared her antifascist beliefs as well. She invited a select few to join her weekly study group, and was pleased to discover how much their experiences and perspectives enriched the group's discussions.

As the weeks passed, she became very fond of her students and worried about the grim economic reality that awaited them upon graduation. No matter how well she taught them, no matter how diligently they toiled or how thoroughly they prepared, the jobs they deserved might not exist when they graduated.

Arvid's situation was proof enough that even the best and brightest could find their professional hopes thwarted, although in his case, politics as much as the poor economy had kept him from attaining a university professorship. Mildred's heart overflowed with love and pride to see him undeterred, uncomplaining, working away at the law firm while continuing to pursue his dream. After organizing a research trip to the Soviet Union for ARPLAN, he had written a detailed report about the factories, farms, and public works they had visited, the officials they had met, and the lectures and cultural events they had attended. After distributing copies to the other members of the group, he had begun writing an economic and cultural guide to the Soviet Union, delineating its unique national character and the workings of its planned economy. "When I finish the manuscript, I'm going to find a publisher," Arvid had told her, yawning through breakfast after another late night toiling over his papers and notes. "A well-received book could finally win me an appointment as a university professor."

Arvid's resolve, her students' determination, and her faith in them all sustained Mildred through that contentious autumn. Then came the November election, and the Nazis' setback helped make the Christmas season of 1932 the merriest she had known since the National Socialists had begun their cruel, clawing struggle for power.

More good news came early in the New Year when Arvid's manuscript was accepted for publication by Rowohlt, one of the largest and most prestigious publishers in Germany. When Arvid insisted that she use half of his advance payment to buy herself a new warm winter coat, she agreed on the condition that he use the other half to replace his glasses, which had an outdated prescription and a broken earpiece held together with glue.

"There's so much to work for in the world nowadays," Mildred wrote to her mother in late January after sharing Arvid's happy news. "Never have there been more glorious prospects. I'm thirty years old and I have the work I want, and there are no insurmountable obstacles to my advancement. Life is good."

The following evening, bundled warmly in her new wool coat and a scarf Arvid's mother had knitted for her, she walked to the Berlin Abendgymnasium only to find several of her students waiting for her outside the front entrance, their expressions grim.

"Have you heard?" asked Karl Behrens, a metalworker who aspired to be a mechanical engineer. "Hindenburg has appointed Hitler chancellor."

Mildred's heart plummeted. "Are you sure?"

"I know a clerk on the president's staff," said Paul Thomas. "Hindenburg's people tried to form a coalition backed by the army, but when that failed, they began negotiations with the National Socialists. The Nazis convinced Hindenburg that their conservative members will be able to constrain Hitler's more extreme impulses, and so—" He gestured angrily with his single arm. "The Old Gentleman went ahead and did it."

"Chancellor Adolf Hitler," said Mildred, testing the words. They rang alarmingly false. "This can't be."

"But it is," said another student, clutching her books to her chest. "What do we do now?"

At the moment Mildred had no idea if there was anything they *could* do, but she would not discourage her students after they had turned to her for hope. "We go to class," she said firmly, gesturing to the entrance. "We carry on as always, but watchfully. Your education is still as important today as it was yesterday."

By sheer force of will, Mildred focused her thoughts and conducted the class as if it were an ordinary evening. Judging by her students' expressions, they seemed equally divided between those who regarded the news of Hitler's rise with dread and those who exultantly welcomed it. The latter snatched up their books and raced from the room as soon as class ended, while most of the former stayed behind. Mildred offered them what encouragement she could as they commiserated and speculated about what this sudden and dramatic shift might mean for the future.

When the class finally dispersed, she was surprised to discover Arvid waiting for her outside the front entrance. With him was his eighteen-year-old stepnephew Wolfgang Havemann, a law student at the University of Berlin. Arvid's sister Inge had remarried the year before; Wolfgang was the son of her new husband, the concert violinist and conservatory professor Gustav Havemann.

"Wolfgang and I were walking by and we thought we would see you home," Arvid said, greeting her with a kiss on the cheek.

"The university has been crackling with tension ever since the news broke," said Wolfgang. "The Communists are going to protest Hitler's appointment outside the Chancellery."

"We thought we might go to observe," said Arvid, "and to show the Nazis that not only the Communists oppose them."

Mildred ignored a pang of apprehension. "Lead on."

As they approached the Reichskanzlei, they found no discernible presence of the opposition, but only throngs of Nazi enthusiasts lining the sidewalks, men and women, jovial and menacing with their broad smiles and swastika flags. Most of them gazed up at a window on the second floor of the Reichskanzlei, their faces bright with eager reverence, while others craned their necks to look down Wilhelmstrasse.

At the sound of distant cheers and marching feet, Mildred seized Arvid's hand and pulled him to a stop. Wolfgang too halted, and as the crowd stirred with excitement all around them, they glimpsed a red, flickering glow down the boulevard, steadily rising in intensity as it moved toward them.

"Fire?" said Wolfgang.

Arvid nodded. "Torches."

Soon the marchers appeared, Brownshirts in front, torches held aloft, smoke rising to the winter sky. Then came black-clad SA, metal insignia gleaming in the torchlight. "*Deutschland erwache!*" someone in the crowd shouted, and another man took up the cry, and then on both sides of the street, voices rang out in song, *"Deutschland, Deutschland über Alles!"*

Row after row of marchers passed, faces stern and proud and triumphant, a flood of black and brown uniforms, torchlight and gleaming metal. Suddenly the voices swelled to a roar. When Arvid turned toward the Reichskanzlei, Mildred followed his gaze and discovered that a pair of tall windows on the second floor had opened and a man stood silhouetted against the bright electric lights blazing in the room behind him. She recognized him immediately, his slight stature and favored salute—right arm outstretched stiffly, palm facing down— straight brown hair parted low on the left and combed over, the unfashionable square of a mustache between his nose and upper lip.

"Meet our new chancellor," Wolfgang muttered in disgust as Hitler saluted one section of the crowd and then another, drinking in their adulation.

"It doesn't seem real," said Mildred, sick at heart. She could not bear to watch the new chancellor beam and gloat, but the scene below his window was no better. Ordinary men and women, her neighbors and fellow citizens, cheered him with stunning fervor. All the while, the parade of SA and SS men went on, twenty thousand marchers or more, their faces proud and sinister in the torchlight.

"Mark them well, these men with their straps fastened and daggers polished," Arvid said to his nephew, his gaze shifting from the new chancellor to the officers saluting him. "They're bloodthirsty and capable of anything. You'll see. With those torches they'll first set Germany ablaze, and then the rest of Europe. They'll have you in uniform before you know it."

Wolfgang blanched. "Arvid," Mildred chided.

"You'll see," Arvid repeated. He took Mildred's hand and jerked his head to indicate she and Wolfgang should follow him out of the throng. They had all seen enough.

The next day, Mutti Harnack sent word that Arvid's cousin Dietrich Bonhoeffer would be delivering an address on the radio the following evening on a special broadcast about Hitler's unexpected appointment.

As a Lutheran minister, Dietrich had been asked to offer a religious perspective.

On the evening of February 1, Mildred and Arvid invited their progressive discussion group over to listen to Dietrich's address, which he had titled "The Younger Generation's Altered View of the Concept of Führer."

"If they expect my cousin to praise Hitler as a good Christian and admonish everyone to accept his appointment as the will of God, they're in for a surprise," said Arvid as he tuned in the station. As a crescendo of symphony music and the announcer's smooth baritone marked the beginning of the program, he quickly joined Mildred on the sofa while everyone gathered around the radio.

They listened intently as Dietrich spoke, his voice clear, strong, and earnest as he acknowledged that a country needed a leader, but he questioned why German youth, in particular, vested all their hopes in a single charismatic man. "A Führer may be idolized by his followers," Dietrich warned. "They, in their total devotion, can create a climate which exaggerates the Führer's understanding of his authority. This must, at all costs, be resisted, or our leader will eventually become our *mis*leader."

"He already is," said Paul Thomas.

A murmur of agreement fell silent as Dietrich continued.

"To be feared are those who think of the Führer as a higher being, greater than man, unconstrained and omnipotent. The Führer must know that instead, he serves the people." Dietrich's voice rose in intensity. "An individual is responsible to God above all. For most of us, this is obvious. But now there is a movement afoot to unseat God, a plot to install the Führer as the ultimate authority in our lives. Should this happen—"

A burst of static, then silence.

"What's wrong?" asked Sara, alarmed.

Arvid leapt up to check the radio. "Nothing's wrong with the set."

"They must have cut off his microphone," said Karl Behrens. "I hope that's all they did."

Mildred gasped.

"I'm sure Dietrich is fine," said Arvid, but the strain in his voice revealed his uncertainty.

It was not until the following day that Arvid was able to reach his cousin and find out that he was safe and unharmed—and furious. Unaware that someone in the station had switched off his microphone, he had continued for another five minutes, warning the German people not to imbue Adolf Hitler with the qualities of a religious icon.

"Dietrich is determined to get his whole message out, so he's arranging to have it published," Arvid told Mildred afterward. "He's already begun work on a new essay arguing that Christians have a moral and religious obligation to defend the Jews from persecution."

"I hope he changes a lot of minds, and quickly."

"Dietrich isn't alone. Others are speaking out, and we must too, before we lose our opportunity. We must uproot Hitler from his new office now, before he digs himself in too deeply."

But all around were signs that they were running out of time. Two days later, Chancellor Hitler tightened his grip on his newfound authority by convincing President Hindenburg to dissolve the Reichstag and set a new general election for March 5.

Alarmed and outraged, socialists and Communists joined forces to oppose the move. Mildred and Arvid were among two hundred thousand demonstrators who gathered at the Lustgarten on the frosty night of February 7 to protest Hitler's appointment, bearing torches, chanting slogans, singing songs of unity and peace. Shivering in the cold, Mildred was nonetheless heartened by the sheer numbers of protestors filling the plaza, people like her and Arvid and their friends who recognized the danger of the fascist surge and refused to be swept up in it. Some Brownshirts stood about in clusters on the edges of the protest, glaring malevolently, but on that night, greatly outnumbered, they refrained from their usual violence.

It was a triumphant, hopeful protest, but in the days that followed, the SA arrested thousands of political enemies, mostly Communists, dragging them off to makeshift prisons on the slightest of pretexts. By the middle of February, violence in the streets of Berlin surged as Brownshirt mobs attacked members of the Catholic Center Party and trade unionists as well as their usual targets, Communists and Social

Democrats. Some politicians appealed for calm as the election approached, but many prominent officials were strangely silent.

"Everyone knows the Nazis are responsible for the violence," Arvid said. "No reasonable person wants more of this. Surely the German people will vote Hitler and his whole party out of office."

Mildred hoped he was right. The situation was untenable, and in the end, reason and common sense had to prevail. The March 5 election was their chance to get the political situation back on track so they could focus on the economy, on jobs, and on helping the poor.

Then, late in the evening on February 27, just as Mildred was yawning over a pile of student essays and contemplating going to bed, the wailing of a fire engine drew her and Arvid to the cupola windows. Another siren joined the first, and then another, until the cold winter night itself seemed to shriek with alarm.

Off to the northwest the horizon glowed red, and when the wind gusted, it carried the scent of burning. Arvid wanted to go out to see what was ablaze and whether Neukölln was in any danger, but Mildred would not allow it, fearing riots or worse. "Check the radio," she urged, but the few stations still broadcasting at that hour played music as they did on any ordinary night.

Mildred and Arvid lingered near the windows, watching and listening past midnight, until the quieting of the sirens and the absence of fire trucks on Hasenheide convinced them that the fire had been contained. Exhausted, they went to bed and dropped into restless sleep.

In the morning, they learned that the source of the smoke and flame was the Reichstagsgebäude, now a smoldering ruin on the edge of the Tiergarten.

CHAPTER TEN

February–March 1933

Sara

The distant wail of sirens woke Sara in the early morning hours of the last day of February, but after a moment of disorientation in which the sound grew fainter and faded away, she drifted back to sleep, trusting that the unknown danger was too far off to harm her family.

When daylight broke, she learned that she could not have been more wrong.

The morning papers delivered the shocking news. While they slept, the Reichstag building had gone up in flames. Within three hours of the first alarm, firefighters had brought the fire under control and determined that the cause was indisputably arson. Without any evidence to support his claim, Hitler had blamed Communist dissidents for the blaze. He had quickly convinced the ailing President Hindenburg to issue an emergency decree granting him unprecedented powers— ostensibly to enable him to find and apprehend the culprits, but in truth to eliminate the Communists as political rivals.

By early morning, Hitler had already exploited his new authority by ordering the police to arrest more than four thousand Communists. Civil rights guaranteed by the Weimar Constitution were suspended indefinitely. Banished overnight were the rights of habeas corpus, the inviolability of residence, freedom of expression, freedom of the press, freedom from censorship, the rights of correspondence privacy, the right to property, and the rights of assembly and association. The official definition of treason now included the production, dissemination, or possession of written material that called for strikes or other uprisings.

"We must warn Natan," said Sara's mother, blanching. "He's always been too outspoken for his own good. He may unintentionally write something that was tolerated yesterday but is treasonous today."

"Unintentionally?" echoed Sara. "I think it's more likely he'll do so on purpose."

"Sara," her father chided, with a surreptitious look that begged her not to upset her mother. To his wife he added, "I'm sure Natan is well aware of the new regulations."

"I doubt Natan will call for an uprising, but we can't expect him to stop writing about Nazi outrages," said Sara. "A free press is fascism's most dangerous opponent. That's why Hitler wants to discredit and silence it."

"I wouldn't expect Natan to stop reporting the truth," her mother replied, "only to be more circumspect."

"Our Natan is brave but also clever," Sara's father said, taking his wife's hand. "He won't be intimidated into silence, but he won't recklessly provoke enemies either."

Sara thought it took very little to provoke the Nazis, but as she watched her mother fight back tears, she kept the observation to herself.

In a frenzy of activity leading up to the March 5 elections, leftist newspapers were banned, and new National Socialist newspapers and magazines filled the vacant spaces on newsstands. The Nazis tightened their control on state radio, filling the airwaves with party propaganda. With the freedoms of speech and assembly eliminated, it was a simple matter for Hitler to ban political rallies for any party but his own. Communist and Social Democrat politicians hardly dared set foot outside their own homes for fear of attack or arrest.

Since the night of the Reichstag fire, Sara and her parents had seen Natan's byline in the *Berliner Tageblatt* several times, but Sara's parents became increasingly worried when he did not come by the house or phone. When Amalie told them that he had canceled a night out with

Wilhelm, apologizing and blaming the frenetic pace of his work, Sara decided to stop by his apartment after classes to check in. She would get dinner started, study until he came home, and catch up with him while they ate. She doubted he had enjoyed a nourishing meal or a good night's sleep since the Reichstag burned.

On the night before the elections, Sara let herself in with the spare key, calling out her brother's name as she opened the door. His apartment was dark and silent, the stale air suggesting that no one had crossed the threshold in days. She turned on the lights, picked up the mail that had collected on the rug after tumbling through the slot in the door, carried the groceries to the kitchen, and began washing and chopping vegetables.

Before long, she had soup simmering on the stove and had settled down at the kitchen table with her books and notes. It was difficult to focus as twilight descended and her brother still had not appeared, but eventually she became engrossed in her studies.

It was almost midnight when the door opened and her brother walked in, his hair and clothes disheveled, his lower lip cut and bleeding.

"Natan," she exclaimed, bolting from her chair. "What happened?"

He let her take his satchel and help him out of his coat. "The police stopped me on my way home and took me in for questioning."

Setting coat and bag aside, Sara cupped his chin in her hand and examined his split lip. "This is how police question people in Germany now? Did you tell them you were a journalist? Did you threaten to expose them in your paper?"

"That didn't occur to me, but I don't think it would have helped."

"What did they want with you?"

"To find out whether I'm a Communist and if I have any information about who burned the Reichstagsgebäude."

"How would you possibly know that?"

"They know I've written about strikes and protests and that I have contacts within the party. I suggested they check party membership rosters, and they acknowledged that they already had, and hadn't found my name. I asked them if they considered the *Berliner Tageblatt* to be a Communist newspaper, and they admitted that it wasn't." He touched his cut lip gingerly with the back of his hand. "It's possible that they don't really think I'm a Communist, but were just using that as an excuse to intimidate me. Either way, when I didn't confess, they let me go with a warning."

"Some warning." Sara ushered him to the kitchen, where he wearily dropped into a seat as she fetched him a cool, damp cloth for his lip. "Maybe you should get out of town for a while, just until things settle down. You could stay at Schloss Federle."

"If the Nazis want me, they won't overlook my relatives' homes, even if it means going all the way to Minden-Lübbecke. I won't put Amalie, Wilhelm, and the girls in danger." He shook his head, wincing in pain. "I'm not going anywhere before the election. Every vote counts, and I'm not letting those fascists intimidate me away from the polls, or from this story."

On the morning of March 6, the Weitz family learned that despite the Nazi program of intimidation, their firm grip on the media, and the fact that the SA and SS had been assigned to monitor the voting, they had not crushed the opposition. Although the Communists had lost about a quarter of their seats, they had held on to 288. And while the Nazis had won five million more votes than in the previous election and had gained 92 seats in the Reichstag, they claimed just under 44 percent of the vote, which meant that they still lacked a majority in the legislature.

But the next day, the National Socialists announced that they had joined forces with the German National People's Party, forming a coalition that comprised 52 percent of the Reichstag—a majority, albeit a narrow one.

In the days that followed, more Communists were arrested, taken from their homes and workplaces and held without charges in makeshift prisons hastily set up to accommodate the overflow. Natan assured his family that he was probably safe, since he had already been questioned, investigated, and released, but, ever cautious, he asked friends and neighbors to let him know if anyone came by asking questions or demanding to know his whereabouts.

On the evening of March 9, Sara's mother summoned them all together for an unusual midweek family supper. The cook outdid herself, inspired by the homecoming of her darling Amalie and by the presence of Baron von Riechmann, whom she was certain was accustomed to and expected the finest delicacies, despite the many times Sara had assured her that Wilhelm was one of the most amiable, unpretentious people she knew.

Dinner conversation was relaxed and undemanding, in deference to the two young children at the table. Only afterward, as the adults sipped coffee at one end of the drawing room while the girls played with their dolls at the other, did talk turn to politics.

"The military does not support Hitler," Wilhelm assured them emphatically. "The generals despise him, and many believe Hindenburg betrayed them by appointing Hitler chancellor. General Ludendorff accused him of handing over our sacred German homeland to a demagogue, and he predicted that unimaginable suffering will result. He declared that future generations would curse Hindenburg in his grave for this action."

Sparing a glance for her granddaughters, Sara's mother turned up the radio slightly so their conversation would not be overheard. "I hope the general's prediction of suffering is wrong, but I'm terrified that it isn't."

"We may not be through the worst of it, but Hitler's coalition will eventually fall apart," Sara's father insisted. "The Nazis can sow hatred and violence, but they cannot govern."

Natan frowned. "They don't have to be competent leaders to do a lot of damage with hatred and violence in a short amount of time."

"Son, please," his father said. "You'll upset your mother."

"Will you all stop worrying about upsetting me?" Sara's mother exclaimed. "Of course I'm upset. I'd be a fool not to be." She fixed her husband with a firm look. "My dear, I cannot agree with you that Hitler and his Nazis and these dreadful times are going to fade away like a bad dream if we're simply watchful and patient. I believe we should be realistic and plan for the worst." She inhaled deeply and squared her shoulders. "Perhaps we should consider emigrating."

"I don't want to leave Germany," Sara broke in, thinking of the university, her study group, and Dieter.

"We won't have to," said her father. "The rabbis assure us that if we mind our own business and prove ourselves law-abiding citizens, the crisis will pass."

Her mother sighed. "And so the discussion ends before it begins."

"You won't have to emigrate," said Wilhelm, taking Amalie's hand and looking around at everyone. "I'll do everything in my power to protect the family. You must know that."

"I know you mean well, Wilhelm, but what do you think you can do?" asked Natan. "Being married to a Christian might protect Amalie for a while, but she and the girls are still Jews, and—"

His last words were drowned out by the radio as the musical program was interrupted for a news bulletin. Sara listened with rising alarm as the announcer reported that the Communist delegates had been declared invalid. When the new Reichstag opened, they had not been seated.

"How can one party simply declare that members of an opposing party weren't really elected?" asked Sara, bewildered. "The votes were counted and the results were published. Everyone knows what really happened."

"The Nazis command the police," said Natan, rising. "They have the Brownshirts. God help us all if they ever take control of the military. Please excuse me, everyone, but I have to call on a few prominent Communists I know. Perhaps they'll contradict that report."

"It's too dangerous to go out now," his mother protested. "Wait until morning."

Natan paused halfway to the door and gave her a rueful grin. "Mutti, you know I have a job to do."

Wilhelm stood. "I'll come with you."

"I appreciate the offer, but the people I intend to see won't tell me what I need to know if I bring a Wehrmacht officer along."

Frowning, Wilhelm nodded and sat down. Amalie immediately clasped his hand in both of her own as if to hold him there.

"Then I'll come," said Sara, bounding to her feet.

"I'm sorry, Sara, but Mutti would never forgive me if I let you tag along."

"Indeed I would not," their mother said.

Grumbling under her breath, Sara too dropped back into her chair, exchanging a quick commiserating look with Wilhelm. All they could do was wait for news, stay calm, and hope for the best.

Natan returned two hours later, grim and somber. Not only had the Communist delegates been forbidden to take their seats in the Reichstag, but warrants had been issued for their arrest. Those who had eluded capture had fled the country or gone underground.

CHAPTER ELEVEN

March 1933

Mildred

From the moment the crackdown on avowed and suspected Communists began, Mildred feared for Arvid's safety. His publications and lectures made his academic interest in the Soviet Union's Five-Year Plan a matter of public record, and his recent travels there and the founding of ARPLAN provided more evidence against him. People often erroneously assumed he was a Communist until he set them straight, but the National Socialists were unlikely to give him the benefit of the doubt.

As reports of arrests and violence flew through Berlin, Mildred persuaded Arvid to leave the city immediately after he cast his ballot. Pretending they had been called to Jena on a family emergency, they took a room at a remote country inn on the outskirts of Berlin, where they could study, write, and follow the news of the election returns in anonymous safety.

They worried about their outspoken friends and family who had not taken such precautions. Arvid's cousin Dietrich Bonhoeffer continued to preach against fascism and to publish essays criticizing the Nazis and the fanatics who followed them. His brother Klaus, a lawyer, had publicly questioned the legality of the Nazis' refusal to allow the Communist delegates to be seated in the Reichstag. Their father Karl Bonhoeffer, a prominent psychiatrist and neurologist at the University of Berlin, regularly discussed Adolf Hitler's disturbing behavior and possible symptoms of mental illness with professional colleagues. The Harnacks, the Bonhoeffers, the Dohnányis, the Delbrücks—the entire clan was united in their abhorrence of Hitler and the Nazis. The only exception was Inge's husband, Gustav, who made family gatherings uncomfortable and infuriated his son Wolfgang with his increasingly ardent praise for the National Socialists' so-called accomplishments. Mildred and Arvid agreed that Gustav would be safe from persecution, and probably Inge and even Wolfgang by extension, but many other members of their extended family were in danger of arrest.

Three days after the election, wondering what her family back in America might have read about the turmoil in Germany, brooding over what indiscreet remarks they might put in letters that would soon land in her unattended mailbox, Mildred wrote to her mother to let her know they had temporarily left the city.

"We have come to a little country hotel in the woods outside Berlin where it is quieter," she wrote. "Our curious ideas are not known here. We are safe, very well, and happy. Who would bother about two students sitting off in a corner and thinking thoughts about the future of the world? So don't worry about us at all." Then she added a note of caution. "And best keep still. If anyone asks you about us, we are not interested in the world from a political but from a scientific standpoint. That's all you need to say."

With the right to privacy of correspondence abolished, Mildred could not be certain when she might again be able to write to her mother more frankly than that.

She and Arvid could not remain at the inn indefinitely without burning through their savings and losing their jobs, so when the immediate danger faded, they returned home, wary that they might be walking into a trap. Their apprehensions eased as the days passed and Arvid was not arrested at the office, nor did the SA pound on their door in the dead of night. Many of Mildred's students were anxious, and when they met in the privacy of the Harnacks' flat, the study group could speak of little else but what would become of Germany now that the unthinkable had happened and Hitler had become chancellor.

When Sara Weitz mentioned that her mother wanted to emigrate, other Jews in the group nodded somberly, admitting that they too had considered leaving the country. But where would they go, and why should they leave? They were Germans. They had been born in Germany, as had their parents before them. For some, their German heritage stretched back more generations than they could recall. Politicians came and went; Hitler was ascending now but he would fall out of favor eventually. Besides, if all of Hitler's opponents fled, who would remain to defend the country they loved?

One evening a fortnight after the election, Mildred returned home from her classes at the Berlin Abendgymnasium to find Arvid seated in the cupola, staring out of the window. He had hung his coat in its usual place by the door, but he had forgotten to remove his hat.

"Darling?" she called anxiously as she locked the door behind her. "Is something wrong?"

He turned away from the window, removed his glasses, and rubbed his eyes. "I heard from Rowohlt today."

"Your publisher?" Mildred hung up her coat beside Arvid's and joined him in the cupola. She sat on the armrest of his chair, gently removed his hat, and smoothed his hair back in place. "What did they want?"

"They're canceling my book."

"But it's coming out next month!"

"They say they have no choice." He reached for her hand. "No one dares publish a book about communism or the Soviet Union now. It's too controversial, too dangerous. They fear that everyone in the publishing house would be thrown into prison."

"Oh, Arvid. I'm so sorry."

"They've already destroyed the printing plates." His voice was dull with exhaustion and resignation. "They're letting me keep the advance."

"That's the least they could do," said Mildred. "Anyway, they couldn't get it back. We've spent it."

"Mildred, darling, I'm so sorry. This book—" He interlaced his fingers through hers and brought her hand to his lips, but he could not meet her gaze. "I was counting on this book to get me a position as a university professor at last. We could have stopped living from hand to mouth—"

"What about your second book? The manuscript's finished, and I think it's even stronger than your first. Since it's based upon your graduate research at the UW, I'm sure Professor Commons would write a foreword. Perhaps Rowohlt would publish this book in place of the one on the Soviet Union."

"I don't think they'll consider the Marxist labor movement in the United States any less dangerous a topic than the one they've rejected." He shook his head, pensive. "Perhaps I should burn the manuscript."

"You mustn't," Mildred protested. "It's a powerful, important book, representing years of research and analysis."

"But if the police raid our flat—"

Mildred thought quickly. "You could give the manuscript to Reverend Turner at the American Church. I'm sure he'd keep it safe for you until the political winds shift."

"By that time, my research may no longer be relevant."

Nevertheless, the next morning, Arvid carefully packed up the manuscript and took it to the minister for safekeeping.

Mildred meant to spend the day writing and preparing for her evening classes, but she felt restless and uneasy, watching from the cupola windows for the police truck she feared would soon appear at the curb below. When Arvid finally came home from work, her relief faded at the sight of his stricken expression. Over dinner, he told her that after leaving his manuscript with Reverend Turner, instead of going to the office he had gone to the home of his ARPLAN colleague Paul Massing, a sociologist actively involved with the Communist Party in Berlin. "He was not there," Arvid said. "His girlfriend said he had been taken to a detention center across from the Tempelhof airfield. When she went to visit him, she was told that he had been sent to a prison camp in Oranienburg."

"On what grounds? What prison camp exists for someone who hasn't been tried and convicted?"

"A concentration camp for political prisoners, from the sound of it." Arvid pushed his food around on his plate, then set down his fork without taking a bite. "I left in haste, in case his flat was being watched. When I arrived at the office, I phoned Friedrich Lenz at the University of Giessen. I thought that as president of ARPLAN, he should be informed."

Mildred studied the lines of tension in her husband's face. "Professor Lenz already knew?"

"Not specifically about Massing, but he'd had his own encounters with the local Schutzstaffel. The Blackshirts raided Massing's house, and apparently they found something that suggested he has close ties to Moscow. They denounced him as a Communist and perpetrator of Marxist ideas, and the university responded by suspending his lectures."

"How has he managed to avoid arrest?"

"I don't know. A good number of our members aren't waiting to see if they'll be next. They've fled the country." Arvid's gaze turned inward, and when he spoke again, his voice was quiet and resigned. "Professor Lenz and I agreed to disband ARPLAN. We've notified everyone we could, and I've destroyed the membership list."

"I'm sorry, darling." She reached across the table and took his hand. "It's a shame, but I think you made the prudent choice."

"It was the only choice," he said wearily, but he managed a thin, reassuring smile as he took up his fork again and tried to eat.

Her heart went out to him, full of love and sorrow and pride. How well he bore it, seeing so much of his life's work destroyed or undone, all in a matter of days! A lesser man would have crumbled beneath the weight of so much disappointment, but not her Arvid.

"I hope you know how much I love you," she said.

He responded with a look full of warmth and thankfulness.

His dreams of an academic career thwarted, Arvid resolved to find other work in economics, if not in the university, then in government. In the meantime, his cousin Klaus helped him find a more lucrative position as a lawyer with Lufthansa, where Klaus was the corporate counsel. Arvid worked as his cousin's assistant by day, and in the evenings he prepared for the state examinations to qualify for the civil service.

Soon after Arvid's first day at Lufthansa, on March 23, the new Reichstag convened at the former Kroll Opera House, on the Königsplatz across from the ruins of the former Reichstagsgebäude. There the National Socialist coalition pushed through a measure that essentially abolished what remained of the Weimar Constitution. The "Law to Remedy the Distress of People and Reich" granted Chancellor Hitler and his cabinet the authority to enact laws without any oversight or involvement of the legislature. The Social Democrats voted against it, but it passed regardless. The Nazis celebrated their victory by banning the Social Democrat party altogether, eliminating them as rivals as they had the Communists before them. The political parties that remained, fearing that they would be next, quickly disbanded rather than risk imprisonment in Oranienburg or at the new concentration camp that had opened at Dachau only two days before.

In a single day, the Reichstag had rendered itself obsolete.

Swiftly, inexplicably, willingly, the people of Germany had voted themselves out of a democratic republic and into a dictatorship.

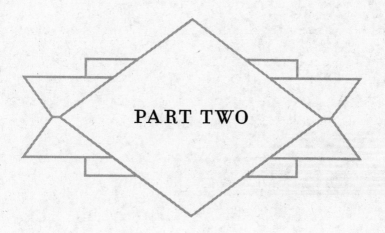

PART TWO

CHAPTER TWELVE

March–April 1933

Greta

On the morning after the last vestiges of the Weimar Republic crumbled, Greta strode to campus with her shoulders squared and jaw set, seething with outrage she dared not express. How could her fellow citizens have been so reckless as to hand over their country to a ranting madman? Was it ignorance or malice that had compelled them to embrace fascism?

As she passed other men and women on the streets going about the business of an ordinary day, she wondered if they were as horror-struck as she was or if their impassive expressions masked jubilation. Unless they bore the swastika on an armband or lapel pin, or strutted triumphantly in the uniform of SS or SA, her searching gaze revealed nothing. Outward appearances betrayed little of the truth of someone's heart, whether one secretly raged and lamented, or hated Jews, women, and Communists and was bursting with satisfaction that soon they all would get what the Nazis promised they had coming.

When Greta arrived at Professor Mannheim's office, she found him seated at his desk, gazing out the window over the rims of his glasses, shoulders slumped in resignation. When she shut the door behind her, he nodded in greeting and began arranging papers on his desktop without truly looking at them. His face was gray and haggard, as if he had not slept in days.

"It's a grim day for Germany," she said, going to the bookshelves to pick up her work where she had left off the day before. "My academic training never prepared me for this."

He strangled out a laugh. "I understand. As a sociologist, I recognized the ominous signs, and yet somehow I still believed that ultimately the German people would reject fascism, that we would choose liberty, equality, and progress. And yet—" He gestured to the window, to the newly unfathomable world beyond it. "Here we are."

"Here we are," Greta echoed, wondering where that was exactly, where this sudden, drastic shifting of the axis of life as she knew it would tumble them.

"Miss Lorke, I have a proposition." Professor Mannheim fixed her with an appraising look. "You enjoy traveling abroad, do you not?"

"Yes, very much." With a pang of wistfulness, she thought of the Henrichs' lovely home in Zurich, of dinners with the Friday Niters at the University Club in Madison. How distant they seemed to her now, how warm and safe and welcoming, how inaccessible.

"You're fluent in English?"

Honesty compelled her to admit, "I've fallen out of practice since I left America, but I'm sure I could quickly regain whatever fluency I've lost."

"I've received an offer to join the faculty of the London School of Economics," he said. "Recent events have convinced me to accept."

"I see." Greta struggled to conceal her distress. What would this mean for her, for her work, for her dissertation? "When will you be leaving?"

"As quickly as it can be arranged."

She nodded, heart plummeting. Too soon for her to complete her degree, then.

"I had hoped that you might assist me," he continued. "I have many details to sort out here—selling my home, settling accounts, preparing my family, packing, visas—" He closed his eyes and shook his head as if to clear it of noise. "I'd like to send you on ahead to London, if you're willing, to set up my office, find a suitable residence, and otherwise prepare for my family's immigration."

She listened, speechless, as he set out the terms—departure date, an increase in salary, room and board gratis until he arrived in London, expedited enrollment in his new department if she wished to complete her doctorate there. Even if she did prefer to return to Frankfurt after he was settled in London, she could still continue to work on her dissertation in the meantime, with all the resources of the London School of Economics at her disposal.

When he suggested that she take a few days to think it over, she found her voice. "That won't be necessary," she said, overwhelmed by relief and hope and the sudden shift in her fortunes. "I accept."

After a brief trip to Frankfurt an der Oder to visit her family, Greta traveled by train to Calais and from there by ship across the Channel to Dover. On the train to London, as overlapping conversations in English seemed to come at her from every direction, she was struck by a jarring sensation of reliving a slightly distorted memory from her own past, the strange dissonance of hearing her native tongue again upon her return to Germany from the United States.

After a few days in London, immersing herself in English as she completed the long list of tasks Professor Mannheim had entrusted to her, Greta felt nearly as comfortable in conversation as she had in Madison. The city deeply impressed her, its history, its charming boroughs, the people's passion for turning even the smallest patch of earth into an abundant and orderly garden. If the food was not as satisfying and flavorful as German cooking, it was plentiful, and her cheerful landlady kept her well supplied with tea and biscuits in the parlor of her Covent Garden boardinghouse.

Greta quickly became familiar with Clare Market in Westminster where the school was located, and as she strolled the streets between her boardinghouse and campus, she could well imagine remaining in London to complete her doctorate, as Professor Mannheim had suggested. She felt as if she had left a heavy burden of wariness behind her on the pier at Calais, and that once again she could think and speak freely without fear of repercussions. No swastika flags flapped in the wind off the Thames, no Brownshirts paraded on Pall Mall, and a rational if imperfect gentleman with strong ties to the labor movement served as prime minister.

In the absence of the pleasant distractions of her friends and her study group, she resolved to make steady progress on her dissertation. At first, every evening after a full day of work, she dutifully settled down to her books and papers in her boardinghouse room, taking notes and writing a few pages. But outside her window the West End beckoned, and after a few days the enticement of the theater proved irresistible. She scrimped on meals and walked everywhere, saving her wages for cheap tickets to the Theatre Royal Drury Lane, the Prince Edward, the Adelphi, the Phoenix. She enjoyed the cinema too, indulging in comedies and musicals as well as dramas and literary adaptations. And when the newsreels played alarming reports of growing fascism in Germany, she found comfort in the indignant murmurs of the audience, a sense of vindication that her worries and her anger were justified, not products of an overactive imagination or a zealous liberal mind-set.

One night after a screening of *Shanghai Express* at the Carlton Theatre, Greta was walking home, lost in thought about Marlene Dietrich's marvelous performance, when she heard someone call her name. Glancing about, she spotted a choreographer she had known in Berlin hurrying across the street to meet her. They embraced, marveled at their unlikely encounter so far from home, and quickly decided to catch up over tea and cake at a nearby café.

Anna's news from Berlin was unsettling. "German theater is dead," she said flatly, stirring sugar into her tea. "The geniuses who created our golden age—whether Jews, Communists, or simply opponents of fascism—have fled the country or have fallen silent. Their only other choice is to conform to the new regime, which I believe is a fate worse than death."

The renowned playwright and director Bertolt Brecht had left a hospital bed to flee to Prague with his wife and eight-year-old son, leaving their two-year-old daughter behind in hopes that relatives could bring her to them later. The celebrated Jewish filmmaker and stage director Max Reinhardt had escaped to his native Austria. The Jewish and socialist producer Leopold Jessner, to whom Adam had introduced Greta at the Internationaler Theaterkongresse, had gone to New York. Erwin Piscator, an outspoken member of the Communist Party, had found refuge in Moscow.

"Günther Weisenborn has more courage than the rest of us combined," said Anna. "His play *Warum lacht Frau Balsam?* premiered last month at the Deutsches Künstlertheater as scheduled, but word had gotten out that it was antifascist, and Nazis rioted at the theater. The show closed that night and the play was immediately banned. God only knows when Weisenborn will be able to produce a play in Berlin again."

"Such a loss," Greta murmured. Günther Weisenborn was exceptionally gifted—as was everyone Anna had mentioned. "With Jessner gone, what will become of the Staatstheater?"

"Nothing good, I'm sure. Franz Ulbricht is in charge now, and he's made no secret of his admiration for Hitler and Mussolini." Anna shuddered and bent over her teacup as if to draw strength from its warmth. "I for one shall never work there again."

"And what of Adam Kuckhoff?" Greta inquired, too casually.

Anna regarded her knowingly. "He's received many offers to join theaters elsewhere in Europe, but he seems determined to stay put. He told me that as someone who is neither a Communist nor a Jew, he's one of the few politically engaged writers in Germany who is not under attack either racially or politically. He's able to stay, and so he's obliged to stay, to fight fascism from within."

Greta felt a rush of warmth and pride. That was so like Adam, so brave and selfless—and reckless. "I hope he manages to stay out of those new prison camps."

Anna held her gaze for a moment before glancing away. "His brother-in-law, Hans Otto, does not get along well with Ulbricht. He's received invitations from theaters in Vienna, Zurich, and Prague, but he seems as reluctant to leave Germany as Kuckhoff is."

Greta nodded, understanding what Anna was trying to say. If Otto would not leave, then his wife would surely remain as well, as would Armin-Gerd, Marie's son by Adam. If the rest of the family stayed in Germany, it was very likely that Gertrud—Marie's sister and Adam's wife—would too. Adam's domestic situation would remain as complicated as ever.

"You're better off here," said Anna suddenly, reaching across the table to clasp her hand. "We both are."

"My friends from the university in Frankfurt say the same. They tell me how lucky I am to be able to breathe freely and write, and that I shouldn't even think of returning for several months."

"And yet?" Anna prompted.

"Germany is my home," said Greta, impassioned. "I agree with Adam. If we can stay and fight, we should. Jews and Communists— yes, they should flee if they can. They wear targets on their backs. But as for the rest of us—" She shook her head. "Who will remain to resist the Nazis if all decent people run away?"

"Well, this decent person is staying in London until she's sure it's safe to go home." Anna studied her. "You must realize that if you go back, it may cost you your career, your freedom, even your life."

Greta's heart thudded, but her friend's anxiety compelled her to shrug and force a smile. "Maybe. You're very persuasive. Why shouldn't I stay here to plug away at my dissertation and to enjoy as much of the West End as I can afford? What difference could one woman make, especially one as utterly unqualified for politics as I am?"

Some of the worry left Anna's eyes. "When I write home to friends," she said carefully, "should I say that you asked about Kuckhoff?"

Greta waved a hand dismissively. "It doesn't matter. I asked about a lot of people. There's no need to mention Kuckhoff unless you mention them too."

Anna shrugged and sipped her tea as if it were of little consequence, but Greta suspected it would not be long until Adam knew she was in London.

A week later, Professor Mannheim arrived in London, exhausted but effusive in his praise and thankfulness for Greta's efforts on his behalf. "This will do nicely," he said. "I feel as if I had been cast adrift on a lifeboat, and the London School of Economics pulled me in to a safe harbor. I wonder if you would recognize the university in Frankfurt anymore, so many faculty have left."

"I feared as much," said Greta. "In his last letter, my father mentioned that he had read in the newspaper that professors throughout Germany are suddenly taking leaves of absence. He said there were six listed from Frankfurt am Main alone."

"Only six? Your father's information is out of date." Professor Mannheim gave a derisive snort. "Leave of absence. What a pretty euphemism. Jews, Communists, and other undesirables are being forcibly excised from academia. Who will be next?"

"Women, I imagine."

The professor regarded her with sympathy over the rims of his glasses. "You must not let that discourage you from completing your degree."

"I won't." Her interest in her dissertation was waning for entirely different reasons.

Any reasonable person would conclude that her only rational choice was to enroll in the London School of Economics, earn her doctorate, and wait out the strife at home. Let others engage in that fight for Germany's soul, people better suited for waging political battles, people like Adam.

A fortnight later, Greta received a letter in care of the Department of Sociology, a letter from Germany she had anticipated ever since her unexpected reunion with Anna Klug.

Adam had not written to her in months. She pocketed the letter and resolved not to read it until later that evening, or perhaps the following morning. She had plans to meet a friend at the British Museum and would not let Adam's words distract or distress her. But her heart pounded fiercely as she walked northwest along Drury Lane, each theater she passed reminding her of him, of their long, engrossing discussions about classic plays and the renaissance of German theater and the role of the artist in society.

She made it to the steps of the museum before she tore open the envelope and withdrew a small sheet of paper.

Adam had written scarcely more than a sentence: "Come—I'm waiting for you."

A mix of emotions flooded her, joy and hope, longing and wariness. Adam was waiting for her, but had he done anything to extricate himself from his marriage? Or was she misreading him entirely, and he only meant that she should return to join the struggle against fascism?

She was apprehensive—she could admit that. Returning to Germany meant willingly accepting uncertainty and danger. Yet Adam's brief message, five simple words, forced her to acknowledge how homesick she truly was. She missed her family and friends, German food and culture, the Berlin theater. She ached with anger and indignation when she thought of Jewish friends suffering under the Nazi regime, friends she could help if she were there.

The more she brooded over it, the more she yearned for home.

Her decision, once made, was firm and immutable. She would return to Germany, but whether Adam would play any role in her life, and whether she wanted him to, was impossible to know.

CHAPTER THIRTEEN

March–April 1933

Sara

Sara could ignore the swastika flags and the Brownshirt recruiting posters proliferating all over the University of Berlin campus, but she froze in terror whenever she came upon storm troopers smashing windows of Jewish-owned shops, destroying merchandise, and roughing up the frightened proprietors. At first city police attempted to intervene, but they were no match for the SA, and over time many began to look the other way, as if it were more important not to muss their green uniforms than to uphold the rule of law.

Natan told Sara that he had seen SA officers stride into courthouses, haul Jewish lawyers and judges out to the street, berate them, beat them, spit on them. Attacks on synagogues were so commonplace that it had become second nature to glance over one's shoulder while walking to Shabbat services.

The outrages received widespread coverage in the international press, and a movement began among Jewish organizations worldwide to boycott German goods in protest. Adolf Hitler denounced German Jews for turning the international press against the Nazis, and in retaliation, he proclaimed a national boycott of Jewish businesses beginning the first day of April.

Sara thought the date was a curious choice, as April 1 was a Saturday and many observant Jews closed their businesses for Shabbat. Perhaps Hitler hoped people would see the darkened windows and assume the intimidated Jews had not bothered to open their doors that morning. Or perhaps he knew that observant Jews did not shop on Shabbat, pre-empting any attempt the Jewish community might have made to offset the boycott with shopping sprees.

Indignant, Sara phoned her sister. "Dieter invited me to a party and I need a new dress," she said. "Want to come shopping with me on Saturday?"

After a moment's hesitation, Amalie agreed. "Don't tell Mother," she warned.

"Of course not! She'd lock me in the house."

On the morning of April 1, Sara and Amalie met in front of the Café Kranzler in Charlottenburg. Amalie was as breathtakingly lovely as ever, her dark hair arranged in a graceful chignon that emphasized her slender neck and high cheekbones, and her clothing, elegant and perfectly tailored, spoke of wealth and excellent taste. Only a tremulous smile betrayed her nervousness.

The sisters linked arms and strolled along Kurfürstendamm, their conversation falling silent at the sight of storm troopers standing menacingly outside shops and businesses unmistakably identified by the symbols painted on their windows and doors, a yellow six-pointed Star of David with *Jude* or *Jüdisches Geschäft* scrawled in black in the center. Posted on walls and lampposts were chilling signs in stark black and white: "Don't Buy from Jews," ordered one, and "The Jews Are Our Misfortune," another. "Germans, defend yourselves against Jewish atrocity propaganda," another warned. "Buy only at German stores!" Black-clad SA men strode along the sidewalks with placards hung around their necks bearing identical warnings in Blackletter: "Germans! Resist! Do not buy from Jews!"

"This is absurd," said Sara in an undertone as they passed two SA men chatting amiably while blocking the entrance to a Jewish-owned department store, one of her mother's favorites. "The Nazis are persecuted? *They* need to resist *us*?"

"Hush. I know," murmured her sister, the picture of serenity.

Sara had expected the most popular shopping district in Berlin to be nearly deserted, but to her surprise, nearly as many people as on any other Saturday strolled the sidewalks, some gawking at the harsh signs and garish symbols, others pretending they did not exist. Several Jewish-owned shops were darkened, the shades drawn, the signs turned to "Closed" in the front windows, but customers passed freely through the doors of those that were open, carrying shopping bags and string-tied parcels, ignoring the glares of the SA.

A stocky blond storm trooper stood outside Amalie's favorite dress shop. "I beg your pardon, ladies," he said as they approached the door. "This is a Jewish shop."

"Yes, thank you, we know," said Amalie, fixing him with a smile so radiant that he blinked stupidly and said nothing more.

The proprietor greeted them with a strained smile. After trying on several pretty frocks, Sara chose a lovely crepe de Chine dress, burgundy with cream pinstripes, with a buttoned, jewel-neck bodice, a peplum waistline, and a flounced hem that swirled just above her ankles when she moved. Amalie put the purchase on Wilhelm's account, and the salesclerk carefully folded the dress in tissue paper and packaged it in a box bearing the store's name.

"Thank you, Amalie," Sara said as they left the store, passing the storm trooper, who studiously looked the other way. "Thank Wilhelm for me too."

"I will, but how are you going to explain this to Mother?"

"I'll hide the box beneath my bed for a few days. She'll never know."

Their simple act of defiance raised their spirits, so they decided to return to the Café Kranzler for an early lunch. Only when they parted company at the Untergrundbahn did Sara feel a stir of trepidation, wondering how she was going to sneak the box into the house and up to her bedroom without her mother noticing. She pondered her options all the way home, but just as she turned onto her own block, she saw her mother approaching from the opposite direction. From her elbow dangled a shopping bag bearing the name of Ernst Kantorowicz's bookshop.

"Mutti," cried Sara as they met at their own front gate, utterly astonished. "You broke the embargo. And on Shabbat!"

Her mother drew herself up. "Do you think only the young can defy authority?"

"Not exactly, but—you're a wife and mother."

"Who more than a wife and mother has a responsibility to make the country equitable and civil for her family?"

Sara had never been prouder of her.

By evening the Nazis had declared victory, claiming the boycott had succeeded so overwhelmingly that there was no need to extend it beyond a single day. Their words did not change the facts. Anyone who had browsed Berlin's popular shopping districts that day knew the truth.

When her study group met a few days later at Mildred Harnack's flat in Neukölln, Sara learned that nearly everyone there had broken the boycott. Sara was deeply impressed when Mildred told them how her husband's ninety-one-year-old great-aunt had imperiously ignored the cordon around KaDeWe, the Jewish-owned department store where she had shopped for decades. The SA had briefly detained her, but had soon released her on account of her age.

"How could anyone arrest a ninety-one-year-old woman for ignoring a boycott?" exclaimed Sara. "She didn't break the law, and at her age, she's earned the right to shop where she pleases."

Mildred smiled. "That's essentially what she told the SA."

Less than a week after the boycott, on April 7, the Reichstag passed the Professional Civil Service Restoration Act, or *Berufsbeamtengesetz*, which required all non-Aryans and members of the Communist Party to retire from the legal profession and civil service. President Hindenburg had objected to the original bill, but he approved it after exemptions were made for veterans of the Great War and those who had lost a father or a son in combat. Even in its amended form, the law meant that thousands of Jewish lawyers, judges, teachers, professors, and government workers suddenly lost their jobs, and when a second law was passed soon thereafter, countless doctors, tax consultants, notaries, and even musicians were thrown out of work too.

"See, Mutti?" said Natan sardonically the next time the family gathered for Shabbat. "I was right to choose journalism over law school."

"They may come for reporters and editors next," she replied.

Sara and Natan deliberately avoided each other's gaze, and Sara offered only the slightest shake of her head to say that she had not told anyone about his arrest and questioning. Why give their mother more reason to worry about her son's occupational hazards when he had resolved not to give up his occupation?

By then the Nazis had arrested more than forty-five thousand of their opponents, nearly all of them Communists and Social Democrats. Day by day, the SA and the SS intensified their attacks on Jewish businesses and synagogues. Four times Sara went to class only to find a stranger at the front of the lecture hall, someone invariably fair-haired and blue-eyed and male. After introducing himself he would explain with righteous condescension that he was taking over as instructor because his predecessor had decided to take a leave of absence.

Sometimes the news met with murmurs of confusion or disgruntlement, sometimes with a smattering of applause, sometimes both. Only once did a student call out, "I spoke with Herr Professor yesterday evening and he said nothing of this."

The new instructor allowed a thin smile. "It was a sudden decision."

"He lent me a book," the young man persisted. "Where shall I return it to him?"

The smile hardened, turned brittle. "Leave the book with the department secretary and we will see that he gets it." Without pausing he began his lecture, and the student sank back in his seat, glowering mutinously.

What will happen next? Sara wondered as policies that would have seemed outrageous a year before were written into law, enforced, obeyed. *What more does Hitler have to do before the German people realize that he is unfit to lead?* Sara and her friends asked one another in hushed whispers when they crossed paths on campus or met for a beer after a long day of study. Mildred urged her to remain watchful, but to let nothing distract her from studying, working, earning her degree. Sara devoted so much of her time to her books that Dieter ruefully lamented that he rarely saw her anymore. Fervently she read and wrote and learned, as if she were running out of time, as if she feared that she too might be banished from academia as nearly all her Jewish professors had been.

And then one day, she nearly was.

On April 25, the Reich government passed the Law Against the Overcrowding of German Schools and Universities—another title with a lie built into it, like "National Socialist," for there was no overcrowding and that was not the situation the law sought to amend. Quotas were established to reduce the number of Jews in German public schools and universities until the percentage fell to that of Jews in the general population. For new admissions, Jews could make up no more than 1.5 percent of the class. Schools that were judged to have more students preparing for a profession than there were jobs available were required to reduce enrollment, with Jews the first to go, until the school reached a maximum of 5 percent non-Aryans.

Sara was brought up short on her way to class by an ugly placard listing the provisions of the new law in dispassionate legalese. Blood rushed to her head, but her panic subsided when she read past Paragraph 4 to the exemption for certain Jews, including "Reich Germans not of Aryan descent whose fathers had fought at the front during the World War for the German Reich." Her father had served and had been decorated for bravery. Thanks to him, Sara could continue her education, for now.

Nevertheless, her entire academic future seemed imperiled, and she felt helpless outrage for her fellow students and friends who had been expelled. She wanted to resist, to fight back, but how? What could one undergraduate do against such crushing opposition?

Her parents urged caution, warning her not to jeopardize her own precarious position. "This is not the same as ignoring a boycott," her father said over dinner two days after the law was announced.

"It's very much the same," Sara countered. "What if they come for bankers next? What if you lose your job?"

"Mr. Panofsky would never comply with orders to fire his fellow Jews."

"And if the Nazis close down the bank entirely?"

"I doubt anyone will harm Mr. Panofsky or his interests," her father replied. "He has a plan to protect himself and his family from the Nazis. It will require the unwitting cooperation of the American ambassador, but if it succeeds, *when* it succeeds, not even the most zealous SA man will harass him. And if Mr. Panofsky is protected, he will protect his employees."

Sara's mother shook her head, puzzled. "The ambassador left Germany last month after their new president was inaugurated."

"I meant his successor, whoever he may be. Mr. Roosevelt will surely appoint a new ambassador soon."

"Let's hope nothing happens to Mr. Panofsky in the meantime," said Sara's mother.

Despite her father's certainty that his job was secure, Sara could not shake off pervasive anxiety about her future. One evening, as she and Dieter strolled hand in hand through the Tiergarten after seeing *42nd Street* at the cinema, her worries about potential new restrictions upon Jewish students spilled from her, until he twice had to plead with her to lower her voice, as she was attracting curious stares.

"I'm sorry I'm so upset," she said, swallowing hard, blinking back tears, "but the thought that I might be expelled from the university all because of my religion terrifies me."

"You don't have to worry," Dieter said. "Your father is a veteran. You're exempt from the quotas. The law says so."

"What if the law changes? We Jews face more restrictions every day. Although I'm exempt now, that may change tomorrow. And what about all the other Jews whose fathers didn't serve? How can I sit in the lecture hall, smug and satisfied, when my friends have been shut out?"

"Sara, listen." Halting on the footpath, he took both of her hands in his. "I don't think the University of Berlin is foolish enough to let a bright student like you slip away—"

She choked out a laugh. "They let Herr Professor Einstein get away. He's at Princeton now. If they don't bend the rules to keep *him*—"

"That was their mistake, and surely they've learned from it. If you do have to leave the university, it doesn't have to be the end of your education. You can study on your own, as I did."

"If they don't ban Jews from libraries next."

"If they do, I'll buy you every book you need." Dieter raised her hands to his lips and kissed them. "Darling, I promise to love you and protect you every day for the rest of my life."

A new warmth in his voice gave her pause. "Thank you, Dieter," she said, uncertain. She thought it would be rude to explain that she wanted to be able to stand on her own, in need of no one's protection.

"I thought this would be a happier evening," he said wryly, "but I can't delay on that account, not when I might put some of your fears to rest." Still clasping her hands, he knelt upon one knee. "Sara, darling, when I said I promise to love and protect you, I meant that I want to do so as your husband. Will you do me the honor of becoming my wife?"

Sara gazed down at him, speechless. She was angry, she was upset, she was frustrated—not at him, of course, but all the same—and he wanted her to think about love and promises and forever. The sudden, wrenching shift rendered her dizzy. "I'm sorry," she managed to say. "What?"

He reached into his breast pocket and pulled out a small box. "Sara, my love, will you marry me?"

He opened the box to reveal a beautiful ring, a sparking diamond in a cluster of small emeralds.

She inhaled deeply, silently berating herself for not feeling the over-whelming joy that a young woman ought to feel at such a significant moment, but wishing instead that he had waited for a happier, more romantic occasion. "Have you spoken to my parents?" she said in a small voice.

"You're a modern young woman. I wanted to ask you first. If you accept me, then I'll go to your parents."

She liked that; she smiled, her anger and worries receding. "I accept," she said, tears springing into her eyes. "Yes, I'll marry you."

He rose, slipped the ring on her finger, and kissed her, and in that moment she did feel safe and protected. The love they shared was precious and powerful. All the Nazis knew how to do was rage and destroy, but together she and Dieter would build something stronger than all of them.

For all his hatred, for all his misused authority, Hitler could not diminish their love or legislate it away.

CHAPTER FOURTEEN

April–May 1933

Mildred

Hitler's new Aryan Laws provoked outrage and indignation not only from Jews but from all Germans who could not abide the oppression of their fellow citizens. With increasing dismay, Mildred encouraged her Jewish students to persevere and bade sad farewells to colleagues who had decided to leave Germany rather than lived in dread of dismissal or arrest.

Not everyone who wanted to emigrate could. One day in late April, Samson Knoll, a student Mildred had known at the University of Berlin, appealed to her on behalf of Alfred Futran, a Jewish bookseller and journalist whose father had been shot by right-wing extremists in 1920 during an attempted coup. "Futran has to leave the country," said Samson. "You have contacts at the American embassy. Would you help my friend get to America?"

"The U.S. has immigration quotas," Mildred cautioned, though her heart went out to him. "Your friend might have to wait years until his case comes to the top of the list."

"It would be enough to help him get out of Germany." Samson grasped her hand in both of his. "Please. I wouldn't ask if it weren't urgent."

Deeply affected, Mildred promised to speak to a friend at the embassy. That friend was U.S. consul George Messersmith, but although he sympathized, he could not expedite Futran's immigration to the United States. "The best I can do is to get him to Paris," he said.

Mildred thanked him profusely, and in the days that followed, she made similar requests for other friends. Messersmith always did what he could.

As an American in a country increasingly hostile to foreigners, she sometimes wondered if she too ought to leave Germany. At the end of March, three American men visiting Berlin on business had been confronted by a group of Brownshirts after they had failed to offer the Nazi salute to Hitler's motorcade. Arrested by the SA, they had been taken to headquarters, stripped, and left to shiver in a cold cell overnight. In the morning they had been beaten into unconsciousness and dumped on the street. Soon thereafter, a United Press International correspondent had been arrested without charge, but after Messersmith made repeated inquiries, he had been released unharmed.

Mildred believed that she did not stand out as a foreigner the way American businessmen and journalists did, but she visited the U.S. embassy frequently and was active in the American Women's Club, so perhaps she was fooling herself. But even if she were, how could she contemplate leaving Germany, where she had built a life for herself among beloved family and friends? Arvid did not want to emigrate, and she could not bear to go without him. To a casual observer, she appeared German. Surely she would be safe as long as she did nothing to draw the attention of anti-American thugs.

"We need a strong ambassador to deal with these Nazi outrages," Messersmith confided to Mildred after the UPI correspondent's release. "Let's hope the new president sends one soon."

In the meantime, many of the ambassador's duties fell to Messersmith and Counselor of Embassy George Gordon, including securing the release of Americans rounded up by the new state secret police, the Geheime Staatspolizei, Gestapo for short. The censored press reported almost nothing about attacks on Americans, but anxious rumors spread swiftly among the small expatriate community. Since it was well known that Mildred and Messersmith were friends, she was often asked to confirm shocking reports of arrests or assaults. Whenever the American Women's Club met in its comfortable suite on the Belle-vuestrasse near the consulate for lunches, lectures, games of bridge, or teas, she endured a barrage of questions for which, over time, it became increasingly difficult to find reassuring answers.

For everyone who opposed the Nazis, discretion became paramount as the government imposed *Gleichschaltung* on the country, forcibly bringing all aspects of German society into alignment with Nazi ideology. Schools were an essential early target of this "synchronizing." Throughout Germany, teachers and staff were investigated, and those considered non-Aryan or politically questionable were permanently suspended.

Mildred was not surprised when the Berlin Abendgymnasium, a progressive institution founded by the Social Democrats, came under particular scrutiny. After the Easter recess, she returned to school only to discover that the break would be extended indefinitely while the Nazis conducted a thorough inspection. A secretary confided that the administration was resigned to making whatever distasteful concessions were required to keep the school open.

"I don't stand a chance," said Mildred, pacing in their flat while Arvid studied in his favorite chair in the cupola. "I'm the only woman on the faculty and a foreigner. All they have to do is ask Herr Schönemann why he dismissed me from the University of Berlin and I'll be fired for sure."

Arvid tried to keep her spirits up, but she was so certain her dismissal was imminent that when she received a letter announcing the date the school would reopen, she was unsure whether she would be expected to teach or to clean out her desk. The first day back would be for faculty only, an all-day meeting to address issues raised during the inspection. Perhaps they intended to fire her in person.

The appointed day came, and upon her arrival, Mildred was shocked to learn that although she had somehow held on to her job, half of the faculty had been dismissed, including the principal and the four tenured professors who prepared and proctored graduation exams. Dr. Stecher, the student adviser, had been appointed the interim director. Mildred fought to keep her expression impassive during his opening remarks, wherein he denounced the school's "outspoken liberal-democratic tradition" and "faded ideology," and declared that the momentous historical events of 1933 had propelled the school into a great new age of "powerful becoming." As soon as he concluded—to tepid, perfunctory applause—his assistants scrambled to reassign students to the twelve remaining instructors. Immediately thereafter, a chapter of the National Socialist German Students' Association was established at the school in order to encourage students to conform to the ideals of the new state. Classes resumed, and by the time final exams began, every trace of the Berlin Abendgymnasium's Social Democratic origin and philosophy had been expunged.

The first day of May was traditionally a time when German trade unions celebrated their solidarity with parades and speeches, but that year the Nazis appropriated May Day for their own purposes, declaring it "National Labor Day" and making it a paid holiday in an effort to win over the workers. Enormous rallies and festivals were held throughout the country, but the largest was in Berlin, where even previously skeptical labor organizations joined in the spectacle. Tens of thousands of people marched past Mildred and Arvid's windows overlooking Hasenheide, singing, shouting slogans, holding banners high en route to the Tempelhof airfield, where more than a million performers and enthusiastic onlookers packed the grounds. As swastika banners unfurled overhead, twelve large blocks of uniformed marchers went through their paces with crisp military precision, evoking ecstatic cheers from most of the crowd and sickening dread from others.

"How beautiful it was," Mildred wrote to her mother the next day, adopting a simple code she trusted her mother would understand, saying the exact opposite of what she meant. "Thousands upon thousands of people marched in order, singing and playing through the majestic streets which radiate from our home. I thought of the preparedness parades in our country at the beginning of the Great War. There is a great impulse in masses of people which can be roused—a very great and beautiful impulse. You know that I thought this impulse was directed rightly in the war and I think it is being directed rightly in the same way now. It is a very beautiful and serious thing—as serious as death."

Later, Mildred learned that even as she was putting pen to paper, the Nazis were executing a coordinated strike on Social Democrat trade unions throughout the country, breaking into their offices, shutting down their publications, seizing their funds. Union leaders were arrested and held in protective custody in concentration camps—except for those who were killed outright, allegedly for resisting arrest.

"One day the Nazis celebrate the worker," said Arvid, "and the next they destroy him."

"Surely the German people see the same pattern we do," said Mildred. "They can't be distracted by rallies and entertainments forever. Eventually it's going to come down to right and wrong, common sense versus nonsense."

Arvid said nothing.

"Don't you think so?" Mildred prompted. "Things can't keep going on this way. Eventually the people are going to say enough is enough."

"Which people?" said Arvid. "The Communists and labor organizers in prison camps? The German Jews being stripped of their civil rights day by day? The hungry students swept up in Hitler's enthusiasm because they want easy answers and someone to blame?"

"Rational people," said Mildred. "People who act out of decency, compassion, and respect for the rule of law rather than hatred and fear. That is the real Germany, not—" Standing in the cupola, she made a sweeping gesture from the street below their window toward the Tempelhof airfield. "Not that frenzy of lies we saw yesterday."

"Are you sure there are more of us than there are of them?"

"There must be."

"I once thought so. I'm not so sure anymore. But even if our numbers are small, I can't jettison my most deeply held convictions just to go along with the majority."

"I can't either."

"Then we won't." Arvid took her hands in his. "We'll remain true to ourselves, but we must be careful."

Mildred knew this all too well. As *Gleichschaltung* inexorably took hold all around her, she had begun to feel too anxious to speak freely on political matters except in the private homes of friends and family. In the classroom, she guarded her words even among members of their progressive study group, in case an unsympathetic person lurked within earshot.

The presence of the National Socialist German Students' Association steadily transformed the character of the Berlin Abendgymnasium. Although Mildred fought to keep the group's influence out of her classroom, she could not avoid the placards posted in the hallways listing their Twelve Theses for restoring the purity of German language and literature. Most were demands to purge German culture of "Jewish intellectualism" and get back to the "pure and unadulterated" expression of its folk traditions. "Our most dangerous enemy is the Jew and those who are his slaves," the fourth thesis shrilled, and the fifth began, "A Jew can only think Jewish. If he writes in German, he is lying."

There was no logic to the Twelve Theses, only hatred and rage, and it sickened Mildred to see students reading the placards and discussing them earnestly as if they were truths meriting intellectual inquiry rather than so much garbage interlaced with invective. Her heart ached to see some of her own students eagerly preparing for the "Action Against the Un-German Spirit" called for by the association's Main Office for Press and Propaganda. Chapters were encouraged to compile blacklists of "degenerate" authors, write articles denouncing the Jewish influence on German literary culture, and submit the documents to their local press and radio. Their publicity campaign would culminate on May 10 in a vast, nationwide *Säuberung*—a literary cleansing by fire.

As twilight descended that fateful night, Mildred stood at the cupola windows pensively watching lights come on in windows up and down Hasenheide. Arvid found her there and gently embraced her from behind. "We don't have to go," he said, gazing over her shoulder to the scene outside. "Imagining it is bad enough. You don't have to watch it happen."

"No, I do." Mildred inhaled deeply, turned in the circle of his arms, and kissed him. "I have to see with my own eyes just how desperate things have become, or I won't believe it."

Pulling on a warm sweater to fend off the cool spring night, she followed Arvid downstairs and outside, where the sweet aromas of *Kuchen* and vanilla still wafted from the patisserie though it had closed hours before. She took Arvid's arm as they walked quickly to the University of Berlin, where his cousin Dietrich Bonhoeffer waited for them outside his office building.

"Students have been building the pyre for four days," he said as they walked toward the Opernplatz, where thousands of students, citizens, and a few professors in robes and caps milled about, jittery with anticipation. "They started by emptying the entire library of the Institut für Sexualwissenschaft, and since then countless other books have followed, works by Freud, Einstein, Mann—"

Dietrich broke off at the sound of shouts and cheers and singing. As they turned to look down the street, Mildred's heart sank at the sight of the familiar flickering red glare lighting up the elegant buildings along Unter der Linden.

"Yet another parade," muttered Arvid, taking Mildred's hand, his gaze fixed on the approaching marchers. "More torches."

"But this time, the torches that light their way will also plunge them into darkness," said Dietrich quietly. "The darkness of intolerance and ignorance, more dangerous than the darkest night."

Students, SA, SS, Hitler Youth—toward the Opernplatz they marched, row after row of them, their faces sinister in the garish light. In their arms were books seized from school libraries, from bookshops, from shelves in homes where Mildred imagined bewildered parents lamenting the strange fanaticism that had transformed their beloved children into frightening strangers. A thunderous roar of voices drew her attention back to the square, where torches were flung upon the pile of books, smoldering, smoking, rising into flame.

As the marchers approached the pyre to throw more books onto the blaze, Mildred felt a cold, sickening shiver run up her spine as tens of thousands of voices began chanting a litany of Fire Oaths—first, the offense against German language and literature; next, what must succeed it; and last, the author to be consigned to oblivion. "*Against* class struggle and materialism," they chanted. "*For* national community and an idealistic way of life. Marx and Kautsky!"

An earsplitting roar followed as the men's books were thrown onto the pyre.

"*Against* decadence and moral decay. *For* discipline and decency in family and state. Mann, Glaeser, and Kästner!"

The acrid smoke stung Mildred's eyes and her breath caught in her throat. So many works by authors she respected and admired, whose brilliant words she taught to her students. Erich Remarque's autobiographical novel of the Great War, *All Quiet on the Western Front*. Works by Theodor Wolff and Georg Bernhard. For their corrupting foreign influence, Ernest Hemingway and Jack London. For pacifism, for advocating for the disabled, for seeking better conditions for workers and women's rights, Helen Keller.

Reich Minister of Propaganda Joseph Goebbels addressed the crowd from a podium draped with a swastika banner, his usually resonant tenor raspy from smoke or overuse. "The era of extreme Jewish intellectualism has come to an end, and the German revolution has again opened the way for the true essence of being German," he declaimed, each word precisely enunciated. "Over the past fourteen years, you students have had to suffer in silent shame the humiliations of the Weimar Republic. Your libraries were inundated with the trash and filth of Jewish literati. The old past lies in flames. The new times will arise from the flame that burns in our hearts!"

On and on he went, stirring the crowd into a frenzy of exultant anger. Clasping Arvid's hand so tightly her fingers ached, Mildred watched, horrified and dismayed, as the most cherished works of some of the world's most celebrated authors turned to ash and smoke.

Then, a jolt of recognition so sharp it left her breathless.

Among the marchers, clad in SA brown, one of her former students filed past, not two feet from where she stood. His gaze fixed ardently upon the towering pyre, he did not recognize her, but she knew him, and she knew the book tucked under his arm—a collection of plays by the renowned nineteenth-century poet Heinrich Heine, a German Jew.

As she watched him march off to destroy the book, Mildred knew that at universities throughout Germany, other disgruntled, angry, vengeful students were destroying the very books that could teach them that this was wrong, that this would create nothing but ash and loss. It would not bring them joy, or find them work, or fill their bellies.

It would not erase the wisdom that resonated from the author's mind to the reader's heart.

As flame and smoke rose to the sky, a line from Heine's play *Almansor* drifted into her thoughts: "*Dort, wo man Bücher verbrennt, verbrennt man am Ende auch Menschen.*"

Where they burn books, in the end they will also burn people.

CHAPTER FIFTEEN

May 1933

Greta

Greta did not respond to Adam's note to tell him she was returning to Germany. She was not entirely sure why. Perhaps she did not want him to think she was coming back for his sake rather than her country's; fighting the rise of fascism in her homeland was more important to her than their ill-fated romance. Perhaps she wanted the option to change her mind if she decided at the last minute that she could not see him.

She arrived in Frankfurt am Main two days after tens of thousands of books had gone up in flames in city squares throughout Germany. Students from the Universität Frankfurt had staged their own cleansing by fire in Römerberg in front of city hall. By the time Greta passed through the square, the pile of ash was gone, cleared away by rain or an assiduous street sweeper. Somehow it seemed that the stink of burning lingered, like a ghost from the past or a foreboding vision of the future.

Before setting out from Dover, she had bought a newspaper at a stand near the pier. On the front page was an open letter to the Student Body of Germany from Helen Keller, the famous blind and deaf American author and advocate. "History has taught you nothing if you think you can kill ideas," she had written. "Tyrants have tried to do that often before, and the ideas have risen up in their might and destroyed them. You can burn my books and the books of the best minds in Europe, but the ideas in them have seeped through a million channels and will continue to quicken other minds." She reminded them that years before, out of love and compassion for the German people, she had arranged for all the royalties from her book sales to go to the care of German soldiers blinded during the Great War, but she concluded with a warning: "Do not imagine that your barbarities to the Jews are unknown here. God sleepeth not, and He will visit His judgment upon you. Better were it for you to have a millstone hung around your neck and sink into the sea than to be hated and despised of all men."

The stirring words had heartened Greta even as the winds off the Channel threatened to tear the newspaper from her grasp, but once she arrived in Frankfurt, the oppressive weight of the Reich fell upon her shoulders like a lead cloak, compelling her to walk with her eyes downcast and shoulders slightly bent, curved protectively around her heart. She forced herself to lift her chin and stride with confidence, suitcases in hand, not seeking out the gaze of SA and SS men but not averting her eyes either. She refused to let the Nazis make her regret returning to Germany. She loved her homeland and would not abandon it to fascist barbarians without a fight.

When she entered her boardinghouse room, at first she found nothing amiss. She had asked her landlady to collect her mail and water the plants in her absence, but as she unpacked, she realized that some items on her dresser had been moved, and the stack of mail on the table near the door was thinner than it should have been. When her gaze fell on her disordered desk, she discovered that her typewriter was missing.

Greta hurried downstairs and knocked on her landlady's door. "Did you borrow my typewriter?" she asked as soon as the older woman answered.

"Well, hello to you too," the landlady replied. "I wasn't sure you were coming back."

"Did you borrow my typewriter?" Greta asked again, keeping her voice steady. "It's all right if you did, but I need it back, please."

"I don't have it." The older woman's voice quavered. "The SA came around asking questions about you. I had to let them search your room. How could I refuse?"

"The SA took my typewriter? Did they say why?"

"No, but I'm to call them if you come back. I suppose I can wait a day—"

"No need for that. I'll go see them right now."

The older woman blanched. "Are you sure that's wise?"

"How else will I get my typewriter back?"

Glancing about for eavesdroppers, her landlady argued against it. When Greta's resolve did not waver, she sighed, withdrew into her room, and returned with a card the SA officer had left behind.

When Greta arrived at the SA headquarters near the Rathaus on the Römerberg, the clerk studied some papers, grimaced, and ordered her to follow him down a corridor. He halted before a small, windowless room furnished with a wooden table and two chairs placed on opposite sides. "Sit," the clerk ordered, gesturing into the chamber. She obeyed, her stomach lurching when he remained in the hall and locked her in.

Heart pounding, she stood and paced the chamber, wishing she had never come. She tested the doorknob, but she had scarcely touched it when someone began to turn it from the other side. Quickly she returned to her chair and composed herself as two black-clad SA men entered, one young and tall, the other older and stocky, both regarding her severely.

The older man carried a folder, which he opened upon the table as he seated himself. The younger man planted himself between the table and the door. "Name?" the older man asked, his voice clipped.

Greta assumed that information was in the file, but she said, "Greta Lorke."

He eyed her, frowning. "Full name?"

"Margaretha Lorke."

"Place and date of birth?"

"Frankfurt an der Oder, December 14, 1902." She watched as he checked off two items on the first paper in the file. "I beg your pardon, but I've come to collect my typewriter. One of your officers took it from my apartment, and I would like it back, please."

"Why do you need it?"

"I'm a graduate student, and I use it to write papers, correspondence, the usual things."

"And flyers summoning your comrades to treasonous gatherings?"

Greta started. "Of course not."

"Did you help the Jew Karl Mannheim escape to England?"

"Escape? Why would Professor Mannheim need to escape?"

He slammed a fist on the table. "Did you or did you not assist him?"

"I assisted him in his move to the United Kingdom," Greta replied, shaken. "He hired me to do so. My confusion is regarding the word 'escape.' Herr Mannheim left Frankfurt to join the faculty of the London School of Economics, not for any nefarious purpose."

"Where did you learn to fly?" the younger officer demanded. "In the United States?"

Greta looked from him to the older man and back. "I don't understand."

"Do you deny going to the United States?" asked the older officer, incredulous.

"Of course not. I attended graduate school at the University of Wisconsin. I'm proud of my achievement and I certainly make no secret of it."

The younger officer planted his hands on the table and loomed over her. "Where is your airplane?"

Greta inhaled deeply and held his gaze. "I honestly have no idea what you're talking about. I've never flown in an airplane. I'm just here for my typewriter."

"The typewriter you used to produce this?" The older officer took a page from the file and placed it on the table before her. "Will you deny that you posted these throughout the university's Department of Sociology?" He indicated her name, handwritten in the lower right corner. "That is your signature, yes?"

Greta stared at the paper, dumbfounded. "Yes, but—"

"*Fliegergruppe?*" the younger officer barked, jabbing a long finger at the title phrase. "A flying group with a zeppelin?"

"Where is your aircraft?" the elder officer demanded.

Greta burst into laughter. The two officers gaped at her, shocked.

"I'm sorry," she gasped, fighting to suppress her wild mirth. "I mean no disrespect. Yes, I did create these flyers and post them on the department's bulletin boards. The *Fliegergruppe* is only a study group. We call it our flying group because we fly from one topic and location to another; from one meeting to the next. You must be new to Frankfurt or you would have heard of Zeppelinallee—it's a street just west of campus." She shook her head and pressed her lips together, aware that their bewilderment might quickly give way to anger. "We discuss topics in sociology, collaborate on papers, study for exams. I swear to you, there isn't a single pilot among us."

The older officer regarded her sourly. "You would do well to choose another name for your group."

"Yes, I see that now. I'll suggest that at our next meeting."

"There may be no need." The younger officer straightened and clasped his hands behind his back. "While you were abroad, so many of your professors decided to take leaves of absence that your entire department has been closed down."

Greta studied him, uncertain. "I hadn't heard that."

"What will you do now, Fräulein Lorke?" he asked, feigning sorrow. "Go back to England, to the Jew Mannheim?"

"I suppose—" Greta's thoughts raced to come up with an answer that would please them. "I will go home to Frankfurt an der Oder, to care for my aging parents."

The older officer nodded. "And once you're settled at home, you should marry. *Kinder, Kirche, Küche!*"

She nodded and bowed her head in false submission. "I'm grateful to you both for your patience. Now that we've cleared up this misunderstanding, may I have my typewriter, please?"

"Why should you need it, if you are no longer going to be a student?" asked the younger officer, feigning puzzlement.

"For correspondence, for conducting household business for my parents . . ." Greta shrugged. "It is mine, after all, and I've done nothing wrong, nothing to warrant having my property confiscated."

"I think you will be better off without the temptation of a typewriter, Fräulein Lorke." The older officer closed his file and stood. "We will put it to good use in service of the Reich."

She pressed her lips together to hold back a furious retort. She could not afford to buy a new typewriter every time a Nazi became confused.

Silently fuming, she allowed the younger officer to escort her to the door, where she nodded curtly instead of returning his sharp, one-armed salute. She went directly to the university, where she confirmed that the Sociology Department was essentially defunct. Professor Mannheim had left just in time.

Nothing remained to hold her in Frankfurt. She gave notice to her landlady, closed accounts and settled bills, and packed up her belongings. Two days later, she boarded the morning train for Berlin.

Greta's first task was to find a place to stay. With only a small amount of savings and no certainty of finding work soon, she eschewed convenience and luxury and instead sublet a room in a boathouse on the Havel in Pichelswerder, a far western suburb just north of Grunewald.

Next, she left a message for Adam at the Staatstheater: If he wished to see her, she would be at the Romanisches Café at three o'clock the following afternoon.

He came, as she had known he would; unexpectedly, he arrived first. When she entered, he left his table and crossed the room to meet her. He grasped her hands, pulled her close, kissed her cheek, and murmured words of welcome and endearment, all with an intense, almost feverish energy.

They sat down and ordered *Kaffee und Kuchen*. "Are you merely visiting or have you come to stay?" he asked.

"I plan to stay." Honesty compelled her to add, "For now." If her savings ran out before she found work, she might have to return home to her parents after all.

"You've returned to a very different city than the one you left."

"I saw that as soon as I got off the train." Suppressing a shudder, Greta sipped her coffee and glanced out the window, where swastika banners hung from the windows and balconies of the building across the street. "Anna Klug insists that German theater is dead. Please tell me she's wrong."

He grimaced. "I wish I could."

The Staatstheater had become almost intolerable under its new management, he explained, as she savored the sound of his voice, his familiar expressions and gestures. The director had not renewed the contract of Adam's brother-in-law, Hans Otto, despite the acclaim he had received for his magnificent performance in *Faust, Part II*. Otto's occasional costar, the beautiful and popular Elisabeth Bergner, a Jew, had fled Germany. Adam's frequent collaborator, the author Armin Wegner, had disappeared into the Gestapo's prison camp system after writing an impassioned letter denouncing antisemitism and mailing it to Hitler in care of Nazi headquarters in Munich. Other friends and colleagues had been arrested, or had fled the country, or had chosen cautious silence, which provoked Adam's disgust.

"I can't shirk my responsibility to remain politically active," he said emphatically, arousing both Greta's admiration and her unease. "You must become politically engaged too. Abandon your social scientist's professional detachment and get involved. Don't just stand at a distance and observe, analyze, and report. Write. Speak out. Protest."

"I intend to," she replied, a trifle defensively. "Why else do you think I came back? But I'm going to be smart about it. I'm not going to send Adolf Hitler heartfelt letters imploring him to stop hating the Jews."

"Yes, you're right, discretion can be the better part of valor when one is overmatched. But in this fight, everyone must take a side. Whoever does not actively oppose the Nazis abets them."

"I will never abet them," she shot back, her voice low and fierce. Their eyes met over the table. His gaze was warm and admiring, and a searing rush of love and desire flooded her, wonderful and terrifying, until she had to tear her gaze away before she was swept up in it and lost.

A long moment passed in silence. She sipped her coffee, which was cooling in the cup, and took a small bite of cake.

"Are you working?" he eventually asked. "Are you going to finish your doctorate at the University of Berlin?"

"When they're forcing students out? I can't imagine they'd let me in." Greta shook her head. "I thought I'd look for freelance editing and tutoring. I got by on such piecework before. I'm sure I could again."

"I'll ask around for you, if you like. Some of my theater friends might need an assistant."

"Thank you." She took a pencil and notepad from her purse, jotted down her new address and telephone number, tore the paper free, and slid it across the table to him. "I appreciate your help."

He reached across the table for the paper, but took her hand instead. "Greta, you told me to call you when I was single. I'm not."

Her heart sank. "When you wrote to me, I hoped that meant your situation had changed."

"If I divorce Gertrud, Marie will never let me see my son again."

"So you've said."

"Gertrud and I have an understanding."

"I'm not like you and Gertrud and Marie and Otto. You may call me bourgeoise or old-fashioned, but I could never be happy in such an arrangement. I don't have to be married, but I need to know that my man is mine and mine alone."

His hand tightened around hers. "I would be. I love you more than I've ever loved anyone. I swear to you, I would be yours, no one else's."

Reluctantly, she slipped her hand from his grasp. "Think it over—deeply, honestly. When you're certain, only then make me a promise I can believe."

"Greta—"

"Think it over, Adam." Quickly she rose and left the café before her resolve crumbled and she took back every word rather than risk losing him forever.

Two blocks from the café, she heard a man call her name, and at first she was torn between elation and dismay that Adam had not taken more time to consider her ultimatum. Then she turned and spotted a tall, slender man with blond hair and round wire-rimmed glasses raising a hand in greeting as he hurried to catch up with her.

"Arvid?" she gasped. "Arvid Harnack?"

"Greta Lorke. It *is* you." Astonished, he seized her hand and shook it. "I hardly believe it. You haven't changed a bit."

She laughed a bit shakily. "Oh, but I have."

"What have you been doing all these years? When did you leave Wisconsin?" He shook his head and smiled. "So many questions, but Mildred will want to hear the answers too. Come home with me and dine with us. It isn't far."

Mildred. At the sound of her old friend's name, Greta felt a pang of fondness and yearning so acute that her breath caught in her throat.

"I'd love to see Mildred," she said. "Should we call ahead and let her know I'm coming?"

"No, no, let it be a surprise." Smiling, he offered her his arm, and after the barest hesitation, she took it. "Where there's enough for two, there's enough for three."

Considering the number of advanced degrees Arvid had accumulated and his family connections, Greta was astonished to learn that he and Mildred resided in Neukölln, the grim lower-class neighborhood Greta remembered well from her student work-study job at the orphanage. "Darling?" Arvid called out as he unlocked the door to the Harnacks' flat on the fifth floor of 61 Hasenheide and motioned for Greta to proceed him inside. "Come see whom I found walking around Gendarmenmarkt."

Smiling, Mildred entered from an adjacent room. She was even slimmer than Greta remembered, her clothes neat and flattering though a trifle faded and discreetly made over, but her golden blond hair, kind smile, and open, welcoming gaze were exactly as Greta remembered.

"Greta!" Mildred cried, hurrying to embrace her old friend, kissing her on both cheeks. "I can't believe it. It's been too long."

"Much too long," said Greta. "I've missed you terribly."

Over a hearty cabbage, potato, and sausage soup, they shared stories of where life had taken them since they had parted company four years earlier. The frugal meal and the location of the flat had raised Greta's suspicions that the couple was not particularly well off, and yet she was taken aback to learn that Arvid had been unable to get a university appointment.

"At least you completed your degree," said Greta, chagrined to admit failure to her former rival. "Despite all my time and study, I still haven't earned my doctorate."

"Neither have I," said Mildred ruefully. "I'm still toiling away on my dissertation."

"My student days are over," said Greta. "I hope to find work in theater or journalism instead."

"Journalism is a dangerous profession these days," said Arvid, "unless you're willing to hold your nose and write for the Nazi press."

"Never," Greta retorted.

"In the meantime, you should join our literary salon," said Mildred. "We've put together a lively crowd of writers, editors, publishers, journalists, and intellectuals for discussing literature and publishing. It's an artistic group, not political. You could join our progressive study group for something closer to the Friday Niters."

"I do miss the Friday Niters." Greta sighed, wistful. "And sodas at Rennebohm's, and Bascom Hill, and walking the path along Lake Mendota in autumn."

As twilight descended, they reminisced about their favorite places in Madison and mutual friends—John Commons, William Ellery Leonard, Clara Leiser, Rudolf and Franziska Heberle, and others. The time flew by until Greta realized with a start that it was quite late.

"Promise you'll come to our next salon," Mildred said as she and Arvid saw her to the door.

"I will." Greta embraced her friend once more before hurrying away, grateful for their reunion, an interlude of joy in a bleak season.

It was after midnight when she finally reached Pichelswerder, but she felt perfectly safe. Her unexpected reunion with the Harnacks had diminished the pain of her bittersweet meeting with Adam. The streetlights illuminated the way ahead, and other couples and groups of friends were strolling the sidewalks, their quiet conversations and occasional bursts of laughter reminding her that there was much to cherish in life even in those uncertain times. Only when she reached the boathouse and saw a shadow shift near the front entrance did she halt, instantly wary, and wish that she were not alone.

Then the figure stepped into the light, and she recognized Adam, his hat pushed back, hands thrust into his pockets, mouth set determinedly. "You told me to come when I was certain," he said, drawing closer. "I told Gertrud I want a divorce. She swore that she would never consent."

Her hopes plummeted just as they had begun to rise. "I see."

"I'll keep trying. Maybe someday she'll fall in love with someone and release me." He took her hands. "You deserve better, but if you can accept this wretched situation, and accept me with all my imperfections, you'll be the only woman I'll ever love for the rest of my life. I promise."

Tears sprang to her eyes. She wanted more, but in such ugly, uncertain times, she would be a fool to let any chance of happiness with the man she loved slip through her fingers.

"I believe you," she said, and she kissed him.

CHAPTER SIXTEEN

June 1933

Sara

Sara offered to accompany Dieter when he asked her parents for their blessing, but he preferred to speak to them alone. She waited in the garden while they met in the parlor, imagining their joyful surprise, her father's proud smiles, her mother's happy tears. But as the minutes dragged by, she become increasingly nervous, pacing beneath the linden trees, absently chewing on a thumbnail, a childhood habit that unfortunately reappeared at particularly anxious moments. Exasperated with herself, she thrust her hands into the pockets of her dress and kept them there until she heard the sunroom door open and voices murmur. She hurried back to the house, her heart racing with anticipation, but her parents' expressions brought her to an abrupt halt. Dieter beamed happily, but her father's face was curiously stoic, her mother's in constant motion as it shifted between distress and a tearful smile.

They congratulated her, kissed her, and wished her and Dieter every happiness. And yet in the days that followed, they did not ask when she and Dieter planned to marry, nor did they announce the engagement to their friends. Sara tried not to take offense. Several years before, although her parents had been very fond of Wilhelm, Amalie's engagement had rendered them more regretful than happy. Their reluctance had eased after Amalie convinced them that she would not convert,

Wilhelm would respect their traditions, and their children would be raised in the Jewish faith. Even so, the gossip provoked by the unusual intermarriage had annoyed them greatly, and sometimes Sara's mother had wept alone, unaware that afterward her red eyes and pale face betrayed her secret grief.

Several years had passed. The gossip had faded, the blissfully happy newlyweds had become devoted parents, and Wilhelm had become part of the family. Sara had assumed that her sister's happiness would make it easier for her parents to accept her own marriage to a Christian. Instead, they seemed to have greater misgivings about her engagement than they had ever shown for Amalie's.

Could something else be troubling them, something that had nothing to do with religion or their dismay at the prospect of becoming the subjects of pity and gossip again?

One day in mid-June, Sara packed a basket with sandwiches, fruit, and a large flask of strong coffee and went to see her brother at the *Berliner Tageblatt*. He could not spare the time for a picnic in the Tiergarten, so they shared lunch in his office instead, clearing a space on his cluttered desk for a table, closing the door to keep harried copy clerks from rushing in and out.

Natan sat back, propped his feet up on a stack of books, took a bite of sandwich, and raised his eyebrows at her in a silent, good-humored inquiry.

"I don't think Mama and Papa want me to marry Dieter," Sara began, recognizing her cue. "I don't know if they object because Dieter isn't Jewish or some other reason." She sighed and picked a bit of bread crust from her sandwich. "Do you like Dieter?"

"I don't *dis*like him. How old are you, nineteen? Amalie didn't get married until she was twenty-four. What's your rush?"

"There's no rush. Dieter and I agreed not to marry until I finish my education."

"Good. I strongly endorse any plan that involves a long engagement—the longer, the better."

"If you think I'm making a terrible mistake, I wish you would just tell me."

He took another bite of sandwich and eyed her thoughtfully as he chewed and swallowed, stalling for time. "Maybe Dieter isn't the man I would have chosen for you, but as long as you're happy and he's good to you, I'm satisfied."

"Why wouldn't you have chosen him?"

"You don't seem to have much in common. I know he's good-looking, especially if you like Aryan features——"

"I wouldn't marry someone just because he's handsome." Then understanding dawned. "Aryan features. So that *is* the problem. Dieter isn't Jewish."

"It isn't a problem for me, but it might eventually become a problem for Dieter that you aren't Christian."

"Amalie and Wilhelm——"

"Wilhelm is a man of integrity and honor, a rare example of an aristocrat whose wealth and power haven't corrupted him. Dieter, on the other hand——" Natan gestured as if trying to grasp a handful of smoke. "He seems . . . insubstantial. He's one of the most amiable, inoffensive men I know, but that's because he shapes himself to his companions. Who is he, on his own? What does he stand for?"

"Would you rather have him argumentative and disagreeable?"

"If he disagrees with me, yes, I would. I'd rather have a good, honest argument than empty pleasantries any day." Natan drained the last of his coffee. "But that may just be me. Occupational hazard."

"Maybe Dieter's occupation has hazards too. A businessman has to know how to get along pleasantly with all sorts of people, regardless of his personal opinions. When you get to know him better, I'm sure you'll find many things to argue about."

"I'd almost welcome that. Listen, if you love him and he's good to you, I can't complain."

"But I want you to like him. I want you to be friends, the way you and Wilhelm are friends."

"I haven't ruled it out."

Sara knew she could not ask more than that. "Do you think Mutti and Papa feel as you do about Dieter?"

"We haven't discussed it," said Natan. "Maybe they believe no man is good enough for their daughter. They'd hardly be the first parents in history to feel that way about their daughter's fiancé."

Sara managed a wan smile, appreciating his attempt to reassure her, although it fell short.

The next day, Sara's mother suggested that they invite Dieter and his mother for supper so the parents could become better acquainted. Sara suspected that Natan was behind it; she had not sworn him to secrecy and the timing fit too well to be a coincidence. Even so, she agreed, and after some back-and-forth with Dieter, they settled on the following Sunday.

Sara scarcely knew Frau Koch, having met her only once. One spring afternoon a few months after she and Dieter began dating, Frau Koch had invited Sara to their small flat for *Kaffee und Kuchen*. She was a quiet, unsmiling woman, thin but with squared shoulders and a ramrod spine, her hands and face aged a decade beyond her forty-some years. Sara knew from Dieter's stories that his mother had had a difficult life even before his father was killed in the Great War, and that he attributed all his success to her unrelenting devotion.

Sara brought her flowers in a cut-glass vase, did her utmost to be pleasant and polite, and complimented her on the butter cake, which truly was excellent. In return Frau Koch offered faint smiles and courteous murmurs, but aside from a few hard, appraising looks she gave Sara when she thought herself unnoticed, the focus of her attention was Dieter, who carried the burden of conversation as if unaware how uncomfortable his companions seemed.

Now that Sara and Dieter were engaged, she could only hope that her future mother-in-law had a warm, friendly side she had not revealed in their first meeting.

Dieter and his mother arrived promptly at six o'clock, and as Sara's parents escorted their guests to the parlor, Frau Koch's gaze darted this way and that, taking in the crystal chandelier in the foyer, the Renoir and the Monet in the gallery, the tastefully elegant furnishings, the warmth of ample light. "You have a lovely home," she said as she seated herself in the chair Sara's father offered. "They say your kind is prosperous, and I see that it's so."

Sara stiffened, but her mother only raised her eyebrows in polite inquiry.

"Mother wanted me to go into banking," Dieter quickly added, "but my apprenticeship led me elsewhere."

Sara smiled, relieved. Frau Koch meant bankers, not Jews. Given the political climate, the Weitzes could be forgiven for assuming the worst.

Frau Koch declined a cocktail, but Dieter accepted. The parents' conversation turned to Sara and Dieter, who offered faint protests as amusing, sometimes embarrassing stories from their childhoods were shared. Over dinner, after the first course was cleared and the second was placed before them, Sara's mother turned to Frau Koch and said, "I must say we're pleased that Dieter and Sara are going to be married. Your son is a fine young man and we trust they'll be very happy together."

Frau Koch's face took on a pinched look. "I hope so, but they haven't chosen an easy path, have they?"

"I'm not sure what you mean," said Sara's mother, no less pleasantly than before.

"I've raised Dieter to love the Lord." Frau Koch's brow furrowed as if the hazards were so evident they needed no explanation. "I gather Sara has no plans to convert, but I hope my son can change her mind."

"I told you, Mutti," said Dieter amiably, "we're planning on a civil ceremony."

"A marriage that isn't blessed by the church isn't a true marriage." Frau Koch's gaze darted to Sara's parents. "No offense intended."

Sara's father inclined his head, expressionless.

Frau Koch turned back to her son. "And what about the children? Will they be baptized? Will they know the scriptures?" Her gaze lit upon Sara for a moment before returning to Dieter. "Have you given that any thought at all?"

Sara's throat constricted. In what she now realized was a glaring oversight, she and Dieter had never discussed whose religion they would pass on to their children. Sara had never posed the question because to her, the answer was obvious; in her tradition, children born of a Jewish mother were Jewish. But perhaps Dieter had different traditions that were equally obvious to him.

"It's true Sara and I have much to discuss before the wedding." Dieter reached for Sara's hand, and squeezed it once in a private message of reassurance. Looking around the table, he added, "We'll come to you often for advice. We'll respect your opinions. However, in the end, all decisions about our children will be ours alone."

He spoke so reasonably that he disarmed any argument before it could be raised. Overwhelmed, Sara lowered her eyes and pressed her napkin to her lips to hide her distress. What if her own parents objected as strongly as Frau Koch, and for similar reasons, but were keeping silent out of respect for her right to make her own decisions?

The rest of the evening passed without incident, but when Dieter bade Sara good night, he left her with a kiss and the unsettled feeling that more objections were likely to appear before the first were resolved. Pleading a headache, she thanked her parents for hosting the dinner, kissed them good night, and hurried upstairs to her room.

She prepared for bed and settled down with a well-worn copy of *The Call of the Wild* that Mildred Harnack had lent her, which Sara dared not read anywhere but at home since Jack London's works were among those burned and banned in the *Verbrennungstakt* of May 10. Always before, his evocative prose had swiftly transported her into the vast Yukon wilderness, but on that night she brooded over the concerns raised at dinner and those yet unspoken. She set the book aside and turned off the light, but sleep eluded her. Eventually she flung off the covers, drew on her dressing gown, and went to make herself a cup of chamomile tea to calm her churning thoughts. She moved quietly to avoid waking her parents, but from the top of the staircase she glimpsed light coming from the parlor and realized they were still awake.

A good, honest conversation would ease her mind better than any cup of tea, so she descended the stairs and went to meet them. Just as she was about to rap gently on the open door, she heard her father say, "Everything will be fine. He's not an unpleasant young man, or cruel, or in any way objectionable."

"Then why do we object?" her mother replied.

Sara's heart thudded. She inhaled deeply, silently, straining her ears to hear more.

"Object?" said her father. "A strong word for a small uncertainty."

"Natan calls him an empty suit."

"Natan has very high expectations for the young men who pursue his sisters."

"He always has," said her mother. "Sara loves Dieter. Shouldn't that be enough for us?"

"I suppose." Her father sighed. "We should think of all the good that may come from this marriage. He's advancing in his career and he will surely be a good provider."

"Yes, and he's very handsome, so our grandchildren will be beautiful."

"Beautiful Jews or beautiful Christians? I think Sara's mother-in-law will have the last word."

"Jakob—"

"Yes, yes, focus on the good." A chair creaked as if her father had risen and had begun to pace the room. "He'll give her an Aryan last name. That might protect her from Nazi harassment."

"And he travels abroad often. If Sara needs to flee the country, he should be able to organize a quick escape."

Their voices faded to murmurs, but Sara had heard enough. She crept back upstairs to bed, her tea forgotten. She lay under the covers, heartsick and confused, until she heard her parents climb the stairs and retire to their room down the hall. Only then was she able to drift off to sleep.

The next morning, nagged by guilt for eavesdropping, she said nothing to her parents about what she had overheard. If they sensed her downcast spirits, they hid it well. And yet Sara's mother unexpectedly followed her to the door and hugged her as she was leaving for her first class. "It's true that you and Dieter have much to discuss before you marry," she said, "but all couples do. Take heart, my dear."

"Thanks, Mutti," said Sara, blinking back tears and kissing her cheek.

Later that afternoon, instead of going directly home after her last class, Sara took the Untergrundbahn to her sister's neighborhood. She arrived at their home just as Amalie and the nanny were coming outside with the children, adorable in their matching dresses and dark brown braids. "Would you like to come to the park with us?" Amalie asked, but after she took in Sara's expression, her smile faded. "Or perhaps Mrs. Gruen can take the girls, and you and I can stay here for a cup of coffee and a good chat."

When Sara nodded, fighting back tears, her sister quickly kissed the girls goodbye, murmured instructions to Mrs. Gruen, and sent them on their way. Putting an arm around Sara's shoulders, she led her inside to the kitchen, directed her to sit, and put on a pot of coffee. "Now then," she said when they both had steaming cups in hand and a plate of English biscuits on the table between them, "why don't you tell me what's troubling you?"

Out spilled the entire story—Natan's remarks, Frau Koch's concerns, their parents' valiant attempts to find a silver lining in Sara's engagement. "I don't know what to do," Sara lamented. "I was happy, and now——" She lifted her hands and let them fall to her lap. "Everyone is anxious, and I hate that I've upset Mama and Papa, and I just want everyone to like Dieter and be happy for us."

"I like Dieter," said Amalie. "I'm happy for you. I know Wilhelm is too."

Sara felt a rush of gratitude. "Really?"

"Yes, really." Amalie reached for Sara's hand and clasped it on top of the table. "I won't pretend that the religious differences aren't significant, because of course they are. So are questions about how you'll raise your children. Wilhelm and I went through this too before we married." She smiled, but her brows drew together in concern. "Don't shy away from the difficult, uncomfortable questions. Those are the ones you most need to answer. You can't possibly prepare for every challenge that might come up in a marriage, but the question of your children's religion is one you must resolve *before* you marry. Don't imagine things will sort themselves out after your children are born. Whatever you decide, you both must be sure you can abide by that decision without harboring any secret hopes that the other will change their mind."

Reluctantly, Sara forced herself to ask, "You don't think I should break off the engagement?"

"Of course not. No one has suggested that, not even Frau Koch." Amalie studied her intently. "Unless you're suggesting it now. Are you?"

"No, not at all," said Sara quickly, shaking her head. "I love Dieter with all my heart. I want to marry him."

"Then you should." Amalie smiled, but her eyes glistened. "Oh, Sara, there's so much hatred and fear in the world right now that if you're fortunate enough to find true love, you should embrace it, cherish it, as a rare and precious gift."

Sara smiled through her tears and clasped her sister's hand tightly. She hoped that what she and Dieter had was true love. Was there really any way to know until a love was tested and either grew stronger or shattered?

"Cherish love, Sara." Amalie's voice was a soft, fierce whisper. "Only love will sustain us in these dark times. Fear can't do that. Worry can't. Only love."

CHAPTER SEVENTEEN

July 1933

Martha

The sea was calm and beautiful throughout the Dodd family's eight-day voyage from New York to Hamburg, so although Martha grieved for all she had left behind in America—the family's comfortable home on Blackstone Avenue in Hyde Park, her job as assistant literary editor at the *Chicago Tribune*, dear friends like Carl Sandburg and Thornton Wilder, who encouraged her writing—her sorrow lessened day by day. She passed the hours strolling the decks of the *Washington* with her mother, enjoying the sunshine and breezes; playing cards and cracking wise with her older brother, Bill Jr.; and dutifully listening while her father read aloud from a German history textbook for an hour every day so she would become familiar with the language. In the evenings, she drank champagne and danced with Franklin D. Roosevelt Jr., the president's second-youngest son, who by a delightful coincidence happened to be on board the same ship as his father's new ambassador to Germany.

Months before, when rumors first began swirling that William Dodd was being considered for a position in President Roosevelt's administration, he confided to his family that he hoped for an appointment to Belgium or Holland, where his role would be prestigious but his duties light enough so he could continue his academic life's work, a comprehensive history of the Old South. Then, in early June, Mr. Roosevelt phoned his office at the University of Chicago to offer him the embassy in Berlin. "I want an American liberal in Germany as a standing example," the president said, and gave him two hours to decide.

Naturally he accepted, once his wife gave her reluctant consent. William Dodd was not the sort of man to refuse a direct request from his president to serve his country.

Martha's father had invited her and Bill to come along, promising them the adventure of a lifetime. Martha could assist her mother in her role as official embassy hostess, and Bill could pursue his doctorate. Whereas Martha thought it would be a lark, full of embassy parties, cocktails with foreign diplomats, and a waltz with a prince or two, Bill said he most looked forward to experiencing German culture on the precipice of historic transformation. She teased him for his foreboding tone, the same one he used whenever he mentioned the Nazis. From the little she had read about the National Socialist movement, it sounded wonderfully exciting, youthful and vigorous and strong and noble, much like their own American Revolution. How thrilling it would be to witness the rejuvenation of Germany firsthand, and from such a vantage point as the American embassy! All that she would experience in the year ahead would invigorate her writing like nothing else.

A breathtaking glimpse of Ireland from afar—an enchanting vision of brilliant emerald hills, lush and wild in the golden dawn—heralded the end of their ocean crossing. Many passengers disembarked at Southampton a few hours later, while still more, including the young Mr. Roosevelt, went ashore at Le Havre. The Dodd family remained aboard for the dull, slow sail up the Elbe to Hamburg, where they docked at long last on July 13.

Martha had eagerly anticipated taking the famous "Flying Hamburger" express train to Berlin, but when Counselor of Embassy George Gordon met the Dodds at the pier, they discovered that no arrangements had been made to transport them to the capital. Complicating matters was the Dodds' reliable old Chevrolet, which Martha's father had insisted upon bringing along so he could drive himself rather than indulge in the customary extravagance of a chauffeur. Bill agreed to drive the car to Berlin, and while he worked his way through the mountain of paperwork required to get the car from the ship's hold onto German soil, Gordon scrambled to book two compartments aboard a disappointingly ordinary train for Martha, her parents, and himself. In the meantime, the new ambassador fielded questions from a throng of reporters, his shy wife and smiling daughter standing by his side, their arms full of bouquets presented to them by various officials and organizations.

Before long their train departed. At first, they all gathered in one compartment so that Gordon could brief them on what they could expect upon their arrival in Berlin. Martha listened politely, but she soon began to develop an intense dislike for the embassy's second in command and passionately wished she were motoring along with her brother instead. George Gordon was a gentleman of the old school, impeccably attired in an elegant, finely tailored suit more expensive than any her father had ever owned, complete with gloves, stick, and a proper hat. He had a ruddy complexion and gray-white hair, and the tips of his mustache curled upward as if to approximate the smile he had yet to offer. He spoke in a clipped, formal, and unmistakably condescending accent, and he was clearly rendered aghast by the Dodds' lack of pretension and uniformed servants. President Roosevelt had heartily endorsed her father's plan to live modestly and limit expenditures, but apparently no one had told Gordon. Most ambassadors were men of means who entertained foreign dignitaries lavishly, paying from their own pocket when they inevitably went over budget. If Gordon expected a man as principled as William Dodd to continue in that style while millions of unemployed Americans were going hungry, he was in for a rude awakening.

Finally Gordon announced that he had important political developments to discuss with the ambassador in strict confidence. Recognizing their cue, Martha and her mother left the two men alone to talk, slipping gratefully into the relative peace and quiet of the other compartment, fragrant with the flowers that had been presented to them at the pier.

"What an insufferable fellow," said Martha, moving aside a pile of bouquets and settling down in a seat by the window.

"He's only doing his job," her mother replied mildly, but her face was drawn, as if Gordon's demeanor had confirmed her worst fears of what the European dignitaries would expect of her as the ambassador's wife.

"I suppose so," Martha conceded. "Let's just hope he lets Dad do his."

She gazed at the passing scenery for a while, murmuring reassuring replies when her mother worried aloud about the duties facing her, the sudden and dramatic disruption to the comfortable pattern of her days. Eventually the rocking of the train and the rumble of the wheels upon the track lulled Martha to sleep.

She woke with a start three hours later when the train shrieked to a halt at the Lehrter Bahnhof, the majestic train station on the Spree in central Berlin. Stiff and yawning, she barely had time to rub the sleep from her eyes and put on her hat before she and her parents were ushered outside to the platform, where a crowd of people speaking in German and English awaited them. Gordon pointed out a few representatives from the U.S. embassy standing near the front, while several officials from the German foreign bureau were easily identified by their swastika armbands and lapel pins. Perfectly placed to observe the scene was a crush of newspaper reporters and photographers. Their flashbulbs popped blindingly until Martha could no longer discern faces through the spots before her eyes, but she gamely smiled first this way and then that as people called to her.

Eventually the furor subsided and a smiling man of medium height bounded forward to introduce himself as George Messersmith, the counsel general. Martha immediately recognized his name; her father had mentioned reading his dispatches to Washington describing the state of affairs in Germany. Martha took an instant liking to him as he courteously brought forward prominent members of the crowd who wished to meet the ambassador and his family—German officials, American expatriates, and representatives from other foreign embassies. Martha was most pleased to meet the leader of the American Women's Club, a lovely blonde, slender and tall, with large, serious gray-blue eyes and a manner that suggested thoughtful contemplation of her words before she spoke. The club presented Martha and her mother with a lovely bouquet, and before long so many other groups had showered them in beautiful roses, orchids, and other blossoms that their arms became too full to accept any more.

At a word from Messersmith, Martha's father took the press corps aside, read some brief prepared remarks, and invited questions. After a few moments, a plump, golden-haired woman who looked to be around forty approached Martha and her mother and offered to help carry their flowers. "Thank you," said Martha, inclining her head toward her mother.

"It's the least I can do for a coworker," the woman remarked as she took on more than half of Mrs. Dodd's burden. She seemed just about Martha's height, five foot three, with an impish face and a tenacious gleam in her blue eyes. "Sigrid Schultz, the *Tribune*'s correspondent in chief for Central Europe."

"Yes, of course," said Martha. "I've read your work, and I've seen your photo in the office."

"What are your first impressions of Berlin?" Sigrid asked Martha's mother.

"That depends," Martha interjected before her mother could reply, with a teasing smile to soften the sting. "Is this an interview?"

"If I let you off the hook now, would you grant me an exclusive later?"

"We'd be delighted to have you over for tea and a chat, Miss Schultz," said Martha's mother graciously. "Just as soon as we're settled."

"Fair enough."

The crowd had begun to disperse, and Gordon was gesturing toward a nearby curb where two gleaming black Mercedes-Benzes waited, presumably to carry the Dodds, their luggage, and their escorts to their lodgings. As Martha and her mother bade the lingering well-wishers goodbye, Sigrid touched Martha's arm. "Don't leave just yet." Cupping her hands around her mouth, she called to the tall slender blonde from the American Women's Club. "Mildred, do you have a moment?"

The woman nodded, then exchanged a few words with her companions and returned to the platform. "Hello, Sigrid," she said, her voice warm and mellifluous. "Mrs. Dodd, Miss Dodd."

"Please call me Martha," she said, though it was a relief to hear herself referred to as Miss Dodd again. If she had her way, no one in Germany would ever know her married name. Her divorce would surely be wrapped up soon, so why not reclaim her maiden name now?

"You two really ought to know each other better," said Sigrid. "You're both midwesterners, and you share a love of literature and writing."

"You're a writer?" asked Martha, pleased. "I used to write for the *Tribune*, like Sigrid here, but just book reviews, author profiles, and publishing news. Nothing as glamorous as news reports from around the globe."

"I wish I were so prolific," said Mildred, smiling. "I'd like to write more poetry and fiction, but teaching, studying, and working on my doctoral dissertation consumes all my time."

"So you're a scholar as well as a writer," said Martha. "You and my father would get along wonderfully. You must come to lunch at the embassy so I can properly introduce you."

Mildred said she would be delighted and gave Martha her card, but their conversation ended abruptly when Counselor Gordon strode over and announced that the cars were ready to depart.

Martha assumed she would ride with her mother while her father went off with the embassy officers, but there was much bustle and confusion, worsened by the press corps shouting questions. Martha was led to a car already occupied by an embassy officer Messersmith introduced as the family's *Protokol* secretary. At first she was pleased—the officer was rather good-looking, young, blond, broad-shouldered—but she was startled when Messersmith suddenly closed the door before anyone else climbed in. As their driver pulled into traffic, she craned her neck just in time to glimpse her parents packed into the other car with Messersmith, his wife, and Gordon.

They drove south, crossing a bridge over the Spree and proceeding down long, straight boulevards into the city. The orderly grid reminded her of Chicago, but little else she glimpsed through the windows did. Instead of the familiar skyscrapers of the Loop or the tall brownstones of Hyde Park, the buildings were rather low, rarely more than five stories tall, with charming stone buildings centuries old set beside modern structures with glass walls, curved façades, and flat roofs. The energy of the streets also reminded her of home—the sidewalks bustling with businessmen and shoppers, the streets full of omnibuses, electric trams, and autos, a swift river of color and chrome.

The *Protokol* officer pointed out various landmarks as they passed, which Martha understood as an invitation to consider him her tour guide. She asked him about this building and that street, until her incessant curiosity apparently got the better of him and his voice became strained, his replies increasingly brusque.

"That, of course, is the Reichstagsgebäude," he said as they passed an enormous sandstone building on an open plaza, an imposing Italianate Renaissance structure with towers two hundred feet tall at the four corners.

"I thought it had burned down," Martha exclaimed. From what she had read in the papers, she had expected a pile of rubble and ash, but the towers stood tall and the walls seemed undamaged. "It looks all right to me. Tell me what happened."

Suddenly the *Protokol* officer leaned toward her, his face scarlet. "Sssh!" he hissed. "Young lady, you must learn to be seen and not heard. You mustn't say so much and ask so many questions. This isn't America and you can't say all the things you think!"

Astonished, Martha pressed her lips together, glared indignantly, and turned back to the window. She would have expected more courtesy from a diplomat. Perhaps she had been a bit overly enthusiastic, but he clearly was in the wrong line of work if he could not handle a few questions from the new ambassador's daughter on her first visit to Berlin.

It was a frosty ride the rest of the way to the Esplanade, the luxurious hotel on Bellevuestrasse where the embassy had arranged for the Dodds to stay. As soon as the car was parked and the driver opened her door, Martha bounded out and rejoined her parents without a single parting word for the insolent *Protokol* secretary. While bellhops sorted their luggage, Messersmith and Gordon escorted the family through the glamorous lobby and past the Palm Courtyard—an elegant restaurant, Martha surmised from the quick glance she managed in passing, a stone courtyard enclosed by a high glass ceiling, with crystal chandeliers, spotless white linen tablecloths, and gleaming silver and china. An elevator carried them to the Imperial Suite, where their escorts insisted upon showing them around to be sure everything was satisfactory.

"It'll do nicely," Martha managed to say, hoping that no one had seen her jaw drop when she crossed the threshold. University professors' families were not accustomed to such magnificence. The Imperial Suite was bigger than their home in Hyde Park—three bedrooms with baths, a drawing room, a conference room, and two reception rooms with high ceilings, walls lined with satin brocades, tapestried furniture, and marble tables. Every room overflowed with the loveliest flowers. So many well-wishers had sent floral arrangements—orchids, rare scented lilies, blooms of every imaginable variety—that there was scarcely space to move in.

Martha's mother took in the size of the rooms, the opulent decor, and the breathtaking views through the floor-to-ceiling windows, stifling gasps as she discovered new splendors everywhere she turned. "We'll have to mortgage our souls to pay for all this," she murmured, somewhat dazed.

Before Martha could reply, she overheard her father speaking in an adjacent room. "I'm sorry you went to so much trouble, Messersmith," he said sternly, "but before we left the United States, I told the State Department that I wanted modest quarters in a modest hotel. This is certainly not that."

"The Germans would find that very strange, even offensive," replied Messersmith. "An ambassador is expected to meet a certain standard of extravagance."

"Even in the midst of a depression? When we landed in Hamburg, the manager of the Adlon hotel wired to offer us a suite free of charge. I'm inclined to accept."

"You mustn't, sir," Gordon broke in. "State Department officials and American diplomats always stay at the Esplanade. If we leave, it will be an atrocious breach of protocol."

"If you're going to break precedent, I'd advise you not to choose a competing hotel," said Messersmith.

Martha's father sighed, considering. "I can't abide spending taxpayer dollars on opulence when people back home are going hungry. We'll find a private home to rent, but we won't stay here."

Messersmith acquiesced, Gordon too, though far less readily. With that sorted, the embassy officials bade the Dodds good evening and left them on their own. Martha's father retired to his room with a book to rest before dinner, while Martha and her mother tried to make themselves at home in the grand drawing room, overawed by their glamorous surroundings.

"I don't think we need to rush into house hunting," said Martha, kicking off her shoes and stretching out luxuriously on a tapestried sofa. "Can't we enjoy being spoiled for a while? Haven't we earned it after all those days and nights in a tiny cabin aboard ship?"

Her mother raised her eyebrows, but before she could chide Martha for embracing extravagance, she was interrupted by a knock on the door—a bellhop with another delivery of flowers and cards welcoming the family to Germany. Martha had no sooner found a place for them when another knock on the door sounded, and two more bouquets were presented. Again and again the bellhop returned, until at last the flow of deliveries ceased just in time for them to dress for dinner. Bill himself brought in the last bouquet.

Martha's father was in excellent spirits as they went downstairs to the hotel dining room and were seated at one of the finest tables. His wife and children exchanged amused glances as he tested his German on the waiters and staff, asking questions, making jokes, and generally not behaving at all as a properly stuffy, arrogant ambassador ought. They enjoyed a delicious, authentic German dinner, and Martha tasted her first real German beer and declared it quite perfect.

Afterward, they decided to go for a walk to stretch their legs and relax before calling it a night. They strolled the length of the Siegesallee, a broad boulevard lined with lovely trees and ponderous statues of Germany's former rulers and statesmen. Martha's father paused before each one and offered his family a brief historical sketch of the man, his era, his accomplishments, and his character. He seemed utterly in his element, and Martha was so happy for him that her heart overflowed with joy and love.

How thankful she was that her father had invited her to share in his adventure! It was a lovely night, the streets softly lit, and all was serene, romantic, unfamiliar, nostalgic. She delighted in the warmth and friendliness of the people, the caress of the summer air perfumed with the fragrance of flowers and trees, the charm of the Old World buildings of stone and brick, so different from the skyscraper canyons of Chicago and New York.

If first impressions counted for anything, the American press had badly maligned Germany. She could not wait to see what other unexpected delights awaited her.

CHAPTER EIGHTEEN

July 1933

Greta

Berlin was sublime in summer, the Tiergarten green and blooming, the breezes soft, the sunshine warm and beneficent. Restaurants and theaters thrived; fashionable men and women laughed and drank and smoked at cafés. Neighbors gossiped and carefree children played underfoot. The poor still struggled, but there was a sense that better times lay just around the corner. As for the marching SA in their ill-fitting brown uniforms, and the SS in their more impressive tailored black, unless one was their enemy, their appearances brought a thrill of excitement to an otherwise ordinary day. The National Socialist anthems and chants raised hopes and renewed pride in a nation beleaguered by economic depression and humiliation that still lingered years after the end of the Great War.

Or so Greta observed in neighbors and acquaintances who had fallen in line with the Nazi doctrine with an ardent swiftness that defied understanding. What she felt was a vague, unsettled dread punctuated by alarm and horror. Almost daily she heard of new atrocities dealt to the Nazis' political rivals, Jews, and unwitting tourists who had eluded the process of *Gleichschaltung* and did not realize they had committed a crime until a Brownshirt knocked them to the pavement with a rubber truncheon or the butt of a rifle. Attacks on Americans—

Jews, or people perceived as Jews, or tourists who eschewed the Hitler salute—were reported almost every day, terrifying in their randomness and violence. Greta was deeply concerned that Mildred, in her American naiveté and optimism, would stumble into danger even though she had lived in Germany for several years.

But as dangerous as Germany had become for Americans, countless thousands of German citizens endured even worse treatment at the hands of their own government. Americans who stumbled into trouble had the influential U.S. consulate to advocate for them. German Jews, Communists, and outspoken opponents of the Reich had no one.

Although Greta had returned from London to a very different Germany than she had left, she could not agree that German theater was dead. Certainly its people had been scattered and diminished by arrests, desertions, and emigration. Yet subversive remnants persisted, not only in the irreverent, dissolute cabarets but in the most renowned theater circles. Adam introduced Greta to playwrights, actors, and producers who drank and dined with Nazi officials one night and condemned them in scathing satire and allegory the next. Offstage, Adam and some trusted friends surreptitiously produced and distributed flyers denouncing the Nazis and calling for Social Democrats and Communists to unite in opposing them. It was dangerous work, as anyone caught in possession of anti-Nazi literature was severely punished with imprisonment and harsh beatings. Although Greta feared for Adam's safety, it was a relief to meet people undaunted and defiant when so many other Germans had fallen under the spell of Nazi propaganda or had slipped into a state of passive oblivion. As long as some Germans resisted, Nazi dominion was not absolute.

Adam urged Greta to join the fight. "Because I love you, I must have you at my side in this political struggle," he told her one evening as she typed and proofread an antifascist pamphlet he and Hans Otto had written together. When she raised her eyebrows at him and gestured to the pages she was preparing for the mimeograph, he added, "Not mere clerical work. A woman of your intelligence could, and must, contribute so much more."

She glowed from his praise, but what more could she do? She had no power, no influence, few resources. She barely had work from one day to the next, patching together a living from freelance writing and editing jobs. Some offers came from Adam's colleagues, but most she had picked up through connections made at Mildred and Arvid's literary salon, a friendly and loyal group of intellectuals, writers, editors, and artists who gathered at their flat a few times a month for suppers and Saturday afternoon teas. Mildred made the rooms cozy with candles and artful arrangements of pussy willows and alpenrosen, and she passed around plates of liverwurst sandwiches, thinly sliced bread, cheese, sausage, and tomatoes, but it was the conversation and company that most enlivened the senses. Greta observed in the other guests' expressions what she herself felt, that the Harnack flat had become a sanctuary for dissenters and antifascists, a place where one could breathe deeply, speak freely.

One Wednesday evening in late July, Greta arrived at the salon too late for dinner—Adam had asked her to observe a run-through of a new play at the Staatstheater and it had taken longer than expected—but just in time for coffee and dessert. She found friends and colleagues mingling and talking, some murmuring intently with heads bent close together, others smiling as they debated animatedly, and one brave or reckless soul loudly declaring that Goebbels was a vile bastard and Himmler an utter fool.

Greta made her way to the kitchen, claimed a cup of coffee and a slice of *Apfelkuchen*, and wandered into the front room to search for Mildred. She found Arvid instead. "It's not the University Club, but it'll do," he said by way of greeting, taking in the crowded room, offering her a wry smile.

A pang of nostalgia struck. She imagined herself back in Madison, ascending the stone staircase and passing through the arches to the front entrance of the gracious redbrick building on the corner of Murray and State streets on the Library Mall at the foot of Bascom Hill. Inside, the sounds of laughter and animated conversation beckoned her downstairs to a private dining room where about two dozen men and women mingled around three tables, some holding cigarettes, others with newspapers or books tucked under their arms—the Friday Niters, professors and graduate students meeting to study and discuss the imperative matters of the day, confident in their belief that well-meaning people in academia and government could work together to make the world better, safer, more equitable for all. How long ago and far away it seemed.

"I can only imagine what Professor Commons and the rest of our old friends think of what has become of Germany," said Greta.

"Perhaps Germany will serve as a warning," said Arvid. "May they learn from us to snuff out fascism in America when the first sparks arise and not delay until democracy goes up in flames all around them."

"This could never happen in America. A nation that elected Franklin Delano Roosevelt would never elect a madman populist."

"A few years ago, I was equally certain that Germany would never repeat the mistakes of fascist Italy or Spain." Arvid shook his head, pensive. "The question is, what nation does Hitler seek to emulate now? Not Spain anymore, certainly not America. Ancient Rome, perhaps. I worry that Hitler will declare war on the Soviet Union to gain *Lebensraum* in the east."

"Surely not. He and Stalin are allies."

"How can that alliance endure? Communists and fascists are on opposite ends of the political spectrum."

Greta could not deny that, but the thought of war was so dreadful that she had to refute it. "Even if that is what Hitler wants, he'll be out of power long before he could ever organize for war. And even if the Reichstag is in his pocket, Hindenburg would never sanction it." Suddenly a horrible, sinking dread flooded her. "Unless the Soviet Union attacks us first. Do you think Hitler would deliberately provoke them?"

"It's up to rational Germans like us to see that he doesn't. We must resist. We have to cross all lines that currently divide us—class, political party, religion—and unite to bring down the Nazis before they lead Germany any further down this road to self-destruction."

Greta nodded, thinking of Adam and his comrades working in isolation to produce their pamphlets and flyers. If they could connect to a larger network of opponents of the regime, they could vastly increase their influence.

Arvid drew closer and lowered his voice. "I have connections to groups that produce antifascist literature. Their purpose is to warn the workers not to be deceived by Nazi propaganda. With your ties to the working class, we can expand our reach."

"I'm not sure what ties you mean."

"Mildred told me that when you were in London, you spoke to workers' unions to warn them about fascism."

"I did, and I'm willing to do the same here, but don't fool yourself that I have any special influence with the workers just because my family is poor."

"I meant no offense, Greta. If you have no connections, that's unfortunate, but you can fix it. You're looking for work. Why not find a job that would allow you to develop such connections?"

The condescending manner she had always found so annoying rankled her anew. "Why me?" she countered. "Why not do it yourself? Why not ask Mildred?"

"Mildred has already found her role." A fond smile appeared as he glanced past Greta to scan the room for his wife. "She's teaching her students to recognize and refute propaganda, how to defend themselves against it with reason and logic. She recruits the brightest and most courageous of her students to join our group. And she's using her connections at the American embassy to get visas for Jewish acquaintances so they can get out of the country. But you—" He shrugged, chagrined. "You seem to be still searching for your place."

For a moment she let her old rival stew in his embarrassment. "You aren't wrong," she admitted. "I'm just tired of being told that I must do something before I figure out for myself what that should be."

At that moment Mildred approached them. "Don't let Arvid bully you," she said in English, kissing her husband's cheek and resting a hand on Greta's shoulder. In German she added, "He only recruits people he trusts and respects, but you mustn't feel pressured to do more than you can."

"I'm honored to have your trust and respect," Greta told Arvid, and she meant it sincerely. "I'll think about what you've said."

Arvid looked as if he might say more, but when someone called his name, he glanced over his shoulder, excused himself, and left Greta and Mildred to themselves. Greta's thoughts raced. First there was Adam's urging, then Arvid's, and now these revelations that Mildred had been helping Jews escape Germany. Greta wanted to do her part too, but what?

"Mildred—" she began, but found herself at a loss for words.

Somehow, Mildred understood. "Why don't we meet tomorrow, just the two of us, so we can talk uninterrupted?"

The following afternoon, they met at the Brandenburg Gate for a walk through the Tiergarten. The paths they wandered along took them over a bridge to Luiseninsel, where they admired the memorials, statuary, and blooming rose gardens before crossing another footbridge over the Tiergartenwässer and turning north. Greta had spent most of the day mulling over Arvid's words and marveling at Mildred's courage and generosity. Mildred could lose her job, her freedom, and possibly her life if a malicious person informed the Gestapo that she was teaching her students to resist Nazi propaganda. Greta knew from her own ugly encounter in Frankfurt that helping Jews emigrate provoked the wrath of the SA. If Mildred could risk so much for her adopted land, how could Greta, a German by birth, do any less?

"I have a confession to make," she said as they diverted onto a more secluded path. "I know it will make you think poorly of me, but I owe you the truth if I expect you and Arvid to continue to trust me."

"What is it?"

"I'm involved with someone. More than that. We're in love." Greta steeled herself and plunged ahead. "He's married."

"Married? Oh, Greta, no."

"His wife knows about us. She doesn't object." When Mildred looked skeptical, Greta quickly explained Adam's complicated relationship with the Viehmeyer sisters. "I know what you're thinking. If he truly loved me, he would divorce Gertrud and marry me. He asked, and she refused."

"Perhaps she thinks he'll tire of you and come back to her."

"He won't."

"How can you be sure?" Mildred placed a hand on Greta's arm to bring her to a stop. "Is it possible that you're not the first? Maybe he strayed before and went back to her."

"It's not like that." Greta shook her head, eyes downcast, hating to see herself diminished in her friend's eyes. "It's true that I wish he weren't married, but I love him, and I'd rather have him this way than not at all." She managed a short laugh. "I understand what you must think of me. You've always been so virtuous, so true. How can some-one as perfect as you remain friends with someone as morally dubious as me?"

"Oh, Greta—"

"You know you're thinking it."

"I'm not. I'm really not." Mildred bit the inside of her lower lip, her eyes glistening. "I'm not perfect. Far from it."

"You'd have every right—"

"No. Listen." Mildred tucked her hands into her pockets and shook her head, sad and apprehensive. "I have a confession to make too, and when you hear it, *you* may be the one who can't bear to stay friends with *me*."

"What's the worst you've ever done? Forgot to make your bed one morning?"

"I joined the National Socialist Teachers League."

"You can't be serious."

Mildred nodded bleakly.

"But why? Why would you do such a thing?"

"In June, a few days before graduation, the principal informed me and the other holdouts among the faculty that if we wanted to con-tinue working at the Berlin Abendgymnasium after the summer recess, we had to join." Mildred pressed a hand to her waist. "I walked home in a daze, sick to my stomach, thoughts churning. I couldn't afford to lose my job. Arvid and I are barely getting by as it is. But I couldn't bear to have any affiliation with racist, authoritarian brutes who burn books and persecute Jews. Signing my name to their roster would give tacit approval to beliefs and practices I find morally abhorrent."

"Then why didn't you resign in protest?"

"And what then? I would have faced the same requirement at every other school I might apply to. My choices were to join the league or give up teaching." Mildred's gaze fell upon a nearby bench, and with a heavy sigh, she sank down upon it. "Of course I joined in name only. I'll never attend a meeting or participate in their activities. Arvid says the Nazis are wrong to make this a condition of my employment and they deserve to be deceived."

"He's right. You had no choice."

"There's always a choice." Mildred clasped her hands together in her lap, pensive. "I'm not certain I made the right one."

Greta sat down beside her. "I've no doubt that every other teacher on the faculty made the same decision."

"They did," Mildred acknowledged, "but you wouldn't have. You would have told them what they could do with their job and their unreasonable requirements."

"And I would have found myself out of work and under increased scrutiny from the Gestapo, or placed into their so-called protective custody."

"But you would have known that you had done the right thing."

"What a great comfort my moral superiority would have been to me as I toiled in a work camp."

"Yes, exactly." Mildred seemed to have missed Greta's sarcasm. "So as you see, I'm far from perfect myself."

"If you say so." Greta sighed and sat back against the bench. "Mildred, I didn't tell you about Adam to unburden my soul or to prompt a confession from you."

"No?"

Greta shook her head. "I've thought carefully about what Arvid said regarding expanding our circles of acquaintances, of joining smaller, isolated opposition groups into a larger network."

She fell silent as a heavyset man strolled past, a small white dog on a leash preceding him.

Mildred regarded her intently, waiting for her to continue.

"Adam and Arvid have a lot in common," Greta said when they were alone once more. "I think they should meet."

CHAPTER NINETEEN

August 1933

Martha

On the first day of August, Martha's father informed his family that he had taken a fully furnished house on Tiergartenstrasse, a short, pleasant walk away from the American chancery on Bendlerstrasse. The owner, Alfred Panofsky, a partner with Jacquier and Securius Bank, had offered it at the astonishingly low rent of about 150 U.S. dollars a month.

Martha and her mother exchanged a look, unable to imagine what could be found at that price on a street known for gracious, elegant homes. The old carriage house of a luxurious mansion converted into flats? Servants' quarters in an attic? Martha was afraid to ask. Her father was exceedingly proud of the great bargain he had struck, so she prepared herself for the worst.

She was in no hurry to relocate. She adored the Esplanade, her comfortable bedroom and the elegant reception halls where the family had already entertained many fascinating foreign dignitaries and handsome, exciting men—including Louis Ferdinand, Prince of Prussia and second in line of succession to the recently abolished German throne; Ernst Hanfstaengl, the German foreign press chief, who cheerfully urged Martha to call him by his nickname, Putzi; and Boris Vinogradov, the first secretary of the Soviet embassy, a particularly intriguing new acquaintance.

Then there was Rudolf Diels, the young, compelling, and sinister chief of the Gestapo. His penetrating eyes could convey warmth or malevolence, but it was what lay behind those eyes that had earned him the sobriquet Prince of Darkness. He seemed to take a vicious joy in his mystique, which for Martha only enhanced the allure of his lovely full lips, his luxuriant black hair, and even the cruel, broken beauty of his scarred face. A long, shallow V marred his right cheek, a deep crescent the left, and smaller arcs cut across his chin and near his mouth— dueling scars, or so the rumors told. He was also said to possess great charm and sexual prowess—rumors Martha hoped to confirm for herself before long.

Martha winced with chagrin whenever she imagined entertaining a guest like Rudolf Diels or hosting a banquet for high-ranking German officials and aristocratic foreign emissaries in a cheap flat. Her father's determination to drive their own Chevrolet was an endearing quirk. His decision to rent the least expensive residence on the market could prove to be an embarrassment or worse.

The next day, Martha, Bill, and their mother went to see Tiergartenstrasse 27a for themselves. The street ran along the southern edge of the park, offering them a lovely view of lush greenery and flowers as they walked along. When they reached the correct address, their doubt gave way to amazement. Their new home was a four-story stone mansion enclosed by a tall, ornate iron fence, with leafy trees rising above beautiful cultivated flower gardens in the front yard. The front façade curved gracefully, and through the foliage Martha glimpsed the main entrance near the northwest corner, at the base of a rounded tower rising the entire height of the building. Near the street, the driveway passed through a high gate with an elaborate ironwork arch and ended beneath a porte cochère. Above that rose a gallery one and a half stories tall with many windows to let in the light.

Perhaps Martha's father did not object to luxury after all, as long as it came at the right price.

When they knocked on the front door, the butler, a stocky blond in his midforties, answered. Herr and Frau Panofsky were not at home, he informed them, but it would be his pleasure to give them a tour of the house.

The residence was as impressive inside as it was from the outside. The main entrance led into a large foyer with coatrooms on opposite sides and a grand staircase at one end, drawing visitors above and away from the functional rooms that took up the rest of the first floor—the kitchen, pantry, laundry, ice room, various storage and supply areas, and the servants' quarters. The second floor boasted two reception rooms, an expansive dining room with walls covered in red tapestry, and a ballroom with a gleaming oval dance floor and a grand piano, upon which sat a crystal vase filled with flowers.

Several graciously appointed bedrooms were on the third floor. The master bath was immense, larger than some apartments Martha had known back in Chicago. The floors and walls glimmered with gold and mosaics of multicolored tiles, and the massive bathtub stood on a raised platform like an altar to some pagan god of cleanliness.

Martha nudged her brother. "On weekends we could sublet the tub to the German Olympic swim team."

As Bill guffawed, Fritz frowned primly and led the Dodds to the library. The walls were covered in dark wood and rich red damask and lined with bookshelves filled with a vast array of tempting volumes. A glass table held a vase abundant with flowers and a few artfully arranged rare books and manuscripts. At one end of the room stood a great stone fireplace with an elaborately carved mantel and a pair of comfortable leather chairs and a large leather sofa arranged before it. Light streamed in through tall windows with stained glass at the top, and the smells of old paper, leather, and flowers gave the library a familiar, welcoming atmosphere, beckoning Martha to choose a book and settle down for a long, indulgent read far from the cares of the outside world.

Lastly Fritz took them to the *Wintergarten*, a glass-enclosed sunroom on the south end of the main floor that opened onto a terrace overlooking the garden. "Frau Panofsky would insist that you take refreshments before you go," he said, and when they demurred, reluctant to impose, he bowed silently and departed. He soon returned with coffee and cake, which he served to them at a wrought-iron table on the terrace. With another slight bow, he left them.

"Here's to Dad," Martha said, raising her teacup in a toast. "I'm sorry I doubted him."

"This is really quite a place," said Bill, enjoying a hearty bite of cake. "And this cake is marvelous."

"You'll be pleased to know that the cook and the rest of the staff will remain," their mother said, pursing her lips as she gazed out at the verdant garden. "Mr. Panofsky was most insistent that they be allowed to stay, and your father was happy to agree."

Martha studied her. "That's a rather sad face for such good news."

"I only wonder why the Panofskys are charging us so little for so much. How could they part with such a beautiful home and everything in it?"

"Maybe they're going abroad for a while but intend to return," said Martha. "Maybe they're tired of these beautiful things and want to buy new ones. Maybe they're extraordinarily wealthy—"

"Or extraordinarily desperate," Bill broke in. "If the Panofskys are Jewish, they may be preparing to flee Germany."

"Surely not." Martha gestured from the garden to the beautiful house. "Herr Panofsky clearly has money, and money equals power and influence no matter who runs the government."

"Not in Germany, not if you're a Jew." Bill leaned forward and lowered his voice. "Money, power, prestige—they offer scant protection now. A rich Jew is subject to the Aryan Laws as much as a poor Jew. The only exception is for veterans of the Great War and their immediate families, and who knows how long those provisions will last."

Martha raised her eyebrows at her brother. "What a grim appraisal."

"Grim but accurate. About fifty thousand Jews have left Germany since Hitler took over as chancellor. Others probably would too, if they could afford it and if they had somewhere to go."

"I hope you're wrong," said their mother. "This home is lovely, but I don't want to benefit from someone else's misfortune."

That evening over dinner, their father confirmed some of what Bill had surmised. The Panofskys were Jews, but as far as he knew, the family did not intend to leave Germany. "They aren't even leaving the house," he said. "Mr. Panofsky's wife and two children have gone to the countryside, but he and his mother are staying. They're keeping the entire fourth floor and use of the elevator for themselves."

"I imagine it would be difficult to retreat to the attic while strangers enjoy your luxurious home," said Martha's mother, concern clouding her expression.

"Herr Panofsky must think it will suit them," said Martha's father. "Perhaps he and his mother intend to join the rest of the family in the countryside soon."

When the Dodds moved in a few days later, they discovered beautiful floral arrangements throughout the house and a gracious letter from Herr Panofsky welcoming the family to his home, which he hoped they would consider their own for as long as they remained in Berlin. He expressed his admiration for America and encouraged them to come to him if they had any questions about Berlin or needed any recommendations for businesses and services.

"It seems our landlord enjoys the novelty of hosting the American ambassador's family," Martha's father remarked after he finished reading the letter aloud.

"Perhaps that accounts for the low rent and their attic quarters," Martha mused. Her father smiled, and her mother admitted that she made a fair point, but Bill merely shook his head, unconvinced.

A week after the Dodds moved into Tiergartenstrasse 27a, they decided to take a road trip to see more of the country. They planned to drive south from Berlin to Leipzig, where Martha's parents would linger for a few days so her father could visit his favorite old haunts from his graduate student days. Meanwhile, Martha and Bill would continue on all the way to Austria.

As they were planning their route and debating what sights to see, Bill asked if he might bring a friend along. "Fine by me," said Martha, tempted to suggest Rudolf Diels, who would surely prove to be as fascinating a guide as he was a dinner companion. Or perhaps Boris Vinogradov, whom she had been getting to know at various embassy functions. He was tall and blond with gorgeous blue-green eyes, a charming if inelegant dancer and quite the flirt. He spoke little English, and she spoke no Russian, but they managed to stumble along well enough in German.

But Rudolf and Boris were her friends, not Bill's, and Martha was well pleased with his choice—Quentin Reynolds, a journalist, formerly a sports reporter with the *New York Telegram* and recently appointed an associate editor of *Collier's Weekly*. He was tall, burly, and quite handsome, with curly red hair, blue eyes, and a ready grin. Martha was not entirely disappointed that flirting with the Prince of Darkness and the Russian first secretary would have to wait until she returned to Berlin.

Since Bill was bringing a friend, Martha suggested inviting Mildred Harnack too. Soon after the Dodds' arrival in Berlin, Martha had asked Mildred to join her for lunch at the Palm Courtyard at the Esplanade, and they had become fast friends over their mutual love of literature and writing. They shared many favorite authors in common, and they eagerly recommended novels, new and classic, to one another. Mildred had asked Martha to join her literary salon, and at Martha's invitation, Mildred had attended several teas and other functions at the embassy. Mildred spoke German perfectly and would have been excellent company on the road. Unfortunately, she had to decline, as their three-week itinerary would prevent her from returning to Berlin in time for the start of the new school term.

Thus it was a party of five rather than six that departed Berlin on a warm, sunny Sunday morning. Bill drove the old family Chevrolet, their father took the front passenger seat beside him, and Martha sat in back between her mother and Quentin. Martha soon teased out of him that he was a native New Yorker of Irish ancestry, he despised the Nazis, and he hoped to write a novel or two someday. He would make a fine traveling companion, she thought, smiling to herself as she settled back to enjoy the ride.

As they drove south through picturesque countryside and charming villages, Quentin asked Martha's father how he was settling into his new job. After taking the precaution of declaring his remarks off the record, Martha's father explained that he would not be officially recognized as the American ambassador to Germany until he could present his credentials to the president. However, Hindenburg had withdrawn to his estate at Neudeck in East Prussia to recuperate from an undefined illness and was not expected to return to the capital until the end of August. Until then, Martha's father kept busy organizing his office, meeting his staff, briefing American news correspondents, and handling routine diplomatic issues. He had also lodged official protests with the German government regarding the violent attacks on Americans. "Foreign citizens are under no obligation to offer this *Hitlergruss*, this Hitler salute," he said. "If the current administration can't establish that as official policy, I may have no choice but to urge the State Department to issue a travel warning."

Quentin's eyebrows rose. "The German government would find that offensive, deeply humiliating."

"Indeed, which is why I'm confident they'll do whatever is necessary to avoid it."

It was almost eleven o'clock when they arrived in Wittenberg, where their first stop was the Schlosskirche. It was there that in 1517, Martin Luther had nailed his Ninety-five Theses to the door of the church's main portal, sparking the Protestant Reformation.

"I sometimes attended services here when I was a student," Martha's father reminisced as they climbed the front steps, but when he tried to open the door so they could look around, he found it locked. Disappointed, they descended the stairs just as a Nazi parade emerged around the corner of an adjacent street. While Martha looked on eagerly, the others exchanged wary glances, and by unspoken agreement, they quickly departed in the opposite direction.

They spent an hour strolling around Wittenberg before climbing back aboard the Chevrolet and continuing south to Leipzig. They reached the city at one o'clock and went immediately to Auerbachs Keller, one of the most famous restaurants in Germany and a particular favorite of Goethe. "Do you recall the scene from *Faust* that took place in this very room?" Martha's father asked as they sat around a long table awaiting their meal. "Faust and Mephistopheles met here, and the demon's wine turned to fire."

"I'm glad I chose beer, then," remarked Quentin, raising his stein and beckoning for a refill. Laughing, Bill and Martha raised theirs too and cheered, while their parents, who had kept to water and tea, looked on indulgently.

After the meal, Martha, Bill, and Quentin suggested a walking tour to settle their heads before they resumed their journey. Martha's father agreed, and he eagerly showed them around the city he had loved as a young scholar, pointing out his old favorite haunts as well as places of more historic significance.

By midafternoon, Bill was ready to take the wheel again, so the younger set parted company with Martha's parents at their hotel and set out for Nuremberg. Quentin moved to the front seat, Martha had plenty of room to stretch out in the back, and they chatted about writing as they drove along, except when they paused to admire a particularly lovely scene outside the window. Bill drove swiftly through the countryside but slowed to a more sedate pace whenever the road passed through a village, not only to ease the jolting of the wheels over the cobblestones but to let them better admire the architecture and the occasional villager clad in colorful regional attire, lederhosen and dirndl. In nearly every town they encountered an SA parade, men of all ages and sizes clad in brown uniforms, marching, singing, chanting slogans, holding aloft red banners bearing the white circle and black *Hakenkreuz*. Whenever Bill slowed the car to a crawl to avoid the crowds and to better navigate the winding, narrow medieval streets, SA members, SS officers, and ordinary citizens would snap out the *Hitlergruss* and shout "Heil Hitler!" at them.

"Heil Hitler!" Martha cried out the window, saluting them back.

"Would you stop doing that?" Bill asked irritably. "You're an American. You don't have to."

"I might not have to, but when in Rome—" She offered another salute to several boys clad in short-pant versions of the men's brown uniforms. "Why do the people keep saluting us, anyway? They aren't shouting at other cars."

"It's the license plate," said Quentin. "More important individuals are given lower numbers, and by custom the American ambassador is assigned number thirteen. They probably assume we're some hotshot Nazi official's family."

"Great," said Bill sarcastically.

Quentin grinned. "I'm not flattered by the mistake any more than you are."

"Stop being such spoilsports," said Martha, offering the salute and a smile to a pair of Brownshirts idling on a street corner. "I don't know why you can't appreciate the excitement and vigor of the new Germany. I find it marvelous. We could use some of this optimism back in the States."

"I'll take Roosevelt's New Deal over Hitler's Aryan Laws any day," said Quentin.

"Hear, hear," said Bill.

Martha let out a long, exaggerated sigh, so comical that Quentin guffawed and even Bill cracked a smile.

They encountered fewer marches as the afternoon wore on, and by the time twilight descended, the villages had turned peaceful and quaint again, looking as they might have one hundred years before except for the Nazi banners unfurled before government buildings.

"Most of Nuremberg will be tucked in bed fast asleep when we arrive," Quentin warned when they reached the outskirts of the city. "Fingers crossed we can still find a decent pub where we can get a hot meal."

"And a drink," said Bill.

It was nearly midnight by the time they reached their hotel, but the town was still very much awake, the sidewalks full of lively, smiling people, the atmosphere festive.

"Are you sure you've been here before?" Martha teased Quentin as they unloaded their luggage. "Your description of the nightlife is a bit off the mark."

He shrugged. "Must be a local holiday or something."

When they went inside to check in, Quentin asked the registration clerk, in fairly decent German, if a festival was going on. The clerk laughed so vigorously that the tips of his curved mustache trembled. "Not a festival," he replied in English. "A sort of parade. Someone needs to learn a lesson."

"A lesson?" echoed Martha, but the clerk merely smiled and shrugged.

After arranging for their luggage to be sent up to their rooms, Martha, Bill, and Quentin ventured out in search of supper. The streets were even more crowded than before, and everywhere Martha looked she saw people milling about the square, laughing and talking in the friendliest manner. As the people began lining up on either side of the street, Martha heard distant music and the swelling roar of laughter and cheers. She wove through the crowd and claimed a spot right on the curb, the better to see the parade. She recognized the familiar red glow of torchlight, and her heartbeat quickened as she realized this was likely no festival but yet another Nazi demonstration—and sometimes those turned violent.

She would have backed away, but the crowd pressed in closer, blocking her retreat. Fortunately, Bill and Quentin were right behind her, and Martha knew they would not let her be shoved into the street. She went up on tiptoe, craning her neck as the first rows of marching Brownshirts appeared, banners and torches held aloft. The crowd roared approval as they passed, and here and there people frantically waved small Nazi flags.

The music of the brass band grew louder, but it was nearly drowned out by jeers and coarse laughter. Bewildered, Martha looked past the columns of marchers and saw that following immediately afterward were two very large storm troopers, half carrying, half dragging a small, barefoot human figure between them.

Martha stared, transfixed with disbelief that swiftly gave way to horror. The figure was a woman, her blouse and skirt disheveled, her head shaved and lolling on her shoulder, her face and scalp covered with a white powder. All around, the crowd erupted in an earsplitting barrage of taunts, insults, and epithets.

Then Martha spied the placard hanging around the woman's neck. "What does it say?" she asked Quentin.

"'I have offered myself to a Jew,'" he read aloud.

"We have to help her," said Bill, pushing forward.

Quentin seized his arm and yanked him back. "What can we do? Look at this crowd. We'd be torn to pieces."

Martha's vision blurred with tears of outrage as the gruesome parade passed and the crowd surged into the street to follow after. She, Bill, and Quentin managed to avoid being swept along as the shouting, cheering throng continued down the street, immobilizing the few vehicles whose drivers had unwittingly turned into their path. Passengers on the top level of a double-decker bus whistled and shouted, pointing at the girl from above. The two large storm troopers lifted up the semiconscious woman so they could have a better look, so high that her feet dangled lifelessly above the ground.

The parade fell apart into one seething mass of hatred and vengeful glee. As Martha was jostled back and forth by fiercely grinning revelers, she seized Bill's arm. "Let's go back to our rooms," she implored. He nodded, but to their dismay, the large storm troopers propelled the woman into the lobby of their own hotel. The band reassembled on the sidewalk outside and struck up a raucous tune, and as they reached the last refrain, the storm troopers emerged and hauled their victim to the hotel next door. At that moment the band struck up the "Horst Wessel Lied," the Nazi Party anthem. Immediately the people around them halted in place, thrust their arms into the air in the *Hitlergruss*, and began singing along loudly and ardently.

"I need a drink," said Bill, his voice low and thick with disgust. Staying close together, they wove their way through the crowd back to their hotel, where they withdrew to the bar and sank wearily down at a table in the corner. Blood pounded in Martha's ears, and when she closed her eyes she saw the small woman, her head slumping to one side, her arms pale and slender in the storm troopers' grip, her unshod feet dangling helplessly.

"I don't know about the rest of you," said Quentin, "but I intend to get extremely drunk."

He pushed himself away from the table and went to the bar, where he placed an order and engaged the bartender in a quick, whispered conversation. Martha and Bill sat in silence until he returned with a tray of three foaming beers, a thick loaf of dark bread, sliced cold sausages, and cheese. Though Martha had been ravenous before the parade, at the sight of food bile rose in her throat and she had to look away.

"Her name is Anna Rath," Quentin said. "She's a local girl, Aryan, and she apparently intends to marry her Jewish fiancé."

"What's the problem?" asked Martha. "Is she already married?"

Bill grabbed one of the steins and drank deeply. "Didn't you know? The Nazis disapprove of marriages between Aryans and Jews."

"That's absurd."

"It's a fact."

Quentin leaned forward and rested his arms on the table. "The press has been reporting Nazi atrocities for months, secondhand tales cobbled together from observers' accounts. This time I'm an eyewitness."

"You can't mean you're going to write about this," protested Martha. "That's not fair. It's an isolated incident—terrible, of course, but it doesn't represent the real Germany."

"You've been in the country a month," said Quentin. "I've been here for years. Believe me, this is no isolated incident."

"Would you condemn all Americans for the violence committed by a few members of the KKK?"

"Sorry, sis, but you really don't know what you're talking about," said Bill. "You should spend less time at parties drinking champagne with aristocrats and more time walking around Berlin, talking to ordinary people and observing what's really going on."

"Please don't file this story," Martha implored. "When people hear that Bill and I were involved, my father will be dragged into an ugly controversy just as he's trying to establish his credibility with the German government."

Quentin ran a hand over his jaw. "Fine. I'll tell my editor I have two unimpeachable witnesses, but I'll leave your names out of it."

Martha knew better than to press her luck. Resigned, she took a drink, sat back in her chair, and said nothing more, wishing she could blot out the image of poor Anna Rath from her memory.

CHAPTER TWENTY

September–October 1933

Mildred

Mildred was only a week into the fall term at the Berlin Abendgymnasium when Martha returned from her driving tour and attended the Harnacks' literary salon. Mildred was pleased to see her new friend again, but as she led her around the flat making introductions, she detected tension around Martha's eyes, a puzzling forced jollity in her voice. She knew Martha was eager to meet other writers, editors, and literati in Berlin, and her interest in their conversation seemed unfeigned, but something was clearly troubling her.

Later, when Martha took Mildred aside and told her about the shocking events she had witnessed in Nuremberg, Mildred understood. As promised, Quentin Reynolds had not named Martha or her brother in his article, but after German foreign press chief Ernst Hanfstaengl accused him of fabricating the entire tale, he had been obliged to identify his fellow eyewitnesses. Their names were not made public, but afterward even Reich Minister of Propaganda Joseph Goebbels could not deny the truth. And yet when confronted by international reporters at a press conference, he dismissed it as an isolated incident and made excuses for the Brownshirts' brutality even as he promised that the men involved would be punished.

"Just yesterday, an official from the German Foreign Office pri vately apologized to me," said Martha. "They regret that I was upset by what I saw. But where is the apology for Anna Rath? Where is her justice? When I asked Rudolf, he just gave me a cryptic smile and told me not to hold my breath."

"Rudolf?"

"Rudolf Diels." Martha's mouth curved in a secretive smile. "We've become friends—intimate friends."

"Martha—" Mildred grasped for the proper words. "Be careful with that one. The things I've heard—"

"Don't worry. I know what I'm doing."

Mildred was not so sure.

Later, Martha revealed that her father had finally presented his credentials to Hindenburg upon his return to Berlin, and also that he had declined Hitler's invitation to attend the annual Nazi Party rally in Nuremberg. "Since it wasn't an official state event, my father thought it would be inappropriate for him to attend," Martha explained, "just as it would be wrong for the German ambassador to attend a Democratic or Republican national convention back home."

"Well done, Ambassador Dodd," said Mildred, pleased.

"He didn't want Goebbels to portray his presence as an official endorsement of the Nazi regime. He secretly convinced the ambassadors of Great Britain, France, and Spain to decline their invitations too."

"Not very secretly, if you heard of it."

Mildred nudged her playfully, but her smile quickly faded. "My father has made several formal protests about all these attacks on Americans, but nothing's improved. He says that the Germans are concerned about negative press back in the States. You'd think that would be enough to compel the government to keep the SA and SS in line."

"Maybe they're confident their censors will keep negative stories from getting out."

"They didn't stop Quentin." Martha shook her head as if clearing it of distressing thoughts. "Speaking of journalism, I've been thinking you and I ought to write something together."

What she had in mind was something for English speakers living in Germany—a column for *Berlin Topics*, the lone English-language newspaper in Berlin. They both loved to write, Martha had experience in journalism, and Mildred had connections throughout the Berlin literary community. But what form should their column take? Martha had to steer clear of politics and controversial subjects due to her father's position, and neither of them wanted to cover the usual territory women were relegated to, housekeeping and beauty tips. Eventually they struck upon the perfect idea for two devoted bibliophiles: a book review.

The executive editor was thrilled to welcome a pair of writers with their credentials to the staff. Soon thereafter, when their first column, "Brief Reviews," was published, Mildred enjoyed seeing her name in a byline again after such a long hiatus. She was also grateful for her share of their modest payment.

Although neither was accustomed to writing with a partner, they quickly figured out an efficient method. Together they chose two books for each column, and Mildred would write the review for one and Martha the other. They met weekly at Martha's home to revise and edit their reviews, working in the library on cool, rainy days and in the *Wintergarten* or on the terrace when the sun shone. They took turns typing up the final version from their marked-up pages and scrawled notes. After they submitted the finished column to their editor, they chose two books for the next column.

One lovely Sunday afternoon, Mildred and Martha were drinking coffee on the Dodds' terrace and debating whether to review the English translation of Hans Fallada's latest novel when a happy shriek from the garden below interrupted them. Mildred craned her neck and spotted two children darting about on the footpaths, a dark-haired boy of about seven and a little girl a few years younger. Rising, Martha called down to the children in cheerful but halting German that if they went to the kitchen, they would find some "*sehr leckere Kekse*" that the cook had baked earlier that afternoon. As the children thanked her and darted back into the house, Martha returned to her seat, satisfied. "That should keep them quiet for a while."

Mildred regarded her, amused. "Care to explain why you're offering cookies to two German children running around your garden?"

"Actually, it's their garden. That was Hans and Ruth Panofsky."

Mildred immediately recognized the surname of their resident land-lord, the banker. "I thought only Herr Panofsky and his mother were still living here."

"That was the original arrangement." Martha sighed and set down her pen. "About two weeks ago, Mr. Panofsky brought in a team of carpenters to remodel the attic. When my father asked him what all the distracting hammering and sawing and banging was about, Mr. Panofsky told him that his wife, children, and a few servants were returning from the countryside. They needed to adapt their living quarters to make everyone more comfortable."

"I didn't think Mr. Panofsky's wife and children meant to return to Berlin."

"Neither did we. Mr. Panofsky assured my parents that we wouldn't be inconvenienced, but my father was not appeased. He told Mr. Panofsky that while he was happy the family had reunited, he was concerned that the children would suffer, since they no longer had free run of their home. He also made it clear that if he had known Mr. Panofsky's plans, he would have taken lodgings elsewhere."

"Are you going to break the lease?"

"I don't think so. This place is perfect for entertaining, and we can't beat the price or the location. For now my father is willing to wait and see." Martha shrugged. "My mother and I think Hans and Ruth are adorable, and the two Mrs. Panofskys are so discreet that you wouldn't know they were here, but my father grumbles about the children's noise, and he was much annoyed the other night when they burst in on a dinner he was hosting for some important diplomats."

Mildred wistfully thought that it would be wonderful to have a pair of happy, healthy children—or even one precious only child—at home to interrupt her work.

"In my opinion," Martha continued, "which sadly does not carry much weight around here, while my father is at the embassy, Hans and Ruth ought to go wherever they please. You can't keep children shut up in an attic when there's a perfectly wonderful garden outside. But my father—well, he thinks it was Mr. Panofsky's plan all along to lure us here, and once we were comfortably settled—"

"*Lure* you here, with a luxurious home, low rent, ideal location—"

Martha laughed. "Exactly. What a cruel trap he set for us! And all because he knew that our presence would offer his family some protection against the Nazis."

Now the astonishingly low rent made perfect sense, for what Mr. Panofsky needed most was not extra income, but security. Surely the SS and SA would not risk an international incident by storming into the American ambassador's residence in order to seize Jews living in the attic. It was a clever plan, but Mr. Panofsky could still be arrested at his bank or on the streets if the Nazis wanted him badly enough.

"In Mr. Panofsky's place," Mildred ventured, "wouldn't you do whatever was necessary to protect the ones you love?"

"In his place, I'd leave Germany," said Martha, taking pen in hand again. "I wouldn't stay here another day. I'd gather my children and get out."

In early October, Martha invited Mildred and Arvid to a birthday party she was throwing for herself at Tiergartenstrasse 27a. Mildred readily accepted, but she almost regretted it in the days that followed when she learned that it would be a rather lavish affair, the guest list crowded with royals, nobles, the offspring of foreign diplomats, and young government officials. Mildred had only two dresses suitable for parties, neither of them formal enough for Martha's gala, but when she confided to Arvid's sister Inge that she was tempted to cancel, Inge immediately led her to her own closet, pulled out a lovely blue crepe de Chine dress, and insisted that Mildred take it.

On the night of October 8, Arvid put on his best dark suit and escorted Mildred, feeling lovely and carefree in her new gown, to the ambassador's residence, where the party was already well under way. In the ballroom, guests chatted as jazz played on the Victrola and the butler and a maid circulated with trays of drinks. Martha was clearly enjoying herself as she mingled among her guests, sipping champagne, introducing an American to a German here, flirting with a debonair young officer there. Little Hans and Ruth were nowhere to be seen, and over the music, Mildred could not hear them either.

"I see friendly faces over there," said Mildred as she glimpsed Quentin Reynolds chatting with Sigrid Schultz on the other side of the dance floor. "Let's say hello."

She and Arvid made their way to the pair, who were engrossed in conversation with another man, slight and dark, with keen, glowering eyes and a pipe clenched firmly between his teeth. They spoke earnestly in low voices, and every so often one would glance casually over a shoulder as if keeping watch for eavesdroppers. At the sight of Mildred and Arvid approaching, the third man abruptly fell silent.

"Don't worry about these two," Sigrid told him. "They're all right." Quickly she introduced Mildred and Arvid to Norman Ebbutt, a correspondent with the London *Times*. "We're holding a wake for journalistic freedom in Germany."

"I thought that died in March," said Arvid. "Hitler murdered it with the Reichstag Fire Decree."

Sigrid sighed and sipped her wine. "True enough, but the *Schriftleitergesetz* that the rubber-stamp Reichstag passed four days ago put the final nail in its coffin."

"This Editors Law forbids non-Aryans to work in journalism," said Ebbutt, his British accent mitigating none of his disgust. "When it goes into effect on January first, no Jew, and no one married to a Jew, will be permitted to work as a journalist or editor. And editors will be required to cut any story, any statement, that might, and I quote, 'weaken the strength of the Reich' here in Germany or abroad."

Sigrid shrugged. "If they don't want us to write about the bad things they do, they shouldn't do bad things."

Mildred knew the details of the law well thanks to Sara Weitz, who had analyzed it thoroughly for their study group the day before it went up for a vote in the Reichstag. Sara's brother was an editor at the *Berliner Tageblatt*, and she was deeply concerned about what the new restrictions would mean for him.

"It was only a matter of time," said Quentin. "Hitler knows that nothing poses a greater danger to a fascist regime than the free press. He and Goebbels are determined to put us in a chokehold, silencing our voices, discrediting whatever stories we manage to get past their censors."

"'Our voices'?" echoed Mildred. "The law applies to foreign correspondents too?"

"That remains to be seen," said Ebbutt. "I'm not terribly optimistic."

Even if foreign correspondents were exempt, Mildred knew many editors and writers who would suffer under the law—Sara's brother, former colleagues from the University of Berlin, as well as a significant proportion of their literary salon.

They commiserated a while longer, until Quentin and Ebbutt wandered off in search of another drink and Sigrid excused herself to hunt down a certain Nazi official whom she hoped would give her a quote for a story.

Just then, Mildred and Arvid spotted Martha coming their way on the arm of a tall man in his early forties with receding blond hair, shrewd blue eyes, and a mouth pursed in a contemplative frown. She introduced him as Hans Thomsen, an official who served as a liaison between the Chancellery and the Foreign Ministry. Thomsen's eyebrows rose when he learned that Mildred was an American, an academic, and an expert in American literature. "I'm very interested in contemporary American authors," he said, a faint Scandinavian accent coloring his English. "I'm especially curious to know which writers have the most influence with the American people."

"You'll have to ask her later," said Martha, smiling as she linked her arm through Mildred's. "I have to borrow Frau Harnack for a moment. In the meantime, Dr. Harnack is a brilliant economist, and if you ask nicely, I'm sure he'll explain his plan for saving the German economy."

Thomsen regarded Arvid with new interest. "Do you indeed have a plan, or is Miss Dodd giving me false hope?"

"I have a few ideas," Arvid acknowledged.

"Then you could be just the man the Reich needs."

"We'll leave you to it." As Martha led Mildred away, she added in an undertone, "Here's hoping they become fast friends. With a word to the right person, Herr Thomsen could help Arvid get a job at the Economics Ministry."

"I doubt they'll hit it off," murmured Mildred. "Thomsen's a Nazi."

"Yes, and very well placed. He and Hitler are quite close. It'll be fine. Tommy's not one of the fanatical ones. My father considers him relatively reasonable."

"Tommy?" Mildred echoed, amused. "Another romantic conquest?"

"Not one of mine. He's enamored with Elmina Rangabe, the Greek minister's daughter." Martha nodded toward the fireplace, where a beautiful dark-haired young woman in an emerald satin gown was holding court. "If you knew who I'm currently seeing, you'd never approve."

"I do know, and I don't approve. The chief of the Gestapo is—"

"Not Rudolf." Martha waved a hand dismissively, but there was a note of regret in her voice. "That's history. You know what they say, the hottest flames burn the swiftest, until only embers remain." She fanned herself with her hand. "We're still friends, though."

"That's fortunate, since he would be a very dangerous enemy. Who's your new fellow?"

"Oh, no. You're not getting that out of me. If my father knew—" Martha shook her head, then brightened as an enormous black-haired man burst into the ballroom and was met by a chorus of welcomes. He was well over six feet tall and looked to be around 250 pounds, and when he greeted his friends, his voice boomed like a baritone roll of thunder above the din of the party. "Oh, you have to meet Putzi Hanfstaengl."

A memory stirred as Mildred looked from her friend to the giant and back. "Is he your—"

"Putzi? Oh, God, no." Martha laughed. "Just a friend. But he's loads of fun. Don't let appearances deceive you. He's a Harvard man, and was quite the star of the Hasty Pudding Club as a student. He plays piano and sings too." She rose up on tiptoe and waved to the newcomer, who spotted her, beamed, and began making his way through the crowd to them. "In his student days he became good friends with Theodore Roosevelt Jr., a classmate, and he visited the White House often. Once he played the piano in the White House basement with such vigor that he broke seven strings."

Suddenly Mildred remembered why his surname sounded familiar.

"Is Putzi Hanfstaengl related to Ernst Hanfstaengl, the Nazi who gave Quentin such a hard time about his article?"

"One and the same. Putzi's a nickname. He's not just Hitler's foreign press chief. They're longtime friends, very close." Martha said the last in a hurried whisper as the man reached them. There were greetings and introductions, and although the big man was charming and spoke at a more civilized volume at close range, by the time he was called away to meet other friends, Mildred felt quite overwhelmed. She was relieved when Martha left to circulate among her guests and she could return to Arvid, who had not, as it happened, become best pals with Hans Thomsen, although Thomsen had found his economic theories intriguing.

Some time later, Mildred and Arvid were chatting with a young couple who were thinking about attending graduate school in the United States when the record on the Victrola began skipping.

"Put on Schubert's *Unfinished Symphony*," Putzi Hanfstaengl boomed.

"I know a tune you'll like even better," said Martha merrily as she crossed the room, graceful and swift, to change the record. After a moment of searching through the stack on a nearby shelf, she chose one, set it on the spindle, and lowered the needle. "This will get all you Germans singing."

A moment later, the bright notes of brass filled the room, and after the first few measures Mildred recognized the "Horst Wessel Lied," the Nazi Party anthem. How in the world had such a record ended up in the collection of the Dodd family? It couldn't possibly belong to Alfred Panofsky.

As the lively march played on, Putzi Hanfstaengl and a few others raised their voices in song and the Nazi officers snapped out the *Hitlergruss*. Suddenly Hans Thomsen strode across the room and switched off the record player.

"What's the matter?" protested Martha, smiling uncertainly, bewildered. "Don't you like it?"

"This is not the sort of music to be played in mixed gatherings and in a flippant manner," he snapped. "I won't have you play our anthem, with its significance, at a social party."

"The rest of us were enjoying it," said Hanfstaengl. His grin carried a hint of warning. "It's Martha's birthday, her party, and her house. She can play what she likes."

Martha's cheeks had flushed red with surprise, but as Hanfstaengl spoke, she frowned at Thomsen, a challenge in her eyes.

"I won't allow it," said Thomsen shortly. He removed the record from the Victrola, slipped it into its cardboard sleeve, and returned it to the shelf.

Hanfstaengl shrugged and murmured a joke to the people standing nearest to him. As they stifled nervous laughter, he sat down at the piano, flexed his fingers, and began playing Schubert's *Unfinished Symphony*.

The festive mood of the party was spoiled, but as the evening passed, Mildred admired Martha for the cheerful, vivacious way she went about trying to restore it. Hans Thomsen left early with Elmina Rangabe on his arm, easing the tension considerably.

Later, as Mildred and Arvid were preparing to leave, they came upon Hanfstaengl offering Martha a few kind words of reassurance. "No harm was done," he said in flawless English. "Find it in your heart to forgive him if you can."

"Why should I?" Martha retorted. "I thought you would enjoy it. I certainly meant no insult. His reaction was totally out of proportion."

"Perhaps, but some people have blind spots and no sense of humor regarding certain matters." Hanfstaengl gently placed his enormous paws on Martha's shoulders and bent to catch her eye. "One must be careful not to offend their sensitive souls."

Softly Mildred cleared her throat to warn them they were not alone, and they quickly stepped apart. Arvid shook Hanfstaengl's hand, Mildred kissed Martha on the cheek, and they both wished her a happy birthday.

"One must be careful not to offend the Nazis' sensitive souls," said Arvid acerbically when he and Mildred were alone on the sidewalk outside Tiergartenstrasse 27a. "They're as precious and fragile as butterfly wings."

"But of course," said Mildred, taking his arm. "Nazis are known around the world for their delicate, sensitive, artistic souls."

Arvid smiled wryly, and as they headed home, Mildred felt a small, guilty twinge of satisfaction. She was sorry that Martha had been embarrassed by a guest at her own birthday party, but if the insult helped shatter her illusions about the nobility and wisdom of the Nazis, Mildred could not regret it.

CHAPTER TWENTY-ONE

October–December 1933

Martha

On the evening of Saturday, October 14, Martha carefully applied her favorite red lipstick, fluffed her short dark waves with her fingers, and smiled winsomely at herself in the mirror before pulling on her most flattering autumn coat and snatching up her purse. By that time her escort ought to be parked a block away, glancing at his watch with impatient hope and willing her to hurry. Any other fellow would have waited for her in the drawing room, enduring appraising looks from her mother and the third degree from her father, but this particular date was so fraught with political tension that she thought it best if she just slipped quietly out the front door.

She found Boris Vinogradov's black Ford convertible parked exactly where he had promised to wait, the top up in deference to the season. She gracefully slipped into the front passenger seat, allowing him a quick, not-quite-accidental glimpse of thigh before smoothing her skirt down demurely.

Boris's gaze flicked from her legs to her face. "Good evening, Miss Dodd. I thought you might have changed your mind."

She shrugged. "No better offer came along, so here I am."

He smiled and started the engine. "I'm honored that you spent so much time primping for me that it made you late."

"Don't flatter yourself," she teased. "I just threw on the first thing I grabbed from my closet and ran a comb through my hair."

"When you bade your parents goodbye, did your father mention what he thinks of Chancellor Hitler's decision to withdraw Germany from the League of Nations and the World Disarmament Conference?"

She arched her eyebrows at him. "Who's asking? Boris, my charming dinner companion, or Comrade Vinogradov, first secretary of the Soviet embassy?"

His only reply was a grin and a shrug.

"You'll have to ask him yourself," she replied airily. "As I've told you, my father never discusses diplomatic matters with me."

She gazed out the window, pretending to admire the lights in the Tiergarten, her smile fading. After the shocking announcement earlier that day, her father had warned the family that with a single decision, Hitler had rendered the League of Nations impotent.

"They might as well tear up the Treaty of Versailles," Bill had said. "The only possible explanation is that Hitler intends to rebuild the German military."

"The other members of the League won't permit that," their father replied. "They would have no choice but to respond with force while they still have the power to subdue him. We'd have another war."

"Impossible," Martha protested. "No one wants another war in Europe."

"The German people don't want war, even if certain irrational leaders do," Martha's father had said. "Everything depends upon whether the will of the people will constrain Hitler, or whether Hitler will reshape the will of the people."

In spite of the rising tensions, Martha's father, his counterparts in the German diplomatic corps, and other foreign ambassadors were expected to conduct business on behalf of their governments as always, and that meant mixing cordially with Nazi officials at embassy dinners and other functions. Martha skipped the duller affairs unless her mother specifically asked her to attend, but if the invitation mentioned drinks and dancing, or if the guest list included particularly handsome and charming men, she happily accepted.

One Saturday evening in late October, Martha attended a cocktail party at the Italian embassy. It was a joy to forget her cares for a few hours, drinking and dancing in the ballroom with the young people while their elders talked somberly in little groups in the drawing room. Boris was not there, which disappointed Martha because he had promised to come, but Putzi attended, and they had a jolly time.

After two glasses of champagne, Putzi confided that Hitler's recent decisions troubled him. "His erratic temper is bad for the Reich," he grumbled. "But what can I do? He's surrounded by ambitious, unscrupulous men. He needs a good influence to counteract the bad."

Martha shrugged and drained her glass. "He should spend more time with my father. You couldn't find a more decent, honorable man, not in Germany and not in the States."

"That's a lot to ask of your father." Suddenly Putzi brightened. "What Hitler needs is a woman."

"That's not what I've heard. They say he's completely indifferent to women, although he's been involved with a few rather young girls—"

"Hush!" Putzi seized her elbow and steered her away from the others. "Don't you care who might be listening?"

"Are you kidding? My father knows you've tapped the phones at the embassy and our residence. Don't you already know everything I think and say?"

"I didn't tap your phones."

"I didn't mean you personally." Martha took a fresh glass of champagne from a passing waiter's tray. "Some entry-level spook did it for you."

Putzi heaved a sigh. "Martha, listen. I'm serious. All Hitler needs is the love of a good woman and he'll calm down and become more reasonable. The right woman could transform the destiny of Europe."

Martha raised her glass. "I wish her good luck and Godspeed."

"Martha, you are the woman!"

She regarded him for a moment, uncertain whether to laugh or to be insulted. "I really don't think so."

Undeterred, Putzi cajoled and argued his way through the rest of the evening. When they parted company later that night, he must have imagined he detected some equivocation in her refusal, for he began calling her once or twice a day, until she found herself wavering. Perhaps it wasn't such a crazy idea. Putzi considered Hitler a friend, so he must have some redeeming qualities.

After thinking it over and getting her parents' reluctant consent, Martha called Putzi and agreed that he could play matchmaker.

Martha had no idea what to wear for the date Putzi arranged, lunch at the Kaiserhof, a grand hotel seven blocks away on Wilhelmplatz, just southeast of the Tiergarten. She understood that Nazis preferred women to be seen and not heard, to be demure and lovely ornaments on the arms of great men. Wives were expected to be meticulous housekeepers and fecund mothers, but Martha would definitely break it off before it went that far.

Still undecided with only one day to go, when Mildred came over to work on their column, Martha begged her to help her choose the perfect dress and accessories for a very important date. "You know what German men like," she said. "You married one."

Mildred smiled and set down her pen. "Who is this special fellow?" she asked as they went upstairs. "Putzi Hanfstaengl?"

"For the last time, no. Putzi is just a friend. You probably wouldn't approve, but—" Martha shook her head. "Never mind."

"Never mind? You can't leave it at that."

"Well—" Martha glanced over her shoulder. Her family had begun to suspect that Fritz sympathized with the Nazis, and one couldn't be too careful. She waited until they were alone in her room before taking a deep breath and plunging ahead. "Putzi thinks Hitler needs a girlfriend to make him a more pleasant, reasonable person, so . . . he arranged a date. With me."

Mildred recoiled, horrified. "You can't mean it. A date with that fascist monster? How could you agree to that? You know what he is, what he stands for!"

"It's only lunch," said Martha, defensive. "I haven't agreed to be his concubine."

Mildred grimaced and pressed a hand to her stomach. "Now I really do feel ill. I don't understand. Hitler's odious, vile, cruel. What will your parents say when they find out?"

"They already know, and anyway, if my father knew who the alternative was, he'd push me into the chancellor's arms."

"I can't believe that. Anyone would be better than Hitler."

"If I tell you, you have to swear to tell no one, not even Arvid."

Mildred frowned and nodded, marking an X over her heart with a finger.

"Boris Vinogradov."

For a moment Mildred could only stare at her. "The first secretary of the Soviet embassy?"

"So you see my problem." Martha dropped onto the bed, her hands in her lap. "The United States hasn't officially recognized the Soviet Union. It would put my father in a very difficult position if word got out that I'm seeing one of their diplomats."

"That's not your only problem," said Mildred. "Arvid has friends at the Soviet embassy, and—I don't have any proof, but Boris Vinogradov almost certainly works for the NKVD." When Martha barely shrugged, she added, "That's the Soviet intelligence division. It's quite possible that he isn't trying to romance you, but to recruit you."

"All the more reason for me to see other men."

"Agreed, but *this* man?"

Martha threw her hands in the air, exasperated. "The last time I saw Carl Sandburg before leaving for Germany, he told me that I should take notes on anything and everything. He urged me to 'find out what this man Hitler is made of, what makes his brain go round, what his bones and blood are made of.'"

"So you're saying you'd date Adolf Hitler because you think it would be good research for a future book?"

"If you were single, wouldn't you?"

"Absolutely not. The very idea makes my skin crawl."

"Then my books are destined to be more exciting than yours," Martha replied. "Now, are you still willing to help me decide what to wear?"

After a moment Mildred nodded, but it was obvious she hoped

Martha would find nothing suitable and would have no choice but to cancel the date.

"Nothing too glamorous or revealing," mused Martha as they studied her closet. "And yet still elegant and alluring. If I'm going to change the course of European history, I'd better look the part."

They settled on a pearlescent light mauve crepe de Chine suit and a hat with a tiny veil that added modesty without concealing any of her enticing features. "You look very pretty," said Mildred as Martha turned and posed in front of the mirror. "Too pretty."

"I know you disapprove," said Martha, turning her back to the mirror, "but if there's even the slightest chance that Putzi is right, and I could influence the chancellor for the better, shouldn't I try?"

"I don't know. Just be careful," she begged, and Martha promised she would.

The next day, Martha dressed, fixed her hair, and studied her face in the mirror, frowning slightly. She had worn almost no makeup as befitted the Nazi ideal, and she was not happy about it. But she had no time for second thoughts about her appearance, for Putzi arrived fifteen minutes early to drive her to the Kaiserhof. He seemed even more anxious than she was for the date to go well.

Putzi escorted her to the elegant Kaiserhof tearoom, where they met another lunch guest, the famous Polish singer Jan Kiepura. "Where's the chancellor?" Martha asked Putzi after they were seated and a quick glance around revealed that her date was not in the room.

"He's coming," Putzi replied. "Not to worry."

The three chatted and drank tea for quite some time, and Martha was just beginning to wonder if she had been stood up when she heard a commotion near the front entrance, the scrape of chairs against the floor, and shouts of "Heil Hitler!" Moments later, Hitler entered the room with his usual entourage of Nazi Party men, bodyguards, and beloved chauffeur, a set of companions Boris contemptuously referred to as the Chauffeureska.

Martha smiled and tried to catch the chancellor's eye, but to her surprise, he never glanced her way as the maître d' led his group to a nearby table. As Hitler and the Chauffeureska seated themselves and began perusing their menus, Martha raised her eyebrows at Putzi in a significant glance and picked up her own menu.

The men at the chancellor's table ordered lunch; Martha and her two companions ordered theirs. After the first course, one of Hitler's aides came over to their table and invited Jan Kiepura to meet the chancellor. Martha feigned indifference, but she could not help feeling slighted as Hitler invited the singer to be seated and the two men conversed earnestly throughout the second course.

"Kiepura is a Jew on his mother's side," Putzi murmured. "I don't think Hitler knows."

"I hope you aren't planning to tell him."

"Of course not," Putzi replied, wounded. "It's none of my business."

Martha managed a tight smile, wondering why she was there when her ostensible date seemed to have no interest in acknowledging her existence. The food was excellent, so at least there was that.

As the second course was cleared, Putzi excused himself, walked over to Hitler's table, and spoke briefly, bending close to his ear. Soon he returned to Martha and said that Hitler had consented to be introduced to her.

Martha rose, hiding her surprise, for she had assumed consent had already been given. She followed Putzi to the other table and remained standing while he made a formal introduction. Hitler rose, took her hand, and kissed it politely. He murmured a few phrases in German that she did not quite catch, so she smiled and nodded in reply, wishing Putzi would translate for her.

It occurred to her that Hitler's little mustache did not look as ridiculous in person as it did in photographs. His face was unexpectedly soft and weak, with pouches under his eyes and fleshy lips. His hands were small and surprisingly feminine. His only distinctive feature was his eyes, which Martha found startling—very pale blue, intense, unwavering, even hypnotic.

The chancellor spoke again in German, his tone polite and perhaps a bit embarrassed, and Martha smiled back, though she grasped only every third word or so and he could have been rudely propositioning her for all she knew. After a brief time he shook her hand, and raised it to his lips for another kiss, which Martha assumed was his way of bidding her goodbye, for as soon as he released her hand, Putzi escorted her back to their table.

"Are you going to translate any of that for me?" she murmured.

"Just the usual pleasantries," he replied quietly, pulling out her chair. "He thinks you're very pretty, sufficiently Aryan despite your dark hair."

Martha bit back a derisive laugh and sat down. Over dessert and coffee, she and Putzi chatted idly, while at the other table, Hitler and Kiepura resumed their conversation, sober and intent.

"What are they talking about?" Martha asked Putzi in an undertone.

"Music," Putzi replied. "What else?"

What else indeed. Martha muffled a sigh and finished her cake. From time to time, Hitler gave her a few curious, abashed stares, but they never exchanged another word, not even when the chancellor and his Chauffeureska rose and departed.

Martha watched him go, bemused. Most men she met tried a little harder to impress her. Considering his position, perhaps he thought the burden was upon her to impress him.

Putzi seemed jubilant as he drove her home, which Martha did not understand in the least, because she could not imagine that she had made a very good impression. She had no idea what sort of woman it would take to inspire romance from Chancellor Hitler.

It came as no surprise when the days passed without an invitation from Hitler to meet again, or even a perfunctory, impersonal note from the chancellor's office acknowledging their meeting, which an ambassador's daughter might have expected.

Putzi seemed disappointed at first, but he got over it by mid-November. The most enduring outcome of the date was the jealousy it provoked from Boris—which was quite thrilling, and added another element of excitement to their clandestine relationship. The United States officially recognized the Soviet Union on November 16, but even after Martha's father paid his first official visit to the Soviet embassy, the couple remained utterly platonic in public. Their romance, if it became widely known, would displease Martha's parents, Boris's superiors, and the innumerable Nazi officials who spotted threats and conspiracy in every chance meeting between foreign diplomats—and their daughters too, apparently. Martha was certain the Gestapo shadowed her and Boris on walks through the Tiergarten to admire the autumn foliage, and at private dinners at discreet restaurants. Fortunately, Tiergartenstrasse 27a had many rooms, and her parents preferred to turn in early. How fortunate it was, too, that she had obtained a diaphragm back in Chicago during her brief stint as a married woman. It would have been all but impossible to get one as a single girl in Berlin.

The Dodds' first Thanksgiving abroad passed, and winter followed swiftly after with starry nights and gentle snow showers. It seemed to Martha that no one celebrated Christmas more merrily than Germans. Even in those troubled times, candles shone in the windows of every home and electric lights in every storefront, their illumination reflected in the streets and sidewalks, wet from melted snow. Strings of electric bulbs adorned the tall evergreen trees in public parks and squares, and shoppers bustled about purchasing delicacies for neighborhood parties and family feasts.

"I find the German enthusiasm for Christmas absolutely extraordinary," Martha's father told his family a few days before the holiday. "Christmas trees at public squares and in every house I've entered. One might be led to think that Germans believe in Jesus and practice his teachings."

When his wife gently reminded him that many Germans did, Martha's father acknowledged that he was wrong to conflate all Germans and the Nazis.

"Never mind, Dad. We've all made that mistake," said Martha, with a sudden flare of sympathy for the Harnacks, for Greta Lorke, for other Germans she knew who strongly opposed the regime, an increasingly shrinking minority in a country increasingly intolerant of dissent.

CHAPTER TWENTY-TWO

January–June 1934

Sara

On the first day of the New Year, Sara's brother and many of his colleagues were abruptly thrown out of work when the Editors Law went into effect. Foreign correspondents were exempt, but all German writers and editors were required to present church records or civil documentation to prove that they were Aryan. If they could not, they were forbidden to register with the Reich Press Chamber, and unregistered journalists caught writing or editing faced up to a year in prison. Jews who had served in the Great War, who had lost a son in battle, or who wrote for Jewish newspapers were exempt, but very few slipped through those loopholes. Natan was one who did not.

Their father offered to ask Mr. Panofsky if there were any clerical posts available for him at the bank, but Natan said he would prefer to look for something that better suited his talents. Their mother reminded him that he could always move back home to save on rent until a new job came along. Natan thanked her but declined; he had been putting money aside ever since the law was announced in October, and he could afford to keep his apartment for now.

Sara thought her brother was being remarkably stoic for someone whose career had been stolen from him. Natan had been forced to give up work he thrived on, and his circle of friends diminished as colleagues and competitors, newly unemployed and with most other professions closed to them, decided to emigrate. Some found their plans thwarted by bureaucracy. When Natan mentioned that some journalists he knew struggled to get visas, Sara asked for their names, ages, and addresses. He regarded her appraisingly but asked no questions, and two days later he produced a list of about a dozen journalists. At the next meeting of her study group, Sara took Mildred aside, gave her the folded paper, and asked if she could convince her contacts at the U.S. embassy to intervene.

Mildred scanned the list. "I don't see your brother's name."

"He's not leaving. I almost wish he would, except I'd miss him, and my parents would be heartbroken."

Mildred smiled understandingly, folded the paper, and slipped it into her pocket. She made no promises, but in early February, Natan told Sara that the obstacles preventing his friends from emigrating had inexplicably vanished. "I don't know what you did," he said, embracing her in a bear hug that lifted her feet nearly off the ground, "but thank you."

"All I did was pass on a list."

"To those men and their families, that was everything."

As winter passed, Sara continued her studies, dreading that any day her exemption would be revoked and she would be expelled from the university. Her father's job seemed secure as long as Mr. Panofsky remained in charge, and with the American ambassador's family residing in his home, the Gestapo surely would not risk an international incident by harassing him. Natan said very little about his job search, but it seemed to Sara that it had stalled, if it had ever truly started. She stopped reading the *Berliner Tageblatt* in protest, but Natan, amused, reminded her that it was not the publishers' fault he was no longer permitted to work for them. "Depriving yourself of the best news reporting in the city won't get me my job back," he pointed out. "I still read the *Berliner Tageblatt* and I intend to continue."

"How can you be so loyal?" she asked. "The publishers didn't fight to keep you. They've already replaced you. I've seen the new bylines."

He shrugged. "They have to keep the paper going, and they can't do that without reporters."

Sara marveled at his forbearance. In his place, she would resent every new reporter who had accepted a job unwillingly vacated by a Jew. Surely they knew they were profiting from the misery of Natan and his former colleagues.

When she shared her feelings with Dieter, he sided with Natan. "If your brother and your parents still read the *Berliner Tageblatt*, why shouldn't you?" he asked reasonably. "Some of these new writers are really quite good."

"They can't be as good as Natan," she retorted, and Dieter quickly replied that of course they weren't, he hadn't meant that at all. Natan had been wronged and the paper suffered for it, but he was resourceful and Dieter was confident that he would figure out something.

Eventually Sara acquiesced, but when she resumed reading the paper, she insisted that it was not as good as before. "Some of the new reporters write fairly well," she conceded one morning when Natan asked her for her honest opinion. He had joined the family for breakfast, something he indulged in more often lately, now that his schedule permitted. "This M. A. Holtzer, for example, has a fluid style."

"I'll let you in on a secret," said Natan. "M. A. stands for Mathilda Alisz."

"A woman?" their mother remarked. "And she's not trapped on the society page? How marvelous!"

Sara scanned the front page until her gaze lit upon another newly familiar name. "Konrad Dressler is quite good too. Informative, but never didactic or sensationalist. A graceful, yet straightforward style. And yet—"

Natan's eyebrows rose. "A complaint?"

"No, a concern. Criticism of the Nazis is woven through everything he writes, so subtly that he wouldn't be condemned for it, yet readers who agree with him couldn't mistake his true meaning." Sara spread the paper out flat and held Natan's gaze over the table. "Do you know him well enough to warn him to be careful?"

"I do, and I could, but I don't think he'll change."

"So he's as stubborn as you?"

"He should be. I taught him everything he knows."

Sara smiled sweetly and pointed at the second paragraph of Dressler's editorial. "Including this rather eccentric use of the dative construction instead of the genitive?"

"What?" Natan spun the paper around and studied it, frowning. "How did that happen?"

"As editor, you would have caught that error. Say what you will, the paper isn't as good as it once was."

"They're doing the best they can in difficult circumstances. We all are."

"Then why don't you let Papa find you a job at the bank? Why don't you move back home before you use up all your savings?"

"Why not indeed?" said their mother.

"What if you need that money to—" Sara could not bring herself to say that he might need it to emigrate. "For something important?"

Natan rested his elbows on the table and looked her straight in the eye. "Don't worry about me. I pick up odd jobs here and there. I'll be fine." His gaze shifted to his parents. "I promise that if the choice is move back home or starve, you'll find me back in my old room in a heartbeat."

Sara had to accept that, but it frustrated and angered her that he had to resort to odd jobs while someone more Aryan sat in his old office doing his work half as well.

Winter faded and spring bloomed, green and fresh, the days gently sunny and warm, belying the political tempest raging through Berlin. Sara and Dieter once again walked hand in hand through the Tiergarten, avoiding political topics because Dieter did not like to see her upset over things she could not change and Sara did not think he took current events seriously enough.

In April, the brilliance of the lush, verdant spring diminished as seasonal rain showers held off and temperatures climbed. At the end of the month, as foliage withered in the Tiergarten and grasses faded to brown, Reich officials revealed that President Hindenburg was gravely ill and was not expected to survive the summer. Immediately the question of who would succeed him became an urgent matter. Natan thought that Chancellor Hitler was the strongest contender for the role, but he faced a formidable challenge from his erstwhile friend Captain Ernst Röhm, the head of the Sturmabteilung. The Brownshirts had increased in number so rapidly that Röhm now commanded more storm troopers than were in the entire Reichswehr, which the Treaty of Versailles limited to one hundred thousand troops. If Hitler defied the treaty, as he seemed eager to do, he would gain parity of numbers with Röhm, since the army was controlled by the defense minister, a loyal member of his cabinet.

"According to my sources," Natan told Sara in mid-May over a lunch-time picnic of sandwiches made from leftovers from the Weitz family's supper, "Röhm has told a number of foreign diplomats that he wants to incorporate the Sturmabteilung into the Reichswehr, with himself in charge of the new, unified military. Captain Röhm already has many enemies, and he seems determined to make another of Hitler."

"You still have sources?" asked Sara. "You didn't have to turn them over to your replacement?"

"Dressler can find his own sources."

"How do you think it will end?" asked Sara, trying to sound less anxious than she really felt. If Natan suspected his reports frightened her, he might stop sharing them. "Is there a chance that they might fight and bring each other down?"

"It's more likely that one man will destroy the other." He finished his sandwich and brushed crumbs from his fingertips. "As long as Hindenburg is at least nominally in charge, I still have hope for Germany."

As the drought persisted into summer and concerns rose that the year's harvest might be lost, gossip about conflicts in the Nazi hierarchy flew through Berlin. One compelling rumor said that President Hindenburg blamed Hitler for the rising tensions in Germany and that his downfall was imminent, prompting debate about who might replace him—perhaps Heinrich Brüning or General Kurt von Schleicher, both former chancellors. Another, more foreboding rumor insisted that Hitler could be neither uprooted nor constrained, and that he was merely waiting for an opportune moment to crush Röhm and remove the threat of his SA once and for all.

Dieter remained resolutely neutral, noting that his business's clientele came from all walks of life and he could not afford to offend anyone by publicly siding with one faction or another. Sara chided him that when something was demonstrably morally wrong, one had an obligation to disavow it. Her words had little effect. Dieter was so determined to see the virtues of every group that Sara gave up trying to discuss anything with him other than the weather, their family and mutual friends, and his business.

Even their engagement became an uncomfortable subject. Every time Sara brought up unresolved issues, such as what to do about their children's religious upbringing and how to handle his mother's increasingly querulous inquiries about Sara's interest in converting, he would either list a variety of valid opinions without clarifying his own or defer the discussion for another day. She would have suspected that his interest in marriage was waning if not for his increasing ardor when they were alone. At first she enjoyed it, but when he began urging her to go further than she wanted, murmuring breathlessly between kisses that they were going to be married anyway so there was no reason to refrain, and he didn't need her to be a virgin on their wedding night as long as he was the only man she had been with, she became annoyed and unhappy. What if she got pregnant? What if something happened and they didn't marry after all? He assured her nothing would go awry, but the world was veering sharply toward the wrong and no one knew for certain what the future would bring. She still loved Dieter, but she found guilty comfort in their decision not to marry until she finished her education, and in the fact that it took years to earn a doctorate.

With Dieter proving a poor conversationalist, Sara relied on Mildred's study group for engrossing political conversation, Amalie for long heart-to-heart talks about her hopes for the future. But for someone without a job, Natan was curiously unavailable. He still met Sara for weekly lunches, but he stopped coming around for breakfast and declined an invitation to spend a weekend with the family at Amalie and Wilhelm's estate in Minden-Lübbecke. Then, one Wednesday in late June, Natan failed to show up for their weekly lunch, and the following Saturday, he did not come home for Shabbat.

"He always lets me know if he has to cancel," Sara's mother said, a deep groove of worry appearing between her brows.

"I'm sure he's fine," said Sara's father. "Perhaps something came up at the last minute."

"Perhaps he's met a nice young woman, and he's celebrating Shabbat with her family tonight," said Amalie, smiling brightly for her daughters. Sylvie and Leah smiled back, but Sara knew no one else at the table believed it.

The next morning, when Natan did not answer his phone, Sara decided to go see him. The Untergrundbahn seemed to make the trip across the city more slowly than it ever had, but eventually Sara was racing up the stairs to Natan's flat, knocking on the door, and calling his name.

He did not answer.

She tried again, and when he did not reply, she checked under the loose piece of carpet below the door hinge for his spare key. It was gone. Heart pounding, she peered through the mail slot and saw a few envelopes scattered in the entry.

She rose, thoughts racing. Many of his friends had emigrated, and she was not sure how to reach those who remained.

Then she realized exactly where to start searching.

Fifteen minutes later, she arrived at the offices of the *Berliner Tageblatt*. She had visited Natan at work frequently through the years, but she did not recognize the pretty young blonde sitting at the receptionist's desk. "I beg your pardon," Sara asked, as calmly as she could. "Is Natan Weitz in today?"

The young woman frowned, thoughtful. "I don't believe he works here anymore."

"Perhaps he's here visiting a friend."

She shook her head. "I didn't see him come in."

Sara searched her memory. "Is his boss here? Simon Auerbach?"

"Herr Auerbach resigned two weeks ago."

"Would you phone him for me, please?" Sara heard the rising panic in her voice and took a deep breath. "Or give me his number and I'll call him from home? Whatever is easier for you."

"I'm sorry, but he moved to Canada. I could give you his address——"

"No, thank you." Then a thought struck. "Konrad Dressler. May I speak with Konrad Dressler?"

"Miss Weitz?"

Turning, Sara discovered a trim man in a fine suit studying her with concern. "Yes?"

He shook her hand. "Karl Meinholz, senior editor."

"Oh, yes, of course." Natan had always spoken well of him. "I'm looking for my brother. Have you seen him recently?"

In reply, Meinholz invited Sara to accompany him to his office. She accepted the chair he offered, but before she could say anything, he held up a finger, shut the door, and sat down behind his desk. Only then did he speak. "I regret that Natan Weitz is no longer on the staff of the *Berliner Tageblatt*. That would be against the law."

"Yes, I know, but Natan has so many friends here, and I haven't been able to reach him."

His brow furrowed. "When he stopped coming around, I assumed he had left Germany."

"Natan has no intention of leaving. I last saw him almost two weeks ago. He isn't at his apartment, and he isn't answering his phone. That's why I came here, to see if any of his friends know where he is."

"You asked to see Konrad Dressler."

She nodded. "Natan mentioned him, and I know he still works here."

"Miss Weitz—" Meinholz paused. "There is no Konrad Dressler."

"But I've seen his byline."

"Yes, his byline, but your brother's words."

"You mean . . ." Sara studied him. "My brother is Konrad Dressler?" Meinholz nodded.

"Then Natan violated the Editors Law. If the Gestapo figured it out—"

"No one here would have breathed a word," Meinholz assured her. "Betraying him would put us all in danger."

But a jealous rival could have informed on Natan nonetheless, or the Gestapo could have found out another way. They could have followed him from his flat to work, or recognized his writing style. Regardless, he had broken the law and had put himself in terrible danger.

Sara murmured her thanks and quickly left Meinholz's office. She ran back to Natan's flat, tried the door again, roused his landlord, and convinced him to unlock the door for her. She was afraid to ask if anyone else had come by looking for Natan—Gestapo or Brownshirts or police.

The landlord fumbled with the key in the lock, but eventually he opened the door and waved her inside. The spare key sat on the table in the entryway.

"Thank you," she said, managing a shaky smile as she stooped to pick up Natan's scattered mail. "I'll lock up when I go."

Grumbling, he left her. Immediately she closed and locked the door.

She left the mail beside the key on the table and searched the flat. The bed was made. Breakfast dishes were piled in the sink. A hand towel near the washbasin was perfectly dry. The air was still and stale, the plants on the windowsill unwatered. Natan's suitcase sat on the floor of his closet beneath a half-full laundry basket.

Natan was gone, but if he had fled Germany, he had told no one and had taken nothing with him.

CHAPTER TWENTY-THREE

June–July 1934

Martha

Early on the morning of Saturday, June 30, Martha gave her father a jaunty wave and her mother a quick peck on the cheek before snatching up her bag and her wide-brimmed hat and darting out the door to meet Boris, who was waiting in the driveway at the wheel of his Ford convertible with the top down. "Shall we go?" she asked as she climbed in and slung her bag into the back next to a folded blanket and a picnic hamper. She slipped on her sunglasses and considered putting on the hat too, but she tossed it on top of her bag instead, the better to enjoy the wind in her hair.

Boris started the car, a corner of his mouth turning inquisitively. "You hope to make a quick getaway before your parents discover who is driving away with their daughter?"

"Don't be silly." She had confessed that she was seeing Boris shortly after her strange date with Chancellor Hitler. There was already too much deceit poisoning the world. "They know I'm with you."

"And they still let you leave?"

Martha laughed lightly, and as he turned the car onto Tiergartenstrasse, Boris grinned back. They both knew there was very little her parents could do to prevent her from doing as she pleased.

Exhibit A: her upcoming tour of the Soviet Union. Her parents were vehemently opposed to the trip, even though she had explained that it was not admiration for communism that compelled her but love for Boris. As much as she adored him, she could not ignore her nagging worries that their romance was doomed. She needed to learn more about him, his beliefs, and his country before she could possibly know whether they had a chance at a future together. And she needed to know. Every day, as her feelings for him grew stronger, so too did her concerns that the differences between their two worlds were irreconcilable, and she ought to get out now rather than set herself up for worse heartbreak later.

She did not confess her worries to Boris, but she suspected he knew. "I could show you the Soviet Union," he had protested when she first announced her trip. "You'll get a much better sense of my country that way than on an official government tour, with everything scripted and curated to impress."

"If you're there, you might influence me even without meaning to," she had said, running a hand through his hair and kissing his cheek to soften the blow. "I have to reach my own conclusions."

He had nodded grudgingly, but they argued about it later, spoiling a lovely evening walk through the Tiergarten with baseless accusations and biting retorts. They were both such passionate people that their relationship inevitably shifted dramatically through peaks of great joy, valleys of anger when they declared it was over between them, and the muted middle ground of remorse and reconciliation. Mildred, who disapproved of Boris only slightly less than Martha's parents did, called it the "Russian roller coaster" and encouraged Martha to disembark. Martha laughed off her friend's warnings even as she secretly thought she probably ought to heed them. Could she really marry Boris and make a life with him in the Soviet Union, a country so unlike America? Her trip would help her decide one way or the other.

But that journey was a week away, and she refused to let any worries about the future of their relationship spoil their outing. The night's coolness had burned off with the dawn, and the bright sunshine and cloudless skies promised a hot, sultry day, perfect for swimming and sunbathing.

They drove about twenty kilometers west to Gross Glienicker See, a beautiful serene lake with secluded coves and sandy beaches surrounded by lush forest. In a private spot on the northern shore, they spread their blanket in the sunshine, stripped down to the swimsuits they had worn beneath their clothes, and plunged into the cool, pristine lake, refreshed and exhilarated by the sensuous touch of the water upon their skin, their mutual desire, and the anticipation of pleasure. By unspoken agreement they said nothing of Nazis or politics but luxuriated in idleness, speaking little and then only of the fine weather and the beautiful scenery. They glided together and apart, closing their eyes and lifting their faces to the sky, sighing as the concerns of Berlin and of the future were washed away.

When they tired of swimming they lay in each other's arms on the blanket, baking in the sun, plunging into the lake again when the heat became unbearable. When they were fatigued, they dozed; when they were hungry, they moved their blanket into the shade, unpacked the picnic hamper, and dined on sandwiches, beer, and vodka. Martha had not felt so content since she had arrived in Berlin, with the crystal lake shimmering in the sunlight, the blue sky above endless and serene, and Boris, lacing his fingers through hers, smiling as he smoothed her windblown curls from her face, pressing his lips to hers and lingering there, his mouth warm and hungry and tasting faintly of beer and mustard.

The temperature continued to rise throughout that glorious, lazy, sunbaked day, and they agreed that it was probably unendurable in the city and they were clever to have escaped it. But they were obliged to return, so at five o'clock they reluctantly dressed, shook the sand from the blanket, packed up the Ford, and headed back to Berlin.

As they left the lake behind, Martha sighed contentedly, relaxed into her seat, and pulled up her skirt to the bottom of her bathing suit to soak in the last sunbeams and enjoy the cooling breezes stirred up by the car's swift passage. From the corner of her eye, she noticed Boris glancing frequently at her sun-kissed thighs. "Keep your eyes on the road or we'll end up in a ditch," she teased.

"How can I?" he retorted, his voice a low, thrilling growl. "You're the most delicious distraction."

She smiled and tilted her head back, enjoying his attention.

The car sped from cool shade into patches of brilliant sunshine where the scent of pine and earth came to her sharp and pungent. They passed between bicyclists traveling in both directions, men and women alike, some carrying small children in little wagons on the side or in baskets on the front. Occasionally a motorcycle sped noisily past them, the riders' faces obscured by leather helmets and thick goggles. Others traveled on foot, women in pairs, strolling leisurely with a basket dangling from an elbow or with armfuls of flowers, sturdy men striding along with knapsacks. Martha's heart warmed to the German country folk, so simple, friendly, and earnest as they enjoyed the beauty of their land.

It was nearly six o'clock when they reached Berlin, and, knowing that she might be recognized, Martha pulled down her skirts and sat up straight as befit an ambassador's daughter. Boris said something in Russian, a mournful complaint understandable in any language. Martha laughed, so charmed by his admiration that a few minutes passed before she realized that the streets were curiously empty for a balmy Saturday evening—no couples strolling arm in arm, no stout gentlemen walking their dogs, no friendly groups meeting up outside restaurants or theaters. Martha spotted a few sparse clusters of men on street corners, but they were strangely static, turned inward, sometimes glancing warily over their shoulders at the police, who seemed to be out in greater numbers than usual.

Beside her, Boris shifted in his seat and inhaled deeply, and she knew he sensed the unsettling, electric tension in the air too.

As they approached the heart of the city, Martha's heart sank with dismay at the sight of heavy army trucks, machine guns, soldiers posted here and there, black-clad SS officers marching, and more police, their green uniforms standing out against the stone buildings.

"Where are the SA?" said Boris, slowing the car to give way to a heavy military truck turning onto the boulevard before them.

Martha's breath caught in her throat as she looked around. There was not a Brownshirt to be seen.

Traffic slowed to a crawl, and when they reached the Tiergarten, they discovered more military trucks loaded with soldiers and what

Martha guessed were stores of weapons. Armed soldiers had taken up positions on the sidewalks and in the park, and some streets were blocked off and heavily guarded. Her heart thudded as they approached a checkpoint, but the soldier scrutinized the diplomatic plate on Boris's Ford and waved them through.

"Boris," she said shakily, "what's going on?"

"I don't know." He inched the car along, nodding politely to the soldiers who made way for them. "Stay calm."

She nodded and clasped her hands together in her lap, willing her features into a dispassionate mask. At last Tiergartenstrasse 27a came into view, but her breath caught in her throat at the sight of more trucks, soldiers, and armaments arranged across the street before it. Not far away, Standartenstrasse was entirely roped off, a cordon of green-uniformed police barring passage to all.

"I have to get to my embassy," Boris said as they drew closer to the residence.

"I know. Just drop me off at the end of the driveway."

"Are you sure?"

She inhaled deeply and nodded. Keeping one hand on the wheel and his eyes on the streets and soldiers, Boris reached for her hand and squeezed it. She clasped it in both of hers and held on tightly until he brought the car to a halt in front of the residence. There was no time for parting endearments; she snatched up her bag and hat, darted from the car, and ran down the driveway to the front entrance without looking back.

Hurrying inside and shutting the door hard behind her, Martha was momentarily blinded by the darkness of the foyer, dizzied by the sudden coolness of the air after hours of blazing sunshine. Dropping her belongings, she stumbled up the stairs to the main floor, her breath coming in quick gasps.

"Martha, is that you?" she heard her brother call. A moment later he held her by the arms and was peering into her face, his expression drawn and tense. "Where have you been? We've been worried sick."

"Traffic," she managed to say. "Trucks and soldiers and SS everywhere. What's going on? Has there been a coup?"

"Schleicher has been shot and killed." Bill led her into the green reception room. "We don't know what's happening. Martial law has been declared in Berlin."

For a moment she turned over the name in her thoughts without recognition, until suddenly she remembered—General Kurt von Schleicher, Adolf Hitler's predecessor as chancellor, well regarded as an officer and a gentleman and a shrewd politician. Though he had resigned months before, he retained a great deal of influence in the Reichswehr and was feared by the Nazis, who saw in him a potential rival to Hitler.

"Why did they shoot him?" Martha sank into a soft chair away from the window, distressed. "What has he done? Hitler can't shoot everyone who opposes him or there won't be anyone left to run the country."

"They killed Schleicher's wife too." Bill's words came in a rush, strained and harried. "From what I've been told, several of Göring's police appeared at their front door and demanded to speak with him. When a servant said he was out in the garden, the police stormed into the house, through his office, and out the back door. They found Schleicher walking with his wife in the garden, facing away from the house. The police didn't even call out a warning before firing multiple times into their backs."

"Oh my God." Martha pressed a hand to her mouth, head spinning. It was cold-blooded murder, and for what? Schleicher was a potential political rival even in retirement, but what crime had he committed? And Frau von Schleicher—how could anyone justify killing her?

Just then Martha's mother rushed into the room. "Martha, dear," she exclaimed tearfully. "Thank God you're home! Are you hurt?"

"I'm fine," said Martha, rising to embrace her. Her thoughts flew to Boris. She hoped he had made it safely to the Soviet embassy, and she wondered what he had learned there.

After shutting the door firmly against eavesdropping servants, Martha's mother said that her father was in his office preparing telegrams for the State Department and fielding phone calls from anxious diplomats. Then Bill explained what he had learned from his friends in the press and the diplomatic corps of the events of the day and the previous night.

It was a harrowing tale. The Schleichers were only two of at least twenty-five and perhaps as many as several hundred people killed by the Nazis that day, and at that very moment the death toll continued to rise as assassination squads prowled the country carrying out peremptory executions. Karl Ernst, the chief of the Berlin SA, had been dragged off a ship in Bremen as he prepared to embark on his honeymoon. Erich Klausener, the leader of Catholic Action and an outspoken critic of the Nazi regime, had been murdered in his office. Many Jews had been shot simply for being Jews. Vice Chancellor Franz von Papen, who only days before had infuriated Hitler by making a speech in Marburg denouncing authoritarianism and calling for greater democracy in government, had been arrested. His speechwriter and press secretary had been killed outright. Captain Röhm, apprehended at a resort in Munich while in bed with a young SA paramour, had been arrested and dragged off to prison still declaring his loyalty to Hitler even as the insignia was torn from his uniform. His fate was unknown.

At three o'clock, Hermann Göring had given a press conference at the Reich Chancellery, where he had announced that the strike's purpose was to quash an imminent putsch by the SA, plotted by Captain Röhm with the complicity of an unnamed foreign power.

"Everyone presumed he meant France," added Bill. "When the reporters asked what connection people like Schleicher and Klausener could possibly have to an SA putsch, Göring grinned and claimed they had plotted against the regime."

"This is all too horrible," their mother murmured. "Where will it end—"

They started as the door opened and Fritz entered, paler than usual, to announce more phone calls and letters received. Bill quickly got rid of him and shut the door again, but the obsequious butler frequently returned, interrupting their hushed conversation with new messages or to inquire after their needs. Other servants too entered the room on any pretext, their faces white and scared. Martha suspected they were afraid and yet eager to learn what the Nazis had done, but her family dared not trust them with their secrets.

As notes and phone calls flooded the residence in the tense hours and anxious days that followed, the horrifying extent of the purge gradually sank in. One of Bill's friends in the diplomatic corps came by the house, visibly shaken, and after conferring privately with the ambassador, he told Bill and Martha that Lichterfield, a prison in a Berlin suburb, had been turned into a veritable shooting gallery, with human bodies as targets.

"Why doesn't the army fight back?" Martha asked in a whisper, glancing over her shoulder for Fritz, who seemed to be perpetually lurking about. "So many officers in the Reichswehr have been murdered. Why doesn't the army avenge them?"

"The army hates the Brownshirts more than they resent the insult to their own," Bill's friend said. "They may be willing to sacrifice a few of their officers if it means the utter destruction of the SA."

Martha shook her head, sickened. Even if only a few of those killed were army officers, how could that not be enough to compel their leadership to intervene? The official death toll released by the German government was less than 100, but the reports Martha's father received from American consulates in other German cities put the total at 235, although an SS officer had told the consul in Brandenburg that 500 had been killed and 1,500 arrested. It was impossible to know for certain.

By Sunday evening, Martha's father had confirmed that Captain Röhm was dead. Röhm had been confined at Stadelheim Prison since his arrest, as Hitler had struggled to give the order to execute his old friend. Eventually Röhm had been given a loaded gun, a newspaper describing recent events in order to crush his last vestiges of hope, and time alone in his cell, but he had refused to oblige his captors by taking his own life. According to one account, when the impatient SS men checked in on him, Röhm had declared, "If I am to be killed, let Adolf do it himself." The officers relieved him of the gun and shot him on the spot.

Early the next morning, the Dodds learned that Reich Minister of Propaganda Joseph Goebbels had scheduled a radio address for that evening. "We expect him to offer an official account of the events of the past forty-eight hours," said Martha's father, his voice thin with strain, his face gray, his hands trembling from exhaustion. He had hardly slept since the purge began. "Although how anyone can justify such brutality, the outright murder of men and women who have been neither charged with a crime nor proven guilty is beyond my comprehension."

As word of Goebbel's radio address spread, another flurry of messages and phone calls arrived from American expatriates and foreign diplomats who urgently wished to listen to the speech at the American embassy. Perhaps they felt safer there, more able to speak freely. Martha certainly did. She had come to loathe and fear the Nazis as much as she had once admired them. How could she have been so blind?

The guests included several of her own friends, whom she hoped would have information about mutual acquaintances yet unaccounted for. As twilight fell, she welcomed friends with the new greeting that Berliners had swiftly adopted during those shocking, harrowing days—spoken ironically, with a slight smirk or an arched eyebrow to mask one's fear: "*Lebst du noch?*"

Are you still among the living?

CHAPTER TWENTY-FOUR

July 1934

Mildred

On the afternoon of July 4, Mildred and Arvid were among the three hundred Americans, embassy and consulate staff, members of the press, German officials, and foreign diplomats invited to attend the American embassy's annual Independence Day celebration.

"One might have expected Mr. and Mrs. Dodd to cancel the party in the aftermath of such horror," said Arvid as they dressed.

"They wouldn't." Inspecting herself in the mirror, Mildred tucked a loose strand of golden hair back into her chignon. "It's not just a party anymore but a reminder of American democracy and freedom, of the refuge our country offers to those fleeing oppression."

"And the refuge it offers expatriates." He took her hand and raised it to his lips, his gaze warm and understanding. "Whatever turmoil goes on outside the embassy doors, for a few hours you'll be on American soil among your own people. Perhaps . . . perhaps you should enjoy that sense of belonging and security every day."

"I don't think Martha wants a roommate."

"You know what I mean. You could go home to the U.S. and return when things are better here."

It was true that the harrowing events had intensified Mildred's homesickness for Wisconsin and her family, but she knew from experience that a prolonged separation from Arvid would be even more difficult to bear. "My home is wherever you are," she said, kissing him, "and you and your family and our friends are my people."

And yet, for the day at least, she welcomed the promised respite from Nazi rule. The bloody purge had left her badly shaken, weighed down by a heavy sense of dread. The killings had ceased, or so the public was told, but rumors and revelations about the extent of the carnage heightened her worry that the slaughter continued somewhere out of sight.

Only the day before, the chancellor's cabinet had enacted a law retroactively making all executions carried out over the weekend legal, as actions conducted "in emergency defense of the state." Mildred felt as if Germany had crossed into a dangerous shadowland where the letter of the law had never been more strictly enforced even as the rule of law had become arbitrary. The Independence Day celebration would be the first formal occasion after the purge where Americans and Germans would mingle socially. She could not imagine how they would be able to carry on as if their world had not fundamentally changed.

The afternoon was warm and overcast, but Tiergartenstrasse 27a was pleasantly cool as Mildred and Arvid climbed the foyer stairs to the main floor, beckoned by the sounds of conversation, laughter, and music. They found the Dodd family receiving their guests at the ballroom entrance. Mrs. Dodd looked lovely in a long, flowing blue-and-white dress, her hair pure silver and radiant in the subdued light, her voice as ever soft and gracious, enhanced by the notes of her native Virginia. Only the unusually bright flush to her fair skin and a certain keen look in her dark eyes suggested that her thoughts were troubled or that her mind was anywhere but on the pleasant light conversation she made with each guest.

The ambassador concealed his strain better than his wife did. He greeted Mildred and Arvid with affable good humor and just a hint of irony, enough for her to know that he was sincere when he said he was pleased they had come.

Next in the receiving line, Bill welcomed them almost too heartily, his jaw clenched when he smiled and lines of tension around his eyes, but Martha made no pretense of her true feelings. "*Lebst du noch?*" she asked sardonically as she kissed Mildred's cheek and nodded to Arvid.

"For now," said Arvid. "The day is young."

Martha laughed shortly, but Mildred suppressed a shudder. "You two and your gallows humor," she said, managing a smile as she took Arvid's arm and led him away.

The ballroom and reception rooms were beautifully decorated for the holiday, with abundant red, white, and blue floral arrangements and small American flags adorning the tables and mantelpieces. In the ballroom, an orchestra performed traditional American favorites and lively jazz tunes. Mildred and Arvid lingered to listen until tempted away by delicious aromas wafting from the dining room, where they found a banquet table generously laden with plates of enticing food and drink. After serving themselves, they found seats at a table near a window that offered a lovely view of the Tiergarten in one direction and the receiving line in the other. Mildred noticed that on several occasions, a diplomat or a correspondent would draw Mr. Dodd away from the line for a brief hushed, intense conversation, interrupting the flow of arriving guests until the ambassador could return to his place between his wife and son.

Mildred and Arvid had almost finished eating when the stocky blond butler approached Martha and murmured in her ear. After exchanging a quick word with her mother, Martha hurried off down the grand staircase. Mildred assumed her friend was dealing with some calamity in the kitchen, but when she did not promptly return, Mildred knew something more urgent had called her away.

As Mildred kept an eye out for Martha, she and Arvid mingled among the other guests, conversing in guarded murmurs with close friends, limiting themselves to light pleasantries with everyone else. An electric tension pervaded the gathering as the Americans, Germans, and diplomats of other nations wandered about the ballroom and reception rooms, onto the terrace, or through the gardens, exploring the gravel paths and lingering in the cooling shade. The guests chatted and gossiped, enjoyed food and drink, bantered and laughed with such ostensible ease that the scene probably resembled the Independence Day celebrations going on at American embassies throughout Europe—and yet behind their smiles the Germans seemed tense, the foreign diplomats anxious.

Mildred and Arvid were strolling through the garden when, more than an hour after Martha had broken away from the receiving line, they spotted her on the terrace above, her eyes bright, a slight flush to her cheeks. She caught sight of them, gave a little wave, and descended toward the stairs. Mildred and Arvid exchanged a knowing look and went to meet her.

"Are you enjoying the party?" Martha asked, an ironic lilt in her voice.

"Indeed, as much as we expected to," Mildred replied as Martha linked arms with her and led her and Arvid to a secluded corner away from the other guests. "How is Comrade Boris?"

"You think I was off on some tryst?" said Martha, wounded. "I went to meet Franzie von Papen. His entire family is under house arrest. The SS is tapping their phones and censoring their mail, and guards have been posted inside and out. They only let Franzie leave so that he could take his final exams. By now I'm sure he's returned to his prison."

"How is the vice chancellor?" asked Arvid.

"He's still alive, but Franzie says the SS have made it clear that he could be shot at any moment." Martha clasped her shoulders as if warding off a chill. "He's been charged with conspiring with Röhm and Schleicher to overthrow Hitler. Franzie insists that his father was not involved in any plot. He despised Röhm and mistrusted Schleicher's ambitions, and wouldn't have had anything to do with either man. It's a complete lie."

"I don't think the truth matters anymore," said Mildred.

"Franzie believes that his father would have been executed days ago if President Hindenburg weren't so fond of him. That friendship is all that shields him from death—"

Martha broke off abruptly as Hans Thomsen strolled past nearby, Elmina Rangabe, the Greek minister's beautiful dark-haired daughter, on his arm. Mildred was surprised to see the *Kanzlei* liaison there after the way he had rebuked Martha for playing the Nazi anthem at her birthday party, but apparently Ambassador Dodd still considered him a valuable ally.

"The longer they delay Papen's execution, the more likely it is that he'll survive the purge," said Arvid after the couple moved on.

"I hope you're right," said Martha. "As for me, I'll never trust the Nazis again. How deluded I was, thinking their political coup was some noble and glorious revolution. For that, we'll have to look to the Soviet Union."

"Then you're going ahead with your tour?" asked Mildred.

Martha nodded, her gaze darting from Hans Thomsen to other guests in Nazi regalia strolling through the garden, serpents uncoiling in Eden. "If nothing else, it will get me out of Germany for a while. I've had enough blood and terror to last me the rest of my life."

"Haven't we all?" said Mildred softly, reaching for Arvid's hand.

Gleichschaltung had swept over the nation so relentlessly that Mildred feared it would soon demolish every last good and true thing that stood in its way. She and Arvid loved the old Germany of literature, reason, and the rule of law, but Berlin was a diverse and modern city in an increasingly fascist realm. They knew Germany well, but even they were sometimes confounded by the increasingly unfamiliar country that confronted them daily. How much more inscrutable Germany must seem to a recently arrived ambassador and the far-distant president who had appointed him.

Some developments were so obviously foreboding that Mildred could not understand why the American government showed so little concern. Germany had left the League of Nations. The Treaty of Versailles seemed powerless to constrain Hitler's ambition. And although Hitler repeatedly insisted that he wanted peace and even hinted that he might support a nonaggression pact with France and Great Britain, in the countryside all around Berlin, unemployed men had been hired for vast new construction projects—administrative buildings, airfields, barracks, training grounds, antiaircraft bunkers. Soldiers drilled in the forests and meadows; Hitler Youth marched, trained with rifles, and played vigorous war games that usually ended in bloody fistfights between opposing teams, a quick, efficient means to toughen them up.

Everything pointed to one malignant ambition.

Visiting Americans—members of the press, diplomats, businessmen—observed these troubling signs and carried warnings home to Washington, where, as far as Mildred could tell, they were promptly dismissed and forgotten.

More than a week after the party, on the evening of July 13, Mildred and Arvid gathered with other members of the extended family at his cousin Klaus Bonhoeffer's house to tune in on the radio as Chancellor Hitler addressed the Reichstag at the Kroll Opera House. In the first official account of the violent purge, Hitler proclaimed his hope that the events would endure in German history for all time as both a sad reminder and a warning. He blamed the crisis upon "a few isolated fools and criminals" who had sought to impose communism and anarchy upon the fledgling Reich, a revolt of mutineers who had briefly gained possession of the government.

On and on he went, accusing Röhm and other treacherous Germans of conspiring with an unnamed foreign power to overthrow the government. He described in great detail how the Reich had responded, acknowledged that their intervention had been "ruthless and bloody," and explained why such extreme measures had been necessary. Once he veered off on a tangent to denounce the press, especially foreign correspondents who had "flooded the world with untrue and incorrect assertions and reports in the absence of any kind of objective and just reporting," but he soon returned to his main thrust, justifying his actions during the horrific bloody hours he called the Night of the Long Knives.

Throughout the long, vehement speech his audience often burst into applause and thunderous shouts of approval, culminating in a deafening, uncanny roar when he declared himself solely responsible for every decision made, every blow struck. Hitler's vile words were enough to make Mildred sick to her stomach, but the crowd's rapturous cheers were somehow even worse.

Three weeks passed, fraught with tension that eased almost imperceptibly day by day. The sanctioned bloodshed had ceased, or so it appeared. Roving gangs of SA no longer prowled the city beating Communists, breaking the windows of Jewish shops, or assaulting foreigners who failed to offer the Nazi salute. On the streets Mildred heard murmurs of relief and tentative expressions of hope that they had survived the worst and better days were coming.

But on August 2, the government announced that President Hindenburg had died at his country estate. The last impediment to Adolf Hitler's ascendancy was gone.

Hitler moved swiftly. In honor of the late beloved statesman who had served Germany so long, he vowed that the title of president would never be borne by another. Laws were quickly enacted merging the roles of president and chancellor. Hitler assumed the title of *Führer und Reichskanzler*—leader and chancellor—and became at once both Germany's head of state and its head of government.

Gleichschaltung was complete. The last checks and balances on National Socialist power had been extinguished. Adolf Hitler had established totalitarian control of Germany.

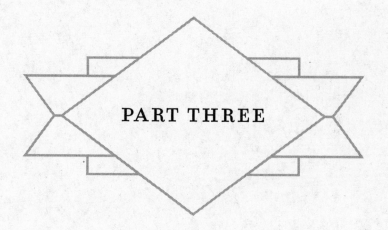

PART THREE

CHAPTER TWENTY-FIVE

August 1934

Greta

Just before noon on August 7, Greta walked alone through the Tiergarten on her way to meet Adam at the Staatstheater. People strolled by as calmly as ever, as if they were insensible to the somber tolling of bells filling the air with the melancholy proclamation of President Hindenburg's funeral, which had begun at eleven o'clock that morning nearly six hundred kilometers to the east at the Tannenberg Memorial in Hohenstein. The late president would have strongly disapproved of Hitler's arrangements. Before his death, he had publicly stated that he did not want to be buried at the site of his great military victory of 1914 but in his family plot in Hanover. But Hindenburg was dead, unable to protest, and who would deny Führer und Reichskanzler Hitler the pomp and circumstance he demanded?

The funeral bells were still tolling when Greta reached the Gendarmenmarkt. From across the *Platz* she paused to take in the elegant classical structure of the Staatstheater, the six Ionic pillars and the ornamental crowning of the portico rising dramatically above a central staircase. As always its beauty moved her, even as she reflected mournfully upon the recent suffering of artists who had once considered it a second home. So many eminent lights of the German stage had been snuffed out, none more horrifically than Hans Otto, Adam's brother-in-law, his first wife's second husband.

After his abrupt dismissal from the Staatstheater in February 1933, Otto could have followed many of his colleagues into exile, but he had insisted upon remaining in Berlin to try to piece back together the decimated remains of the Communist Party. Eight months later, five storm troopers had burst into the small café on Viktoria-Luise-Platz where he had been meeting with Gerhard Hinze, a fellow Communist activist and actor. Otto and Hinze had been arrested and hauled off to an SS retreat outside Berlin, where they had been flogged, kicked, and beaten as their captors demanded the names of their compatriots. When Otto had refused to talk, they had slammed his head into a wall.

For days the two men had been tortured and interrogated, frequently transported from one filthy, vermin-ridden, overcrowded basement or cellblock to another, each smelling of blood and urine and fear. Ultimately they had been taken to the SA barracks on Volkstrasse back in the city, where they were separated. As Hinze later told Marie, the last time he had seen her husband, Otto had been beaten into unconsciousness. Water had been thrown upon him, but when he failed to revive, the SA officers had dragged him away.

Otto was found soon thereafter dumped on a city sidewalk, barely alive. He was taken to a public hospital, where on November 24, 1933, he died from his injuries.

The Gestapo had informed Marie that Otto had committed suicide by leaping to his death from a window on the top floor of the barracks building. Goebbels himself had personally attested to that version of events. If Hinze had not been released and told what he witnessed, Otto's grieving widow might never have learned the truth.

In the days following Otto's death, the Nazis had warned his family and close associates that any mention of his death in the press was forbidden and that attending his funeral would be considered an offense against the Reich. Adam risked it anyway, although he insisted that Greta stay home. He was among only a handful of family and friends who dare attend, and the description he gave afterward was harrowing—the shocked and grieving mourners, the watchful Gestapo agents lurking about the cemetery, the heartfelt eulogies. But if the Nazis had hoped to keep Hans Otto's death a secret, they failed. He was too beloved and admired as an actor simply to fade from public memory.

Months had passed since Otto's horrifying murder. Adam told Greta that if not for their son, he feared Marie might lose her will to live. Her sister was one source of strength and comfort, Adam another. Perhaps the sisters were too preoccupied with their loss to care about petty jealousies, but they welcomed Greta too into their unusual little family without bitterness. Adam had always said that they would, but she had not believed him. She still felt awkward in the sisters' presence, although Marie and Gertrud both seemed perfectly comfortable around her.

Once Marie and Gertrud had accepted her, their extended family in the theater community had too. Now Greta felt as much a part of the close-knit circle as she had the Friday Niters, so long ago and far away.

They were waiting for her even now. Greta crossed the Gendarmenmarkt, turned down an alley, and entered the theater through the stage door, where the sound of voices drew her to the largest dressing room. She found the props master turning the dial on an old radio, actors distractedly leafing through scripts, dancers with towels draped over their necks working out kinks in sore muscles. Adam was engrossed in an intense discussion with one of the producers, but when he glanced up and spotted Greta in the doorway, he broke off, smiled, and waved her over.

How good it was to be among like-minded friends in such dreadful times, friends who shared her love not only for theater and literature and the arts, but for freedom, liberty, democracy. Sick with anguish for her homeland, which had undergone a tectonic shift into the horrifying and surreal, Greta turned her gaze longingly to the democratic West, to Roosevelt and the New Deal, to Madison, the Friday Niters, and the Wisconsin Idea. She could not comprehend how Germany, a country of great philosophers, artists, and intellectual achievement, could have succumbed to the poisonous allure of populism.

For years Greta, Adam, Mildred, Arvid, and their friends had fought the rise of fascism by resisting *Gleichschaltung* and educating others about the threat confronting them, but their efforts had failed.

Totalitarianism had crept up on them steadily, menacingly, and then, with one swift lunge, it had seized them around the throats. Adolf Hitler controlled every branch of government—and now the military as well, having compelled all military officers to swear personal allegiance to him rather than the country. "I swear before God to give my unconditional obedience to Adolf Hitler, Führer of the Reich and of the German people, supreme commander of the Wehrmacht," they were obliged to vow if they wished to keep their posts, "and I pledge my word as a brave soldier to observe this oath always, even at peril of my life."

It was a nightmare, incomprehensible, and yet it was happening.

Although they knew they must be more circumspect than ever to avoid attracting the attention of the Gestapo, they were resolved not to abandon their resistance activities. If anything, they were determined to redouble them. They would never give up, not while any chance remained that they might prevail.

CHAPTER TWENTY-SIX

August 1934

Sara

"I have a sworn affidavit from senior editor Karl Meinholz confirming that my brother was not employed by the *Berliner Tageblatt* after December thirty-first of last year." Sara took the document from her folder and placed it on the attorney's desk. The editor had taken a risk by putting his signature to the carefully phrased assertions, and her hopes rose when Herr Mandelbaum picked up the letter and studied it. Of the last six lawyers she had visited, two had recoiled at the sight of the paper, three had ignored it, and one had demanded that she take it away immediately. Four other attorneys had not even let her get that far, but had asked her to leave as soon as she explained that she needed their help securing Natan's release from a Nazi work camp.

"From the time the law went into effect through the day my brother was arrested, his byline doesn't appear in the paper even once," Sara added, encouraged by Herr Mandelbaum's studious frown as he examined Meinholz's letter. She clasped her hands together in her lap, silently willing him to help her. She had to find someone to take Natan's case. A legal challenge was his last and best hope for release, if he yet lived. Natan was forbidden visitors and his only letter had been smuggled out six weeks before, so all they had left was hope—

Sara's heart cinched as Mandelbaum sighed, shook his head, and returned the affidavit. "I'm sorry, Fraulein Weitz, but as you surely know, as a Jew I'm forbidden to practice law anymore. I could be arrested merely for advising you."

Tears of frustration and disappointment threatened, but Sara kept her voice steady. "Then why did you agree to meet with me?"

"Out of respect for your father." Chagrin clouded his expression. "I suggest you retain an Aryan lawyer."

"I've tried." Even longtime friends of the family had declined the case.

Mandelbaum studied her in silence for a moment, then took up a pen, tore his letterhead from a piece of creamy ivory stationery, and jotted down three names and addresses. "These gentlemen might be able to help you," he said, holding out the page. "Even if they can't represent your brother, they may be able to arrange for your family to visit him." Sara rose and took the list by the torn edge, but he held on to it a moment longer. "Don't show anyone this paper, and don't say I referred you."

"I won't," Sara promised. With a nod, he released the paper and she slipped it into her bag. Soon she was outside his garden gate stifling a groan of anguish and outrage. Another favor called in for nothing, another meeting that brought her brother no closer to freedom. Even the list in her bag was essentially meaningless. What could these Aryan lawyers—strangers—do for Natan that Wilhelm, with all of his aristocratic and military connections, had been unable to accomplish? It was thanks to Wilhelm that the family knew Natan had been arrested while browsing in a Charlottenburg bookshop, that he had spent five weeks in Columbia Haus, a once obsolete military prison near the Tempelhof airfield recently reopened to accommodate the vast overflow of prisoners from the Gestapo's overcrowded jails. Rumors told that the guards at Columbia Haus specialized in torture and interrogation, and that after every last confession was brutally wrung from their captives, those who survived were shipped off to concentration camps to serve out their sentences. As if to confirm every horror the family imagined, in due course Natan had been transferred to Konzentrationslager Oranienburg, a concentration camp just north of Berlin for political prisoners, homosexuals, and other "undesirables."

The Brownshirts had established KZ Oranienburg in a defunct

brewery more than a year before, but after the SA was wiped out in Hitler's purge, control of the camp had passed to the SS. Prisoners were forced to perform hard labor for the local council, and nearly every day they were marched through the town to and from the worksites. Many times Sara and Amalie had traveled to the town bearing letters and parcels of food and clothing that they hoped to pass to Natan, but although they peered through the fences into the camp perimeter and searched the rows of thin, bedraggled men as they were marched under guard through the center of Oranienburg, they never once glimpsed their beloved brother. They feared that Natan was dead or that he had been transferred to one of the so-called wild camps rumored to exist in the countryside, where anarchy reigned and enemies of the Reich were tortured or killed on a whim, but Wilhelm's friends in the Wehrmacht confirmed that Natan was in Oranienburg and promised to do what they could to see that he was well treated. Sara's mother was frantic, her father haggard and aging beyond his years. No assurances could ease their suffering. Only Natan's release would do that.

Thoughts churning, Sara walked down the sidewalk, clutching her bag to her side. Even if she ran all the way to campus she would arrive too late for her afternoon class. She decided to go to Natan's apartment instead, nagged by the faint hope that she might find something there she had overlooked before, something that would convince the Nazis to release her brother at once.

She paused at a curb to let traffic pass. Glancing to her right through the buildings and vehicles, she glimpsed the green of the Tiergarten a few blocks away and realized she was near Herr Panofsky's beautiful home, where in better days he had hosted lovely parties for his employees and their families. How clever he was to have leased his home to the American ambassador. Even though Panofsky was wealthy, cultured, and powerful, the exact sort of Jew that the Nazis despised most, the Gestapo dared not harass his family, not with such an illustrious tenant there to observe and report on every indignity.

Suddenly, inspiration struck.

All around her, other pedestrians surged forward, carrying her across the street in their current, but her thoughts lingered upon Tiergartenstrasse 27a and the ingenious shield Mr. Panofsky had erected around his home and family. Perhaps she too could contrive a way to convince the Gestapo that even if Natan had committed a crime, it would be in their best interest to leave him alone.

Mildred Harnack would help her. Her influential acquaintance at the American embassy, George Messersmith, had left Germany in May to accept the post of ambassador to Austria, but Ambassador Dodd had hired Mildred to type and edit the manuscript for his history of the Old South and she was close friends with his daughter. Perhaps she could persuade the ambassador to make inquiries on Natan's behalf, as embassy officials had done for numerous Americans and foreign correspondents whom the Nazis had unjustly arrested. Natan was not an American citizen, but if the Americans took up his cause, perhaps the Nazis would release him rather than risk worsening Germany's already strained relations with the United States.

As she turned toward Neukölln, Sara felt her spirits rise for the first time since Natan had been arrested. Mildred would convince the ambassador to help them. She would persuade the ambassador, and the ambassador would persuade the Nazis, and Natan would come home to his family, safe and sound. This was Sara's last hope. What might happen if it failed was too terrible to contemplate.

CHAPTER TWENTY-SEVEN

August–December 1934

Martha

A year and a month into her father's tenure as ambassador, Martha could not mistake the signs of his increasing pessimism as the United States remained firmly isolationist contrary to the best interests of America and of the world. Time and again he wrote to his superiors at the State Department warning them of Hitler's ravenous ambitions, but it seemed that all he accomplished was to give his enemies within the diplomatic corps evidence that he was philosophically unsuited for his post and ought to be replaced.

Sometimes Martha suspected her father might welcome that, especially on days when his efforts seemed especially futile and he contemplated asking for leave so he might visit Stoneleigh, his beloved 385-acre farm in Round Hill, Virginia. Although the rest of the family much preferred the comforts and modern conveniences of their Chicago brownstone, rustic Stoneleigh was the home of her father's heart. As autumn approached, Martha knew he yearned to be harvesting Pippin and Cortland apples from his thriving orchards, or driving his two dozen Guernsey heifers out to graze in the pastures, or riding one of his four horses through the gently rolling Appalachians.

Martha could not give him that, but whenever he sank too far into despondency, she would pull him away from his desk and invite him for a stroll through the Tiergarten. Once or twice a week they walked together, and as they admired the late summer flowers of August and then the first autumnal tints of September, he acknowledged his increasing frustration with his colleagues in Washington and his revulsion for his counterparts in Berlin.

"It's humiliating to be obliged to shake hands with known and confessed murderers," he told her. "Murderers, moreover, who are plotting for war."

Martha's heart quickened. "Do you really think so?"

Her father nodded soberly. "There's ample evidence that the Reich government is preparing for a massive struggle. It's only a question of time. The German military is arming and drilling more than a million and a half men, all of whom are constantly indoctrinated in the belief that continental Europe must be subordinated to them."

Martha took her father's arm. "You're the president's eyes and ears in Berlin. Why won't the State Department heed your warnings?"

"They fervently hope I'm wrong and can't bear to admit I may be right. Congress wants us to stay out of any European conflicts, and so does the majority of the American people. As for me, I'm convinced we must abandon our isolationism, and I've written to Army Chief of Staff Douglas MacArthur to tell him so."

"I hope he'll listen."

"I hope so too, but I have grave doubts." Her father heaved a sigh and patted her hand. "I'm afraid I must resign myself to the delicate work of watching and carefully doing nothing."

Martha knew her father was hardly "doing nothing." In addition to continuously briefing Washington about the irrefutable signs of impending conflict and advocating for Americans who ran afoul of the Reich, he also helped persecuted Jews, in the limited fashion his office permitted. Mildred frequently asked him to facilitate a Jewish friend's visa application or emigration to a more hospitable European nation, but one afternoon she approached Martha with a more unusual request. A Jewish journalist, the brother of one of her students, had been arrested more than three months before for violating the Editors Law and was being held in KZ Oranienburg. He had not been able to obtain legal counsel, and his family's anxious pleas for visiting rights had been rejected.

"Has he been convicted of anything?" Martha asked.

"He hasn't even been granted a trial," said Mildred. "Do you think you could ask your father to intercede on his behalf? His sister is one of my favorite students and a dear friend. You've met her—Sara Weitz."

Martha searched her memory and conjured up the image of a petite, dark-haired, pretty young woman, with expressive hazel eyes, luminous skin, and light brown hair. "Sure, I remember. She seemed like a sweet girl, smart too. I liked her."

"Then will you help?"

"If Sara's brother was an American, I'm sure my father would pull out all the stops," she said, hesitant. "But since Natan is a German citizen, I don't think the embassy can intervene."

Mildred's face fell. "I see."

"Not to worry," said Martha. "Even if the embassy can't get involved, I know someone else who might, as a special favor to me."

As soon as Mildred left, Martha phoned the offices of the *Regierungspräsident* of Cologne, 580 kilometers west of Berlin in the Rhineland. Her call was put through to newly appointed administrative president Rudolf Diels so quickly that she briefly indulged in the flattering notion that her name was on a short list of intimate friends for whom his secretaries had been instructed to interrupt all other work. When Martha asked Rudolf to come to Berlin to see her as soon as possible, he agreed to meet her the next day.

Rudolf had once been chief of the Gestapo, but he had been removed from office in April after his superiors decided he was not ruthless enough to suppress the SA. Two months later, he narrowly escaped losing his life in Hitler's bloody purge after Reichstag president Hermann Göring, a close friend, had warned him that enemies were conspiring against him. Rudolf had fled to Switzerland, where he remained for several weeks until passions cooled. Upon his return to Germany, he served briefly as deputy police president of Berlin until he was appointed *Regierungspräsident* of Cologne. Though he had been knocked down a few rungs in the Nazi hierarchy, he remained very powerful, for he possessed influential friends, a vast intelligence network, and files of incriminating evidence on his political enemies, entrusted to an associate in Zurich who had orders to publish if Rudolf met with foul play.

The following evening, Martha arrived at the rooftop club of the Eden Hotel to find Rudolf waiting for her at their favorite table. Most of the other tables were occupied by businessmen in expensive suits, Nazis in full regalia, and ladies in gorgeous dresses and sparkling jewelry. Couples danced as Oskar Joost's orchestra played a lively fox-trot, drowning out the fine patter of rain on the adjustable glass roof overhead.

Martha saw the maître d' at Rudolf's side, bending deferentially to better hear his confidential instructions, but he was otherwise alone. Although none of the guests openly stared, Rudolf nonetheless commanded the room, as if a dark energy radiated out from him, evoking tension and wariness in those within its range. Crossing the room to join him, Martha felt anew the pull of his charisma and the dark beauty of his scarred face. Once she had sat on his lap and kissed his scars, one by one, as he wryly explained how he had earned them fighting duels years before, when he was a hotheaded student proving his manhood to other, equally hotheaded schoolmates.

Rudolf rose with sinuous grace, kissed her hand, and guided her gracefully into a chair adjacent to his. "What a great pleasure it is to see you again," he said as he seated himself. "You are as exquisite as I remember."

His smooth baritone sent an enticing shiver up her neck, but she dared not be tempted. "Oh, come on," she said lightly. "It hasn't been that long since we last met."

"It was before you went on your tour of the Soviet Union." He studied her, smiling faintly. "Did you find communism in practice as impressive as in theory?"

"It met my expectations," she said, offering a little shrug. Her departure had been covered widely in the press, and many had interpreted it as a public declaration of her opposition to the Nazi regime. They were not wrong, but whether Rudolf saw it that way or believed, as her parents did, that she had gone impulsively out of starry-eyed infatuation for Boris, she could only guess.

"Tepid praise," said Rudolf. "Are you still seeing the Russian?"

"You know I am."

"Yes, I know," he acknowledged. "As for myself, I rarely see Vino-gradov these days."

"I suppose not. I understand things have become rather chilly be-tween Moscow and Berlin since the Night of the Long Knives." Martha had seen for herself that few German officials attended parties at the Soviet embassy anymore. Nazi agents posted outside the consulate kept a watchful eye on all who came and went, noting license plate numbers and the frequency and duration of visits.

"Chilly?" Rudolf shook his head, amused. "Hitler and Stalin do not see eye to eye on everything, but there is no reason why they should not continue to cooperate on matters of mutual interest."

They paused as the waiter approached bearing an excellent bottle of champagne and a silver dish of ripe, plump strawberries, his demeanor betraying a hint of terror that he had either arrived too soon and had in-terrupted an important moment, or had not arrived promptly enough. As he poured, Martha's eyes met Rudolf's and she smiled, pleased that he remembered her tastes. She almost regretted that things had not worked out between them. If not for Boris, she might be tempted to give him another try.

When the waiter departed, Martha nibbled a strawberry and sipped her champagne, sighing with pleasure as the orchestra struck up a buoyant swing tune. "We should dance later," she said, watching other couples circling the dance floor. "After we finish this bottle. Do you still prefer slow dances?"

"Is that why you asked to meet me, so we could dance?"

"No, but now that I'm here, it seems like a fine idea."

He smiled, his gaze penetrating. "Are we here to discuss German and Soviet relations? Perhaps you're gathering intelligence for your father."

She was so surprised she laughed. "That'll be the day." She toyed with her glass, resisting the temptation to drain it in one gulp. "I'm here on a personal matter."

His eyebrows rose. "Personal?" he echoed lightly, deftly infusing the word with countless delicious possibilities.

She nodded. "A favor for a friend."

Briefly she explained the situation, deliberately nonchalant, as if it were all a simple mistake that could easily be sorted out, with no harm done and no hard feelings afterward. Rudolf listened without comment as she spoke, his expression one of polite interest, as if she were describing a rather ordinary shopping excursion or the weather. She knew him, though, and she knew his mind was working swiftly in the depths, though not a ripple betrayed him on the surface.

"What is this Herr Weitz to you?" he asked when she finished, refilling her glass. "A new lover?"

She leaned forward to take her glass in hand, teasing him with a glimpse of décolletage. "Why? Are you jealous?"

"Certainly."

"Well, you needn't be. I've never met him. He's a friend of a friend."

"Then why should you care what becomes of him? He's just another Jew journalist, no one of any consequence."

"Then it shouldn't be any bother to release him." She took another strawberry and closed her eyes as she savored a bite, her knee brushing Rudolf's beneath the table. "Honestly, I don't care about this fellow, but I do care about my friend, and she's distraught. Can't you pull some strings?"

"He broke the law."

"You don't really know that, do you? He hasn't even had a trial." Martha shook her head, frowning in feigned bewilderment. "Isn't that illegal? It sure is in the States."

Rudolf smiled, amused. "We are not in the States."

"Darling, I know that if you said the word, he could walk out of that camp tonight."

"And if every prisoner with an alluring advocate is permitted to walk out of prison before serving their sentences . . . ?"

"Then you might have to shut down those camps, which might not be such a bad thing, since I hear they're pretty horrible." She sipped her champagne, enjoying the bubbling warmth as it spread through her. "You just admitted that you still find me alluring."

"That is hardly a secret."

She set down her glass and reached for his hand. "Tell me you'll see what you can do."

He sighed and interlaced his fingers through hers. "I'll see what I can do."

"And say that you'll dance with me."

"I will." He inclined his head toward the bandstand. "The next slow song."

"Naturally." Resting her elbow on the table and her chin in her free hand, she smiled dreamily at the orchestra. "What is this song? 'When man something something—'"

"*Wenn man sucht wird man finden*," Rudolf corrected. "When one seeks, one will find."

"Do you believe that's true?"

"It depends. What one finds is often not what one had sought." He caressed the back of her hand with his thumb. "When you tire of your Russian boyfriend, perhaps you will seek me."

"Darling, you know I can't. You're married."

"That never bothered you before."

"Maybe I've mended my ways."

"Then honor compels me to warn you that Vinogradov is married too, and he has a young child."

"Yes, I know. A daughter. We've met." Martha also knew, as apparently Rudolf did not, that Boris was seeking a divorce, and that he and Martha had discussed marriage. She smiled, clasped her other hand around Rudolf's, and gave him a teasing, contrite pout. "Let's not worry about the future. Who knows what might happen? We're here together now. Let's enjoy now."

He raised his glass. "To now."

She clinked her glass against his. "To now, and to favors granted."

He regarded her wryly over the rim of his glass, and she let her eyes shine teasingly into his.

A fortnight later, when Mildred came for tea at Tiergartenstrasse 27a, she thanked Martha profusely for whatever she had done on Natan Weitz's behalf. He had not been released, but his family had been granted weekly visits and were permitted to bring him packages of food, clothing, books, and letters. The Gestapo promised to release him if he confessed, but he continued to proclaim his innocence.

"Is he innocent?" asked Martha.

"Sara hasn't said, and I won't ask," said Mildred. "Natan can't admit to breaking the Editors Law without implicating others at the *Berliner Tageblatt*. He doesn't sound like the sort of man who would condemn friends to prison so that he might go free."

"Then for his sake I hope he can stick to his story under pressure."

"So do I." Mildred frowned, pensive. "They rushed him through a disgrace of a trial and sentenced him to eighteen months. The family hopes he'll be permitted to serve it out at Oranienburg where they can easily visit him, but they're powerless to prevent him from being moved to Dachau or another camp even farther away."

Martha nodded, suddenly apprehensive. Was that Rudolf's doing? Surely he could have freed Natan Weitz if he had chosen to do so. Was he sending Martha a message, a reminder that he could do so much more for Sara's brother if only Martha were willing to do more for him?

The weeks passed, and as autumn deepened into winter, Martha saw Boris often and Rudolf not at all, wary of him as she had never been before, thankful for the many kilometers that separated them. She and Boris had begun to discuss marriage more earnestly, and as their intimacy grew, they had become careless about concealing their affection in public. After each slip they vowed to be more discreet, well aware that their affection irritated Boris's superiors, who wanted him to think of Martha as an asset, not a lover. Seduction was a tool with which Boris was meant to control her. He was not supposed to fall under its spell himself.

In early December, at a luncheon at the Soviet embassy where the vodka flowed freely and lively music and boisterous laughter filled the halls, Boris rose unsteadily to his feet and raised a toast to her, calling her "Martha, my wife." More than a little tipsy herself, Martha nevertheless noticed the disapproving looks his superiors exchanged, and she quietly warned him to behave himself, hoping he was sober enough to heed her advice.

A week later, as Martha and her mother were decorating the embassy for Christmas, Boris came to Tiergartenstrasse 27a and asked to speak to her alone. For a heartstopping moment she thought he was about to go down on one knee and propose, but instead he told her, pale with anguish, that he had been transferred to Moscow.

"They cannot keep us apart," he vowed, seizing her hands, kissing her again and again. "No distance can diminish our love."

She wanted to believe him, and they parted with promises to arrange rendezvous in France or Switzerland as often as possible. But almost as soon as Boris left Berlin, Martha sensed that their last embraces had been infused with a desperate sorrow, a defiant refusal to accept the inevitable.

CHAPTER TWENTY-EIGHT

January 1935

Mildred

Mildred and Arvid welcomed the New Year in a new flat on the third floor of Woyrschstrasse 16, two blocks south of the Tiergarten and about five kilometers northwest of their old place. For more than two years they had enjoyed living in Neukölln, but the neighborhood had come under increased scrutiny by the Gestapo due to its long-standing hospitality to workers, immigrants, and Communists. When forced to choose between ending their study groups and salons or moving to a more discreet neighborhood, they had bidden a sad farewell to Neukölln.

Their new flat was small but modern, with a spacious front room, a galley kitchen, an en suite bath, and a balcony with just enough room for a table and two chairs. There were two bedrooms, but when Mildred and Arvid set up the smaller one as an office, they made none of the usual optimistic predictions that it would make a fine nursery someday. After more than eight years of marriage, countless attempts, and fleeting hopes and crushing disappointment, Mildred could no longer bear to arrange her home or her life around a dream that seemed unlikely to be fulfilled.

There were days she found some consolation in reflecting that perhaps it was better not to bring an innocent child into a world that had turned so ugly, so full of fear and hatred.

Even without a child, their lives and hearts were full. She and Arvid had each other. They had many dear friends, although their once vibrant salons had diminished with the emigration of so many gifted writers, editors, and scholars. They had fulfilling work. Arvid was busy practicing law and studying for the arduous exams that would qualify him to work in the civil service. Mildred continued to write by day and teach at the Abendgymnasium at night, avoiding as best she could the ubiquitous scrutiny of the National Socialist German Students' Association.

In recent months she had struggled to publish anything of significant academic value, a problem that had plagued her colleagues and writer friends for more than a year, ever since Joseph Goebbels's Reich Chamber of Culture had issued a multitude of regulations intended to impose Aryan uniformity on all publishing in Germany. Mildred had managed to slip a few subversive pieces of literary criticism past the censors, including an essay in the *Berliner Tageblatt* that deftly ignored the Nazi reverence for *Blut und Boden* by offering a sympathetic analysis of racial issues in Faulkner's fiction, but for the most part she had been restricted to picturesque reminiscences of her Wisconsin girlhood. Her most promising long-term project was a translation of *Lust for Life*, Irving Stone's biographical novel of Vincent van Gogh. Since Universitas Publishers had already accepted the manuscript, she had reasonable expectations that the book would see print, but she knew an overzealous censor could quash the project at any time.

Once Mildred had hoped that this sort of quiet resistance would be enough. Enlightening her students, inoculating them against Nazi propaganda, writing essays that inspired a better vision of humanity—these dangerous activities would earn her the outrage of the Nazis if she were exposed. She could lose her job, or face arrest or even deportation. Yet the severity of the punishments she faced seemed wildly out of proportion to the damage she was inflicting upon the Nazi regime. She felt as if she were stubbornly flinging pebbles against a vast stone fortress—a nuisance, nothing more. Only when she helped Jewish friends escape the Reich did she feel that she was accomplishing any real good.

Arvid shared her frustration, that infuriating sense of powerlessness before the Nazi juggernaut. Quietly, obliquely, he spoke with friends who shared their antifascist beliefs, hoping to build a discreet opposition network, sharing ideas and information. "There is strength in numbers," he often said, "and power in knowledge."

One evening, Arvid returned home from work with an unusual lightness in his step, the carefully benign mask he wore on the streets falling away to reveal cautious anticipation. "Rudolf Heberle came to see me today," he said. "I invited him to join us for supper, but he couldn't come."

"Oh, I wish he had," said Mildred as she set the table. "We haven't visited with him and Franziska in ages. It would be so lovely to talk over old times in Madison."

Like Arvid, Rudolf had come to the University of Wisconsin as a Rockefeller Fellow to study with Professor John R. Commons, and the two couples had become friends through the Friday Niters. Rudolf was a *Privatdozent* in sociology at the University of Kiel, but also like Arvid, he had been denied a professorship because of his political beliefs. His most recent book, a study of the rise of National Socialism amid the rural population of Schleswig-Holstein, was unlikely ever to be published in Germany while the Nazis remained in power.

"Rudolf agrees that opposition to the Reich is too weak, too scattered and directionless," Arvid said.

"Yes, but how do we unite when anyone we approach might be a Gestapo agent?"

"We begin with friends we trust, and then friends of friends. Franziska has a second cousin in the intelligence office of the Air Ministry."

"And we should start with *him*?"

"I know it sounds unlikely, but apparently he despises the Nazis as much as we do. Rudolf suggests we collaborate."

Arvid explained that he had agreed to meet with Franziska's cousin, Harro Schulze-Boysen, at their flat the following evening. "He and I shouldn't be seen together in public, in case we need to deny knowing each other later," Arvid explained. "I want you to meet him too, *Liebling*. If your intuition tells you we can't trust him, I won't."

Mildred's intuition told her she could trust Franziska and Rudolf, but Arvid's matter-of-fact acknowledgment of the new risks he was prepared to accept sent a shiver up her spine. She consented, but through-out the next day, as she cleaned the flat and baked an *Apfelkuchen* from Mutti Harnack's recipe, her hopes warred with apprehension, and she was tempted to phone Arvid and beg him to call off the meeting. Instead she busied herself with work, translating paragraphs of Stone's *Lust for Life* until Van Gogh's world seemed more vivid than her own.

The sound of Arvid's key turning in the lock broke the spell. She set aside her books and papers and hurried to meet him, but they had only a few minutes to confer before a knock sounded on the door, precisely at the appointed hour. When Mildred answered, Rudolf quickly led a tall man in his midtwenties into the foyer. Although he wore black slacks and a black sweater beneath his black wool topcoat rather than a uniform, Harro Schulze-Boysen otherwise could have stepped right out of a Luftwaffe recruiting poster. He had broad shoulders and a military bearing that seemed to add inches to his height; handsome, patrician features; a strong chin and a confident smile; dark blond hair, a bit thin but not a strand out of place; and a keen blue-eyed gaze that, Mildred suspected, missed nothing. When he removed his hat, she quickly hid her surprise—part of his right ear was missing.

Rudolf waited until she had locked the door behind them to greet her fondly, but it was a brief, insufficient reunion, with little time to spare for family news. Mildred showed them into the sitting room where Arvid waited. Rudolf made introductions, Arvid and Harro shook hands heartily, and as they seated themselves, Mildred returned to the kitchen for *Kaffee und Kuchen*. By the time she returned, the men were so engrossed in their conversation that they scarcely glanced her way when she poured a cup of coffee for herself and took a seat. Arvid had asked her to observe and evaluate the Luftwaffe officer and she intended to do so.

She soon concluded that Harro despised the Nazis with such palpable antipathy that it could not possibly be a ruse. Although he was an avowed Communist, his patriotism sprang from an illustrious family military tradition; his great-uncle was the renowned Grand Admiral von Tirpitz, and in the Great War, his father, Commander Edgar Schulze, had served in Belgium as chief of staff to the German naval commander. Harro explained that he had joined Göring's intelligence office not to serve the Reich but to hasten its demise, preserving Germany as a sovereign nation, governed by Germans. He was deeply concerned that Hitler's overreaching ambitions could provoke another world war, and if the Reich fell, the nations of Europe would install their own puppet government in its place.

Mildred did not doubt Harro's opposition to the Nazis, but as he cheerfully recounted his exploits to prove his bona fides, she began to have grave concerns about his judgment. Several years before, as the outspoken editor of the banned radical opposition magazine *Gegner*, he had tried to unite the Right and Left against the fascists, holding boisterous meetings in restaurants and rallying his comrades to march in May Day parades. He deliberately sought attention, hoping to inspire others to join his cause, but in March 1933, a squad of SS had burst into a *Gegner* editorial meeting and arrested the entire staff.

"Our prison was a cellar, our bed a cold stone floor strewn with hay," said Harro, his mouth set in a grim, defiant smile. "Some of my colleagues were soon released, but a friend and I were stripped naked and ordered to run a gauntlet of guards armed with lead-weighted whips. Three times they ordered us to pass between their ranks while they beat us with all their strength."

Sickened, Mildred pressed her lips together to hold back a gasp.

"After the third time through, my friend collapsed, unconscious, and later he would die of his injuries." Harro absently fingered his scarred right ear. "I suffered injuries too, but anger kept me on my feet. I staggered, bruised and bleeding, to the starting point, clicked my heels together, and shouted, 'Reporting for duty! Orders carried out plus one more for luck!'"

Rudolf nodded approvingly, but Arvid's brow furrowed. "After all you had suffered, you mocked them to their faces?"

Harro shrugged. "Mockery was the only weapon at my disposal. It seemed to impress them. They declined to send me through the gauntlet again, and the leader told me admiringly that I belonged with them."

Prevailing upon influential friends of Harro's father, his mother had managed to get him released, half-starved, ill, with thick ropes of scars from the whips on his back and swastikas knife-carved into his thigh. He had required weeks to heal and regain his strength, but as soon as he was able, he had resumed his opposition work, though more covertly. Obtaining a post in the Luftwaffe Ministry was unlikely for someone with Harro's record, and indeed, at first the personnel chief had declined his application for a commission. But soon thereafter, Reichsminister Hermann Göring had personally overruled the decision, impressed by Harro's military lineage, persuaded by powerful mutual friends, and charmed by Harro's aristocratic wife, Libertas, the beautiful, captivating, flirtatious granddaughter of Prince Philipp zu Eulenburg-Hertefeld.

As Harro described his professional duties, it seemed to Mildred that Arvid and Rudolf could barely contain their excitement. Fluent in five languages, Harro reviewed and summarized reports on foreign air forces for Göring, handled intelligence reports from Luftwaffe officers serving abroad, and disseminated confidential documents throughout the Air Ministry. There was no question that he had access to extremely valuable military intelligence, but when Mildred and Arvid exchanged a surreptitious glance, she knew her husband was wondering, as she was, what price the resistance might ultimately be forced to pay for it.

When the interview ended, the men wished one another good luck and courage, and Rudolf and Harro departed. Pretending to adjust the curtains, Mildred watched from the window as the men emerged from the building a few minutes apart and walked off in separate directions.

"What did you make of him?" asked Arvid, hugging her from behind and resting his chin on her shoulder.

Sighing, she turned in the circle of his arms and cupped his cheek in her hand. "His zeal is impressive, and when I think of the state secrets that cross his desk on any given day, I can't imagine any better place to have an ally. And yet . . ."

"He's reckless," Arvid finished for her. "He's intelligent and courageous, but impulsive, and he's already too well known to the Gestapo."

"Do you think you could rein him in?" asked Mildred. "Teach him discretion?"

"I don't think discretion is in his nature. One careless moment of bravado could bring down the entire group."

"We don't have a group, not yet," Mildred reminded him. "With his connections, Harro could help us develop one."

"Or he could get us thrown into a prison camp." Arvid shook his head, frowning. "I hate to let his access to military intelligence slip through our fingers, but I'm not convinced it would be worth the risk."

A few days later, Arvid returned home from work just as Mildred was leaving for the Abendgymnasium. Rudolf had come by the law firm that morning to ask if he should arrange a second meeting.

"I asked him to tell Harro that I appreciate his time and trust, but although I'm very interested, I can't see him again," said Arvid. "It's simply too dangerous."

Mildred agreed. It was some consolation to know that Harro would continue his opposition work with or without them. She wished him success, for they were on the same side even if they dared not work together.

CHAPTER TWENTY-NINE

January–February 1935

Sara

The first time Sara, Amalie, and their parents were permitted to visit Natan at KZ Oranienburg, they were escorted into a small office with one wooden chair and bars on the windows. Twenty anxious minutes later, Natan was brought stumbling into the room—handcuffed, filthy, unshaven, held upright by two guards, one on each arm. Bursting into tears, Sara's mother hurried to ease him into the chair.

For a moment, Natan blinked at his family in disbelief. "Good to see you," he said hoarsely, as if he were welcoming them to his flat and not to hell on earth. "Glad you could come." A fit of coughing prevented him from saying more, but he managed a slow, ironic grin, revealing the gap of two missing teeth.

A guard remained in the room with them throughout their visit, but when Sara and Amalie pleaded, he unlocked Natan's handcuffs so that he could eat some of the food his mother had packed. He chewed and swallowed slowly, carefully, as if his jaw pained him, but he saved most of the food to take back to his cell, along with the clean, warm clothes they had brought, several books, and a packet of letters from friends. Most were unsigned, with subtle clues only Natan would recognize to identify the authors, full of good cheer, innocuous enough to pass the censors.

While Natan ate, they shared news of the family and the neighborhood, carefully editing the facts for the guard's ears. Natan said very little about the conditions he endured in the prison, but his thin, disheveled appearance confirmed their worst fears. His hair had been hacked off, his clothes were threadbare and stained, and a faint sour odor clung to his skin. Even so, his bloodshot eyes were alert, and he never cringed when the guards shifted their weight or touched the rubber truncheons on their belts. All the while, he held his left arm close to his side, and when Sara embraced him, he stiffened in pain.

Abruptly and all too soon, the guards ended the interview, but before they shackled Natan's hands again, Sara darted forward to murmur in his ear, "We'll be back to see you soon. We're going to get you out of here."

"Don't bring Mutti next time," he said, his voice barely audible. "Don't let her see me like this."

The guards took him away before Sara could vow that next time he would leave the prison camp with them. It was just as well that she had not given him false hope. A fortnight passed and a second visit was granted, but although Mildred's contacts at the American embassy continued to pressure the commandant, he would not release Natan.

It was also just as well that Sara had not promised Natan to convince their mother to stay at home. When she tentatively suggested it, her mother drew herself up, pale and dignified. "Of course I'm going to see my boy," she said. "Nothing would keep me away."

The weeks passed. Twice each month Sara and her parents were granted an hour with Natan, and they were permitted to give him one small carton of food and clothing and necessities, carefully inspected at the entrance for contraband. Sara's father learned to leave a bottle of schnapps or a tin of caviar on top as a bribe for the guard at the gate, swiftly pocketed as the family was waved through.

Weeks turned into months. Natan's hair was hacked off again, and once he was given a rough, careless shave, leaving him with patches of stubble and skin scraped raw. His cough worsened as winter deepened, and he continued to lose weight, and they soon realized he shared the food they brought him with the other prisoners. "What would you have me do? Watch them starve?" he replied when they begged him to keep more for himself. "In my place, could you?"

One day the family passed the camp commandant in the corridor as the guards escorted them to the small, bare office. He watched them pass, frowning imperiously, and afterward, he intercepted them as they were being led to the exit. "You are Herr Weitz, the banker, are you not?" he inquired crisply.

Sara's father clasped his hat in front of his chest and offered a small, formal bow. "I am, Herr Kommandant."

"You served in the Great War?"

"I did, sir. I was wounded at Verdun."

The commandant's eyebrows rose. "That was a bad business."

"Yes, Herr Kommandant, it was."

"How does your son know Regierungspräsident Diels?"

Sara's father shrugged deferentially. "I was not aware they were acquainted."

"You're regrettably ignorant where your son is concerned. Even so, perhaps you can tell me why the Americans are so interested in one Jew journalist. What is he to them?"

"Who can say why Americans do anything?"

"Quite right." The commandant nodded to the guards. "Take these Jews away."

Sara felt a surge of panic, but when the guards merely led them to the exit, she took a deep, shuddering breath and willed her heart to stop racing. In the backseat of Wilhelm's car, she and Amalie held hands tightly until the driver left her and her parents at home.

Mildred promised that Martha Dodd would not let her father forget Natan, and that Martha's contact would see to it that he would be well treated. Sara was sickened to imagine what poor treatment looked like if what Natan received was considered better.

As winter passed, Sara saw Dieter only rarely. Business took him out of the country for weeks at a time, but it was almost a relief to have him gone. In recent weeks, their infrequent, tense, and uncomfortable discussions about what their married life would look like retraced the same circular arguments and resolved nothing. "Perhaps this is a sign that as much as you love each other, this marriage is simply not meant to be," Amalie had gently suggested after Sara had tearfully confessed her frustration. Perhaps Amalie was right, but Sara did not know what to do. If she broke off the engagement, she would lose Dieter forever, and what if all they needed was a little more time to work things out? For now, postponing the wedding while the family focused on obtaining Natan's release was the most she could do.

For his part, Dieter assured Sara that he understood the reason for her distance and distraction, but she was guiltily certain that he did not know all that she felt and feared. "Tell me how to help Natan and I'll do it," he said, but she had no idea what more he could do aside from providing the imported luxuries they used to bribe the guards. His boss often distributed overstocked items or slightly damaged packages unsuitable for store shelves among his employees, and Dieter had always been generous with his share.

Then, in late February, Sara's parents received a letter from the SS announcing that Natan would be released early on account of good behavior. Since he never would have confessed which of his colleagues at the *Berliner Tageblatt* had helped him defy the Editors Law, Sara knew that at last Mildred's American friends had prevailed.

On the appointed day, she feared it was all a cruel Nazi trick, or a mistake in the paperwork, and they would arrive at the prison camp only to discover that it was just another visit, and afterward Natan would be torn from their arms and led back to his cell. When the guards at the front gate stalled before admitting them despite the usual parcel and bribe, she mentally composed arguments, threats, pleas. Only when they had Natan in their car wrapped in warm blankets and they were speeding away from Oranienburg could she breathe deeply, lightheaded, clutching his hand, murmuring assurances that all would be well. He nodded and managed a grin, unable to speak for the deep, wet coughs racking his thin frame.

They went directly to their longtime physician, a Jew who was no longer permitted to practice medicine, but nonetheless saw Jewish patients in secret at his home. After examining Natan thoroughly, the physician reported that he was severely malnourished and suffering from pneumonia. His left arm had been broken three months earlier and had been set badly, but it would do more harm than good to break it again and reset it. A program of strengthening exercises would help him regain full use of the arm in time. He had also contracted skin infections and lice. The doctor provided a cream for the first affliction and recommended Natan shave his head for the second.

Sara and her parents took Natan home—not to his flat, which Sara and Amalie had cleared out months before, but to his childhood bedroom. Sara and her mother prepared him a simple, nourishing meal of potato soup and bread while he bathed and shaved, at first refusing his father's help, and then admitting he required it. Afterward his cough was worse, but the medicine had eased his fever, and he looked so much better clean, freshly shaven, and even bald that tears came to Sara's eyes. After he ate—carefully, sparingly, following the doctor's warning—he dragged himself upstairs and collapsed into bed. He slept for eighteen hours.

When he woke, he was ravenous. Clad in warm flannel pajamas and a dressing gown, he came downstairs to the kitchen, where the cook prepared him a hot breakfast of coffee, oatmeal, and toast. He asked to read the *Berliner Tageblatt* while he ate. Sara brought it to him, poured herself a cup of coffee, and seated herself at the table, ready to fetch him anything else he wanted, or to talk if he felt up to it.

Instead he studied the paper with a burning intensity, nodding approval at one article, muttering disparagingly at another. "This is such ingratiating propaganda that Goebbels himself might have written it," he grumbled once, smacking an article with the back of his fingers. His brow furrowed at the many unfamiliar bylines, and his concern deepened as he realized how many names of former colleagues were absent. Eventually he pushed the paper aside, rested his arms on the table, and regarded Sara as if he expected an argument. "I have to find work."

"You have to regain your strength."

"After that. I have to find work. I have to write."

"Natan, no," she protested, glancing over her shoulder for their parents. "You can't. The Gestapo will be watching you. The moment you break the law again, they'll throw you into a worse camp than Oranienburg. You won't survive."

"It's not against the law for a Jew to write for Jewish newspapers. I'll convince a Jewish newspaper to hire me, or I'll start my own."

"I don't understand why you have to go looking for trouble."

"The trouble's already here. I'm just going to write about it."

She decided not to tell their parents, in the hope that Natan would change his mind. Still, although she worried, she could not help admiring him for his determination, his undaunted courage. She was just a literature student, her only form of protest her participation in Mildred's study group. Natan's work, when he resumed it, would actually make a difference.

A few days after Natan came home, Dieter phoned to ask if he could see her, if a visit would not impose upon the family. She invited him to come for tea that afternoon, guiltily mindful of the many dates she had canceled as the family prepared for Natan's release. In two days Dieter would be leaving for Australia on business and would not return for four months. She had to see him before he left, and this might be their only chance.

"Maybe you should go with Dieter to Australia," said Natan, lingering in the doorway as she tidied the living room.

"He's going on a business trip, not a vacation. Anyway, we're not married yet. Mother and Father would never allow it."

"I think they might. Maybe they should go too, and you all should . . . stay. Indefinitely."

"You mean emigrate." Shaking her head, Sara plumped a pillow vigorously and set it back down on the sofa. "How could we leave you and Amalie behind?"

"You could return when the Nazis are out of power."

"And that would be when?"

"Or we could join you in Australia." Natan heaved a sigh and turned away. "Just think about it."

There was no point in thinking about it; Dieter was leaving in two days and she could never make arrangements to accompany him on such short notice. Nor would she leave the university so close to earning her degree. Natan was just being an overprotective elder brother, she told herself as the doorbell rang and she hurried off to welcome Dieter.

"Sara, darling, it's so good to see you," he said when she opened the door. He was bundled up in a heavy wool coat and a hat, his cheeks red from the cold, and he carried a large box she assumed held imported delicacies. "How is Natan?"

"Getting stronger every day." She opened the door wider and beckoned him inside.

Dieter shifted the box as he drew closer, and when he did, a glint of metal on his lapel caught her attention. "What are you wearing?" she asked, sickened, although she knew exactly what it was.

Dieter set down the box and scrambled to remove the swastika from his lapel. "It's just a pin. It's nothing."

"It's not nothing."

"Sara—" He shoved the pin into his pocket. "I'm not a Nazi. You know that."

"Then why would you wear—" She gestured to his pocket, anger surging. "That thing, that horrible symbol? Do you usually wear it whenever I'm not around to see?"

"I didn't want to offend you." He reached for her hand, but she recoiled. "I wear it for business. My boss expects it. Our customers appreciate it. It means nothing. You know how it is. I have to go along to get along."

"That's no excuse," she said, incredulous. "How *could* you? These are the people who held my brother in a concentration camp. You know what they think of Jews, of my family, of me. You know what they are. And yet you wear their symbol because it's good for business?"

"Sara, please, let's talk." He took a few steps toward her, arm outstretched, but he halted when she backed away. "I'm leaving in a couple of days. Let's not part like this. We're going to be married."

She tried to speak, but words failed her. She shook her head, blinked tears from her eyes, and closed the door on him, ignoring the pleas and apologies he sent after her, first contritely and then with rising frustration, until he fell silent.

Twenty minutes later, when she cautiously drew back a curtain and glanced outside, the box was on the doorstep, but Dieter was gone. Her heart ached with regret, but somehow she felt more relief than sorrow.

CHAPTER THIRTY

April–May 1935

Greta

In April, Mildred threw a small party for Arvid when he passed his last qualifying exam for the civil service. Soon thereafter, with the help of one of Greta's childhood friends, he was offered an excellent job within the Ministry of Economics.

"I can't thank you enough," he told Greta soon after he accepted the position, surprising her at her boathouse flat with a small basket packed with decadent treats. "I hope this expresses my gratitude more eloquently."

"This wasn't necessary," Greta protested, marveling as she peered inside and discovered a bottle of Russian vodka, a tin of Russian caviar, South American coffee, and her favorite Swiss chocolates. "You shouldn't have squandered your first paycheck on me—unless all this came from your friends at the Soviet embassy?"

"Neither," Arvid admitted. "Mildred received this from one of her students to thank her for helping arrange her brother's release from a prison camp."

"You mean Sara Weitz."

"Yes. Mildred demurred, but Sara insisted. I hope that doesn't make my gift seem any less sincere."

"Not at all." With an appreciative sigh, Greta closed the box. "This is too good to refuse, but I don't need a gift for helping a friend. It's reward enough to know that the great Arvid Harnack, prince of academic royalty, needed my help to get a job."

They shared a smile. Over the years their old rivalry had mellowed into friendly banter. With more menacing enemies threatening them both, it made no sense not to be allies.

Then Arvid's smile faded. "Before I'm allowed to start work, I have to attend a Nazi boot camp. It's meant to toughen me up physically and bludgeon my political beliefs into proper alignment."

"That's dreadful. How long must you be away?"

"A week. One week too many."

Greta wondered how Arvid would be able to conceal his true feelings from officers trained to detect and snuff out dissent. "By Wednesday you'll be cursing me for getting you the job," she said with false levity. "You're going to demand this gift back."

"The vodka, anyway," he deadpanned, but his expression was bleak.

Greta next saw Mildred a few days after Arvid returned home from his indoctrination. They had met for a walk in the Tiergarten, one of the few places they could talk without fear of listening devices picking up their conversation. When Greta asked if the camp had been as terrible as Arvid had expected, Mildred shook her head. "Worse, much worse," she said, a tremor in her voice. "He refuses to tell me the details because he says he wants to spare me the grim images that he can never forget."

Greta shuddered. "Poor Arvid."

"He came home uninjured and undaunted, so whatever he went through, it wasn't as horrible as what Natan Weitz suffered. The experience only strengthened Arvid's antipathy for the Nazis. He's stronger than they are, with their propaganda and calisthenics and false science. They tried to make him one of their own and they failed."

"Some people simply can't conform upon command," said Greta. "I'm thankful I'm one of them."

"So am I," said Mildred fervently. "Anyway, Arvid is home now, nursing sore muscles and preparing to start work at the Ministry of Economics—while we work at the American embassy."

Greta nodded. Ambassador and Mrs. Dodd were hosting a tea on

May 8 in honor of the American novelist Thomas Wolfe, who had come to Berlin to promote Rowohlt's German translation of his renowned novel *Look Homeward, Angel*. The Dodds had already invited many American dignitaries and members of the press corps, but Martha had asked Mildred to select the German guests, "intellectuals who are both brilliant enough to impress Thomas Wolfe and brave enough to attend," as she put it. In recent months, as Mr. Dodd's antipathy for the Nazi regime had become more apparent, German diplomats had begun avoiding the American embassy, returning marked "out of town" invitations to various events. Loath to embarrass their honored guest with a flop of a party, Martha had begged Mildred to create a guest list on the ambassador's behalf. Mildred was perfect for the job, Martha insisted. Not only did she and Arvid know the German literati exceptionally well, but she had also published several scholarly articles and had given numerous lectures about Wolfe's work.

After conferring with Arvid, Mildred had decided to invite only known and suspected opponents of the regime. At the tea, she, Greta, and Adam would circulate among the journalists, authors, and editors, carefully evaluating their political beliefs and establishing contact with those who seemed suitable candidates for a literary resistance. Forging ties to other groups would help them evaluate the strength and extent of the anti-Nazi movement, and eventually to share information and collaborate on resistance actions.

But first, the guest list.

Linking arms as they strolled, pretending to be engrossed in the rosy buds and pale green flush of spring that had recently swept over the park, Greta and Mildred quietly suggested names, debated them, rejected some, added a select few to their mental list. Once, in a secluded grove of linden, Mildred suggested they sit for a while, but the only bench in sight was painted yellow to indicate that it was reserved for Jews. Not surprisingly, no one sat upon it.

"Shameful," Greta muttered, turning away as anger boiled up inside her. What would the Nazis ruin next? Whenever Greta thought they had exhausted all the possible ways to humiliate German Jews, they surprised her with something new, something more cruel.

Greta and Mildred walked on until they were satisfied with their guest list, parting with a mix of hope and apprehension for how their fates might intertwine in the days to come.

On the afternoon of the tea, Adam met Greta at her flat and they went off to Tiergartenstrasse 27a together. "Arvid won't be attending," Greta told him as they approached the luxurious residence, where several cars were lined up in the driveway. Each driver paused at the gate, where a guard examined their invitation before allowing them to pass beneath the elaborate ironwork arch. "He thought it would be unwise to mingle publicly with Americans so soon after accepting his new post."

"He's married to an American. That ought to be excuse enough," said Adam. "He shouldn't have taken the job if it meant shunning his friends."

"Except that he wants to keep a roof over their heads and food on their table," said Greta. "He doesn't have the luxury of turning down work. And now he'll have access to invaluable financial and economic information—where the Nazis are keeping their money, how they're spending it, what their intentions may be. Would you really have him walk away from that?"

Grudgingly, Adam admitted that he would not.

At the front entrance, Greta and Adam were shown inside by Fritz, the stocky blond butler. Although she had never heard him utter a single "Heil Hitler," Fritz struck Greta as a burgeoning fascist, sly and suspicious, increasingly grim-faced as relations soured between the Reich and the homeland of the people he served. She could not give a reason for her instinctive distrust, but she would not discount it either.

Adam offered Greta his arm and escorted her up the grand staircase to the main hall, where Martha and her mother met them. Martha, bright-eyed and smiling, was smartly dressed in a pale mauve suit with white satin trim and a flared skirt. Beside her, white-haired Mrs. Dodd seemed small, wan, and very tired, but she was unfailingly gracious as she greeted each new arrival.

"I'm counting on you to help loosen up some of the tension around here," Martha confided to Greta. "I asked Mildred to invite interesting and intriguing people, but I haven't seen a grimmer bunch of Germans gathered in one place since the Night of the Long Knives."

Greta glanced around the room. "I'm sure everyone's just anxious for Thomas Wolfe to arrive."

"I hope you're right. I wanted amusing conversation, an exchange of stimulating views, not miserable scowls better suited for a funeral."

As Martha turned to welcome another guest, Adam and Greta moved on. "Something tells me Martha doesn't know how interesting and intriguing these particular guests are," he said in a wry undertone as they joined the crowd.

"That's because Mildred and I didn't explain our criteria for choosing them," said Greta. "Mildred wanted to, but Arvid and I thought she would be a more convincing hostess if she had nothing to hide."

She exchanged a smile across the ballroom with Bella Fromm, formerly the diplomatic reporter for the *Vossische Zeitung*, now with the *Continental Post*. Glancing to her right, Greta nodded discreetly to Max Tau, the renowned German-Norwegian editor and author. As a Jew, he had taken to prefacing his job titles with "erstwhile" whenever he was obliged to mention them in mixed company. She hoped he continued to work in secret.

Greta and Adam separated to mingle through the crowd, the better to gather more impressions to compare later. Adam immediately went to his friend John Sieg, the former editor of the *Rote Fahne*, a Communist newspaper officially forbidden by the Nazis but still published clandestinely by the Communist underground. In 1933, Sieg had been caught up in a wave of Nazi arrests and had spent four months in an SA prison, but that had not deterred him. With his connections to the underground, he would be a valuable ally.

Wandering the rooms, Greta soon found Mildred, radiant in her blue crepe de Chine dress, her golden hair woven into a bun. They conferred quietly before parting to work the crowd. Everything was in place. All around them, Germans and Americans chatted in lively groups or in somber pairs while liveried footmen circulated with trays of hors d'oeuvres and cocktails for those who craved something stronger than tea.

An hour passed as Greta wandered through the ballroom, the dining room, the *Wintergarten*, and the terrace, slipping easily into some conversations, eavesdropping on others as she accepted a cup of tea or nibbled on a canapé. Some guests revealed themselves less averse to the Reich than Greta and Mildred had believed. Others, though more circumspect, were unquestionably opposed, although whether they would be brave enough to join the burgeoning resistance was more difficult to ascertain. A few were so guarded and noncommittal that Greta could only guess where they truly stood. She imagined Arvid nodding approval and declaring that they should all be so careful and stoic, even among those they believed to be sympathetic to their cause. Studying them, marveling at how little they revealed of themselves, she wondered if they were more cautious because they already belonged to resistance circles and had more to lose if they were discovered.

Suddenly, a commotion near the top of the grand staircase heralded the arrival of the guest of honor. From across the hall Greta watched as the towering, dark-haired American shook hands with the Dodds. As his German publisher guided him through a swiftly gathering crowd of admirers, Thomas Wolfe tried to shake all the hands thrust at him, smiling and thanking his well-wishers, appearing somewhat embarrassed and yet still enjoying the attention. He had to be around six feet five inches tall, with rich, alert brown eyes, a boyish mouth, a small nose, and rounded cheeks. A moment later, Martha was at his side, her head barely reaching his shoulder as she tilted her face quite far back in order to grin up at him. Something in the proprietorial way she rested her hand upon his arm told Greta that Wolfe was yet another one of Martha's conquests, or soon would be.

Only after observing the author from a distance for a while did Greta give in to the intrigue of his celebrity and introduce herself. She had read *Look Homeward, Angel* and his most recent book, *Of Time and the River*, in the original English, so they had a brief, pleasant chat about his work, mostly Greta complimenting his writing and Wolfe accepting her compliments. Her strongest impressions of him came later, growing out of what she overheard him say to others. He was affable and courteous, even when the crowd pressed too close, and he modestly deflected the unceasing flow of compliments Greta thought he honestly deserved. She quite liked him for that, and was amused by the way his thoughts often seemed to tumble from him in an unrestrained, disorderly flow. He took an immediate liking to Mildred, which to Greta suggested excellent judgment. She was flattered when she overheard him confide to Ambassador Dodd that he considered the Germans to be the kindest, most warmhearted, and most honorable people of all he had met in Europe

And yet other remarks left her feeling disappointed and repulsed. He expressed too much enthusiasm for what he described as the strength, vigor, and "noble spirit of freedom" of Nazi Germany. When Bella Fromm, visibly taken aback, reminded him of the Aryan Laws, Wolfe tossed back a drink, grinned, and said, "Seems to me the Nazis are simply showing the normal hostility toward the Jews."

Some of his listeners grinned, but far more frowned in bewilderment or disapproval. Disgusted, Greta turned and left the room, certain that she would never again be able to enjoy his novels as she once had.

When she and Mildred met the following Saturday morning in the Tiergarten, they compared notes and found that they had reached strikingly similar opinions about most of the German guests. After they narrowed down the list to those they would approach about the resistance, Greta brought the subject around to the tea's guest of honor. Mildred too had been dismayed by some of his behavior, especially a callous joke he had made about Jews influencing President Roosevelt's administration, and his distorted, idealized notion of what Germany had become under Nazi rule. "His naïve enthusiasm reminds me of Martha's when she first arrived," Mildred said. "After she lived here awhile, her eyes opened and she saw the Reich for the horror it is. I can only hope Thomas Wolfe will undergo the same transformation."

"That's not likely to happen if he spends his entire visit attending parties and meeting fans," said Greta, dubious. "That would have to be a whirlwind of change in a very brief time."

"That's true. He's setting sail for New York at the end of June." Mildred allowed a small conspiratorial smile. "He's promised me a lengthy, detailed, thoroughly honest interview before he departs."

"Mildred, that's wonderful," Greta exclaimed. Switching to English, she said, "That's quite a—what's the phrase?—a scoop."

Mildred laughed. "Yes, it is—or it will be, if I can publish it."

"I'm very happy for you," said Greta sincerely. No one more deserved a bit of publishing luck than Mildred. As Goebbels's Reichskulturkammer had tightened its chokehold upon the publishing industry, her "Brief Reviews" column had been canceled and permission to publish scholarly articles had become increasingly difficult to obtain. An exclusive interview with an acclaimed author whose works passed Nazi restrictions and sold exceptionally well in Germany could create new opportunities for her—and the income would surely be gratefully received.

Later that month, Adolf Hitler addressed the Reichstag, speaking earnestly of Germany's desire for peace, understanding, and justice for all. Hitler repudiated the very thought of war—a senseless horror that would accomplish nothing—and insisted that Germans had no interest whatsoever in conquering other peoples. "The principal effect of every war is to destroy the flower of the nation," he declared as he offered thirteen specific proposals to secure peace in Europe. "Germany needs peace and desires peace!"

In the days that followed, newspapers around the world tentatively praised Hitler's overtures, although several European leaders asked for reassurances regarding certain military matters. Hitler's replies apparently diminished their fears, but although tensions eased, the tone of the foreign press remained watchful and wary.

"Of course Hitler wants peace," said Adam. "He wants peace to buy himself time to prepare for war. And I think he'll get it. The world wants peace so desperately that they'd prefer to be lulled into complacency than to challenge him."

Greta hoped Adam was wrong, but she feared he was right. World leaders, men who ought to be more skeptical, clung to what Hitler said and ignored what he did. Even as the Führer promised peace, the Reich government passed laws requiring air raid shelters to be constructed in all public buildings. Why would he squander time and money on bunkers if he did not expect to need them?

CHAPTER THIRTY-ONE

June–July 1935

Mildred

Thomas Wolfe had brought a whirlwind of excitement to Berlin, and Mildred, longing for a respite from the steadily worsening constraints of the Reich, had allowed herself to be swept up in it. Wolfe had granted her a lengthy interview at the St. Pauli bar on the Rankestrasse, unabashedly candid as he described his creative process, his feelings about the South of his childhood and the present day, his opinion of other authors, and his collaboration with his editor, Max Perkins. In the days that followed, on several long walks through the Tiergarten, the paths shaded by abundant foliage and the air fragrant with masses of pansies in full bloom, he confided in her more deeply about his writing, his fears, and his childhood.

"I was made to believe that whatever I did that didn't put money into my pocket was wrong," he said, a corner of his mouth turning wryly. "Even today I feel that if I didn't make any money on my books I'd believe I was a failure. But I know that isn't a good thing. The best things are not done for money. Don't you believe that?"

Mildred agreed, but she vehemently disagreed when he praised the National Socialists, and with equal frankness told him what life was really like in Hitler's Germany—the oppression, the stifling of writers and artists, the protestations of peaceful intent belied by the ongoing militarization of the country. He listened willingly, unafraid to challenge his own opinions, and eventually acknowledged that he may have misjudged the Nazis and would be more skeptical in the future.

But his visit was not all deep, heartfelt conversations on long, companionable strolls. Martha escorted Wolfe all around Berlin on a merry, boisterous dash of parties, dinners, teas, newspaper interviews, radio broadcasts, photo shoots, lectures, and all-night drinking bouts. Mildred and Bill often accompanied them, but it soon became evident that Martha and Wolfe were spending a great deal of time together in private as well.

"Wolfe's practically moved into the embassy," Bill grumbled as he and Mildred sat observing the towering author and his petite, flirtatious partner make a comically unlikely pair on the dance floor. "You know how Martha is with a new conquest. Our parents look the other way but I'm sure our mother is distressed. I wish Martha would settle down."

"With whom? Thomas Wolfe?" Mildred watched them dance, dubious. "Are they in love?"

"I think they imagine themselves to be. Don't tell Martha I said this, but I think her heart still belongs to the Russian. She and Wolfe fight a lot, with shouting and tears on both sides. Martha accuses Wolfe of drinking too much and wasting his talent. Wolfe doesn't know why it's any of her business, since they've only just met."

"They must shout rather loudly for you to pick up all that."

"That they do," said Bill shortly. "Never mind. This is just a fling. It won't last."

Mildred was quite sure it would not, and not only because Wolfe planned to stay in Germany a mere six weeks. In the meantime, if a brief, torrid affair helped Martha get over the heartbreak of losing Boris, Mildred supposed some good might come of it.

When Wolfe left Berlin at the end of June, he seemed to take all the color and light and breath of their literary society with him. In his absence, Mildred transformed his abundant revelations into a two-part interview for the *Continental Post* and an essay for the *Berliner Tageblatt*, which received considerable acclaim and provoked both admiration and jealousy from the American press corps. As Greta had predicted, the interviews turned out to be a wonderful literary scoop.

But as the heady warmth of her journalistic triumph faded, Mildred felt restless and discouraged. New regulations out of Goebbels's Reichskulturkammer held editors responsible for anything disparaging to the Reich that passed through their offices, so they had become increasingly anxious, excessively wary of putting into print anything that might offend. "The only safe topics anymore are the weather, gardens, and butterflies," Mildred complained to Martha, knowing a fellow writer would commiserate.

Martha sympathized, but she was not constrained in the same suffocating way. Lately other pleasures had distracted her from writing, but she hinted that she was working on a memoir. "It's inspired by my experiences in Berlin, but it's no mere travelogue," she once said, smiling coyly. When Mildred nervously asked how much she might divulge about her friends' secrets, Martha quickly assured her that although Mildred would definitely recognize herself in it, she could alter certain details so that no one else would. She did not intend to publish her book until after her family returned to the United States, when she would be free from the restrictions of both her father's position and the Nazi censors.

Reluctant to squander precious time writing articles and literary criticism that were unlikely to see print, Mildred focused her attention on her translation of *Lust for Life*, which was nearly complete and scheduled for publication in less than a year. One afternoon in mid-July, she had just finished a particularly challenging chapter when Arvid returned home from the Economics Ministry, his expression pensive.

"What's wrong?" she asked, quickly shutting the door and locking it behind him.

"Perhaps nothing. Perhaps this will turn out to be a momentous day." He hung up his hat and took her in his arms for a lingering kiss. "An old friend met me as I was on my way home from work, and not by chance."

"Who?"

"Alexander Hirschfeld."

Mildred searched her memory. "The Soviet official who advised ARPLAN years ago?"

"He's first secretary of the Soviet embassy now." Slipping an arm around her shoulders, Arvid led her into the front room and to a seat beside him on the sofa. "He wants to meet with me to discuss the possibility of helping the Soviet Union bring down the Reich."

"Help them how?"

"I assume by providing them with intelligence, the same economic information you've been passing on to Ambassador Dodd ever since I started working at the ministry."

"But that's different," said Mildred. "I'm giving information to the Americans, to my own country."

"I understand, but the Americans don't seem to be doing anything with it. Ambassador Dodd tells you he passes my reports on to the State Department—"

"And I believe him."

"I do too, but apparently once the information arrives in Washington, it's promptly shelved and forgotten." Arvid took her hand. "I know you suspect Stalin is no better than Hitler, but I have no reason to distrust Alexander Hirschfeld. If providing him with economic intelligence will help bring down the Reich, I must do it."

"I suppose it wouldn't hurt to meet with him, if only to find out what he has in mind."

Arvid raised her hand to his lips, then pulled her close into an embrace. "I'm glad you agree," he murmured, kissing her cheek and the hollow behind her earlobe.

The two men met the following evening in the Tiergarten. At the Abendgymnasium, Mildred could hardly keep her mind on her lectures as she imagined Arvid and Hirschfeld strolling the forested paths, conferring quietly, avoiding strangers. There was no question why the Soviets would be eager for the proprietary financial information only Arvid could give them, but how would they use that intelligence to bring down the Third Reich? Would they expect to seize control of Germany afterward? And if Arvid became their informant, what could they do to ensure his safety? It had never occurred to Mildred to ask the same questions of the American embassy. She knew Ambassador Dodd was a man of indisputable honor and integrity, and she had great faith in the progressive, democratic administration he represented. She could not say the same for Alexander Hirschfeld, whom she barely knew and whose government lied to foreign observers and its own citizens with impunity.

After her last class, Mildred hurried home only to find their flat empty. She made tea and tried to settle down to grading student essays, but she often caught herself staring into space wondering where Arvid was, or pacing out to the balcony to search the sidewalks below for him.

When he finally came home, there was an eager light in his eyes, and he seemed both invigorated and wary. He had agreed to provide the Soviets with intelligence from the Ministry of Economics, details about the German economy and currency, Germany's foreign investments, the national debt, and trade agreements with foreign nations. What he refused to do, despite Hirschfeld's emphatic requests, was abandon his resistance activities.

"Hirschfeld urged me to break off all contact with German Communists and stop working with the resistance," he said. "That includes no longer helping Jews. The Soviets insist I'll be more useful to them if I don't expose myself to unnecessary dangers."

"Useful to *them*?" echoed Mildred. "The point of the resistance is to oust Hitler and save Germany, not to promote the Soviet Union."

"Exactly. I told Hirschfeld I had no interest in becoming a Soviet spy. My goal is to bring down the Nazis and to help the people they persecute. If giving economic intelligence to the Soviets will help me accomplish that, then I'll work with them." He shook his head. "I'm not going to stop helping Jews, or my Communist friends, or anyone else who desperately needs me."

In the end, Hirschfeld accepted Arvid's terms. Arvid would be a source, not an agent, but only as long as helping the Soviets also helped the resistance restore democracy to Germany.

CHAPTER THIRTY-TWO

August 1935

Greta

Steadily and surely, Greta and Adam added threads to the fine web of their resistance network. Soon after the tea for Thomas Wolfe at Tiergartenstrasse 27a, John Sieg agreed to collaborate with them, but he introduced Adam to barely a handful of his comrades in the Communist underground, the better to preserve both circles' security.

Adam had many contacts of his own among Communist workers, and after appraising their suitability, he approached the most intelligent, reliable, and discreet about joining the resistance. Of the few he invited, only three agreed to join. The others he swore to silence.

By mid-August, Adam had spun out a thread of strong steel to Adolf Grimme, the former prominent Social Democratic politician who had served as the minister of science, art, and education for Prussia until July 1932, when he had been thrown out of office after Chancellor Papen dissolved the Prussian government. Adam and Grimme, who had been friends since their student days, agreed that their network should focus on gathering intelligence and inciting civil disobedience to destabilize the Reich from within. This would unsettle the Nazis and hearten their opponents by proving that Hitler's control was not absolute.

Greta urged Adam to invite his friend and occasional collaborator

Günther Weisenborn to join their group, but the gifted playwright had plunged into a deep depression after his plays and novel were thrown onto the pyres during the *Verbrennungstakt* two years before. "I don't think he's in any condition to help us," said Adam. "He's still writing under pseudonyms, but I'm not sure how long he can persist."

"What a loss to German literature it would be if he set down his pen," said Greta. But would anyone beyond the arts community even notice? So much brilliance had already been snuffed out. What was one more fading ember when the hearth was buried in ashes?

"When I last spoke with him," said Adam, "he mentioned that he might go to America."

"If it's the only way he can continue to work, perhaps he should."

Adam thrust his hands into his pockets and scowled. Greta muffled a sigh, stretched out her hand to him, and held it there until he took it and she could pull him close and soothe him with a kiss. He had no patience for anyone who left Germany unless their life was in immediate danger. For Adam, the only courage that mattered was the courage to stay and fight.

All the while, the Harnacks too were expanding their resistance network. Arvid's family connections infiltrated nearly every university and government ministry, although for security reasons, Mildred and Arvid divulged very little regarding who was involved and what they were doing. Arvid also strengthened his ties with the Soviets and cautiously sought out allies within the Ministry of Economics. Mildred had her contacts within the American embassy and the expatriate community, and she recruited students from the Abendgymnasium and her study group. These members included Sara Weitz, who in turn brought in her brother. Greta knew that Natan Weitz was extending threads of the web to other antifascist journalists and editors, but like John Sieg, Natan did not disclose their identities. They were all safer if each of them knew no one beyond their own immediate circle, unless they themselves were the link to another group.

One morning in the last week of August, Greta arrived at the Tiergarten to meet Mildred for their usual walk and conference, only to find that her friend was not alone. Studying the stranger at Mildred's side, Greta fixed a benign expression in place to conceal a sudden pang

of wariness. Something about the woman struck Greta as familiar—
her straight, wheat-brown hair cut short beneath a small, fashionable
hat, her slim figure and assured stance—

"Clara," she said, scarcely believing her eyes. "Clara Leiser."

Beaming, Clara laughed and embraced her. "Greta, it's so good to
see you," she said in English, her midwestern vowels startlingly delightful, like a fresh breeze off Lake Mendota. "You look exactly as you
did back in Madison."

"And you're just as full of flattery," said Greta, smiling back. She
knew worry had chiseled her face too thin and had etched fine lines
around her mouth and between her eyebrows. "How have you been all
these years? What are you doing in Berlin?"

Clara's elation dimmed. "I'm working for the New York court system now. I'm here as an official observer of these mass trials the Nazis
are so fond of."

"They know about them in America?" said Greta.

"Oh, yes," said Clara. "They're a matter of grave concern."

Greta and Mildred exchanged a look, and Greta saw her own muted
hope reflected in her friend's eyes. "That's encouraging," said Mildred,
as if she hardly dared believe it. "Sometimes it seems as if the United
States is determined to ignore all the terrible things happening here,
despite the warnings we send, despite the evidence they ought to see
clearly even an ocean away."

"Most Americans remain firmly isolationist," Clara admitted, "but
there's been enough public outcry in New York over reports of injus-
tices that the authorities decided they must gather more information.
Sometimes local governments can get involved when it would be im-
politic for the federal government to do so."

"If you want to see injustice, you came to the right place," said
Greta.

"I've been granted permission to witness two mass trials and to
tour two prisons," said Clara. "I'll ask to see more, but it wasn't easy
to wring even that much out of the Nazis. They'll probably turn me
down."

"I know someone who was recently released from KZ Oranienburg," said Mildred. "A Jewish journalist arrested for violating the

Editors Law. He was sentenced in a sham trial to eighteen months, and he suffered horribly. His imprisonment was an egregious violation of his civil rights."

"And of basic human decency," Greta broke in, instinctively lowering her voice and glancing over her shoulder for eavesdroppers. "We've heard his story only secondhand, through his sister. I can only imagine how harrowing the full truth would be, offered to an impartial third party."

"Do you think he would speak with me?" asked Clara. "I could withhold his name from the official record if he's afraid of repercussions."

Greta shook her head. "You'd have to withhold more than that, or I'm sure the Gestapo would be able to identify him."

"I think he would speak to you anyway," said Mildred. "He's very brave, and as a journalist, he would want the truth to be told."

Greta had misgivings, but she trusted that her two American friends understood their judicial system better than she did. If they believed Natan Weitz would not find himself thrown back into a prison camp for speaking with a representative of the New York courts, she would not protest. There was always a chance the Gestapo would never know.

Mildred set up a meeting through Sara. Natan agreed to speak to Clara alone, as long as his name and all other identifying details were omitted from the record so that he would not put his family at risk. After they met, all Clara would reveal to Greta and Mildred was that his story had been a revelation and his experience a nightmare.

The rest of Clara's mission brought mixed results. For the two prisons she was permitted to tour, the Gestapo had chosen institutions for citizens convicted of ordinary crimes—theft, forgery, murder—not for political prisoners like Natan and the countless thousands of others arrested simply for being Communists, Social Democrats, or Jews. Clara's Nazi escorts refused to allow her to speak alone with prisoners and rejected her requests to inspect Oranienburg and Dachau. They would not allow her even to approach the front gate of Plötzensee, where a female political prisoner of particular interest to the New York courts awaited execution.

When the time came for Clara to observe the two trials, she invited

Greta and Mildred to accompany her, passing them off as her assistant and translator. The first trial was for eight Communists charged with manslaughter for allegedly shooting a restaurateur four years before. That the man had died was certain, but the entire proceeding reeked of artifice, and Greta had to carefully arrange her features to conceal her profound skepticism. There had been one gun, one shot, no eyewitness testimony, and yet eight men, who all happened to be Communists, were found guilty and sentenced to five years at Dachau.

The second trial was for seventeen men and boys accused of high treason for distributing literature critical of the Reich and for organizing meetings where "subversive sentiments" were expressed. Greta sat almost motionless through the hours of testimony, scarcely able to breathe, feeling as if a rough hand were tightening around her throat. The men and boys in the dock—pale, defiant, tearful, angry—had done nothing she, Adam, Mildred, and Arvid had not also done. When the defendants were sentenced to die for their crimes, Mildred seized her hand. They clutched each other so tightly that Greta's fingertips went numb.

In the days that followed, Greta and Mildred helped Clara acquire more information that they hoped would be useful to the New York courts. What they might do with the information back in the States, Greta could only guess, but if it helped shake the Americans out of their complacency, the effort would be time well spent.

The day before Clara departed Berlin, the three friends met at the Palast-Café for a farewell lunch and one last walk through the Tiergarten. "You should leave Germany, both of you," Clara urged as they were parting at the Brandenburg Gate. "It's too dangerous here. You've gotten used to it so maybe you don't see just how horrifying it is."

"Mildred could go, but it's not so simple for me," said Greta. "I would have to get immigration papers, and there are quotas and a very long line ahead of me. Even if I could get a student visa—somehow, if someone at the University of Wisconsin would do a favor for an alumna—eventually it would run out and I'd have to come home." She stopped herself before blurting out that she could not bear to leave Adam, or to be even farther from her aging parents in Frankfurt an der

Oder, or to abandon the resistance network when it had barely begun and by every indication was becoming more crucial every day.

Clara fixed her gaze firmly on Mildred. "Just you, then, Mildred. You're an American. Come home."

Mildred shook her head. "I can't leave Arvid."

"Convince him to come with you."

"He wouldn't. His family is here, his work—"

"Then come without him. I know you don't want to leave him, but he would want you to be safe."

"He would," Greta interjected, not because she wanted Mildred to go, but because it was true.

"It's not his decision, but mine," said Mildred. "Clara, I know the answer seems so obvious—we should get out now before things get worse. But some of us feel we have to stay to keep an eye on developments."

Greta nodded. How could they flee? How could they abandon Germany to evil men who were determined to destroy everything good about it?

Clara took a deep, shaky breath and told them she understood. "This isn't goodbye," she vowed, embracing each of them in turn. "We'll meet again, in better days."

Greta wanted to believe her, but better days seemed very far away.

CHAPTER THIRTY-THREE

June–September 1935

Sara

A few weeks after Dieter arrived in Australia, he sent Sara a gift—a boomerang, a graceful curve of smooth dark wood, polished to a high sheen and painted with black geometric designs that Sara guessed were tribal insignia. He had enclosed a letter in the package, contrite, imploring, full of apologies and explanations. He was no Nazi, he insisted, and if Sara knew him at all she ought to know that. He was wrong to have worn the swastika pin for the sake of diplomacy in business and he would never wear it again, even if it cost him his last commission. Better to lose his job than Sara's respect.

"Even your favorite instructor had to join the National Socialist Teachers League to keep her job," Dieter wrote. "If you could forgive Frau Harnack, then surely you can forgive me."

If they had not been separated by almost ten thousand miles, Sara would have retorted that Mildred had joined the league only with great reluctance after agonizing over the consequences. Dieter had willingly pinned that swastika to his lapel to convince clients he was a Nazi in order to make sales. His motives and complicity and Mildred's were nothing alike. The only reason Sara would ever want to see Dieter again would be to tell him so, and to return his ill-considered gift—and the engagement ring.

She could not bear to wait until he returned from Australia to settle the matter once and for all. She mailed him a heartfelt letter breaking off their engagement, trying as best she could to be gentle and kind. Then she carefully tucked the ring and the boomerang in a box—only those, it would have been spiteful to return every gift he had given her through the years—and set out for Dieter's apartment.

His mother answered the knock, pursing her mouth and narrowing her eyes as her gaze traveled from Sara's face to the box in her arms. "What's this about?" she asked.

"Would you please see that Dieter gets this?" As Frau Koch accepted the parcel, she added, "Please keep it somewhere safe. It's . . . valuable."

A faint triumphant gleam lit up Frau Koch's eyes. "Does this mean what I hope it means?"

"I don't know what you hope."

"Then it's true. He finally ended it."

Sara saw no reason to clarify the finer points of their breakup. "The marriage is off, yes."

"Praise God!" Frau Koch clutched the box to her chest and gazed heavenward. "This is an answer to a poor mother's prayers."

"Yes, well—" Sara forced a tight smile and stepped away from the door. "Goodbye."

"He's better off with his own kind," Frau Koch called after her as she left. "You both are."

Sara broke the news to her family the next time they gathered for Shabbat. Wilhelm and the girls were off at the Riechmann ancestral estate in Minden-Lübbecke, but her parents and siblings absorbed the news with obvious relief. Everyone expressed their sympathy in careful phrases, but no one seemed surprised or regretful.

Soon thereafter, Amalie tremulously made a far more upsetting announcement: She, Wilhelm, and their daughters were leaving Germany indefinitely.

"But why?" their father protested.

Because recent events and rumors in military circles had convinced Wilhelm that withdrawing to Schloss Federle would offer Amalie and the girls scant protection in the days to come. He intended to move the family to Switzerland until the Nazis fell from power and the persecution of Jews ceased. He had already resigned from the Wehrmacht and was getting their affairs in order, preparing their homes and household staff for a lengthy absence.

Tears filled Sara's eyes as she embraced her sister. "I'll miss you so much! I feel like my heart is breaking."

"I'm sorry, Sara, but Wilhelm insists."

"Wilhelm's right," said their mother. "You must get out while you still can."

Sara and Amalie broke off their embrace and turned to her, startled.

"Far be it for me to complain that Wilhelm is *too* devoted and protective," said their father, shaking his head, "but I believe he's overreacting. Surely the Nazis have already done their worst. If we go about our lives, do our work, pay our debts, and cause no trouble, they will leave us alone."

"The way they left Natan alone?" Sara said, incredulous.

Her father fixed her with a look of pained reproof. "Natan broke the law."

"A law so unjust that the only proper response was to break it," said Natan.

"Please, let's not argue," Amalie begged. "Wilhelm is worried for me and the girls, and he won't change his mind. As soon as he can make arrangements, we're going, and we urge you all to come with us."

"Sara and Natan, you should go," said their mother. "I would too, but I won't go without your father."

He reached for her hand. "There is no need. We are German. This is our home."

"I can't leave," said Sara, thinking of the resistance, deliberately avoiding Natan's gaze. "I won't interrupt my studies."

"I won't leave," said Natan. "I just got a job. I have too much to do."

"You could write for another paper at least as good as the *Judische Nachrichtenblatt* in Switzerland," said Amalie, but her despondent expression revealed that she knew it was a lost cause.

Within days, Amalie, Wilhelm, and their daughters left for Switzerland. Amalie invited the family to visit them at the chateau Wilhelm had taken in Geneva, but Sara missed her sister terribly and not even the hope of a brief reunion comforted her.

In the second week of September, Natan attempted to rouse Sara out of her unhappiness by inviting her to accompany him on a trip to Nuremberg to cover the annual Nazi Party rally for the *Judische Nachrichtenblatt*.

"That's an odd choice for a cheerful distraction," said Sara.

"I didn't say it would be cheerful, but it won't be boring."

Sara mulled it over. Perhaps she might observe something at the rally that would benefit the resistance, something worth enduring several days in the company of tens of thousands of fanatical Nazis. She decided to go, although her parents had strong misgivings and begged her never to leave her brother's side when they were out in public.

On September 10, Natan and Sara took the train to Nuremberg, squeezing into the crowded third-class compartment, each carrying one small suitcase and Natan his typewriter case as well. They were still standing in the aisle when the train unexpectedly lurched forward. Sara instinctively grabbed the nearest seat with her free hand and managed to keep her feet, but Natan stumbled and the corner of his typewriter case nudged another man in the back.

"I beg your pardon," said Natan. In reply, the man shot him a withering glare over his shoulder.

As the train picked up speed, Natan and Sara tumbled into a seat, but they had barely gotten settled when she felt eyes boring into the back of her head. A surreptitious glance revealed the same man two rows back and across the aisle, fixing her and Natan with a hard stare.

Sara resolved to ignore him. "They're calling this the *Reichsparteitag der Freiheit*," she said to Natan in an undertone. "The rally for freedom—freedom from what?"

"From the Treaty of Versailles," he replied. "Now that Hitler has reintroduced compulsory military service and has revealed his secret rearmament program to the public, Germany is no longer bound by the treaty's restraints—"

"You there," a voice broke in. "Where are you from?"

Sara and Natan turned in their seats to find the same man glowering at them. Sara quickly looked away, but Natan smiled. "From Berlin, where we boarded," he replied affably.

"That's not what I meant. Are you Jews? You look Jewish."

Natan's smile deepened, but his voice took on an edge. "So what if we are? Anyone is allowed on this car."

"Not for long. You'll see. You'll get what's coming to you."

Heart pounding, Sara squeezed her brother's arm. "Pay no attention to him."

Miraculously, Natan obeyed. The angry man said nothing more to them for the rest of the journey, but Sara was conscious of his malevolence, and of the sidelong suspicious glances from other passengers. In the seat in front of them, two young women about Sara's age murmured to each other and inched as far away from her and Natan as they could. From time to time they glanced over their shoulders, their mouths pursed and noses wrinkled as if they smelled something foul. Cheeks burning, Sara fixed her attention on the scenes passing outside her window, the early autumn hues coloring the countryside, the disheartening sight of picturesque villages draped in swastika flags and banners.

When they reached Nuremberg, Sara and Natan quickly retrieved their luggage and disembarked before anyone else could confront them. First they went to the home of a friend of Natan's, a fellow journalist who had offered them a place to stay since rally attendees had booked every hotel room and boardinghouse in the city. Over supper, their host and his wife repeatedly emphasized that they should avoid drawing attention to themselves and must deny that they were Jews if challenged. As they walked to the site of the rally, six square miles of stadiums, buildings, and parade grounds, Natan handed Sara a stiff paper card. "Keep this in a safe place," he said. "It's your press credential."

"So official," she joked to hide her rising trepidation, but after a closer look, she gasped. "The *Los Angeles Times?*"

"That's right. I'm covering the rally for them as well as the *Judische Nachrichtenblatt*. Under a nom de plume."

"What if the Gestapo finds out?"

"Writing for a non-Jewish newspaper is the *least* offensive crime I plan to commit against the Nazis." His brow furrowed. "You don't expect to bring them down without breaking their rules, do you?"

"No—no, of course not."

She steeled herself as they approached the massive parade grounds. They had missed the arrival of Hitler's motorcade, but throngs of Nazi faithful still milled about excitedly, swastika flags clenched in fists, pins like Dieter's glinting on lapels, arms snapping out the Hitler salute when acquaintances met, impromptu chorales breaking into the "Horst Wessel Lied."

As the crowd pressed upon them, Natan seized Sara's hand and led her through the crush of people into the stadium, where they joined the press corps, a pocket of watchful stoicism amid the frenzy. As Natan conferred with colleagues, Sara took in the scene. The air was electric with expectation and euphoria, the seats filled with men and women in various Nazi regalia from simple armbands to full uniforms, their rapt gazes fixed upon the parade grounds, where more than 150,000 marchers paraded in precise geometric formations. Boys clad in the uniforms of the Hitler Youth performed on drums and trumpets; girls in the middy blouses and full, dark blue skirts of the Bund Deutscher Mädel sang anthems to the Führer and the Fatherland. Transfixed with foreboding, Sara felt herself shrinking inwardly the more the audience roared approval. She knew the spectacle was designed to inspire Hitler's worshippers and intimidate everyone else, and she hated to feel its power working upon herself.

Day by day, the pageant at the parade grounds varied little—marchers, songs, speeches by party dignitaries, displays of reinvigorated military might—but on the evening of September 15, the rally would culminate in the much-anticipated announcement of new party policies.

Natan managed to claim two places for them in the press box at Congress Hall, modeled after the Colosseum in Rome, with seating for more than fifty thousand. As they awaited the first speaker, Sara quietly debated the possibilities with a few members of the foreign press she had befriended. As their predictions grew more and more dire, they concluded that whatever Hitler and his inner circle had devised would inevitably be worse than anything they had yet imagined.

Before long, Göring took the stage. After a brief preface, he began to praise the Weimar flag, calling it "the symbol of national glory in the days before the war," which even afterward had remained "encased in glory." In the future the Nazis expected the old Imperial flag to be treated with respect, but, he noted, tapping the podium with a forefinger for emphasis, "in the struggles for the regeneration of Germany the swastika has become for us a holy symbol." For that reason, the current German flag would be retired, superseded by the swastika banner of the National Socialists.

"Well, why not?" said Natan ironically. "The Nazi Party has become the state and the state is the party."

"It's wrong," said Sara, indignant. "Germany and the Nazi Party are not one and the same."

But even as she spoke, she wondered if that were true anymore.

Then Göring announced two additional laws, cruel and chilling, his words so unbelievable and wrong that they pinned her in place, trembling, unable to cover her ears or look away.

The first was the Reich Citizenship Law, which redefined citizenship based upon parentage rather than birthplace. Jews were identified as "not of German blood" and were thereby stripped of their citizenship and all associated civil rights, including the right to vote. Even Jews who had converted to Christianity were bound by the decree.

Then Göring announced the Law for the Protection of German Blood and German Honor.

"In bygone years, the German people have suffered much from the unpardonable sin of racial impurity," he shouted, to a thunderous roar of accord from the audience. "German women must be protected against racial contamination."

To that end, marriages between Germans and Jews were henceforth forbidden. Marriages made in violation of the law were declared void, and extramarital relations between Germans and "non-Aryans" were prohibited. Marriages conducted abroad with the intention of circumventing the decree would not be recognized in Germany. In order to prevent the defilement of German domestic servants by Jewish employers, Jews could no longer hire German women under the age of forty-five years. Violators were subject to punishments including fines, imprisonment, or, in the most egregious circumstances, hard labor at a concentration camp.

Sickened, Sara forgot to take notes, her hands clenched around her pad and pencil until her knuckles turned white and her fingers ached. It did not matter. Every provision of the abhorrent new laws was seared into her memory.

Eventually the rally ended. Sara and Natan collected their luggage from his friend's home and traveled back to Berlin. Unnerved and shaken, Sara felt as if she had aged a year since she had last sat aboard a train. Only a few days before, she was German, a citizen of the country of her birth. Now, following a rubber-stamp vote in the Reichstag and the stroke of a pen, she was stateless, a woman without a homeland. Or so the law decreed, although she felt no less German than before.

Reports of the new laws had already been widely published by the time Sara and Natan arrived home, and yet their parents hastened to meet them in the foyer, ashen-faced, seeking verification, hoping in vain that the press had misrepresented the new decrees. Natan confirmed their worst fears and divulged something they had not yet read in the papers: The new laws revoked all exemptions for Jewish veterans of the Great War. The modest protection their father's past honorable service had provided the Weitz family was no more.

"I fought for this country," Sara's father said, pained and bewildered, sinking heavily into a chair. "I bled for this country. I was willing to give my life for it. How can anyone deny that I am a citizen?"

As his breathing became labored, Sara and her mother flew to his side, loosened his necktie, and offered soothing reassurances they did not themselves believe. When calm was restored, Sara's mother ventured that perhaps it would be prudent for them to stay with Amalie in Switzerland until the implications of the new laws became clear.

One implication was perfectly clear to Sara: She could not marry Dieter now, even if she wanted to with all her heart.

The next day when Sara returned to school, the atmosphere on campus was tense and expectant, with undercurrents of malevolence and apprehension sweeping through the quadrangles and corridors. Some of her professors excised politics from their lectures so completely that one could almost believe they were unaware of what had taken place. Others wove the rally and the Nuremberg Laws into their lectures, some in outrage, others in jubilation. After one lecture in which a venerable professor praised the Führer and waxed rhapsodic about cleansing the university of the poison of Jewish influence, Sara and several Jewish classmates instinctively drew together as the students streamed from the hall.

They gathered outside a discreet distance away to share information, ponder rumors, worry aloud about their Jewish friends who had stopped attending classes—"We thought we had lost you too," one classmate told Sara—and speculate about what their loss of citizenship would mean for their status at the university. Would they be expelled? Would Jews be forbidden to practice the few occupations remaining open to them? Would intermarried couples be required to live apart? Would Jews be forced to emigrate from the country of their birth, the only homeland they knew?

German Jews no longer had any voice in the political process. Would those who had not been silenced speak for them, or would they look the other way and count their blessings that it was the Jews who suffered and not themselves?

Sara and her friends had no answers and little hope, only questions, anger, and fear.

CHAPTER THIRTY-FOUR

March–May 1936

Mildred

Every day, reports describing in assiduous detail the budget priorities of Hitler's regime crossed Arvid's desk at the Ministry of Economics. Mildred marveled at the documents he smuggled home to copy and pass on to Alexander Hirschfeld and her own contacts at the American embassy, indisputable evidence that despite Hitler's protests to the contrary, he was rebuilding the German military. Surely this intelligence would compel other nations of Europe as well as the isolationist United States into action, dowsing the smoldering embers of war before they ignited and scorched the entire continent.

In the first week of March, Arvid came home from work badly shaken. He drew Mildred away from the door and murmured, "Funds are being dispensed to the Wehrmacht in a way that can only mean Hitler intends to mobilize troops."

Mildred felt a cold fist tighten in her chest. "Where?" she mouthed, barely breathing the word. "When?"

He shrugged and shook his head.

It was wretched having so little to go on, a handful of facts adding up to a vague, undefined threat. Mildred scanned the newspapers, seeking a careless aside that might inadvertently reveal the truth, but it was like hearing an ominous rumble of thunder, searching the skies for the storm cloud, and finding endless, unbroken blue.

Then, on March 7, Hitler sent thirty thousand German troops into the Rhineland, the territory between the Rhine River in western Germany and the borders of the Netherlands, Belgium, Luxembourg, France, and Switzerland. Even though Mildred had expected the army to move, she was still shocked by the egregious violation of the 1919 Treaty of Versailles, which had banned Germany from establishing any military presence in the region and explicitly stated that the Allies would regard any violation as a threat to world peace. Six years after that, in 1925, Germany had joined France, Britain, and Italy in signing the Locarno Treaties, confirming the border between France and Germany, making permanent the demilitarization of the Rhineland, and declaring that if either France or Germany attacked the other, Britain and Italy would be required to assist the nation under assault.

A demilitarized Rhineland had been the single greatest bulwark maintaining peace in Europe, and now it was over.

Mildred waited anxiously to see how the nations of Europe would counter Germany's aggressive move, but a month passed, and then another, and they did nothing but issue statements of condemnation. She imagined outraged, confounded men debating in council rooms in London, Brussels, and Paris—and when their anger was spent, throwing their hands helplessly into the air and deciding yet again to wait and see. Mildred could almost hear their rationalizations: Hitler had long regarded the imposed demilitarization as shameful and degrading to the German people. Perhaps occupying the Rhineland would satisfy him. Why put their own troops in harm's way and jeopardize the peace and stability of Europe by provoking Hitler if he wanted no more than what he had already taken?

"He will always want more," said Arvid as Mildred lay in his arms in bed one morning in early May, both of them reluctant to get up and face the day. "The Rhineland, the constant adulation of the people, the timid acquiescence of the great leaders of Europe—none of it will ever be enough to fill the void where his soul should be."

Mildred imagined a dusty, echoing hollow in Hitler's chest, empty of all compassion and empathy. Strange that such a cold, dark place should be the source of so much heated rhetoric and fiery hatred for the Jews. How much more would Germany's Jews be able to endure? Only a few days before, Sara had turned up at the Harnacks' flat tearful and distressed, having just been informed that Jews would no longer be permitted to sit for doctoral exams.

"I've worked so hard for so many years," Sara had lamented, choking back tears, "and just when my degree is within reach, it's snatched away. What am I to do now?"

Mildred had comforted her young friend as best she could, plying her with *Kaffee und Kuchen* and offering pragmatic advice—to secure a copy of her transcript, obtain letters of recommendation from favorite professors, create a portfolio of her papers and research, and continue to read and study on her own so she would not lose ground while she arranged to transfer to a university abroad.

"Ambassador Dodd has influence at the University of Chicago," said Mildred. "Martha would put in a good word for you with her father. I myself have contacts at the University of Wisconsin—"

"I can't leave Germany now," said Sara, startled out of her tears. Shaking her head, she took a handkerchief from her book bag and wiped her eyes. "You need me."

She meant the resistance needed her, but she was clever enough not to say so aloud, not even in the presumed security of the Harnacks' flat. "We could spare you for the sake of your future," said Mildred.

"What future will I have if I don't do my part to stop my country from hurtling toward its own destruction?" Sara gestured as if indicating the edge of a precipice. "I don't see you packing up and heading back to America, even though all you have to do is buy a ticket and brandish your American passport, and you're halfway home."

Mildred shrugged noncommittally to hide her chagrin. Arvid alone knew that a month after the German army occupied the Rhineland, she had written to William Ellery Leonard, her former mentor at the University of Wisconsin, to inquire about joining the faculty of the English Department. His reply, regretful and yet oddly sanguine given her circumstances, described state budgets severely tightened due to the Great Depression, staffing cutbacks, and a surplus of unemployed academics. Unlike most scholars competing for scarce positions in academia, Mildred had not earned her doctorate, which put her at a distinct disadvantage. She seemed to have found her niche in Berlin introducing great works of American and British literature to Germans, he wrote condescendingly. Perhaps she should resolve to find greater satisfaction in that.

"Even for me, leaving wouldn't be as easy as you might think," Mildred told Sara. First and foremost, she could not bear to leave Arvid. In Berlin she had a job and a higher purpose in the fledgling resistance. If she returned to America, safer but heartbroken, she would be entirely dependent upon the generosity of her siblings until she found work—*if* she found work, when millions of others were unemployed and struggling.

Mildred was grateful for her job at the Abendgymnasium, which remained fulfilling despite the Nazi influence over the curriculum and admissions policies. Although the National Socialists constantly boasted about Germany's miraculous economic recovery, the economy had improved only slightly under Hitler's rule. It was true that many men had found decent jobs thanks to public works schemes like the National Labor Service—building roads, digging irrigation ditches for farms, planting trees—but the dramatically improved unemployment statistics Hitler boasted about were illusory. Women, who were not supposed to be working outside the home at all but attending to "*Kinder, Kirche, Küche*," were no longer included in the official count of the unemployed. Although Jews had been driven from the workforce in vast numbers, they were not counted either because they were not considered citizens. The reinstatement of the draft had shifted many young men from the unemployment rolls to the military, and other men hired to work in the factories built to turn out equipment for the troops improved the statistics even more. Arvid, uniquely positioned to understand the real state of things, acknowledged that the economy had shown some genuine growth. "But to declare a swift and complete restoration, and to attribute it to Hitler's financial genius?" He shook his head. "Propaganda, nothing more."

Hitler lied with impunity, Mildred thought grimly one evening in early June as she walked to the Abendgymnasium. Why shouldn't he, when he suffered no ill consequences, when his fanatical admirers disregarded all evidence that contradicted him? She wondered sometimes if the Führer believed his own lies, but she suspected the answer was much simpler, that he was ruthlessly calculating—

Her train of thought abruptly broke when, from a block away, she spotted two gleaming black cars parked in front of the Abendgymnasium, swastika banners on the front grilles and fenders. Two SS officers flanked the entrance to the building.

Ignoring the impulse to flee, she forced herself to approach with her usual smooth, brisk stride. Surprise inspections of schools had become commonplace. She had no reason to believe the Gestapo had come for her.

She greeted the officers with a demure nod as she passed between them. Inside, the halls buzzed with tension as students and faculty hurried between offices and classrooms, some pausing in alcoves to exchange furtive whispers, glancing nervously over their shoulders and swiftly dispersing. Mildred saw her own apprehension reflected in some faces, but others were lit up with the gleam of zealotry. Just ahead, a familiar burly figure emerged from the throng, an instructor from the History Department she knew to be no friend to the Nazis. "Einhard," she said, catching hold of his arm, "what's going on?"

"The SS received an anonymous report," he said, looking warily past her to the students racing off to class as if he believed the accuser mingled among them—which, Mildred supposed, could very well be true. "An accusation of seditious teachings. We're supposed to carry on as usual, but each member of the faculty will be pulled from class at some point and questioned. Those officers by the front door are there to remind us not to leave early."

Mildred managed a smile. "How fortunate for me that I have a room on the ground floor, with accommodating windows."

Einhard strangled out a laugh. "I might pay you a visit if this goes on too late." He briefly rested a hand on her shoulder before hurrying off to the stairwell.

Steeling herself, Mildred continued on to her classroom only to find Karl Behrens waiting for her outside the door. "Whatever they accuse you of, deny everything," he said, his voice low and furious. "We'll all vouch for what a perfect Nazi *Frau* you are."

"Thank you, Karl," she murmured, gesturing to the door. "Let's not arouse suspicions by whispering in doorways."

He nodded and preceded her into the room. Feigning serenity, she waited for a few stragglers to take their seats before beginning the evening's lesson. Her heart thudded with such force she marveled that she could speak at all. One glance at her syllabus would reveal that she taught antifascist literature, and although she did not have her students read banned books—it had become impossible to acquire copies—she discussed several *verboten* authors in her lectures. But if the informant had accused her in particular, why had the SS not confronted her directly? Why put the entire school through this frightening ordeal— unless it was to terrify them, to turn them against one another to save themselves?

Forty minutes later, a knock sounded on the door. Before Mildred could answer, Dr. Stecher peered in and asked her to accompany him to his office. "Certainly," she said, smiling briefly as she turned back to her students. "Emil, would you please lead the class in a discussion of chapter seven?" Emil Kortmann nodded and approached the podium. He was one of her brightest pupils, a member of the school's English Club as well as her private study group, eminently trustworthy, and less likely than Karl to lead the students in outright revolt.

On the short walk to Dr. Stecher's office, the principal betrayed not a single flicker of emotion to indicate what might await her. When they reached his office, he opened the door and gestured for her to enter alone, and he closed it firmly behind her after she did.

A Gestapo officer sat behind the principal's desk, his black uniform immaculate, his blue eyes appraising, his dark hair graying at the temples. "Frau Harnack," he greeted her, glancing at a file lying open on the desktop—her employment records. "Please be seated."

She obeyed, back straight, hands clasped in her lap, gaze calm and level.

"I deeply regret that an accusation of subversion and disloyalty to the Reich has been made against the Abendgymnasium." His brow furrowed as he studied her. "Do you have anything you wish to disclose?"

"No, sir, I do not."

"Are you certain? These are very serious charges."

She feigned puzzlement. "I'm not sure how you think I can help you."

She half expected him to pull her syllabus from the file, slam it onto the desk, and demand that she explain herself. Instead he regarded her with something resembling sympathy. "I know it isn't easy to betray the confidences of a friend, but sometimes, for the greater good, it becomes necessary. Don't you agree?"

"I suppose on certain occasions it could be."

"We have arrived at one of those occasions." He sat back in Dr. Stecher's chair. "Frau Harnack, are you aware of any Jews on the faculty?"

"I—I'm quite sure there are none," she said. "Several Jewish instructors were dismissed after Easter recess three years ago, and as far as I know, none remain."

"You are not yourself Jewish?"

"No," she replied, taken aback. "I'm American, as I'm sure you were informed, but my heritage is English."

"Dr. Stecher assures me you are entirely Aryan, and I'm inclined to agree." His eyes narrowed as his gaze took in her blue eyes and blond hair. "You look more Aryan than I do. But appearances can deceive. Can you prove that you are indeed fully Aryan?"

Mildred's thoughts raced. "My mother has researched our family genealogy. We were accepted into the Daughters of the American Revolution based upon the records she found. I have copies—"

"Good. Bring them to Gestapo headquarters tomorrow so we may verify them ourselves."

She agreed, and he dismissed her. Hiding her astonishment, she rose on trembling legs and hurried off before he decided to examine her file more carefully. When she returned to her classroom, the discussion immediately broke into a flurry of anxious questions. She tried to offer reassuring yet truthful answers, but she was not sure she succeeded.

The interrogations were still going on when her last class ended, but the students and all of the faculty who had already been questioned were permitted to leave. Mildred looked for Einhard in the halls but did not see him. It seemed unwise to linger, so she set out for home. Just around the corner out of sight of the Abendgymnasium, she found several colleagues who had ducked into an alley to compare notes. One, a professor of French, had been forced to justify his entire field of study—the inferior language and culture of an inferior people, the SS officer had disparaged it. Another, a history professor, had been sharply rebuked for using an older textbook, one that preceded the Reich and thus did not provide the new official version of German history. All had been ordered to prove that they were of pure Aryan descent.

"Was anyone arrested?" Mildred asked, glancing over her shoulder and drawing nearer to hear the answer. But they did not know. No one had heard any commotion in the halls redolent of a prisoner dragged off under duress, but that confirmed nothing.

The following morning, Mildred sorted her genealogy documents, hoping that copies would suffice since her mother had kept the originals. Arvid offered to escort her, but she declined, unwilling for him to miss work or to invite the scrutiny of the Gestapo or the SS. "One Harnack under suspicion is more than enough," she said lightly, but Arvid's frown of worry only deepened. In the end he agreed that she should go alone.

The Gestapo made their headquarters at Prinz-Albrecht-Strasse 8, a former art school adjacent to the SS headquarters in the Hotel Prinz Albrecht and a block away from the Prinz-Albrecht-Palais, which housed the SS intelligence service. An aspect of menace seemed to shroud the marble walls and pillared lobby, but she told herself it was only her imagination, not the ghosts of forgotten artists lamenting that their temple of creativity and artistic aspiration had become the lair of fascists. Mildred knew Heinrich Himmler kept an office on the top floor, and as she was directed from a main desk to a smaller office and to meet one particular clerk, curiosity compelled her to watch for him.

The clerk made her wait in an uncomfortable chair before beckoning her forward to query her about the purpose of her visit and to examine her documents. "Everything appears to be in order," he finally said, stamping several pages with an official seal. "There's no question that you're pure Aryan, although surely you will soon give up teaching and take up the more noble career of motherhood?"

Pained, Mildred forced a demure smile. "One can only hope."

He nodded, satisfied, and told her she was free to go. She waited a moment for him to return her documents, but when it became clear he had no intention of doing so, she inclined her head and departed, hardly daring to believe her ordeal was over, unable to breathe a sigh of relief until she stood outside on the pavement.

That evening, she arrived early for her first class, anxious to learn what had happened after she had left the Abendgymnasium the previous night. To her relief, she found Einhard in his classroom, still shaken from the interrogation and no wiser than she about what, if anything, the Gestapo had concluded. "If some of our colleagues don't show up to teach today, I suppose that will tell us something," he said gloomily, but as best as she could determine from hasty exchanges with other instructors during passing periods, everyone was accounted for.

After her last class, Mildred longed to hurry home to Arvid, but it was the night for the weekly meeting of the English Club, and they were well into rehearsals for their upcoming production of *Richard III*. For a brief, blissful two hours, she lost herself in the beauty of Shakespeare's language and the joy of helping talented, dedicated students bring his timeless drama to life. It was quite late by the time rehearsal ended, but when Mildred left the building with Emil, Karl, and a few other students who had lingered to discuss their characters, they stepped into a balmy twilight, strangely peaceful and reassuring after the pervasive dread of the past few days.

The group broke up at the street corner, but Emil was heading in the same direction as Mildred, so they walked along together, chatting about blocking and costumes and whether they ought to risk using real swords in act five. Emil was all for it, Mildred against. "If we use real swords, we may be expected to use real horses too," she teased as they walked along Tauentzienstrasse toward the Bahnhof Zoo.

Emil's face lit up, but before he could reply, a swarm of SS were upon them, as suddenly as if they had risen from hidden fissures in the earth. Instinctively Mildred reached for Emil's arm, but the black-clad officers swept them and other hapless passersby along before them, a wave cresting toward the UFA Filmpalast. Frantic, Mildred tried to tear herself free, certain they had been caught up in a raid, but when they reached the sidewalk in front of the entrance to the theater, the SS suddenly halted, penning them in.

"Frau Harnack!" called Emil, struggling to make his way to her side, but just as he reached her, the enormous double doors swung open and Adolf Hitler strode out, surrounded by his usual entourage. A murmur rippled through the crowd and swelled into a roar as all around arms flung out in the *Hitlergruss* and shouts of "Heil Hitler!" rose to the sky. As the SS shoved the crowd back to clear a path from the door to the Führer's automobile, his flaccid face and piercing eyes turned to one side and then the other as he accepted the people's worship, returning their salutes with a rather affected one of his own, his elbow bent at his side, his right hand flung up by his ear, palm facing forward. Almost, Mildred thought fleetingly, as if he were shooing away a persistent fly.

It was all over in a moment. Hitler climbed into his car and was swiftly driven away with several SS staff cars as escort. "What a historic moment," an old woman cried, her thin voice rising above the excited hum of the crowd. "How thankful I am to have lived long enough to see our great leader!"

Emil muttered disparagingly under his breath, but Mildred was shocked into silence as she watched the old woman tremble in tearful ecstasy. Sickened, she turned her gaze to the faces of the people surrounding them. They looked like men and women she might see strolling through the Tiergarten on a Sunday or waiting in a queue at the market or opening a hymnal at church. But now these perfectly ordinary people turned beatific faces toward the departing cars, a feverish light in their eyes. They behaved as if a god had briefly come to earth to walk among mortals, and they, the fortunate few, had witnessed his divine majesty and would never be the same.

Mildred's gaze found Emil's, and she saw her own dismay reflected in his eyes. How could the resistance persuade such devout followers that the Nazis were leading them toward destruction? How could reason overcome such ardent, irrational veneration?

A week later, Dr. Stecher called an all-school assembly.

There, trembling and watery-eyed, he bravely announced that although the accusations of seditious teaching and disloyalty to the Reich had not been proven, the Gestapo had decided to close the Abendgymnasium. The students' dismay and outrage struck the hapless principal with such force that he stepped backward. Raising his hands for silence, he shouted back empty reassurances that they would receive full credit for their incomplete courses and assistance transferring to universities and trade schools. It was only as she was clearing out her desk that Mildred learned the faculty would receive no severance pay, no help finding new jobs, nothing.

"Why would they close the school when they found no evidence of subversion?" Mildred lamented to Arvid. "The Nazis boast about creating jobs and lowering unemployment, and the Abendgymnasium helps students move on to better careers and higher education. Why shut us down when we're accomplishing work they themselves insist is important?"

"The Abendgymnasium was founded by the Social Democrats," said Arvid. "Anything created by the previous administration, however beneficial to the German people, must be swept away."

"It's stupid and wrong," said Mildred, close to tears.

Arvid brushed her hair away from her face and kissed her, but the gesture gave her no comfort.

The Gestapo could shut down her school, but they could not prevent her from meeting elsewhere with her students. She would find another job—something, somehow—but she was a teacher, and she would never relinquish her responsibility to her students. As long as they wanted to learn, she would teach them.

CHAPTER THIRTY-FIVE

June–August 1936

Martha

Martha relished the thrill of athletic competition as much as anyone, but it was difficult not to regard the Berlin Olympics cynically as a massive state-sponsored public relations campaign. The new facilities included a magnificent art deco track and field stadium with room for one hundred thousand spectators, a natatorium for ten thousand, and a state-of-the-art 130-acre Olympic Village for housing the athletes. Arranged in the shape of a map of Germany, it boasted houses fitted with the latest modern conveniences, a post office, a bank, and training facilities including a 400-meter oval track and a regulation size indoor swimming pool. The director of construction, Captain Wolfgang Fürstner, had promised that these were the most excellent accommodations ever provided for Olympic athletes. From what Martha had seen, she would be hard pressed to disagree.

The ten-mile road connecting the Alexanderplatz to the Olympic complex just north of Berlin was lavishly adorned with banners and flags bearing the swastika and the Olympic rings. Whenever Martha drove along it, she had the strange sensation of participating in a caesar's triumphal procession in ancient Rome. If only someone would assign a staff officer to follow Hitler around whispering, "Remember you are mortal."

The Olympiastadion and the Via Triumphalis were the most impressive refurbishments Hitler had ordered in honor of the Games, but they were hardly the only ones. For months, conscripted workers had remade nearly every visible surface of Berlin, painting houses, patching roads, restoring decrepit railway stations, banishing litter, pruning and polishing as required. It seemed to Martha that even the oldest cobblestone streets gleamed as if they had been swept and scrubbed.

The economy continued to improve steadily, but more important to Hitler was the *appearance* of prosperity. Pamphlets were distributed to every household encouraging citizens to grow flowers rather than vegetables in their gardens and window boxes. Vacant shops and offices on main thoroughfares were leased at significantly below-market cost, with additional subsidies available so that proprietors could spruce up their new storefronts. Unsightly Roma camps were demolished overnight, although none of Martha's Nazi acquaintances would tell her what had become of the Roma themselves. Then, in the last few weeks before foreign tourists would descend upon Berlin, familiar tokens of the new Germany began quietly disappearing. The ubiquitous signs in store windows declaring *"Juden unerwünscht"* were removed. Newsstand racks reserved for the rabidly antisemitic newspaper *Der Stürmer* were refilled with foreign papers. Many of the same books that the Nazis had thrown onto the pyres returned to bookstore shelves. Posters announcing the Nuremberg Laws and other regulations stripping Jews of their civil rights were torn down, every trace of paste and paper scrubbed from the brick.

"Germany primps for the tourists like a debutant for her coming out," Martha remarked to her mother one afternoon as they were shopping on the Kurfürstendamm.

"No amount of fresh makeup can conceal such gross disfigurement," her mother replied, an edge to her voice. "I'll believe in the Nazis' Olympic spirit of peace and fellowship when they close the concentration camps and send the prisoners home to their families, and not a moment before."

It was her mother's public vehemence rather than her beliefs that took Martha by surprise. Her mother and Bill had been skeptical of the Nazis from the very beginning, while Martha's father was suspending judgment and Martha was enamored with their noble revolution, or whatever she had called it. Her cheeks flushed with shame when she remembered how enthralled she had been by the glamour and spectacle, how she had once cheerfully echoed every "Heil Hitler" sent her way.

Now the Germans were rehearsing their best behavior for when the world came to Berlin for the Games. Martha hardly dared hope their rehabilitation would be permanent, but at least for the moment the humiliation and abuse of the Jews had significantly diminished.

A few days before the opening ceremonies, as Martha was reading on the terrace, Fritz approached her to announce a visitor. His prim, sour expression kindled a memory, and for an electrifying moment she thought Boris had returned. Setting her book aside, she leapt up from her chair and followed Fritz into the house, quickly outpacing him on the way to the green reception room.

A large, dark-haired man stood at the window, his back to her, engrossed in the view of the Tiergarten.

"Why, Thomas Wolfe," Martha exclaimed, swiftly crossing the room to greet him. "What a wonderful surprise. Are you here for the Olympics or for me?"

"Both." Thomas swept her up in an embrace and kissed her soundly on both cheeks. "And also because Herr Hitler won't let me take the royalties for my German translations out of the country. I had to come to Germany to spend them."

"I can certainly help you with that. Germany isn't as much fun as it used to be, but we can still find good champagne, extravagant dinners, and great music to dance to."

"So it's not all military marches, Wagner, and the 'Horst Wessel Lied'?"

"Not yet."

"Then I'd be happy to indulge you." With a playful grin, he bent low, his face so close to hers that their noses almost touched. "And what would I get in return?"

She smiled, amused. "Name your price."

"Tickets to the Games."

"Oh, that's easy." She waved a hand dismissively. "You can join us in the embassy box, but the competition will be an international scandal, in my opinion. The Olympic Games are supposed to bring together the greatest athletes in the world. It's pathetic that some of Germany's best won't be allowed to compete because they're not Aryan."

He straightened, eyebrows rising. "Hitler would deny Germany a chance at a medal just to keep the Jews out?"

"Of course. How can he argue that Aryans are the master race if a Jew trounces them in a boxing match or what have you?"

"He can't exclude all non-Aryans. The American team is full of 'em."

Martha raised an imaginary champagne glass. "Then here's to the American non-Aryans. May they leave the master race in the dust."

Thomas grinned and mimed clinking his own glass against hers. "Hear, hear."

She regarded him, amused. "You're certainly singing a different tune. The last time you were in Berlin, you weren't exactly rushing to the Jews' defense."

"I'm no antisemite," he protested. "I have lots of Jewish friends. Don't lump me in with these blasted Nazis over a few careless remarks. That's not fair."

"Maybe, maybe not." She took his arm. "Let's debate it as we spend your hard-earned royalties."

They began with a late lunch at the Taverne, an Italian bistro run by a gruff German and his shy Belgian wife, a favorite gathering spot for American journalists and their spouses. Martha always found a place at the *Stammtisch*, the table reserved for regulars, and during his previous visit Thomas had been welcomed even more heartily. They moved on from there to his favorite watering holes, one after another, enjoying reunions with old acquaintances, drinking and dancing until the early hours of the morning when they declared themselves incapable of downing a single drop more.

Staggering out of the Kakadu and onto Joachimstalerstrasse, Thomas hailed a cab to take them to Tiergartenstrasse 27a. "You must stay the night," Martha said as they helped each other stumble to the front door. "No, for your entire visit. I insist. We have plenty of room."

"I'm delighted to accept," said Thomas, his breath thick with the scent of whiskey. "Especially since I can't recall the name of my hotel."

She burst out laughing and sank down upon the doorstep. Choking back laughter, Thomas took her key and attempted to fit it in the lock, but before he could, the door swung open. "*Kaffee*, Fraulein Dodd?" Fritz said, eyeing them dourly as Thomas hauled Martha to her feet and helped her inside. "Aspirin?"

"No to the former, yes to the latter." Head spinning, Martha seized Thomas's hand and tugged to compel him to follow her to the kitchen. "Never mind. I'll get it myself. We're going to need a whole bottle."

"Apiece," Thomas added, and she exploded with laughter again.

When she woke the next morning, bleary-eyed and aching, she discovered that however many aspirin she had taken, it had not been enough. Her head throbbed and she had no memory of finding her way to her room and collapsing on her bed, fully clothed. And yet it must have happened, for there she was.

With a groan she sat up, judging by the harsh light streaming through the windows that it was almost noon. She hoped Thomas had found his way to a guest room and was not passed out in the hallway outside her door.

After a soothing shower, a change of clothes, and fresh makeup, she descended to the kitchen to find Thomas seated with a cup of steaming coffee and a plate of fried eggs and buttered toast. "You must have a liver made of steel," she remarked, envious.

"I'm twice your size and I've built up a tolerance." He gestured to an adjacent chair, and as she sank into it, he gallantly rose and poured her a cup of coffee. "Anything to eat?"

"God, no." She closed her hands around the cup and took a deep, restorative drink. "Maybe in a bit. How much of last night do you remember?"

"All of it. You?"

"Nearly all." She sipped her coffee. "I seem to recall you holding many whispered conferences in dark corners. Plotting something?"

"Not yet." His grin faded. "I lost count of how many friends took me aside to confide the Nazi horrors that haunt their nightmares."

"Ah, yes." She set down her cup with a sigh, willing her headache to recede. "Reality encroaches upon our fun despite our attempts to drown it."

"I once thought the rise of the Nazis was about politics. I don't anymore." Thomas rubbed at his jaw, his gaze distant. "It's something deeper, more sinister, going well beyond mere racial prejudice. The German people are desperately ill with some dread malady of the soul." He leaned forward and folded his arms on the table. "Think of it. An entire nation has become infected with an ever-present hatred and fear, twisting and blighting all human relations."

Martha wished she could deny it with a careless laugh, but he was right. It was little wonder her mother's anxiety increased with each passing month, that her father spoke wistfully of resigning and returning to Chicago and his beloved farm in Virginia. But as long as President Roosevelt wanted him to stay on as ambassador, Martha's father would do his duty. And as long as her parents remained in Berlin, Martha would too.

After a piece of dry toast and some hair of the dog, Martha felt much better, so they decided to join the opening ceremonies in progress. They had slept through numerous official events—religious services, a wreath laying at the Tomb of the Unknown Soldier, synchronized athletic displays by thousands of German schoolchildren, Goebbels's speech at the Old Museum for International Olympic Committee guests and thirty thousand members of the Hitler Youth—but Martha and Thomas agreed they were quite happy to have avoided those. The more compelling events were yet to come.

Thomas had arranged for a driver, but they made it only a few miles down the Via Triumphalis before they were forced to divert to a side street to clear the way for the official procession. From what Martha had seen, it appeared that the entire route was guarded by vast numbers of SS, SA, officers of the Berlin police force, and members of the National Socialist Motor Corps. Filling the sidewalks behind them, tens of thousands of citizens awaited the parade of dignitaries, shifting about and craning their necks in hope of finding an unimpeded view.

At the Reichssportfeld, guards were posted at every stadium entrance, vending booths were shuttered, and nearby restaurants and bars were closed. "I hear they put the international press corps near the Honor Loge to discourage protestors from planting a bomb beneath

Hitler's chair," Martha remarked as they made their way to their seats in the embassy box a few rows behind the Führer's.

Hitler's state box was empty, she noted as she exchanged greetings with friends and embassy officials, some of whom had been there since one o'clock, when the gates had opened so that spectators could be seated well before the Führer made his grand entrance. To keep the crowd entertained in the meantime, the Berlin Philharmonic, the National Orchestra, and the Bayreuth Wagner Festival choir were presenting a joint concert. "Wagner, of course," said Thomas, cocking an ear, giving Martha a little nudge as they settled into their seats.

"What's a Nazi spectacle without a bit of Wagner?" Shading her eyes with her hand, Martha turned her gaze skyward, marveling at the giant zeppelin *Hindenburg* as it cruised back and forth, an Olympic banner trailing from the gondola. The airship was a symbol of German engineering genius and a source of considerable national pride, and she was not at all surprised to see it on display, impressing the international audience with every graceful pass over the stadium.

A few minutes before four o'clock, a trumpet fanfare and the raising of the *Führerstandarte*, a red swastika on a purple field, announced Hitler's arrival. Upon spotting their Führer entering the stadium through the Marathon Gate with a few IOC executives, the vast majority of the hundred thousand spectators leapt to their feet, thrust out their right arms, and roared thunderous approval. Instinctively Martha covered her ears, but she still felt the prolonged wave of frenzied cheering as a rattle in her spine.

As the roar subsided from its peak, the combined Olympic Symphony Orchestra struck up Wagner's "March of Honor" as Hitler and his entourage strode across the field. They paused halfway across so that Hitler could accept a *Hitlergruss*, a bouquet of flowers, and a pretty curtsey from an adorable young girl, blond-haired and probably blue-eyed. Martha rolled her eyes when Hitler took the child's hand and briefly knelt to speak with her, all paternal warmth and kindness, melting the heart of every Aryan mother present.

Thomas leaned close so she could hear him beneath the din. "Aren't you sorry now that your first date didn't lead to more?"

"Not one bit," she retorted.

When Hitler and the other dignitaries finally took their places, Martha was pleased by Thomas's sardonic delight that for the rest of the Games they would enjoy an excellent view of the back of the Führer's head. Immediately thereafter, the orchestra struck up the German national anthem and the flags of the participating nations were slowly raised up fifty-two flagpoles. Next the solemn, deep tolling of the Olympic bell heralded the traditional march of the national teams into the stadium. Leading the procession was Greece, the birthplace of the Olympiad, followed by the other nations in alphabetical order, except for the host nation, which customarily entered last. Hitler and the dignitaries stood throughout to receive the salute of each nation as its athletes passed before the Honor Loge.

It quickly became apparent to Martha that the predominantly German audience applauded each country not only according to long-standing sentimental ties, but also commensurate with the degree of deference they appeared to show the Führer. The Austrians received resounding cheers for offering the *Hitlergruss* as their flag bearer dipped their standard to Hitler when they passed in review. So too did the Italians, whose *Hitlergruss* may also have come in tribute to Hitler's burgeoning friendship with Mussolini. The Turks, who held the Nazi salute for the entire procession, received a roar of approval, as did the Bulgarians, who added a goose-step to their fascist salute for good measure.

To Martha's surprise, the French also received hearty applause, even though they acknowledged the Honor Loge not with the *Hitlergruss*, with the arm raised to the front, but with the traditional Olympic salute, with the right arm lifted to the side.

"It's unfortunate the two salutes look so much alike," Martha said to Thomas. "The Nazis will interpret it as they please."

The United Kingdom avoided any misunderstanding. Their athletes kept their arms at their sides, swinging in time with the march, and when they passed before the Führer, in union they acknowledged him with a crisp "eyes right." A faint smattering of applause was nearly drowned out by jeers, but as far as Martha could tell Hitler betrayed no reaction.

Then came the United States, the penultimate team before the host country. The Americans eschewed the traditional salute and did not dip their flag to Hitler in passing, but rather removed their boater hats, held them over their hearts, and kept their eyes fixed on the Stars and Stripes. A harsh roar of protests and catcalls rained down from the stands, but the American athletes strode on without flinching, proud and purposeful.

Martha clapped until her hands stung, as did everyone else in the embassy box, ignoring the grumbles and sidelong looks of those seated around them.

"What did the Nazis expect?" said Thomas. "If the Yanks didn't dip the flag to the British king at the London Games in 1908, they certainly weren't going to do it for Herr Hitler today."

The crowd's disgruntlement quickly gave way to exultation as the German team marched in behind a large swastika banner. The orchestra played the German national anthem again, followed immediately by the "Horst Wessel Lied," to thunderous applause and ecstatic cheers from the home crowd.

"Sport as political theater," Thomas drawled as the ceremonies continued, through a lengthy speech by the president of the German Olympic Committee to the swift and triumphant entrance of the last Olympic torchbearer. "When the Games are through, everyone will carry home the impression that Germany is the most hospitable, peace-loving nation on earth, if you can overlook all the martial flourishes."

Martha shared his wary disgust, but in the days that followed, that was not enough to keep either of them away from the competitions. She invited several other friends to join them in the embassy box, and Mildred often accepted. The recent publication of her translation of Irving Stone's *Lust for Life* had taken some of the sting out of the closing of the Abendgymnasium, but Martha knew she worried about finding a new job. Martha hoped the Olympics would provide a restorative distraction.

Mildred was very glad to see Thomas again, and he seemed even more delighted to reunite with her—as he should be, Martha thought, given the glowing articles Mildred had written about him. As the days passed, the three friends observed and quietly discussed Hitler at least as much as the sporting events. Hitler evidently enjoyed track and field, for he attended nearly every day. Whenever a German athlete won, he beamed, slapped his thighs, and applauded with great enthusiasm. When the gold medalists approached his box to be congratulated, as was the custom, he sprang to his feet and received them with warmth and good humor.

Not so when athletes from other nations took the gold.

On one particularly successful day for the United States, the Stars and Stripes were raised at least five times, almost in succession, and everyone in the stadium was obliged to stand for "The Star-Spangled Banner"—including the Führer, who saluted with his arm outstretched and a surly expression that worsened with each repetition, even more so if the victor was colored. Day after day Hitler was subjected to marvelous performances by American athletes, including thrilling races won by Jesse Owens, the Alabama native who had broken three world records and tied a fourth as a student at Ohio State. His astonishing speed and physical prowess quickly won over the crowd, but whenever Owens or another colored American athlete won, the Führer conveniently managed to be away from his box when they came to receive his congratulations.

This had not escaped the notice of Martha and her friends, and they fixed the Führer with hard, indignant looks as he left his box soon after Owens won the gold medal in the 100 meters. "The Americans should be ashamed of themselves, letting Negroes win their medals for them," Hitler remarked to his *Gruppenführer* Baldur von Schirach, leader of the Hitler Youth, as they strode past the embassy box, or so Mildred translated for her friends. "I shall not shake hands with this Negro. Do you really think that I will allow myself to be photographed shaking hands with a Negro?"

Later, after Jesse Owens took his third gold medal, Hitler suddenly hastened away on what Martha acidly assumed was another invented errand. Along the way, he spoke earnestly to his companion, whom Martha recognized from an embassy dinner as Albert Speer, the architect.

As Hitler passed their box, Mildred drew in a breath sharply.

"What's wrong?" Martha asked.

Mildred hesitated. "Hitler is . . . very annoyed by Owens's victories."

"Obviously, but what did he say?"

"I'd rather not repeat it."

"Come on," Martha implored. "Don't I deserve to know, if only for getting you that great seat?"

"He said—" Mildred hesitated, pained. "He said that people whose ancestors came from the jungle are primitive. He says that their physiques are stronger than those of civilized whites, and therefore they should be excluded from future Games."

"That's damn foolishness," said Thomas. "I wish Jesse Owens could win a fourth gold medal just to spite him."

Later, he seemed poised to do exactly that.

As the runners for the first heat of the men's 4-by-100 meter relay took their places on the track, Martha gasped. "Isn't that Owens in the lead leg?"

"That's him all right," said Thomas. A faint roar surged through the crowd as if everyone else had simultaneously made the same observation. "And that's Ralph Metcalfe lining up to run second."

Martha checked the program. "They weren't originally in this relay. The coach must have made a last-minute substitution."

"They're replacing Marty Glickman and Sam Stoller," said Mildred, studying her program. "They're Jews. Do you suppose the Nazis pressured the U.S. Olympic Committee to replace them? Or perhaps the coach wanted to avoid offending Hitler?"

"I certainly hope not," said Martha. "However, as much as Hitler hates Negroes, he hates Jews more."

"That probably has nothing to do with it," said Thomas. "Owens took the gold and Metcalfe the silver in the hundred meters. It's a strategic decision."

"The original team was already heavily favored to win," Mildred pointed out. "Why fix what wasn't broken?"

"Well, now the odds have improved even more," said Thomas, but he frowned slightly as if he too wondered about ulterior motives.

Martha leaned forward as the runners settled in their lanes. She jumped at the sharp crack of the starter's pistol, her heart beating faster and faster as Jesse Owens pulled away from the other runners and flew around the first curve, his feet seeming barely to touch the ground. A blink of an eye, a flawless baton exchange, and suddenly Owens was gradually slowing as Metcalfe sped away, down the straightaway to Foy Draper, who took the second curve with the Italian runner on his heels. As the roar of the crowd rose, louder and louder, Frank Wyckoff carried the baton down the final stretch with an Italian barely a second behind him. And then it was over. The United States and Italy, first and second, would advance to the finals.

Exultant, Thomas leapt to his feet, cupped his hands around his mouth, and let out an earsplitting war whoop. Hitler twisted in his seat, fixed him with a furious gaze, glaring with stark hatred. If looks could kill, Thomas would have been finished. Martha seized his left arm and Mildred his right, and they pulled him back into his seat.

"What the hell," he protested, laughing. "It's the Olympics and our team won. Owens was wonderful. I'm proud, so I yelled."

"Maybe not so loudly at the back of the Führer's head next time," Martha advised, but she smiled, not at all sorry that Jesse Owens had spoiled both Hitler's fun and his theory of Aryan supremacy.

The German team won the third heat, much to Hitler's jubilation, but in the finals the Americans triumphed yet again, with the Italian team taking the silver and the Germans the bronze. Thomas celebrated the victory, but less ostentatiously, so Martha did not have to worry that he might spark an international incident. This time the Führer remained in the Honor Loge as the medals were awarded, possibly out of loyalty to the third-place Germans. But if he ever shook the hand of Jesse Owens or the other men on the American relay team, Martha did not see it.

"He is such a child," Martha said to Mildred and Thomas later as they left the stadium. "Throughout the Games, he hasn't shown the slightest indication that he understands good sportsmanship, or that he has any appreciation of sport for its own sake."

"His sportsmanship is the least of our worries," said Mildred. "If he's a child, with a child's impulsiveness and irrationality, then he's an extremely dangerous one, powerful and cruel, able to act on any hateful whim with the full force of the German military and millions of devoted fanatics."

Sobered, Martha made no reply. Of course there was no question that to Hitler the Berlin Games had nothing to do with the Olympic ideals of international friendship, peace, solidarity, and fair play. They were an entirely Germanic affair, pure and simple, meant to demonstrate German superiority, might, and peaceful intentions to the world, regardless of the truth.

And in that, Martha feared, he had triumphed.

CHAPTER THIRTY-SIX

August–December 1936

Greta

After the Olympics, the international tourists went home impressed by the unprecedented magnificence of the Games and much reassured that Hitler's intentions were peaceful, that he would make Germany great again without any peril to its neighbors. But as the eyes of the world turned away from Berlin, Greta and her friends braced themselves for the Nazi persecution of the Jews to resume with a vengeance.

Almost immediately, the signs announcing *"Juden unerwünscht"* returned to the front windows of shops and businesses. Arrests for the slightest offenses, or merely the suspicion of offenses, redoubled. Storm troopers resumed their arbitrary attacks on Jews in the streets of Berlin. The Reich Ministry of Education banned Jewish teachers from the public schools. And two days after the Games concluded, Captain Wolfgang Fürstner, designer of the much-lauded Olympic Village, committed suicide after he was dismissed from the military because of his Jewish ancestry. The Nazis claimed he had died in a car accident and interred him with full military honors, but drawing upon his network of informants, Natan Weitz swiftly uncovered the truth. Unfortunately, even after his report was picked up by the international press, millions of ardent Nazis insisted upon believing the lie.

Greta fumed with anger and frustration that the world could be so easily duped by the spectacle of the Olympics. She understood the yearning to believe that Hitler was a man of peace, that Germany was ready to rejoin the fold of civilized nations after the horrors of the Great War, but wanting desperately for something to be true did not make it so. The flame of the Olympic torch, the fanfare of trumpets, the inspiring display of physical perfection, and the glitter of gold medals had distracted attention away from the battered Treaty of Versailles, ground under the boots of the German military as they marched into the Rhineland. What more evidence of Hitler's expansionist intentions did world leaders require?

The resistance had to keep writing, keep speaking, keep bearing witness to what was really happening in Germany. They had no arms, no tanks, no storm troopers. Their only weapon was the truth, but Greta had to believe that in the end, the truth would always defeat a lie.

Earlier that year, she had moved from her sublet room in Pichelswerder into a modest flat on Scharnweberstrasse a few blocks north of the Volkspark Rehberge. Her new place was only six kilometers away from Adam's home on Dortmunder Strasse, more anonymous than the boathouse and more convenient for Adam's overnight visits.

"You know what would be even easier?" he asked wryly. "If you just moved in with me."

She demurred, as he must have known she would. Even though he was no longer living with his estranged wife, Greta did not want to share a home with him while he was still married to someone else. She knew she invited mockery for holding this line when she had already crossed so many others, but she did not care. She loved Adam and wanted to be with him, but she would not relinquish her independence for someone who would not fully commit to her and her alone.

Greta's new landlady, Ruth Levinsohn, was half-Jewish on her father's side, a widow with two grown daughters, both of whom had recently emigrated to Poland to avoid Nazi persecution. Perhaps it was out of loneliness for them that she took a special interest in Greta, not prying into her affairs, but always ready with a cup of tea, a morsel of something sweet, and news from the neighborhood if they happened to cross paths in the lobby. She was intelligent and well-read, a former rare books librarian who had been forced into early retirement in the purge of Jewish professors from the University of Berlin.

Frau Levinsohn knew Greta earned a living from a patchwork of freelance writing and editing, and one evening after Greta returned from delivering a proofread manuscript to Rowohlt, she met her at the door. "I may have found a job for you," she said, her dark eyes keen with expectation.

Intrigued, Greta followed her into her office, where Frau Levinsohn poured her a cup of coffee and told her about another tenant, an Irishman named James Murphy, a professional translator and author. "He did the English translation of Max Planck's latest book for a prominent London publisher."

Greta's eyebrows rose at the Nobel laureate's name. "*Where Is Science Going?*"

"Yes, that's the one. And just last year, Dr. Murphy translated Edwin Schrödinger's book *Science and the Human Temperament*." Frau Levinsohn peered at Greta over the rims of her glasses. "Dr. Murphy is a dedicated scholar and his work is very highly regarded."

"I would imagine so."

"For the past few months, Dr. Murphy has been working on another project, perhaps his most important book yet. Unfortunately, he has fallen ill, and he needs an assistant to help him complete the manuscript. When I told him about your qualifications, he asked to meet you as soon as possible—if you're interested."

"I'm definitely interested," said Greta. "What book is he translating?"

"Dr. Murphy wanted to explain that himself." Frau Levinsohn glanced to Greta's cup to make sure she had finished her coffee. "If you wouldn't mind waiting in the lobby, I'll bring him down to meet you."

Greta agreed, and as her landlady hurried off, she settled into a chair in a quiet corner away from the front door, mulling over the possibilities. Was the project the collected works of Albert Einstein? Unlikely, since the Jewish genius had lived in America since 1933. A comprehensive study of quantum mechanics by Werner Heisenberg? Was he even still in Berlin? So many renowned scientists had fled the Reich that it was difficult to remember who remained. Whoever the author was, Greta knew she would have to read deeply in his field of study in order to make her translation as rich and accurate as possible.

Before long Frau Levinsohn returned with a gentleman in his middle fifties attired in a well-cut suit and tie, walking a trifle unsteadily, perhaps, but looking very little like an invalid. He had to be more than two meters tall and at least one hundred kilograms, and he carried himself with regal dignity that commanded respect. He had full cheeks, a deeply cleft chin, and a wispy fringe of fair hair clinging defiantly to the back of his head. Although his gaze was intelligent, his eyes were bloodshot and the skin around his nose was flushed from capillaries spreading like fine red roots toward his cheeks.

Greta rose to meet them, and after Frau Levinsohn made introductions, they sat down for a chat. "Frau Levinsohn recommends you very highly," Dr. Murphy said in flawless German, with only a trace of a charming Irish lilt. "I understand that you're a freelance writer and editor, and that you've studied in the United States and at the London School of Economics."

"I was only in London for a few months, but otherwise that's correct," she replied in English. "Frau Levinsohn told me about some of your previous translations, and I confess I'm quite impressed."

Pleased, he smiled and briefly described his translation process, how he tried to be true not only to the literal meaning of the author's words but also to the intent and emotion behind each phrase. He did not explicitly state his political views—wisely so, as other residents and visitors occasionally passed through the lobby on their way to the elevator—but as he spoke, certain words and allusions convinced Greta that he was no Nazi sympathizer. Even before he finished describing her responsibilities and schedule, and the wages he could provide, she had decided that she would accept the job.

"If my terms are acceptable, I'd like you to begin tomorrow," he said, "but before you decide, I feel obliged to tell you what the project is."

Greta prepared herself to hear the title of a challenging work full of specialized technical language. "I'm very eager to know," she said, smiling.

"The Ministry of Propaganda has hired me to produce an unabridged English version of *Mein Kampf*."

Greta recoiled. "Why?"

He shrugged and ran a hand over his scalp. "Goebbels didn't say, precisely. Perhaps they want to have an English edition ready to release when they feel the time is right."

"When would that be, exactly?" Greta quickly composed herself. "What I meant was, why would you translate such a vile, wretched book?"

Frau Levinsohn cleared her throat and glanced significantly to the front door and along the length of the lobby.

"Hitler's autobiography is a manifesto of hate," Greta continued, lowering her voice. "He advocates genocide and *Lebensraum*. Why would you choose to introduce his racist ideology to millions of new readers?"

"There are already a few English versions in print, all of them severely expurgated. The best of a bad lot came out three years ago, only a third as long as the original, with the most offensive, most revealing passages omitted. A reader would have no idea what Hitler really thinks, what he intends for Germany, for Europe, for the Jews, for the world."

"And you believe an unexpurgated edition would reveal him as the monster he truly is."

"Exactly."

Greta sat back in her chair, thoughts churning. Hitler's autobiography had become an enormous bestseller since being published in two volumes in 1925 and 1926, earning him millions of Reichsmarks. After he became chancellor, he had compelled the government to buy millions of copies and distribute them as gifts to every newlywed couple in Germany. "Your translation would be an authorized edition," she pointed out. "Hitler will earn royalties from it."

Grimacing, Dr. Murphy acknowledged that this was so.

A trifle sharply, she said, "I for one am loath to do anything that would put a single mark into that man's pocket."

"Miss Lorke, please keep your voice down," Frau Levinsohn murmured.

"No, no, she has a right to express herself," said Dr. Murphy.

She regarded him in utter disbelief. "No, I really don't, not here, not anymore. This isn't Ireland. Surely you can see that if the Ministry of Propaganda is *for* something, good people should be *against* it."

"Goebbels's purpose may be nefarious, but mine isn't."

"And yet you're still giving the Nazis what they want, which is aiding and abetting them, even if you don't know their intentions." To spread their repellent ideology in England and the United States was the glaringly obvious answer, but she would not be surprised if Hitler had something even worse in mind.

Dr. Murphy leaned forward and rested his elbows on his knees, his gaze earnest and deadly serious. "The world beyond Germany's borders will never grasp what this man stands for if they read a sanitized version of his manifesto."

"I understand that. I just don't know which is worse, to say nothing or to say too much."

"Your ethical concerns prove that you're the right person for this work. Don't refuse until you're absolutely certain you can't do it. Take a few days and think it over."

Greta pressed her lips together and nodded. They parted with a handshake, Dr. Murphy's large hand warm and solid and reassuring around hers.

She slept restlessly that night, her mind churning over his proposal. She wished Adam were there to kiss her, stroke her head, and calm her frenzied thoughts until sleep came. She wished he would be there in the morning, to hold her as she unburdened herself, asking questions and offering insight until she sorted out her conflicted feelings and made a decision.

She was tired of spending so many troubled nights alone.

For the next two days, she slipped in and out of the apartment building furtively, reluctant to run into Dr. Murphy or Frau Levinsohn until she decided. She did not have a chance to discuss the job with Adam until the evening of the second night, when she met him, John Sieg, and John's wife, Sophie, at the Siegs' apartment in Neukölln to sort a new batch of pamphlets for distribution. It was a reprint of a joint statement by prominent German Communists, Social Democrats, and expatriate intellectuals living in Paris, a call to unity published earlier that summer in the international edition of the *Rote Fahne*. The banner headline sent a surge of energy through Greta whenever she saw it—"Be United, United Against Hitler! A People's Front to Rescue Germany from the Catastrophe of War"—and she found herself turning her gaze to it whenever she found her confidence flagging. If these rival political factions joined together, as they should have done before the National Socialists seized complete control, their combined strength could yet be enough to bring down the Reich. In the shadow of fascism, the disputes that had once divided them seemed insignificant now.

John Sieg was a Communist and an American citizen, born in Detroit to German immigrants, educated alternately in Germany and America, depending upon the wishes of his relatives and the restrictions of the Great War. Sophie was Polish by birth, petite and pretty, with dark ringlets and the alluring gaze of a film star. They had left the United States when the Great Depression had closed the factories, driving John and millions of others out of work. He had not fared much better in Germany, and he now earned a living through sporadic day labor. Sophie had worked as a stenographer and law clerk in a posh office on Potsdamer Strasse until her employer, a Jewish lawyer, had been barred from the profession. The Siegs were poor, but very much in love and happily married. Greta often envied them and reproved herself for it.

On that humid night, as thunder rumbled faintly and the open windows let in the scent of distant rain, Adam, John, and Sophie listened intently as Greta described the interview, her conflicted feelings, her hopes for the good that could come of the project, and her apprehensions for all that could go awry.

"In your place I would do it," said Adam, his expression telling her that he knew it was her decision alone. "It's part of our mission to tell the world the truth about Hitler."

"But does his autobiography qualify as the truth?"

"It's his truth, what he is and what he intends."

"The German people have read his so-called truth," said Sophie. "They didn't recoil in horror. They embraced it. They made him their Führer."

"The Americans and the British would view *Lebensraum* entirely differently than German nationalists do," said Adam. "They wouldn't be inspired by this book, but forewarned."

Greta nodded. "Ideally, that's what Murphy's translation would accomplish, but—"

"You must do it, Greta," John broke in. "Do you know of Ivan Maisky?"

Adam shrugged, brow furrowing; Greta and Sophie shook their heads.

"He's the Russian ambassador to the United Kingdom. I've never met him, but we have mutual friends through the party. Maisky told one of my comrades about an exchange he had with David Lloyd George."

Adam's eyebrows rose. "The prime minister?"

"Former prime minister, but yes, the same fellow. According to my comrade, Maisky persistently warned Lloyd George that Hitler was a fascist with dangerous expansionist intentions. He urged him to read Hitler's book and take all necessary precautions before it was too late. Eventually Lloyd George retorted, 'I don't know why you tell me all these things are in *Mein Kampf*. I've read it and they aren't.'"

"Oh, my," breathed Sophie.

"You must help these people prepare, Greta," said John. "Get that book into English."

Adam placed a hand on her shoulder. "Darling, if you're involved—"

"I can make sure nothing essential is omitted this time." Greta inhaled deeply, steeling herself. "I'll do it. What other choice is there?"

The next morning, Greta went to her landlady's office and told her she would accept the job. Visibly relieved, Frau Levinsohn promptly escorted her upstairs to the Murphys' flat. After Greta and Dr. Murphy shook hands and made it official, he introduced her to his wife, Mary, and to his secretary, Daphne French, a young Englishwoman about Greta's age. Greta felt as if she were joining another resistance cell, but a disconcertingly overt and jolly one, with the official sanction of the Ministry of Propaganda and promises of tea and biscuits when she reported for work the next morning.

In the weeks that followed, Greta came every day except Sundays to work on Dr. Murphy's manuscript, sometimes editing his drafts, occasionally translating one chapter while he worked on another. Before long she came to know him, his wife, and Daphne quite well. They were all strongly antifascist, fond of German music and literature, and nostalgic for the Germany that once was. Daphne was an excellent secretary, but although she could type flawless copies of German documents as perfectly as if it were her first language, she spoke it haltingly. Mrs. Murphy was clever, tolerant, and encouraging, and she had a dry sense of humor that Greta found delightful, especially when Nazi officials were the target of her satirical barbs.

As for Dr. Murphy, he was intelligent, skilled, and as deft with German as he was English, and fluent in French and Italian as well. In conversations over a great many lunches, he revealed an impressive knowledge of science, art, and literature. Sometimes Mrs. Murphy and Daphne joined them for coffee breaks or to help sort documents and organize files, but it was usually just Dr. Murphy and Greta from morning to night in the parlor, in the study, or at the kitchen table, writing, revising drafts, and debating the best phrase for a particular concept.

It was absorbing, grueling, important work, but it did not come without conflict. It took a few weeks, but Greta eventually realized that the cause of Dr. Murphy's unexplained illness was alcohol. He always appeared perfectly sober when his wife was around, but when she was abroad visiting family and friends in County Cork, Greta would arrive in the morning to find him already intoxicated. And yet he concealed it well, never drinking in front of her and Daphne or producing inferior work. Often Greta and Daphne conferred worriedly about what, if anything, they should do, if they should confront him respectfully, if they should tell Mrs. Murphy. In the end they reluctantly concluded that Mrs. Murphy surely already knew, and if Dr. Murphy could refrain from drinking when she was present, he must still be in control. So they said nothing and pretended not to notice his bloodshot eyes, the faint slurring of his consonants. Greta found silence and pretense deeply unsatisfying, but she did not know what else to do.

Their frequent disagreements about the text, on the other hand, were impossible to ignore. Dr. Murphy prided himself on his eloquence, and with good reason, for Greta herself envied his ability to turn a phrase. But it irritated her when he would return a page to her, one he had written and she had painstakingly edited, with complaints that she had altered it too much.

"You've coarsened the language," he protested, pointing to one phrase and then another.

"No, I restored its original roughness," she retorted. "You polished it too much, made it too pretty."

"But this is vulgar!"

"Yes, exactly as it was in Hitler's original."

On other occasions, as he read over her drafts, he would shake his head and mutter under his breath until she clenched her teeth in irritation as she awaited his verdict. "You have to do this over," he would say, indignant. "It borders on incoherence."

"Just like the source," she replied sharply. "The readers should see for themselves how convoluted his arguments are. It's wrong— reprehensible, even—to make him seem more rational than he is. That's Goebbels's job, not mine."

In those moments she knew Dr. Murphy was just as annoyed with her as she was with him. Sometimes he would listen to her and let something that offended his standards for good English stand, but ultimately it was his book and his name that would be on the cover, and he had the last word.

Greta chose her battles wisely and stood firm when she knew the integrity of the work depended upon it. She won more arguments than she lost.

The work continued throughout the autumn and into the winter. As Germany's Jews found their lives increasingly constricted, as Protestant pastors were arrested for protesting the Aryan Laws, as Jehovah's Witnesses were rounded up and sent to concentration camps, Greta wrote, edited, and revised with greater urgency. Nothing she would ever write would be more important than this.

They had to make the truth known, the truth that no one in England or America wanted to believe, the truth that Hitler's Games had obscured. And time was running out.

CHAPTER THIRTY-SEVEN

December 1936–January 1937

Sara

Dieter had played such a small role in what had emerged as the most important aspects of Sara's life that when he was finally, truly gone, her days passed almost as they always had, unchanged but for the small knot of pain and anger that tightened in her chest whenever a stray thought drifted his way.

It was a small mercy that this happened less often as time went by.

She knew she was better off without someone so ethically malleable. She also knew that she was fortunate to have discovered Dieter's fatal flaw before they married rather than afterward. The truth was she grieved the loss of her doctorate more.

Sara had taken Mildred's advice and had assembled the necessary documents so she could transfer to a university abroad, eventually, someday. She continued to study and work on her dissertation, which was nearly complete, and she also began a new research project, an analysis of female archetypes in the works of Nathaniel Hawthorne. Increasingly, however, she filled her hours assisting Natan with his investigative journalism, meeting with the study group, and surreptitiously distributing Greta's leaflets on campus and in nearby cafés and bookshops frequented by students, where thanks to her age she could easily blend in, not only as a student but as an Aryan. No actual living person resembled the caricatures of Jews in Nazi posters, and Sara's light brown hair and hazel eyes had thus far rendered her immune to the hostile, suspicious, lingering looks her brother often drew with his dark hair and eyes and olive complexion.

Often she felt an ache of loss when she strolled through the University of Berlin campus, the venerated ground that had once felt like home to her but had cast her out. The administrators could prevent her from sitting for her exams and defending her dissertation, but as long as she could pass for a student, she would keep coming back.

She was absolutely certain that the group's illicit flyers and pamphlets were essential to bringing down the Reich. The uninformed and uncertain people of Germany must be made aware of the horrors of fascism. The ambivalent and reluctant had to be warned that the same tactics used to persecute the Jews, Communists, and Roma could be turned upon them next. The antifascists who felt increasingly isolated and powerless needed to know that they were not alone. And the oppressed must be reassured that they had allies even within the country that had disowned them.

Her parents had no idea how she spent her days. They knew she kept up with her studies and helped Natan, but otherwise they did not ask her to account for her time. Perhaps they respected that she was a grown woman, capable of making her own decisions. Perhaps they figured whatever she did was fine, as long as she wasn't moping around the house weeping over Dieter's old letters.

Once her mother asked if she had considered finding a job. "I'd take one if I could find anything suitable," Sara replied truthfully. "Everything I've trained for is barred to me."

She was a Jew and she was a woman. The Reich did not want her in the workforce. In fact, they did not want her anywhere. They wanted her not to be.

Questions about her future plans came almost exclusively from her mother, as well as from Amalie, whose every letter included a heartfelt plea to come for a visit and stay as long as she liked. Sara was tempted. Switzerland was beautiful, she missed her darling nieces, and Geneva boasted an excellent university where she might be able to complete her doctorate. Although she demurred, she held on to that possibility like a gold coin tucked safely away in a pocketbook for emergencies. For now, she had important work to do in Germany.

Sara's father cared as much as her mother did about her future, but he was distracted by serious matters at work and accepted her assurances that she was fine with a nod and an absentminded pat on the shoulder. Since *Gleichschaltung* had begun years before, the Nazis had imposed the Aryanization of Jewish-owned businesses with increasing force. At Jacquier and Securius Bank, one Jewish partner who had been with the firm since 1919 had been forced out, and those who remained had been ordered to accept two Aryan investors as majority stakeholders. Mr. Panofsky retained his title and salary, but he had been barred from performing his managerial duties and had to answer to the Aryan newcomers. "It would be a blow to any man's pride," Sara had overheard her father tell her mother, "but what else can he do? His employees and clients depend upon him to keep the bank open."

In recent months, the struggle to keep the bank solvent had been taking a toll on the partners and managers. Although the economy was improving, many of their employees and customers suffered under the increasing restrictions placed upon Jews, and nervous investors were moving their funds elsewhere. According to Sara's father, Mr. Panofsky still believed his family would be safe from Nazi persecution as long as Ambassador Dodd's family remained his tenants, but beyond the gates of Tiergartenstrasse 27a, the ground was steadily eroding beneath them.

Sara understood that the Weitz family depended upon Mr. Panofsky and the bank, not only for her father's livelihood but for the intangible benefit of his association with the American ambassador. Now, as Mr. Panofsky's position seemed less tenable day by day, she felt that small measure of protection slipping away. She wondered if it had ever truly existed, or if that was just a story they had told themselves to quell their increasing dread.

As the end of January drew near, Sara's father suggested they invite the Panofsky family to join them on a holiday at the Riechmann estate in Minden-Lübbecke. "January thirtieth is their son's eleventh birthday," Sara's father said. "What better way to celebrate than with horseback riding, ice skating, snowshoe walks in the forest, and plenty of fresh air and good food?"

"We could all use some time away from the city," said Sara's mother, some of the tension leaving her face. "And Amalie and Wilhelm did ask us to look after things in their absence."

At first Natan demurred, citing work and other vague obligations, but his parents' disappointment was so obvious that he fell silent, chagrined. "It won't be much of a family vacation without you," said Sara, pressing her advantage, and Natan conceded.

An invitation was sent to the Panofskys, arrangements were made in a series of phone calls with the estate staff, and at the end of January, the two families drove in tandem about 400 kilometers west of Berlin through forests, villages, snow-covered pastures, and dormant fields of barley and alfalfa. Twice they had to pull off the road to allow convoys of military vehicles to pass, presumably on their way to the Rhineland, but those were brief, jarring interludes in an otherwise scenic journey to Wilhelm's ancestral estate.

Schloss Federle took Sara's breath away every time she glimpsed it through the trees growing on the banks of the broad encircling moat, ice-choked now but no less a formidable barrier, traversable by a single stone bridge at the foot of a long garden in front of the residence. Although the original castle dated back to the thirteenth century, the residence as it now stood had been constructed around 1780, with significant refurbishments to the interior made just before the Great War. The large main building and two perpendicular wings stood three stories tall and were fashioned of white stone and golden stucco. Curved single-story galleries connected the east and west wings to the main building, facing each other across a long oval garden encircled by the driveway, snow-dusted now, but bursting with lush greenery and colorful, fragrant flowers from spring through autumn. Tall rectangular windows framed by green shutters filled the walls, and teardrop-shaped rust-colored tiles covered the mansard roof and numerous dormers. And yet for all its grandeur, it was warm and welcoming, steadfast and strong.

Several members of the household staff hurried out to greet them as the cars halted before the main entrance. As the footmen carried their luggage indoors and her parents introduced the Panofskys to the housekeeper and butler, Sara turned to admire the view back the way they had come. The day was crisp and clear, and in the distance she could just make out the frosty blur of the Wiehen Hills in the distance. If only Amalie and her family were there, everything would be perfect.

The Panofsky party included Mr. Panofsky, his wife, his silver-haired mother, and the two children—Hans, one day shy of eleven, and his younger sister, Ruth. All was happy chaos as the two families called out cheerful greetings to one another, stretching their legs, inhaling deeply the cold, pine-scented air. The children darted about, leaving tracks in the snow and shrieking with delight, while the adults chatted and looked on indulgently. Sara felt a knot of worry loosen in the pit of her stomach, and as she drank in the familiar, beloved sights of her sister's home, she was struck by overwhelming relief at the absence of a single swastika or black-clad SS officer. She had not understood how depressed her spirits had become by the ubiquitous presence of Nazi symbols until they no longer obstructed her view.

"It is so quiet and peaceful here," marveled Mrs. Panofsky. "The perfect remote country retreat."

"And yet we're only about one hundred twenty kilometers from the Dutch border," said Sara's father. "In ninety minutes, we could be in the Netherlands."

Mr. Panofsky, his wife, and his mother nodded thoughtfully.

Eventually the adults grew too cold to linger outdoors, so when the children wore themselves out from scrambling through snowdrifts, they all headed inside to warm themselves by the fireplace in the great hall before supper. A whirling snowstorm descended while they dined, and afterward, the intermittent scour of snow crystals on the window-panes followed them as the Weitzes led the Panofskys on a tour of the castle. Hans and Ruth enjoyed the way their voices echoed down the marble halls, and they were very impressed by the suits of armor in the north gallery. Their parents were more interested in the antique Persian rugs, the vast library, and the art collection, not only the portraits of Wilhelm's illustrious ancestors displayed in gilded frames throughout the public rooms, but the modern paintings and sculptures he and Amalie had acquired on their international travels. "Magnificent," proclaimed Mr. Panofsky as he examined a cubist painting of musical instruments. "Picasso, I assume?" Natan confirmed that it was.

As they went along, Sara shared some of the fascinating stories her brother-in-law had told her about the history of various rooms, distinctive antiques, and illustrious or notorious visitors from the past. In the conservatory, when her gaze turned to the beautiful, gleaming black Steinway with some of Amalie's sheet music still poised upon the stand, she felt a pang of longing for her sister so acute that tears sprang into her eyes. It was painful and strange to be in Amalie's home without her, paradoxically drawing her closer and emphasizing the vast distance between them. When she heard her mother's soft sigh and felt her touch upon her shoulder, Sara knew she felt the same.

After the tour, they returned to the great hall for stories and games before Mrs. Panofsky put the children to bed. Then it was time for *Kaffee* before the blazing hearth, as well as schnapps for those who wanted something stronger. They toasted their absent benefactors, Amalie and Wilhelm, and the conversation turned from fond reminiscences about happier occasions they had spent together at Schloss Federle to recent news the young family had sent from Geneva.

"Switzerland is lovely," said Mrs. Panofsky, with a significant glance for her husband. "We have friends in Zurich, and your old classmate says his bank in Basel is growing."

Mr. Panofsky regarded her fondly. "Last week you preferred London."

"London, Zurich, New York—" Mrs. Panofsky waved a hand. "Whichever city will welcome us, I'll happily make it our home."

"Have you decided to emigrate?" asked Sara.

"I didn't want to spoil our holiday with talk of business," said Mr. Panofsky reluctantly. "However, since the partners intend to make a public announcement soon, it could do no harm to confide in you now, in appreciation for your hospitality."

Sara and Natan exchanged wary glances as their father frowned pensively and shifted in his chair. "Nothing you say will leave this room, of course," he said.

"The Jacquier and Securius Bank cannot continue as it has under the Reich," said Mr. Panofsky, spreading his hands, letting them fall to his lap. "The partners hope to sell the bank, and if that fails, we'll liquidate the assets and close our doors."

"It's not right that you should have to close an institution that has thrived for more than one hundred years," said Natan.

"I quite agree," said Mr. Panofsky.

"Afterward, yes, we intend to emigrate," said Mrs. Panofsky, a tremor in her voice. "After restricting ourselves to the attic of our own home for all these years, I've simply had enough—" She broke off, and when her husband reached for her hand, she managed an apologetic smile. "I don't mean to complain. Our arrangement has kept us safe so far, and the Dodds are pleasant people."

"We understand," said Sara's mother kindly. "Your feelings are perfectly reasonable."

"Liquidating the bank won't be easy, dear," said Mr. Panofsky. "Nor will emigration."

Tears filled Mrs. Panofsky's eyes, but she blinked them away. "I know."

They all knew. For a country that wanted to rid itself of Jews, the German government seemed determined to thrust daunting obstacles in the path of those who wanted to go. Jews who intended to emigrate had to relinquish the titles to their homes and businesses and were required to pay staggering emigration taxes. Their personal possessions and financial savings were considered German property and very little could be taken with them. Severe restrictions were placed upon the amount of money that could be transferred from German banks into foreign accounts, and travelers were permitted to carry only ten Reichsmarks with them when they left the country. None of this applied to Wilhelm, as he was Aryan and had not officially emigrated but was merely residing in Switzerland indefinitely, as was a wealthy baron's prerogative. For the Panofskys, however—and the Weitzes, if they ever chose that path—emigration meant sacrificing homes, livelihoods, and everything they owned and starting over in a new country utterly impoverished.

Sara knew none of that mattered unless they could convince another country to accept them. The most desirable nations subjected would-be immigrants to arduous application processes, requiring German Jews to provide detailed information about themselves and their family, extracted with great difficulty from physicians, banks, and the German police. The United States was particularly difficult to enter, for potential immigrants must provide affidavits from American citizens willing to become their sponsors. They also had to secure a place on the waiting list within the quota permitted for each country of origin, and with thousands of German Jews desperate to escape to America, the competition was fierce. The uncertainty obliged them to apply to several different countries at once, creating an exhausting and expensive bureaucratic snarl with no guarantee of success.

From his contacts in the international press, Natan had learned that the United States, Canada, and Great Britain were reluctant to increase their quotas and allow more impoverished people to flood their shores when they were already struggling with unprecedented unemployment, poverty, and widespread hunger due to the Great Depression. He had heard rumors that the number of German Jews allowed to enter the United States was actually far below what the quota stipulated. "Antisemitism isn't exclusive to Germany," he had told Sara the previous autumn, little guessing how crushed and bewildered his offhand remark had rendered her. Her entire academic career had been devoted to American and English literature. Every American she had ever met had been kind and generous, although it was true that she hadn't met very many. Even so, she could not bear to think that the country she had admired from afar for so many years, a country founded on liberty and religious freedom, would reject her and her family simply because they were Jews.

The next morning dawned sunny and clear, with a sparkling white blanket of snow covering the landscape outside Sara's window. Smiling at the muffled laughter of the children as they played somewhere downstairs, she quickly washed, dressed warmly, and hurried to the dining room where the families were gathering. After breakfast, Sara's parents offered to show Mr. and Mrs. Panofsky and Mr. Panofsky's mother around the grounds while Natan and Sara took the children sledding. Natan, caught off guard, looked so wary that Sara had to laugh, but the children were fairly bouncing in their chairs from excitement, so he smiled and agreed.

After an hour outside in the clear, crisp winter air, Sara knew her brother did not regret being conscripted to entertain the children rather than spending the day clattering away on his typewriter. The nearest hills were either too tame for Hans or too steep for Ruth, so instead of racing downhill, Sara pulled Ruth on one sled while Natan pulled Hans on the other, escorting them on their own tour of the estate, over the bridge and into the woods, singing and laughing, pausing to study the tracks forest creatures had left in the snow. They deduced from the paths traced through the drifts that the older set had made the rounds of the orangery, the greenhouse, the stables and indoor riding arena, and the gardener's cottage before returning indoors to a warm fire.

Late in the morning, Sara and Natan hauled the children up a long, gentle rise and paused at the top to catch their breath and to admire the view of the entire Riechmann estate spread out below all around them.

"See that man down there?" Natan said, his cheeks red from cold as he knelt between the two sleds and pointed to a frozen pond at the northern edge of the forest, fed by the same creek as the moat. "That fellow is Mr. Albrecht, the groundskeeper. He's clearing the ice for us so we can skate after lunch."

Hans let out a cheer and Ruth clapped her mittened hands together in delight. Then Natan's last words sank in and both children suddenly realized they were hungry. Her own stomach rumbling, Sara swung Ruth's sled around and followed the trail Natan broke through the drifts down the slope, careful not to let the children's sleds get away from them.

The children's grandmother met them at the back door and quickly ushered them indoors, smiling as she noted their rosy cheeks and shining eyes. As she helped them out of their coats, boots, mittens, and scarves, Natan quickly shrugged off his own winter gear and hurried away, whistling, no doubt intent on typing a few paragraphs before lunch. As the elder Mrs. Panofsky took charge of her grandchildren, Sara hung up her things and went upstairs to change, rubbing her hands together to warm them.

Just as she passed the library, she heard Mr. Panofsky say, "But are you certain the staff is absolutely loyal?"

Curious, she paused in the doorway and found Mr. Panofsky and her father seated in adjacent chairs before the fireplace. As she entered, they looked up and immediately fell silent. "Is something wrong, Mr. Panofsky?" she asked. "Do you need help from the staff?"

After the barest hesitation, he smiled and patted his stomach. "Only lunch," he replied. "Our tour of the estate left me with a hearty appetite."

"Sledding with the children had the same effect on me. I'm sure lunch will be ready soon, but if there's anything you need in the meantime—"

"Thank you, child," her father broke in, shaking his head wryly at his friend. "Rest assured, Frau Osthaus would never allow a guest to starve between meals."

Satisfied that nothing was amiss, Sara excused herself and continued upstairs to her room.

Later, after lunch, while Mrs. Panofsky bundled up the children for ice skating and Natan stole away to his room to write, Sara curled up on a sofa in the drawing room with a new novel, a blanket, and a steaming cup of tea. Midway through the first chapter, she glanced outside the window and saw her father and Mr. Panofsky trudging through the snow away from the house. Mystified, she watched them until they disappeared behind a stand of fir trees. They were heading too far north to be going to meet the children at the skating pond, and the only outbuildings that lay before them were the stables and the riding arena, which Mr. Panofsky had already seen. Perhaps they wanted to ride, Sara thought, although it seemed unlikely, as her father had not sat a horse since he was wounded in the leg in the Great War.

At supper the two gentlemen said nothing about their excursion, but instead joked about a contentious game of chess that they claimed had consumed the better part of the afternoon. Taken aback, Sara did not contradict the falsehood, but she could not help watching them more closely afterward.

As the days passed, full of playful romps in the snow with the children, quiet snowshoe hikes through the woods, leisurely afternoons with games and books, and so many delicious meals that Sara was not sure her skirts would fit by the time they returned to Berlin, her father and Mr. Panofsky often slipped away on their own, with no explanation for anyone. Nor did their wives ever mention their absences or wonder aloud where their husbands had disappeared to.

On the last day of their country idyll, Sara came upon the gentlemen at the riding arena just as she was leading Amalie's horse back to the stable. She caught them by surprise at the foot of the staircase, either on their way up to the offices on the second floor or descending from above. "Papa?" she interrupted, suddenly, inexplicably anxious. "What are you doing here?"

"Another tour," Mr. Panofsky said. "Your father promised to show me everything and I intend to take him at his word."

Her father nodded agreement, but then both men simply stood there, smiling politely, apparently unwilling to speak or move until she departed. "Well," she said uncertainly, "enjoy yourselves."

They assured her they would, and she tugged gently on the horse's lead and continued on to the stables, wondering.

Later, after supper, she managed to get her brother alone and asked him if he had noticed their father and Mr. Panofsky behaving strangely. "Actually," he said, rubbing at his jaw, "yesterday I was trying to edit a story but my concentration kept being broken by this strange banging sound. I traced it to its source and found them upstairs in the attic, stomping on the floors and peering out of the windows."

Quickly she told him what she had observed over the previous few days. "Have they gone mad?" she asked.

"No," he said slowly. "I think they're entirely sane."

Jerking his head to indicate that she should follow him, he strode off to the library, where they found the two gentlemen poring over a map of Europe spread out upon the broad oak desk, various objects holding down the curling corners.

"Papa," said Natan as they entered, a hint of exasperation in the endearment, "when are you going to tell us what you're planning? Does Mutti know? Does Wilhelm?"

The older men looked up, startled, but then their father straightened, resigned. "It was Wilhelm's idea," he said. "And of course both your mother and Mrs. Panofsky know."

"And you didn't think to enlist my help?"

"We didn't want Sara to worry, and we knew you would tell her."

Sighing, their father nodded in her direction. "As you clearly have already done."

"He hasn't told me anything," Sara said, instinctively rushing to her brother's defense, although she had only the vaguest idea what she was defending him against.

"Sara didn't need me to tell her. She's the one who noticed you two acting suspiciously."

"What is going on?" Sara asked, although suddenly she was sure she knew.

"We're evaluating several locations on the estate for their suitability as a hiding place for our family and the Panofskys," came her father's reluctant confession.

"Just in case," Mr. Panofsky hastened to add. "Nothing has been decided. We haven't given up hope that we will be able to emigrate."

"But failing that," her father said, "if the worst should befall us, we want to be prepared to go into hiding."

Sara stared at them, heart thudding. "If the worst should befall us," she echoed. "How much worse could it possibly get?"

As all three men regarded her bleakly, her throat constricted, choking off the desperate questions she was suddenly too afraid to ask.

CHAPTER THIRTY-EIGHT

March–August 1937

Greta

In early spring, Greta and Adam celebrated the publication of his novel, *Der Deutsche von Bayencourt*, adapted from an antiwar play he had written in the early 1920s. The story, set from late July to early October 1914, featured a German-born farmer living in France whose loyalties were tested in the midst of the Great War. When a German patrol became stranded near his village, the farmer, torn between his German patriotism and loyalty to his French neighbors, offered the soldiers refuge. After the French authorities discovered what he had done, he was arrested, tried, and executed. The farmer's son, a pacifist, denounced his father's sentence, declaring that the nation's real enemies were the warmongers and profiteers on both sides of the conflict who fomented "the boundless horror of this war."

Greta thought it was a brilliant work, deftly and subtly crafted, a compelling entreaty for social justice in the guise of a suspenseful war drama. Even so, she was surprised when Rowohlt offered to publish it, because the novel's prevailing theme—that one's ethical obligations could conflict with one's loyalties to the state—would surely provoke outrage from Nazi censors. Greta understood that Adam saw the publication of his novel as an act of resistance, a way to sharpen his readers' political awareness and focus their gaze. She wondered whether

Rowohlt had published the book because of its subversive themes or in spite of them.

Adam and Greta had prepared themselves for a backlash when the novel appeared on bookstore shelves, so they were guardedly pleased by glowing early reviews and steadily rising sales. To their astonishment, positive reviews also appeared in intensely partisan Nazi newspapers and cultural journals, but Adam's delight soon gave way to ire. "These fascists see Bernard's choice as a patriotic sacrifice for the Fatherland and completely ignore his son's calls for peace," he complained, crumpling up a newspaper and shoving it aside. "They call it my masterwork, but they've completely missed the point."

"Isn't it better that way?" asked Greta. "Otherwise they might have thrown you into a concentration camp to punish you for seditious writings."

He ran a hand through his hair, distracted and upset. "But will everyone miss the point?"

"No, darling." She placed her hands on his face and turned his gaze to meet hers. "They'll understand that your novel is a plea for decency and humanity in times of horror. The Nazis see only a story about the Great War. The vast majority of readers will know you're also writing about our times."

Her words seemed to comfort him, but when producers began inquiring about the film rights, he proceeded with a wariness that swerved toward the bellicose. Adam had seen how Joseph Goebbels, Leni Riefenstahl, and others had transformed innocuous and even antifascist source material into propaganda for the Third Reich. "I refuse to allow anyone to twist my novel into a cheap piece of melodrama whose sole purpose is to justify declaring war on France," he grumbled.

"Then don't sell the rights," she told him. "You don't need the money. The novel is selling well, you have other work, and more opportunities will come. It's your book and they can't take it from you by force."

If only Greta could have said the same for the book that had consumed so much of her own time and effort, a book she considered even more important to the resistance.

With her help, Dr. Murphy had completed the translation of *Mein*

Kampf on schedule and with growing confidence that it would transform the way Great Britain and the United States regarded the Nazi threat. Together he and Greta meticulously polished the final version, and then waited eagerly while Daphne typed it up and made a carbon copy. Then, in early April, just as they were preparing to submit the manuscript for publication, the Ministry of Propaganda informed Dr. Murphy that the book had been canceled. They ordered him to gather all his manuscripts, drafts, and notes and surrender them to the ministry immediately.

"They offered no explanation," Dr. Murphy said hoarsely after he broke the devastating news. His hands trembled and he repeatedly glanced down the hall to his bedroom, where Greta and Daphne suspected he kept a bottle hidden beneath a floorboard. "Perhaps they finally realized what we've known all along, that Hitler's vile, racist pronouncements will turn the world against him."

Heartsick, Greta sank into a chair and buried her face in her hands, struggling to compose herself. "We don't have to obey," she finally said. "No German publisher would defy Goebbels's orders, but you could smuggle the manuscript to London or Edinburgh and publish it there."

"No other publisher would touch it as long as Eher Verlag owns the copyright. The legal challenges would keep the book tied up in the courts for years. And if we don't give the ministry what they've asked for, they may demand that I repay the advance, and it's already spent." He heaved a sigh and ran a hand over his face, his shoulders slumped. "I'm sorry, Greta, but it's over."

In silence they gathered up the pristine version of the final manuscript, their handwritten notes, the marked-up drafts, every scrap. Greta did not notice until the loathsome task was nearly complete that at some point Dr. Murphy had quietly slipped off to his bedroom and had shut the door, leaving the work to her and Daphne.

"Should we draw straws to decide which of us gets to deliver this?" Greta asked bitterly when all the evidence of their months of toil was neatly packaged and ready to go.

"I'll take it on my way home," said Daphne. "It's not far out of my way. Besides, I'm afraid that if you run into Goebbels, you might slap him."

"Don't tempt me," Greta retorted. "What do you think they're going to do with all this? File it? Burn it?"

"File it," said Daphne, hefting the box and balancing it on her hip. "Burn the sacred utterings of their Führer? Never."

They fell silent for a moment, listening for any sound from Dr. Murphy's bedroom that might suggest he was on the phone with the publisher or the ministry or his lawyers fighting to proceed with the book. When only silence followed, Greta held open the door for Daphne and followed her out of the apartment, doubting she would ever return. It was not until later that evening that she realized she should have shared a more meaningful farewell with Daphne, for it was unlikely they would see each other again.

But a few days later, as she was heating up some soup for her supper, Greta answered a knock on her door to find Daphne standing in the hall. "Do you have a moment?" she asked, glancing furtively over her shoulder, clutching her bag tightly to her side.

Greta nodded and beckoned her inside, guessing that she had come directly from Dr. Murphy's. As soon as Greta closed and locked the door behind her, Daphne took a deep breath and blurted, "The orders were to give them all manuscripts, drafts, and notes. They said nothing about carbon copies."

"You don't mean—"

Daphne nodded and patted her bag, her eyes wide and frightened. "I forgot that it was in my typewriter case. What should I do with it?"

"Does Dr. Murphy know you have it?"

"I don't know. I believe Mrs. Murphy saw me put it in my bag. She said nothing to me, but she might have told him."

Greta's thoughts raced. "Do you have a safe place to hide it?" Her heart sank a bit when Daphne said she had an ideal place, because Greta would have liked to have taken charge of it herself. In rapid whispers, they agreed to say nothing of the carbon copy to anyone, not even Dr. Murphy, but to keep it hidden away until an opportunity to publish came along. If Daphne returned to England, she would take it with her; if her hiding place became compromised, she would give the copy to Greta.

Although the book was no closer to appearing on bookstore shelves, simply knowing that the manuscript existed raised Greta's spirits. It was difficult keeping such an important secret from Adam, and that, coupled with her disappointment over the canceled publication and the loss of her job, had rendered her unusually tearful and moody. She had been feeling increasingly tired and out of sorts, easily nauseated and lightheaded. Mildred urged her to get out in the sunlight and eat more fresh vegetables and greens, but while walks through the Tiergarten with her attentive friend did make her feel better, the very thought of vegetables turned her stomach. On most days, all she could keep down was plain bread and yogurt.

It was early May before she realized she had been keeping another secret from Adam, and from herself.

A week passed, and then another, before she summoned up the courage to tell him. By then she had seen her doctor, who confirmed that she had not misinterpreted her symptoms. She had also resolved to have the child even if Adam wanted nothing to do with it. She was not a fool; she knew it would be difficult to raise a child on her own. She might have no choice but to return in shame to Frankfurt an der Oder, but after her parents got over their initial shock and distress, they would take her in, and they would love her child.

She summoned up her courage as she and Adam lay in bed together one glorious spring morning, a Sunday, with sunlight streaming through the open window and the white curtains stirring in a breeze fragrant with linden blossoms and freshly cut grass. "Don't get up yet," she told him, grasping his arm when he kissed her and climbed out of bed to go start the coffee, their usual routine when he stayed over. "You should be sitting down for this."

He sank down on the edge of the bed, studying her warily. "So this is it. You've finally had enough. You're leaving me."

She laughed. "God, no." Then she realized he was serious. "No, Adam. That's the last thing I want."

"Then what is it?"

"I'm pregnant."

He opened his mouth to speak, then closed it again. His expression was pained, disbelieving, which broke her heart a little. "Are you sure?" he managed to say after too long a silence.

"Yes, I'm sure. I wouldn't have said so otherwise."

"Of course you wouldn't have," he said, apologetic. "How are you feeling?"

"Better now than at first." Because he had not thought to ask, there was an edge to her voice when she added, "The baby is due in January."

"The baby," he echoed, almost to himself. "Holy Christ, a baby."

"Our baby," she emphasized. "Yours and mine."

"Greta——" He grimaced, took her hand and held it in both of his. "Let's stop and think. Is it right to bring an innocent child into a world full of hate and violence?"

"There's more to the world than hate and violence," she said. "There's also love, and friendship, and literature and music. And right or wrong, it's happening."

"It doesn't have to."

She slipped her hand from his grasp. "I am not getting rid of this child. I can't believe you'd even suggest such a thing."

"We need to be realistic," he said steadily. "These are dangerous times. Friends are being snatched off the streets and thrown into concentration camps every day. The child would be utterly dependent upon you for years. What if something happened to you? What if you were arrested?"

"We would make arrangements for a legal guardian ahead of time, as all good parents should." She climbed out of bed and threw on her dressing gown. "I'm thirty-four, and the Nazis might cling to power for years. If I wait until they're gone and all is right with the world, it might be too late for me. Anyway, it doesn't matter, because I'm having this baby. The only question is if it will be with you or without you."

"Of course it will be with me." He rose, came around to her side of the bed, and stood facing her, his hands on her shoulders. "Do you think I'd abandon you? I missed too much of Armin-Gerd's childhood. I won't make that mistake again."

She rested her head on his chest, eyes welling up with tears, at a loss for words. A moment ago he was hinting that she should get an abortion. Was it really so ridiculous to think that he might walk out on her? "I don't want to live apart after the child is born," she said. He tensed for a moment, then stroked her hair away from her face and kissed the top of her head.

She was not sure what he meant by the wordless gesture, but a few days later, he told her that he believed it would be best for the child if they married.

"I think Gertrud would have something to say about that," Greta said lightly, managing a smile.

"She's deferred the inevitable long enough," said Adam. "We *will* divorce."

At the end of May, Greta met Mildred for a walk through the Tiergarten and their usual discussion of political developments and resistance-circle activities. As a teacher, Mildred was outraged by the mayor of Berlin's recent decree banning Jewish children from the public schools, and as a wife, she was distressed by the new employment regulations making membership in the Nazi Party all but mandatory for members of the civil service. Against every one of his scruples, Arvid had joined rather than lose his job.

"He had no choice," Greta consoled her. "Not even the Nazis consider people in Arvid's situation to be true believers. You've heard what is said about them—they're like undercooked meat, Nazi brown on the outside and Communist red at the center. It won't mean anything to people who truly know him."

Mildred looked taken aback. "Adam didn't tell you?"

"Tell me what?"

"Adam and Arvid met by chance on the street not long ago when Arvid was on his way home from work. When Adam saw the Nazi emblem on Arvid's buttonhole, he called him an unprincipled careerist and boxed his ears."

"He did that?"

"Right there on the pavement, in plain sight of dozens of passersby. It was humiliating, but Arvid didn't even try to defend himself."

"I'm so sorry, Mildred," said Greta, appalled. "I'll talk to him. He should know better than to doubt Arvid's integrity."

"His family knows the truth, but I think they would have preferred for him to refuse the job and go off to England like his cousin Dietrich." Mildred hesitated. "By now, I think—I hope—most of our true friends have convinced themselves that he joined only to conspire against the Nazis."

"You shouldn't tell them how right they are. You'd put them at risk."

"But please do tell Adam. He must know he can trust Arvid, if we're going to continue to work together."

"I will." Greta braced herself. "Mildred, there's something else I need to tell you."

As gently as she could, she explained that she was pregnant and that she and Adam were going to marry.

For a moment, Mildred looked pained, stricken, and her eyes filled with tears. A heartbeat later, she was smiling radiantly and embracing her. "I'm so happy for you," she said. "You'll be a wise and wonderful mother. What a lucky little child this will be!"

Greta's heart went out to Mildred, who had longed for a baby for so many years and had borne disappointment so bravely, without ever succumbing to bitterness. Greta broke down in tears, overcome by the profound injustice of the world, that what Mildred desired with all her heart would be denied her, and yet had come to Greta unexpectedly and unsought, a disruption rather than a joy.

Soon more generosity of spirit came to Greta from an unexpected source. Gertrud did not contest the divorce, but wished Adam and Greta well and signed the papers as soon as they were delivered. Only then did they begin planning their wedding. It angered and offended them that they were required to obtain an *Ariernachweis*, a certification of their Aryan purity, before they would be permitted to wed. Resenting the necessity, they nevertheless scrambled to collect proof of their ancestry from family members, church records, and government archives.

On August 28, Greta and Adam married in a civil ceremony surrounded by their family and dearest friends. The guests included Mildred and Arvid; Rudolf and Franziska Heberle, another couple Greta had first met in Wisconsin; several of Greta's childhood friends and university classmates; Adam's son Armin-Gerd, accompanied by Marie and Gertrud; dozens of luminaries from the German theater, close friends of the groom; and a few members of their resistance circle who did not fit into any of the other groups but were scattered among them, revealing as little about themselves as possible.

The two witnesses of the ceremony were Hans Hartenstein, a prominent official at the Ministry of Economics whom Greta had known since her school days, and Adam's good friend Adolfe Grimme, the former Prussian minister of culture. Greta had to suppress her laughter at the reaction of the officious registrar, a stout little fellow who went wide-eyed and tongue-tied when he recognized the two very distinguished men who stood before him.

"He's duly impressed," Greta murmured to Adam, concealing her smile behind her bouquet.

"Apparently no one told him that they were both sacked for refusing to join the Nazi Party," he replied.

"Hans wasn't sacked. He resigned."

"Fair point."

Then they could say no more, because the registrar, in accordance with protocol, ordered the two witnesses to attention, snapping out the one-armed salute and a shrill "Heil Hitler!" The two men regarded him mildly and did not return the perfunctory greeting, nor did anyone else in the company. Flustered, cheeks scarlet, the registrar stammered and sweated his way through the rest of the ceremony, clearly at a loss for what else to do. It was too important and happy an occasion to spoil with irritation or annoyance, so by unspoken agreement the wedding party decided to regard the registrar with amusement instead.

They soon forgot him as they strolled a block down the street to their reception, where Greta danced and ate and laughed and accepted warm wishes and congratulations from new friends and old, all the people she loved best in the world. It was a wonderful day in a bleak season, when the promise of love lit up the world in a golden glow and the air tasted as sweet as wine.

CHAPTER THIRTY-NINE

October–December 1937

Martha

On October 29, Bill drove Martha and their mother in their reliable old Chevrolet to the Lehrter Bahnhof to meet their father's train from Hamburg, where his ship from New York had docked earlier that morning. His lengthy absence had been hardest on his wife. As Martha watched her mother clutch her purse in her lap, her lips pressed together anxiously as she gazed out the window, she wished once more that her mother could have accompanied her father to the United States. She needed a respite from Berlin almost as much as Martha's father had.

The previous year had been the most arduous, stressful, and frustrating of Ambassador Dodd's life. He had watched, powerless to intervene, as German troops marched into the Rhineland in defiance of the Treaty of Versailles. He had observed Hitler mock the Olympic ideals at the Berlin Games, the Führer's assurances of peaceful intentions in sharp contrast to Germany's growing military might. As before, her father had shunned the annual Nazi Party rally in Nuremberg, noting with horror and disgust that the German people increasingly revered Hitler as a god. Women wept tears of joy when his motorcade passed. Men dug up the soil he had walked upon and preserved vials of it as sacred relics. Young boys in crisp brown uniforms marched, trained, and sang songs glorifying blood spilled on the battlefield in defense of the Fatherland. To a young American woman raised on democracy and rational thought, it was repulsive and disturbing, but Martha found it impossible to tear her gaze away.

One day soon after the 1936 rally, Martha went looking for her father only to find his study empty, a draft of a letter marked "Personal and Confidential" on his desk. Naturally she stole a glance.

"With armies increasing in size and efficiency every day; with thousands of airplanes ready on a moment's notice to drop bombs and spread poison gas over great cities; and with all other countries, little and great, arming as never before, one cannot feel safe anywhere," her father had written to Secretary of State Cordell Hull. "What mistakes and blunders have been made since 1917, and especially during the past twelve months—and democratic peoples do nothing, impose no economic or moral penalties, to halt the process!"

Martha stopped reading there, deeply troubled by her father's grim, foreboding assessment. After that, his frequent wistful reminiscences about Chicago and Stoneleigh took on a new significance. A month later, as they wandered through the garden of Tiergartenstrasse 27a admiring the changing autumn hues, her father confided that he was suffering from severe headaches and digestive troubles, which his physician attributed to stress. "You mustn't mention this to anyone, but I don't see how I can continue in this atmosphere longer than next spring," he said, oblivious to her rising fear at the thought of her indomitable father brought down by the pressure of impossible demands. "I can't render my country any useful service with my hands tied with red tape, and the stress of always doing nothing is too much to bear."

Martha kept his confidence, divulging nothing to anyone, not even Bill or her mother, and certainly not Boris. She had no doubt that the letters she sent him at his new post in Poland were opened by Nazi censors before they crossed the border. Even on the few occasions when, to her parents' consternation, she slipped away to Warsaw to meet him, she limited their conversations to the local nightlife, gossip about mutual acquaintances in Berlin, sex, and—although he had begun to show an infuriating lack of enthusiasm for the subject—marriage. Not that Boris needed her to tell him anything about conflict within the

American embassy. Boris still had contacts in Berlin, and he probably knew more about the challenges her father faced than she did.

She would have poured out her heart to Mildred, except they rarely saw each other anymore. Martha and Bill were under almost constant surveillance by the Gestapo and Soviet intelligence. If she and Mildred met other than at official embassy events, they would have been observed, endangering their entire resistance network. Martha wished she dared risk it. Kind, sympathetic Mildred would have found the words to comfort her.

Her father's circumstances worsened throughout the winter, and spring brought his most difficult ordeal yet. Helmut Hirsch, a twenty-one-year-old German Jew and antifascist, had been sentenced to death for his part in a thwarted plot to bomb sites in Nuremberg, with Nazi Party headquarters and the offices of *Der Stürmer* among the suspected targets. Although Hirsch had never been to the United States, he held American citizenship through his father, and the State Department instructed Martha's father to demand a new, fair, and legitimate trial. Outraged that the young man had been condemned to die although no bombing had occurred and no evidence connecting him to any plot had been produced, Martha's father fought vigorously for clemency.

On April 27, in the midst of intense negotiations about Hirsch's fate, her parents hosted a luncheon at Tiergartenstrasse 27a for members of the German Foreign Office. In the middle of the soup course, the doughy official seated beside Martha leaned closer to her and, breath thickly scented with alcohol, said, "You should warn your father that he is wasting his time."

Martha regarded him archly. "What do you mean?"

"Helmut Hirsch, the American Jew who wanted to kill the Führer, cannot be let off with life imprisonment. He must be executed even though he did not actually commit the crime."

"What sort of justice is that?" Martha asked, taken aback, but the official merely shrugged and took another drink of wine. As soon as their guests departed, Martha passed on the warning to her father, but he could not explain how Hirsch's charges of a plot to bomb buildings in Nuremberg had been conflated with an attempt to assassinate Hitler.

Undaunted, her father continued to fight for Hirsch's life. At the end of May, informed that Hirsch could be shown no leniency, he convinced two important Reich ministers, Otto Meissner and Konstantin von Neurath, to appeal personally to Hitler, warning him of the repercussions that would follow if they killed an American citizen under such questionable circumstances.

But her father's tireless efforts were in vain. At sunrise on the morning of June 4, Helmut Hirsch was executed by guillotine.

Although Martha's father had exhausted every option, his failure to save the young man struck him a bitter blow. His headaches increased in severity and duration until he suffered continuous pain for days without respite. Once Martha overheard him complain to his physician that intense pain spread over the nerve connections between his stomach, shoulders, and brain until he found it impossible to sleep. By early summer, the problems with his digestive tract had worsened so drastically that eating became torturous, forcing him on one occasion to go without food for thirty hours straight. Through it all, he kept up his rigorous schedule at the embassy, until Martha and her mother worried that he might literally work himself to death.

"Please, please, for our sakes, if not your own, take better care of yourself," Martha's mother begged. He promised to try.

Finally, in late July, Martha's father was granted a three-month leave so he could rest and recover his health. Why their mother had not insisted upon accompanying him home to the United States, Martha and Bill could only wonder. Their parents were usually inseparable, and other embassy officials or their wives could have filled in for their mother at ceremonial occasions. Then, one afternoon, Martha ran into Mrs. Panofsky when she was returning from an outing with her son and daughter. They chatted briefly, long enough for Martha to observe the dark circles under Mrs. Panofsky's eyes and the lines of tension around her mouth. As she led the two children to the elevator and up to their attic home, Martha suddenly understood why her parents were so keen to maintain an American presence at Tiergartenstrasse 27a.

But since Martha's mother had remained behind, she was powerless to enforce the doctor's orders. The family hoped he would rest, but soon his letters from America told a different story. Ambassador Dodd described the late summer beauty of Stoneleigh and the abundant harvest, regular checkups with his doctor, and fond reunions with old friends, but also meetings with President Roosevelt at the White House and conferences with State Department officials, some of them contentious. In mid-August he wrote that the president had urged him to deliver lectures on the state of affairs in Germany while he was in the States, to "speak the truth about things" as often and as emphatically as he could. These demands were hardly conducive to allowing a sixty-five-year-old overworked man to regain his strength and peace of mind, but Martha knew her father would endeavor to do whatever his president asked of him.

Not everyone appreciated his loyalty and perseverance. Her father was besieged on all sides by obnoxious political enemies trying to push him out of office—not only Hitler's men but Americans too, petty bureaucrats who complained that her father's antipathy for the Nazis rendered him unfit for his post. Martha and Bill firmly believed that anyone who was *not* repulsed by Hitler and his Nazi regime was unqualified to represent the United States in Germany, on the grounds of intellectual weakness or moral bankruptcy or both. Their father, unimpressed by fascist spectacle, ethically incorruptible, was absolutely the best man for the job, but they worried that President Roosevelt could not perceive this from so far away. They feared even more that the job would put their father into an early grave.

Thus when they first glimpsed him descending from the train to the platform at the Lehrter Bahnhof, well rested and vigorous, they exchanged relieved glances and blinked back tears before making their way through the crowd to his side. He was smiling again, Martha observed, and how immeasurably grateful she was to see it. The haunted look had left his eyes, and he had acquired a healthy tan from hours basking in the Virginia sunshine as he puttered about his farm.

At long last, they were all together again, safe and sound. Embracing joyfully, they complimented him on his appearance and teased that he had come back just in time to save Germany from itself. "I'm not so sure about that," he replied, rueful. "As we sailed down the Elbe, I spotted an astonishing number of army trucks on the roads hauling arms and equipment. My heart sank to see them, and all the other signs of the coming catastrophe."

"Those awful instruments of death and destruction," Martha's mother said, shuddering as she took her husband's arm. "Is there no possible way to stop men and nations from destroying each other?"

"What kind of talk is this for a family reunion?" Bill protested, draping his arms over his parents' shoulders. "Let's save the gloom and doom for tomorrow."

Martha chimed in her agreement, and her father good-naturedly consented. His time back home in the States had apparently restored his energy and optimism, just as his family had hoped. As soon as they arrived at Tiergartenstrasse 27a, he took a book from his valise and proudly presented it to his wife. "How wonderful," she exclaimed, holding out the book so that Martha could read the title, *The Old South: Struggles for Democracy.* "Congratulations, my dear."

"Yes, congrats, Dad," said Martha, rising up on tiptoe to kiss his cheek. "How marvelous it must be to hold a finished copy of your own book, your life's work." She hoped she would know that feeling herself someday.

"This is only volume one of my life's work," he corrected, smiling. "My publisher is eager for me to begin the second volume."

Martha and her mother exchanged pensive glances. "Will your duties at the embassy leave you any time to write?" her mother asked. "You've only just regained your health. Promise me you won't exhaust yourself from overwork."

"I won't, dear," he said, clasping her hand. "I had several good conversations with the president, and he has agreed that I may resign in March."

Martha's mother cried out, surprised and thankful. Bill grinned and clapped their father on the back. But Martha felt her heart sink. She too felt homesick for America from time to time, and she had become thoroughly sick and tired of the oppressive Third Reich, but she could not help the resistance from Chicago. And how would her romance with Boris survive if they were an ocean apart? She already sensed his interest in marriage dwindling, and he was only in Warsaw.

Well, Martha thought, that's it for dallying. They had until March to resolve things once and for all. Perhaps the thought of losing her forever would finally prompt Boris to propose.

"Why March?" asked Bill. "Why not now?"

"President Roosevelt asked me to stay on until spring to give him time to find the right man to succeed me. I also want to tie up some loose ends to smooth the transition." He hesitated, wincing. "Also, if I left any sooner, it would give the impression that my rivals and critics, American and German alike, had succeeded in their efforts to have me removed."

Martha nodded. The appearance that he had been abruptly fired would humiliate her father. A few more months at his post was a small price to pay for his dignity.

In the days that followed, Martha's father resumed his duties with a new resolve to serve, as President Roosevelt had charged him to do more than four years before, as a steadfast example of American liberalism against fascism. To Martha, it seemed an increasingly futile task. She sensed dangerous forces at work in Germany, strengthening every day, driving the whole world toward an abyss. Although people like her father, the Harnacks, and her friends in the international press corps perceived the gaping emptiness ahead, no one with the power to act seemed willing or able to stop the inexorable rush into the darkness.

Then, on the afternoon of November 23, Martha was reading in the library when she heard her mother cry out. Racing to see what was the matter, she found her parents at the top of the grand staircase, her father home early from the embassy, pale and haggard, her mother taking his arm and guiding him to a chair. "What is it?" Martha asked, hurrying over.

"I've been relieved of my duties," her father said, his voice strangely flat and distant.

"No, you resigned," said Martha, bewildered. "You and the president agreed."

Her father reached into his breast pocket and withdrew a folded telegram. Wordlessly he passed it to her, and although it was marked "Strictly Confidential," Martha opened it. "It's from Secretary Hull," she told her mother. "'Much as the President regrets any personal inconvenience which may be occasioned to you, he desires me to request that you arrange to leave Berlin if possible by December 15 and in any event not later than Christmas, because of the complications with which you are familiar and which threaten to increase.' Complications? What is he talking about?"

Her father shook his head and held out his hand for the telegram. "I'll protest, of course. I'll remind Hull of my agreement with President Roosevelt. But I doubt it will do any good."

"Unbelievable," fumed Martha. "After all you've done for your country—"

"Perhaps it's for the best," her mother interrupted. "Now we can go home, where you want to be anyway. You can continue to recover your health and finish your book."

"But important work remains to be done here."

"Other men can do it," she replied sharply, but then her voice softened. "Decide what is best and what you want most, dear, and I'll be content."

But other men had already decided for him. His protests went unheeded, and he realized that the forces arrayed against him were stronger and greater in number than he had suspected. Reconciling himself to the inevitable, he booked passage home.

He could not yet step down from his post, however, and when word of his imminent departure spread, he was inundated with invitations to dinners and luncheons with sympathetic ambassadors from other nations. Diplomats urgently sought his intervention on various matters while he still had the power to help them. Universities requested campus lectures, events that caused a greater stir of anticipation than they would have only a few months before, since he was now free to speak his mind without fear of repercussions. Privately Martha and Bill called it their father's farewell tour, hiding their disgust that this show of approval had come too late to save his job.

Martha had farewells of her own to make.

Soon after her father had received the curt telegram from Washington, she went to Warsaw to break the bad news to Boris in person. He was dismayed—more than she had expected, which was rather satisfying—and their brief hours together were more passionate than ever, infused with the sweet melancholy of their inevitable parting.

Martha supposed, unhappily, that the rendezvous would be their last, but in mid-December, Boris unexpectedly appeared at the front door of Tiergartenstrasse 27a. He carried a bottle of vodka in one large hand and a bouquet of flowers in the other, but he managed to hold on to them both as he took her in his arms and pulled her close.

She spent the night with him at his hotel rather than add more turmoil to the household by inviting him to stay. She was astonished to learn that he had left his post without permission in order to see her one last time, and the thought that he would risk so much for her sake delighted and aroused her. "I want to marry you," she told him as they lay in bed together, their limbs intertwined.

"It is impossible," he said, sighing heavily. "It always was. Now it is even more so."

"You don't know that."

"Darling, let's forget about the future and just enjoy this time together. I'll certainly pay dearly for it when I return."

Their stolen days were glorious and heartbreaking and over too soon. Martha refused to believe that they might never see each other again, and she waited for Boris's letter from Warsaw humorously describing the reprimand he had earned for her sake. She hoped against all reason that he might somehow manage another visit, just one more, to hold her over until they could meet again in better days.

Martha postponed saying goodbye to Mildred until the last possible moment. Mildred had been her truest, dearest friend throughout the four and a half years she had spent in Berlin, from the moment Mildred had met her family's train at the Lehrter Bahnhof bearing flowers from the American Women's Club.

A few days before Martha's departure, she and Mildred met at a restaurant near the Harnacks' flat where they were unlikely to run into any Nazi officials. They chose an inconspicuous table away from the front windows and lingered over lunch, reminiscing wistfully about their literary column, Mildred's fascinating salons, mutual friends who had already left Berlin, Thomas Wolfe, their observations of Hitler at the Olympic Games. Only then did Martha realize how many of her memories of Germany were indelibly marked by Mildred's presence.

They chatted about books, their dread of fascism, and their hopes for the future. "You must write to me now and then," Martha said, when the hour grew late and she was overdue to help her mother finish packing.

"I'll have to be circumspect," said Mildred. "Don't expect too many specific details."

"Anything you can sneak past the censors will be good enough for me."

"Agreed," said Mildred. "You must promise to write back. Send me chapters of your book."

"I haven't even begun writing it yet. Besides, what I have to say would definitely get held up by the censors."

They laughed together, but then Mildred abruptly stopped. "How can we joke about having our mail censored, as if it's a perfectly ordinary inconvenience? What has happened to us? Five years ago, we would have been shocked and outraged by the very idea."

"I'm still shocked and outraged."

"Are you really?" Mildred shook her head. "I'm afraid we've all become acclimated to cruelty and injustice by being exposed to it in steadily increasing doses through the years. Intolerable wrongs we accept now as a matter of course would have provoked marches in the streets and calls for new elections only a few years ago."

Martha reached across the table and took her hand. "Not you, Mildred. You don't accept injustice any more now than you did when we first met. You could never be cruel or tolerate cruelty. And you are not alone."

Reminded of their brave friends, Mildred allowed a small smile. Someday, they agreed, Germany would emerge from this nightmare of fascism and become a just, tolerant, and wise nation again, at peace with itself and the world.

They left the restaurant and parted with a quick kiss and promises to stay in touch. After they went their separate ways, Martha suddenly halted and turned around, eager for one more glimpse of her friend, hoping she would glance over her shoulder and offer one last smile, a parting wave. But Mildred had already disappeared into the crowd.

With a sharp pang of loneliness, Martha continued on to Tiergartenstrasse 27a. She would miss Mildred terribly, but she felt none of the bitter unhappiness of her parting from Boris, whom she suspected she would never see again. Surely she and Mildred would reunite someday back in America, perhaps not soon, but eventually.

Until then, they would share letters and memories.

On December 14, Martha took a train to Hamburg, where she boarded the SS *Manhattan* bound for New York. As the ship sailed slowly up the Elbe, Martha stood at the railing on an upper deck and took in her last views of Germany, marveling at how beautiful it became at a distance, as the swastika flags diminished and became indistinct, blending into the background of quaint villages and rich farmland and deep forests until she could almost convince herself that they were not there at all.

CHAPTER FORTY

January–June 1938

Mildred

When Greta and Adam welcomed their son into the world in early January, Mildred and Arvid were among the first to meet him. Little Ule Kuckhoff had his father's broad face and his mother's dark, wavy hair and dark eyes, solemn and pensive, as if he knew that courage and sacrifice would be required of him soon.

Greta wrapped him in the soft blue-and-white-striped blanket Mildred had knit for him and placed him in Mildred's arms. "This is your Tante Mildred," she said softly, "and though you've only just met, she already loves you."

"It's true, dear one," said Mildred softly. She eased herself into Greta's chair and gently rocked the tiny newborn, her joy for her friends tempered by her incessant yearning for a child of her own. She was already an aunt several times over, but although she found much consolation in the role, it could not fulfill her heart's desire.

Greta's mother had come to help the new parents through the first few weeks, but Greta had endured a difficult labor and when her recovery came slowly, her mother's visit stretched into a month and then two. Mildred visited as often as she could to help, and once, when they were alone, Greta confessed her frustration that her resistance work had come to an abrupt halt. "Adam and his comrades toil over their pamphlets and posters, and what do I do?" she fretted. "Nothing. I lie around the flat doing nothing while people suffer."

"You're regaining your strength and caring for your baby," Mildred protested. "What could be more important?"

"Bringing down the Reich," Greta retorted, but quietly so her mother would not overhear. "Speaking the truth. Refuting their lies. I have to make a better world for Ule."

Mildred assured her that she would be able to resume her work soon, but Greta's frustration mirrored her own. Ambassador Dodd, her most important American contact, had been recalled to the United States, and no one else had emerged as someone she could trust with the intelligence Arvid gathered from the Economics Ministry. Worse yet, acquaintances among the embassy staff had told her that Mr. Dodd's successor, a career diplomat named Hugh Wilson, had resolved to take a more cordial approach to the Nazi regime. Improved relations between their two countries could only benefit American businesses, he had declared in more than one meeting, and after one junior official had presented reports of Gestapo abuses, Wilson rejected his offer to draft a stern condemnation. "We do not love or hate, we do not judge or condemn," he had admonished the younger man. "We observe, we reflect, and we report."

Even as Mildred's contacts at the American embassy were diminishing in number, Arvid was losing his among the Soviet delegation. Stalin, apparently determined to rid the Soviet Union of every conceivable threat, had ordered sweeping, violent purges of his political enemies. Rumors abounded that within the past few years, nearly five million Soviet intellectuals, military officers, Communist party officials, police chiefs, and others had been arrested. Of these, nearly a million had been executed, and one could only assume that countless others had suffered and died in prison camps, with more deaths every day.

The sheer number of estimated dead was almost too vast to comprehend, but Mildred's amorphous dread came into sharp focus when, without warning, many Soviet diplomats and attachés stationed in Berlin were ordered to return to Moscow. Among those recalled was Sergei Bessonov, a prominent economist assigned to the Russian trade mission who had helped Arvid set up ARPLAN. In the years since, he and Arvid had become close, and Arvid and Mildred had frequently invited him to their home for supper. Bessonov had left Berlin so suddenly that Arvid had no chance to offer help or say goodbye.

They heard nothing more of Bessonov until early March, when the newspapers listed him as a defendant in the Trial of the Twenty-One. Prosecutors claimed that he belonged to a "Bloc of Rightists and Trotskyites" who had conspired to assassinate Lenin and Stalin, to commit espionage, and to collude with the governments of Germany and Japan in order to overthrow the Soviet Union. Arvid was deeply upset by the news. Bessonov was a good friend, and Arvid knew he was already lost. No defendant was ever acquitted in Stalin's show trials.

Two days after Bessonov's trial began, Mildred was reading the *Berliner Tageblatt* over breakfast when a familiar name leapt out at her from a column on international diplomacy. "Boris Vinogradov has been recalled to Moscow," she said, dismayed. "He's been accused of collaborating with the Nazis."

"Poor fellow." Arvid sighed, removed his glasses, and rubbed the bridge of his nose as if warding off a headache. "He put a target on his own back with that foolhardy visit to Martha in December."

Mildred nodded soberly, searching the column for more details, finding none. The last time she had seen Boris's name in the German papers had been shortly before Christmas, when the German press reported on that same ill-fated unauthorized trip. While Boris had been away from his post, the NKVD had raided the Warsaw embassy and had found incriminating documents in his office, or so they claimed. "I wonder why the Soviets waited so long to recall him."

"Perhaps all their jail cells were full. Perhaps he was still useful to them for a while. I hope he disobeyed the order and fled. He must know that if he returns to Moscow, he would be signing his own death warrant."

From what Mildred knew of Boris, he did not fear his superiors and would have readily obeyed their summons. "Martha always said that he was unshakably loyal to the Soviet Union," she mused aloud. "I can't imagine he betrayed their secrets to the Nazis."

"If he believes his innocence will protect him, I'm afraid his trust is misplaced." Arvid's voice turned bitter. "My friend Bessonov was loyal, for all the good that does him now."

"I wonder if Martha knows." With a sudden pang, Mildred realized that it was her responsibility as Martha's friend to break the bad news to her before the American press did. "I'll write and tell her."

"There's no need. Martha has probably forgotten him by now."

"Nonsense," Mildred protested. "I think she truly loves him. She wanted to marry him."

"I'm sure she did at the time, but I wouldn't be surprised if she's already found someone new."

"Oh, Arvid, that's unkind."

"I'm sorry, *Liebling*. I'm not feeling particularly kind today." He rose from the table and kissed her on the forehead. "Forgive me."

"Of course," she said, watching as he headed down the hallway to their bedroom. She tidied the kitchen as he got ready for work and kissed him tenderly when they parted at the door. She knew he was not as cold or unfeeling as his words suggested. It was his frustration coming out, his anger at his powerlessness to help his doomed friend.

Alone in the flat, with only the distant sounds of traffic passing outside and other tenants moving about the building to keep her company, Mildred poured herself a second cup of coffee and settled down with a notepad, a pen, and the *New York Times*. The paper was several days out of date, but it was the most recent edition she had and it was essential for her work. Earlier that year, the Berlin publisher Rütten & Loening had hired her as a reader and consultant, advising them on American novels they might wish to acquire for translation. This often involved scanning American newspapers for book reviews and announcements of newly released works, copies of which publishers eagerly sent her, all for the price of a stamp and an official request on Rütten & Loening stationery. Her astute recommendations must have impressed her employers, for they soon began offering her translation projects as well, with a commensurate increase in pay. She missed teaching, but her new job was intellectually stimulating, it filled her hours, and it supplemented their household income, and for that she was grateful.

She was at home working on a translation of Walter Edmonds's *Drums Along the Mohawk* when a radio announcer interrupted the musical program to announce that German troops were marching into Austria.

In public speeches, in the press, in radio addresses redolent with the historic significance of the day, every German official who spoke publicly on the annexation of Austria was careful not to call it an invasion. Uniting the two nations into a Greater Germany had been contemplated since the nineteenth century, they pointed out, although they neglected to add that far more recently, the union had been expressly prohibited by the Treaty of Versailles and the Treaty of Saint-Germain. They referenced polls and referenda to prove that the *Anschluss* was overwhelmingly popular in Austria, and indeed, newsreels showed thousands of Austrians lining the streets, cheering, waving swastika flags, and offering the Hitler salute as German tanks rolled across the border and into Austrian villages. Girls and young women, their blond hair in pretty braids and ribbons, presented soldiers with bouquets of flowers as they marched past.

As all the Berlin newspapers reported in the days that followed, on the afternoon of March 12, Hitler and an entourage of bodyguards four thousand strong received a hero's welcome at his birthplace, Braunau am Inn, just over the border. A triumphant four-day tour of Austria culminated in a rally at the Heldenplatz in Vienna, where two hundred thousand exultant Austrians gathered to celebrate as their Führer declared their once independent country to be "the newest bastion of the German Reich." *Ein Volk, ein Reich, ein Führer*, the Nazis declared: One People, One Nation, One Leader.

Arvid had known the *Anschluss* was coming. He had observed the steady flow of money for months, and then the sudden rush in the days before the troops moved across the border. It had all come about with the collusion of Austrian Nazis, but that did not make it any less a violation of international treaties. In the days that followed, Arvid, Mildred, and their friends tuned their radios to foreign broadcasts and waited, hopeful and expectant, for news of a strong, united response from the free nations of Europe and America. Statements were released. Condemnation was expressed. But in the end, not even the most vehement opponents of the annexation—Britain, France, Italy, and Mexico—did anything but talk. Meanwhile, in Germany, Hitler had never been more popular.

Although Mildred was disappointed with the ongoing reluctance of the United States to take an unambiguously firm stand, the *Anschluss* and the rising militaristic fervor permeating Germany compelled her to draw closer to the American expatriate community. Although the Dodds were gone and membership in the American Women's Club had diminished as husbands resigned posts or arranged transfers to safer regions, she found comfort and companionship at embassy events and club meetings. American accents, foods, and stories felt like letters from home, a soft, warm shawl draped over her shoulders on a chilly morning.

On Sunday, April 17, she attended an Easter tea with the American Women's Club at its fashionable suite on the Bellevuestrasse. She missed seeing Martha and her mother there, but she enjoyed catching up with other friends, grateful for each who remained. She met a rare newcomer, too, when the chairwoman introduced her to Louise Heath, the vivacious brown-haired wife of the new first secretary and monetary attaché, Donald Heath.

"Monetary attaché?" Mildred remarked, smiling. "Is he an economist?"

"Not really," replied Louise. "He was a newspaper reporter in Kansas before the war, and after serving in the army he became the White House correspondent for the United Press. Before long he joined the State Department, and that led us here. The reason he's working for the Treasury Department as well as State is because, thanks to budget cuts, the Treasury Department couldn't afford to hire a second man."

"So your husband has to do the work of two?"

"Yes, for the price of one, unfortunately." Louise sipped her tea, her blue eyes bright with mirth. "You know what bothers me most? The Treasury Department, of all places, ought to know how to squeeze one more salary out of even the tightest budget."

"That might explain something about our country's financial woes."

"My thought exactly."

"Economist or not, as the monetary attaché, your husband probably has a lot in common with mine," said Mildred. "He works in the Ministry of Economics and will happily talk fiscal policy for hours on end."

Louise's eyebrows rose. "The Germans hired an American to work in the Economics Ministry?"

"Oh, no. Arvid is German. We met as graduate students at the University of Wisconsin."

"How marvelous," said Louise, her gaze keen. "We'll have to introduce them. Donald needs some German friends." Leaning closer, she murmured, "Just between us, he's not inclined to make any among the 'Sieg Heil' set."

"I like him already," said Mildred, and Louise smiled knowingly.

As it turned out, they did not need to introduce their husbands. As Mildred learned afterward, Donald was so delighted to hear that his wife's new friend's German husband had studied in the United States that a few days later he called on Arvid at the Economics Ministry and invited him to lunch. Intrigued, Arvid had accepted.

"I'm glad you've become friends," said Mildred, smiling as she set the table for supper, charmed by his enthusiasm.

"He's more than a friend, *Liebling*. We're going to be partners."

After lunch the men had taken a walk through the Tiergarten, the only place where one could speak without danger of wiretaps or hidden recording devices. There Heath had revealed that his role in Berlin involved far more than his job titles disclosed. He was also an intelligence officer assigned to obtain vital economic information about the Reich, including the state of the German treasury, the Reichsbank, money markets, national debt, gold, foreign exchange—all subjects squarely in Arvid's purview. Arvid had agreed to provide him with the information the Americans sought.

Mildred nodded as he spoke, her heart thudding. She knew this was exactly the sort of work they wanted to do, reopening the flow of vital intelligence that had been choked off with Ambassador Dodd's departure and the loss of their contacts at the Soviet embassy. But the Reich had declared the delivery of economic information to foreigners to be treason, punishable by death. Arvid knew almost nothing of Donald Heath, nothing to ensure them that he would value his informants' lives as much as his mission.

"Are you sure Heath can be trusted?" she asked. "Will he protect you?"

"I have no idea. My instinct is to trust him, but we've only just met." Arvid shrugged. "You liked his wife."

In spite of herself, Mildred laughed. "That's hardly an exhaustive background check."

He smiled, but then he grew solemn again. "My instincts tell me to trust him, and everyone else who could get him this information is loyal to the Nazis. It has to be me."

She knew he was right. As the chief of trade policy, Arvid was in nearly daily contact with the Foreign Office and the desk chiefs for individual nations. Since it was his responsibility to monitor Germany's economic capacity, production levels, financial reserves, and foreign trade, he knew more about the state of the German economy than almost anyone. And, as he had recently been promoted to government counselor, he was required to confer with his counterparts from other nations. He could meet publicly with Heath without raising any suspicions.

He did not need Mildred's approval, but she knew he wanted her support. And so she suppressed her worries, put her arms around him, and murmured, "Promise me you'll be careful."

He held her close, and only then did she realize how hard his heart was pounding.

As spring bloomed, green and fragrant and warm, Arvid and Heath became trusted partners, and before long the two couples became good friends. Mildred and Louise met often for lunch, teas at the embassy, or events with the American Women's Club, and they frequently enjoyed dinners out together or evenings at home playing cards and listening to the radio. On sunny weekend afternoons, the Heaths' ten-year-old son, Donald Jr., would join them for walks through the Tiergarten or on picnics by the lake in Wannsee. Any observer inclined toward suspicion would see only an innocent family friendship between three expatriate Americans and one indulgent German husband. Mildred did not ask what Heath did with the information Arvid risked his life to give him, but she fervently hoped that it would compel the United States to take bold measures to constrain Hitler's military expansion before catastrophe struck.

Then, in late June, Mildred received a letter from another American friend.

It was only her second letter from Martha since the Dodds had returned to the United States, a reply to Mildred's letting her know that Boris had been recalled to Moscow under suspicion of collaborating with the Nazis. "You're a dear to be concerned," Martha had written, "but I'm sure Boris is fine. Last month I received a letter from him, dated April 29 and sent from Moscow. It was very warm and affectionate, and he had lots of nice things to say about our last meeting in Berlin. He spoke of our eternal love, which, I have to say, was very flattering but impossible, because—Are you sitting down?—I'm going to be married!"

Mildred was so startled she had to start over at the beginning and read the letter again.

She had not misunderstood. Soon after Martha arrived in New York, she had met Alfred Stern—tall, handsome, ten years older than she, and wonderfully wealthy thanks to a generous divorce settlement he had received from his defunct marriage to a Sears Roebuck heiress. After a whirlwind romance, Alfred had proposed and Martha had accepted. They planned a large celebration at the family farm in Round Hill, Virginia, on September 4, and Mildred and Arvid were very welcome to attend if they could possibly make it.

"I suppose I must tell Boris," Martha wrote, with a trace of chagrin. "What an awful letter that will be to write, nearly as bad as it would be to receive!"

Mildred felt more than a little chagrined herself. Apparently Arvid had been right all along about her friend's fickle heart. She hoped his judgment was equally sound about Donald Heath, and that the embassy's new first secretary would prove to be as shrewdly intelligent, cautious, and deserving of their trust as he seemed. Their lives depended on it.

CHAPTER FORTY-ONE

March–September 1938

Sara

For Austria's Jews, the *Anschluss* became a swiftly unfolding nightmare.

In the aftermath of the annexation, the Nazis immediately imposed the same restrictions upon Jews, Gypsies, and other undesirables that they had honed to cruel perfection in Germany. *Ein Volk, ein Reich, ein Führer*, one hatred. Jewish shops and businesses were looted, the proprietors hauled out to the sidewalks and beaten. Throughout Austria, the front windows of Jewish-owned stores and restaurants were marked in yellow paint, *Jude* and the Star of David, warning Aryans to avoid them. In Austrian cities, Jews were forced to scrub city streets; laborers, lawyers, and clerks toiled on their hands and knees with coarse brushes and buckets of soapy water under the watchful gaze of armed storm troopers and hundreds of curious onlookers. In Vienna, Jewish actresses were made to scrub public toilets.

Sara and her family followed the news from Austria with a cold, sinking dread that outwardly might have appeared stoic. All of it was horrifying, none of it unexpected. To Sara the rumors spreading through the Jewish community and the reports in the Jewish press bore a grotesque veneer of familiarity. Everything that was happening to the Austrian Jews—the public humiliations, the loss of rights, the chilling certainty that any passing Aryan could inflict whatever violence they wanted upon you and the authorities would do nothing—had been a part of their daily lives for years.

By late spring, the hiding place at Schloss Federle was nearly complete, five rooms in the attic of the west wing accessible only by a narrow staircase leading from a spare room used to store old furniture, some of which was dusted off and hauled upstairs. Mr. and Mrs. Panofsky stocked a large closet with canned and dried food and other necessities, purchased in modest amounts over time to avoid drawing attention. Sara's father and Natan rerouted pipes to provide running water for a sink, shower, and toilet. Though the dormer windows faced the forest, Sara and her mother covered them with heavy blackout curtains, and made up the beds and put down rugs, not only for comfort, but to muffle their footsteps.

They did all of the work themselves. They could not risk entrusting their secret to contractors, strangers who might betray them later out of carelessness or malice. The household staff, whose integrity and loyalty Wilhelm swore was secure, treated their suddenly more frequent visits as perfectly unremarkable and pretended not to notice the sporadic bursts of activity in the castle's least-used wing.

"We may never need to spend a single night here," Sara's father told her mother. "Let us hope our hard work will prove unnecessary."

Her mother smiled wanly and agreed.

Then, in late June, Mr. and Mrs. Panofsky suddenly changed their plans. Germany had become too dangerous for Hans and Ruth, they told Sara's parents. Since Mr. Dodd and his family no longer resided at Tiergartenstrasse 27a, the children were not safe even in their own home. Friends in Great Britain had agreed to take them in, and although the thought of splitting up the family was hardly bearable, it would be a relief to have the children out of harm's way. And perhaps the family would not be separated for long. On March 1, two Aryan partners had officially taken over Jacquier and Securius, releasing Mr. Panofsky from his commitments to the bank. With nothing to hold them in Berlin any longer, they planned to emigrate to Great Britain as soon as it could be arranged. They had reached the top of the waiting list and it was only a matter of time until they were granted visas. The Panofskys reconciled themselves to the hard fact that as a condition of their emigration, they must relinquish nearly everything they possessed to the Reich and start over in a strange country with almost nothing.

"You've made the right decision," Sara's mother told Mrs. Panofsky, embracing her as she fought back tears. "One couldn't take such young children into hiding. They need to run and play and go to school."

"You should leave too," Mr. Panofsky urged Sara's father. "Nothing here is worth sacrificing your lives. Leave everything behind if you must, but get out before the door closes."

To Sara, it seemed the door was already barely ajar, open only wide enough for children like Hans and Ruth to slip through. The Weitzes had completed the emigration forms and filled out more as new regulations required. They were on waiting lists for Switzerland, Great Britain, the United States, and Canada. In the meantime, they had little choice but to keep their heads down in public, plan their escape to Schloss Federle if they were forced to go into hiding, and hope for the best.

And in the quiet shadows, Sara and Natan would continue the work of the resistance, although they privately agreed it seemed increasingly unlikely that Hitler would be brought down from within.

One evening in September, Sara went to the Harnacks' apartment for a meeting of the progressive study group. Mildred met her at the door, her face pale, stricken, her eyes red-rimmed. Immediately Sara assumed something terrible had happened to Arvid, but when she asked, Mildred pressed her lips together, shook her head, and gestured toward the living room. Anxious, Sara joined the other students, and in a quick exchange of whispers she learned that no one knew why Mildred was upset, although everyone in that room had good reason to be.

When the last student had arrived, Mildred took her usual chair at the top of the circle. "I apologize for my distress, and for worrying you," she said, lowering her gaze. "Arvid and I are fine, but I've had distressing news from America. An author I deeply admire, a friend—" She took a deep, steadying breath. "It grieves me to say that two days ago, Thomas Wolfe passed away."

The cause was miliary tuberculosis, Mildred told them, her voice catching in her throat. He had died a few weeks before his thirty-eighth birthday.

Even those who had not met Wolfe when he had visited Berlin were shocked and saddened by the news. Abandoning the evening's assigned reading, they instead contemplated Wolfe's work, the transformation of his understanding of the Nazis over time, the tragedy of a profound voice silenced too soon. That led them to sober reflections upon other voices that had fallen silent, lost to emigration, imprisonment, or death. Those who remained, determined to speak out through allegory or in the underground press, often found themselves muffled by censorship or drowned out by the loud, angry voices preaching intolerance and hate.

Earlier that month, the annual Nazi Party rally at Nuremberg had once again been a showcase for such vitriol. Excerpts from Hitler's speeches and descriptions of the rapturous cheers of his audience had appeared in German newspapers, but the students were skeptical of the Nazi-controlled press and urged Sara to share her impressions. As in years past, she had attended the rally to help Natan cover the events for the *Judische Nachrichtenblatt* and the underground press, and her fellow students hung on her every word as she described what she had witnessed. A rumble of disgust followed her account of Hitler's closing speech at the rally, in which he had attacked the president of Czechoslovakia and denounced what he called the oppression and humiliation of nearly three and a half million ethnic Germans living in the Sudetenland, a suppressed minority placed by the Treaty of Versailles "at the mercy of an alien power they hate."

Karl Behrens glowered. "Can there be any doubt that Hitler intends to invade the Sudetenland next?"

"Time will tell," Mildred said simply, and although the group exchanged uneasy glances, no one urged her to say more. Sara understood why Mildred did not disclose whatever her husband might have confided to her about a potential invasion. Although everyone in the study group was antifascist, not all were members of the resistance.

After the meeting, Mildred drew Sara aside as the other students packed up their books and left the apartment, singly and in pairs several minutes apart, to avoid suspicion. "Arvid recently came across disturbing information about Hitler's construction plans for Berlin," Mildred told Sara as soon as they were alone.

"There's nothing about that project that *isn't* disturbing," Sara replied. Within the past year, Hitler had spoken of reconstructing Berlin as the capital of the new Grossdeutsches Reich, the Aryan race, and civilization itself. "These buildings of ours should not be conceived for the year 1940," he had proclaimed in one public speech, "no, no, not for the year 2000, but like the cathedrals of our past, they shall stretch into the millennia of the future." It was said that Hitler's chief architect took him quite literally and intended to design this new German world capital so that it would be more beautiful and awe-inspiring than Paris and Vienna when it was newly complete, and as glorious as the ruins of Athens and Rome when Berlin too had experienced centuries of decay. The idea that Nazis would be in power long enough to sculpt the landscape of Berlin for even a decade filled Sara with revulsion, but to the Nazis, their Thousand-Year Reich was already a certainty.

"The architect's grandiose plans call for the demolition of older buildings in order to make room for the new," Mildred said, her gaze fixed steadily on Sara's. "As a result, many people will lose their houses and apartments. The architect recommends that Jews living outside the construction zone should be evicted from their homes to make room for displaced Aryans."

"Where are the Jews supposed to go?" asked Sara, aghast. "Will they be compensated?"

"As far as Arvid knows, the details haven't been worked out yet." Mildred took Sara's hand and gave it a gentle squeeze. "But I wanted you to be forewarned."

Sara nodded and murmured her thanks, her throat constricting as she imagined her mother's grief if she were forced from her beloved home. Their house was spacious, beautifully decorated, and in a desirable neighborhood—too good for Jews, she imagined the Nazi bureaucrats declaring. Would they be given sufficient notice to pack and find a new home on their own instead of accepting whatever the Reich assigned them? Or would the storm troopers come in the night, drag them from their beds, throw them into the street with nothing but the clothes on their backs?

"Your neighborhood might not be chosen for evictions," Mildred said, her gaze searching Sara's face and surely finding every fear and worry written there. "It might not happen at all."

"Maybe not, but we should prepare." Sara inhaled deeply to steady her nerves, dreading the thought of telling her parents. Perhaps she should urge them to sell their home before it was taken from them. They could always retreat to the Riechmann estate if they lost their home and if their visas failed to come through, but what of all the other Jews in Berlin?

"There's something else I wanted to—" Mildred's gaze flicked to the door, and they both fell silent at the sound of footsteps in the hall. When a key turned in the lock and Arvid entered, Mildred sighed with relief.

"Something else?" Sara prompted.

Mildred hesitated. "Greta and I plan to take Ule around the Tiergarten on Wednesday afternoon. Do you want to join us?"

Sara quickly agreed, eager to know what Mildred had been about to tell her before they were interrupted.

Two days later, she met Mildred, Greta, and eight-month-old Ule at the Englischer Garten in the northern section of the Tiergarten. As they headed toward the zoo, Mildred and Sara flanking Greta as she pushed Ule in his pram, Mildred quietly shared Arvid's latest news from the Economics Ministry. Hitler's vision of *Lebensraum* did indeed include the annexation of the Sudetenland—but as dreadful as it sounded, some good might come of it.

"One of Arvid's cousins at the Ministry of Justice has organized a conspiracy among certain German military officers and other prominent men," Mildred said, her voice barely above a murmur. "They intend to declare him unfit for office and remove him from power."

Essential preliminary measures had already been accomplished. Arvid's cousin Hans von Dohnányi had assembled a dossier documenting Hitler's criminal activities. An uncle, Karl Bonhoeffer, an eminent psychiatrist, was prepared to certify that Hitler was mentally ill. A high-ranking officer in military intelligence was in place to arrest him at a moment's notice, and a general, who until recently had served as a chief of staff, would handle relations with the military.

All the plan required to be set in motion was for Hitler to commit a reckless act of aggression, a breach of international law so outrageous that the democratic nations of Europe would be compelled to retaliate with united force. "This would disgrace him in the eyes of the German people and embolden his opponents," said Mildred. "When Hitler is vulnerable, Arvid's cousin and his group will take him into custody, remove him from office, and, with the cooperation of the military, restore democracy."

Sara felt a thrill of hope, but beside her, Greta walked steadily ahead, pushing the pram and frowning pensively. "Europe and America did nothing but complain when the Nazis sent tanks and troops into the Rhineland. Then came the *Anschluss*, and still they did nothing but protest from a distance. Why should anyone expect them to spring into action now?"

"If the German army invades Czechoslovakia, Great Britain would be obliged to go to war on their behalf," said Mildred.

"The same way they were obliged to go to war when Germany violated the Treaty of Versailles the first two times?"

"This would be different," said Sara, her excitement rising. "The Rhineland is within Germany's borders. The majority of Austrians welcomed annexation. But this would be the invasion of a foreign country that has no interest in becoming part of the Reich."

"I agree with your premises but not your conclusions," said Greta. "Yes, it would be an escalation of Hitler's aggression, but the response from the rest of the world would be the same."

"You don't know that," said Sara.

"Let's say for the sake of argument that Germany invades Czechoslovakia, and in return, Britain and France attack Germany," said Greta. "Why does Arvid's cousin assume this would turn the German people *against* Hitler rather than inspire them to rally *to* him?"

Mildred hesitated. "I suppose we must trust the expertise of the military officers among the conspirators."

"I want to believe it could work," said Greta, reaching into the pram to stroke Ule's dark curls. "Truly, I would. But if this plan depends upon intervention from the Allies, it will never happen."

In the days that followed, tensions heightened throughout Europe as heated, frenzied negotiations took place, concessions were offered, ultimatums issued. Hitler would not relent. On September 24, he declared that Czechoslovakia must cede its German-speaking regions to him within four days or he would take them by force.

For years Sara had prayed that war would be avoided, but now, knowing that Arvid's cousin and his coconspirators were poised to force Hitler from office if Britain and France were provoked into military action, she found herself wishing for it.

As September drew to a close, Hitler invited representatives of the other three most powerful nations of Europe—Neville Chamberlain of Great Britain, Benito Mussolini of Italy, and Édouard Daladier of France—to a summit in Munich to resolve the Sudeten crisis once and for all. Sara imagined the summit as a vigorous shouting match, with Hitler screaming and spitting on one side of the table, Mussolini seconding every declaration, Chamberlain and Daladier coolly regarding them from the opposite side, resolute in their refusal to let Hitler snatch up whatever parts of Europe caught his eye and tuck them into his pocket.

Then, on September 29, an announcement came from Munich: The four nations had reached an agreement. The German army could occupy the Sudetenland by October 10, and Great Britain, France, and Italy would not intervene. Czechoslovakia could submit to the German invasion or resist, but if they chose war, they would fight alone.

The next morning, recognizing the futility of their circumstances, the Czech government acquiesced. Later that day, Chamberlain and Hitler signed a peace treaty between Great Britain and Germany that Chamberlain proudly declared from 10 Downing Street would offer them "peace in our time."

Just as Greta had predicted, Hitler's aggression provoked no military response. The conspiracy led by Arvid's cousin fell apart.

Sara realized then what Greta had surely figured out long before: No one was coming from afar to save them. They had only one another, and they were on their own.

CHAPTER FORTY-TWO

October–November 1938

Greta

Greta had always believed that the Allies would not go to war over the Sudetenland if Hitler invaded, but she never could have predicted that the leaders of Great Britain and France would capitulate before a single German tank rumbled into the disputed territory. How could they believe that the Sudetenland would be enough for Hitler? The more of Europe he greedily consumed, the more ravenous he would become to devour the rest of it. They were deluding themselves if they thought otherwise. Greta could not understand why they treated Hitler as if he were a legitimate statesman. No one could believe any promise he made when he had already broken so many.

The Munich Pact had staggered the resistance, rendering them demoralized and shaken. For years they had watched in dismay as the vast majority of their fellow Germans embraced *Gleichschaltung*, adopting an unshakable belief in Aryan superiority and open hostility toward the Jews, the same people they had once considered friends, neighbors, and coworkers. It frightened Greta to see how quickly ordinary, reasonable people had become glassy-eyed, flag-waving, slogan-shouting fanatics. Then there were Germans who did not beat Jews in the streets or paint graffiti on synagogues but stood by passively, watching it happen, convincing themselves that it was none of their business. To Greta, they were no better than the Nazis who declared themselves with armbands and lapel pins.

The resistance would rally. They must, or everything they once loved about their country would be gone forever. Hitler's triumph in Munich and his seizure of the Sudetenland emboldened the Nazis to increase their oppression of the Jews, legislating spite and racism through a series of new restrictive laws. In early October, Jews' passports were declared invalid until they were surrendered to the authorities and returned to them stamped with a red J. By January 1, Jews whose names did not clearly indicate their heritage were required to add "Israel" or "Sara" to them, and all were required to carry identification cards noting their status as Jews. And if it were not already clear that the Nazis wanted to make life so miserable for the Jews that they would voluntarily emigrate even if it meant becoming impoverished refugees, the word *Judenfrei* began appearing in speeches and in the press, used almost wistfully to describe a purely Aryan Germany, entirely free of Jews.

At the end of October, dissatisfied with the pace of voluntary emigration, the Gestapo forcibly expelled roughly seventeen thousand Polish Jews, compelling them, often at gunpoint, to illegally cross the Polish border. When the government of Poland refused to let them enter, they were left stranded in a no-man's-land between the two countries. Many refugees made their way farther east, congregating around the Polish town of Zbąszyń about one hundred kilometers east of Frankfurt an der Oder, but others were so traumatized by deportation that they committed suicide.

"I could hardly believe my own eyes and ears," Greta's brother Hans wrote to her from her old hometown soon thereafter. "Hundreds of our fellow citizens lined the streets, shouting 'Out with the Jews! Off to Palestine!' as thousands passed through our city on trains and trucks, to be dumped like so much rubbish just over the border. They cannot stay, they will not be taken in. What will become of them?"

Although he dared not express his feelings more openly than that in a letter, Greta detected her brother's anger and disgust in the jagged strokes of his pen. She shared it. In some regions, the Gestapo had rounded up only the men, assuming that their wives and children would voluntarily follow after them, but elsewhere in Germany, entire families had been snatched up—men, woman, children, infants in arms. Many elderly deportees, frail and distraught, died before they reached their destination.

In the days that followed, Adam's Communist sources in Poland sent word that the Red Cross was feeding Jews stranded along the border, but they had no shelters and conditions were dire. International Jewish relief organizations had established a refugee camp near Zbąszyń and were pressuring the Polish government to allow some Jews to settle permanently in Poland and to help others obtain visas so they could emigrate elsewhere. Although Greta was relieved that some aid was being provided, it seemed woefully insufficient. She also feared that Poland's initial refusal to accept the Polish Jews, many of whom held Polish citizenship and passports, would echo in other countries as desperate German Jews were forced to flee the Reich and seek sanctuary in foreign lands.

Then, on November 7, news from France scorched radio wires throughout Europe. A seventeen-year-old named Herschel Grynszpan—a German-born Jew of Polish heritage residing with an uncle in France—had become distraught upon hearing that his elderly parents had been expelled from Germany and confined to a refugee camp. He had entered the German embassy in Paris and had shot a diplomat, seriously wounding him. At that moment, the diplomat was in critical condition and Grynszpan was in the custody of the French police.

"What did this diplomat have to do with the deportation order?" Greta asked Adam.

"Nothing, as far as I know," he replied. "Herschel Grynszpan is probably just a desperate, frightened young man, frantic about his parents. Maybe he wanted to draw attention to the plight of the Polish Jews living as refugees in the country of their birth. Maybe he didn't think it through, but struck back the only way he knew how."

Greta studied her husband, taken aback by the grim approval in his tone. "I don't see how any good can come of this. The Nazis will twist this attack to their own purposes as they always do."

"They might," Adam acknowledged, gently lifting their sleeping son from her arms. "But at least one Jew struck a blow."

"But at what cost?" Greta asked softly so she did not wake the baby. If Adam heard, he did not reply.

Two days later, they learned that Grynszpan's blow had proven fatal. Despite the valiant efforts of Hitler's personal physician, the German diplomat, Ernst vom Rath, had died of his wounds.

Later that evening, Greta and Adam left Ule in the care of a neighbor—Erika von Brockdorff, a countess married to an artist and the mother of a young daughter—so they could attend an important dress rehearsal for a revival of Friedrich Schiller's *Kabale und Liebe* at the Schiller Theater in Charlottenburg. For more than a year, the theater had been closed while the building underwent significant renovations, and the first night of *Kabale und Liebe* would mark the gala reopening. Adolf Hitler was scheduled to attend, and he would view the show from the *Führerloge*, a luxurious state box constructed especially for him. Under the circumstances, the theater could not be opened for the usual previews, so acquaintances from the theater world, friends who would not mind the construction dust, had been invited for a private showing to help the cast and crew prepare for the important night.

Adam had some misgivings about attending. He was barely on speaking terms with the director—Heinrich George, a former Communist turned Nazi collaborator who worked on several Reich propaganda films—but he had several friends in the cast and he owed the stage manager a favor. At the last minute, Adam accepted the invitation and suggested he and Greta make a night on the town of it.

Although Greta missed little Ule, she enjoyed the indulgence of an evening out with Adam alone, dressing up, savoring a leisurely meal at a fine restaurant rather than gobbling down something quick between feeding the baby and changing his diaper, conversing without interruption, seeing a play rather than collapsing on the sofa and taking turns trying to coax the baby to sleep.

The performance was going quite well, Greta and Adam agreed as they strolled to the lobby during intermission. They both noted only a few stumbles near the end of the first act, nothing the cast could not correct before opening night. But as she sipped a cocktail, Greta realized that most of the conversation around them was not about the show at all but rumors out of Munich.

That night marked the fifteenth anniversary of the Beer Hall Putsch, Hitler's failed coup attempt that had earned him a charge of high treason and eight months in jail. November 9 had become the Nazi equivalent of a Holy Day of Obligation, and National Socialist party leaders had gathered in Munich to commemorate the occasion. From what Greta and Adam overheard, other members of the audience had heard from friends in Munich that Goebbels had made a tempestuous speech accusing "World Jewry" of conspiracy in Grynszpan's assassination of Rath. The minister of propaganda had announced to the assembly that the Führer had decided the party should not prepare or organize any protests, but if demonstrations erupted spontaneously, they should not be thwarted.

"That's a rather poorly disguised call for violence," said Adam as blinking lights reminded the audience that the second act would begin shortly. As Greta and Adam returned to their seats, her heart sank as she recognized one Jewish friend sitting a few rows behind them, and another across the aisle. It was not a good night for Jews to be out and about in the city, not that any night was safe. She hoped they would not run into any storm troopers on their way home.

She was too distracted to enjoy the second act, impatient for it to end so they could return home to Ule. In the lobby, when Adam helped her into her coat and asked her what she thought of the show, she murmured a few compliments for the lead actress and the ensemble, but her thoughts were elsewhere.

They emerged from the theater onto Bismarckstrasse, still bustling despite the late hour. "Do you want to stop for a nightcap on the way home?" Adam asked, but his last words were drowned out by the wail of a siren.

At that same moment, Greta smelled smoke.

Quickly Adam seized her hand and strode off through the crowd, which only then Greta realized was mostly young men, jostling startled bystanders as they jogged along, shouting to one another. Her hand held fast in his, she hurried after Adam toward the Knie, the curve in the junction of five streets between Bismarckstrasse and Hardenburgstrasse. Suddenly just beside her a grinning young man flung a brick through a storefront window, shattering the glass.

Instinctively she turned her head away and raised her free arm to protect her eyes, but Adam was pulling her along, urging her to hurry. The smell of smoke intensified; the air carried shouts of *"Juda verrecke!"* and strains of the "Horst Wessel Lied." She glimpsed a yellow Star of David painted on a bookshop window, but as they hurried past, three young men bearing short clubs rushed forward and smashed it, sending a shower of crystal shards over them. Greta's cheek stung; as Adam quickened their pace, she wiped her cheek with the back of her hand and brought away a smear of blood.

Smoke billowed out of an alley just ahead. "This way," Adam shouted, turning sharply. Glass shards ground underfoot as she stumbled to keep up with him. They were headed south, she realized, opposite to the direction of home, but before she could urge Adam to turn back, they rounded a corner and discovered a tall building engulfed in flames.

Coughing, disoriented, Greta needed a moment to recognize the Fasanenstrasse Synagogue. Shock brought her to a sudden halt and her hand slipped from Adam's grasp. On the street before the synagogue, a dozen firefighters stood idle, smoking and laughing with a crowd of onlookers as flames consumed the temple. Others unleashed their hoses full force upon adjoining buildings to keep the fire from spreading, but the synagogue was allowed to burn freely.

The hateful laughter, the jubilant shouts, the roar of the flames, the wail of sirens filled Greta's ears as she stood and watched, her eyes tearing up from the smoke and the heat of the blaze. She felt Adam's arm around her shoulders. "We must get home before this gets any worse," he spoke loudly into her ear.

She nodded, her heart in her throat, a cold rush of fear coursing through her as she imagined the riot in their own neighborhood, fire threatening Ule. Taking Adam's hand, she ran alongside him for the trolley, but they found it packed full and at a dead stop in the middle of an intersection as a flood of rioters swept around it. Turning again, they glimpsed a sign for the Untergrundbahn and hurried toward it, but the crowd thickened between them and the entrance, forcing them to change direction twice more and work their way against the crowd until they were in the clear. Out of breath, they slowed their pace and went three blocks more until they reached another station. Everywhere they passed broken storefront windows of Jewish shops and businesses. Everywhere shattered glass littered the streets and sidewalks, glittering in the lamplight.

Eventually they made it back to their neighborhood, breathless, their clothes in disarray, their hair smelling of smoke. They found Erika waiting up for them, anxious and alarmed, little Ule slumbering peacefully in the cradle beside her daughter. "Greta, you're bleeding," Erika gasped, hurrying off to fetch a damp washcloth. Inspecting Greta's face, Adam called after Erika to bring a pair of tweezers too, and as he picked small fragments of glass from the narrow cut across her cheekbone, they told their horrified friend what they had witnessed.

When Greta's wound was cleaned and bandaged, they gathered up Ule and went home. Safe inside their own apartment, Greta laid the baby in his crib and returned to the living room to find Adam at the open window, gazing out into the night. The smell of smoke had grown fainter, but the sirens and shouting persisted—louder, perhaps, unless that was an illusion sparked by exhaustion and fear.

They cleaned themselves up, checked on Ule once more, and went off to bed, where they both lay awake listening to the fading sounds of the riot. Greta's thoughts churned with questions—whether they were safe in their apartment, if they should take Ule and flee, where they might go, what tomorrow would bring. Eventually she drifted off to sleep.

The next day Greta stayed home minding Ule and listening pensively to the radio. Adam ventured out, but he returned home early in the middle of the afternoon, outraged and shaken. Tens of thousands of Jews had been arrested, he told her, dragged from their homes, paraded through the streets, and eventually forced into trucks and hauled off to concentration camps. Jewish businesses were forbidden to reopen unless they were managed by an Aryan. Curfews had been imposed upon Jews, restricting them to their homes from nine o'clock in the evening until five in the morning. Almost every synagogue in Berlin had been desecrated and severely damaged, or destroyed utterly, after their archives had been stolen and turned over to the Sicherheitsdienst. What the Security Service intended to do with the records, one could only imagine.

"The official story is that these were spontaneous demonstrations, rising up from the *Volk*," said Adam as he dropped wearily into a chair. "Observe, the Nazis say, how almost no one in the mobs wore uniforms."

"I would argue that the absence of uniformed Nazis makes it even more suspicious," said Greta.

Adam nodded grim agreement, "The truth as far as my comrades understand it is that the regional Nazi Party leaders organized the riots in response to Goebbels's speech. They ordered the SA and the Hitler Youth not to wear their uniforms to create the illusion of a popular uprising."

A fuller picture of the nightmare came out in the days that followed. Nearly one hundred Jews had been killed and hundreds more injured. Throughout Germany, more than a thousand synagogues had been burned, and seventy-five hundred Jewish businesses had been destroyed. Jewish cemeteries and schools had been vandalized. And more than thirty thousand Jews had been arrested and sent to concentration camps, convicted of no crime, accused of nothing more than simply being Jewish.

On November 13, Mildred unexpectedly appeared at Greta's door. The Harnacks did not have a phone because Arvid was wary of wiretaps, so when Greta missed their usual weekly walk in the Tiergarten—in all the turmoil, she had completely forgotten the day—Mildred decided to check in to make sure they were all right.

When Mildred coaxed her to bring Ule out for a walk, Greta reluctantly agreed. She was surprised to find that most of the shattered glass had been swept up from the streets and pavements, although many broken storefront windows had yet to be repaired. Some had been boarded over, but many more stood gaping open, accusing mouths with sharp glass teeth silently demanding justice. Greta could hardly bear to look at them as she pushed Ule steadily along in his pram, Mildred beside her, neither of them speaking

"Walther Funk is calling it *Kristallnacht*," Mildred suddenly said. "Derisively, as one might expect, to make light of the Jews' suffering."

"Walther Funk?"

"The Reich minister of economics. Yesterday Hermann Göring held a meeting of top Nazi officials—himself, Goebbels, Reinhard Heydrich, Funk—"

"Arvid?"

Mildred allowed a small smile. "Not Arvid. He only heard about it later. The purpose of the meeting was to assess the damage and determine who was responsible for it."

"Responsible?" said Greta sharply. "Is there any doubt? Obviously Goebbels deserves the blame, although perhaps he would say he earned the credit."

"They're sticking with the story that this was a spontaneous protest, and therefore the Jews are to blame." Mildred sighed. "The real problem, as Göring sees it, is that Aryan insurance companies are now obliged to pay Jews for the damage done to their shops and businesses."

"That's some small measure of justice, at least."

"I'm afraid not. They've ruled to fine the Jews one billion marks to cover the cost of repairs. The six million marks the insurance companies have already paid for the broken windows must be turned over to the Reich."

"That's madness," said Greta, her voice low and flat. "How can they blame the Jews for the crimes committed against them? How do they expect to collect this outrageous fine?"

"I have no idea. Arvid is trying to find out." Mildred hesitated. "Something else came out at the meeting, though, and it's been troubling me ever since Arvid mentioned it."

Steeling herself, Greta adjusted Ule's blanket, tucking it more snugly around him. "And that is?"

"At the meeting, Göring announced that he had just received a letter written at Hitler's command, requesting that 'the Jewish question be now, once and for all, coordinated and solved one way or another.'"

"The Jewish question?" echoed Greta. "What's that supposed to mean? Coordinated and solved how?"

"That," said Mildred, "is what keeps me up at night."

Greta inhaled deeply and let out a long, shaky breath. Whatever it was, it meant suffering and death, she was sure of it.

The next time Greta and Mildred met was on the morning the news broke in the German papers that in protest to the pogroms, the United States had recalled its ambassador to Germany. Only a small staff, including Donald Heath, would remain behind to monitor American interests in Berlin. In response, Germany promptly withdrew its ambassador to the United States.

For years the resistance had hoped the United States and the nations of Europe would shake off their isolationist lethargy and join the fight to defeat fascism in Germany. Now they could only watch in dismay as one by one, potential allies withdrew from their country, leaving the resistance to struggle on alone.

CHAPTER FORTY-THREE

November 1938–April 1939

Sara

After Mildred told Sara that Jews might be forced from their homes to make room for Aryans displaced by Albert Speer's construction projects, Sara and Natan urged their parents to put their home up for sale before it was taken from them. "Get every mark you can for this place while you have the chance," said Natan. "You know if the Nazis seize it they'll give you nothing in return."

"But this is our home," their mother protested. "You children grew up here. We built our lives here."

"We're planning to emigrate anyway," Sara said. "If we move out now, we'll be ready to leave the moment our visas come through."

"*If* they come through," her mother countered, but eventually Sara and Natan convinced their parents to put their home on the market. Their father reminded them that moving the proceeds from the sale out of Germany would be a formidable challenge, but they would worry about that later.

A few people toured the house soon after it went up for sale, but they were more curious than serious, and made no offers. Then, in the middle of October, a couple in their late thirties came for a showing, first just the two of them, and then again with their three young children. On a third visit, the Wagners made an offer—reasonable, yet far less than Sara's parents would have considered were they not so eager to sell, especially since the purchase included most of the furniture.

As if worried the low bid would insult them, the Wagners hastily, apologetically explained their circumstances. Although they had both lived in Germany for nearly twenty years, by birth he was Austrian and his wife was Polish. Their current home was in a predominantly immigrant neighborhood with many other Poles, but given the recent disagreement between their two countries, it seemed prudent, for the sake of their children, not to draw too much attention to their Polish heritage, and to move as soon as possible.

"Earlier this year, my wife inherited a sizable trust from her late grandmother," Herr Wagner said, reaching for his wife's hand. "We could write you a cheque today for the entire amount, but the trust is held in a bank in Kraków, and we would be obliged to pay you in złoty."

"Usually most people turn us down at this point," said Frau Wagner with an anxious, self-deprecating smile.

Sara's father mulled it over. "As long as your bank confirms that the funds are available, I see no reason why the location of your trust should be an issue."

In the week that followed, Sara's parents and the Wagners haggled briefly over the price but soon reached an agreement. As Sara's parents waited for the Kraków bank to confirm that Frau Wagner's trust held sufficient funds, Wilhelm set up an account in his father-in-law's name with a bank in Geneva. After the Wagners' payment went through, Herr Wagner and Sara's father signed the paperwork, shook hands, and congratulated one another on a good deal fairly struck. The sale was complete, the income safe in a Swiss bank a short drive from Amalie and Wilhelm's chateau. Now all the Weitzes had to do was get to Geneva to claim it.

"Actually, from Switzerland the money could be transferred to any bank in the world, wherever we decide to settle," Sara remarked to her mother as they packed the belongings they planned to take along to the flat they had rented in Friedenau, a few blocks from the Kuckhoffs' place. Valuable artworks and family heirlooms not included in the sale had already been carefully wrapped, crated, and loaded onto a truck Natan had borrowed from a friend. Earlier that day, Sara's father and Natan had driven everything to Schloss Federle for safekeeping. They could have returned by nightfall, but they had decided to stay a few days to work on the hiding place and take inventory of their supplies.

That was November 8.

When the pogrom erupted, Sara's father and Natan could not risk driving back to Berlin, even though they were frantic with worry when their phone calls home did not go through. On the morning of November 10, when the SA swept through the city arresting Jews and the inevitable pounding on their own front door came, Sara's mother ordered her to run upstairs and hide.

"What about you?" Sara asked as her mother began pulling open kitchen drawers and closing them, searching for something.

"Go," her mother ordered, snatching up an apron and cap their former housekeeper had left behind. Her voice was iron. Sara turned and fled.

Crouching on the floor of the closet in Amalie's old room, Sara heard her mother open the front door and calmly greet the officers. Even when they demanded to see Natan, her manner remained briskly efficient as she replied that he was not there.

"He is a convicted criminal," one officer said. "We have his release papers identifying this as his permanent residence. His parole has been revoked. Bring him to us at once."

"As I said, I cannot."

"This is the home of his father, the Jew banker Jakob Weitz," said another officer, his voice hoarse as if he had been shouting for hours.

"Officers, you are mistaken," Sara's mother replied, feigning puzzlement. "This is the home of the Austrian businessman, Herr Ernst Wagner. He bought this house from Herr Weitz last month."

"Jakob Weitz! Natan Weitz!" the hoarse man called into the far reaches of the house. "Present yourselves immediately or we cannot guarantee the safety of anyone in this house."

"Goodness," Sara's mother exclaimed. "If you're going to make threats, just come in and look around. While you're in the study, please take note of the papers on the desk. You'll see I'm telling the truth. The Wagners own this house now. Herr Weitz and his son are not here."

When Sara heard boots crossing the foyer floor, she inched back into the depths of the closet and held perfectly still, hardly daring to breathe. While the men strode through the house, her mother pleaded for them to be careful. "My mistress is very particular," she said, begging the officers to mind this piece of furniture or that one, thus warning Sara where the men were.

They must have found the paperwork on the desk, for they abruptly called off the search. With no apologies for disturbing the household, they ordered Sara's mother to call the Gestapo immediately if the Weitzes should return. The front door slammed, the house fell silent, but Sara waited ten minutes more before she left the closet and crept downstairs.

She found her mother sitting at the kitchen table clad in the housekeeper's cap and apron, her head in her hands, her shoulders trembling as she wept without making a sound. Choking back sobs, Sara ran to her, knelt beside her chair, and embraced her.

"I was terrified," her mother confessed.

"You were brave. So very brave."

"They thought I was the housekeeper."

"Yes, I know. You fooled them."

"*I* was the fool. How stupid of me. What if they had asked my name, or for proof of my identity? What if they had found my passport? It was in the top desk drawer, right below the papers I told them to examine. What if they had bothered to ask the neighbors who lives here?"

"They didn't. Your ruse worked. We're safe." Suddenly Sara felt hysterical laughter bubbling up inside her. "Next time I'll be a housemaid and you be the cook."

"May there never be a next time," said her mother fervently. "It was only their impatience that spared us. They're cruel, but they aren't stupid. If they come to search again, they'll be more thorough."

Sara knew her family had to be long gone before then.

When Sara's father and Natan returned to Berlin after the violence subsided, they embraced Sara and her mother as if they had not expected to find them safe at home. Quickly Sara and her mother finished the little packing that remained while Natan loaded the borrowed truck. They left the house in such haste that Sara had no time for nostalgic farewells, for pausing in doorways and reminiscing about the happy moments she had spent in each room. By suppertime they were unloading their boxes and suitcases in the new flat in Friedenau.

As she prepared for bed that night, Sara tried to shake off the uncomfortable sensation that she was an itinerant guest in a stranger's home. To clear away the stale air in a room too long closed up, she opened the window and craned her neck to take in the view along the block. Cars passed on the street below. Several young men Sara's age strolled by, teasing one of their group about a girl who had spurned him at a bar they had just left. Through the windows of a restaurant down the street, she glimpsed couples dining by candlelight. In the gutters and alleyways, a few traces of broken glass glistened in the lamplight.

The mid-November night was too cold to leave the window open long, but before she closed it, Sara thought she detected the faint scent of char. She assumed it came from one of the two restaurants visible from her room, but the next morning Natan told her the source was probably the Synagogue Prinzregentenstrasse two blocks away, now a gutted ruin choked with ashes.

As the Weitzes were unpacking and settling in, the Nazis issued a series of punitive decrees apparently designed to prevent Jews from living anything resembling a normal life. To the mass arrests, deportations, and enormous fines to pay for the destruction of *Kristallnacht*, the Reich added a new obligation for Jews to keep their businesses shuttered, but to pay their employees nonetheless and make repairs at their own expense. Beginning January 1, Jews would no longer be allowed to run retail, handicraft, or mail-order businesses, nor could they serve in any position in which they managed personnel. Jewish executives within corporations must be given six weeks' notice and dismissed. And if the Jews wanted to forget their troubles for a while by enjoying some entertainment, they were on their own, for they were banned from theaters, cinemas, concert halls, museums, sports facilities, and similar public places.

The restrictions kept coming, onerous and unrelenting. The *Juden-*

bann was extended to include restaurants that were not run by Jews. In the first week of December, Jews were prohibited to enter government buildings or even to live nearby. In the same decree, they were forbidden to own or operate automobiles or motorcycles. All German Jews were ordered to turn in their driving permits and automobile registration papers by the last day of the year.

"How will we escape to Schloss Federle if we can't drive?" Sara asked Natan.

"Our plans haven't changed," said Natan. "If the police pull us over while we're fleeing for our lives, being caught without a driving permit will be the least of our problems."

"But we're not even allowed to own a car anymore," said Sara, struggling to contain her rising panic. "Jews have to turn in their registrations. What reason could there be for the Nazis to collect all that paperwork except to let them know where to confiscate the cars?"

Natan thought for a moment. "I have a friend, an auto mechanic. I'll ask him to keep our car at his garage. If the Nazis come looking for it, we'll explain that we sold it."

But even as he was making arrangements, a worse blow fell.

Effective immediately, Jews would be excluded from most of the west side of Berlin, including the Tiergarten and important thoroughfares such as Unter den Linden, Wilhelmstrasse, Leipzigerstrasse, Kurfürstendamm, and Friedrichstrasse. They would need a police permit to travel through the area, and therefore Jews with homes in the area were encouraged to trade residences with Aryan Germans living elsewhere. The ban would not cover neighborhoods in central and northern Berlin, poorer blocks already heavily populated by Jews, creating a ghetto roughly defined by Linienstrasse and Grenadierstrasse.

The Weitzes found little comfort in knowing that their flat in Friedenau fell just outside the *Judenfrei* zone. A ban, once created, could easily be expanded.

On the last day of the year, the Weitzes relinquished their driving permits, but they entrusted the car registration and ownership papers to Natan's mechanic friend. There were no more drives through the countryside to admire the snowy landscape, no impromptu trips to

Schloss Federle to restore themselves in a remote haven free of swastikas and black-clad SS. The city Sara had always cherished as her modern, sophisticated, intellectual hometown had become steadily more oppressive as her movements were restricted, constraining her tighter and tighter until she felt as if it were a struggle just to breathe. The new apartment felt cramped compared to the comfortable, elegant home they had left behind, but she was so grateful that her family was together and safe that she never complained. The hiding place at Schloss Federle would be smaller yet, and she knew the day might come when she longed for the relative spaciousness of Friedenau.

In January, after Mildred warned her that Arvid had heard rumors that additional housing restrictions for Jews might be issued as early as spring, Sara broke the news to her family with a heavy heart. "Perhaps we should begin looking for an apartment in the ghetto," her mother suggested, dividing the last of the evening's supper between her husband's plate and Natan's. "This way we can choose for ourselves before the best places are taken, and before the Nazis choose for us."

Since traversing the city while avoiding areas from which Jews were banned had become an arduous ordeal, Sara and Natan urged their parents to stay home while they looked into a few places Natan's friends in the area had recommended. Their parents gratefully accepted, relieved to avoid a chance encounter with storm troopers who might demand to see their identity cards and, upon seeing the red Js, publicly humiliate them, or worse.

It took Sara and Natan nearly two hours to navigate the new topography of Berlin between Friedenau in the southwest suburbs and the ghetto in the northeastern part of the city, but to Sara, the destination was worse than the journey. She struggled to hide her dismay as they toured one vacant apartment after another, unable to imagine their family living in any one of them. Wordlessly she noted peeling paint, rusty pipes, water-stained ceilings, lingering odors of cabbage and onions and sometimes urine, stairwells littered with debris, drafty rooms so cold she assumed a window had been left open until a closer look told her otherwise.

Sara was both disappointed and relieved when they left the last apartment on Natan's list. "You know," he remarked as they stopped at a small Jewish café to warm themselves with coffee and a piece of *Kuchen* to share, "many people have lived in this neighborhood happily for years, and they didn't need the Nazis to force them here."

Sara's cheeks flushed. "I don't mean to be a snob," she said in an undertone, "but can you imagine Mutti being content in any of the places we saw today?"

"My old place wasn't much better."

"You know that's not true."

"Okay, maybe not. But you saw how nicely Mutti fixed up our retreat in the country. She'd do the same with one of these apartments." Before Sara could argue that the hiding place in Schloss Federle had started out in much better structural condition than the apartments, Natan added, "I'm more worried about Papa. He'll be crushed to see how far we've fallen."

"It's not his fault."

"Of course not, but he's always provided so well for his family. It's a blow to a man's pride when he no longer can. You and I would get along fine here, but our parents?" He shook his head.

They agreed that they could not return home with nothing to show for their search, so they chose the best of the vacant apartments and planned how they would describe it to their parents—honestly, but with optimism, promising that it would be easy to refurbish it themselves. Later, over supper, their parents listened with interest, but Sara doubted they were fooled.

Natan returned to the ghetto a few times throughout January and February as he received tips about new vacancies, but otherwise the Weitzes settled into the Friedenau flat as if they intended to stay. Restrained by the curfew, Sara spent most of her evenings in her room with her books or listening to the radio with her parents, but occasionally she went to Greta's flat for *Kaffee und Kuchen*, or to mind the baby while Greta ran errands for her freelance work or the resistance.

Travel restrictions imposed on Jews meant that Sara saw Mildred even less frequently than she saw Greta. She could no longer accompany her friends and one-year-old Ule on walks through the Tiergarten, nor could she join her former classmates for friendly debates at any of the cafés near campus. Increasingly isolated, she lingered at Mildred's flat after a study group meeting even though she risked being caught on the streets after curfew, just so she could pour out her heart to her sympathetic teacher and friend.

"Is emigration any more likely?" asked Mildred.

"We could leave Germany tomorrow if we had anyplace to go," Sara said, fighting back tears. "We haven't been able to get entry visas."

Mildred nodded and drank the last of her coffee. Then she fixed her calm blue-eyed gaze on Sara and said, "How would your family feel about Norway?"

Sara's heart leapt as she recalled how Mildred had helped the Jewish editor Max Tau escape to Norway in the weeks after *Kristallnacht*. Mildred had divulged few details, and she probably would have said nothing at all except to ease Natan's worries. The two men were friends, and in the aftermath of *Kristallnacht* when Max Tau had disappeared, Natan had searched in vain for him, fearing he had perished in a concentration camp.

"I've always wanted to see Norway. I've heard it's beautiful. But—" Sara hesitated. "Switzerland would be better."

Mildred smiled. "Of course. Let me see what I can do."

"What can you do? Ambassador Dodd is gone. The American embassy is nearly empty."

"But not entirely so." Mildred glanced at the clock. "You should be on your way, unless you'd like to spend the night?"

Sara thanked her but refused, knowing her parents would worry. Impulsively she hugged Mildred and darted out the door, and as she hurried home through a flurry of icy snow quickly turning into slush beneath her boots, she decided not to mention anything rather than give her family false hope.

She sustained her own hopes, alone, as the winter passed without any word from Mildred's contacts. In March the winds softened and the days lengthened, and she imagined the first buds of spring appearing on the trees and in flower beds in the Tiergarten. She longed to stroll there one last time, but doubted she ever would.

Then, at the end of March, Mildred surprised her by turning up at her family's apartment, eyes shining. When Mildred invited her for a walk, Sara quickly threw on a sweater and accompanied her outside.

Sara was banned from the nearby parks, so they kept to the sidewalks, saying little until they came to a small *Platz* and sat down upon an empty bench where they would see anyone approaching. "I have entrance visas for Switzerland," Mildred told her.

"Really?" Sara gasped. "Oh, Mildred, how will I ever thank you?"

"Sara—" Mildred hesitated. "I'm so sorry. I'm afraid I could only get two."

Sara's breath caught in her throat. "Oh. I see."

"I might be able to get two more in a few months."

"Two is better than none." Sara clasped her hands together in her lap and squeezed her eyes shut, suddenly lightheaded. "My parents will insist that my brother and I take them. My brother will insist that my mother and I do."

"The choice is yours. I'm sorry to give you this burden. I wish—"

"It's not a burden. This is a gift, a great blessing. Two of us are going to get out."

And two would be left behind.

As they walked back to Sara's apartment, Mildred promised to keep trying to acquire more visas, and Sara promised not to lose hope.

She needed only two days and one heated debate with her brother to confirm the choice, which in truth she had made moments after she and Mildred parted. She only wanted her brother's blessing first.

Her parents were overjoyed when Sara announced that within a month they would be in Geneva with Amalie and their grandchildren. Natan offered to book the train tickets to give them more time to tie up loose ends and bid old friends farewell.

"How thankful I am that we won't need our country retreat after all," Sara's mother said with a sigh on the eve of their departure, as they lingered over a late supper. Four suitcases and two trunks were already packed and waiting by the front door. Their precious family heirlooms would remain at Schloss Federle for safekeeping.

The next day, April 20, dawned bright and sunny, bursting with the full, verdant beauty of spring. Sunshine from cloudless blue skies bathed the city in warmth and light. On the radio they were calling it *Führerwetter*, as if nature itself had joined in the national holiday celebrating Adolf Hitler's fiftieth birthday. Every German household had been ordered to fly the swastika flag in honor of the occasion—Jews were prohibited from doing so—and more than fifty thousand troops would march in a grand parade before an anticipated two million spectators. It was expected to be the greatest event the Nazis had ever staged, an elaborate spectacle of historic significance, and the Weitzes were all too happy to miss it.

They tried to hail a cab; several sped past without slowing down, discouraged either by their luggage or their suspect Jewish appearance. Eventually one halted and they piled in, and as they drove to the station, Sara's mother inclined her head toward the ubiquitous swastika banners they passed. Leaning closer to Sara, she murmured, "I certainly won't miss all this."

Sara pressed her lips together to hold back a sob and forced a smile, turning quickly away so her mother would not see her tears.

All too soon they were standing on the platform, awaiting the arrival of the train. Natan paced nearby, his hands thrust in his pockets, working off his agitation. A distant whistle caught his attention, and the announcement that their train was approaching brought him to a halt. He threw Sara a despondent look, and she knew it was time.

"The tickets," Sara's mother exclaimed suddenly, clutching her pocketbook to her side. "Sara, do you have them?"

"I have them," said Natan, taking from his coat pocket a thick envelope, which he gave to his father. "The visas are here too. You should carry them the rest of the way." He raised his eyebrows at Sara, urging her to speak, as they had planned, before time ran out.

"Papa, Mutti—" Sara cleared her throat. "First, I love you both very, very much. Second, I'm sorry I couldn't tell you the truth any earlier than this. Third—"

"She could only get two visas," Natan broke in, impatient. To Sara he added, "They'll miss the train if you drag this out any longer."

For a moment her parents stared at her, dumbfounded, until realization dawned. "So, this is goodbye," her father said, with false heartiness. He came forward and embraced her. "That's fine. We'll be all right. Kiss your sister for me."

"No, Papa. The visas are for you and Mutti. You two are going. Natan and I are staying here."

Their parents protested, as Sara and Natan had known they would. As the conductor called all aboard, Sara quickly explained that she might be able to get two more visas soon, but not before the two they already had would expire. They must go in pairs. It was the only way. Then their father and mother pressed the visas and tickets upon their children, and Sara had to point out that they were in their parents' names. No one else could use them. Even the suitcases belonging to Sara and Natan held their mother's and father's clothing. Sara had emptied and repacked them the night before while their parents slept.

"You did all of this without our knowledge or consent," her mother said tearfully.

"Yes, because otherwise you wouldn't go." Sara embraced her. "You have to go. Now. You can't miss this train. We'll see you again in Switzerland."

Natan hauled their luggage toward the train, his jaw set as if he were prepared to carry his parents aboard too if he must. With minutes to spare, they embraced on the platform, distraught parents and resolute children saying farewell for no one knew how long.

At the last moment, Sara's mother gripped her tightly by the shoulders. "Sell the silver. The utensils and smaller pieces are stored in two brown leather cases at Schloss Federle with the other heirlooms. Phone Herr Albrecht, the groundskeeper, and arrange for him to deliver them to you. It was going to be yours someday anyway. Sell it piece by piece. Find a good, safe place to live and don't let yourself go hungry." She released Sara and turned to embrace her son. "Please watch over her. She has a way of stumbling into trouble."

"Don't I know it," Natan replied gruffly, holding his mother close and kissing the top of her head.

The whistle blew. Their parents hurried aboard the train and quickly appeared at a window. They waved, their eyes bright with tears, until the train pulled too far ahead and Sara and Natan could not see them anymore.

"They might forgive you someday," Natan remarked as the train disappeared into a tunnel.

"Will you?"

He pulled a face. "There's nothing to forgive. You did the right thing. Like I said in the ghetto, you and I can survive here. They couldn't. And now, thanks to you, they won't have to."

Thanks to Mildred and her mysterious contact, Sara almost added, but she kept silent. She could tell from bystanders' sidelong glances and curious stares that their tearful parting had attracted notice. Natan must have sensed it too, for he put his arm around her shoulders and quickly ushered her from the platform.

She tried not to brood over the onlookers' hostile, curious stares as she and her brother made their way back to Friedenau. Just as they turned onto their street, a mechanical roar thundered overhead. Shading her eyes with her hand, Sara looked up and spotted airplanes flying in precise military formation toward the northeast, wave after wave of aircraft, dark, angular shapes stark and swift against the cerulean sky.

"Heinkels and Messerschmitts," said Natan. "The Luftwaffe's on their way to the Brandenburg Gate to send old Adolf best wishes on his birthday."

"May he never see another," Sara retorted, her gaze fixed on the soaring aircraft, heedless of who might overhear.

CHAPTER FORTY-FOUR

May–August 1939

Mildred

Although the American presence in Germany had greatly diminished, as long as Donald Heath remained at his post, Arvid and Mildred trusted that the State Department knew what was going on in Germany. What the United States government would do with that information was another question entirely.

On long, deceptively sedate walks through the Tiergarten, embraced by gentle breezes carrying the fragrance of fresh blossoms and the music of songbirds, the two men walked a few paces ahead, their voices quietly urgent as they discussed what Germany's finances revealed about Hitler's plans for the future. Mildred and Louise followed after with Don Jr., keeping a lookout for anyone who might be trailing them or observing them too keenly as they passed.

By late spring, Arvid was convinced that Hitler intended to invade Poland. He was equally certain that if France and Great Britain stood united in strong opposition, imposing strict economic sanctions or sending in troops to curtail Hitler's plans for expansion, the damage to his prestige could be enough to bring down the Nazi regime from within. Arvid also told Heath that the resistance distrusted Neville Chamberlain and suspected he sympathized with Hitler. "Chamberlain suffers under the illusion that Hitler's ambition is limited to Eastern Europe and that he can be appeased with some gifts of territory here and there," Arvid said. "My friends and I aren't fooled. We place our trust in Roosevelt and in his democratic ideals. We believe in him. We only hope he believes in us."

Mildred and Arvid had no doubt that Heath trusted the intelligence Arvid provided, but as summer approached, they began to suspect that the United States government would never understand the perilous urgency of the situation unless they heard it from Arvid himself.

Unexpectedly, an opportunity arose to test their theory.

In July, the Economics Ministry sent Arvid to Washington to meet with U.S. trade officials. His official assignment was to secure copper and aluminum supplies for Germany's factories, but he had a second, secret mission of his own to offer to help the United States against the Third Reich. Heath had arranged for him to meet with several trusted colleagues in the Treasury Department, and he assured Arvid that if they were impressed with his interview, they would take his offer to the secretary of state.

Mildred accompanied Arvid as he sailed from Hamburg to New York, but while he continued on to Washington, she remained in New York to visit friends, after which she would embark on a lecture tour of several universities in the Northeast and Midwest. Since it was *verboten* to take enough money as she needed out of Germany, her friend Clara Leiser had invited her to stay with her while she was in the city.

Mildred had not seen Clara since she had visited Berlin in August 1935 on behalf of the New York courts. As Mildred unpacked her suitcase in the guest room, Clara sat cross-legged on the floor and asked if the grim reports out of Germany were accurate.

"Whatever you've learned from the American press," Mildred replied wearily, "the reality is far worse."

"Why haven't you put any of this in your letters?" Clara protested. "The Nazis haven't turned you, have they?"

"Of course not," Mildred replied, taken aback. "Our mail is censored, and the Gestapo isn't constrained by ordinary laws. They can arrest anyone on a whim, condemn anyone to prison or a concentration camp without even the pretense of a trial."

"Ah, yes, their trials." Clara sighed. "I remember them well. I wish more had come of my work in Berlin than a stern condemnation of the farcical Nazi judicial system from the New York judiciary. I was so annoyed by their silence that I started a book, a collection of quotes from Hitler and other prominent Nazis. Let them condemn themselves with their own words." Suddenly she brightened. "You could help me. You could send me anecdotes and quotes from Berlin, choice bits that don't make it into the papers."

"I'd like to help, but . . ." Mildred put her last blouse on a hanger and shut the closet. "As I told you, our mail is censored. A letter containing disparaging stories about prominent Nazis would probably never make it out of the country. Worse yet, anything I put in a letter could be used against me, or against Arvid."

Clara studied her, frowning. "Wouldn't it be worth it, to make the American people aware of what they're really like?"

"Worth my life? I'm sorry, Clara, but if I'm going to risk my life, and Arvid's, and his family's—" She shook her head. "It will have to be to accomplish something no one else can do, and in no other way."

Disappointed, Clara shrugged and let the subject drop, but as the days passed, Mildred sometimes caught her old friend studying her, worry and suspicion in her eyes.

It was the first, but regrettably not the last, uncomfortable exchange of Mildred's visit. In their Madison days Clara had been confident and outspoken, but over the years she had become more blunt and less thoughtful, quicker to judge and unwilling to temper her criticism. On one occasion, when Mildred mentioned that she planned to inquire about faculty positions at the universities she visited on her lecture tour, Clara winced and said, "I don't mean to be cruel, but don't you realize that people who have been teaching American literature for years, and are already living on this side of the Atlantic, *and* have earned their doctorates haven't been able to find work?"

"I understand jobs are scarce," said Mildred, "but it wouldn't hurt to ask."

"Why waste your time? You know you'd never leave Arvid, not for the best faculty job in America."

"No, I probably wouldn't," Mildred conceded, forcing a smile. She had no intention of leaving him. If she were fortunate enough to land a faculty position in the States, she would convince him to return with her or she would decline the offer. Still, she thought it unkind of her longtime friend to imply that it was presumptuous of her to inquire.

Of all the friends she had hoped to see while she was in New York, after Clara, Martha had been at the top of the list. As soon as Arvid booked their tickets, Mildred had written to Martha at her new address on Central Park West to let her know when she would be in the city. No reply came before they sailed, but eight days after her arrival, a small package arrived for her at Clara's apartment. It was dense and solid, wrapped in heavy brown paper with a postmark from Ridgefield, Connecticut. Unwrapping it, Mildred discovered a book with a red cover and the title and author printed in gold type on the spine. "*Through Embassy Eyes*," Mildred read aloud, "by Martha Dodd."

Astonished and apprehensive in equal measure, Mildred settled down in a chair by the window and opened the book. Inside the front cover she found an ivory-colored envelope holding a letter written on ivory stationery with a black border, which she recognized as the same one Martha had used in May 1938 when she had shared the sorrowful news of her mother's unexpected death from heart failure.

"I'm sorry I won't be able to see you while you're in the city," Martha had written. "I so wanted to introduce you to my darling Alfred and to hear all the news from Berlin, and to see the expression on your face when I handed you my book. Can you believe it? After all my talk about my audacious ambition, I finally did it. It's part memoir, part juicy exposé. If I have to be a bit indiscreet to open people's eyes about what's going on in Nazi Germany, then so be it."

Mildred's heart plummeted. How indiscreet had Martha been? Surely she would not have been so eager to drive up book sales and settle old scores that she would have put the lives of her friends in the resistance in jeopardy.

Steeling herself, Mildred read on.

"You'll recognize yourself in these pages, I have no doubt," Martha continued. "But never fear. I named no names—well, I named plenty of names, as you'll see, but not yours and not Arvid's. I refer to you once as 'a German married to an American' and another time as 'a lovely German woman who detests the terror of Nazi Germany.' No one will ever guess I meant you."

Mildred hoped with all her heart that Martha was right.

"I'm afraid you'll have to finish the book before your return journey, because it's been banned in Germany," Martha added. "Those tender, sensitive Nazis couldn't bear to have unflattering—but utterly truthful—portrayals of themselves flying off bookstore shelves from Hamburg to Munich. So read through to the end before you go back to Berlin, or, better yet, don't go back at all. I know what it's like, and as your true friend I urge you not to return. If money is the issue, you can stay with me and Alfred in New York or our estate in Connecticut. If you're worried that Arvid will object, don't. I'm sure he cares for your safety above all else."

He did, Mildred reflected. She was rather surprised that he had not suggested she stay in America too, unless he was saving that argument for when they reunited after her tour.

"Please write to me before you return to Germany so I'll receive at least one letter in which you can speak freely without fear of the censors," Martha urged. "It's frustrating to know so little and worry so much about our mutual friends. Please take good care of yourself. Be safe and know that I'm doing what I can on this side of the Atlantic by telling the truth of what I witnessed there."

Perhaps Martha's book would help change minds, Mildred thought as she returned the letter to its envelope. As the former ambassador's daughter and an eyewitness to the rising Nazi menace, she was well placed to refute the angry shouts of the "America First" movement.

Mildred read *Through Embassy Eyes* in two days. Although it was forthcoming and detailed, she found it more gossipy than intellectual, but she still hoped it would enlighten American readers. She was relieved to find that Martha had protected her sources in the resistance well, although she had not done the same for certain Nazi officials who deserved censure. "If there were any logic or objectivity in Nazi sterilization laws Dr. Goebbels would have been sterilized quite some time ago," she had written archly in a profile of the propaganda minister, and if Adolf Hitler ever read Martha's description of their lunch date, he would surely explode in a fit of outrage and humiliation. It was little wonder the book had been banned throughout the Third Reich.

On her last day in New York, Mildred began her lecture tour at New York University. Clara and several other academic friends were in the audience, which appeared to number more than two hundred. In her presentation, titled "The German Relation to Current American Literature," she spoke of how renowned American authors such as Theodore Dreiser, Jack London, Carl Sandburg, and Thomas Wolfe were regarded in Europe. As she discussed various political and social themes in the authors' works, she spoke candidly about the Nazi blacklisting of "degenerate" authors and the massive book burnings of May 1933. "I not only witnessed important works of literature turning to ash," she told them, "but also the absolute suppression of dissenting voices that followed."

Her remarks met with enthusiastic and sustained applause. Several professors and students approached her afterward with questions about literature or the state of affairs in Germany, which she answered as thoughtfully and thoroughly as she could. Most of these conversations were cordial and interesting, but two stood out as oddly strained, even confrontational. The first was with a man—dressed almost entirely in brown except for his black boots, an outfit disconcertingly reminiscent of the Brownshirts—who wanted her opinion on the "rhetorical genius" of Joseph Goebbels. The other was with three smiling young blond women clad in nearly identical black skirts and white blouses who expressed admiration for her work and wanted to know how, as a wife and mother, she found time for a career. "I have no children," she said simply, nodding politely when they expressed their abundant pity. She refrained from pointing out that no one ever asked her husband or any other man how, as a husband and father, he managed to find time for a career.

She tried to forget those brief unpleasant moments and simply enjoy her success. That evening, Clara threw her a combination farewell party and celebratory reception, crowding into her apartment about four dozen old acquaintances Mildred had not seen in years and who had come into the city especially to see her. Several had attended her lecture, and most congratulated her warmly, but one former colleague from her brief stint at Goucher College peered at her over the rim of his glass, took a deep drink, and remarked, "You were awfully friendly with that bunch from the Bund."

"The Bund?" Mildred echoed.

"The German American Bund. Surely you didn't miss the uniforms. That fellow in the jackboots and the girls in the black-and-white getups and blond braids." He took another drink, regarding her quizzically as if he was not sure whether her confusion was genuine. "The Bund is an American pro-Nazi organization, if that's not a contradiction in terms. They number in the thousands across the country, holding pro-Hitler rallies, waving their swastika flags, putting their little boys in summer camps like the Hitler Youth. It's all rather disgusting."

"I couldn't agree more." Mildred pressed a hand to her stomach, suddenly nauseous. Had she said anything that could put her friends or Arvid's family in danger should those Bund people report it to the Gestapo? "I wonder why they came to my lecture."

"I was wondering the same thing," he said flatly, draining his whiskey sour in one last gulp and moving off into the crowd.

After that, Mildred guarded her words, plagued by thoughts of storm troopers apprehending Greta as she strolled with Ule in the Tiergarten, or hauling Arvid's brother Falk out of a classroom in Munich, or dragging his mother away from her easel at her home in Jena. What might they do to the people she loved in retaliation for anything offensive she said or did? What might they do to her and Arvid the moment they disembarked from their ship at Hamburg?

More than once, as the evening passed, she caught herself glancing over her shoulder in midsentence and turning back to find the person she was conversing with watching her, bemused. These were old friends, she admonished herself. None of them corresponded with Nazis. And yet she could not shake off her cautious reserve. Any hope she might have had that no one noticed was dispelled when, just as she was about to enter the kitchen, she overheard someone within telling a companion that she feared Mildred had "gone Nazi." Rather than enter the room and calmly reassure them that she had not, she silently withdrew.

It was with heartbreaking relief the next morning that she packed her bags, tucked Martha's book carefully in with her academic papers, thanked Clara for her hospitality, and departed for Penn Station. She caught the midmorning train to Philadelphia and from there traveled on northwest of the city, where later that evening she spoke at Haverford College. There the reception to her lecture was even more enthusiastic than in New York. "You discussed these contemporary trends in European literature with a charm, power, and vividness that I have rarely seen equaled," declared one philosophy professor when he and several other faculty members joined her onstage afterward as the audience filed from the auditorium. "You have almost restored my ebbing faith in the function of the interpretive lecture."

Mildred could hardly have asked for higher praise than that, but her glow of gratitude diminished when she glimpsed members of the German American Bund congregating in one of the aisles, watching her expectantly, no doubt hoping to speak with her on her way out. Fortunately, her hosts instead led her backstage and out a side door to a cab, which quickly whisked her off to the charming inn where they had arranged for her to spend the night.

A similar scene played out at the University of Chicago, except that four men in derivative Brownshirt uniforms approached her podium before her host could escort her away. They asked, politely and in very good German, if she and her chaperone would do them the honor of joining them for dinner. Before Mildred could respond, the event host, a silver-haired professor of Germanic languages, answered in flawless German that Frau Harnack must offer her regrets due to a prior engagement for which she was already five minutes late. "You didn't look like you wanted to go with them," she said in an undertone after the men walked away disappointed. "I certainly didn't, and it would have been inappropriate for you to go alone."

"Thank you," Mildred murmured back. "I'd much rather have dinner with you, if you're free."

Mildred suggested a restaurant she had visited years before, but the professor insisted upon treating her to a home-cooked meal. Quite serendipitously, Mildred found herself sharing a delicious supper with the professor, her husband, and their eldest granddaughter, and spending the night in their redbrick town house on South Blackstone Avenue in

Hyde Park, less than a block away from where the Dodds had lived when Mr. Dodd was on the university faculty.

By the time her tour brought her to Madison, she had learned to spot members of the Bund at a glance even when they were not clad in their full regalia, and to evade their pointed questions.

The lecture at the University of Wisconsin was the event she had most looked forward to, and it proved to be a wonderful homecoming. Many friends and former teachers and colleagues were in the audience, as well as her brother and his family. Her former mentor, William Ellery Leonard, also attended—but he provided the lone disappointing moment of the evening. He damned her with faint praise when a group of former classmates cheerfully asked for his review of her lecture, saying with a shrug that it was precisely what he had expected it to be. Mildred concealed her embarrassment with a smile, but she could not maintain the pretense later when he took her aside and told her that there were no faculty positions available for her in Madison. "You have many splendid achievements as wife, as *Frau Professorin*, and as an ambassador of American literature, since you've mastered a foreign language well enough to translate our nation's great works for that wonderful culture," he said, smiling indulgently with only the barest trace of regret. "But unfortunately, we don't need this in Madison in these wretched days."

"I understand completely," Mildred said, smiling, pleasant, professional. "I trust you'll let me know if circumstances change."

She was not surprised to hear that the UW English Department had no faculty positions available; none of the other universities on her tour were hiring either. What troubled her most was Leonard's dismissive, condescending tone. She did not understand what she had done to disappoint him, but apparently her former mentor no longer believed in her. Perhaps it was the simple fact that she had never completed her doctorate. That, at least, she could put right. As soon as she returned to Berlin, she would resume work on her dissertation in earnest and not stop until she had earned her degree. Even if she could no longer count on Leonard for a letter of recommendation, she would have a much better chance of finding a university position with her doctorate in hand.

Although her job search had proven fruitless, and her encounters with the German American Bund unsettling, she did not regret her tour. Her lectures had been well received, and she had met several fascinating scholars with whom she hoped to keep in touch. She had reunited with old friends, which had been lovely, most of the time. After the Madison event, she spent several days at her brother Bob's farm south of Madison, enjoying his company and that of her sister Marion, their spouses, and their children. Surrounded by loved ones on the beautiful, rich land thriving beneath the capricious midwestern skies, she felt truly at home for the first time since she had returned to America. But when she walked through the apple orchard where she and Arvid had married, she longed for him so intensely that tears came to her eyes.

Even more urgently than Martha had done, her brother and sister begged her not to return to Germany. They offered her and Arvid a place to stay until they found work and could get back on their feet.

"If we can't earn a living, we can't stay," she said after explaining her futile job search. "Also, we have important work to do back home."

Her siblings exchanged a look. "You called Germany home," Marion said sadly.

"Wherever Arvid is, that's home," she replied, and when they glanced at their own spouses, she knew they understood.

The visit restored her spirits more than she could have imagined possible. In early August, as she traveled by train east to Washington where Arvid waited for her, she was able to appreciate and admire her country as she had not when she was caught up in the stress of the tour. She admired the pastoral landscape speeding past her window, farms and small towns, creeks and forests. Times were still tough, but thanks to Roosevelt's New Deal—which the Friday Niters had strongly influenced—people were going back to work. Bridges were being built, roads repaired, art created for public places. There was an air of renewal, of hope and restored confidence. Perhaps the American economy was not rebounding from the Great Depression as quickly as was Germany's, but no one had to be denied citizenship to improve America's unemployment statistics. People did not have to be kicked out of professions by the tens of thousands to create jobs for others.

Compassion and respect could build an economy too—not overnight, but steadily, and with more enduring results.

Mildred delighted anew in all the things she had missed about America. Overheard conversations and jokes in regional accents. Newspapers free to present the facts as reporters discovered them, with editorials representing a broad political spectrum. Bookstores full of works that uplifted and questioned and instructed and challenged. Baseball. Jazz. City blocks where whites and Jews and Negroes and immigrants lived side by side, if not always in friendship, then at least in mutual respect. The rule of law. Due process. The Bill of Rights. Every mile brought a new reflection, something lost to Germany, rediscovered in the land of her birth.

When her train pulled into the station in Washington, Arvid met her on the platform, swept her into an embrace, and kissed her cheek, murmuring endearments in English and German. They spent the night at the Willard Hotel two blocks from the White House, dining and dancing in the evening, ordering a hearty breakfast in their room the following morning—all expenses paid by the Economics Ministry, since Arvid was officially traveling on business.

Arvid too seemed more relaxed than when they had left Germany. "I feel like a houseplant neglected in a pot on the windowsill, shriveled and drooping, and suddenly some kind *Hausfrau* emptied the watering can over me," he said in English as they strolled hand in hand along the Washington Mall.

Mildred had to laugh. "What an image."

He smiled and squeezed her hand. She was happy to see him cheerful again, when he had good reason to be discouraged. His meeting with Heath's colleagues had gone about as well as her job search. Arvid had warned the Treasury Department officials of Hitler's intention to invade Poland and had provided copies of incriminating financial records as evidence. Warning them that war was imminent, he had listed significant hidden German assets the United States should be prepared to seize when the day came. The officials had listened politely, examined the documents he had smuggled out of Germany at enormous risk to himself, and promptly dismissed him. His letter to the State Department offering his services in the inevitable fight against the Third Reich would almost certainly never be delivered.

After another day in the nation's capital, Mildred and Arvid went to Maryland to spend time with Mildred's eldest sister, Harriette, her husband and children, and their mother. It was a joyful reunion, at least on Mildred's part, but on the eve of their departure, Harriette took her aside and asked if she would not prefer to stay and let Arvid go home alone. "He can't make you go back," she said firmly. "We'll all stand with you."

"What are you saying?" asked Mildred, astonished. "He would never *make* me go back, or make me go anywhere."

"Mildred, I'm your sister. You can be honest with me." Harriette fixed her with a loving but stern gaze. "Arvid's changed. We never had the chance to get to know him well, but now we can see he's a typical German. He's a Nazi."

"That's not true. He joined the party because he had to, but he's no Nazi." He's in the resistance, she almost blurted, and I am too. But she couldn't. The risk was too great. "Please trust me. He's a good man. I wouldn't stay with him if he weren't."

Harriette studied her for a moment in silence, but eventually she nodded, still dubious.

It was an unhappy note to mark their parting, and the uncomfortable reticence lingered as Mildred and Arvid bade the family goodbye and boarded the train for New York. Someday, Mildred silently assured herself, when the Reich was no more and Arvid's role in the resistance could be made known, her family would realize their mistake. Perhaps as soon as their next visit, she and Arvid would both be welcomed back with warm embraces.

In mid-August, they departed on a ship bound for Hamburg, dispirited and doubtful that Arvid's warnings would be heeded by the United States, apprehensive about what awaited them back in Germany. They were together, Mildred reminded herself, and that would be enough to get her through whatever might come next.

CHAPTER FORTY-FIVE

August–September 1939

Greta

Late one August night while Adam worked on a screenplay in the living room, Greta put Ule to bed, tidied the kitchen, folded the laundry, answered her son's plea for a drink of water, soothed him back to sleep again, and then—only then, exhausted and tempted to give up and go to bed—settled down at the kitchen table to the work she had set out hours before.

It was not recent, the speech she intended to translate for a flyer to distribute around Neukölln, the universities, and perhaps the ghetto too, if she could scrounge up enough paper. President Roosevelt had delivered the speech the previous October, but she had received the transcript only recently from a friend in the foreign press corps. And yet, with the Gestapo squeezing Berlin's Jews into a few overcrowded, dilapidated blocks and the Wehrmacht going through maneuvers along the border with Poland, Mr. Roosevelt's words remained sharply relevant. The Ministry of Propaganda controlled the flow of information within the Reich so absolutely that most Germans had no idea what the leaders of other nations said about their country. Most Germans probably did not care, content to believe whatever Goebbels told them to think. But for those people like herself who hated fascism, loved democracy, and longed for reassurance that the free world had not forgotten them, an inspiring speech from a leader like President Roosevelt could make the difference between sustaining hope and succumbing to despair.

"It is becoming increasingly clear that peace by fear has no higher or more enduring quality than peace by the sword," she murmured aloud, tapping her knee with her pencil, searching for the perfect German phrases to capture Mr. Roosevelt's eloquent balance of authority and compassion. "There can be no peace if the reign of law is to be replaced by a recurrent sanctification of sheer force."

The American president did not need to mention Hitler by name for the subject of his speech to be perfectly clear. Greta firmly believed that the German people needed to know that not every Western leader had been duped by Hitler's hollow claims that he wanted peace. Some Germans would find that a heartening revelation, others an existential threat.

Greta wrote steadily, translating the phrases, referring to her well-worn German-English dictionary, circling a word she knew was not quite right to remind herself to choose a better synonym later. Mildred would know, but the Harnacks had no telephone, and at that hour she was probably asleep anyway.

"'There can be no peace if national policy adopts as a deliberate instrument the threat of war,'" Greta read aloud, carrying the transcript in one hand as she went to put the kettle on, yawning until her eyes watered. She ought to go to bed, but Ule was so busy and bright and curious all day long that late nights and early mornings were the only times she could get any work done. "'There can be no peace if national policy adopts as a deliberate instrument the dispersion all over the world of millions of helpless and persecuted wanderers with no place to lay their heads.'"

"Greta?" Adam called from the living room.

Sighing, she set the kettle on the burner, tossed the transcript on the table next to her notes, and went to the living room, where she found Adam turning up the volume on the radio.

"Are you deliberately trying to wake up Ule?" she asked wearily, wiping perspiration from her forehead with the back of her hand. Despite the late hour, the heat of the day had barely diminished with the sunset.

"Come listen," he urged, without turning away from the radio.

An announcer had interrupted the scheduled classical music program with a news bulletin, but since Greta had missed the beginning, at first she did not understand what he was saying. Sickening dread filled her when she realized that the German minister for foreign affairs was en route to Moscow to sign a nonaggression pact with the Soviet Union.

"How can this be?" asked Greta. "Fascists and Communists, allies? They're on opposite sides of the political spectrum. The Nazis have been persecuting German Communists for years. How could Stalin form an alliance with their tormentor?"

"Think of poor Poland, trapped between them in a pincer grip." Adam ran a hand over his jaw, grimacing. "Just a few days ago, Harnack was trying to convince me that Hitler would eventually attack the Soviet Union, that he'd send the Wehrmacht toward the Caucasus to secure a steady supply of oil for the Reich. Now he won't have to. He just gained access to the Soviet Union's raw materials without firing a shot."

"But what does Stalin get out of it?"

"I don't know. Maybe he's buying time. Maybe he and Hitler have agreed to divide up Poland between them."

To Greta that seemed all too likely. Apparently Hitler had fooled Stalin as easily as he had Chamberlain and Daladier.

They stayed up for another hour, hoping to learn more, but the music resumed without interruption. Greta went off to bed shortly after midnight, but Adam decided to stay up another hour, just in case.

In the morning, Adam told her that nothing more had been announced before he had come to bed at two o'clock. The Nazi press had been busy overnight, though, for all the major papers had put out extra editions hailing the German-Soviet Nonaggression Pact as a tremendous diplomatic victory over Great Britain, shattering their ongoing negotiations with France and Russia for an alliance that would have left Germany encircled by its rivals. Jubilant editorials proclaimed that a resolution of the matter of Poland would soon follow. "The world stands before a towering fact," enthused *Der Angriff*, the Nazi paper Goebbels had founded when Hitler was just beginning to ascend to power. "Two peoples have placed themselves on the basis of a common foreign policy which during a long and traditional friendship produced a foundation for a common understanding."

"Long and traditional friendship," retorted Adam, giving the paper a shake. "It's ten hours old and as abnormal a friendship as the world has ever known."

Later that morning, when Adam phoned Arvid at his office and suggested they meet, Arvid invited him and Greta for supper that evening. The Kuckhoffs brought food and wine, Mildred provided dessert and coffee, and while little Ule played at their feet or tumbled from lap to lap, squealing and giggling, they pooled their information, which was frustratingly meager.

Arvid was adamant that the friendship between Hitler and Stalin would be short-lived. "It's absolutely clear that Hitler will now prepare even more determinedly for war against the Soviet Union," he said.

"You've seen a draft of a declaration of war?" Greta asked archly, annoyed by his didactic certainty.

"Economically, he's not yet prepared," Arvid replied, ignoring her tone. "He'll try to gain control of other countries' raw materials and production facilities as quickly as possible."

"Poland will be the first," said Mildred.

"But not the last. The longer this fragile pact between Germany and Russia lasts, the more of Europe Hitler will consume."

"Maybe Stalin is smarter than you give him credit for," said Adam. "I know you despise him, and you have good reason. He killed your friends. But hear me out. What if Hitler *intends* to provoke a war between Germany and the West? In the resulting chaos, the Bolsheviks could step in and impose communism upon the countries involved—"

"Or what's left of them," said Mildred.

"Or," said Greta, "perhaps Stalin isn't smart at all. Hitler has broken every international agreement he's ever made. Didn't this very pact with Russia shatter an understanding Germany had with Japan? Just five years ago, Hitler made a similar pact with Poland, and you see how he disregards that now. When Hitler has wrung everything he wants out of Russia, this so-called friendship will be obsolete."

Arvid's eyebrows rose. "So you agree with me rather than your husband."

"I didn't mean to," said Greta, but then she gave him a wry smile. Sometimes their old rivalry resurfaced in moments of tension, inconvenient and childish. She had to do better.

Arvid briefly returned her smile, but it soon faded. "For now, our primary goal should be to gather information. I suspect things are going to unravel quickly, and we need to stay one step ahead."

But in the days that followed, Greta felt as if they were racing to catch up from behind.

Rumors of impending conflict sizzled and sparked through Berlin as the military requisitioned private automobiles and installed antiaircraft weapons on the rooftops of strategic buildings along Unter den Linden. On August 24, as German bombers flew over the city almost without respite all day, Greta was startled by a loud pounding on her door. It was a friend of Adam's, Jon Cutting, a member of the British press corps and an aspiring playwright. Breathless, apologizing profusely for disturbing her, he asked for Adam.

"I'm sorry, but he's not home." She held open the door wider. "Would you like to wait? He should be back soon."

"Sorry, no time. Might I beg a favor?" He held out a set of keys. "Our embassy has ordered all British correspondents to leave for Denmark tonight. Would you ask Adam to take charge of my car while I'm away?"

Startled, Greta took the keys. "Of course."

"It's parked out front, with a full tank," he said, inclining his head toward the window. "I don't expect to be gone very long—ten days, perhaps, until the embassy gives us the all-clear to return to do our jobs."

Greta promised they would take good care of his car, the first step being to move it someplace more discreet. He thanked her and dashed off before she had a chance to ask him if anything in particular had prompted the British embassy to urge them to leave the country.

Two days later, when she and Mildred met in the Tiergarten for a walk with Ule, Mildred revealed that earlier that morning, the United States embassy had issued a statement urging all Americans whose presence was not absolutely necessary to leave Germany immediately. "Most businesses and correspondents have already sent their wives and children away," Mildred said, taking a turn pushing Ule's stroller. "They've chartered two trains to take the rest to Denmark later this week."

"Will you be on one of them?" Greta asked.

Mildred shook her head. "Arvid wants me to go. When he couldn't persuade me, he asked Donald Heath to try. But I won't leave Arvid, and Arvid won't leave Germany to the Nazis."

"You should go."

Mildred gave her a sidelong smile. "You don't really want me to leave, do you?"

"It's for your own good," Greta countered, but of course Mildred was right. She did not want to lose her dearest friend.

Early the next day, the news broke that beginning Monday, August 28, the government would begin rationing essentials including food, soap, shoes, clothing, and coal. The announcement sent a shock rippling through Berlin, dredging up distressing memories of rationing during the Great War, when more than a million German civilians had perished from malnutrition. If she had not been so uneasy, Greta might have laughed at the newspaper articles that accompanied the announcement, column after column describing in excessive detail the abundance of the nation's food reserves. "Starving is impossible!" one report claimed, which Greta and Adam sardonically agreed was hardly a confirmed scientific fact.

That same morning, before ration cards were issued, before purchases were restricted, Greta left Ule with her neighbor and fellow resistance woman Erika von Brockdorff and hurried out to the shops to stock up on essentials, joining thousands of other Berliners similarly inspired. Quickly, before the shelves were emptied, she snatched up kitchen staples and nonperishable goods, and after dropping the cartloads off at home, she set out again in search of warm winter coats for herself and Adam, winter boots for herself, and entire wardrobes for Ule, enough clothes in increasing sizes to see him through the next two years. She depleted almost all of their household cash and in the end resorted to credit, but instinct told her this was no time to be frugal.

She could not take the chance that by the time Ule outgrew his clothes, she would be able to buy him what he needed. She could not say exactly what she thought might prevent Berlin's shopkeepers from restocking their wares, but there were only a few reasons a nation might impose rationing upon its citizens, and none of them inspired confidence in the future.

At the end of her long day of shopping—waiting in overcrowded queues, noting the swiftly multiplying empty spaces on store shelves, fearing that she might have forgotten something important, avoiding eye contact with other shoppers out of a vague shame for their implied covetousness and pessimism—Greta collected Ule, arranged to watch little Saskia the next day so Erika could shop, and went home, exhausted. When she turned on the radio to listen to the news while she prepared supper, she heard a description of the rationing system, which seemed so convoluted that Greta wondered how it could possibly succeed. All German citizens and permanent residents would be divided into three categories based upon the physical demands of their work—normal consumer, heavy worker, and very heavy worker—and would be allotted rations accordingly, with additional categories for infants, children, and adolescents. Special arrangements were made for Jews. Their allotments would be drastically smaller, and they would be forbidden to shop except during certain times of the day, typically the last half hour before the shops closed. If what Greta had witnessed in the stores that day was any indication, by the time the Jews were allowed to shop, there might be nothing left to buy.

When Greta took Ule and Saskia out for a walk through the Tiergarten on the morning of August 29, the day was sunny and warm, but the mood in Berlin was dejected and somber. Troops flowed through the city in a steady stream from west to east, but with none of the glamour of the parades made to feed Hitler's vanity. Some soldiers rode in troop transports, but others were packed into commercial moving vans and grocery trucks, proving that expediency had become more important than military protocol.

Diplomatic talks were ongoing, Greta knew, no doubt at an increasingly frenzied pace as the days passed. She wanted to believe that the recent spectacle of war preparations—the rationing, the bold proclamations in the press, the flight maneuvers, the rapid shifting of troops in the direction of the Polish border, the official assurances to Belgium, the Netherlands, Luxembourg, and Switzerland that Germany would respect their neutrality in case of war—was a show staged to intimidate Great Britain and France, and that ultimately no war would come. Judging by the apprehensive expressions and slumped shoulders of the people Greta passed on the streets of Berlin, the thought of imminent war filled them with dread.

In the last days of August, strange reports appeared in the press of Polish terrorists crossing the border to attack German troops. "I don't believe it," said Adam, incredulous and angry, after they read of an alleged attack on a radio station in the German border town of Gleiwitz. "If these stories aren't complete fabrications, then the incidents must have been staged."

Greta agreed. Poland had no reason to provoke their increasingly aggressive neighbor, whereas Hitler was strongly motivated to create evidence to justify a strike against Poland. If they required any more reason to doubt the truth of the official accounts of what was happening on the Polish border, they need only consider the fact that Hitler was a proven liar, a master of propaganda and manipulation.

The next morning, Greta woke to a hand on her shoulder, the faint aroma of coffee, an urgent voice. "Greta." Adam shook her gently. "Greta, wake up."

She blinked at him, then at the clock. Adam always rose first and started breakfast, minding Ule and allowing her to sleep undisturbed as long as she could. But although it was past dawn—"What's wrong?" It was too early. She scrambled to sit up. "Is Ule—"

"Ule is fine," he said quickly. "He's fine."

"Thank God. But what—"

"Greta, it's happened. This morning at dawn, Germany invaded Poland."

CHAPTER FORTY-SIX

September–October 1939

Mildred

All German radio stations carried the same announcement: At four o'clock that morning, German troops had crossed the Polish frontier and were advancing toward the east. In this valiant counterattack against Polish terrorists who had repeatedly assaulted innocent German civilians, force would be met with force. German honor would be defended.

"Counterattack?" echoed Mildred, incredulous. "This is a flagrant, unprovoked act of aggression! Surely no one believes this nonsense."

"Those who want to believe it, will," said Arvid. He turned the dial from one station to another, but each announcer only repeated the same bare sketch of the invasion, the same nationalist platitudes.

Eventually they remembered their breakfasts cooling on the table. Dazed, a knot in her stomach, Mildred finished her coffee but could barely swallow a piece of toast. "I suppose I'll go to work," Arvid said as they cleared the dishes, uncertain. It seemed strange to carry on as if it were an ordinary day, as if they were not at war.

It was a beautiful morning—abundant sunshine, a cool, gentle breeze carrying the first hint of autumn. Unable to settle down to her work, Mildred went for a walk in the Tiergarten to clear her head. She found Berlin outwardly unchanged—quieter, perhaps, more subdued, with slightly less traffic on the streets. On her way home, when throngs of delighted children passed her as they dashed along the sidewalks in their school uniforms, their knapsacks bouncing as they ran and skipped, she realized school must have closed early.

She arrived home at ten o'clock and turned on the radio just in time to hear Hitler address a special session of the Reichstag. She sank into a chair to listen, imagining Arvid gathered with his coworkers around a radio at the Economics Ministry, carefully concealing his emotions or feigning those expected of a loyal Nazi.

Hitler sounded more tired than usual, hoarse, even hesitant, but as he spoke, his voice gradually took on its usual vigor as he blamed Poland for starting the conflict with terrorist provocations and refusing to negotiate a peaceful settlement. The struggle would demand sacrifice of the German people, Hitler declared, the same sacrifice he had been willing to make as a soldier in the Great War, the same he was willing to make for the Fatherland now. His words met with thunderous cheers and an earsplitting chorus of "Sieg Heil," which continued unabated until the announcer broke in to say that Hitler had left the chamber.

Sick to her stomach, Mildred was tempted to turn off the radio, but she paused with her hand on the dial as the announcer read off specific sacrifices the government now required of the German people. Ration cards would be distributed that day. Hoarding was forbidden and would be severely punished. In Berlin, residents must stack sandbags around cellar and ground-floor windows for protection from potential bomb blasts. Beginning that evening, blackout regulations would be strictly enforced: Every source of light in the city must be extinguished, filtered, or shaded during hours of darkness. All windows and doors must be shuttered or curtained, skylights and basement vents sealed with waxed paper. If lights in railway stations, buses, and trams could not be switched off entirely, they were to be shielded with blue filters.

Mildred could hardly believe her ears when the announcer noted that while these regulations would be strictly enforced, they would prove unnecessary. German military defenses would never allow a Polish, French, or British bomber to get anywhere near Berlin.

Berlin could be bombed, Mildred thought, staring at the radio, pressing a hand to her mouth. Their own apartment block could be struck. That was what happened in a war. That was what was happening to the people of Poland at that very moment, although she could not hear the roar of aircraft or feel the shudder of impact or smell the acrid smoke. It all seemed very far away and not quite real.

Eventually she turned off the radio.

She felt tremulous and fragile as she gathered her purse and sweater and set out to collect their ration cards. The queue at the office was predictably long, the people waiting subdued and silent. Eventually Mildred reached the front and was given seven color-coded ration cards—blue for meat, orange for bread, green for eggs, pink for flour, rice, and oatmeal, and so on—printed on heavy paper, perforated so that coupons could be torn off with each purchase. The *Marken* would be valid for four weeks, after which new cards would be issued.

As Mildred stepped aside to tuck the ration cards into her purse, the next person in line, a younger woman holding the hand of a little boy about four years old, stepped up to the counter. The clerk, who had been perfectly courteous and efficient moments before, spoke to the woman so harshly that Mildred instinctively glanced up to see what was the matter. The woman kept her voice low and demure, and as the clerk continued to query her about her paperwork, she pulled the little boy closer, inch by inch, until he clung to her leg. Eventually the clerk heaved a sigh and shoved the woman's *Marken* across the counter. The woman released her son's hand long enough to gather up the cards, but before she could put them away, Mildred saw that they were over-printed with red Js. The woman quickly took the boy's hand again and led him away from the queue. For a moment her gaze locked on Mildred's—tense, haunted—but then she pressed her lips together, tore her gaze away, and gently tugged on her son's hand to urge him to hurry. Then they were gone.

Mildred walked home, struck by the somber resignation on the faces of the people she passed. The shops were busy, crowded with tense customers making use of their new ration cards, puzzling out the restrictions, confounded by the point system established for the purchase of clothing. She overheard some grumbling, but more surprising was the absence of any enthusiasm for the invasion. The *An-*

schluss had provoked celebrations on the street, great smiles and songs and abundant national pride, but Mildred observed none of that now.

When she reached her own block, she was brought up short by the sight of an enormous pile of sand dumped in the courtyard of the building next door. A few young children climbed upon the mound or pushed toy trucks and trains through the spillage near the bottom, while older teens and adults worked busily, women sewing hessian cloth into bags, men filling the bags with sand for others to haul away and stack near ground-floor windows. The knot in Mildred's stomach tightened as she hurried upstairs to leave her purse and collect her sewing kit before returning to join one of the sewing circles. She recognized a few residents of her own building, but most were strangers.

"Did you hear that as of today it's illegal to listen to foreign broadcasts?" one young woman piped up. Her hair was cut short in a sleek dark bob, and her hands were pale and slender with perfectly lacquered nails. "If you're found guilty of intentionally listening, you'll go to prison. If you're convicted of spreading around what you heard and undermining German morale, you'll be executed."

Mildred kept her expression carefully neutral. She and Arvid listened to the BBC several times a day, both the English and German broadcasts out of London.

"How are they going to enforce that?" scoffed an older, stouter woman keeping one eye on her work and the other on a pair of rambunctious boys scrambling around the sand pile. "How could they know who's listening to what? Will they send men to every home in Berlin to listen at doors?"

"They'll rely on denunciations, of course," said a white-haired woman, peering intently through her glasses as she threaded a needle. "Neighbors will inform on neighbors. Hitler Youth will inform on their own parents to their group leaders. You'll see."

A few of the women exchanged uneasy glances. "Who wants to listen to foreign broadcasts anyway?" said one pretty young woman whose infant slept beside her in a bassinet. "They're nothing but lies invented by Jews."

There were a few murmurs of assent, but the conversation trailed off into an uneasy silence. "Those two," the stout woman suddenly grumbled, exasperated. "They'll take half the sand home with them in their shoes and trousers if they don't settle down." Gathering up her things, she strode over to the pile and spoke vigorously to a pair of tousle-haired boys, then glanced warily around the courtyard and joined a different sewing circle some distance away.

Mildred sewed until midafternoon, when she returned home to start supper and prepare for the blackout. She listened to German radio as she worked, but eventually, repulsed by rapturous descriptions of the Wehrmacht's swift and merciless pulverization of Poland, she lowered the volume and tuned to the BBC. The announcer described the on-going attack in far more somber tones, the relentless forward march of German troops, villages and farms bombed into utter ruin, the destruction of the Polish air force, courageous but futile charges of the Polish cavalry upon German tanks.

Mildred hung on every word, but she heard nothing of a British or French response. She knew both nations were bound by treaty to go to Poland's defense, but whether they would honor their commitment remained to be seen.

When Arvid returned home, he turned down the volume until it was barely audible. Over supper he said that he had observed the same despondent mood on the streets as she had, very different from the jubilation and confidence he remembered from the commencement of the Great War. "Perhaps it's different in the countryside, in villages and small towns," he reflected. "Berliners are worldly, and their memories are too full of the last war to embrace a new one with reckless abandon. But if Germany can take Poland swiftly and France and Britain do nothing, even Berliners will rally to the cause. Nothing seduces like victory."

They lingered at the table, saying little but finding comfort in each other's company. Later they settled down in the living room, Arvid with a stack of economic reports, Mildred with the revised draft of her dissertation. Knowing how close she was to completing her life's goal sent a thrill of pride and relief through her, and yet she knew she would miss the engrossing distraction the work provided. She hoped to submit a polished and perfected dissertation to her professor by late September, and if all went well, she would defend it in early October and have her doctorate in hand soon thereafter. Surely then American universities would find her a more promising candidate, when the economy improved and they began hiring again.

At seven o'clock, an earsplitting wail shattered the night skies.

"Air raid," Arvid barked, bounding from his chair, snatching up his attaché case with one hand and the flashlight from the mantel with the other. Mildred barely had time to put on her shoes before Arvid took her arm and swiftly guided her into the hallway, pushing her toward the stairwell as he paused to lock the door. Racing downstairs, fighting back terror when slower residents blocked her way, she glanced over her shoulder and felt her heart constrict when she glimpsed Arvid a flight above. He gestured for her to proceed, so she did, crowding into the basement with other couples, families with small children, a few elderly men and women. The block warden had organized the shelter months before, and all residents had been required to participate in drills, but this was different, the semidarkness disorienting, the shriek of the sirens filling her ears and drowning out every sense but terror.

She found a seat on a bench near the wall but could not breathe easily until Arvid joined her there. With his arm around her shoulders, she shivered in the cool dark, her gaze fixed on the half window above, a faint outline on the opposite wall, sandbags barely visible through the glass. The air was dank and thick with the smell of fear and sweat, perfume and soiled diapers, stale cigarettes. A baby fretted. The minutes stretched out endlessly, and eventually speculation broke out whether it was the Poles, the Brits, or the French coming to bomb them, or if it was all just an unannounced drill, or why they bothered to cower in a basement anyway since the building would never withstand a direct hit. A few people hissed at that remark, and one man ordered the speaker to shut up before he frightened the children.

Mildred strained her ears, listening for explosions in the distance, but she heard only sirens and, infrequent and almost inaudible, a man issuing commands over a loudspeaker. Eventually the all-clear sounded, and Mildred and Arvid made their way back upstairs. "A false alarm, I suppose," she said with false bravado as he unlocked the door to their apartment.

"Or a propaganda exercise," he replied. "That would be my guess."

The radio reported nothing, and in the morning, the papers praised the exemplary responses of the block wardens and citizens without disclosing the reason for the alarm. Rumors flew through the city all day, a few concurring with Arvid that it had been orchestrated for propaganda purposes, some that a careless officer had set off the sirens by mistake, and others who claimed that a single plane straying too close to the capital had provoked the air raid warning.

Throughout that beautiful, sunny autumn day, enthusiastic reports of artillery bombardments, military advances, and Polish treachery filled the airwaves, punctuated by occasional references to ongoing negotiations between British ambassador Sir Nevile Henderson and his counterparts in the German Foreign Ministry. From an illicit BBC broadcast, Mildred learned that President Roosevelt had urged the leaders of every nation involved in the conflict to affirm that its armed forces would not bomb civilian populations from the air. Mildred thought it was a noble appeal, and she fervently hoped it would succeed, but she could not imagine Hitler agreeing to anything that might bind his hands.

The air raid sirens remained silent that night, but in the morning she and Arvid learned that Henderson had delivered an ultimatum to the Reich Chancellery. If Germany did not immediately cease all aggressive action against Poland and withdraw its troops by eleven o'clock, a state of war would exist between Great Britain and Germany.

Shortly after the deadline, the British ambassador returned to the Wilhelmstrasse and received Hitler's reply in the form of a memo. Germany rejected the ultimatum. Germany and Great Britain were at war.

Mildred learned the dreadful news as she was on her way to deliver an edited manuscript to Rütten & Loening, halting on the sidewalk amid other pedestrians as Hitler's speech was broadcast over loudspeakers throughout the city. Rousing herself from her shock, she hurried on her way, wishing she could leave the strident voice behind, but as soon as it began to fade she would approach another *Platz* with more loudspeakers, and so the madman dogged her steps all the way to the publisher's office.

The next day, the British and French embassies closed and their diplomats and families left Berlin, scenes to Mildred painfully reminiscent of the partial closure of the American embassy. It seemed that every friendly nation, every potential ally of the resistance, was leaving Germany as swiftly as their chartered trains could carry them away.

In the days that followed, if Mildred did not turn on the radio and hear the exultant reports of the Luftwaffe raining down destruction upon Poland as the Wehrmacht marched inexorably eastward, she could almost believe that the nation was not at war. Early in the morning of September 9, an air raid siren again broke the predawn silence, but the all-clear sounded soon enough and it was evident Berlin had never been in danger. The British had sent twenty-five planes to bomb Wilhelmshaven and had dropped leaflets over the Rhineland, but if the reports were true, not a single shot had been fired along the western front. Mildred and Arvid heard halfhearted jokes around the city that they were engaged in a "phony war," and indeed, except for the rationing and the blackouts, life went on almost as it ever had. Restaurants and shops were open, theaters and concert halls and cinemas enjoyed full houses. Rumors that a peace accord with France and Great Britain was imminent alternated with reports that Russia was preparing to invade Poland from the east. From what Arvid observed in the Economics Ministry, he found the latter far more plausible than the former.

He was right. On September 17, the Soviet army invaded eastern Poland. Ten days later, after relentless artillery bombardments, Warsaw surrendered to Germany.

In the first week of October, on the same day that Mildred successfully defended her dissertation and earned her doctorate at long last, Adolf Hitler appeared before the Reichstag to announce a peace proposal for Great Britain and France. Essentially he offered the two countries peace in the West if they did not interfere with Germany's plans to acquire *Lebensraum* in Eastern Europe. Bitter experience must have taught their leaders to put no trust in Hitler's promises, for this time they did not concede.

If only they had given this strong, united response years ago, Mildred thought. Now it seemed that another world war was inevitable, and her dread of what might befall them was infused with a deep sense of failure. For years the resistance had worked to oust Hitler in order to avoid war, to end suffering. Now Hitler was more powerful than ever, and although the Allies had met the terms of their treaty with Poland by declaring war on Germany, they seemed reluctant to engage in battle.

"You should have stayed in the United States," Arvid told Mildred one evening as they fixed the blackout curtains in place. "I wish I would have insisted."

"It would have broken my heart to disobey you," said Mildred lightly. "I wouldn't have stayed without you, and I couldn't have stayed without a way to support myself."

"Your sisters and brother offered you a place to stay."

"I refuse to become a burden to them. They have enough mouths to feed."

But she did often wish that she and Arvid were safe in America. So many other friends had fled. With renewed confidence thanks to her doctorate, and with little to lose, Mildred sent out another round of inquiries and applied for Rockefeller and Guggenheim fellowships. She arranged for all replies to be sent to Donald Heath at the American embassy, for it would jeopardize Arvid's position in the Economics Ministry if it became known that his wife was trying to leave the country.

In the meantime, preparations for war went on. On the western front, British and French forces built fortifications on one side of the Rhine in plain view of German defenses on the other, but no shots were fired. Children were swiftly packed off to relatives in the countryside for their safety, despite official assurances that it was impossible for enemy planes to get past German defenses and bomb Berlin. Death notices began appearing in the papers, poignant tributes by bereft parents mourning sons killed in battle in Poland.

One afternoon in mid-October, Arvid came home unexpectedly early from work and barely paused to greet her in his haste to pack a bag. He was going to Jena, he called over his shoulder on his way to their bedroom. His mother had been arrested.

"I'm coming with you," said Mildred, quickly following.

As they threw clothing and money and ration cards into their suitcases, Arvid explained that an hour ago, his sister Inge had called him at his office to give him the terrible news. She was waiting outside with her husband's car. Falk was already en route from Weimar.

Inge, pale and trembling, slid over to let Arvid take the wheel as he and Mildred loaded their suitcases in the trunk and took their seats. As they sped southwest from Berlin, she explained what had happened. That morning, Mutti Clara had been out for her daily walk when she passed a park where several children were playing. When she overheard them singing songs from the Hitler Youth and Jungmädelbund, she asked if they knew that there were better songs to sing—German *Volkslieder*, for example. As the children eagerly gathered around so she could teach them a traditional tune about a little bluebird, an outraged passerby stormed off to report her to the Gestapo.

"What has this world come to that an elderly woman can be thrown into prison for teaching children an innocent song?" said Inge, fighting back tears.

When they reached the Gestapo's main office in Thuringia, they found Falk speaking with a disgruntled, impatient officer, arguing and cajoling by turns for his mother's release. With tangible relief, he let his older brother take over. Arvid quickly assessed the facts of the case, the charges against his mother, and the evidence, which seemed to consist solely of the informant's testimony and Mutti Clara's "confession" that she had indeed taught the children the song.

While Arvid reasoned with the official, Inge and Mildred were allowed into the cellblock to see Mutti Clara. To their relief, they found her in good health and spirits, bemused by all the fuss and annoyed at the inconvenience. "I wasn't teaching them 'La Marseillaise,' for heaven's sake," she said, wringing her hands in agitation.

Mildred suspected it was not the *Volkslied* but the implication that Nazi songs were inferior that had prompted her mother-in-law's arrest, and when she and Inge rejoined Arvid and Falk, the brothers were addressing that very point with the Gestapo officer assigned to the case. "By discouraging the children to renounce their Hitlerjugend and Jungmädelbund songs, Frau Harnack was undermining the authority of their leaders, and by extension, that of the Reich," the officer said, his faint flush belying his firm tone. Was he angry, or was he embarrassed by the absurdity of prosecuting an elderly woman for such a trivial misdeed?

"She wasn't asking them to renounce anything, but rather to add *Volkslieder* to their repertoire," said Arvid. "Surely you agree with our Führer that children should learn the songs of the *Volk*?"

"Certainly, but a woman of her advanced years should know better than to question the children's instruction."

"A woman of her advanced years is easily confused," said Arvid. "You know how the older generation is affected by talk of war, having such vivid memories of the last one. She has been deeply upset by the bombings in Poland, and it has affected her mind."

The officer appeared to soften at this. Out of respect for Arvid's high rank in the Economics Ministry, he agreed to take the matter up with his superior, but for the present, Frau Harnack must remain in prison. When Inge begged him to permit her mother her paints, easel, and brushes, the officer hesitated, but eventually agreed.

The next day, they returned to the prison to visit Mutti Clara and plead her case to any official who would see them. After four days, Mildred, Falk, and Inge remained in Thuringia, but Arvid was obliged to return to the ministry. He continued to work from his office for his mother's release, calling in favors, finding advocates in the Nazi hierarchy for whom the Harnack name still carried weight. Finally, after a harrowing fortnight, Mutti Clara was released on the condition that she leave Jena. She reluctantly consented, and even more reluctantly, her children decided to admit her to a sanatorium for the aged in the countryside for her own safety.

Soon after Mutti Clara was settled in her new home—temporarily, they all hoped—Mildred received word that her applications for the Rockefeller and Guggenheim fellowships had been rejected.

"I'm sorry, *Liebling*," said Arvid, embracing her. "They're fools not to recognize your genius."

Despite her crushing disappointment, Mildred had to laugh. "How could I ever leave such a sweet and loyal husband?" she asked, kissing him.

Arvid managed a halfhearted smile, but as the days passed, she sometimes caught him watching her, guilt and torment in his eyes.

"I cannot bear that you're subjecting yourself to an ominous future for my sake," he told her once, and the next Saturday, as they walked through the Tiergarten with the Heath family, he again asked Donald to persuade Mildred to return to the United States.

"If you can't convince her, I don't know why you think I could," Donald said, while Louise reached out and squeezed Mildred's hand in sympathy.

A few days later, when Arvid returned home from work, he took a thick envelope from his attaché case and gave it to Mildred. "Keep this with you at all times," he said, not quite meeting her gaze.

"What is it?"

"I booked you passage from Hamburg to New York with United States Lines."

"Arvid, no," she protested, tossing the envelope on the table and planting her hands on her hips.

"Mildred, listen. It's good on any of their ships, at any time. I'm not sending you away tomorrow, but should it ever become necessary, I want you to be able to leave Germany at a moment's notice."

"Where's *your* ticket?" she asked, already sure he had not purchased one for himself. When he shook his head sadly, she studied him for a long moment in silence before agreeing to keep the envelope in her purse.

She could not imagine using the ticket. How could she ever leave her beloved Arvid behind to an uncertain fate? If she fled to the United States, the Gestapo would immediately suspect him of disloyalty to the Reich and place him under close scrutiny, jeopardizing his job in the ministry, his work with the resistance, his very life. She could not abandon him to that. They would go together or not at all.

CHAPTER FORTY-SEVEN

November 1939–March 1940

Sara

Sara and Natan received one letter from their parents at the apartment in Friedenau letting them know they had arrived safely and assuring them of their love, understanding, and gratitude. Without mentioning their destination by name, they urged Sara and Natan to join them there soon.

In reply, Natan wrote a letter addressed to Wilhelm, purportedly from Adam Kuckhoff, reminding him of their meeting on September 5—Sara's birthday—and the theatrical production they had discussed. "Kuckhoff" hoped he was still interested in producing a new biographical play about Ludwig van Beethoven, and if so, he should respond by return mail at his earliest convenience.

Adam took wry pleasure in his role in the subterfuge, and it was not long until Greta presented Sara with another letter from her parents, albeit in Wilhelm's handwriting and bearing his signature. He was eager to produce the play, he had written, and the enclosed cheque should be considered his first investment. Perhaps Kuckhoff would consider perfecting the play in Geneva before introducing it to Berlin's more discriminating audiences.

Their improvised code evolved as they sent letters back and forth. Natan was called the playwright, Sara the stage manager. Their parents were the Swiss investors, Amalie their secretary, her children their staff. It was a necessary artifice, frustrating in its obliqueness. Although sometimes Sara and Natan could not puzzle out what their parents meant by a certain theatrical metaphor, they were grateful to have any communication at all. Natan once joked that the more they wrote about their nonexistent Beethoven biography, the more he liked the idea. "Kuckhoff and I should go in on it together," he said, "especially if Mutti and Papa are willing to fund it."

The money their parents sent had become essential. Sara had no paying work, and Natan's freelance, pseudonymous journalism assignments had diminished as his contacts in the German press became too apprehensive to employ an incognito Jew. Sara had sold off pieces of the family silver as her mother had instructed, but her frequent visits to pawnshops drew unwanted attention. Inevitably, a proprietor would realize that she was Jewish, size up her desperation, and offer her a small fraction of what an Aryan would have expected to receive for the same items. She hated to let precious family heirlooms go for a few marks and an earful of insults. As long as the Swiss investors continued to fund Kuckhoff's play, she would not have to.

"Natan and I are grateful for your help," Sara told Greta one afternoon when she came by to babysit little Ule, a slight but strong boy of almost two years. Greta had added translation to her freelance editing jobs, and between that, her resistance work, and tending Ule, she toiled almost every waking hour. "We know what risks you're taking for our sake, not only with our correspondence but simply by associating with us."

Greta gazed heavenward and shook her head. "I'm not going to give up my Jewish friends just because Hitler says I should."

"Perhaps you should, for your own safety. Most of my Aryan friends have cut off contact with me."

"That's their loss." Greta kissed Ule's cheek and fixed Sara with a look of fond resolve. "Do you know how hard it is to find a reliable babysitter these days? I'm not giving up Ule's favorite without a fight."

Smiling, Sara resolved to put her faithless friends out of mind. Greta at least would never abandon her. Sara had witnessed her generosity to other Jews too often to believe her capable of it. She gave free English lessons to Jewish families awaiting visas to Great Britain and the United States. Before the war, she had traveled to London to help sort out thorny Jewish immigration issues and to meet with colleagues in British trade unions, marshaling their support and soliciting donations for Jewish relief. She and Adam—and the Harnacks too—saved portions of their rations to share with Jewish neighbors whose allotments were never enough to assuage their hunger. Greta's instinctive acts of kindness, her refusal to learn hatred and exclusion, gave Sara hope.

Sara gathered hope wherever she could find it, from her friends' perilous generosity, from antifascist graffiti that sprang up overnight on buildings and railways cars, and from rare, startling subversive acts that disrupted the Nazi myth of a German *Volk* united in solidarity behind Hitler. In September, bombs were detonated outside the police headquarters in Alexanderplatz and the Air Ministry. In November, the office of Hitler's personal photographer was vandalized, the shop windows where portraits of the Führer were displayed shattered. No one in Sara's resistance circle was responsible, prompting Natan to note, "This proves we're not alone."

Hope, however slender the thread, sustained Sara as winter descended, for as the days grew colder and the nights longer, the blackout became more oppressive, more isolating. Crime soared in the darkness—prostitution, murders, thefts, rapes. To make navigating the city at night less hazardous, curbs, street corners, crossings, steps, and sidewalk obstructions were marked with phosphorescent paint, and arrows indicating the way to air raid shelters were painted on walls. Pedestrians carried electric torches screened with the necessary filters and wore phosphorescent badges on their lapels to avoid colliding with one another. Even so, accidents soared throughout Berlin. People making their way home from work in the darkness tumbled into gutters or tripped over cracks in the sidewalk. With vehicle headlights reduced to screened rectangular openings no larger than five by eight centimeters, traffic moved through the city at a crawl, other cars and trucks barely visible as narrow slits of headlights, pedestrians entirely obscured. Drivers became disoriented without familiar landmarks and street signs, running off the road or crashing into one another. Trains sped past dimmed warning signals and plowed into the backs of other railcars. As the death toll rose, officials insisted that matters were well in hand and the German people only needed time to get used to the new conditions. Sara avoided the worst of the hazards by staying indoors after twilight, but she worried about Natan, who ignored the curfew imposed on Jews and kept his own schedule as he always had.

In December, despite the blackout and rationing, despite the gloom and depression and uneasy expectation that British bombs might fall upon the cities or fighting break out along the western front, most Germans began preparing for Christmas. Sara had always felt somewhat estranged from the Christian majority during their festive season, but that year was more isolating than any she remembered. She observed her fellow Berliners hauling home *Tannenbäume*, putting up candles and wreaths, and singing carols with forced good cheer as the Reich scheduled Christmas concerts and pageants to improve morale. High-ranking Nazis made a show of visiting the troops on the front lines, to shake hands or to share a holiday feast.

Such displays of patriotism seemed to please most Berliners, but Sara was careful to keep her expression impassive when she overheard grumbling about other Nazi intrusions upon the holiday. Rationing and the scarcity of goods made shopping for gifts frustrating, if not impossible, and devout Christians took offense at wrapping paper printed with swastikas and Christmas carols revised to include Nazi themes. Sara too was taken aback when she first heard the updated version of the beloved "Stille Nacht":

Silent night, holy night,
All is calm, all is bright.
Adolf Hitler is Germany's star,
Showing us greatness and glory afar.
Bringing us Germans the might.
Bringing us Germans the might!

The most ardent Nazis did not celebrate Christmas at all that year, but a newly contrived holiday called *Julfest*, a time to reflect upon one's

Aryan ancestors and honor soldiers who had sacrificed their lives in service to the Fatherland. As a Jew, Sara found it all strange and surreal and menacing. She could only imagine how it felt to those German Christians who still revered Jesus more than Hitler.

She woke on the first morning of 1940 to find a fresh blanket of snow covering Berlin, soft and white and clean, concealing all its recent ugliness, restoring the charm and beauty she recalled from winters past. She ached with longing for her parents and sister, for their home in the Grunewald, for family suppers and her nieces' laughter and Amalie's beautiful music rising from the piano.

When Natan found her staring out the window with tears in her eyes, he seized her by the hands and pulled her up from her chair. "Bundle up," he ordered. "We're going out. Leave your identification card here."

"Why?"

"Because I'm your older brother and I said so."

Dutiful, curious, she put on her warm coat, boots, hat, and mittens and followed him outside, along sidewalks that storekeepers were busily clearing of slush. "Where are we going?" she asked when they reached the entrance to the Untergrundbahn.

"You'll find out."

Although he gave her no hints, she could make an educated guess based upon the direction they were traveling, and her suspicions were confirmed when he gestured for her to get out at the Bahnhof Zoo. "Natan, no," she said, even as she followed him outside.

"Why not?"

"Because—" She lowered her voice as she hurried to keep up with him. "Because Jews aren't allowed in the Tiergarten."

"Who's going to know? It's not like we're wearing a sign."

Somehow they always know, Sara thought, but as they caught sight of the bare-limbed, snow-covered trees just ahead, a knot of resolve in her chest hardened and she strode ahead.

"Not so fierce," Natan said, muffling laughter. "You're just an ordinary German *Fraulein* enjoying a New Year's Day stroll, remember?"

Sara took a deep breath and let her shoulders relax.

Snow and ice had transformed the Tiergarten into a magical realm of stark beauty. Together Sara and Natan walked the snowy paths, breathing deeply the crisp, cold air, jumping out of the way as a group of young boys rushed past pulling a toboggan. Smiling, Sara closed her eyes and lifted her face to the sky as a gust of wind blew a shower of snow down from the treetops. "Do you remember when you taught me to ski?" she asked her brother. Grinning, he nodded, and one reminiscence prompted another, until her cheeks ached from smiling.

All was joyous until they passed a group of Nazi soldiers at rest, smoking and passing a flask back and forth, rifles slung idly over their shoulders. Abruptly the spell was broken. "Let's go home," Sara murmured, clutching her brother's sleeve.

"Why, are you too cold? Do you want my scarf?"

She took a step backward, her gaze fixed on the soldiers. "No, let's just go."

He looked as if he might argue, but something in her expression stopped him. "All right," he said, slinging an arm casually over her shoulders and turning her away from the soldiers. "We'll come back another time."

Sara doubted they ever would.

As January passed, bitter cold descended upon Berlin, the worst Sara could remember. For days on end, daytime temperatures struggled to rise above $-5°C$, plunging even deeper in the night. Canals, ponds, and lakes froze over, and when one heavy snowfall after another buried the city—one storm dumped almost a meter within eight hours—and high winds carved the snow into deep drifts, travel became so difficult it was rarely worth the attempt. Strict snow removal policies were enacted for homeowners, and work teams of Hitler Youth, drafted citizens, and conscripted Jews were assigned to clear sidewalks, roads, and public thoroughfares. Despite these efforts, it was almost impossible to keep up with the snow, which fell almost without respite upon the beleaguered residents.

Sara thought rationing was bad enough when there were things to buy, but as winter dragged on, shortages of food and fuel made difficult circumstances nearly unendurable. Frozen canals prevented coal barges from reaching the city, and when shipments managed to arrive by rail, they sold out almost before merchants had time to announce they had restocked. Schools were instructed to return all coal over a fortnight's supply to their distributors so that it could be made available for the public, while churches were ordered to surrender all of their coal supplies and make do without heat until the crisis passed. Factories engaged in war production were promised an adequate supply, but others received none. Sara and Natan adapted by heating only the living room and wearing thick layers of clothing indoors, but then municipal authorities mandated the shutdown of all domestic central heating boilers so that hot water was available only on weekends. To be cold and hungry and anxious, and then to be unable to enjoy the comfort and necessity of a hot shower—it was a terrible blow.

Natan and Sara were creative in their attempts to stay warm, braving the cold streets to seek out the few heated public places where Jews were still permitted. One bleak February day, they walked to a hotel where they intended to order two cups of ersatz coffee and sip slowly in a discreet corner of the lobby. "See that?" Natan said, nudging her until she glanced up at one of the ubiquitous placards that had been posted all over the city: *Niemand hungert oder friert in Deutschland!* "No one goes hungry or freezes in Germany, so we have nothing to worry about."

"Good to know," Sara managed to say, clenching her jaw to keep her teeth from chattering.

It was the coldest winter in northern Germany for more than a century, but eventually it too, like all things, yielded to the inexorable force of time. In the first week of March, their icebound world began to thaw, flooding gutters with meltwater and creating icicles, some more than a meter in length, hanging precariously from eaves and rooftops. The sunlight on Sara's face created the illusion of spring even when the temperatures lingered only a few degrees above freezing. She craved fresh vegetables and fruit, and the first time she glimpsed a few scrawny sticks of asparagus and rhubarb at the bottom of a bin when she was permitted to enter the market at the end of the day, she snatched them up and triumphantly handed over her ration cards and Reichsmarks as if the handful of vegetables would suffice for a feast.

She longed for a small patch of earth to cultivate, and although it was risky to draw attention to herself, she considered suggesting to their landlord that the concrete in the sunniest part of their building's courtyard be removed so that it could be made into a community garden. But before she could, she and Natan returned home from a walk to discover a notice tacked to their apartment door.

Natan snatched it down and read it in silence, his frown deepening.

"What is it?" Sara asked, afraid to know.

He unlocked the door, motioned for her to enter, and waited until they were safely inside before he answered. "We've been evicted." He crumpled the notice into a ball and threw it toward the empty coal scuttle. "Another Aryan family lost their home to Speer's construction projects. They need our apartment, and we can go to hell."

"Where *will* we go, really?" asked Sara, her voice small and anxious like that of a much younger girl. When her brother looked at her bleakly without saying a word, she knew the answer.

CHAPTER FORTY-EIGHT

March–June 1940

Greta

As the harsh winter relented and the icebound city thawed, the oppressive sense that Berlin was under siege began to lift. If not for the blackout, the rationing, the antiaircraft weapons on the rooftops of strategic buildings, and the absence of millions of young men who had been called into military service, one could almost forget that Germany was at war. Or so it felt to Aryans, sighing with relief as they shed layers of clothing and opened windows to fresh spring breezes. Greta suspected Jews felt increasingly tense and frightened as their existence in Germany grew more precarious day by day.

Greta's trip to London had yielded positive results, not only generous donations to Jewish relief efforts but also the priceless gift of increased support for Jewish immigration to Great Britain. While there, she had visited a favorite bookstore and had been thrilled to discover James Murphy's translation of *Mein Kampf* on the shelf. She wondered how Daphne had managed to get the carbon copy of the manuscript out of Germany, and she fervently hoped that the translation would serve as a warning to anyone who still doubted Hitler's sinister motives. She wished everyone in the American government would study it well.

In the third week of March, when only a few stubborn, ice-crusted snowbanks lingered in the shadiest parts of the Tiergarten, Greta took

Ule with her to meet a young couple in Neukölln for an English lesson. They were discouragingly low on the British emigration list, but both husband and wife were apt pupils, grasping idiom as deftly as if they had been studying the language for years. But when she reached their apartment building, their brass nameplate was missing from the list at the entrance, and inside, no one responded when she knocked upon their door.

"Lazar?" she called out, knocking again. "Jutta?" Still nothing.

Uneasy, she considered what to do. The couple had never missed a lesson before, and it was rather late in the morning for them to have overslept, especially since they had an infant son. She pressed her ear to the door, but no one stirred within.

At a sudden sound behind her, she turned to find a woman about ten years older than herself peering out from another apartment farther down the hallway. "Are you looking for the Gittelmans?" she asked, frowning slightly as she eyed Greta and little Ule, who tugged on his mother's hand in his impatience to go inside and play.

"Yes," said Greta. "They were expecting me. Would you know if they've gone out for the day?"

"They've gone for good." The woman folded her thick arms across her chest. "They moved out two days ago. Scurried out before dawn carrying everything they owned."

Greta's heart sank. "Did they leave a forwarding address?"

"Not with me. You could ask around the ghetto. Where else would they have gone?" The woman shrugged. "They weren't bad neighbors, even though they were Jews. Maybe it's for the best. This way the boy can grow up among his own kind."

Greta felt her expression freeze in place. "Thanks for your help." Before Ule could protest, she led him down the hall and away, ignoring the curious stare the neighbor gave her in passing.

That evening when she told Adam what had happened, he sighed, torn between sympathy and impatience. "I hate to see you break your heart over and over again," he said.

"What would you have me do, simply stop caring?"

"As if you could," he said. "Just remember that assisting a few Jews here and there won't solve the real problem. The only way we're going to stop the suffering once and for all is to overthrow Hitler and bring down the Reich."

"I don't see why we have to abandon one effort to serve the other." Why must he belittle her work? What she could do, she did. "People need food and hope now. You can't expect them to wait until the Nazis are brought down. They'll starve first."

"I understand that, but we have to stay focused on our main objective. We can't afford distractions."

Bristling, she turned away before she said something she regretted. In recent months, Adam and John Sieg had developed the profoundly annoying habit of dismissing her contributions to the resistance as inconsequential, and that was when they acknowledged her at all. For years she had written and edited flyers, translated documents, typed and copied, arranged meetings, and acted as a courier, risking her freedom and her life as much as any man. Yet from the time of Ule's birth, they had increasingly excluded her, shutting themselves away in Adam's study instead of holding their meetings in the living room as they once had. When she protested, they explained that they could no longer speak freely in front of Ule, since children often innocently repeated anything they overheard. When she suggested leaving him with a neighbor, they objected, insisting that this would draw attention to their meetings. They had an excuse for everything.

One evening when they were alone, she confronted Adam about his infuriating transformation. "Do you remember what you told me when I returned from London years ago?" she asked. "You said a woman of my intelligence should not be relegated to mere clerical work, but that I could and must contribute more."

"That was then, but now——" Adam inclined his head toward the room where their son slept. "Now it's better that you not know too much, for your sake and Ule's, in case our circle is betrayed."

"If we're discovered, the Gestapo would never believe I'm innocent." Greta gestured to the desk where translations and drafts of flyers were neatly sorted in locked drawers, out of sight but not out of reach, her handwriting on every page. She indicated the bookcases along the walls, where beside Adam's scripts and novels and her own cherished volumes sat dozens of banned books entrusted to them by nervous friends who had purged their own shelves of illicit literature. "I'm already involved up to my neck. There's no point in shutting me out."

Adam was a fool if he believed being a woman and a mother gave her some natural immunity against Nazi violence. Did the Nazis spare Jewish women? Communist women? The wives of their political enemies? Even before the Night of the Long Knives, women had paid the price for their own insurgence as well as that of their husbands. Why pretend otherwise?

"We bear all the risks the men do, but our opinions matter half as much," Greta complained to Mildred a few days later while they washed and dried the supper dishes in the Harnacks' tiny kitchenette. Arvid had invited the Kuckhoffs over, but although they discussed politics and strategy as equals over the meal, afterward the men went to the living room to continue the conversation while the women cleared the table and tidied up. "They want to shield me from their resistance activities because I'm a mother. If they believe the Gestapo could search our apartment and not immediately know that I'm as guilty as they are, they're fooling themselves. And it's precisely because I *am* a mother that I'm committed to the resistance. I have to make the world better for Ule. Did you know that next month, participation in the Hitler Youth becomes compulsory for all boys aged ten through eighteen?"

Mildred nodded soberly. "Yes, I know."

"I won't allow it." Greta shook her head as she furiously wiped a plate dry. "I won't let them make him into a little Nazi automaton, worshipping Hitler and singing cheerful tunes about blood and soil."

"Ule has eight years before he would be old enough. God help us all if Hitler is still in power then."

"Exactly, which is why the resistance needs every one of us. Not just the men. Everyone who is willing and able, including mothers. Including me." Scowling, Greta draped the dishtowel over her shoulder while Mildred scrubbed the last pan. "I'm the only mother in our circle, and so they treat me differently than they treat you, or Sophie Sieg—"

"Greta—"

"I get up before dawn and stay up late for my resistance work. I never neglect Ule, not one moment."

"Of course you don't. No one would ever accuse you of that. But Greta, listen—" Mildred hesitated, rinsed the soap from her hands, and plucked the dishtowel from Greta's shoulder to dry them. "You're not going to be the only mother in our circle for long."

"You mean Sophie—"

Mildred shook her head, eyes shining.

"Mildred, you?" Greta exclaimed, and when Mildred nodded, Greta embraced her. "How wonderful! How far along?"

"Six weeks." Mildred's face glowed with joy. "I know it's still early, which is why we haven't told anyone yet. Except you."

Suddenly Greta's words came rushing back to her. "Mildred, you mustn't worry that the men will put you aside once you become a mother. They can't afford to lose you, not with your contacts among the Americans."

"They can't afford to lose you either, even if they don't always realize it."

Greta smiled, heartened by her friend's encouragement, delighted beyond measure that Mildred's long-cherished dream to have a child was at last coming true. She would not think of spoiling her friend's happiness with cautions about how difficult it was to raise children in the Reich, not only because of rationing and shortages and the pervasive fear that at any moment this strange *Sitzkrieg*, the "phony war," would suddenly burst forth like a long-held breath into all-out warfare, with British bombs laying waste to Berlin as Germany's bombs had done to Warsaw. It was the poisonous influence of Nazi propaganda and scenes of arbitrary violence Greta feared most, and the older Ule grew, the more difficult it would be to shield him.

With the return of fair weather, Greta had resumed taking Ule on outings to the Tiergarten for fresh air and sunshine. She had hidden her dismay as he had admired older boys marching past in their crisp uniforms of the Hitler Youth, singing songs in praise of the Führer and banging upon drums. Whenever Ule saw other little children waving small swastika flags, he begged Greta for one of his own. "We don't have a ration coupon for a new flag," she usually told him, which was true, but only because no coupon was needed.

One lovely spring evening after Greta and Adam had taken Ule for a walk around the neighborhood, savoring the longer days that allowed them more time to enjoy the outdoors between supper and the blackout, Ule had brought his hand out from behind his back and proudly showed them a swastika flag he had found lying on the sidewalk. "It was lost," he said, his voice sweet with happiness. "I found it, Mama."

"I see," she said noncommittally, sickened by the sight of her innocent boy waving about that symbol of hatred and cruelty. When her eyes met Adam's over their son's head, she knew he shared her anger, her disgust and frustration. But what could they do? If they took the flag from him and he told his friends, and their parents overheard, they could be reported.

Then Adam stooped down beside Ule, pretending to admire the flag. "It's a bit on the small side. Why don't you go outside and plant it in the garden so it can grow into a larger one?"

Ule's face had lit up. He had fetched his toy pail and shovel, seized Adam's hand, and pulled him to the door to go outside and bury the flag. Greta had watched them go, impressed by her husband's cleverness— although until they returned, she had paced through the apartment half in a panic that a vigilant neighbor would witness the scene and promptly call the Gestapo.

But she saw no reason to trouble Mildred with such worries. It would be years before the Harnacks' child would walk and talk and covet other children's swastika flags. Greta had to believe Hitler would be gone by then.

Greta's determination to persist in resisting the Reich any way she could strengthened as spring passed and the German army marched on Europe. On April 9, Nazi forces occupied Norway and Denmark—for their own good, the Reich insisted in an official statement, to protect their freedom and independence from the Allies, who were determined to "spread the war" and would never respect the two countries' declared neutrality. Rejecting the Nazis' unsought, unwanted, dubious protection, the Norwegians put up a fight, but eventually were forced to surrender.

The *Sitzkrieg* was over. Nothing was phony about the war now.

A month later, at dawn on May 10, the German army invaded Belgium, Luxembourg, and the Netherlands. In his order to the troops, Hitler proclaimed, "The battle beginning today will decide the future of the German nation for the next thousand years." Police forces in Luxembourg fought back against the German troops, but by noon their capital city was overrun. Four days later, the Dutch army capitulated. The Belgians fought on with their British and French allies a fortnight longer, until King Leopold surrendered on May 28.

Then German tanks rolled into France, capturing Paris, driving Allied troops so far back that British and some French troops were forced to make a desperate evacuation across the Channel at Dunkirk, resorting to a civilian fleet of British commercial ferries, fishing boats, and leisure craft to rescue hundreds of thousands of men. Many tens of thousands more remained behind, with no choice but to surrender to the German army.

On June 21, in a clearing in the forest of Compiègne, the precise spot where nearly twenty-two years before the armistice that ended the Great War had been signed, Adolf Hitler presented his armistice terms to France. In the preamble to the document, he declared that he had not chosen the site out of revenge, but merely to right an old wrong. Even if that were true, it made no difference to the French. Their humiliation was complete.

A three-day public holiday was declared throughout the Reich to celebrate the fall of Paris. There were massive parades, proud speeches, grand processions. Church bells rang and flags waved. Hitler's popularity soared. Germany had confronted Great Britain and France on the field of battle and emerged triumphant. The unbridled jubilation in the streets of Berlin sickened and angered Greta so much that unless she had absolutely no choice but to go out, she stayed at home with the windows closed and the radio tuned to the BBC.

But as the holiday ran its course and she witnessed the surging pride and newly invigorated confidence of devoted Nazis and everyday Germans alike, she felt her resolve hardening. The beleaguered resistance had to intensify their efforts. There was no time to nurse wounds, to sit at home dazed from shock that the Allies had been so swiftly and thoroughly overwhelmed.

Their resistance circle had to expand in size and scope, and Greta knew where to begin.

Earlier that spring, she and Adam had attended a dinner party at the home of Herbert Engelsing, an executive producer at the Tobias Film Company and a prominent figure in the German film industry. His work gave him entree into the highest levels of the Nazi hierarchy, where he mingled with men like Propaganda Minister Joseph Goebbels and Hermann Göring, drawn to him because they recognized the power of the movies and celebrity to influence public opinion. Engelsing and his half-Jewish wife, Ingeborg, owed their marriage to Göring, who had personally given Hitler their request for a dispensation to marry. "I'll decide who's a Jew and who's not," Göring had said after he emerged triumphant with the Führer's permission for them to wed. Göring probably would not have been so helpful had he known that Engelsing used his position and influence to help Jews and other enemies of the Reich.

At the dinner party at the Engelsings' luxurious home in the Grunewald, Greta and Adam were introduced to another couple, Harro and Libertas Schulze-Boysen. A Luftwaffe officer serving in the intelligence division of Göring's Air Ministry, Harro was tall, vigorous, and handsome, fluent in five languages, the scion of a celebrated military family. His wife was a vivacious, sensual, stunningly attractive aristocrat, educated at the finest Swiss finishing schools, the granddaughter of a Prussian prince. When they first met, Greta had liked Harro immediately but had found Libertas's youthful exuberance and flirtatiousness annoying. She had felt a sharp sting of envy when Libertas passed around photos of Schloss Liebenberg, the imposing ancestral estate where she had grown up, to recommend it as a shooting location for one of Engelsing's films. That feeling had given way to surprise when she learned that despite Libertas's privilege and wealth, she held down a job as a press agent with Metro-Goldwyn-Mayer's Berlin office.

Greta listened intently as Libertas described blistering phone calls her office had received from various Reich officials outraged by a recent MGM film, *The Mortal Storm*. Set in 1933 Germany, the picture starred Margaret Sullavan as a beautiful German Jew who breaks off her engagement to a Nazi officer when she realizes how abhorrent his political views truly are. She falls in love with an antifascist childhood friend played by James Stewart, and the two eventually attempt to flee Germany. "Goebbels is furious and he's making threats," Libertas said airily, but with an underlying note of worry. "I'm bracing myself for another deluge after *Escape* comes out later this fall. Robert Taylor plays an American trying to rescue his actress mother from a Nazi concentration camp. It will send Hitler and Göring into apoplexies. Many of the cast and crew refuse to have their names in the credits to protect their relatives in Europe from retribution."

"That's show business," said Harro sardonically.

As the evening passed, Greta observed the couple closely, certain that they were strongly opposed to the Reich. Given Harro's position in the Air Ministry, she would not have expected this, but it was intriguing.

She took Adam aside for a quick private chat. "What do you think of the Schulze-Boysens?" she murmured. "Do you think we could be friends?"

"Arvid mentioned Harro to me once, long ago," he replied in an undertone. "About five years ago, one of your friends from Wisconsin urged Arvid to work with him, but although Arvid was impressed, he decided Harro was too reckless."

"Of course Arvid would think so," said Greta, exasperated. "Anyone not as excessively cautious as himself is reckless. Anyway, times have changed. What might have seemed too reckless five years ago may be exactly what we need today."

At home later that night, while Ule slept soundly in the other room, Greta and Adam mulled over whether they should bring Harro Schulze-Boysen into their confidence. He had been fighting fascism for years, so they had every reason to believe he was still on their side, leading a resistance cell of his own. Harro undoubtedly would be a valuable ally. The intelligence he could obtain from the Air Ministry would complement and verify what Arvid learned in the Ministry of Economics. As for Arvid's original objections, perhaps he could teach Harro caution, focus, and discipline, and in return, Harro could invigorate their circle with his confidence and daring.

The next day, Adam approached Harro to gauge his interest in linking their resistance circles. "He remembers Arvid well," Adam told Greta afterward. "Harro's more than willing to collaborate with our group, but how do we convince Arvid?"

"Leave that to me," Greta replied.

She invited Mildred and Libertas to join her for a week's holiday in Saxony. Anyone who observed them would have seen three good friends enjoying a girls' week away from their husbands, hiking, swimming, sunbathing, and dining together, happy and carefree. But alone on the forested trails or behind the locked doors of their hotel rooms, they discussed in carefully imprecise terms their work, the reach of their resistance circles, and their contacts. Mildred and Libertas took to one another quickly, and after several quiet, lengthy, intense discussions, Greta convinced them that their groups should join forces. When they parted at the end of the week, Mildred agreed to urge Arvid to meet with Harro again to discuss the possibilities.

A few days after the women returned to Berlin, their husbands met at the Harnacks' apartment. Greta waited impatiently at home with Ule, unable to settle down either to work or play. When Adam returned home nearly an hour later than expected, she flew to the door as soon as she heard his key in the lock.

Holding a finger to his lips, he entered the apartment, closed the door, and locked it behind him. "Arvid consents," he said, a broad grin spreading across his face. "Greta, the things Harro knows, the information he has access to—this could change everything for us."

Sighing with relief, Greta flung her arms around him and kissed his cheek. Her hopes soared as she considered the many ways their stronger, more extensive resistance network would allow them to undermine the Nazi regime and help the Jews.

But even as she allowed herself to dream, a voice in the back of her thoughts murmured caution. A bigger network meant increased danger of discovery or betrayal. Bolder risks could mean greater rewards, or swift and more severe punishments.

They might not know which lay ahead of them—or what crept up on them from behind—until it was too late.

CHAPTER FORTY-NINE

July–September 1940

Mildred

On the afternoon of July 6, a brass band and a massive crowd met Adolf Hitler's heavily guarded private train when he returned to Berlin from the forest of Compiègne. Thousands of exultant Germans bearing flowers and swastika flags lined the mile-long drive from the Anhalter Bahnhof to the Chancellery, shouting, cheering, weeping, working themselves into frantic hysteria as the Führer's car sedately passed. Before it walked young women clad in the white blouses and blue skirts of the Bund Deutscher Mädel, strewing so many flowers in the vehicle's path that the gray street was entirely covered in colorful blossoms, the crushed petals releasing their fragrance until the warm summer air was thick with their perfume.

Eleven days later, an even larger spectacle greeted the victorious troops upon their return to the capital. A public holiday had been declared, grandstands had been erected on Pariserplatz, and Goebbels had issued a statement urging the German people to offer a "tumultuous welcome for your sons, husbands, fathers and brothers who won the great victories in Poland and France." Mildred perceived an implicit threat in the directive, but when the troops marched through the city—hardened by battle, proud in victory, strong, tanned, disciplined—the spectators' unrestrained jubilation seemed fiercely genuine.

As the military paraded through the Brandenburger Tor and goose-stepped before the review stand, tens of thousands of jubilant Germans lined the streets, weeping for joy, shouting themselves hoarse, tossing flowers, bursting into spontaneous song. Church bells that had not been confiscated and melted down for their copper rang and rang, filling the sun-drenched skies with a song of triumph and warning.

Observing the scenes as if from across a vast chasm, Mildred was both repulsed and astounded. The German people seemed to believe that the war was essentially over, that their loved ones would soon be released from military service, that rationing would cease as material goods from conquered nations flowed into the Reich—metal ores, grain, silk stockings, chocolate. And while it was true that Germany was still officially at war with Great Britain, the British troops had been soundly thrashed. In their retreat they had left acres of arms and equipment behind at Dunkirk, materiel they could not swiftly replace. Surely their surrender was both inevitable and imminent.

The following evening, in an address to the Reichstag at the Kroll Opera House broadcast around the world, Hitler warned Great Britain that only by accepting his peace terms would they avert their own destruction. He openly taunted Winston Churchill, who had replaced Neville Chamberlain as prime minister, for presuming to fight on when the most likely outcome was the complete annihilation of their empire.

Mildred saw no reason why any sensible person would believe anything Hitler said. Even as he spoke of peace, German bombers flew over England and fighters strafed British ships at sea. Hitler's peace would be an untenable détente that would leave him in control over formerly sovereign nations, the conquerer of Europe. It would mean the enslavement of millions and the deaths of millions more.

Great Britain had not yet responded to Hitler's dubious peace offer when Arvid's younger brother Falk visited them from Munich, where he was involved with the student resistance movement. He had brought along a heavy wooden crate, and when he pried off the lid, Mildred gasped to see a wonderful assortment of fresh vegetables—greens, tomatoes, summer squash, cabbages, peppers—that Mutti Harnack had grown in her garden at the sanatorium.

"Mutti said to tell you that these vegetables are for you and her grandchild," Falk told Mildred, smiling. "She admires your generosity to the less fortunate, but you're under strict orders to eat more than you give away."

"I agree with our mother," said Arvid, putting an arm around Mildred's shoulders as he peered into the crate. "You need to eat more."

"We all need to eat more," she pointed out, having already made up her mind to divide up the bounty with Sara and Natan. She did not change her mind even after Falk unpacked the crate and she discovered that it contained fewer vegetables than she had assumed, because beneath them Falk had concealed a wonderful, dangerous gift: a powerful shortwave radio.

When the brothers set up the device away from the windows and walls adjoining other apartments, and the BBC came in as clearly as if it were broadcast from Wilhelmstrasse, Mildred impulsively kissed Falk on the cheek to thank him. "Now it will be so much easier to tune in to foreign broadcasts," she said. "It will help our group's work and our morale to get news we can trust, untainted by the Ministry of Propaganda."

"Be careful on the streets never to reveal how much you know," Falk cautioned. "Goebbels is waging his own private war against radio crime. A single slip of the tongue could betray you to an informant."

Mildred knew her brother-in-law did not exaggerate. Earlier that spring, a friend in the American press corps had told her of an incident the Nazi censors had forbidden him to include in his radio broadcast. The Luftwaffe had informed the mother of a German pilot that her son's plane had been shot down over France and that he was missing and presumed dead. A few days later, unbeknownst to the grieving mother, her son's name was included in a weekly BBC broadcast listing the names of Germans recently captured by the British. The next day, the mother received eight letters from friends and acquaintances assuring her that her son was alive but held prisoner in England. No doubt the mother rejoiced, but soon thereafter she reported all eight friends to the SS, and they were promptly arrested for listening to foreign radio broadcasts.

"Prime Minister Churchill delivered this speech to the House of Commons in June after the Dunkirk evacuation." Reaching into a pocket concealed in the lining of his suit jacket, Falk took out a few sheets of folded paper and handed them to Mildred. "It wasn't recorded, but afterward the BBC read portions of it over the air. I thought you might want to translate it for one of your newsletters, in case anyone doubts the British resolve."

Unfolding the pages, Mildred seated herself and read the transcript, which began with Mr. Churchill's vivid, harrowing account of the battles in France and Belgium that had culminated in the British and French retreat and evacuation at Dunkirk. She was not surprised to discover a very different version of events from the Nazis' official account. More than 335,000 troops had been safely brought to England, where they were preparing to defend their island home. "We shall go on to the end," Churchill had vowed. "We shall fight in France, we shall fight on the seas and oceans, we shall fight with growing confidence and growing strength in the air, we shall defend our island, whatever the cost may be. We shall fight on the beaches, we shall fight on the landing grounds, we shall fight in the fields and in the streets, we shall fight in the hills; we shall never surrender."

Two days later, on July 22, Foreign Secretary Lord Halifax delivered Great Britain's response to Hitler's offer of a compromised peace: a firm, unequivocal refusal.

Hitler had flown into a rage at the news, Arvid learned from ministry colleagues who had witnessed the scene, but his anger quickly found an outlet. As the conquered nations of Europe were brought into the bureaucratic management of the Reich, propaganda campaigns against their stubborn enemy across the Channel intensified. Whereas before the Nazi press had refused to address the subject of civilian casualties, the papers and radio waves now crackled with outraged reports of Royal Air Force raids on Bremen, Hamburg, Paderborn, Hagen, and Bochum, attacks that, the Nazis claimed, indiscriminately killed defenseless civilians.

"Does Goebbels really expect the German people to believe the British are targeting peaceful, sleepy villages and not the tank factories and military installations on their outskirts?" asked Mildred, incredulous.

"If the Führer says it's true, it must be true, however preposterous," came Arvid's sardonic reply.

Since July, the Luftwaffe had been bombing the British Isles, concentrating its attacks on shipping lanes and strategic ports on the coast, but as Harro Schulze-Boysen informed them, with the rejection of Hitler's peace offer, the focus shifted to achieving superiority over the Royal Air Force by attacking airfields, command posts, and aircraft factories. The British responded by attacking Nazi military targets in northern Germany and its conquered territories, dropping leaflets as well as bombs. But to Mildred—and apparently to most Berliners, since life in the capital went on as usual—the danger seemed real but distant.

Harro had warned Arvid that the Luftwaffe was preparing for a more intense campaign, and in mid-August the Germans launched a massive air campaign against Great Britain. It was unsettling to listen to *verboten* foreign radio broadcasts and learn of the destruction of British airfields and factories, each loss a setback the Allies could scarcely afford, each seeming to add years to the duration of the Reich.

Then, early in the morning of August 24, Mildred and Arvid tuned in the BBC and learned that beleaguered Portsmouth in Hampshire had again been bombed, leaving one hundred dead and three hundred injured. As if that shocking death toll were not enough for one night, twelve German bombers, ostensibly on a mission to destroy oil tanks and aircraft factories in the London suburbs, had instead dropped their bombs on the financial district and Oxford Street in the West End, a place devoid of military targets in the heart of the city.

Mildred turned to Arvid, horror-stricken, her hand upon her abdomen in an instinctive and futile gesture to protect her unborn child. He understood her unspoken question. "Whether it was a navigation error or a deliberate attack on civilians, Churchill will retaliate," he said somberly. "We should expect the worst."

That night, the shriek of air raid sirens jolted them from sleep. Swiftly they dressed in the darkness, snatched up their evacuation bags, and fled downstairs to the bomb shelter. For hours they huddled in the darkness among strangers, straining their ears for the distant rumble of bombs exploding elsewhere in the city, flinching at the relentless pounding of antiaircraft fire, frighteningly near. "We're safe," one anxious, trembling woman repeated over and over as the hours passed in stark terror. "Göring promised the RAF could not reach us."

It was nearly half past three o'clock before the all-clear sounded and they were allowed to drag themselves back upstairs and collapse exhausted into bed to steal a few hours of sleep before morning.

The next day, lightheaded from lack of sleep, Mildred and Arvid nonetheless rose at the usual hour, compelled to find out how badly the city had been damaged. As expected, Nazi radio announcers condemned British perfidy and reported a tangle of contradictions, in one breath jeering that the hapless, ineffectual RAF had been driven off by the superior German military, and in the next denouncing them for slaughtering helpless German women and children asleep in their beds.

Reluctant to leave Mildred alone on such a fraught morning, Arvid gave her a lingering kiss at the door, placing his hand gently upon her abdomen and urging her to take care. After he departed for the ministry, she ventured out and discovered that the city apparently had suffered only minimal damage, although it was difficult to be sure, since the authorities had roped off several streets to prevent anyone from approaching as the rubble was cleared away.

Although Mildred thought they had gotten off lightly compared to the citizens of Warsaw, Paris, and London, the people of Berlin reeled from shock and disbelief. Mildred understood why. From the moment the war had begun, Göring had assured them that no enemy planes would ever break through the antiaircraft defenses encircling the capital. When the sirens had gone off the night before, thousands of citizens had not even bothered to take shelter, so wholeheartedly had they trusted the *Reichsminister*'s assurances. In the morning word quickly spread that not only had the Royal Air Force easily swept through the skies above Berlin, but German gunners had not brought down a single British plane.

The myth of Berlin's invulnerability had been shattered by a single raid. When Arvid returned home from work that evening, he told Mildred that Hitler was furious, Göring humiliated. "The leaders of the Wehrmacht vow that it will never happen again," Arvid said. "I don't know anyone who believes it."

They went to bed early that night, desperate to catch up on lost sleep. But shortly after midnight, the air raid sirens wailed again, jolting them out of bed and sending them racing downstairs for the shelter. The night passed in sleepless terror, and in the morning they learned that ten people had been killed and twenty-nine wounded, Berlin's first civilian casualties of the war. The papers raged against the brutality of the RAF, denouncing the "cowardly British air pirates" for acting on Churchill's personal orders to "massacre the population of Berlin."

"Fine bit of hyperbole, that," said Arvid wearily, pushing aside the paper as he rose to get ready for work. Suddenly he halted, frowning as he studied her face. "Are you feeling all right?"

"I'm just tired," she said, smiling to reassure him. "Like everyone else in Berlin."

"Don't work yourself too hard today," he said, stroking her hair back from her face and kissing her softly. "Get some rest."

She promised him she would, and in the afternoon when weariness overcame her, she climbed into bed and slept for three hours.

That night and the next, the air raid sirens remained silent, but on September 1, the pealing wails again roused Mildred and Arvid from bed to hastily dress and stumble bleary-eyed and dazed down to the shelter. Then two quiet nights granted them unbroken sleep, but on September 4 the sirens shrieked again at promptly fifteen minutes past midnight, a time Mildred had already learned to dread. For two hours British bombers roared high above Berlin while the German antiaircraft guns frantically thundered back. The next day, rumors spread that the German gunners could not find the British planes because they were coated with invisibility paint. Another more credible story making the rounds proved true: A bomb had fallen upon the Tiergarten, killing a policeman.

Night after night the air raids came. In public speeches, Hitler angrily declared that if the British continued to attack Germany's cities, he would raze their cities to the ground. Mildred knew from the BBC that the Luftwaffe was already attempting exactly that. Despite Hitler's claims to the contrary, German bombers had been targeting the center of London for more than two weeks.

The days passed in a blur of sleeplessness and terror. Mildred rested when she could, but her nerves were on edge. The sleep she managed to find during the sunlit hours was restless and haunted by nightmares, and even on the nights the sirens were silent, she found herself bolting awake shortly after midnight, heart pounding, straining her ears for the piercing shriek that warned of impending attack, the distant low rumble of bombs as they struck in the distance, the pounding of the rooftop guns.

Then, one night in early September, she woke not to sirens or from nightmares but to pain, a sudden, relentless cramping so intense it took her breath away. When she tried to sit up in bed, her hand brushed the bedcovers and came away warm and damp.

"Arvid," she called out, her voice breaking with grief and terror. "Arvid, help me."

Not this, she thought frantically as Arvid woke and saw the blood and ran to a neighbor's apartment to phone for an ambulance.

She knew before the doctors confirmed it that she had lost the child. She imagined that she had felt the tiny soul leaving her, letting go with a gentle, wistful sigh as if to say it had already learned enough of the world to know it dared not linger.

She wept until she had no more tears left. She nodded mutely when the doctors assured her that she was in good health, if a bit underweight, and that once she regained her strength, there was no reason why they should not try again to conceive. No reason, Mildred thought, except that she had tried and failed for many years with nothing to show for it but disappointment and heartbreak.

After she was discharged from the hospital, Arvid urged her to recover her health at some quiet retreat in the countryside. When she demurred, Falk and Inge chimed in too, until eventually, exhausted and grieving, she consented.

She spent her thirty-eighth birthday at a spa in Marienbad, taking the cure of the celebrated mineral springs, finding comfort for her broken heart in easy walks through forests and gardens, soothing her sorrow with the poetry of Goethe. The food was fresh, plentiful, and nourishing, and at night her sleep was undisturbed by sirens and bombs.

In the last week of September, Mildred returned to Berlin, healing but carrying a sorrow so deep and constant it felt infused into her very bones. Arvid offered tender embraces and loving words and evaded her questions about the resistance work he had carried out in her absence.

"Don't shut me out," she finally told him, thinking of Greta. She wanted to work. She needed purpose. If she could not nurture her own child, at least she could make the world better for other women's children.

Acquiescing, Arvid told her about several curious and foreboding reports he had seen in the Economics Ministry and the Luftwaffe's ongoing merciless pounding of London. Then he hesitated. "There's something else," he said, taking her hand. "While you were away, I had an interesting visitor—the third secretary of the Soviet embassy, Alexander Erdberg."

"An alias and a cover, I assume."

Arvid nodded. "He claimed to be a friend of Alexander Hirschfeld, and he wants me to help him as I once helped Hirschfeld."

"Hirschfeld was a trusted friend long before he asked you to provide him with intelligence," Mildred pointed out. "How do you know this Erdberg can be trusted? You haven't heard from the Soviets in years, not since Stalin's purge began. Why would Moscow contact you now?"

For the same reason any other nation wanted intelligence from the Reich, Arvid explained, because Hitler could not be trusted and his unchecked ambition threatened to engulf the continent. Arvid had investigated Erdberg thoroughly and had confirmed that he was not an agent provocateur. Mindful of the purges that had claimed the lives of friends and acquaintances who once worked at the Soviet embassy, at first Arvid had declined, but eventually he had agreed to help them. Disinterested idealism was his only motive. He refused their offers of payment, and made it clear that he did not share their ideology. His only desire was to bring down Hitler and the Reich. If providing intelligence to the Soviets would help him accomplish that goal, then he would do it.

Mildred muffled a sigh. Once again, Arvid was not seeking her permission, but informing her of the way things would be. "Be careful," she said. She hoped this Alexander Erdberg would prove worthy of his trust.

At the end of September, as bombs hammered London and the British relentlessly attacked German ports in order to delay the invasion of the British Isles, Arvid provided his new Soviet contact with his first intelligence report.

In defiance of the nonaggression pact between Hitler and Stalin, and contrary to the prevailing opinion that Hitler would never risk a two-front war, Nazi high command was secretly devising a plan to attack the Soviet Union.

CHAPTER FIFTY

October 1940–January 1941

Sara

As a courier, Sara often did not know the contents of the documents she carried between members of the resistance circle, but one October afternoon, Arvid invited her to read his latest intelligence report before she delivered it to a secluded dead drop in the University of Berlin library.

"If you're caught with this, the punishment will be severe," Arvid said as he handed her the typewritten page. "You deserve to know why you're risking your life."

Her heart thudded at the reminder of the danger, but of course she read the report. She would suffer the consequences either way, so she might as well satisfy her curiosity.

An officer of the Oberkommando der Wehrmacht had told Arvid that by early 1941, Germany would be prepared to go to war with the Soviet Union. The campaign's objective was to advance to a line from the port of Archangel in northern Russia to the port of Astrakhan on the Caspian Sea. Creating a vassal state from captured territory would bring most of the Soviet population and economic resources under control of the Reich. As an important preliminary measure, the German military would occupy Romania. The officer had hinted that preparations for the incursion into that country would require a postponement of the invasion of Great Britain.

Sara's thoughts raced as she slipped the report into a secret pouch in her old student satchel. In late September, Germany, Italy, and Japan had signed a pact agreeing to assist one another if any of the three were attacked by a country not involved in the current conflicts. One article specifically stated that the Tripartite Pact did not affect the political status existing between any of their countries and the Soviet Union, but Hitler's invasion plans revealed how tenuous relations between Germany and the USSR truly were. If Stalin knew Hitler already intended to betray him, he might abandon the nonaggression pact of 1939, which, unbeknownst to him, Germany had already violated. The Soviets would almost certainly cut off the steady flow of raw materials from the Soviet Union into Germany rather than sustain the production of war materiel that might be turned against them. Perhaps—however improbable it seemed—the Soviets might even form an alliance with Great Britain in order to defeat Germany.

Sara knew the Harnacks had already provided copies of the report to their contacts at the embassies of the Soviet Union and the United States, but she had no idea who would come for the copy she left at the dead drop. Could it be someone she had known from her student days, a former classmate or professor? It seemed so long ago that she had studied there, that she had dreamed of earning her doctorate and winning a fellowship to study in the United States. Her life had turned out nothing like she had imagined it when she passed through the front gates of the university on her first day as a student, so thrilled, so hopeful, so full of anticipation for all that she would learn and do.

By now the students she had studied with had all moved on, graduated or forced out like herself. There were only a handful of people who might recognize her on campus, but she blended in so well that it was unlikely anyone would notice her. And if someone did suspect she was a Jew wandering about where she was forbidden, she would show them the false identity papers the Kuckhoffs had procured for her. They showed that she was Annemarie Hannemann, a student from Frankfurt, with all the rights and privileges accorded to any other Aryan citizen of the Reich.

But no one would catch her. Sara walked with purpose, as if her thoughts were fixed on important matters and she belonged exactly where she was. No one ever questioned her. Sometimes a few young men tried to catch her eye or chat her up, but she offered only polite smiles and quiet demurrals in reply. How lovely it might be to enjoy a brief flirtation with a handsome stranger, like any other young woman could—somewhere else in a time of peace, but not in Berlin in 1940, not when one was a Jew in the resistance, not when it was impossible to tell at a glance who was an inveterate Nazi, who was a friend, and who was a *Mitläufer*, one of the vast number of Germans who went along with the Reich's atrocities, not actively persecuting anyone but refusing to intervene on behalf of the oppressed.

Was Dieter still a *Mitläufer*, Sara wondered, or had he fully assimilated into the Reich for the sake of his precious business? He might be dead for all she knew. Bombs had fallen in the neighborhood where he and his mother had lived, though not on their apartment building. Or he could have been conscripted, and might be encamped somewhere in conquered France or lying in a battlefield grave. Unsettled, she pushed the images aside. She did not want to brood over Dieter's fate, or to think of him at all. If he ever spared a thought for her, it could only be to pray that no one remembered he had once been engaged to a Jew.

Thus far the British bombers had spared the block where Sara and Natan moved after being evicted from the apartment in Friedenau. The cramped studio they shared was on Grenadierstrasse on the eastern edge of the ghetto, a dilapidated building already overcrowded with poor Aryans and immigrants from elsewhere in the Reich. They resented their new Jewish neighbors, who were usually better educated, more cultured, better dressed, and profoundly disconsolate, as if they considered themselves too good for the place. Never mind that most of the Jews were unemployed and constantly hungry from subsisting on much smaller rations. Never mind that they were all poor now, all threatened by the same British bombs.

Whenever the air raid sirens wailed, the German residents made a mad rush for the shelter in the cellar, but Jews were forbidden to enter. Instead Sara, Natan, and a few dozen others descended to the ground floor and waited out the terrifying hours in the central hallway, bracing themselves against the walls, avoiding the windows at either end, covering their heads with their arms when the roar of British planes intensified.

"We should paint 'Jews Here' on the roof so that the British know to drop their bombs elsewhere," Natan said wearily the morning after a long, harrowing, sleepless night in mid-October. "Why should they kill us? We hate the Nazis even more than they do."

"I don't think that would help," Sara replied, stifling a yawn, trying to ignore the gnawing ache in her empty stomach. "The Americans painted 'USA' on the roof of their embassy, but they still have to put out fires when incendiaries land in their gardens."

"In their *gardens*," Natan said, raising a finger for emphasis, "not on their roof."

Sara managed a wan laugh. "I still say your signal is a very bad idea. If the British don't bomb us, the Luftwaffe will."

As autumn passed into a winter of long nights, overcast skies, and frigid cold, Berlin's air raid sirens blared almost every night, interrupting sleep and sending terrified residents scrambling for shelter. In September the RAF bombed the capital about four times every week, but in October the number of raids dropped slightly, and in November Berlin was struck only eight times. But although the frequency of attacks had diminished, they were no less destructive—on both sides, for the German defenses had improved dramatically and had brought down many British planes. By the first snowfall of December, almost every district in Berlin had been struck at least once. The Reichstag building, the Propaganda Ministry, the criminal courts at Moabit, the Berlin Zoo, and the palace at Charlottenburg all had sustained damage. So many factories, military sites, and railroads had been destroyed that Sara sustained a faint hope that the German military would be immobilized and the war would grind to a halt. But it was a small flame, quickly extinguished when she observed how swiftly the Nazis cleared away the rubble and made repairs.

In the last week of December, when Sara stopped by the Harnacks' apartment on a courier run, Mildred told her that a few days before, Hitler had signed a secret directive officially ordering the attack on the Soviet Union. Operation Barbarossa called for the German military to crush the Soviet Union in a swift, decisive campaign before the war upon Britain was concluded. Preparations were to be completed by May 15, 1941.

Sara felt a stirring of hope and fear. "Arvid and Harro have said that a two-front war would be disastrous for Hitler."

"It could be," said Mildred guardedly, "but if Germany defeats the Soviet Union and assimilates their resources and materiel, it will be disastrous for Great Britain."

"And for us," said Sara, meaning the resistance, the Jews, every enemy of the Reich.

"And the United States," said Mildred. "They'll be forced to fight in the end. I only wish they would see that and intervene now. The sooner they do, the more lives will be saved, I'm sure of it."

Sara understood Mildred's frustration. The Harnacks had been passing military and economic secrets to the U.S. government for years, apparently to no avail. They could only hope that plans were developing behind the scenes, that the risks they took were not for nothing.

In January, as bitter cold enveloped northern Germany, Harro Schulze-Boysen and the rest of the executive staff were transferred to the Luftwaffe's wartime headquarters in Wildpark-Werder near Potsdam. His new post gave Harro access to confidential information about the Axis air forces as well as secret diplomatic and military reports from German consulates and embassies. Within his first few days, he learned that the Luftwaffe was planning photographic reconnaissance flights over Soviet territory, and he also met several experts on the Soviet Union who had recently been reassigned from the Air Ministry to Göring's operations planning staff. Soon thereafter, Arvid learned that the German high command had ordered the Military Economic Department to prepare a map of Soviet industrial flights. If Hitler's secret Directive Number 21 was not evidence enough, these activities proved that Operation Barbarossa was real and under way.

Thanks to the resistance, the Soviet Union would be forewarned. It would have months to prepare, and when the German attack finally came in spring, the Soviet defenses would utterly overwhelm the Wehrmacht and Luftwaffe. With its military crushed, the Reich would fall.

But spring was months away, and as persecution of Jews made their lives unbearable and food and fuel grew scarce even for Aryans, Sara began to worry that she and Natan might not make it through the winter. Their ghetto apartment was old and poorly insulated, so even though it was small—merely one bedroom where Sara slept, a living room where Natan made his bed on the sofa, and a kitchenette comprised of a sink, an icebox, a small cupboard, and a hot plate—they could never keep it tolerably warm. Real coffee had disappeared from markets long before, but as in the previous winter, meat, fresh vegetables, and even salt and pepper became scarce. Sara spent her days waiting impatiently, stomach growling, for the appointed hour when Jews were permitted to shop, then set off with her shopping basket praying that she would find enough left on the shelves to put together a meal. She went from shop to shop searching for potatoes and carrots and bread, enduring long queues and anxious pushy crowds. There was never enough for everyone. Sara always had more ration coupons left over than there was food to buy.

She was always tired, always thinking of food, of how she might turn yesterday's potato peelings into a broth that would sustain them through the day. Natan never complained, but his eyes glittered from hunger and his face had become gaunt. She knew from the way her clothes hung loosely upon her that she had become too thin as well. Once Natan brought home a piece of cheese, a gift from a friend, scarcely enough for a sandwich and yet she cried out from joy.

"Enough is enough," he said, his expression hardening. "Tomorrow I'll go to Schloss Federle and bring back enough supplies to see us through the winter."

Sara's mouth watered at the memory of the sacks of rice and beans, the bottles of oil, the cans of fruits and vegetables and everything else they had put away so carefully in the attic of the west wing. "But what if we have to go into hiding?" she asked, instinctively lowering her voice.

"Once we do, we won't be able to help the resistance or claim our immigration visas if our turn comes. As long as any hope remains, we'll take our chances out here. Agreed?"

Wordlessly, Sara nodded. For the same reason, she could not simply disappear into Annemarie Hannemann's identity and wait out the

Reich disguised as an Aryan, as she assumed other Jews who had managed to get false papers had done. Unfortunately, the source who had provided her papers had been arrested before he could make any for Natan.

"We stocked enough supplies to feed two families for several months," Natan reminded her. "Now that it's just the two of us, we could stretch that out for a year, maybe two."

"Or longer," said Sara. But maybe they would not have to. If Arvid and Harro were right, and Germany attacked the Soviet Union in the spring, the war could be over by summer.

Natan intended to make the trip to Schloss Federle alone, but Sara insisted on accompanying him. Not only that, she would drive. "Annemarie Hannemann still has her license," she pointed out. "We only need a good excuse for her to be out on the roads using up her fuel ration."

Early the next morning when they went to the auto repair shop, they discovered that despite the best efforts of Natan's mechanic friend, their parents' luxurious car was gone. The previous March, the army had ordered all but a tiny fraction of car owners to surrender their vehicles' batteries, and a few months later a salvage crew had confiscated the rest for the war effort. Nervous, glancing over his shoulder as he spoke, Natan's friend offered to let them borrow a tow truck for a few hours, but only that one time.

Natan accepted before his friend could change his mind. After pulling a mechanic's coveralls over her clothes and tucking her long dark hair up into a cap, Sara climbed into the driver's seat and familiarized herself with the controls. Natan took the seat beside her, slouching low, ready to drop to the floor if a military convoy passed. They should be fine if they kept moving, but if they were stopped and questioned, they would say that Annemarie Hannemann was on a call for her father's repair shop, and Natan was a conscripted Jewish worker ordered to help her with the heavy lifting. Even as she agreed to her brother's hastily constructed cover story, Sara knew it would never hold up under questioning.

"Just drive carefully," said Natan as she steered the truck from the garage onto the street. "Don't give anyone any reason to pull us over."

She nodded, her eyes fixed on the road ahead. She had not driven her parents' car in more than two years and had never driven anything like the tow truck. Her heart pounded as they made their way out of the city, but the roads were clear of snow and there was little traffic thanks to gas rationing. Even so, she did not breathe easily until they reached the countryside, the thick forests and rolling hills covered in soft white snow exactly as she remembered from winters past, beautiful and enduring, untouched by the war.

They reached Minden-Lübbecke without incident. As they approached the Riechmann estate and Sara caught sight of the familiar white stone and golden stucco walls through the bare-limbed trees, she was flooded by such an intense feeling of relief and safe homecoming that she almost wept. None of the servants came out to meet the truck as they crossed the stone bridge over the broad, encircling moat, but Sara and Natan were not surprised. No one was expecting them, and the day was sunny but bitterly cold, with a sharp wind that stung the skin and sent snow ghosting across the roads. Wilhelm had closed down the east and west wings and several rooms in the main building to conserve fuel while the house was unoccupied. He and Amalie had retained the core household staff, but other employees had been dismissed, or had been taken in the draft, or had left for more lucrative jobs in the wartime economy. Natan had a key, so if no one glanced out the windows and spotted the very conspicuous tow truck parked in the circular drive, he and Sara might be able to slip in and out of the west wing with food and supplies without anyone knowing.

"What would you like for supper tonight?" Sara asked Natan as they walked through the ankle-deep drifts covering the cobblestone path that led from the driveway around the west wing to the rear entrance.

Natan groaned and clutched his stomach with one hand as he dug the key from his pocket with the other. "Anything. Everything," he said, unlocking the door. "Roast potatoes swimming in butter. Fresh bread. Canned peaches. Hot tea with honey."

Sara's stomach rumbled as she followed him inside. "The bread will take too long to rise for me to bake a loaf tonight, but I promise you'll have some for your breakfast tomorrow."

He sighed in anticipation as they carefully locked the door behind them and wiped their shoes on the mat. The stairwell was cold and dark, and when Natan tested the switch, the overhead light failed to come on. "I guess they've shut off the power completely. The water too, probably."

"They'll turn them back on if we go into hiding, right?"

"Of course," Natan said as he raced upstairs. Sara hurried after him, her breath emerging as faint white puffs. When she caught up with him, he was fitting a second key in the door of the spare room, which was as dusty and crowded with old furniture as it had been on their last visit. Single file, they climbed the narrow staircase to the attic, where Natan shoved aside the bookcase covering the low, hidden door. Ducking his head, he entered, and she followed quickly after.

"Take as much as you can comfortably carry," he instructed as he led the way to the large closet they had stocked as a pantry. "We have time for three trips, but then I want to get back on the road."

Nodding agreement, she stood out of the way as he opened the pantry door—revealing empty shelves, a layer of dust, nothing more.

They both stood there for a moment, staring into the pantry. "What the hell," Natan muttered, closing the door and opening it again. It was still empty, of course, and he muttered a curse at his own foolishness. Backing away, he interlaced his fingers and rested them on top of his head. "Is there another pantry I don't know of?"

Sara struggled to think. "I—there's a linen closet next to the bathroom."

She barely had the words out before Natan hurried past her and down the narrow hall. Trailing behind, she found him staring into the smaller closet, once full of spare linens and sanitary items, empty now except for a small package of toilet paper. "Take this," Natan said shortly, snatching it up and tossing it to her.

She quickly left the toilet paper by the exit and met him back at the pantry, where he was straining to reach into the depths of the top shelf. He found a small sack of rice, two tins of sardines, and a bottle of olive oil, which he passed to her, and which she left by the exit. They then began a sweep of the entire hiding place, searching every closet, every drawer, beneath the beds, everywhere. There were still sheets on the mattresses and spare clothing in the wardrobes, but they found no more food, no supplies, no money, although they knew their father had left a lockbox of Reichsmarks and gold coins in his bureau. Even the soft pillows and thick comforters Sara and her mother had arranged upon the beds were gone.

Natan stripped a sheet from one of the mattresses and told her to use it as a sack and fill it with her spare clothing. He did the same with his own clothes and some things of their father's that should fit him. They worked swiftly, without speaking, but Sara felt a rising panic as they gathered all that might be useful and left the hiding place, taking care to replace the bookcase and lock all the doors behind them.

Once outside, they ran to the truck, threw their salvaged belongings inside, and climbed into their seats, expecting any moment for someone to order them to halt. Sara's heart pounded with alarm as she started the engine. When she threw the truck into gear and pulled away, she thought she saw a curtain in a window twitch, but she did not slow the truck long enough to take a second look.

They sped off, across the bridge and away.

"Who—" Sara began, her voice trembling. "It must have been someone on the staff. No one else knew about our hiding place."

"Of course. Papa and Mutti would have told us if they had moved our supplies."

"But Wilhelm and Amalie said most of the servants have been with the family for generations. They trusted them completely."

"Someone obviously didn't deserve their trust." He rubbed at his jaw, glowering out the window. "People change. They become greedy or afraid. They become Nazis, out of convenience or conviction."

"Maybe whoever it was meant us no harm. Maybe they were hungry and thought we weren't ever coming back."

"Maybe," said Natan. "Maybe if we had knocked on the front door and explained the situation, they would have apologized, fixed us a hot meal, and, while we ate, loaded up the truck with everything they had taken. Or maybe they would have called the Gestapo to report two Jews driving a stolen truck, breaking into Baron von Riechmann's castle and robbing the place blind."

Sara pressed her lips together and nodded, a bitter taste in her mouth. Natan was right. They could not trust anyone at Schloss Federle anymore. They had lost not only their supplies but also their hiding place of last resort, and with it the reassurance of knowing that if Berlin became too dangerous, if Jews were banned from every last block in the city, one last sanctuary remained.

Now that too had been taken from them. They could never return, and they had nowhere else to go.

CHAPTER FIFTY-ONE

February–June 1941

Greta

Air raids upon Berlin diminished in the bleak, icy early months of the year, but in March the Royal Air Force resumed its attacks, jolting Greta and Adam out of bed, sending them racing down the hall to snatch up Ule and descend to the basement shelter, hearts pounding, ears straining for the roar of bombers over the thudding of antiaircraft fire.

By early morning, workers had cordoned off damaged areas and were clearing away debris, quickly and efficiently, as if to maintain the illusion that the capital was impervious. Jewish passersby were often conscripted to haul away debris, along with forced laborers from Poland brought to Germany to work on Albert Speer's grandiose Germania architecture projects. They were not prisoners of war, not enemy soldiers, but ordinary citizens enslaved by the Reich. Although most Berliners averted their gaze, it was impossible to miss their squalid camps poorly concealed behind high walls and barbed wire. Whenever Greta encountered the prisoners as they were marched to and from their work sites, she was horrified anew by their tattered clothing, their bleak expressions, their emaciated frames.

The loss of apartment buildings to British bombs and Hitler's dream of a glorious new Reich capital created a housing crisis in Berlin. As always, the Jews were forced to give way. After a flurry of new laws were passed, they lost their few remaining rights as tenants and were forced into *Judenhäuser*, "Jew houses," run-down buildings in the least desirable areas of the city. Two Jews per room was the standard rule, regularly exceeded, as Jewish households already within the ghetto were required to take in the homeless. In late winter, Sara and Natan were ordered to accept a couple with a three-year-old daughter. The siblings took the bedroom, the young family made their beds in the living room, and they all shared the kitchen and bath, trying as best they could to stay out of one another's way. The constant presence of strangers in their home obliged Sara and Natan to be more discreet about their resistance activities, but they did not abandon their work. The need was too great, Sara told Greta wearily, and the alternative—surrender, acceptance of oppression—was too unbearable to contemplate.

As spring arrived, Arvid, Harro, and their contacts within other ministries continued to gather evidence that the German invasion of the Soviet Union was imminent. In mid-April, Erdberg told Adam and Arvid that his superiors wanted him to establish radio contact between their resistance group and Moscow in the event that war cut off other channels of communication.

At first, Arvid refused. They had not a single trained radio operator in their group. Radio signals could be traced to their source, compromising their entire network. If through accident or betrayal they were found in possession of the equipment, the punishment was summary execution. Greta agreed with Arvid, deeply skeptical that radio communications could be established securely or that it would be worth the risk. But Harro strongly supported the idea, and eventually he and Erdberg wore Arvid down, although Arvid flatly rejected Erdberg's request that he become the radio operator. "I'll encode the messages," he said, "but you'll have to find someone else to transmit them."

Greta saw him glance at Mildred as he spoke, and she knew he was concerned for her safety, not his own. Eventually the role went to sculptor Kurt Schumacher, a longtime member of Harro's resistance circle and former student of Libertas's artist father. Erdberg promised to supply the equipment as soon as it could be smuggled from Moscow.

One evening in early May, Adam returned home from a clandestine meeting with Arvid and Erdberg, his expression tense and troubled. "Moscow has sent two transmitters by diplomatic pouch," he said. "Erdberg would like you to receive one of them the day after tomorrow at the Thielplatz Untergrundbahn station."

Greta's heart thudded. "He asked for me by name?"

Adam nodded.

"Why me?"

"Because he trusts you, because he believes a woman would be less suspicious. The radio is built into a suitcase, so he'll simply hand it off to you, and you'll deliver it to Schumacher's apartment."

Very simple indeed, Greta thought angrily. Adam regularly excluded her from meetings in their own home for her dubious protection, and now he wanted her to do this? "Let's be honest here," she said, her voice tight. "When I fetch this suitcase, I'm sticking my head into the noose."

"Greta—"

"It's not safe. You know that as well as I do. Did Erdberg pick me because I'm less suspicious or because I'm more expendable?"

"My God, what a question." Adam took her by the shoulders. "Do you think you're expendable to me or to Ule?"

Maybe not to them, but she could not say the same for Erdberg. "I'm not convinced that this scheme makes any sense. Do we have enough sources to warrant direct radio contact? Can these transmissions be made safely? Those are two simple questions, and I deserve honest answers."

"Of course we have enough sources, and every detail of the intelligence they provide is essential to bringing down the Reich. Kurt Schumacher and his wife accepted the risk of keeping the transmitter, so that's no concern of yours. However, every moment you spend arguing means less time for technical training and practice."

Stung, Greta reproached him with a look but said no more. She had demanded to be entrusted with responsibilities, and if she refused now they would never ask again. Kurt Schumacher's wife had accepted great risk, presumably without complaint. How could she do any less?

Two days later, at a few minutes after one o'clock, Greta met Erd-

berg at the Thielplatz Untergrundbahn station. As promised, she found
him seated on the bench nearest the newsstand, ostensibly engrossed in
Der Stürmer although she had no doubt he was fully aware of his surroundings. He glanced up at her approach, folded the newspaper, and
set it on the bench beside him. She wondered if the paper contained a
secret message for another contact to pick up as soon as he left.

"How delightful to see you again," he said when she joined him, rising, kissing her cheek as if they were old friends. He picked up the suitcase and offered her his arm, and after the barest hesitation, she took
it. He made cordial conversation as he escorted her out of the station,
but although his cheerful, relaxed demeanor eased some of her anxiety,
her heart thumped when she glimpsed a pair of SS men approaching
from the opposite direction, then four more clustered in front of a café
across the street. She would have stopped short at the sight of a gleaming black Gestapo staff car parked at the curb, except that Erdberg propelled her steadily forward.

"We'll make the handoff at the corner," he murmured. "I'll set down
the suitcase to check my watch, I'll give you a kiss goodbye, you'll pick
up the suitcase, then I'll head north and you head east."

"Let's walk one more block. This one is crawling with SS."

"The next block could be worse." He gave her a sidelong look, and
whatever he glimpsed made him reconsider. "Very well. One more
block."

Greta nodded, stoking her courage as they waited at the curb to
cross the street. The next block was more crowded with pedestrians,
but there were fewer SS men among them. "Whenever you're ready,"
she said.

He glanced over his shoulder. "At the next alley."

She spotted it ahead, two storefronts away. With a slight pressure on
her arm, he steered her toward it, but he took the turn too sharply and
slammed the suitcase on the brick corner of the building. The impact
knocked the handle from his grasp and the suitcase fell to the pavement
with a thud and a tinkle of glass.

Passersby shot curious looks their way. Greta's breath caught in
her throat as Erdberg released her arm and seized the suitcase in both
hands. With a jerk of his head, he signaled for her to follow him into

the alley, and she immediately obeyed. "I think it's broken," she said shakily. "I heard glass shatter."

He gave the suitcase a quick once-over. "It looks fine to me." He glanced into the depths of the alley and back to the street. "Change of plans. Take this home and test it. Keep it safe and hidden, someplace close so you can bring it to the shelter if the sirens go off."

"That wasn't our agreement. I'm supposed to take it to the operator."

"Not yet. If it *is* broken, as you believe, I'll need you to return it to me for repairs. If it's working, you can deliver it as originally planned."

"I can't keep this at home," she whispered fiercely. "I have a child."

"Then for his sake, don't get caught." Erdberg smiled and backed toward the sidewalk. "Please tell your husband that I'm taking his play *Till Eulenspiegel* with me on my next trip to Russia. Perhaps I'll find a theater company to stage it."

Astonished, Greta could only gape at him as he turned and strode from the alley without looking back. She picked up the suitcase and followed, but by the time she reached the sidewalk, he had disappeared.

Trembling with fear and anger, she hurried home only to find the apartment empty. After a heartbeat of stark terror she remembered that Adam had taken Ule to the zoo.

She shoved the suitcase into a closet behind some long coats, closed the door, and sank down upon the sofa. A sob escaped her throat, and before she could restrain them, hot tears spilled over. She had brought this dangerous thing into their home, against her better judgment, because what else could she have done? If the SS found it, she and Adam would be shot, and Ule—what would become of Ule? No doubt he would be given to some childless Aryan family to raise as their own, to bring up as a proper little Nazi.

She choked back her sobs and forced herself to take deep, steadying breaths until she stopped shaking.

That was how Adam found her an hour later when he and Ule came home, windswept and smiling. One glance and Adam sent Ule off to his room to play. "What happened?" he asked, and she gestured to the closet. He opened the door, found the suitcase, and turned to her, his expression stormy. "Why is this here?"

"Because our man in Moscow said so." She told him about Erdberg's clumsy mishap during the handoff. "I should have insisted that he take it back to his embassy and test it himself, but it all happened so fast. I had no choice but to bring the radio home. I couldn't abandon it in the alley."

Grimacing, Adam ran a hand over his jaw. "Let's see if it works, and if it does, I'll deliver it to Schumacher tonight." After checking to make sure the front door was locked, he retrieved the suitcase and carefully opened it on the living room floor. "A manual," he said, taking out a thin booklet.

"I suppose that's Moscow's idea of technical training." Greta drew closer as he turned the pages, glancing between the manual and the device built into the suitcase. It was a transmitter-receiver, and according to the book's diagrams and instructions, it had a range of up to six hundred miles and a battery that lasted two hours between recharges. That was, of course, when the radio functioned. As Adam established after clearing away some unidentifiable shards of broken glass, this one did not.

They waited for Erdberg to inform them how to return the radio, but when he did not contact them, Greta consulted Arvid, who arranged for her to hide it in a shed in Spandau until Edberg could retrieve it. Greta's apprehensions lifted the moment the incriminating suitcase was out of her home, but a few days later when Adam told her the device had been repaired, she summoned up her courage and volunteered to collect it. The second handoff went flawlessly. Suitcase in hand, Greta took a circuitous route to the Schumachers' flat, delivered the radio to Kurt, and went home, almost giddy from relief.

That night, Adam kissed her tenderly and praised her for handling her part of the operation so well, and he assured her that her services would not be required for the second radio. Hans Coppi, the passionate young Communist who had agreed to take charge of it, would receive it directly from Erdberg. "This was a dangerous job, darling, but well worth the risk," Adam said. "These radios are going to be more essential than we realized."

"Because of the invasion?"

"Yes, and because soon the Soviets will be our group's only foreign contact. Donald Heath is leaving Berlin. The U.S. State Department is transferring him to Santiago, Chile."

"What?" Greta exclaimed. "That's insane. He's the Americans' best and most informed analyst of the Reich in Germany. Why would they send him to South America when his expertise is badly needed here?"

Adam had no answer, and neither did Arvid or Mildred. Mildred took the Heath family's departure especially hard, for she and Louise Heath had become dear friends. Greta's heart went out to Mildred. With each American acquaintance who left Berlin, her homeland surely seemed more distant yet.

With the loss of their only remaining contact within the United States government, the Soviets seemed to be the group's last hope. When Adam told Greta that Kurt Schumacher and Hans Coppi were working steadily to establish radio contact with Moscow, she was glad that she had not let fear keep her from doing her part.

In early June, even as Arvid and Harro were gathering reams of evidence that Operation Barbarossa would launch within the month, the group suffered another setback—Schumacher was drafted into the Wehrmacht. Not only would he be forced to fight for the regime he despised, not only had they lost their radio operator, but they must persist in their work knowing that their success could cause their comrade's death. Nor was he the only friend whose life their work put in jeopardy. Arvid's younger brother Falk had been drafted by the Wehrmacht and was stationed in Chemnitz in Saxony, directly in line of a potential Soviet counteroffensive.

In the second week of June, Adam brought Greta another assignment. Harro knew the orders for the German attack upon the Soviet Union, the railroads that would be struck crippling blows, the plan for the advance, town by town. "It's too dangerous to put this down on paper," he said. "If a single page fell into the wrong hands, the Gestapo would know that the resistance has infiltrated the highest levels of the military. I need you to memorize the names of these Russian villages and repeat the list to certain comrades, until they too have it by heart."

Greta agreed. All her years as a diligent student had prepared her well for precisely this sort of task. But try though she might, the names of the towns would not stay fixed in her brain. She thought of the German military massing in the east, of the innocent people, women and children, who had no idea that a vast army was poised to strike and that their villages were in its sights.

After she had struggled for hours to memorize the information, a knock on the door startled her out of the fog of toil. Pulling the curtain over the map of the Soviet Union Adam had hung on the wall, she went to answer, only to find Adam welcoming Libertas Schulze-Boysen inside.

"Adam thought you might need a study partner," she said brightly, "and since thanks to Goebbels I'm currently unemployed, I volunteered."

Greta managed a rueful smile. The Reich had been so outraged by *The Mortal Storm* and *Escape* that the minister of propaganda had ordered the studio's Berlin office closed and had banned all MGM films throughout the Reich. Fortunately, Libertas did not need a steady paycheck.

"Things aren't going well," Greta admitted.

"Not to worry." Libertas took a small brown paper sack from her purse and gave it a little shake. "This will fuel our success."

As Libertas opened the sack, Greta detected a faint rich, nutty aroma. "Coffee," she marveled, bending closer and inhaling deeply. "Real coffee. How? There hasn't been real coffee in Berlin in over a year."

"Not so. You only need to know where to look and whom to ask. Shall I make us some?"

She did not need to ask twice. Soon Greta was savoring her first delicious cup of coffee in ages, studying the map with Libertas, steadily fixing the endangered Russian towns' names in her memory. Fueled by caffeine and urgency, she stayed up hours after her encouraging tutor left for the night, but eventually dropped wearily into bed beside Adam. After a few hours' sleep, she rose the next morning, indulged in another precious cup of coffee, and recited the list perfectly, every last Russian syllable of it.

She took Ule in hand and spent the day calling on the designated members of their circle, repeating the towns' names until each contact knew them by heart. Although the spring days were lengthening, it was nearly twilight by the time she returned home, just in time to place the blackout curtains, but too late to put together anything but a hasty meal of bread, cheese, and some sliced *Mettwurst* for supper.

Greta had just finished tidying the kitchen when Libertas again knocked on their door. "How did it go today?" she asked Greta, tilting her pretty blond head and regarding her expectantly.

"Better than I expected," admitted Greta, wiping her hands on her apron. "Messages delivered and received with no mishaps, no misunderstandings."

"You can't ask for better than that. Even so—" Libertas smiled mischievously and took a bottle of cognac from her purse. "I thought you might want a little something to settle your nerves."

"Libertas, you angel," exclaimed Greta. "Have you been raiding your grandfather's castle?"

"Very droll, darling. Are you as thirsty as you are witty?"

"I'll get three glasses," said Adam, bounding out of his chair.

"No you won't," Libertas declared, offering him her most charming smile, which was irresistible. "You'll fetch us *two* glasses, and then you'll sit right back down in that chair and study your lines or whatever it was you were doing while Greta—who has already had *quite* a day—was cleaning up after serving you a good meal."

Greta expected Adam to glower and sulk, but to her amusement, he shrugged, abashed, and retrieved two glasses from the kitchen.

"It's such a lovely night," said Libertas, turning to Greta. "Shall we drink outside?"

"It won't be so lovely if the RAF comes," said Adam.

"Don't you have air raid sirens in this neighborhood?"

"Let's go to the roof," Greta suggested, nudging Libertas toward the door.

"Save some cognac for me," Adam called.

"No promises," Libertas teased as the door closed behind them.

They settled on the rooftop on two weathered wooden chairs another resident had left there long before. Sipping cognac, breathing deeply of the fresh spring air, they sat for a long moment in silence, the blackout darkness complete except for the quarter moon and the faint light of stars.

"You could almost believe the city wasn't there," said Libertas softly, a note of deep weariness and strain in her voice.

"Almost." Was it the cognac that allowed her friend to let down her guard, or was it because it was just the two of them, with no husbands there to observe and appraise?

"Greta, Hitler must be stopped. He's a monster."

"I know he is."

"You think you do but you don't." Libertas paused to refresh her glass. "Terrible things are happening, worse than your worst nightmares. It began in Poland but it's spreading. Harro has access to the classified reports at Luftwaffe headquarters. The Nazis are committing terrible crimes—enslavement, torture, gruesome killings—"

Despite the warm summer air, Greta went cold. "On enemy soldiers?"

"Soldiers, civilians, Jews—especially Jews. Entire families are marched from their villages into the woods, shot, dumped in mass graves—" Libertas drank deeply, then clutched her glass in both hands just below her chin, shivering. "In my deepest heart, somehow I still cannot believe that the German people are capable of committing such horrific deeds. I know what Harro suffered when he was imprisoned years ago, and poor Hans Otto, and the Jews, and the foreign workers here in Berlin, and countless others. But mass murder, the slaughter of entire peoples—"

She broke down in tears. Greta put her arms around her friend and held her, rocking her gently, stroking her back. "Hitler will fall," she said softly. "His time is almost up. He will pay for his crimes, I promise you."

Perhaps the Soviet army would strike the blow that toppled the Führer from power, and sooner than he could possibly imagine.

As the end of June approached and the German military's preparations entered the final stages, Harro and Arvid compiled one last, meticulously detailed memorandum for Erdberg about Operation Barbarossa. Nine German armies with the force of 150 divisions would begin an offensive at dawn on June 22. The report included a list of the Luftwaffe's primary targets and the plan for the German civilian administration of occupied Soviet territories.

On the evening of June 21, Greta and Adam set the blackout curtains and talked quietly over dinner about Adam's idea for a new novel, a letter Greta had received from her brother, and the clever, amusing things their son had said and done that day. After they put Ule to bed, they settled down on the sofa, his arm around her shoulders, her head resting upon his chest. Together they finished off the bottle of cognac, for despite her teasing, Libertas liked Adam and even in her distress had remembered to save some for him.

Tomorrow Germany would go to war with the Soviet Union, expecting certain victory thanks to the element of surprise and overwhelming force. But the Soviets knew what was coming. The resistance had given them sufficient time to prepare their defenses without alerting their erstwhile Nazi allies that they knew war was imminent. Even now the Soviet military could be taking their positions and waiting for the dawn.

Sunrise would herald a new day, the beginning of the end.

CHAPTER FIFTY-TWO

June–July 1941

Mildred

Mildred woke shortly after dawn on Sunday, June 22, to find Arvid already awake, staring up at the ceiling. "Did you sleep at all?" she asked, snuggling closer, kissing him on the cheek.

"A little." He kissed her forehead and stroked her arm gently, but he radiated tension. "By now the German army has crossed the Soviet frontier. What an ugly surprise the Wehrmacht must have discovered waiting for them—the entire Red Army, firmly entrenched and on high alert."

Mildred shuddered, imagining the bloodshed and chaos. "Let's hope the Soviets took measures to protect civilians in the path of the advance."

"Let's hope." Arvid kissed her and sat up. "Time to face whatever comes."

They washed and dressed, and as Mildred set out breakfast, Arvid turned on the radio. "No news yet," he said, shaking his head as he tuned in one station after another and found only music and a weather report.

"Have you tried the BBC?"

"I could barely get a signal, but it was enough to know they weren't discussing Russia."

"Perhaps it's too early. Word might not have reached London yet."

How disconcerting it was to know they were among a mere handful of Berliners aware that events of monumental importance were unfolding hundreds of miles to the east. Soon the news would crash upon the city like floodwaters after a dam burst, but until then, the serenity of that warm, sunny morning would feel glaring and false, an untenable lie.

"Keep close to home today," Arvid urged after breakfast when they parted at the front door with a kiss.

"Greta is expecting me to meet her for a walk through the Tiergarten," she said. "Don't worry. If the Russian bombers come, we know where the public shelters are."

Arvid looked dubious, but he nodded, kissed her again, and set off for the office. He knew better than to order her to stay home, because if the RAF air raids had taught them anything, it was that no place was safer than any other. Sometimes people who sought refuge in the familiar shelters of their own buildings perished while others away from home survived because they had stayed late at work or had missed their usual train.

Mildred had been waiting at the appointed spot for ten minutes when Greta suddenly arrived, breathless, her hat askew. "Sorry I'm late," she apologized. "Adam and I overslept. How could we oversleep on such a day?"

"Never mind." Mildred smiled and adjusted her friend's hat. "This may be our last quiet morning for a while. Let's enjoy it."

They strolled along their favorite paths, savoring the sunshine, the fresh breezes, the fragrance of summer blossoms. Deliberately avoiding talk of war, they discussed Ule's latest antics, various plays in development for the Berlin stage, and Mildred's new job. The war had extinguished German publishers' interest in translating English and American books, but Mildred had found work teaching English for the Foreign Studies Department at the University of Berlin. She never would have expected to rejoin the university faculty after they had dismissed her so abruptly back in May 1932, but suddenly English classes were in high demand, and she was both a native speaker and an experienced teacher with a doctorate.

The primary purpose of the Foreign Studies Department was to train Nazi officers for the foreign service, and many of Mildred's students were women intending to become interpreters or translators. Apparently the dogma of *Kinder, Kirche, Küche* could be ignored if the menfolk were busy conquering Europe for the Führer. Although the department chair was a major in the SS, several other members of the faculty were with the resistance, including Harro Schulze-Boysen and Arvid's longtime friend Egmont Zechlin. Nor were all of the students inveterate Nazis; Mildred had already recruited a few resolute antifascists for their group.

As Mildred and Greta approached the Rosengarten, they passed a dark-haired, stylishly dressed woman pushing a pram. When their eyes met and the woman smiled, Mildred gave a start of recognition. "Nadia, *zdravstvuyte*," she exclaimed.

"*Guten Tag*, Mildred," Nadia replied in richly accented German. "It's been too long."

"It certainly has." Mildred peered into the pram at a dark-haired baby about four months old, sleeping peacefully with her fist in her mouth. She ached to cuddle her. "Who is this little darling?"

"Allow me to introduce my daughter, Anfisa Ivanovna," Nadia said proudly.

"She's adorable," said Greta warmly, smiling.

With a laugh for her own bad manners, Mildred quickly introduced her two friends, but as they chatted, the baby began to stir and mewl. Nadia smiled apologetically and went on her way, lulling little Anfisa Ivanovna back to sleep before she woke up completely.

A faint worry stirred in the back of Mildred's mind as she and Greta walked on together—not the usual, painful longing inspired by the sight of a more fortunate woman with a child, but something else, a sensation of dread that grew as she mulled it over. "Something's wrong."

As if by instinct, Greta's gaze turned skyward. "What do you hear?"

"No, that's not it." Mildred halted in the middle of the path, thoughts racing. "Nadia seemed very calm and content, don't you think?"

"Anfisa Ivanovna must be a much better sleeper than Ule ever was."

"But how could Nadia be so at ease, on this day of all days?"

Greta's eyes widened as understanding dawned. "She shouldn't be strolling through the Tiergarten. She and her daughter shouldn't even be in Germany. They should have been evacuated days ago."

Mildred turned and headed briskly in the direction of the nearest subway station. "We met at an embassy dinner, but Nadia's husband is a businessman, not a diplomat. He has no official affiliation with the Soviet embassy."

Greta hurried to catch up. "Then the Soviets didn't inform their expatriate citizens of the attack. But why? They're in terrible danger."

"I don't know. Perhaps the Soviets feared that evacuating their citizens would have tipped off the Nazis that they knew an attack was coming."

"I hope that's all it is."

"What do you mean?"

"I'm not sure." Greta quickened her pace. "But I agree—something is very, very wrong."

They parted at the station after deciding that Greta would go home, collect Adam and Ule, and meet Mildred at her apartment, where they would scan the shortwave for news of the invasion. When Mildred arrived home, she was surprised to find Arvid in the living room listening to their old radio. "It's happened," he said, waving her over. "Every German station is broadcasting Goebbels reading an official proclamation from Hitler."

Mildred locked the door and hurried to sit on the floor beside him. "I had an odd encounter in the Tiergarten—" she began, but she fell silent at the sound of the propaganda minister's voice.

"German people! National Socialists!" Goebbels intoned on Hitler's behalf. "Weighed down with heavy cares, condemned to months-long silence, the hour has come when at last I can speak frankly." With that, Goebbels launched into a lengthy denunciation of the British, followed by an unequivocal condemnation of the Soviet Union and their "Jewish Bolshevist rulers." He then announced what by then every German within range of a radio already knew: As of half past five o'clock that morning, Germany and the Soviet Union were at war.

"Arvid, listen," Mildred said at the first pause in the program. "I don't think the Soviet embassy informed their citizens about the attack."

Quickly she described her encounter with Nadia.

"Perhaps her family missed the warning somehow," said Arvid, pensive. "Or perhaps the embassy decided they couldn't risk revealing how much they knew."

"But why not warn their expatriates—or better yet, begin evacuating them—the moment the attack began, when it was no longer a secret?"

Just then the radio announcer cut to a press conference by Foreign Minister Ribbentrop. Mildred and Arvid listened as he delivered an address similar to the one Hitler gave to domestic and international journalists gathered at the Foreign Office. When that concluded, the programming switched to a repeat of Goebbels reading Hitler's proclamation. Realizing that they were unlikely to learn anything of substance from Reich radio, they moved to the bedroom, placed the blackout curtains, and took Falk's shortwave from its hiding place in the wardrobe. Greta, Adam, and Ule arrived just as Arvid tuned in the BBC.

They listened in shock and with increasing horror as the announcer described the German military's devastating assault on the Soviet Union. The Reich had deployed more than three million troops. The Red Army had offered little resistance, and by every indication they had been caught entirely by surprise. The Wehrmacht had marched almost unimpeded deep into Russian territory. The Luftwaffe had bombed miles of Soviet roads and railways, rendering them useless, and had destroyed nearly two thousand Soviet aircraft parked on runways and airfields. One by one towns and villages had been overrun by invaders or leveled by German tanks, and the list of names was devastatingly familiar.

"Everything is unfolding exactly as Harro and Arvid reported to Erdberg," said Greta, appalled. "Where are the defenses? Why weren't those villages evacuated days ago?"

"They didn't believe us," said Mildred, feeling faint. "All those reports, all that intelligence, and Moscow did nothing. They didn't even warn their military."

"Erdberg believed us," said Arvid. "I'm certain."

"A fat lot of good that does those poor, helpless people in the path of the invasion," Greta retorted.

"With so much at stake, how could they have disregarded everything we told them?" asked Adam. "Were our reports too cautious? Did the Soviets not trust us because we weren't motivated by Communist affiliations or financial gain?"

"Stalin probably couldn't believe that his good friend Hitler would ever betray him," said Greta bitterly, folding her arms across her chest. "Honor among dictators, I suppose."

When the BBC began to repeat earlier reports, Arvid tuned in a German station, and at the sound of Hitler's voice, Mildred recoiled as if she had been struck. "German soldiers!" he said, his voice ringing with pride and warning. "You enter a fight that will be both hard and laden with responsibility because the fate of Europe, the future of the German Reich, and the existence of our people rests solely in your hands."

Muttering a curse, Adam reached past Arvid to turn the dial. On another Reich station, an announcer triumphantly described the German military's swift and crushing advance, their courage, discipline, and unparalleled might. Russian troops were fleeing in terror, the announcer jubilantly reported. Victory would be swift and certain. Within weeks the Soviet Union would surrender to avoid total annihilation, Great Britain would have no choice but to sue for peace, and nothing more would prevent the Third Reich from assuming dominion over the earth.

The four friends sat in stunned silence as the radio played on.

"What happens now?" asked Mildred shakily, imagining Nadia at home somewhere in the city, cradling her daughter in her arms, listening to the radio with increasing terror.

"Do you have any way to reach Erdberg?" Adam asked Arvid.

"I'll call him from a public phone," said Arvid. "We won't be able to speak freely, but it's better than nothing."

Arvid left at once, but he returned fifteen minutes later shaking his head. "My call wouldn't go through. I suspect the phone lines have been cut."

"Why don't I just go to the embassy?" asked Greta, rising from her chair. "I'm sure I wouldn't be the only curious spectator."

Arvid regarded her, incredulous. "You do realize the Gestapo has the building under constant surveillance?"

"That's why I should go instead of you or Adam."

"I'll come with you," said Mildred. "We'll pretend we're just out for a Sunday stroll. We'll pause in front of the building to adjust a shoe strap, and with any luck Erdberg will be watching from the window and will follow us to a safe place where we can talk."

"And if he doesn't," Greta added, "we'll knock on the front door and ask to speak to him."

Their husbands protested, but Mildred and Greta parried their objections, and eventually the men's desire for information won out. Mildred and Greta discussed strategy as they walked, but when they arrived at the Soviet embassy, they found the building entirely surrounded by SS units. No one was allowed in or out. Two dozen or so Berliners observed the scene from across the street, but most passersby only stole a quick glance without breaking stride, pretending there was nothing to see.

Their hopes of meeting with Erdberg quashed, Mildred and Greta nonetheless lingered at the edge of the crowd. He would spot them easily if he came to a window, but all the blinds were drawn, and despite the warm, summery weather, a thick plume of gray smoke churned continuously from the chimney. "Do you see that?" Mildred murmured, indicating the chimney with a slight nod. "One flue is connected to flash-burning ovens. I'm sure all hands are busy destroying documents, records, codes, anything the Nazis might find valuable."

Greta eyed the heavily armed SS men stationed around the building. "How long before they storm the embassy?"

"I don't think they dare," said Mildred, thinking again of Nadia and her family, of her few remaining acquaintances at the embassy, wishing they were all safely far away. "Remember, there are German diplomats at the embassy in Moscow, and their fate depends upon what happens here."

It was not until the next day that Mildred read in the papers that the families of Soviet diplomats along with all other Soviet citizens living in Germany had been rounded up. Those in Berlin had been detained briefly at Gestapo headquarters on Prinz-Albrecht-Strasse before being transported to an SS camp on the outskirts of the city, where their compatriots from other cities and towns soon joined them. The roughly 1,150 Soviet men, women, and children would be held until they could be exchanged for the 120 German citizens stranded in Moscow.

Erdberg was not among them, as Mildred and her friends soon learned, but remained with the other diplomats within the heavily guarded embassy. Two days after the invasion, the Soviet first secretary bribed an SS officer with Reichsmarks, Russian caviar, vodka, and cognac to smuggle Erdberg out of the embassy on the pretense that he wished to bid farewell to his German fiancée. As soon as Erdberg was alone, he called the Kuckhoffs from a public phone and asked them to meet him at the Rüdesheimer Platz. Concerned for Greta's safety, Adam took Arvid instead.

"Erdberg and the other Soviet citizens will be deported soon under diplomatic protection," Arvid told Mildred afterward. "He offered me twelve thousand marks and said it was unlikely we would meet again. I reminded him that I wasn't doing this for money, but he insisted that I keep it for our expenses. I'll divide it up among the group."

Erdberg had also taught Arvid and Adam a coding system to use in their radio communications, using the key word "Schraube" and a key book, *Der Kurier aus Spanien*. Arvid would give one copy of the popular novel to Hans Coppi, and Erdberg would give another to the radio receivers in Moscow. It would be a very difficult code to break, even if the Nazis discovered what key book they used, which they were very unlikely to do.

Four days after German tanks rolled into the Soviet Union, Hans Coppi finally managed to get the recalcitrant transmitter functioning. Tuning to the appropriate frequency, he tapped out a traditional greeting, "*1000 Grüsse an alle Freunde*"—A thousand greetings to all friends. When an operator in Moscow immediately replied to confirm that their message had been received, Mildred, Arvid, and their friends could breathe a sigh of relief. Although at midnight on the first day of July, Erdberg and the fifteen hundred other captive Soviet citizens would depart Germany on a special train bound for the Russian border, the resistance would still be able to provide him with valuable intelligence.

The Soviet Union had recklessly squandered its best opportunity to defeat the Nazis on the battlefield, but Mildred hoped the Russians had learned from failure and would not repeat the mistake of ignoring their intelligence sources. For with Donald Heath gone and the United States still committed to isolationism, the USSR, for all its faults, remained the resistance's best hope for bringing down the Reich.

CHAPTER FIFTY-THREE

July–November 1941

Sara

By the middle of July, the Wehrmacht had captured Brest-Litovsk, Pskov, Minsk, Vitebsk, and Smolensk, and Panzer divisions had come within ten miles of Kiev. Sara's heart broke every time word came of another Russian town bombed into submission or sent up in flames. So many innocent lives lost, so unnecessarily. Why had Stalin refused to heed their warnings? Great risk had gone into acquiring and delivering those intelligence reports, so meticulous and detailed that only a fool or a profoundly obstinate person could dismiss them as mere speculation or rumor. Bitterly Sara wondered which type Stalin was.

In the weeks that followed, though they were stunned by how badly the Soviets had squandered their advantage, Harro, Arvid, and their highly placed sources nevertheless continued to gather information about the Nazis' military and economic strategies. Everything Sara discovered chilled her to the core.

As the German army plunged deep into Soviet territory, SS and police units followed in their wake, tasked with suppressing resistance behind the front lines. The foremost of these special units were the Einsatzgruppen—mobile death squads organized by Chief of Reich Security Reinhard Heydrich, who personally selected its commanders from among the best-educated and most fanatical Nazis. By the end of

July, numerous reports had crossed Harro's desk of how the Einsatz-gruppen were carrying out their mission of eliminating Russian Jews, Communists, and other enemies of the Reich whom the Nazis believed would interfere with German governance of the conquered territories. First prominent Communist party leaders were executed, then Jews serving in government posts. Jewish Red Army prisoners of war were killed, in defiance of the Geneva Convention.

Still not satisfied that the threat had been eliminated, Heydrich announced that all Jews in Poland should be considered partisans and ordered that all Jewish males between the ages of eighteen and forty-five must be shot. Then he expanded the order to include women, children, and the elderly—any Jew, all Jews.

At first the Einsatzgruppen maintained some semblance of juris-prudence, reading off criminal charges—looting, sabotage, assault—before executing the helpless victims by firing squad. When that proved inefficient, the Einsatzkommandos began herding large groups of Jews to the outskirts of their villages, lining them up on the edge of mass graves, sometimes no more than ravines or ditches, and slaugh-tering them with automatic weapons, picking off any survivors with pistols. In some regions, Jews were spared death but were forced into ghettos and concentration camps to be exploited as slave labor. As ru-mors of the massacres spread, many Jews fled ahead of the oncoming terror. Heydrich did not interfere, for their desperate exodus helped achieve, at no additional expense, the ultimate goal of making the re-gion *Judenfrei*.

Sara could not believe that the children and the elderly could have committed any of the crimes they had been accused of, nor was it pos-sible that every man between eighteen and forty-five was a partisan. "How can they believe that every single Jew in Russia is a threat to the Reich?" she asked her brother, sickened by the slaughter of so many innocents. "The entire Red Army couldn't defeat the German military. How do they expect untrained, unarmed civilians to do it?"

"Don't count out the Soviet army just yet."

"The Wehrmacht is closing in on Moscow," she reminded him. "Don't avoid the question. Why are they so afraid of the Jews?"

"It's not fear," said Natan. "It's hatred. And don't ask me to explain the logic behind it because there isn't any. We're different and Hitler needs a scapegoat."

His words came back to Sara on the first day of September when Heydrich issued a decree requiring all Jews over the age of six in Germany and its annexed territories to wear a yellow cloth star whenever they were out in public. The *Judenstern*, a Star of David with *"Jude"* embroidered in black in the center, was to be sewn to the left breast of one's outermost garment and must be visible at all times. Any Jew who violated the order or attempted to conceal the star would be subject to a fine or imprisonment.

Sara shrank with embarrassment as *Judenstern* were distributed and she accepted enough for herself and Natan. Over several days, she and Anna Hirsch, the young wife assigned to their apartment, spent hours diligently sewing the yellow stars to dresses, shirts, jackets, and coats before the September 18 deadline. At only four years old, little Elke was not required to wear the star, but one afternoon she darted over to hug her mother while she sewed. "Please, may I have a golden star too?" she asked.

After a moment's hesitation, Anna agreed that she could have one on her sweater. "She's too young to understand what it means," she said after Elke darted off again, "how it's meant to ostracize us, to rob us of our last shred of anonymity."

"And our remaining dignity." Sara paused as a memory stirred. "I remember an American novel I read at university called *The Scarlet Letter*. A Puritan woman convicted of adultery was sentenced to wear a red letter A upon her bodice so that everyone would know she had sinned. She obeyed, but she defied the community's elders by wearing a beautiful, lavishly embroidered letter instead of the small, simple mark of shame they had intended."

"Maybe I should do that," said Anna bitterly. "I'm not ashamed to be a Jew. I won't let them make me feel ashamed."

Sara smiled, momentarily captivated by the idea of flinging Heydrich's order back in his face by creating a gorgeous *Judenstern* for herself of golden satin embellished with beads and elaborately embroidered with ebony silk thread. But her smile quickly faded. In Hester Prynne's seventeenth-century New England town, her daring act had provoked outrage and vicious gossip. In twentieth-century Germany, such defiance could mean death.

And so Sara sewed on the same coarse yellow stars every other Jew did. It was Natan who reminded her to leave a coat and a few dresses unaltered for "Annemarie Hannemann" to wear when she went out.

On September 18, Sara was reluctant to leave the house, but if she did not queue up at the shops with her ration book, she and Natan would not eat that night. As she walked to the market, she kept her gaze fixed on the pavement just ahead, her shoulders curved as if the *Judenstern* were made of lead, pulling her down with its weight. Occasionally she caught glimpses of bright yellow in her peripheral vision, and for a moment she felt as if she were not alone.

But when she left the ghetto, she passed far more Aryans than Jews. A pair of elegantly dressed ladies recoiled when they approached her from the opposite direction; instinctively, Sara stepped aside, and spent the next ten minutes silently berating herself for the show of deference. Later, as she was leaving the market with a small loaf of bread and two potatoes in her basket, a young man jostled her and muttered "Filthy Jewish bitch" as he hurried past. She glared after him, and as she walked on to the butcher shop where she hoped to purchase a cut of beef or even a bone with a few shreds of meat still clinging to it, she kept her eyes front, jaw set. She might have imagined it, but she thought she glimpsed sympathy in the eyes of some of the women she passed, and one older gentleman out walking his dog actually tipped his hat to her and kindly wished her a good day. But the overwhelming number of people she passed seemed to regard her *Judenstern* with profound indifference, almost as if it had granted her the power of invisibility. These Berliners did not see it and they did not see her—but only because they did not wish to.

As Yom Kippur approached, Sara found herself yearning for the reconciliation and renewal of the Day of Atonement more powerfully than she had ever before. Natan was not particularly observant, but even he admitted that he hoped to find solace in the traditional rites, in the sound of many voices reciting the familiar Hebrew prayers, in the presence of other Jews seeking forgiveness for the sins of the community. The Reich could take away their every last civil right and privilege and crowd them into a ghetto where they froze and starved, but the Nazis could not separate them from God.

"At least it will be easy to fast this year," Natan remarked irreverently at sundown on September 30. Anna looked shocked, but her husband grinned. Sara merely sighed and shook her head, feigning exasperation. The day her brother stopped mocking authority, she would know all was lost.

Throughout the next day, she ached with longing for her parents and sister, thinking of how they had observed Yom Kippur together as a family in bygone years, and how she feared they might never again. She imagined them attending a synagogue in Geneva, perhaps on a cobblestone street with a view of the beautiful lake and snowcapped mountains beyond, and then she imagined herself and Natan with them. Perhaps next year.

Sara and Natan decided to attend the evening service of Ne'ila at the synagogue on Levetzowstrasse, one of the largest in Berlin, a simple, elegant classical sandstone building able to accommodate more than two thousand worshippers. It had sustained slight damage during *Kristallnacht* three years before, but in comparison to the many synagogues that had been desecrated, burned, or destroyed, it had survived the pogrom relatively unscathed. To Sara it felt like a comforting, familiar refuge in a country transformed by hate and malice.

After the final prayers of repentance were offered and the shofar was sounded, the congregation departed with peace and joy in their hearts, off to end their fasts. Sara, Natan, and the Hirsches planned to eat together, combining their scarce rations to make a small feast worthy of the holiday.

So many yellow stars, Sara marveled, trailing behind Natan as the crowd flowed toward the front doors, bright *Judenstern* on every coat and jacket. She buttoned her own coat as she stepped outside, but suddenly Natan halted so abruptly that she nearly bumped into him. As the crowd shifted, she saw five Gestapo agents standing at attention at the bottom of the stone stairs, evenly spaced across their width.

"We wish to speak with your rabbi," one of the men announced.

Sara's heart thudded as a stir of apprehension passed through the crowd. Eventually the white-haired, bespectacled rabbi, Leo Baeck, emerged from the synagogue. "I am Rabbi Baeck," he said, his voice both curious and welcoming. He was known for his kindness as much as for his intellectual gifts, and he was greatly beloved in the Jewish community.

"We require the keys to your building," the Gestapo officer said. "You and the other elders are ordered to report to the Gestapo office on Burgstrasse at once."

A murmur of protest quickly fell silent when the rabbi turned and calmly gestured for peace. "Might I ask why?" he asked, turning back to the officer.

"You will find out soon enough." The Gestapo officer strode up the steps, halted before the rabbi, and held out his open palm. "The keys. Now."

The rabbi frowned, but he nodded and sent a boy back into the synagogue to fetch the key ring. In the meantime, several older men gathered around the rabbi, their expressions grave and puzzled. Most of the congregation quickly left, but others lingered, scattered between the officers and the tall, pillared portico at the front entrance, beneath the quote from the Book of Isaiah engraved high above: "O house of Jacob, come ye, and let us walk in the light of the Lord." The Jews had greater numbers, but the Gestapo carried sidearms and had the law on their side, however corrupt it had become.

"I'm going to follow them to the Burgstrasse," Natan murmured in Sara's ear. "I'll meet you back home after I find out what's going on. Save me some supper, if there's enough."

"I'll come with you," Sara protested in a whisper, just as the boy returned with the keys and the Jewish elders reluctantly set off on foot in the direction of Gestapo headquarters.

"It's too dangerous. In the blackout I can move more swiftly alone." Then, as if to prove his point, Natan slipped away and lost himself in the darkness before she could follow.

Frightened, indignant, Sara made her way back to their apartment, where she broke her fast with the Hirsches and anxiously watched the clock and listened for Natan's footsteps in the hallway. When he finally arrived, his expression was so harrowed and grim that her recriminations caught in her throat.

"What is it?" she asked, her voice a breathless whisper. "Tell me."

"The Jews of Berlin are going to be resettled in the east, in the captured regions of Poland and the Soviet Union." He shrugged out of his coat, but as he turned to hang it on the peg by the door, in a sudden burst of rage he flung it to the floor. "Our own elders have been ordered to prepare the lists for deportation. The synagogue on Levetzowstrasse will be used as a transit camp until the deportees can be transported out of Germany."

Anna cried out and clasped a hand to her heart. Her husband, Levi, drew her into his embrace, where she trembled, choking back sobs.

Sara kept her gaze locked on her brother. "What awaits us in the east?" she asked.

"The Gestapo was somewhat vague on the details."

"How much time do we have?"

"Little more than a fortnight. The first group selected for deportation will be notified by mail within the next few days."

"They will take young men first, don't you think?" said Anna, wide-eyed and trembling, glancing toward little Elke, asleep on her makeshift bed on the floor next to the sofa. "Usually they want young, strong men, good workers, because there is always work to do. They won't want children."

"I'm sure you're right," Levi soothed, throwing Natan a sharp look, pleading for reassurance, but he had none to offer.

A few days later, the Hirsch family received notice that they must report to the transit camp on Levetzowstrasse on October 16 in preparation for their emigration two days later.

Anna shrieked and burst into tears, clutching Elke so tightly that the little girl began to cry.

"It might not be so bad," said Levi, holding the letter in one hand and stroking his wife's back with the other. "Look, this letter is from the Berlin Jewish Organization, not the Gestapo. Our own people. Everything seems in order. They provide a list of everything we should bring—warm clothing, underwear, bedding, medicines, umbrellas. Matches and scissors and shaving tools. We're allowed fifty kilograms of luggage apiece. I'm sure you could bring your entire sewing basket if you want to."

Anna sniffed and wiped her eyes, dubious.

"May I see that letter?" Natan asked. After a moment's hesitation, Levi gave it to him. "You have to turn over all family papers," Natan noted after scanning the pages, "including birth, marriage, and death certificates—but you get to keep your passports. Looks like they also want all your cash, jewelry, savings books, bonds, and financial papers."

Anna looked from her husband to Natan and Sara. "Maybe we could leave our valuables with you instead, for safekeeping."

"They will probably follow us on the next transport," said Levi. "What would become of our papers and valuables then?"

Nodding, Anna lowered her gaze and kissed Elke, who had stopped weeping but squirmed in her mother's lap, glaring at Natan as if he were to blame for upsetting her parents.

Over the next few days, Sara helped Anna prepare for their departure, and Anna gradually resigned herself to their circumstances. Rumors swept through the ghetto that the deportees would be settled on a kibbutz modeled after those in Palestine. Although the work would be strenuous, they would have plenty of food and fresh air. "It will be good for Elke to be in the country," Anna remarked as she folded her daughter's clothes into a suitcase. "Away from this wretched ghetto, away from the bombs."

"It sounds lovely," Sara admitted, but that was precisely why she found it so unlikely.

On the night before the Hirsches were to report to the transit camp, Natan took Sara aside. "Say your goodbyes tonight. When the Gestapo comes for them in the morning, we can't be here."

"Why not? We didn't receive a letter."

"They have a quota to fill. If they're running short on Jews, they'll snatch up any they can get their hands on."

Uneasy, Sara did as her brother asked.

The next morning, Natan shook her awake before dawn. They quickly washed and dressed, gathered the bags holding their own papers and valuables, and silently slipped from the apartment. They spent the day walking the city, observing from a distance as Gestapo agents escorted Jews from their homes into waiting trucks, their suitcases properly labeled. Sara was unsettled by how very calmly and efficiently the events unfolded—except at one house on Linienstrasse, where a woman with streaks of gray in her dark hair wept and moaned as two Gestapo agents carried her from her apartment still clinging tightly to the chair from which she had refused to rise when they had come for her.

Late in the afternoon, Natan and Sara risked a stroll past the Levetzowstrasse synagogue and watched from a distance as military trucks, one after another, parked at the curb and unloaded Jews—men, women, and children, the young and the old, healthy and infirm. Obediently, suitcases in hand, they filed into the building where many of them had worshipped not so long before, their prayers overflowing with peace and love. Sara dreaded to imagine what they found within those walls now.

When Sara and Natan returned home, the Hirsches were gone, with only a few abandoned possessions scattered about to prove that they had ever been there.

On the morning of October 18, Natan again woke Sara early. They set out in the pouring rain to witness as one thousand Jews were marched, carrying their luggage, from the Levetzowstrasse synagogue to the Grunewald train station six kilometers away. The very young and the infirm were allowed to ride in open trucks—a small comfort, although they were no less drenched from the storm. At the station the deportees were loaded onto passenger cars, and once everyone was seated, Sara and Natan watched through the windows as each was served a steaming hot drink and given a small cardboard box, which they surmised contained lunch or other supplies.

"Perhaps Anna is right," said Sara as the train chugged out of the station. "Perhaps this won't be so bad."

"Don't fool yourself. They're going into hell."

"You don't know that."

"No, but it's the logical conclusion." He turned and strode off through the rain, hands thrust into his pockets. "This kibbutz in Poland is a fairy tale."

"Then where do you think they're going?" she asked, hurrying to catch up to him. "Another ghetto? A work camp, like those horrible places they have for the foreign workers here in Berlin?"

"I don't know. Maybe. If they're lucky."

"Lucky?" Aghast, Sara seized his arm, bringing him to a halt. "You think that's the best we can hope for?"

His expression softened. "Not you and I, little sister. We can still hope for our visas to Switzerland. Wilhelm and Papa are doing all they can."

But less than a week later, Reichsführer-SS Heinrich Himmler issued a decree forbidding Jews to emigrate from the Greater German Reich. The visas to Switzerland Sara and Natan had desperately sought for so long would never come now.

"If the Nazis want us out of Germany," Sara lamented, heartbroken, "why not let us emigrate as we wish?"

"They want us out of Germany," said Natan, "but they'll decide where we go and what happens to us when we get there."

The Berlin Jewish Organization sent out more letters to Jews selected for deportation. Another transport was arranged for October 24, but again Sara and Natan were omitted from the lists. They had no idea why, whether it was by chance or by some system the Jewish elders had worked out with the Nazis.

When the second train departed for the east, Natan went alone to observe it. Afterward he told Sara that everything had gone as efficiently as before, but this time, although the passengers received the small boxes, no hot beverages had been served. Four days later when another thousand Jews were deported, Sara asked to go with him, hoping to see for herself that all was well. The deportees boarded the trains as calmly and cooperatively as on that first morning, but all the amenities distributed to the first group were absent—no hot drinks, no small boxes.

"At this rate, by February they'll have gotten rid of every last comfort, including the seats," said Natan acidly.

The first transports had gone so smoothly that the Nazis agreed to allow the Jewish community to provide their own *Ordner*, the auxiliaries who collected the deportees from their homes and saw them to the transit camp and aboard the train. It was better for a sympathetic fellow Jew to knock upon one's door and tell them it was time to go, the reasoning went, than a grim, unsmiling, impatient Nazi.

With every trainload of Jews that departed the city, Sara knew the likelihood that she and Natan would appear on the next list sharply increased. She wished she knew how best to prepare for resettlement, for the Berlin Jewish Organization's packing list had provided frustratingly few clues. She received one letter from Anna saying that they had arrived safely in Litzmannstadt, which Sara later learned was the Reich's new name for the Polish town of Łódź. Sara promptly wrote back, full of questions, but several weeks passed and no reply came. She supposed that Anna was too busy to write, or the censors had not cleared her letter.

"I wish we knew what to expect in Litzmannstadt when our turn comes," she fretted one crisp, beautiful day in early November. "A kibbutz? A work camp? It would be less frightening if—"

"Our turn is never coming," Natan interrupted fiercely, taking her by the shoulders. "Listen to me carefully. If our deportation letter comes, we're going to ignore it. Whatever else happens, we are not getting on one of those trains."

CHAPTER FIFTY-FOUR

October–December 1941

Greta

Rain pattered on the windows one evening in late autumn as Greta returned to the living room after putting Ule to bed. She spread out papers and books for a new translation project on the table and settled down to work, all the while glancing at the clock and listening for Adam's key in the door. He had gone out after supper to meet with Arvid, but she had expected him home thirty minutes ago.

She tried not to worry. Usually the men's weeknight meetings began promptly and ended quickly, but sometimes an especially critical matter came up, requiring a lengthier discussion. But she could not discount more ominous possibilities. Navigating the city safely during the blackout was difficult in fair weather and nearly impossible in a cold, driving rain. Any envious acquaintance could become an informant, and no one realized they were being watched by the Gestapo until it was too late.

Shuddering from a sudden chill, Greta banished her anxious thoughts and forced herself to concentrate on her work. Even so, it took her an hour to plow through a fairly straightforward paragraph, and she was on the verge of quitting in frustration when at last Adam returned. Breathing a sigh of relief, she met him at the door, but to her surprise, he lingered in the hallway, rainwater dripping from his hat and coat.

"Will you come with me for a moment?" he asked.

"Where?" she asked, bewildered, glancing past him up and down the hallway to make sure he was alone.

"Up to the roof. I have to tell you something important."

"But it's raining. Why don't you come in and tell me here?"

"Because we can't risk being overheard."

"But—" She glanced over her shoulder toward their son's bedroom. "Ule's asleep. I can't leave him alone."

"He'll be fine. He won't even know you're gone."

"It's not safe. If there's an air raid—"

"Greta, please." His voice was strained. "Put on your coat and come with me."

Mystified, she pulled on her coat and galoshes, grabbing an umbrella for good measure. "Can we make this quick?" she asked as she stepped into the hall and he locked the door behind them. He did not reply. Taking her hand, he led her upstairs, shoved open the rooftop door, and pulled her outside into the storm.

"What's going on?" Greta asked, shivering as drops of rain trickled down her collar and ran down her back before she could duck beneath the umbrella.

"You're not going to like this, but Arvid insisted I tell you." Adam pulled up the collar of his coat, stalling for time. "Moscow has been in touch with us through their intelligence outpost in Brussels."

"Finally! Isn't this good news?"

"Apparently our radio messages haven't been getting through to Moscow." He shifted his weight, tense and agitated. "They've asked Brussels to help them reestablish contact, so one of their men is driving to Berlin to meet with us. He was specifically told to seek out you and me."

"Arvid was right to insist you tell me," said Greta, exasperated. "What would I have done if some stranger showed up at our door claiming to be a friendly Soviet agent?"

"I would hope you'd shut the door in his face if he didn't offer the proper code name. His is Kent."

"Good to know." The strain of keeping her teeth from chattering gave her voice an edge. "Now may we please get out of this rain?"

"Not yet. I don't think you understand."

Greta studied him, taking in his grim frown, his barely contained anger. "Maybe you should try again."

"Kent was told to contact you and me, Adam Kuckhoff and his wife. The message included our address and telephone number. Moscow urged Kent to have me arrange a meeting with Arvid and Harro. If for some reason Kent is unable to reach me, he's instructed to contact Libertas, the wife of Harro Schulze-Boysen, at the address and phone number provided. If that too fails, he should try Elizabeth Schumacher in Marquardt near Potsdam."

"You're telling me," said Greta slowly, sickened, her voice nearly drowned out by the rainstorm, "that Moscow put our names, addresses, and phone numbers in a message that they radioed to Brussels, a message that could have been intercepted by any Reich station in Europe?"

Adam nodded.

"Dear God." She pressed a hand to her chest, heart thudding. "That's not possible. Are they insane or just incredibly stupid?"

"Greta, please. It's not as bad as it sounds."

"Really? I'm delighted to hear that, because it sounds like we're finished!"

"We don't know that the Germans intercepted the message," he said in a soothing tone that did nothing to quell her fears. "If they didn't, we have nothing to worry about. If they did, the message was in code. The Germans don't know our key word and it would be next to impossible for them to guess it at random. They also don't know what key book we're using, and without that, they have almost no chance of deciphering the message."

"Next to impossible," Greta echoed bitterly. "Almost no chance."

"Greta, darling, you're right. I won't deny it. It's not entirely out of the realm of possibility that the Germans could break the code, but the odds that they will are infinitesimal."

She took a deep, steadying breath. Arvid and John Sieg had said as much months earlier when Erdberg had given them the radio and a copy of *Der Kurier aus Spanien*.

"One thing more," said Adam. "They got our address wrong—Wilhelmstrasse 18 instead of Wilhelmshöherstrasse."

Greta choked out a laugh, a wild, strangled sound. "Oh, in that case we're perfectly safe. They'll never find us with only our name and phone number."

"It might buy us time."

"Not enough to make any difference. There are a million ways the Gestapo can find us knowing only our surname. We're in the phone directory, for God's sake." Another thought struck her. "Will Kent be clever enough to figure it out?"

"I've never met the man, but I would expect so."

"After he discovers the error the hard way by knocking on the wrong front door." Greta sighed and clasped a hand to her forehead. "At least they didn't give Arvid's last name."

"Yes, that's good," said Adam, but when their eyes met, the depthless regret she glimpsed there told her what he could not bear to say aloud.

If any member of their resistance network was discovered, they would all be compromised.

As dangerous as it was to be in radio contact with Moscow, Greta understood that severing ties would cost the resistance their most important remaining contact with the outside world—and the situation in Germany had become so desperate that they needed all the help they could get. Every day Arvid and Harro discovered official reports of shocking abuse and mass murders of Jews and Communists in the conquered territories of the Soviet Union, but they suspected this was only a glimpse of even greater horrors not yet disclosed. German Jews were being resettled in the east by the thousands, and the few letters from deportees Greta had received indicated that they had been crowded into ghettos and concentration camps. Although the letters were vague and sparsely detailed to pass the censors, the writers described hardships and hunger, and begged for food and warm clothing. She'd immediately sent several parcels, but she never heard if they had been received.

Greta feared that the deported German Jews, wherever they were, suffered conditions as appalling as those of the foreign conscripted workers in Berlin. The laborers toiling upon Albert Speer's Germania construction projects, and the thousands more who had been brought in from defeated territories to work in other industries, suffered increasingly worse hardships as the autumn days grew colder and winter approached. A few blocks away from John Sieg's Neukölln apartment, the National Cash Register compound at 181–189 Sonnenallee had been converted to a munitions plant, with a factory at one end and rough barracks at the other. The crude structures housed slave laborers from France, Poland, Ukraine, and Russia, including numerous Jews and many women. Whenever Sieg passed the site, he witnessed prisoners clad in rags, freezing, starving, enduring beatings. When the guards were not watching, some compassionate residents of Neukölln found gaps in the fences and passed the prisoners potatoes and bread, warm gloves and soap. Sieg gave them flyers with encouraging messages translated into Polish by his wife, Sophie. But although Greta admired them for offering what comfort they could, their efforts seemed hopelessly inadequate to the enormous need.

To do anything on a larger scale, the resistance needed outside help. That meant continuing to provide information to the Soviets, despite the risks.

Soon thereafter, when "Kent" arrived in Berlin, Greta heard about it only after the fact. Ignoring his instructions, Kent had phoned the Schulze-Boysen residence first and asked to meet with Harro. Libertas had met him at an Untergrundbahn station, and after confirming his identity, had brought him home to meet her husband. For more than four hours, Harro had provided him with detailed military information, including the location of Wolfsschanze, Hitler's headquarters in East Prussia; the Wehrmacht's plans to invade the Caucasus in order to access Soviet oil reserves; Germany's preparations for chemical warfare; and information about aircraft productions and battlefield casualties. He also had revealed that the German military faced severe fuel shortages and their supply lines were stretched dangerously thin. Afterward, Kent had returned to Brussels to transmit Harro's information to Moscow.

"I have a confession," Greta said after Libertas finished her report. They were sitting side by side in the old wooden chairs on the roof of the Kuckhoffs' apartment building, wrapped in blankets to fend off the cool air of late autumn. "I'm relieved Kent contacted you and Harro instead of me and Adam."

"He must have heard we have excellent cognac," Libertas said lightly, but her teasing smile soon faded. "I hope our work makes a difference. Sometimes it's hard to tell. Harro's descriptions of the atrocities were bad enough, but the films I see at work, the photos—"

"What films?" In early November, Libertas had taken a new job as a scriptwriter and press agent in the Deutsche Kulturfilm-Zentrale, the better to acquire information for the resistance. Kulturfilm had been founded after the Great War to produce educational German documentaries, but in 1940 it had been placed under Goebbels's direct control and now mostly churned out Nazi propaganda. "What photos?"

"Images of atrocities. Some taken by Kulturfilm staff, others by soldiers on leave. If the world could see what I've seen, every civilized nation on earth would declare war on Germany and put this horror to an end."

"What have you seen?"

Libertas shot her a challenging look. "Are you sure you want to know?"

Greta felt a denial form on her lips, but she forced herself to nod.

"Come by my office tomorrow and I'll show you. Don't bring Ule, and don't say I didn't warn you."

The next morning, Greta dressed in her best dark blue suit, left Ule with Erika, and went to the Kulturfilm office, wondering how Libertas would explain her visit to her superiors and justify showing her films and photos that Greta presumed were strictly confidential. She dreaded the sights that awaited her there, and yet she felt a compelling responsibility to pay witness to them, to share Libertas's burden. She knew how exhausting it was to carry a painful secret alone.

When she arrived, she gave her name to the receptionist in the lobby, and soon Libertas appeared, dressed in a smart rust-colored suit, smiling and cheerfully greeting colleagues in passing. She welcomed Greta with a kiss on the cheek, linked her arm through hers, and led her off to the elevator, chatting animatedly as if they were off on a shopping trip.

Libertas's façade fell as soon as they were alone in her office. She closed and locked the door, drew the blinds, and retrieved a file from a tall cabinet near the window. "These aren't official records," she said. "No one else at Kulturfilm or within the Reich hierarchy even knows this file exists. If they did, they would order it destroyed, and I'd probably be shot if I couldn't talk my way out of it. Soldiers were strictly forbidden to take photos of these events, but—" She shrugged and added sardonically, "Many did anyway. They're proud of their service to the Reich and want to preserve it for posterity."

Greta fixed her gaze on the file as Libertas opened it, suddenly apprehensive. "The Nazis document their deeds to the point of obsession. Why would they forbid this?"

"You'll see."

Libertas turned photos faceup on her desktop, one after another, snapshots from the front—soldiers holding pistols to other men's heads, torturing victims bound to chairs, smiling arm in arm as they stood before open graves filled with bloody corpses, pulling bayonets from victims whose faces were still contorted in pain, one horror after another after another—

Greta staggered back, pressing a hand to her mouth, dizzy with nausea. "My God," she breathed, when she could speak. "Those poor people! How can you bear it?"

"Most days I can scarcely hold myself together." Libertas's voice was strangely flat as she gathered up the photos and returned them to the file. "I spared you the pictures of murdered children, the dead babies."

"How—" Greta's breath caught in her throat. "How did you manage to get these?"

"Most were given to me by the soldiers themselves—young, grayhaired, and every age in between." Shaking her head, Libertas gathered up the photos and returned the file to the cabinet. "They're eager to brag about their adventures at the front when a pretty young thing flutters her eyelashes and acts impressed. They pull out their photos, and with a little flattery, a little flirtation, I convince them to let me make copies. We have all the necessary equipment—" She gestured vaguely toward the wall separating them from the rest of the department. "They assume—even though such photos are officially *verboten*—that I want them for the Kulturfilm archives or for a Reich propaganda film."

"Instead you're creating your own archive."

"Yes." Sparing a glance for the door, Libertas drew closer. "At first, I used it to discourage young people from joining Nazi organizations by showing them the sort of atrocities they would be expected to perform. Now I'm documenting war crimes."

Someday, when the nightmare was over, the Nazis would be brought to justice, and Libertas resolved to make sure the prosecutors had irrefutable evidence of their offenses. For every photograph and reel of film she gathered, she collected names, addresses, and testimony, although the officers she spoke with would never give that name to it. She simply asked questions in a conversational tone about where they had been, what they had done, and why. As soon as she was alone, she wrote it all down, every incriminating detail.

Greta marveled at her foresight, but she was compelled to warn her friend of the potential danger, the dire consequences she would face if her archive were discovered. "I know the risks," Libertas said, a tremor in her voice, defiance and fear. "I have to do this. If I don't, who will? The only way I can get through the days is by promising myself that someday these monsters will be brought to justice."

Someday, Greta silently echoed, willing that day to come swiftly, knowing it would not unless Germany lost the war.

By late November, thanks to concurring intelligence from Luftwaffe headquarters and the Economics Ministry, their resistance circle knew that the German military had been unable to sustain its advance into the Soviet Union. As the seasons changed, the Wehrmacht's trucks and tanks had become bogged down in thick mud, and winter snows were imminent. With supply lines strained to the limit, food and fuel reserves were running dangerously low. Hitler had expected to be in Moscow before the first snows fell, but now German soldiers on the front lines were digging in for an arduous winter campaign clad in nothing heavier than the uniforms they had worn when the invasion began in June. Most Germans, absorbed in the steady stream of propaganda issuing from the Reich press, had no idea how their sons, husbands, and brothers at the front suffered.

Somehow, even as winter descended, heavy and ominous, the German army struggled on into December, only to come to an abrupt halt barely ten miles from Moscow as the muddy roads turned to ice. Temperatures plummeted to −35°C. Tanks, trucks, and artillery became useless as the oil froze within their mechanisms. Quartermasters had prioritized munitions above food and clothing, so the well-armed, poorly clad soldiers suffered from hunger, frostbite, and despair.

Then, on December 6, Harro risked a phone call from his office at Luftwaffe headquarters to tell Adam and Greta that the Soviet Union had launched a massive counterattack against the icebound German army. One hundred Soviet divisions punched into the center of the invaders' lines. Their forces included eighteen fresh divisions with seventeen hundred tanks and fifteen hundred airplanes brought in as reinforcements from the east—at no small risk, since this rendered the Soviet Union vulnerable to an invasion from its longtime rival Japan. When the newly strengthened Red Army fiercely assaulted the Germans along a two-hundred-mile front, they drove the invaders 240 kilometers back from Moscow. Hitler, furious that his demands to fight to the death for every last inch of ground had not been obeyed, fired the commander in chief of the Wehrmacht and appointed himself in the disgraced officer's place, but this did not turn the tide of the battle.

Greta and Adam did not trust the Nazi propaganda machine to give them accurate reports of the counterattack, so they spent the day with the Harnacks, listening to the BBC on their *verboten* shortwave.

Late the next afternoon they returned, bringing supper and wine and flowers as a token of their thanks. Mildred had spent the day following reports on the shortwave, and over supper she shared what she had learned. Afterward they gathered around the shortwave and tuned in the BBC, turning up the volume as high as they dared. Although the reports of the Soviet counterattack were still preliminary, it seemed evident that the German army had not been able to muster a strong defense and was still falling back.

Suddenly, just before half past seven, an announcer broke in with a news bulletin.

"Japan's long-threatened aggression in the Far East began tonight, with air attacks on United States naval bases in the Pacific," the Englishman said, his voice crisp and urgent. "Fresh reports are coming in every minute. The latest facts of the situation are these: Messages from Tokyo say that Japan has announced a formal declaration of war against both the United States and Britain. The Japanese air raids have been made on the Hawaiian Islands and the Philippines. Observer reports say that an American battleship has been hit, and President Roosevelt has told the army and navy to act on their secret orders."

Stunned, Greta looked first to Adam, and then to Mildred and Arvid. She saw her own shock and disbelief reflected in her friends' faces.

The illusion that distance would keep the United States safely isolated from the war in Europe had been shattered. The Americans were in it now. They no longer had the privilege of choice.

CHAPTER FIFTY-FIVE

December 1941–May 1942

Mildred

The day after the Japanese attacked Pearl Harbor, the United States declared war on Japan.

Four days after the attack, on the morning of December 11, Chargé d'Affaires Leland Morris, the highest-ranking American diplomat remaining in Berlin, was summoned to the office of Foreign Minister Joachim von Ribbentrop, who read him Germany's formal declaration of war. A few hours later, from the balcony above the Piazza Venezia in Rome, Benito Mussolini declared that Italy would join the war "on the side of heroic Japan" against the United States. Soon thereafter, appearing before the Reichstag, Hitler asserted that the Tripartite Pact obliged the Reich to join Italy in the defense of their mutual ally Japan, and he accused the United States of severely and continuously provoking Germany by violating all rules of neutrality to the benefit of the Reich's adversaries from the moment hostilities had broken out in Europe. He had wanted to avoid war with the United States, but the perfidious Americans had given him no choice.

Several hours after, following unanimous votes of approval in the House and the Senate, the United States declared war on Germany and Italy.

As soon as Mildred heard the news, she put on her warmest coat and hat, pocketed an electric torch with a blue filter, and made her way to the American embassy. She counted several friends among the minimal staff still in residence, and she hoped to see them one last time, to learn as much as she could and to bid them farewell. But when she arrived, she found the building surrounded by storm troopers, and no one was allowed to enter. Inside, she knew, the diplomats were burning files and destroying assets they could not allow to fall into Nazi hands. As twilight descended, she stood witness, heart aching, as her fellow Americans were led out the front gates, loaded onto a military truck, and taken away.

She summoned up her courage and approached a storm trooper who stood somewhat apart from the others, smoking a cigarette. "I beg your pardon," she asked, "but do you know where they're taking the Americans?"

Her accent was flawless after so many years in Berlin, and she knew from his indulgent smile that he mistook her for a German. "You have nothing to fear from them, *Fraulein*. They'll be locked up tight at an internment camp at Bad Nauheim until they can be exchanged for the German diplomats stranded in Washington."

Mildred thanked him and left, eager to reach home before the utter darkness of the blackout engulfed the city.

She knew Arvid, Harro, and the others were exultant that the United States had entered the war at last. She too was relieved, although she was dismayed by the circumstances that had brought it about. And yet she also felt bereft and abandoned as the last traces of an official American presence disappeared from Berlin, as if she had been cut off from her homeland in one decisive, irreparable stroke. She knew, logically, that this was not so. She still exchanged letters with friends and family back home—heavily censored letters, but better than none at all.

As she climbed aboard the streetcar, she smiled to herself and pressed a hand to her abdomen, still flat to conceal the secret she had not yet divulged to the folks back home. She had told no one but Arvid, Inge, and Greta that she was again expecting a child, and had sworn them to secrecy. It was still too early and she had been disappointed too many times before to share the good news more widely. And it *was* good news, even though times were grim and the future uncertain.

She longed for a child, and she was already thirty-nine. She and Arvid could not afford to wait.

Perhaps now that the United States had entered the war, peace and prosperity might return sooner than they expected. Mildred dared hope this might be so, but according to the Reich press, by entering the war, the Americans had only sealed their own doom. The Nazi propaganda machine worked overtime to convince the German people that the United States and its "mongrel people of Jews, Negroes, and immigrants" would be crushed beneath the superior Aryan race, their defeat both decisive and inevitable.

Such proclamations rallied the spirits of the majority of Germans, but among Berliners Mildred detected something else beneath the quiet, proud stoicism with which they managed the daily business of work, family, air raids, ration cards, and disappearing neighbors. An undercurrent of profound disquiet manifested in a sidelong scowl at headlines while passing a newsstand or a refusal to smile and nod along with a transparently false radio broadcast played over loudspeakers in a public square. The war with the Soviet Union had declined in popularity as families lost loved ones to bullets, disease, and exposure. Now the United States joining the Allies seemed to kindle a widespread, unspoken fear of the worse hardships and deprivations the coming years might bring.

The German people's faith in their indomitable military was badly shaken when Hitler called upon the citizens of the Reich to donate warm clothing for their soldiers on the Russian front. Propaganda Minister Goebbels was given the unenviable task of announcing the collection drive, which he did in a radio broadcast on the evening of December 20. Appealing to the Christmas spirit of generosity and gratitude, he declared that considering all that the military had accomplished and sacrificed on their behalf, the German people surely could not enjoy the festive season knowing that brave soldiers were unequipped to withstand the rigors of winter cold. "As long as a single object of winter clothing remains in the Fatherland," he proclaimed, "it must go to the front. It would be an exaggeration if I talked of sacrifices at this time. What the homeland has suffered in the war are only inconveniences compared to what our front soldiers have borne daily and hourly, over two years." He read off a lengthy, detailed list of items most urgently needed, everything from boots and earmuffs to blankets and gloves, wrapping up with a statement from the Führer urging universal participation.

Goebbels's announcement spurred donations, but also provoked seething anger. For years citizens of the Reich had been told that their military was the strongest, bravest, most disciplined, best-trained, and best-equipped fighting force in the world. Now, as the entire world plunged into war and enemies faced them on multiple fronts, they learned that their sons, husbands, and brothers were suffering through the brutal Russian winter without so much as hats and gloves.

"Perhaps this will prompt the German people to wonder what other lies their government has told them," Arvid said as he and Mildred packed their suitcases before setting out to spend the holidays with family in Jena. Mildred hoped so, but with suspicious neighbors denouncing one another to the Gestapo for the smallest offenses, sometimes only out of anger, or revenge, or to settle petty scores, a widespread protest against the war seemed beyond imagination.

The New Year began with little hope that 1942 would bring peace, prosperity, or anything else one usually wished for on the holiday. For all the hardships the German people endured, the Jews suffered far worse as the fate of their departed friends remained uncertain and still more constraints upon their lives were imposed. Jews were forbidden to sell their personal property without official permission from the Reich. They were banned from all public baths and forbidden to buy firewood, newspapers, and periodicals. The pace of deportations increased, but the Jews were now marched to the Grunewald station at night, presumably to reduce the number of witnesses. Instead of passenger carriages, the deportees were now crowded into cars used to transport goods or cattle. Sara and Natan had observed a pattern in the most recent transport lists, which seemed overwhelmingly comprised of the elderly and the bedridden. As the Gestapo cleared out hospitals and sanatoriums for the aged, Arvid and Natan surmised that the Nazis wanted to keep healthy young Jews in Berlin so they would be available for conscripted labor, but Mildred and Sara worried that the Nazis were targeting the old and the sick because they were helpless and weak, less likely to fight back and reduce the efficiency of the deportation process. Perhaps both possibilities were true.

What had become of the deported Jews after they left Berlin remained an ominous question. At first, some Jews had sent letters to friends in the capital from ghettos in Litzmannstadt, Minsk, Kaunas, and Riga to say that they had arrived safely but desperately needed food and warm clothes, but before long the flow of letters slowed to a trickle and then ceased. Why would the deportees be forbidden to write home? Complaints and strategic information could be censored. Why cut off communications entirely?

By the middle of February, Mildred knew of no one who had heard from a departed Jewish friend in weeks, and letters sent to the resettlement sites were often returned stamped "Addressee Deceased" or "Address Unknown." Rumors swept through Berlin like snow crystals carried aloft in the cold February winds, whispering that the Jews had died in typhus epidemics or had been murdered outright. The rumors were as ephemeral as snow crystals too, for few Berliners remarked upon their absent neighbors at all. Many people were no doubt afraid to say anything rather than risk appearing disloyal to the Reich. Others were glad to be rid of the Jews and to benefit from the redistribution of the property they had left behind—vacated homes given as rewards to party members, furs and jewels sold in special shops at a fraction of their value. It seemed to Mildred, however, that the vast majority of Germans responded to the plight of the Jews as they had for more than a decade, with profound indifference. As long as they and theirs were exempt from persecution, why should they care what happened to strangers?

Their unfathomable lack of empathy and compassion rendered Mildred heartsick, bewildered, and afraid.

In mid-February, Harro came across documents at Luftwaffe headquarters that chillingly, meticulously revealed a sudden and drastic worsening of Reich policy toward the Jews. According to a conference transcript Harro glimpsed on a superior officer's desk, on January 20, Reinhard Heydrich, Adolf Eichmann, and thirteen other high-ranking officials had met at a villa in the Berlin suburb of Wannsee to discuss "the Final Solution to the Jewish Question." Harro could not have stolen a copy of the transcript without raising the alarm, but he studied it swiftly, intently, when it was left briefly unattended on his superior officer's desk. What he saw was enough to convince him that within the past year, Adolf Hitler had authorized a plan to deliberately and methodically annihilate eleven million European Jews. The purpose of the Wannsee Conference had not been to debate whether such a heinous program of mass murder should be undertaken, for that had already been decided, but how to implement it.

As horrifying as Harro's conclusions were, nothing he described contradicted what the Nazis had done elsewhere to Communists, to labor unionists, to Polish politicians, to Soviet prisoners of war, to Jews in the conquered territories of Eastern Europe. And yet somehow, Mildred could not quite believe it—that was to say, she knew it was true, and yet her brain rejected it as impossible. Representatives from the highest levels of the Nazi Party and the Reich government had convened in a Wannsee villa in order to create a bureaucracy to commit genocide. They had probably sipped coffee and passed around neatly typed documents filled with charts and graphs and statistics, all very rational and logical—and yet every man at that table had to be completely mad or irredeemably evil to engage so readily in preparations for mass murder.

Winter passed in exhaustion and dread, a perpetual storm of horrifying revelations from the Luftwaffe and the Economics Ministry, the terror of nightly air raids, the struggle to find enough at the markets to feed herself and Arvid and have enough left over to share with Jewish friends, the inability to ever feel truly warm and comfortable since there was never enough fuel.

"You're too thin for a woman in your condition," Arvid told her one evening as he cut his own potato in half and placed the larger portion on Mildred's plate. "You need to eat more, for you and the baby."

"Darling, you're just as hungry as I am." She tried to return the potato to his plate, but he refused it, and frowned kindly at her until she ate every last bite. The truth was that she was worried. Her appetite had not returned after the wretched early nausea passed, and her abdomen did not seem as full and round as it ought to have been by then. Sometimes she felt a dull ache on the right side of her pelvis, and rarely, although still enough to concern her, she discovered a light spotting of blood in her underwear after walking or doing housework.

At the end of February, concerned by unusual symptoms and worried that stress and malnutrition were affecting her unborn child, Mildred made an appointment with a gynecologist. He and the nurse said very little during the examination, but after the doctor left and Mildred dressed, something about the nurse's brisk, cheerful manner and inability to make eye contact told her something was very wrong.

The nurse escorted Mildred to the waiting room to fetch Arvid, whose hopeful smile faltered when he saw the tears in her eyes. Hand in hand, they followed the nurse to the doctor's office to receive the diagnosis.

"You have an ectopic pregnancy," the doctor told her gently. The embryo had implanted in her right fallopian tube. There would be no child. The condition was potentially fatal to Mildred and surgery would be required to remove the tissue. The operation would almost certainly render her unable to conceive again.

Devastated, Mildred broke down in sobs, weeping and trembling in Arvid's arms. She felt him shaking too, heard the frisson of grief in his voice when he thanked the doctor and scheduled the surgery and helped her into her coat and scarf and out of the office and home.

Due to wartime circumstances the operation could not take place until the end of March. Her symptoms worsened dangerously throughout the delay, and afterward, due to stress or exhaustion or poor nutrition or unrelenting grief or all of these, her recovery was prolonged and difficult. In April, Arvid begged her to get out of the beleaguered city, to convalesce in the calm serenity of the countryside. He knew the ideal retreat—Schloss Elmau, a sanatorium and artists' colony nestled in the sublime alpine valley of the Wettersteingebirge near Garmisch-Partenkirchen in Bavaria. His late uncle Adolf von Harnack had often summered there.

"I'll visit you in May," Arvid promised, tears in his eyes as they kissed in parting. "By then you'll be healthy and strong again, I promise."

After he had gone, she surrendered herself to the beauty of the mountains and forests, taking comfort from the kindness of the solicitous staff, rebuilding her strength with rest and nourishing food, feeling her strain gradually ease as the days passed blessedly free of air raid sirens and falling bombs. She distracted herself with the pleasant company of other convalescents, with hours spent engaged in lectures by distinguished professors or musical programs and literary discussions. She spent at least a few hours every day in restful solitude, in a chair overlooking a glorious mountain peak or a sparkling crystal lake, losing herself in the poetry of Goethe, her familiar touchstone when the world's burdens lay too heavily upon her shoulders.

This was the Germany Mildred loved, the Germany she was willing to risk her life to save. She would not abandon it to the abyss, not while she had any strength left, not while any chance remained that their cause could prevail.

CHAPTER FIFTY-SIX

May–July 1942

Sara

When Mildred returned to Berlin in May, Sara dressed as Annemarie Hannemann, slipped out the back door of her ghetto tenement, bought a bouquet from a florist shop Jews were not permitted to frequent, and walked along streets from which Jews were banned in order to visit her friend at home.

Mildred looked well, as well as Sara imagined anyone could in her place. Her face had lost its gaunt angularity and her skin had a fresh, soft glow, but an ineffable sadness permeated her usual warm, gentle manner. Sara's heart ached for her, and she wished she knew what to say, what to do, how to bring her comfort. Perhaps it was enough for Mildred to know that she was loved, and that her friends would do anything to take away her pain, if only they could.

"What I want most, now that I've recovered, is to get back to work," Mildred told her. "I have this awful sense that we're running out of time, that soon we'll reach a point of no return where every last good thing about Germany will be forever lost, beyond redemption."

Out of consideration for Mildred's grief, Sara restrained a bitter retort. She believed Germany had passed that point when the Nazis devised their Final Solution, but as long as Mildred needed to believe that her adopted homeland could be saved from itself, Sara would not snuff out her hopes.

The harsh winter had demoralized everyone, but it seemed to Sara that spring brought relief and renewed hope to the Aryans, a lifting of spirits that eluded the Jews. Even so, although their fanatical devotion to the Führer surged as he confronted Churchill and Roosevelt, most Berliners remained deeply ambivalent about the war with the Soviet Union. They had not forgiven their leaders for allowing their beloved soldiers to suffer on the Russian front throughout that punishing winter, nor had they forgotten the broken promise that foreign bombers would never breach their city's defenses. Terrifying air raids had become almost commonplace. Thunder and death rained down from the skies by night, and in the morning, Berliners emerged from their homes and shelters to find rescue workers pulling mangled corpses from smoldering ruins.

The resistance took advantage of the blackouts, meeting at discreet spots to collect antifascist flyers and leaflets and venturing out into the darkness to distribute them throughout the city. They usually traveled in pairs or small groups, pretending to be girlfriends enjoying a daring night out, linking arms and chatting animatedly as they walked along. A casual onlooker would never guess that their purses were stuffed with treasonous materials. Or a young man and woman would pretend to be a couple in love, holding hands, ducking into shadowed doorways for an embrace, their pockets and sleeves stuffed with pamphlets, which they slipped into mailboxes when no one was looking. In the mornings, exasperated green-uniformed city police would be ordered to fan out through the city to collect every last leaflet and scrape the antifascist flyers from the walls.

Once Sara was standing watch while her partner, a handsome Romanian Communist she knew only as Andrei, pasted an antifascist flyer over a Nazi propaganda poster. Suddenly she heard footsteps approaching. "Someone's coming," she whispered, and before she knew it, Andrei had shoved the bundle of flyers and the paste pot into an alley and had swept her into a passionate embrace. Sara clung to Andrei, returning his kiss as a pair of storm troopers passed and disappeared around the corner, snickering and making rude remarks under their breath. Andrei immediately released her and apologized profusely. She assured him somewhat dazedly that it was perfectly fine, rather good thinking on his part.

Natan did not like for Sara to venture out at night. "At least leave your *Judenstern* at home and go out as Annemarie," he urged, and she agreed. The yellow star was too conspicuous anyway. If only she could get ration coupons in Annemarie's name, she would never wear the star again, but it was Sara Weitz who must go to the shops after hours and wait in line and hope for a withered potato or head of cabbage to cook into something vaguely nourishing for herself and her brother.

She and Natan debated going underground, but pretending to be Annemarie occasionally was as deep as she dared go. They would starve unless someone sheltered them and brought them food, but anyone caught hiding Jews would pay for their selflessness with their lives. Escape was a better option. Jews were forbidden to emigrate, but Natan was working his contacts in the Communist underground and foreign press and hoped to get them both smuggled out of the country before winter. Sara did not care where they went, as long as it was beyond the borders of the Reich. Eventually, somehow, they would make their way to Geneva and their family would be reunited at last.

"If we can't be somewhere safe, I'm glad the two of us are together," Sara told Natan one evening over a meal of cabbage, onion, and apples fried in the last of the olive oil. "I couldn't survive one day alone in this hell without you."

For a moment Natan was rendered speechless, but then he grinned. "I love you too, baby sister," he said, reaching across the table to ruffle her hair.

One important objective of the nighttime pamphleting raids was to foment the people's disapproval of the unpopular Soviet war, challenging the infallibility of the Reich, shattering the myth of one German *Volk* unified in support of the Führer. Sara and her comrades realized they were making progress when the Propaganda Ministry launched a campaign to bolster public support. In addition to the usual proclamations and posters, Goebbels arranged a cultural exhibition ironically

titled "The Soviet Paradise." A long, one-story, starkly neoclassical
building was constructed on the Lustgarten and filled with dioramas
and exhibits meant to educate the German people about the "poverty,
misery, depravity, and need" of daily life in the Soviet Union.

On the second day of the exhibition, Sara, as Annamarie Hannemann, attended with Mildred, Greta, and their husbands, joining a vast
throng of men and women wandering the aisles, some with children
in tow. Each visitor was given a booklet describing the various displays—a full-scale replica of a Russian cobbler's squalid hovel, or the
cramped, filthy flat of a Moscow factory worker. The guidebook began
with a lengthy treatise explaining how Marxism and Bolshevism, ide-
ologies devised by Jews, had led to the deaths of millions from political
executions and starvation. "Further proof that the Soviet state belongs
to the Jews is the fact that the people are ruthlessly sacrificed for the
goals of the Jewish world revolution," the author declared, at which
point Sara stopped reading in disgust.

Enormous picture panels lined the walls, depicting life in the Soviet Union as grim, cheerless, and colorless, a miserable existence
in muddy, decrepit villages beneath gray, sunless skies. Half-empty
bottles of liquor were scattered around images of Stalin and Lenin to
emphasize the people's hopelessness and sloth. In a large, darkened
room, a fifteen-minute film played continuously; Libertas, who had
seen rough cuts at the Deutsche Kulturfilm-Zentrale, had warned her
friends that it was not for the faint of heart, but Sara steeled herself and
took a seat in the back between Greta and Mildred. The film claimed
to show the gruesome scenes German troops had encountered as they
marched into the Soviet Union—filthy, emaciated orphans begging
for scraps; desecrated churches; drunkards still clutching their bottles as they sprawled in the dirt beside rusted plows and fallow fields;
town squares littered with the bloody corpses of massacred civilians.
"Where once stood prosperous villages," the narrator intoned, "today
the gray misery of the collective farm predominates. This is where the
Soviet peasant lives as a slave."

"I'd like hard evidence that those atrocities were committed by the
retreating Red Army and not the Germans on their advance," Greta

murmured acidly as they left the room, sickened and angry. "After viewing that, no one will wonder why Germany went to war with the Soviet Union."

"That's the point, isn't it?" Mildred replied in an undertone. "Germany had to betray its erstwhile enemy to save the Soviet people."

"Yes, to save them so that the Einsatzgruppen could kill them."

Nervous, Sara glanced over her shoulder to make sure no one had overheard. All around them, curious, interested sightseers looked from guidebooks to displays, wincing sometimes if their gaze fell upon an especially grisly image, but revealing little of the shock and revulsion and skepticism Sara felt. A cold prickle ran down the back of her neck, and she was suddenly aware that she was surrounded by enemies. An impulse to flee seized her, but she fought it, knowing that panic would betray her and bring them all down upon her like hounds cornering a fox.

Taking shallow, steady breaths to calm herself, she stayed close to Mildred and Greta as they rounded a corner and came upon a large display illustrating the SS response to Soviet partisans. Mildred gasped and Sara felt her throat constricting as her gaze traveled from one gruesome image of death to another—blindfolded men before firing squads, knees buckling, smoke forever frozen in midair at the ends of the rifles. Bodies piled in mass graves. Young women dangling limply from ropes knotted about their necks—

Sickened, Sara pressed a hand to her mouth, closed her eyes, and backed away. Her eyes flew open when she bumped into someone and nearly fell, but a man caught her by the elbow and kept her on her feet. "Are you unwell, *Fraulein?*" he inquired, but she yanked her arm free and hurried away, pushing through the crowd until she reached a quiet aisle almost hidden behind a kiosk displaying the same booklets offered at the front entrance. Blinking away tears, catching her breath, she pretended to browse when suddenly a voice murmured an apology and a hand reached past to grasp a booklet. With a start, Sara turned and discovered a familiar pair of blue eyes staring into hers, shocked and disbelieving.

"My God, Sara," said Dieter. "I thought it was you, when I saw you in the crowd—I can't believe you're here. All this time I haven't known if you were alive or dead, if you were still in Berlin or if you had been—"

"I'm still here." Sara clutched her purse tightly to her side and ducked around the kiosk and into the aisle behind it, searching the crowd for her friends. Dieter was wearing a crisp military uniform and he leaned heavily upon a cane, but otherwise he was almost unchanged, except for the strain around his eyes.

"What are you doing here?" he asked, lowering his voice, drawing closer. "You know Jews aren't allowed in the Lustgarten. Do you want to be hauled off and shot?"

"Are you going to turn me in?"

"Of course not." He spared a quick glance over his shoulder. "Are you all right? I mean, have you been all right?"

"I'm still alive." She gestured to his uniform. "And you? I see you've joined the army."

"Drafted." He grimaced and adjusted his stance, leaning heavily upon the cane with both hands. "When they heard what I did for a living, they pulled me from the infantry and sent me to France attached to a procurement division, acquiring food and other goods to ship back to the Reich."

"Robbing the French to feed the Germans, then."

"You're not wrong, but we have plenty of hungry people here at home, and orders are orders."

With effort, she held back more accusations. "What happened?" she asked instead, indicating his leg.

"Some mad Frenchman drove a truck at high speed through the front wall of our office building. He killed two men, injured four, including me." He managed a grim smile. "At least I got two weeks' leave out of it, enough time to visit my mother and check in on the business."

"What happened to the mad Frenchman?"

Dieter's smiled faded. "He was killed on impact." His gaze traveled to the left breast of her sweater, where he surely noted the absence of the *Judenstern*. "Sara, you're not safe here. Have you gone underground?"

"Think about how you're dressed, and then ask yourself why I should trust you enough to tell you anything."

"Don't tell me if you don't want to, but at least—" He dug around in his shirt pocket and brought out a small velvet pouch. "At least let me help you. Take this. It's yours, it always has been. You can sell it or use it as a bribe."

As he held out the pouch to her, she clasped her hands behind her back, certain it held the diamond engagement ring she had returned to his mother while he was in Australia. "You've been carrying that around all this time?"

"Only when I'm in Berlin."

They stood there for a long moment in silence, eyes locked, his hand with the ring extended toward her. Finally she sighed and said, "You know I can't accept it."

"Don't be stubborn," he said, but his hand fell to his side. "It might save your life someday."

She shook her head, but before she could speak again, Mildred and Greta appeared in the aisle behind Dieter. "There you are," Mildred cried, relieved. "We thought we'd lost you."

"We decided we've had enough fun for one day," said Greta, eyeing Dieter suspiciously as she stepped around him and tucked Sara's hand in the crook of her elbow. "Time to go. Our fellows are waiting."

"Sara, wait," Dieter implored. "Where can I find you?"

"You can't," Sara said as Greta led her away. "Don't try."

They hurried to meet Adam and Arvid at the exit, where they had stationed themselves in case Sara passed or was dragged out by storm troopers.

"He knows your name," said Mildred as they left the exhibition.

"Yes," Sara replied shakily. "I knew him . . . quite well, before."

"Will he report you?"

"I don't think so."

"Are you sure?" asked Arvid. "Your life may depend on it."

Greta scowled at him, but Sara knew he did not mean to frighten her. "He won't," she said, more firmly, and she was suddenly sure of it.

Before they went their separate ways, they conferred quietly, disheartened by all they had witnessed. They agreed that the exhibition probably would convince a great many Berliners that the Reich's attack upon the Soviet Union had been justified, and that the ongoing war, as costly and destructive as it was, deserved the staunch support of the German people.

A few days later, after Harro, Libertas, and others had toured the exhibition, several members of the group met at the Harnacks' apartment to discuss if the resistance should respond, and how.

"This Nazi sideshow is dangerously effective," Harro warned. "We know it's all lies and distortion, but the vast majority of viewers have been conditioned to believe anything Goebbels tells them. We have to undermine the credibility of the exhibition before it becomes fixed in the public mind as proven fact."

"How do you propose we do that?" asked Adam.

"A sticker campaign. Nothing could be easier. We have a rubber stamp set and wax stickers. All we need is a powerful, concise slogan to convey our message. We'll post stickers throughout the city, on walls, telephone booths, public transport, and especially over the posters advertising the exhibition."

A few nods and murmurs of approval went up from the group, but Sara saw Arvid and Adam exchange looks of exasperation.

"Protests of this sort can be counterproductive," said the playwright Günther Weisenborn, who had joined Goebbels's Reich Broadcasting Company in July 1940 and within a year had worked his way into the company's innermost circles. "It would draw more attention to the exhibition while doing nothing to prevent people from seeing it."

"We'd be making an important statement," said Harro. "We'd show the Nazis and the public that the voice of opposition has not fallen silent in Germany."

"Our lives are worth much more than a statement," said Arvid. "You're asking us to take a substantial risk for little potential gain."

Back and forth the argument went, with Harro insisting that they could not allow the lies of "The Soviet Paradise" to go unchallenged, and Arvid, Adam, and several others remaining adamantly opposed. Eventually Harro declared that he was determined to carry out the *Zettelklebeaktion* alone if necessary. Arvid and Adam realized they would never dissuade him, but they refused to give the operation their blessing.

As the meeting broke up, Harro invited anyone who wanted to help to accompany him to plan strategy. Several of the younger members of the group left the apartment with him, including the radio operator Hans Coppi and his wife—and Sara. Harro's operation seemed no riskier than the leafleting campaigns she regularly undertook, and she knew how to maneuver safely in the blackout. If their stickers convinced one wavering Berliner to become more skeptical or if they gave the Nazis even a moment of disquiet, it would be worth it.

Within a day, a young couple in Harro's resistance group printed up hundreds of stickers, a mocking echo of Goebbels's promotional ads for the exhibition:

Permanent Installation
The NAZI PARADISE
War Hunger Lies Gestapo
How Much Longer?

On the night of May 17, Sara and the other volunteers met Harro at the designated spot in an alley a block away from the Lustgarten. Clad in his Luftwaffe uniform and carrying his pistol, Harro divided them into teams, assigned them to zones, and distributed bundles of stickers. Sara partnered with her friend Liane Berkowitz, the nineteen-year-old half-Jewish daughter of a Russian Jewish symphony conductor and a famed singing teacher. After receiving their assignment from their team leaders, the groups dispersed through the city, moving out in concentric circles with the exhibition hall in the center, stealthily plastering their stickers on walls, windows, street signs, and any other highly visible surface, taking special care to lavish them upon posters advertising the exhibition.

Dawn was still several hours away when Sara and Liane placed the last of their stickers in the area between Kurfürstendamm and Uhlandstrasse, checked in with their team leader, and bade each other farewell and good luck. Sara hurried home, a rush of excitement and accomplishment hastening her steps. Exhaustion overcame her only after she slipped quietly through the front door and found Natan sleeping on the living room sofa. He had planned to meet with a journalist from Zürich earlier that evening, she recalled, someone with contacts in the Swiss government who might be able to get them out of Germany. Perhaps he would have good news to share in the morning.

"You were busy last night," Natan remarked when Sara finally emerged from her bedroom just after ten o'clock. "The police are so overwhelmed that they're rounding up Jews to help scrape stickers off a square mile of the city around the Lustgarten."

"Is that why you're still home?" Sara teased as she poured herself a cup of ersatz coffee. After many failed attempts, Natan had hit upon a concoction that was surprisingly palatable. "You didn't want to find yourself in a crew and undo all my hard work?"

"That, and I wanted to see your face when you sat down to breakfast." He gestured to a chair. "So sit."

Bemused, she obeyed. Turning his back to shield the cupboard from her view, Natan withdrew a plate and set it before her with a flourish. Upon it were a half a loaf of rye bread and a gorgeous red apple.

"Natan!" Sara gasped. "Where did you—how—"

"A gift from my Swiss friend." Grinning, he sat down across from her and rested his arms on the table. "Just a taste of things to come."

With a moan of pleasure, Sara tore off a chunk of the bread and devoured it. "You mean—"

"He promises to have false papers and train tickets to Zurich for us by the end of June."

"Oh, Natan, that's wonderful!"

"So we just have to hold on a little while longer." He nudged the plate closer to her. "That's all yours, by the way. I already had mine."

It was the best morning Sara had known in a very long time.

That night she stayed in, unwilling to test her luck two nights in a row, certain that the SS would be on alert and eager to make examples of any Jews caught out after curfew. The next morning, Natan again woke first, but when Sara joined him for a meager breakfast of ersatz coffee and rye bread saved from the previous day's generous loaf, his expression was grave. "Someone bombed the exhibition last night."

"What?"

"They've kept it out of the papers, but a friend of a friend heard the explosions go off. Was this Schulze-Boysen's work?"

"I don't think so," she said. "He's reckless, but if he were going to blow something up, he'd discuss it with the group first, and choose a more valuable target. How badly was it damaged?"

Natan did not know. They agreed to check their separate sources and meet later to share what they learned. Sara hoped that the loathsome exhibition had been completely destroyed.

Unfortunately, Greta and Mildred soon informed her that this was not so. An incendiary device had been set off at the entrance and cloth soaked in phosphorus had been set aflame elsewhere in an attempt to burn down the building, but although a few people had been injured and part of the exhibit had been burned, the fire had not spread, the damage was quickly repaired, and the exhibition had opened on time that morning as if nothing had happened. Greta and Adam had been among the first to enter, and they had noted only a few faint scorch marks on the walls. "People are speculating that the Jews attacked the exhibit because they can't stand the truth," said Greta, disgusted.

"Was it someone from our circle?" Sara asked.

"We have no idea who was responsible," said Mildred. "Let's hope the Gestapo doesn't either."

Four days after the bombing, Natan's sources warned him that the Gestapo had raided several locations in the city and had arrested five Jews, three half-Jews, and four Aryans suspected of carrying out the plot. Investigators had determined that the bombs had been manufactured at the Kaiser Wilhelm Institute, which led them to Herbert Baum, an engineer at Siemens accused of being the cell's ringleader. "A conspiracy of Jews and Communists, exactly as the Nazis suspected," Natan said. "This feeds perfectly into their propaganda narrative. They've snatched triumph out of the ashes of humiliation."

More arrests followed as the investigation continued, but although Harro seemed untroubled, others in their circle became increasingly apprehensive. Sara was among those who worried that the Baum cell's bombing and their group's *Zettelklebeaktion* could become conflated, even though their resistance circles did not overlap. She had never been particularly close to Harro, but she observed mutual friends distance themselves from him. Sometimes, too, she overheard angry grumbling about his recklessness, his willingness to risk all of their lives for little gain.

Then, on June 4, two weeks before the bombing suspects were scheduled to go on trial, Chief of Reich Security Obergruppenführer Reinhard Heydrich—creator of the Einsatzgruppen and architect of the Final Solution—was assassinated in Prague.

The resistance welcomed the news, but Arvid's sources warned that although the two events had occurred 350 kilometers apart, many prominent Nazi officials worried that the Lustgarten bombing had exposed a dangerous breakdown in absolute authority, a show of defiance that had emboldened Heydrich's killers. Every Jew in Berlin was a potential assassin. "I for one do not wish to be shot in the belly by some twenty-two-year-old *Ostjude* like one of those perpetrators of the attack against the anti-Soviet exhibition," Goebbels had reportedly grumbled to a colleague at the Propaganda Ministry.

"There will be reprisals," Arvid cautioned. "Watch your backs."

Within hours, they learned that the reprisals had already begun. Radio reception from Czechoslovakia was sporadic, but Mildred had been monitoring one faint, distant station operated by a Czech resistance cell. Before it fell silent, a desperate operator had reported that more than thirteen thousand Czechs had been arrested, and the entire population of the village of Lidice had been massacred after Gestapo agents incorrectly concluded that the assassins were hiding there. Sara offered to help Mildred regain the signal, but although they took turns at the shortwave painstakingly scanning the airwaves and listening intently until their ears rang from the static, their attempts were fruitless. They were so intent on their work that they did not realize Sara had broken curfew until Arvid returned home from the ministry.

"I should go," Sara said, bolting to her feet.

"You can stay," Mildred offered. "Have supper with us and spend the night."

"I don't want my brother to worry, and it's too dangerous. If anyone finds me here, you'd be in a great deal of trouble."

"There are other things here that would get us in even more trouble," said Arvid, gesturing to the radio.

"I'm not wearing the *Judenstern* and I have my false papers," said Sara. "If I'm stopped on my way home, no one will know that I'm breaking curfew."

Mildred smiled. "In that case, no one will know that you're breaking curfew if you're found here."

Sara wavered a moment longer before agreeing to stay. Natan knew she kept erratic hours and would not worry unless she went missing for more than a day. The Harnacks' quiet, pleasant apartment offered a welcome respite from the noise and the smells and the tangible fear of the ghetto, and she was not quite ready to abandon the search for the Czech radio signal.

She and Mildred tried again after supper, but eventually, too exhausted to continue, they gave up and went to bed. Sara slept well on the sofa in the spare bedroom the Harnacks used as an office, but she rose early and set out for home as soon as she finished helping Mildred wash and dry the breakfast dishes.

It was not yet eight o'clock as she quickly made her way through the city toward the ghetto. The morning air was cool and misty, fragrant with the scents of cut grass and dew and fresh blossoms. Shopkeepers swept the sidewalks in front of their stores, clerks and secretaries hurried past on the way to their offices, and paperboys called out the headlines of the morning editions. There had been no air raids the night before, so the mood on the streets was one of relief and thankfulness beneath the routine of the start of another workday.

The mood shifted the closer Sara came to the ghetto. It always did, as the buildings grew more crowded and decrepit and the *Judenstern* appeared in greater numbers, but this morning she sensed something else, as if an alarm pealed just beyond the range of her hearing. Quickening her pace, she turned onto her own street and discovered trucks parked to block the alleys and intersections, and SS officers pounding on front doors and forcing their way inside and hauling out men wearing the *Judenstern*. She heard women screaming and men shouting and children wailing, and without breaking stride she turned left to cross the street and left again to go back the way she had come and did not stop until she was back among the shopkeepers and clerks preparing for another ordinary day.

Lightheaded and terrified, she boarded a streetcar and rode toward Friedenau, her thoughts racing as she made her way to the Kuckhoffs' flat. Greta answered her knock, took one look at her face, and settled her on the sofa, and before Sara knew it she was holding a hot cup of tea. The rattle of the cup against the saucer told her she was shaking.

After Sara described what she had seen, Greta told her that she must not go home until whatever was happening was over.

"I didn't see Natan," Sara said, her voice breaking.

"Did you see any SS going into your building?" Greta asked, her gaze intent.

Sara shook her head.

"Then for now let's hope for the best. Your brother is exceptionally clever. He probably slipped out the back door five minutes before the SS trucks arrived on the block."

Sara allowed a small smile. "He is rather wily."

She stayed at the Kuckhoffs' apartment all day, trying to make herself useful by playing with Ule so Greta could work on a translation project. In the late afternoon, when Adam returned from a meeting at Kulturfilm that Libertas had set up with some film producers, he insisted upon accompanying her home.

When they reached the ghetto, the trucks were gone, the streets subdued. Adam escorted her into the tenement and upstairs to her flat, where they found the door hanging ajar, a chair overturned, books and papers scattered on the living room floor. The rooms were silent.

Sara pressed a hand to her mouth to hold back a sob. Adam left for a moment, and distantly she heard him knock on a neighbor's door. She walked through the tiny flat again in a daze, searching even though she knew her brother was not there, could not be there, or she would have seen him, he would have called out to her and asked her where she had been.

Adam soon returned. "The woman across the hall says the Gestapo raided the entire block," he said. "They arrested more than two hundred men. Your brother was among them."

Sara nodded, set the chair upright, and sank down upon it.

"Come home with me," Adam urged. "You shouldn't be alone. Arvid and Harro can work their contacts and we'll find out where Natan was taken."

"I can't go. Natan might come back. Someone might send word and I might need to go to him."

"You could leave a note."

She shook her head. "I couldn't leave your name and address for the SS to find."

"Just say you went to consult the dramaturge about the Beethoven play. Natan will understand, but no one else will."

She hesitated, but again she refused. She had to stay in case Natan needed her. When Adam persisted, she agreed to come see him and Greta first thing in the morning, to let them know she was all right and to hear whatever Arvid and Harro had learned from their contacts.

Natan did not come home that night, nor did she receive any word from him. In the morning she washed and dressed, head throbbing from worry. She would have crawled back into bed in despair except for her promise to Adam.

When she reached the Kuckhoffs' flat, she found Mildred and Arvid waiting for her with Greta and Adam, and she was suddenly very afraid.

Greta led her to the sofa. Mildred sat beside her and took her hand. Greta offered her tea and breakfast. The thought of food made her feel faintly ill, but she accepted the tea—real tea, sweetened with sugar. She sipped it gingerly, as if it might suddenly vanish.

Arvid pulled up a chair and gently explained that in response to Heydrich's assassination and the bombing of the exhibition, Goebbels had convinced Hitler to increase the pace of deportations as a preventative measure. The Gestapo had immediately ordered the arrests of somewhere between 250 and 500 Jewish men. Natan's name had been on the list.

"The men were transported to Sachsenhausen concentration camp in Oranienburg, north of Berlin," said Arvid.

Sara nodded. She knew the name. Sachsenhausen had replaced KZ Oranienburg, where Natan had served his sentence for violating the Editors Law. As dreadful as Sachsenhausen surely was, at least Natan had not returned to the horrible place that still haunted his nightmares.

"Do you think I'll be permitted to visit him?" she asked, looking around the circle of friends regarding her so gravely. Mildred's eyes shone with unshed tears. "If not, could I send him food or clothing or blankets?" She had no food to send, but she would get some, somehow.

"Sara." Arvid leaned forward and rested his elbows on his knees, his expression grim and sorrowful. "Upon their arrival, half of the prisoners were shot. The others were transported to other camps, Auschwitz or Mauthausen."

Sara pressed a hand to her stomach. Auschwitz was in Poland, Mauthausen in Austria. Both were hundreds of kilometers from Berlin. "Do you know where Natan went?"

"I'm so sorry, Sara," said Mildred, voice breaking. "Natan was among those killed at Sachsenhausen."

A dull roaring filled Sara's ears. She had known Natan was dead the moment she entered the flat and saw them looking at her with grief and sorrow and rage. She had known, but she had pretended not to, because until someone said the words aloud, the possibility remained that they would never need to be said.

Mildred and Greta begged her not to go back to her apartment. Earlier that morning, an order had gone out to round up the families of the men taken the day before and to transport them immediately to the east. Sara must not be home when the SS came looking for her.

"I won't stay long," she told them. She had to go back. She and Natan had pared down their belongings with every move, but she still kept a few precious mementos that she could not bear to leave behind. She had nothing else left of her brother. She must save his photos, his journals. The Nazis could not take her memories along with everything else they had stolen from her.

She embraced her friends, kissed them, and clung to them, closing her eyes and committing to memory their voices, their scents, the way they felt in her arms. "I hope we meet again in better days," she told them, and then she left.

Alone in the tenement flat, she gathered her most precious belongings, her few remaining valuables, clothing, shoes, a coat—Annemarie Hannemann's, not Sara Weitz's. She packed a small suitcase and put on her dark gray suit, the one Natan teasingly called her "secretary disguise." Had called. Would call no more.

She inhaled deeply, steeling herself. She would let her heart fall apart into broken shards later. Now she had to escape.

The last thing she did before leaving the tenement was to slip her ration card beneath the door of a kindly neighbor with several children. Whether she failed or succeeded, she would not need it again.

She slipped out the rear entrance, watchful and wary, choosing a circuitous route, deftly leaving the ghetto behind. In the east where the German Jews had been resettled, she had heard that there were walls around the ghettos, allowing no one in or out. Perhaps one day the Nazis would build walls around Berlin's ghetto, if there were any Jews left to wall in. She intended to be gone long before then.

For their mutual protection, Natan had never told her the name of his Swiss friend. If he had, Sara could have begged him to hide her until he could obtain the forged documents and tickets to Zurich he had promised. Mildred's contacts had left Germany long ago. Wilhelm, Amalie, and her parents were doing all they could from abroad, but they had been thwarted at every turn. Sara could think of only one other person who might be able to help her.

She remembered the way to Dieter's workplace as if she had last visited weeks before rather than years. If his leave had ended and he had already returned to France, she was undone. She could not sit quietly in her flat until the Gestapo came for her, and she would not incriminate her friends by asking them to shelter her.

Dieter would not recognize the name Sara gave to the receptionist, but she was counting on curiosity to prompt him to come see who it was who claimed to have an appointment.

His face blanched from shock at the sight of her, but he quickly recovered and ushered her into his office. "Did you change your mind about the ring?" he asked, closing the door. "I have it here. It's yours if you want it."

"I'm going to ask much more from you than that," she replied. "Does your company still have a branch office in Basel?"

CHAPTER FIFTY-SEVEN

August–September 1942

Greta

Greta was overcome with relief when Adam received a letter from Wilhelm von Riechmann with important news regarding their biographical play about Beethoven. The Swiss investors had welcomed the stage manager to Geneva, and while they were distraught to learn that the playwright had withdrawn from the production, they were deeply grateful that the stage manager had delivered the news in person.

After so many months of corresponding in code, Greta understood at once that Sara had arrived safely in Geneva and had reunited with her family, with one heartbreaking and irreparable absence.

Sara had left Berlin too suddenly to give her friends more than the barest sketch of her erstwhile fiancé's arrangement to send his new employee Annemarie Hannemann to Basel to facilitate a shipment of chocolate and cheese. Greta suspected that Dieter had helped her not because he had suddenly turned against the Reich, but because he had loved Sara once and wanted to atone for the ways he had failed her. It was unfortunate that he was a *Mitläufer*. He evidently possessed skills that would have been useful to the resistance.

As the summer ripened, Greta, Adam, and their friends continued their clandestine activities with heightened apprehension. The Gestapo arrested an average of fifty Berliners a day. Most arrests were provoked by civilian denunciations, but the result was the same: imprisonment at Gestapo headquarters on Prinz-Albrecht-Strasse, solitary confinement in a cold basement cell, inedible food, and harsh interrogations that began with simple questions but escalated to violence if the officers did not like what they heard. Sometimes, after weeks of relentless questioning apparently designed to drive the prisoners mad, they might suddenly be informed that they were free to go, without ever learning the charges against them or receiving a trial. More often, when the investigating officers believed the prisoner was involved with the resistance or was withholding vital information, they would commence *Verschärfte Vernehmung*—"enhanced interrogation." When this did not result in death, it inevitably left the subject broken in body and mind.

Everyone in their circle was mindful of the dangers—even Harro, whose bravado had convinced Greta that he was impervious to worry. But despite the risks, they could not abandon their cause, not when everything depended upon bringing down the Reich. They all had friends and loved ones in the military—Adam's eldest son, Armin-Gerd, had recently been drafted—and the sooner Hitler was deposed and the Nazis were forced from power, the greater the likelihood they would survive.

And so their work continued.

Although they had not heard from Kent or anyone else from the Brussels outpost in months, they continued to collect intelligence for Moscow, which Arvid painstakingly encoded and Hans Coppi transmitted. After the Wehrmacht launched a second offensive across southern Russia toward the oilfields of the Caucasus precisely as Arvid and Harro had predicted, the Soviets became even more eager for their reports. In early August, Moscow sent two German Communists disguised as soldiers on furlough to Berlin with a new, more powerful transmitter for their group. Mildred arranged a safe house for them along their route in Bad Saarow, about seventy-fives miles southeast of Berlin, and when they finally reached the capital, they stayed with Elizabeth Schumacher. Greta never met them, but afterward, Mildred told her that just as Hirschfeld and Erdberg had done, they too urged their group to abandon their resistance and relief efforts and concentrate on gathering intelligence.

"We don't work for them," said Greta, bristling. "We collaborate with the Soviets because it's in our best interest, but we aren't here to do Moscow's bidding."

"I'll be sure to have Arvid put that into his next report," Mildred teased.

"I wish you would," said Greta, and she was only half joking. Their group was deeply invested in helping the Jews and other victims of the Reich. They were not going to give that up just because the Soviets complained it distracted them from more important work. Greta, especially, was becoming more committed to exposing injustice and atrocities, although she did not always receive unanimous support from the group.

Earlier that summer, Libertas had used her connections at the Kulturfilm center to get Adam a job directing a documentary about the Nazis' ambitious construction projects in the Polish city of Poznań, which Hitler envisioned as a new, majestic gateway to Germany from the east. He intended to have the Royal Castle remodeled as his personal palace, but not far from the depots where tons of rare marble were being shipped to the city, groups of Jewish and Catholic Poles were regularly marched out, lined up before mass graves, and shot. The filming provided Adam with a cover under which he secretly forged contacts for the resistance and collected evidence for Libertas's war crimes archive.

On one occasion, Greta managed to get permission to visit him in Poznań, and she was horrified by what she saw. The city was under martial law, and executions were carried out for the smallest infractions or cases of insubordination, with notices of the death sentences posted on a kiosk in a public square as a warning to others. A brave young woman escorted Greta to a hospital where more than one thousand patients had been slaughtered soon after the invasion. From a safe distance, she pointed out Fort VII, officially known as Konzentrationslager Posen, the first concentration camp established in occupied Poland. Prisoners held in the nineteenth-century fortress were kept in cold, dark, overcrowded cells, sleeping on the stone floor or piles of rotting straw. Women's cells were belowground and often flooded a half meter deep. Food was abysmal, diseases and pestilence rampant. One of the guards' favorite means of torture was the "Stairway of Death," a steep concrete staircase on a hill outside one of the buildings. Prisoners were forced to run up and down the staircase carrying a heavy stone, but sometimes when they reached the top, a bored guard would kick them back down. Arbitrary killings were epidemic, but bullets were inefficient, so SS chemists were experimenting with gas.

Shocked and sickened, upon her return to Berlin, Greta immediately wrote a report describing the inhumane treatment of Jews and Poles in Poznań. After presenting it to her resistance circle, she asked for their help printing copies and distributing them throughout the capital.

Everyone was outraged by what she had learned, and the experiments with gas sparked an intense discussion. In the end, however, Arvid reluctantly said, "This is good reporting, Greta, but we cannot publish it."

"The Nazis are committing mass murder of civilians," she protested. "We must get the word out."

"It's impossible." He sighed, removed his glasses, and rubbed his eyes. "Very few people have access to this information. It would be too easy for the Gestapo to trace this report back to you or to Adam, and then to us. Distributing this report would expose us immediately."

Greta tried to persuade him, but his mind was made up, and his resolve influenced the others. Silently fuming, she acquiesced, and when Mildred urged her to add her report to Libertas's atrocities archive, she pretended to be satisfied with that. She was absolutely certain that if Harro or Günther had presented such incriminating information and had asked for the group to publish it, Arvid would have consented.

For several days thereafter, she privately brooded over the matter—until August 23, when the German armed forces launched a massive bombing campaign against Stalingrad. More than one thousand tons of bombs were dropped, nearly thirty thousand prisoners were captured, and, according to military estimates, more than forty thousand people were killed in the city. German high command expressed optimism that Stalingrad would fall within a few days. Studying Adam's maps,

Greta agonized over what it would mean for the resistance if the Soviet Union were defeated before the end of summer.

And yet somehow Stalingrad defied the onslaught.

The city still had not surrendered more than a week later, on August 31, as Greta prepared to welcome Adam home for a brief visit in honor of his birthday. She had planned a small party, just Greta and Ule, Adam's mother, and his first two wives, the sisters Marie and Gertrud. What a strange gathering it would seem to an outsider, she reflected as she finished preparing the meal. If only Armin-Gerd had been able to get a furlough, the family would have been complete.

When Adam finally arrived home, they all hurried to the door to meet him. Weary from his journey, he gladly returned their embraces, sweeping Ule up in his arms, kissing him and growling like a bear until Ule shrieked with laughter. But while everyone made merry, Greta perceived the tension in the lines around his eyes, the strain in his voice.

After their guests departed and they put Ule to bed, Greta took Adam's hand and led him to the sofa, where he lay down, groaned wearily, and rested his head upon her lap. Stroking his hair, Greta allowed him a few moments to gather his thoughts before she asked him what was wrong.

"Harro disappeared from his office today."

Greta's heart plummeted. "What do you mean, disappeared?"

"I phoned him at his Potsdam office today and was told that he was out. So I called Libertas at her office, and she was acting rather high-strung, even for her. She said that earlier today, his secretary told her that Harro had been ordered to report to his superior officer at once, something about an urgent courier mission to the front. Harro promptly hurried off, leaving his hat, his gloves, and his insignia on his desk. He never returned for them."

"Wouldn't he need them on his mission—the hat and the insignia, at least?"

"One would think."

"That's very strange," said Greta, apprehensive. "Why don't I call Libertas now at home and see if she's heard anything more?"

When Adam agreed, she rang Libertas's Charlottenburg residence and spoke with her housekeeper, who reported that Frau Schulze-

Boysen was at dinner and was unable to come to the phone. Greta said she would call back tomorrow and hung up.

"She's home and safe," Greta said as she resumed her place on the sofa. "And she's apparently not too upset to entertain dinner guests."

"It's probably nothing," murmured Adam, already half asleep.

The next day, Greta waited until midmorning and called Libertas at her office, only to be told that she was on a film site all day and unreachable by phone. In the afternoon, Adam went out to meet Arvid and Günther about resistance matters, and when he returned, he reported that Günther had seen Harro two days before at Wannsee for a sailing party. He had seemed perfectly at ease, not at all as if he suspected the Gestapo was breathing down his neck. Arvid urged them to remain calm and watchful, and to carry on at work and home as if nothing was amiss. It was entirely likely that Harro had indeed been sent off on an important mission for the Luftwaffe, and that his secretary had been mistaken about Harro's forgotten belongings, worrying Libertas unnecessarily.

Greta agreed that the simplest, least sinister explanation was probably the correct one, and yet she felt a rising sense of unease. She wished Adam could extend his visit home, but he was expected at the Kulturfilm office in Prague, and if he suddenly canceled, it would alert anyone who might be observing them.

"Call me as soon as you hear from Libertas," Adam urged as she folded his clothes and set them on the bed for him to pack into his suitcase.

"I will." She inhaled deeply, steadying her nerves. Libertas could be capricious and impulsive, but she knew Greta and Adam were worried about Harro's sudden departure from his office. Although it was reassuring to know that Libertas was hosting dinner parties and working at film shoots, which she would not have done if she were terrified for her husband, it was inexplicably thoughtless of her not to return their messages. "You must call me if you hear from Harro."

"Agreed." He took a carefully folded shirt from her hands, dropped it into his suitcase, and took her in his arms. "I wish I didn't have to go, but this job is important."

"I know." They needed the money, and if he dropped out, Kulturfilm would never give him another assignment, no matter how many strings Libertas pulled.

"Do you know what I've been thinking of all morning?" Adam said, stroking her hair. "Hamburg, the Internationaler Theaterkongresse, and the beautiful, clever French girl I fell in love with there."

Greta smiled. "I had forgotten that you thought I was French."

He kissed her. "I want to go back there with you. When this film is done, we'll leave Ule with my mother and spend a holiday in Hamburg revisiting all our favorite places."

"I do have very fond memories of that hotel."

"As do I." He kissed her again, long and full. "Let's do it. Let's just take a few days to pretend we're an ordinary couple in love enjoying a holiday."

She shook her head at him, amused. "Very well. It's a date."

He grinned. "Good. Now I have to run or I'll miss my train." He kissed her quickly on the cheek. "Take care of my boy. And yourself."

He snatched up his suitcase, put on his hat, and threw her a grin over his shoulder on his way out the door. Just then, Ule called out sleepily from his bed. "Oh, Ule's awake," Greta said, turning toward the sound. "Can you spare a minute to kiss him goodbye?"

But when she turned back, Adam was gone, and the door had already closed between them.

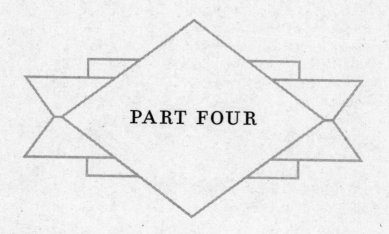

PART FOUR

CHAPTER FIFTY-EIGHT

September—November 1942

Mildred and Greta

Although the United States's entry into the war and the German army's failure to capture Stalingrad had given Mildred and Arvid new hope that it was only a matter of time before the Reich fell, they were exhausted, their nerves strained from constant vigilance. When Egmont and Anneliese Zechlin invited them along on a two-week holiday at the resort town of Preila, they gladly accepted, grateful to escape the stress and danger of Berlin for a little while.

On September 5, a day before their friends, Mildred and Arvid arrived at Preila on the Kurische Nehrung between the Curonian Lagoon and the Baltic Sea. Soothed by the sounds of the waves and the refreshing breezes, they settled into one bedroom of their rented cottage, a charming little place with blue shutters and lovely views of the lagoon. Later they strolled hand in hand across the narrow spit of land to admire the sunset over the Baltic.

Mildred sighed as she gazed across the water. "Sweden is so close," she said, her eyes on the distant horizon. "Perhaps instead of returning to Berlin, we should hire a boat to take us there. Wouldn't it be a relief to wait out the war in a neutral country?"

"I can't leave. My work is too important to the resistance." Arvid raised her hand to his lips. "Yours is too, but I value your safety far more. I wish you would return to America."

"Not without you," she said. "We go together or not at all."

He sighed, rueful. "You've become so stubborn. I blame Greta. She's a bad influence."

Mildred laughed and kissed him.

The next day, they met Egmont and Anneliese at the boat landing in Nidden, and after the Zechlins unpacked at the cottage, they strolled down Preila's main street together, chatting and enjoying the fresh sea breezes. After supper at a charming bistro, they resumed their walk, and in the seclusion of the remote elk marshes, their conversation turned to the war and what might follow. Arvid and Egmont agreed that it was essential to oust Hitler before the Allies defeated Germany in order to preserve German sovereignty. "Otherwise we will be at the mercy of whatever country invades us first," Arvid said, but his last words were drowned out by a deep roll of thunder. Another swiftly followed, and the conversation abruptly ended as they raced back to the cottage steps ahead of a heavy downpour.

Mildred slept peacefully that night in the shelter of Arvid's embrace, but when she woke in the morning, she was alone.

Bright sunshine streamed through the curtains, but beneath the sweet melody of birdsong she heard voices, low and urgent. Stealing to the window, she drew back a corner of the curtain, just enough to glimpse Arvid and Egmont in the yard talking to four men on the other side of the gate.

Trepidation stirred, but the men were dressed in suits and hats, not uniforms, so she supposed they could be other vacationers out for a stroll. She quickly washed and dressed, and when she went to the living room, she found Anneliese observing the men through the front window. "That man in the center showed a badge," she said, her pretty features drawn together in worry. "Who do you think they are? What could they want?"

"I have no idea," Mildred replied. At that moment, the strangers passed through the front gate and followed Arvid and Egmont up the path to the cottage. Anneliese let the curtain fall, and she and Mildred instinctively drew away from the door.

Arvid calmly led the group into the cottage, but Mildred's heart plummeted to see the strain in his expression. "These gentlemen say they are from the police alien registration office."

One officer frowned thinly as he scanned the room. "We've been ordered to tell Oberregierungsrat Harnack that he is needed immediately at the Economics Ministry."

"They could have just sent a wire," said Anneliese, indignant.

Arvid held Mildred's gaze. "I'm sorry, darling, but I must accompany these gentlemen back to Berlin. You should just go ahead with the plans we made when we were admiring the sunset the other night."

Mildred's throat constricted, but she nodded.

"Perhaps I was not clear," said the officer in charge. "Frau Harnack is required too."

"My wife does not work at the ministry," said Arvid. "Why should she have to cut her holiday short?"

"Frau Harnack can remain with us," said Egmont, smiling pleasantly. "None of us have had our coffee, and I'm sure these officers would enjoy a cup. Anneliese, darling, would you make some? We can all drink and talk this over."

Anneliese nodded and darted off.

"You have ten minutes if you wish to pack," the officer told Arvid and Mildred.

Two other officers accompanied them to their bedroom, so they could not speak freely. Blinking back tears, Mildred slowly removed her clothes from the wardrobe, folded them, and placed them into her suitcase. Arvid finished packing first, but he lingered, giving her steady, reassuring looks whenever she glanced his way.

She smelled coffee brewing as she and Arvid returned to the living room, followed closely by the officers. They were Gestapo; they had to be.

"This is all a misunderstanding," Egmont said, looking from Arvid to Mildred and back, forcing a reassuring smile. "I'll meet with the director of the Foreign Studies Department at the university and he'll get this matter sorted out."

Arvid thanked him with a nod.

"Oberregierungsrat Harnack," the officer in charge said sharply, "you are expected at the ministry at once."

Suitcase in hand, Mildred followed Arvid to the door. She threw a glance over her shoulder to Anneliese, who stood in the kitchen doorway watching her helplessly, tears in her eyes.

"Wait," said Egmont, bolting forward. "My wife and I cannot possibly enjoy our holiday knowing our friends' has been spoiled. We'll come with you."

"Professor Zechlin," the officer in charge retorted, "you are too intelligent not to know what is going on here. I am under orders to handle this matter as quietly as possible. You have already interfered too much. I hereby inform you that you are to remain silent about everything you have seen and heard. Otherwise we will arrest you as well." He turned to Anneliese. "Frau Zechlin, the same applies to you."

"The Harnacks are distinguished scholars," Egmont protested. "You cannot prevent me from notifying the university of this outrage."

"This is my final warning, Professor. You are strictly forbidden to tell anyone what has happened here. Any calls you attempt to make will be intercepted."

Egmont looked as if he would say more, but Arvid made a subtle gesture, and he fell silent. As the officers led Mildred and Arvid from the cottage, Egmont took Mildred's hand and kissed it. He gave Arvid a long, wordless look conveying his intention to do everything in his power to help them despite the officer's threats.

"Dear Egmont," said Arvid quietly. "I thank you for everything, for ten years of friendship, and for today." He scarcely had the words out before one of the officers shoved him in the back and forced him stumbling through the doorway, his suitcase banging on the frame. Another officer barked a command close to Mildred's ear, and she hurried after her husband.

They were closely watched all the way back to Berlin, never given a moment alone together, forbidden to speak or to touch. Heart aching, lightheaded with fear, Mildred tried to convey her love through long, wordless looks. Arvid replied with faint smiles and reassuring nods, as if to tell her that all would be well. She longed to believe him, but with every passing hour, her apprehensions rose.

They were taken to Gestapo headquarters at Prinz-Albrecht-Strasse 8, where they were promptly separated. Mildred followed a guard's commands to turn over her valuables, her shoelaces, her belt. Her final destination was the *Hausgefängnis*, one of about three dozen narrow, dank solitary cells in the basement. As the cell door slammed shut with an ominous clang, cutting her off from the world of light and warmth, terror compelled her to disobey orders for silence. "Where is my husband?" she called out, frantic. "Where have you taken him?"

No one answered.

Greta walked home from the Romanisches Café, bemused. It was not like Libertas to miss a date, especially one that had been on their calendar for a fortnight. Greta had waited alone at their favorite table for thirty minutes before hunger compelled her to order lunch. When her *Schweineschnitzel* and *Spätzle* were served, she ate slowly, glancing often to the door, expecting Libertas to appear at any moment, breathless and full of apologies and a good story about whatever Kulturfilm crisis had delayed her. But Greta finished her meal and lingered over her drink for another hour and still Libertas did not appear. Eventually she gave up, paid the bill, and left.

Perhaps Libertas had phoned to cancel at the last minute. Greta had left early to drop off Ule at the kindergarten on the first floor of her apartment building; she might have missed her call. And yet— something was not quite right. Surely if Libertas had tried and failed to reach her at home, she would have left a message at the restaurant.

Uneasy, Greta quickened her pace. As soon as she collected Ule from the kindergarten, she hurried him upstairs, set him down with some toys, and called Libertas's home and office. Libertas's housekeeper and the Kulturfilm receptionist both said that Libertas was traveling, but the receptionist did not know where and the housekeeper refused to say. Perplexed, Greta hung up the phone. Some time earlier Libertas had mentioned that she hoped to travel to Stockholm to visit her sister and brother-in-law, Ottora Maria Countess Douglas and Count Carl Ludvig Douglas. Hermann Göring himself had promised to get her permission to travel as a favor to her grandfather,

Philipp, Prince von Eulenburg, but the last Greta had heard, the permit had been canceled at the last minute, with no explanation.

First Harro had disappeared from his office, or had been sent off on some secret mission for the Luftwaffe, and now Libertas had apparently set off on a mysterious trip without clearing her calendar—

A fist pounded on the door.

Glancing back to make sure Ule was distracted with his toys, Greta answered the knock. When she found two SS men standing in the hall, for a moment she could not breathe. "Yes?" she said, fighting to keep the tremor from her voice. "May I help you?"

"Frau Kuckhoff?"

"Yes?"

"You are wanted for questioning. Come quietly and it will go better for you."

"But—" Greta stumbled out of the way as one of the SS men pushed past her into the room. Her blood ran cold as his gaze traveled around the room and settled on the bookcases filled with classic novels, old scripts, and the great many *verboten* books entrusted to them by nervous friends. "I'm sorry but I can't go with you. I have a child—"

"You should have thought of that before you decided to commit treason."

"What?" she exclaimed. "I've done nothing of the sort. If someone has denounced me, let me confront her face-to-face. Liars inform on neighbors every day out of jealousy and spite. You know that."

The second officer grunted agreement, his head tilted slightly as he read the spines of the books.

"You're coming with us," the first officer said coldly. "You may bring the boy if you like, but I assure you he would be better off here alone."

The second officer lunged and grabbed Greta's arm from behind. "Time to go, *Fraulein*."

"Wait. Let me call my son's grandmother. There's a kindergarten in our building. He could wait there until she can come for him."

The first officer gave his consent, and the second followed her to the phone and listened carefully as she called her mother and explained that she was under arrest and needed her to come for her grandson.

"Will you be all right?" her mother asked, panic in her voice. "Where's Adam?"

"I don't know," Greta replied, just as the second officer grabbed the phone from her hand and hung up.

As slowly as she dared, Greta packed Ule's little knapsack, washed his face and hands, hugged him fiercely, and led him downstairs to the kindergarten. "May Ule wait here until his grandmother arrives?" she asked the teacher. "It may be awhile. She's coming from Frankfurt an der Oder."

"Of course," the teacher replied, concern evident in her tone, though she smiled as she held out her hand to Ule. "Is something wrong?"

The officers had lingered in the foyer, but now Greta heard them approaching. "I'm under arrest," she murmured. "If any of my friends come by asking for me, tell them to run."

Just then the second officer seized her tightly by the arm. "Frau Kuckhoff is mentally ill," he said. "We're taking her to an institution. This nonsense she's speaking is a symptom of the disease. Forget you heard it. Forget we were here."

The teacher's expression tensed and she edged backward, pulling Ule behind her. Greta's last sight of her son was of his sweet face peering up at her from behind his teacher's skirt, his dark eyes confused and shining with unshed tears. "Ule, darling, I love you," she cried as the officers hauled her away.

They put her in the back of a truck, windowless and stifling. Alone, she buried her head in her hands and fought back tears as they jolted along, the frequent stops and starts telling her they had not left the city. All too soon the truck halted and the engine shut down. Two armed guards in brown military uniforms threw open the back and hauled her out, while the first officer ordered them to take her inside. A quick, frantic glance revealed that she was at the police headquarters at Alexanderplatz. Prodded along by the butt of a rifle, she stumbled through the front doors and down a long hallway. She caught fleeting glimpses of people she knew—Elizabeth Schumacher, Erika von Brockdorff—but not Adam or Mildred or Arvid or the Schulze-Boysens or—

But even without her closest friends, there were too many familiar faces, ashen and tear-streaked or stoic or angry, for it not to be certain that their circle had been compromised.

And yet Adam was in Prague, far from all of this. Perhaps the Gestapo did not know. Perhaps one of their friends had been able to get a message to him in time, shouting a warning into the phone while storm troopers broke down their door. Or perhaps her mother had called him before she hurried to Berlin for Ule.

Greta could only hope that word had reached him in time.

Two weeks after Mildred's arrest, she was taken to a large, dark room where she was fingerprinted and photographed, her head held rigidly in a neck brace as they took her photo from the front, in profile, and at three-quarters. By then, the long, harrowing days of endless harsh interrogations without food or water and the agonizing nights of cold, loneliness, and fear had already ravaged her. She had lost weight; the brown prison dress she had been issued on her first day hung from her bent shoulders like a loose shroud. She ached all over from lying on the hard bench in her cell beneath the single barred window, and her flesh was sore and bruised from the slaps and beatings she received under questioning. She was constantly exhausted, her sleep repeatedly interrupted by the discomfort of the cold bench, the screams of other prisoners, nightmares. She felt alternately feverish and chilled, and her chest rattled when she coughed. She was denied medicine, books, visits from loved ones. She had no idea if her family knew where she was.

The only time she saw other prisoners was when she was dragged from her cell to the interrogation room or to the prison yard for her ten minutes of daily exercise. That was how she knew Libertas and Harro were confined to the *Hausgefängnis*, also Adam Kuckhoff and John Sieg, Hans Coppi and Kurt Schumacher. For a while she saw Hilde Coppi nearly every day in the yard, carefully walking with the others, her hands resting upon her rounded abdomen, but then she disappeared; Mildred fervently hoped that she had been released on account of her pregnancy. She never saw Greta, but she once glimpsed Wolfgang Havemann, Arvid's stepnephew. She knew Arvid was near, and she often begged the guards to let her see him, if only for a moment, or at least to tell her which cell was his. They ignored her. The SS officers conducting her interrogations offered to give her time alone with Arvid if she would only make a full confession—such a small thing, really, since they already knew she was guilty—and answer their questions, so many questions about Arvid, the Kuckhoffs, the Schulze-Boysens, the Soviet calling himself Kent and the Soviet intelligence outpost in Brussels and on and on. Increasingly despondent, she responded to every query with denials. She knew nothing of any resistance group. She was a wife and a teacher. Yes, she was an American, but she had no connection to the United States government. Yes, she had been friends with Ambassador Dodd's daughter and other American diplomats and their wives, but those had been innocent friendships, and her American acquaintances had all left Germany long before.

Once, after a particularly intense interrogation, so violent that she had to be carried from the room on a stretcher, she was left for a few minutes in a hallway, lying in a blur of pain and despair, unable to rise or even open her eyes. Thinking her insensible, the guards and officers conversed in passing, and so she learned that more than one hundred members of their group had been rounded up. Most of the women, including Greta, were being held in the prison at Alexanderplatz, but Libertas remained at Prinz-Albrecht-Strasse 8, confined in relative comfort in an open cell because of her aristocratic rank and noble connections.

Weeks later, the guard who brought Mildred her supper—a cup of coffee, two pieces of bread spread with margarine—informed her that Arvid and Adam had finally broken under torture in the Stalin Room, stretched between four beds, wrenched by calf clamps, tormented by thumbscrews. "Your husband wept like a child," he gloated, "but it was Kuckhoff who gave up his friends, John Sieg and Adolf Grimme."

"Who?" Mildred murmured, feigning puzzlement as she forced herself to finish the stale bread. Muttering curses, the guard snatched the tin plate from her hands and struck her upside the head with it. She crumpled, blinded by pain, and over the ringing in her ears she heard him stride from the cell, slam the door, and turn the key.

As her body steadily weakened, her ten minutes of daily exercise in the prison yard became both a respite from the grim isolation of her cell and an ordeal. A guard would take her from her cell and lead her from the *Hausgefängnis* to a pair of heavy iron doors leading to the central courtyard. When the doors opened with a clang of metal, for a moment she would be riveted in place, caressed by sunlight and a sudden rush of cool, fresh air. "No talking," the guard would remind her as he shoved her into the open yard, where other prisoners walked slowly around the perimeter of the gravel courtyard. She was not permitted to fall in step with them, but could only tread a diagonal path between two corners of the high encircling walls, alone. She wondered about the other prisoners. They were not allowed to speak to her, nor she to them. Once, one brave woman dared offer her sympathetic glances, so Mildred took a chance and whispered her name and cell number and begged the woman to remember her.

Ten minutes each day was all she had to walk and breathe beneath an open sky and to remind herself that she was human. By the time her stiff, aching limbs loosened up and she fell into a comfortable rhythm, she would be ordered back to her cell.

An interrogator let slip that she and her friends would be tried, but he did not say when, nor did he explain the charges against her, nor was she permitted to meet with an attorney. She could not imagine who would be brave or foolhardy enough to represent them.

In mid-November, a guard banged on her cell door, startling her out of a wistful reverie—hiking around Lake Mendota in Wisconsin on a late autumn afternoon, her hand in Arvid's, the brilliantly colored leaves dancing overhead as breezes tossed the boughs.

"You see how good behavior is rewarded here," the guard said, entering her cell carrying a small box. "Just think of how much more we could do for you if you would cooperate."

Deliberately, she looked away. He set the box on the floor and nudged it toward her with the side of his boot. She waited for him to leave before she rose unsteadily, went to the box, and peered inside. There was food, bread and cheese and hard sausage and an apple. There was a letter from Arvid's mother. And there was a note from Falk, hastily written from the look of it. "Dear Mildred," he had scrawled in pencil on a scrap of paper, "I was just with our beloved

Arvid. We both send you heartfelt greetings and kisses. Your loyal brother-in-law, Falk."

A tear trickled down her cheek, and she absently wiped it away with the back of her hand. She was not forgotten. Her beloved Arvid was still alive. Surely Arvid's family was doing all they could to get them released.

But as swiftly as her hopes had risen, they plummeted. She and Greta had observed Nazi mass trials with Clara Leiser, and she knew the verdicts were often predetermined. What chance did they have of an acquittal? Whatever the specific charges against them were, the best outcome they could hope for was life imprisonment.

In the days that followed, she reread Mutti Clara's letter and Falk's note so often that the paper became as soft as cloth, but their kindness was not enough to alleviate her suffering. Illness, hunger, isolation, and brutal treatment at the hands of the Gestapo had worn her down to a thin shadow. One night, just as she was drifting off to sleep, a man passed outside her door and hoarsely whispered that John Sieg had hanged himself in his cell rather than betray any of his friends. Once Mildred would have recoiled from the thought of taking her own life, but after more than two months of unendurable horror, she felt death beckoning her. Her strength was faltering, and she knew from the rattle in her chest that she was unlikely to survive a lengthy incarceration. She had withstood interrogation thus far, but if the Gestapo subjected her to the same torture Arvid and Adam had suffered in the Stalin Room, how long could she hold on?

Perhaps it would be wiser and braver to take her own life before she could be forced to reveal the names of her friends.

One morning in late November, or so she believed, having lost track, she woke coughing up blood. The guard took her to the infirmary, which smelled of bleach and iron and seemed too brightly lit for her feeble eyes. She caught a glimpse of herself reflected in a stainless-steel basin and was shocked to see a haggard old woman staring bleakly back at her.

She cringed as moans of anguish came from an adjacent room where the doctor was examining another patient. She caught sight of a tray on the counter beside the sink, upon which several objects were arranged—

wooden tongue depressors, a stethoscope, a container of sewing pins. She stared at the latter, perplexed by the apparent incongruity, focusing on that in an attempt to block out the distressing sounds from the other room. What purpose would sewing pins serve here? she wondered, and suddenly she realized what purpose they *could* serve.

Summoning her strength, she bolted from her chair, reached the counter in two strides, snatched up the pins, and shoved a handful into her throat. She heard the guard shout as she closed her eyes and tried to swallow, but then a hand closed tightly around her shoulder and another seized her throat, and then they were prying her jaw open. Frantic, she thrashed and tried to wrench herself free. Her elbow connected with something that gave way with a strange, sickening crunch followed by a howl of pain, then two men had her on the floor, on her side, with hands squeezing her throat to prevent her from swallowing and two more holding open her mouth and slapping the back of her head until most of the pins tumbled out, fingers plunging into her mouth to sweep the last few free. A boot connected with her rib cage, once, and again, and again.

She wept, overcome with pain and anger and frustration. She had come so close to eluding her tormentors without ever leaving their prison. They would never give her another chance.

Many nights Greta dreamed of playful, sunny romps through the Tiergarten with Ule, only to wake in the morning to the sound of her own weeping.

Would she ever see her precious son again? She was permitted a few letters a week, but no visitors—not that she would want her little boy to see her in that wretched place. Her mother assured her that Ule was healthy and content, but he missed her and Adam very much and asked about them often. His grandmother told him that his Mutti and Papa were traveling on important business and would be home soon. Despondent, Greta wondered how long he would believe it.

Soon after her arrest, an SS officer had informed her that Adam had been captured in Prague a few hours after she had been brought to Alexanderplatz. With every heartbreaking letter, Adam's mother asked if

Greta had any news of him, for he had not written to her. She had gone to Gestapo headquarters begging to see him, only to be turned away. Greta had received no word from him either, although from time to time her interrogators would taunt her with horrifying descriptions of Prinz-Albrecht-Strasse 8. She knew that Adam, Arvid, and the others held captive there had been beaten and tortured, and that after several days of torment, Adam had finally confessed. She was devastated to learn that he had given up John Sieg and Adolf Grimme, but she knew he had held out as long as he could in hopes that a delay would give his friends time to escape. Unfortunately, as the Gestapo men told her with mock sorrow, he had not held out long enough. John Sieg was dead, Adolf Grimme was in the *Hausgefängnis* along with Mildred and Libertas, and their wives languished in the Alexanderplatz prison the same as Greta, the same as most of the resistance women, except those few who had eluded capture.

Greta did not understand why her two dear friends were confined to the *Hausgefängnis* with the men instead of at Alexanderplatz or the women's prison in Charlottenburg. Was it because Libertas was the granddaughter of a prince and Mildred was an American? That defied logic. Shouldn't their status merit preferential treatment, not confinement to hell on earth? There was something else at work, something Greta had not yet worked out, keeping Mildred and Libertas apart from the other resistance women.

Alexanderplatz was not comfortable by any means, but from the ominous details Greta had gathered, it was humane compared to the *Hausgefängnis*. Originally built as a men's military prison, it had been converted when the Reich's mass arrests had created serious over-crowding problems at other facilities. The women had the entire fifth floor to themselves, and they were treated less harshly than the men confined to the lower levels. They were allowed to receive letters and packages of food and other necessities. They were permitted small gatherings and were allowed to sing and converse. The prisoners often stayed up late into the night talking, fending off loneliness and despair with quiet companionship. Those fortunate enough to receive sewing kits or knitting baskets from friends on the outside were allowed to occupy themselves with knitting warm scarves or darning socks, both for themselves and other prisoners, even for men they knew held elsewhere in the compound.

Throughout that grim autumn of pursuits and arrests, Greta met many of her comrades for the first time. For security, most members of the resistance had known only the five or six people within their immediate circle, although those like Greta who participated in overlapping circles knew more. It was disconcerting to pass acquaintances in the prison halls and discover that they had unknowingly been members of the same resistance network all along.

As the long, lonely, agonizing weeks passed, Greta became particularly close to Elizabeth Schumacher, whom she had known fairly well for years, and Marta Wolser Husemann, a young Communist actress whom she had only just met. They often talked late into the night, wondering aloud about their husbands and families, and discussing their impending trials, which they assumed were imminent although they had been told almost nothing. They reminisced about life before the Reich, which appeared to them in the warm, rosy glow of the unattainable past, a time they had not realized while they were living it would prove to be the best of their lives. They sustained one another's hopes even when hope was futile. Together they dared to imagine a future when they would be able to reunite with their loved ones far from the cold, forbidding walls of the prison.

Perhaps that would never come to pass, but if wishful thinking got them through the days, Greta would willingly surrender herself to it.

As the days grew shorter and the nights colder, the fifth floor of the prison became increasingly uncomfortable. Greta, Elizabeth, and Sophie Sieg were called out for interrogations more frequently than the others, but when they compared notes afterward, they could discern no pattern to the investigation other than the Gestapo was convinced of their guilt, and that Hitler seemed furious that so many members of their resistance group belonged to the political and intellectual elite. Treachery from Jews and Communists he could understand and expect, but betrayal by people like the Harnacks and Schulze-Boysens, who stood to benefit significantly from the triumph of the Reich, utterly infuriated him. That was a personal affront, unfathomable, unforgivable.

One afternoon in late November, Greta was brought in for yet more questioning. She calmly and plainly responded to the same questions she had heard hundreds of times before, careful to keep her facts straight, to tell the same stories precisely as she had throughout the previous two months. But this time, the Gestapo officer regarded her with a new avidity, nodding smugly after each response.

"You should be more forthcoming, Frau Kuckhoff," he admonished her.

"I've told you everything I know," she replied, careful to show the proper deference.

"Not everything." His voice rang with triumph. "Your husband, Harro Schulze-Boysen, and Arvid Harnack have already confessed to collusion with agents of the Soviet Union, so those simple, condemning facts are no longer in dispute. You are aware that military espionage is classified as high treason?"

Stricken, Greta nodded.

"And you understand that the penalty for high treason is death?"

She tried to speak but could not. She nodded again.

"That much is settled," the officer said. "Your husband will be tried, he will be found guilty, and he will die. The only question is whether you will die with him."

CHAPTER FIFTY-NINE

December 1942–January 1943

Mildred

In early December, Mildred was informed that she was being transferred to the women's prison at Kantstrasse 79 in Charlottenburg. Desperate for one last glimpse of Arvid, she looked frantically down corridors and through open doorways as the guards escorted her from the *Hausgefängnis* upstairs to the exit, but although she saw Adam from a distance, Arvid was nowhere to be found. Fighting back despair, blinking from the sudden brightness as she was led outside, she turned her face to the winter sky and inhaled deeply, shivering in her coarse prison garb, drawing in as much of the thin sunshine and fresh air as she could before the guards opened the back of a green police van and thrust her inside.

As her eyes adjusted to the darkness, she made out a small blond woman sitting on one of the benches, her shoulders slumped in profound dejection, her hair tousled and matted, her head buried in her hands. "Libertas?" Mildred asked hesitantly.

The woman immediately straightened. "Mildred?" she exclaimed. "Oh my God, Mildred! You're alive!"

As the van started up, they embraced unsteadily, tumbling down upon the bench and clinging to each other as if they were drowning. Tearfully Libertas asked Mildred if she had seen Harro; Mildred shook her head and asked if Libertas had seen Arvid. She had, but only once, in mid-October, walking in the exercise yard, thinner but unbowed.

Quickly, talking over each other in their urgency, they shared their news. Mildred described how she and Arvid had been apprehended in Preila, and Libertas confirmed what Mildred had already guessed, that when Harro had disappeared from his office in late August, the courier mission had been a ruse to conceal his arrest. That same day, the mail carrier in the Schulze-Boysens' apartment building had warned Libertas that the Gestapo had been monitoring their letters. Terrified, fearing the worst for her husband, Libertas had frantically destroyed evidence at her home and in her Kulturfilm office. She had hastily packed a suitcase and had spent the next few days first with one friend, and then another, afraid to return home. Finally, convinced that the Gestapo was watching her at every moment, she had boarded a south-bound train for the Black Forest where Harro's brother had a vacation home. She had intended to catch her breath and plan her escape to France or Switzerland, but the SS had captured her on the train.

Both women gasped as the van came to a sudden halt.

"I didn't mean to betray anyone," Libertas said desperately, clutching Mildred's arm. "I was trying to help. She pretended to be my friend. I didn't know, I swear I didn't know—"

"Who?" Mildred asked, bewildered. "What didn't you know?"

The door swung open and guards reached in to haul them out. Instinctively the women clung to each other, but the guards wrestled them out of the van and onto the pavement, where they were quickly separated. Mildred was led away first, stumbling through the prisoners' entrance while Libertas wept and shrieked her name, her voice abruptly silenced when the door slammed between them.

Mildred was taken to a cell, larger than the one in the *Hausgefängnis*, cleaner, above ground, but although it was fitted with two folding beds, she was alone. Later that afternoon, she was interviewed by the matron, given instructions, and warned about the penalties for disruptive behavior.

In the days that followed, Mildred learned that Oberin Anne Weider was strict, but not sadistic. Nor was she a Nazi, but a former Social Democrat and social worker who had been forced to accept the position by the Reich Ministry of Justice. She granted Mildred permission to write to her mother-in-law, and when Mutti Clara and Falk replied with a package containing letters, food, and vitamins, Mildred was allowed to keep them.

In mid-December, Oberin Weider summoned her to her office and gravely informed her that the trial of the Rote Kapelle would begin in two days.

"Rote Kapelle?" Mildred echoed, bewildered.

"Your resistance cell. That is what you are called, the Red Orchestra." Before Mildred could inquire about the origin of the name, the matron said that the case had been assigned to the Reich Court-Martial, the highest court of the Wehrmacht judicial system.

"Court-martial?" Mildred shook her head, confused. "I have never been in the military."

"But other defendants you will be tried with are," Oberin Weider replied. "Harro Schulze-Boysen. Horst Heilmann. Herbert Gollnow."

Dismayed, Mildred nodded, certain this could not bode well for her case.

Early on the morning of Tuesday, December 15, she was taken from her cell and loaded into the back of a police van. Minutes later, Libertas was helped inside with surprising deference; she cried out at the sight of Mildred and flung herself into her arms. Soon thereafter another woman joined them: Erika von Brockdorff, who had assisted Hans Coppi with his radio operations.

"Have either of you met with a lawyer?" Erika asked as the van started up.

Mildred and Libertas shook their heads. "I don't know if I even have a lawyer," said Mildred.

"Oh, we'll have lawyers, all right," replied Erika. "Principled men who like to tilt at windmills. They won't be allowed to read our complete files or tell us what charges we're facing, but they'll do the best they can."

The van jolted along for a few minutes, but there were no windows, so Mildred had no idea where they were until the van halted, the door opened, and Elizabeth Schumacher was thrust inside. She was being held at the Alexanderplatz prison with Greta, Sophie Sieg, and several others Mildred knew, she told them after they embraced one another. "Has anyone seen Hilde Coppi?" she asked.

"I saw her at Prinz-Albrecht-Strasse 8, but that was in late September," said Mildred, clutching her seat as the van lurched into gear.

"She's at Charlottenburg, or at least she was," said Libertas, raising her voice to be heard over the rumble of the engine. "She gave birth to a son in late November."

"How is she? How is the child?" Elizabeth asked, but Libertas did not know.

Soon the van stopped again, and this time eight men were roughly shoved into the back of the van—among them Harro, Hans Coppi, Kurt Schumacher, and Arvid, gaunt and pale, his eyes shadowed, his expression calm but haggard.

"Arvid," Mildred cried. "I'm here!"

Their eyes met, and as the doors slammed shut and the van started up, he made his way to her side and they fell into each other's arms, their hearts full of joy and remorse. To see Arvid again after so long a separation was wonderful, but to be reunited here, on their way to an uncertain fate—Mildred could barely endure it.

They spoke quickly, in hushed voices, not knowing how soon they would be parted again. They professed their love and bravely assured each other that they were fine despite all appearances to the contrary.

"My sister Inge persuaded Dr. Schwarz to represent us," Arvid said, clasping her hands in his. "Falk has met with him, and he has a strategy. You must let me take the blame for everything."

"Arvid, no."

"Yes, *Liebling.*" He lifted one of her hands and laid it against his cheek. "It's the only way one of us might survive. Do this for me."

She murmured protests, but he only smiled, wistful and loving, and when the van halted moments later, he pressed a folded sheet of paper into her hands and urged her to conceal it. Quickly she tucked it down the front of her dress, hoping she would not be searched.

Mildred, Arvid, and the other prisoners exited the truck in a cobblestone courtyard and were escorted under armed guard into the Reichskriegsgericht building, a four-story courthouse spanning the entire length of the block. Outside the courtroom, Mildred glimpsed a sign in passing: "Secret Trial: Public Not Permitted." Heart pounding, she stayed close to Arvid as they passed through the entrance between two soldiers standing at attention with fixed bayonets. Inside, more soldiers stood guard at the windows and doors, motionless but menacing. The spectators' gallery was empty, as was the jury box. Mildred's attention was drawn to a U-shaped table with seven tall chairs on a dais on the far side of the room. The two seats on either end were occupied, one by a stenographer, the other by a handsome dark-haired man in the uniform of a Luftwaffe colonel. Preternaturally calm as he arranged papers on the table before him, he glanced up and smiled faintly when the defendants entered.

"Hitler's *Bluthund*," Hans Coppi muttered, and Mildred felt a chill. The man was Manfred Roeder, a prosecutor known for his cynicism, brutality, and ruthlessness.

The defendants were led to twelve chairs facing the judge's table, separated from the witness stand by a wooden railing. They had only just seated themselves when the five judges entered the courtroom. Everyone but the defendants snapped out a crisp *Hitlergruss*.

Mildred expected the trial to unfold like the mass trials she had observed with Clara Leiser and Greta years before, but this was a military court, and the pretense of impartiality had been stripped away. She felt increasingly disheartened and afraid as she realized that none of the rights granted to defendants in an American courtroom existed here. As the prosecuting attorney, Roeder directed the proceedings, and he had already submitted to the chamber an indictment for each defendant as well as a report of the evidence. Dr. Schwarz and Dr. Behse, the defense attorneys, were not permitted to examine the evidence, nor were they allowed to consult or advise their clients. There would be no witnesses called for the defense, and when the defendants were questioned, they could respond with only a simple yes or no.

After those dire revelations came another that flooded Mildred with anguish and frustration: the official account of how their resistance network had been discovered. Their downfall had not come about due to Harro's recklessness, or Mildred's recruitment efforts, or Arvid's refusal to abandon resistance work in favor of gathering intelligence, or Greta's determination to help her Jewish friends. Instead they had been brought down by Soviet carelessness, a series of mistakes that had led the Gestapo right to them like a branching path of falling dominoes.

In August 1941, when Moscow had radioed the disastrously imprudent message with their names and addresses to Kent at his station in Brussels, the Germans had intercepted the transmission, just as Mildred and her friends had feared. Although the Abwehr had been unable to decipher the code, they had been alerted to the presence of a Soviet intelligence outpost somewhere in the region and had monitored the airwaves vigilantly thereafter. Three months later, upon returning to Brussels from Berlin, Kent had radioed Harro's lengthy, detailed reports to Moscow, broadcasting for hours at a time, seven nights in a row, ignoring every safety protocol in order to get the crucial intelligence to Moscow as swiftly as possible. Nazi counterintelligence operatives had easily homed in on the conspicuous signal, had recorded the coded messages, and within a month had traced the broadcast back to its source: the lair of the Rote Kapelle, Red Orchestra, named for the illicit "music" they had broadcast to enemies of the Reich.

In December 1941, a year earlier almost to the day, Abwehr agents had raided the Brussels outpost, seizing compromising materials and capturing a young Polish cipherer, Sophie Poznanska, as well as the Belgian housekeeper. Poznanska had committed suicide in prison rather than betray her comrades, but the terrified housekeeper had given her interrogators the titles of three books that she had often seen on Poznanska's desk. On May 17, the Abwehr had found a copy of *Der Kurier aus Spanien* in a used bookstore, and by the middle of July they had decoded Moscow's incautious transmission. The Abwehr had immediately placed the Harnacks, the Kuckhoffs, and the Schulze-Boysens under surveillance, watching and waiting, monitoring visitors, mail, and phone calls, patiently observing the suspects and gathering evidence in hopes of capturing the entire network. Eventually they had pounced.

By the time the first day of hearings was over, Mildred felt exhausted, heartsick, utterly lost, and the trial had only just begun. Parting from Arvid was sheer anguish, but at least she knew she would see him again in the morning.

Until then, she had his letter, which she read as soon as she returned to the lonely solitude of her cell.

My most beloved heart,

If in the last months I have found the strength to be inwardly calm and composed, and if I face what is to come with calm composure, it is due above all to the fact that I feel a strong attachment to the good and beautiful things in this world, and that toward the whole earth I have the feeling that inspires the song of the poet Whitman. As far as people are concerned, it has been those close to me, and especially you, who have embodied these feelings for me.

Despite all the hardships, I am happy to look back on my life so far. The light outweighed the dark, and our marriage was the greatest reason for this. Last night, I let my thoughts roam through many of the most wonderful moments of our marriage, and the more I thought about them, the more I recalled. It was as if I were looking into a starry sky, in which the number of stars increases the more meticulously one looks. Do you still remember Picnic Point, when we became engaged? I sang for joy early the next morning at the club. And before that: our first serious conversation at the restaurant on State Street? That conversation became my guiding star, and has remained so. In the sixteen years that followed, how often we lay our heads on each other's shoulders at night when life had made us weary, either yours on mine or mine on yours, and then everything was fine again. I have done this in my thoughts over the past several weeks and will do the same in those to come. I have also thought regularly of you and all my loved ones at eight o'clock each morning and nine o'clock each night. They all think of both of us at the very same time. Do it as well; then we shall know that our feelings of love are flowing between all of us.

The strain of our work meant that our lives were not easy, and there was no small risk of being overwhelmed, but even so, we remained very much alive as people. This became clear to me during our time on the Grossglockner, and again this year, as we watched the great elk emerge in front of us as we walked through the forest by the sea.

*You are in my heart, and you shall always be within it! My dearest
wish is for you to be happy when you think of me. I am when I think
of you.*

Many, many kisses! I am holding you close.

Your A.

For five days, the defendants were subjected to Roeder's belligerent
and bombastic questioning. Mildred tried not to flinch as he harangued
her, and she struggled to remain calm when he repeatedly interrupted
her. When Dr. Schwarz argued that she was innocent of wrongdoing
because like any good German wife she had simply obeyed her husband's instructions, Roeder barked out a derisive laugh. To Mildred's
astonishment, several of the judges reacted with frowns or reproving
looks, which they concealed so quickly that she was afraid she had
imagined them. But for the first time since she had entered the courtroom, she felt a flicker of hope, even though she was deeply afraid of
what Dr. Schwarz's legal strategy might mean for Arvid.

As the trial unfolded, she endured questioning with as much serene
composure as she could muster, and she silently cheered on her companions when they remained dignified, eloquent, and calm in the face
of Roeder's verbal assaults. Only once did she feel truly hopeless, when
Libertas broke down on the stand and began shouting that she was
innocent, that Harro was to blame for everything, that she wanted a divorce. Harro endured it unflinchingly, but Mildred was sure his wife's
desperate rebuke had wounded him.

After several grueling days the prosecution rested its case, and on
December 19, the verdicts were delivered. For the crimes of preparation
for high treason, war treason, undermining military strength, aiding the
enemy, and espionage, the court sentenced Arvid, Harro, Libertas, Kurt
Schumacher, Elizabeth Schumacher, Hans Coppi, Kurt Schulze, John
Graudenz, and Horst Heilmann to death. Herbert Gollnow received
the death penalty for disobedience in the field and for disclosing state
secrets to the enemy. Erika von Brockdorff was sentenced to ten years
at hard labor for keeping a radio that was used to contact the Soviets.

Lastly, the judges declared that they concurred with Dr. Schwarz that Mildred had acted more from loyalty to her husband than from her own political motives. Despite her exceptional understanding of German literature, as a foreigner, she could not possibly comprehend the implications of disloyalty to the Reich. Therefore, she was sentenced not as a conspirator, but as an accessory to espionage, for which she received six years hard labor.

When Mildred's sentence was read aloud, Arvid smiled at her, his face radiant with joy. He would die, but she would live.

"This is an outrage," Roeder exploded, bolting to his feet. "I demand twelve death sentences! The Führer ordered me to cauterize this sore. He will never approve this decision!"

The judges made no reply, but rose and withdrew to their chambers. Quickly the twelve defendants embraced one another before the guards could pull them apart. Mildred clung to Arvid, resting her head on his chest and choking out sobs, but although Arvid's eyes shone with unshed tears, he could not stop smiling. She knew that he had never dared hope that his own life would be spared, but his beloved wife would live, and that was enough. He could go to his own death at peace with his fate knowing that Mildred would survive him, and that one day she would be free.

On December 20, the day after her trial concluded, Mildred woke to the sound of her cell door opening to find that another prisoner had been assigned to the vacant bunk. She did not know the young woman who entered her cell carrying her few possessions wrapped in a thin blanket, but she recognized her at once, for they had exchanged glances in the prison yard. As soon as the guard closed the cell door, Mildred's new cellmate set down her bundle and the two women fell into each other's arms as if they were long-lost friends.

Her name was Gertrud, and she was a Communist and a member of the resistance awaiting transport to Ravensbrück, a women's concentration camp in northern Germany. Mildred suspected Gertrud had been assigned to her cell to discourage her from making a second suicide attempt, but that was an unnecessary precaution. She had no intention of taking her own life when it meant the world to her beloved Arvid that she should keep it. Also, as the green police van had taken them away from the courthouse, Arvid had held her hands tightly and had assured her that in the German judicial system, several weeks elapsed between sentencing and execution, and his family had undoubtedly already begun filing the paperwork for his appeal. How could she willingly depart this world while Arvid remained in it?

Mildred and Gertrud passed the miserable days talking about their lives, about the loved ones they missed and the places they longed to see again, about why they had joined the resistance. They were not permitted books, so they sang and recited poetry to each other. With her precious stub of a pencil, Mildred wrote down from memory some of Goethe's poems for Gertrud to take with her to Ravensbrück.

Gertrud's companionship made the bleak hours more bearable, but every day Mildred sank deeper into despair. She received no mail, no more packages from Arvid's family, and she confided to Gertrud that she brooded anxiously over how she would endure six years at hard labor.

She begged the director, the guards, anyone who would listen for news of Arvid. She humbly implored Oberin Weider to allow her to see Arvid for Christmas, but the matron told her, not without pity, that it was impossible. Christmas came and went with nothing to mark the holy season except for a few wistful carols echoing down the prison corridors. She wrote a long, loving letter to Arvid, and others to his family and her own back in America, but she had little hope that they would be posted.

The New Year began, cold and bleak, but Mildred stoked her courage by reminding herself that Arvid's family was working fervently on his appeal. Now that the holidays were over and all the bureaucrats had gone back to work, the Harnacks might make swift progress and save his life.

In early January, when the matron summoned Mildred to her office, her spirits rose. Perhaps this was the good news she had been hoping for since that day in late December when they had thought their fates were sealed. But as soon as she stood before Oberin Weider's desk and saw the grim sympathy in her eyes, she knew she must steel herself for yet another devastating blow.

And yet it staggered her when it fell.

Although Adolf Hitler had signed the document confirming the death sentences of Arvid, Harro, and the others, he had refused to confirm the judgments against her and Erika von Brockdorff.

Within a fortnight they would face a new trial in a different chamber of the Reichskriegsgericht. This time, the Führer would surely get the verdict he demanded.

CHAPTER SIXTY

January–February 1943

Greta

In mid-January, nine more members of the Rote Kapelle went on trial before the Reichskriegsgericht, university students and young people who had engaged in widespread anti-Nazi leafleting campaigns but had not provided intelligence to the Soviet Union. Greta had not known any of the nine defendants before her arrest, but in recent weeks she had met several of the resistance women in Alexanderplatz, including the pottery artist Cato Bontjes van Beek and Liane Berkowitz, the nineteen-year-old student who had participated in Harro's "Nazi Paradise" sticker campaign with Sara Weitz. Liane was six months pregnant; her fiancé, Friedrich Rehme, a German army draftee, had been arrested in a military hospital as he recovered from serious wounds he had received on the Russian front. When all nine defendants were found guilty, Manfred Roeder again demanded the death penalty, on the grounds that they had offered aid and comfort to the enemy. Although at first the Reich Court-Martial sentenced all nine to die, they must have had misgivings, for soon thereafter they recommended that Cato and Liane be pardoned.

"I want to live, but I expect to die," Cato murmured to Greta as they walked together in the exercise yard. "Hitler will never show mercy, not even to poor Liane, although I pray they'll at least wait until she delivers her child."

They both looked across the yard to Liane, who placed her feet carefully as she walked, peering forlornly out at the dusty yard through thick, dark, unruly curls, her hands on her abdomen. Even for her age, she was too thin for so late in her second trimester. Her friends shared their rations with her, but it was never enough.

"You mustn't lose hope," Greta urged. "Mildred and Erika were shown some clemency. You and Liane may be too."

Cato shot her a sharp sidelong look, not enough to draw the attention of the guards. "You don't know?"

"Know what?"

"Mildred and Erika were sentenced to die."

"No, you're wrong." Greta shook her head. "I know you're wrong. It was Elizabeth—" Dear Elizabeth, a true friend in the darkest days of her life. "You're thinking of Elizabeth Schumacher and Libertas. They received death sentences in that trial." And where were they now? Charlottenburg? The *Hausgefängnis* at Prinz-Albrecht-Strasse 8? All Greta knew for certain was that they were not at Alexanderplatz. She wished she could get a message to them, a few words of love and comfort, some reassurance that they had not been forgotten.

"I'm so sorry, Greta," said Cato, stricken. "I thought you knew. Hitler rejected those sentences. They were given a new trial, with new charges and contrived evidence, and allegations that Mildred had committed adultery thrown in to turn the judges against her. Mildred and Erika were found guilty of espionage and treason. They were given the death sentence."

Greta felt as if all the air was being forced from her lungs. Her knees buckled; she stumbled and might have collapsed except Cato reached out and steadied her. "Are you sure?" she managed to say. "How do you know?"

"I heard it from one of the guards, the chatty one with the short blond braids. I suppose she could have been lying to torment me."

"Perhaps," said Greta, sick at heart. "But for now, they're still alive?"

"I have no idea." Cato inhaled deeply and squared her shoulders as a whistle shrilled to signal the end of their exercise period. "But now you see why I have little hope that any mercy will be shown to me, or to any of us."

Thanks to Cato, Greta knew what to expect when her own trial came, but on the first day of February when she was led from her cell outside to the police van, her heart plummeted and her legs shook so badly that she had difficulty walking. It took all her willpower to maintain a stoic expression rather than give her captors any pleasure in her suffering, but the mask slipped when she arrived at the Reichskriegsgericht building and a guard told her she would be allowed a few minutes with Adam before the trial.

Inside, the guard escorted her to a waiting room and gestured for her to enter. She quickly obeyed, her gaze taking in seven men in prison attire, passing over Adolf Grimme with a flicker of acknowledgment and at last finding her husband. When Adam's eyes met hers, she instinctively pressed a hand to her mouth to hold back a cry—of joy to see him again, and of shock at his haggard appearance.

As she stood frozen, he hurried to meet her by the door, and soon they were in each other's arms, holding on so tightly that Greta almost couldn't breathe. He had aged years in the nearly five months since she had last seen him. She could only imagine how her own altered appearance shocked and dismayed him.

They spoke rapidly, knowing time was of the essence. Adam was almost never allowed to receive mail, so she quickly shared the most important details from the letters their mothers had sent her, focusing on Ule, the family, herself—but before she could ask what he knew of Mildred or their other friends, he took her hands and said, "Greta, listen. There's something I want you to do."

"Anything, darling. What?"

"I need your help clearing Grimme's name."

She stared at him, uncomprehending. "What do you mean?"

"You and I are both done for, but Grimme was barely involved. He still has a chance to get off with a prison sentence. He's been my friend since our school days. If you confirm his innocence in court, if we keep our stories straight, there's a chance we could save him."

A flicker of anger surged. She was not willing to accept that she was done for, not yet, not until the sentence was pronounced. "Very well," she managed to say. "Grimme knew nothing. He did nothing. We hid our work from him because we knew he would not approve."

He smiled, relieved. "That's my good girl." He drew her close again and kissed her cheek. "Thank you, darling."

She stiffened in his embrace, but knowing that she might never again feel his arms around her, she forced herself to relax, to relent, to forgive. And yet in the back of her mind a plaintive voice lamented that Adam and Grimme could have worked out a story to exonerate her instead. She was Adam's wife, the mother of his youngest son, and yet when he decided to try to save one person, he had chosen someone else.

The guard unlocked the door and barked a command, ending their brief interlude. The eight defendants were escorted into the courtroom and ordered to take their places. The court was called into session, Roeder began the proceedings, and then, so swiftly that Greta would have become outraged if she were not so afraid and overwhelmed, Hitler's Bloodhound flew through all eight prosecutions in a single day.

After the judges retired to their chambers, the eight defendants were escorted back to the waiting room and again permitted to speak freely. Shaken from the courtroom ordeal, Greta seized Adam's hand and tried to draw strength from his firm, familiar grasp. She expected the men to discuss the trial and its possible outcomes, but instead they shared rumors of a staggering German defeat at Stalingrad that had apparently occurred only a few days before. Greta looked from one eager, careworn face to another, marveling at their enthusiasm. Could it be that none of them had reached the same conclusion she had—that Hitler, who always found a scapegoat to blame for every failure, could very well hold the Rote Kapelle responsible for this disastrous loss? They had provided volumes of military and economic intelligence to the Soviets. Hitler would not care if a direct link could not be established. He would not care if the correct people were punished, as long as someone was.

As the men's discussion became increasingly animated, Greta worried that they had abandoned caution, at the Reichskriegsgericht of all places. She glanced surreptitiously toward the guards and was surprised to find them conversing nonchalantly, utterly indifferent to their prisoners' seditious talk. Indeed, why should they care? Greta thought bitterly. To the guards, the defendants were as good as dead. Nothing they said mattered anymore.

All too soon, the defendants were loaded into the police van and taken back to prison. Greta slept poorly that night, and was awakened before dawn by a guard rattling her cell door. Groggily, she rose, dressed, and attended to her face and hair as best she could, determined to appear dignified and respectable before the court, not that it would sway their decision.

Again they were brought before the judges, but this time, they were asked if they wished to make any final statements on their own behalf. Greta's blood roiled with shock and anger as Adolf Grimme reminded the court that he was a man of prominence and renown, that he had served as the Reich minister of culture, that he had received the Goethe Prize from Field Marshal Hindenburg's own hands. He swore that he was no Communist, but a socialist and a man of faith who had succumbed to Adam Kuckhoff's influence.

As he returned to his place, Greta could not bear to look at him, but she was startled to find Adam apparently unsurprised by his friend's denunciation. Perhaps they had worked out Grimme's statement between themselves ahead of time, but Greta still seethed with suppressed fury. How dare Grimme vainly attempt to save his own life by shoving Adam toward the gallows?

The verdicts were read: Greta, Adam, and five others received the death sentence. Grimme was condemned for failing to report an attempt at high treason and was sentenced to three years hard labor.

Afterward, they gathered one last time in the waiting room as the police van was made ready. Greta was too furious to speak to Grimme, who stood abashedly cleaning his glasses so he would not have to look Adam in the eye. Once Adam released her hand so that he could shake Grimme's, and she burned with resentment that he had squandered even those few of their last precious moments together. She wanted to shake him, to scream at him that Grimme would live but she would die, and she, his loyal and loving wife, deserved every second of his time.

But she did not want to part from Adam with anger or resentment lingering between them. With an apologetic frown for Grimme, she pulled Adam aside, knowing she would probably never see him again. They embraced, they kissed, they spoke words of love and encouragement. They talked about Ule, their hearts aching even as they reassured each other that he would be brought up well by Greta's parents. One day he would know that his mother and father had given their lives to a righteous cause.

Then they were separated. Greta returned to Alexanderplatz and prepared to die. She wrote letters to her parents, to Ule, to Adam's mother, letters full of fond reminiscences of their lives together and of her love and her hopes for their futures. She filed an appeal for clemency, as her friends and comrades had done before her, knowing that it was almost certainly futile but refusing to give up without at least making the attempt.

She had always been that way, from her impoverished childhood through her student days and into her ill-fated years as a woman of the resistance, stubbornly persisting long after wiser people acquiesced. That quirk of her nature that endeared her to some and made rivals of others had served her well for forty years, and she would not forsake it now.

CHAPTER SIXTY-ONE

February 15–16, 1943

Mildred

On the evening of February 15, a guard unlocked the door to Mildred's cell and ordered her to gather her belongings.

Mildred's heart plummeted. "May I ask why?" It was after nine o'clock, almost time for lights-out, too late for an interrogation or a meeting with the matron.

"You're being transferred to Plötzensee," the guard replied. "You have five minutes."

"No!" her cellmate cried out. "Not so soon!"

Every prisoner knew that Plötzensee was where the condemned went to die.

Lightheaded with fear, Mildred rose and mechanically collected her few books, her sweater, the letters from Arvid's family, her precious stub of a pencil. She had already entrusted Arvid's last letter to Gertrud, believing that it would be safer with her in Ravensbrück. She already knew every word by heart, and she knew that Mutti Clara would cherish it. Gertrud had promised to get it to her somehow, even if it took years.

As Mildred's cellmate began to sob, Mildred wrapped her belongings in the soft flannel blanket Inge had sent.

"One minute," said the guard.

Mildred and her cellmate embraced, and for a moment, as her friend's tears fell upon her shoulder, Mildred's legs gave out and she would have collapsed if her cellmate had not held her upright.

The guard pulled them apart, cuffed Mildred's hands behind her back, tucked her bundle under one arm, and led her down corridors and outside. An icy, driving rain soaked her hair and dress as she boarded a green police van parked in the courtyard. The doors closed and the van pulled away from the Charlottenburg prison, rumbling over cobblestones and around bomb craters, jolting her roughly as it sped through the blackout.

When the van halted at Plötzensee, she descended with some difficulty and was taken inside to a small office, where another guard removed her handcuffs, gestured to a chair pulled up to a narrow desk, and ordered her to sit. As soon as she was seated, he placed a questionnaire on the desk, set a sharpened pencil above it, and told her to fill it out, honestly and completely.

She obeyed, but as she finished the simple biographical questions and moved on to others asking about her financial assets, career, health, criminal history, and relationships, she began to wonder if it was all a cruel joke. To the query "Are you single? Married? With whom?" she took a deep breath and responded, *It can be assumed that I am widowed. I haven't however received an official letter informing me of the death of my husband, who was supposed to be executed.*

On the next page: "Why are you punished now? Do you admit committing the deed you are charged with? In which circumstances and for what reason did you commit the deed?" Mildred reflected carefully upon Dr. Schwarz's argument at her trial before writing, *Accomplice in treason. I admit being an accomplice in treason because I had to be obedient to my husband.* She disliked maligning Arvid, but it would do none of them any good if she bungled their story now.

The last question was so absurd that she might have laughed if she had not felt so wretched: "What do you plan to do after your release? Do you want to go back to your previous work or devote yourself to another, and which?"

She had been sentenced to die by the Führer himself. Did anyone really believe she thought she might one day be released? She could not put that down, so instead she wrote, *To continue translating the best German poems such as Goethe's for the Anglo-Saxon world.*

When she finished the questionnaire, a guard led her to a small cell on the first floor, cold and windowless, illuminated by a single bulb suspended from the ceiling out of reach. He tossed her bundle onto the bed and departed without a word, but no sooner had he left than an SS officer appeared in the doorway. "Your request for an appeal has been denied," he told her curtly. "You will be executed by guillotine tomorrow evening."

Her chest constricting, she sank onto the bed, blood rushing in her ears. She lay down and curled up on her side, staring straight ahead, too shocked for tears.

She expected the dim lightbulb to be turned off eventually, but when it stayed illuminated, she inhaled deeply, sat up, and untied her bundle. She removed her books, gifts from Mutti Clara, turning each one over in her hands and studying them as if they were precious artifacts from another life. Somehow she was not tired; she supposed she would never sleep again.

She opened her Goethe, turned to "Vermächtnis," and read it once quietly aloud before taking up her pencil and writing an English translation in the margin.

No being can to nothing fall;
The everlasting lives in all.
Sustain yourself in joy with life.
Life is eternal; there are laws
To keep the living treasure's cause
With which the worlds are rife.

She was engrossed in translating Goethe when the prison chaplain came to her cell at daybreak. As Reverend Poelchau entered, she saw herself reflected in his shocked expression and realized how completely imprisonment had transformed her. She had withered, aged beyond her forty years. Illness and hunger had chiseled her thin, and her once thick blond hair had gone brittle and white. Her shoulders were bent, her breathing labored.

She invited him to sit. He offered her a Bible in English, which she accepted. She expected him to urge her to pray or to confess her sins so she could face her Creator with an unblemished conscience, but instead he began to converse with her, easily and kindly. They discussed the Bible, Goethe, and her literary work, almost as if they were two acquaintances passing time at a bus stop rather than a woman who was about to die and her spiritual counsel.

Then his expression turned sorrowful. "Frau Harnack," he said gently, "I regret to inform you, since I believe you have not yet been told, that your husband has preceded you in death."

She felt a stabbing pain in her chest. For a moment her vision blurred with tears, and then they spilled over, trickling down her cheeks. She had long feared he was dead, but now all hope that he lived was truly lost. "How?" she said hoarsely. "When?"

"He was hanged here at Plötzensee on the evening of December twenty-second."

Mildred's head spun. Her beloved husband had been gone for almost two months. Even as she had been pleading to be allowed to see him for Christmas, it had already been too late, and no one had told her. "Was he alone?" she asked, because she could not bear to ask if he had suffered.

"Harro Schulze-Boysen, Kurt Schumacher, and John Graudenz were hanged within minutes of your husband. About an hour later, Horst Heilmann, Hans Coppi, Kurt Schulze, Libertas Schulze-Boysen, and Elizabeth Schumacher were executed by guillotine."

Unbidden, Mildred's hand went to her throat. She knew decapitation was considered more humane because death came swiftly, a suitable method for women and youths. Military men were usually accorded an honorable death by firing squad, but apparently that had been denied Harro. Hanging was regarded as the most degrading form of execution, one last cruel, malicious gesture from their Nazi tormentors.

She would face the guillotine. It was only a matter of hours now.

"Your husband was not alone in the hours leading up to his death, either," Reverend Poelchau continued. "I was with him."

Arvid had spent his last day writing letters to his family and reading Plato's *Defense of Socrates*, the minister told her. He had asked Reverend Poelchau to read the story of the birth of Jesus from the Book of Luke, which his father had recited to the family every Christmas. Then he requested to hear the "Prologue in Heaven" from Goethe's *Faust*, which the minister spoke from memory. In his final moments, he asked the chaplain to join him in singing Bortniansky's hymn "Ich bete an die Macht der Liebe."

"I pray to the power of love," Mildred murmured.

"Dr. Harnack did believe in the power of love," the minister said. "He went to his death bravely and heartened by his belief that your life would be spared."

She was grateful he had had that last comfort, false though it had proven to be.

Reverend Poelchau glanced over his shoulder to confirm they were not being observed through the cell door, then reached into the breast pocket of his coat and took out a small packet and an orange, so colorful and bright in the dim light of the drab cell that she blinked. "From Inge," he said, placing the packet on the table before her and handing her the orange. She took it, marveling at its brilliant hue, its full, round perfection. She lifted it to her face, closed her eyes, and inhaled deeply, then set it on the table so that she could open the packet, uttering a small cry of joy when she beheld several family photographs. She studied each one lovingly, but when she came to one of her mother, her eyes filled with tears and she kissed the photo over and over. Then she set it facedown on the table, picked up her pencil, and wrote carefully on the back, "The face of my mother expresses everything that I want to say at this moment. This face was with me all through these last months. 16.II.43."

She peeled the orange slowly, reluctant to spoil its beauty, and ate it, savoring its sweetness.

Reverend Poelchau left soon thereafter, but he promised to return at the appointed hour. Alone once more, grieving for her lost love, for her own too swiftly passing life, she opened the Bible the minister had given her and turned to 1 Corinthians 13. "If I speak in the tongues of men or of angels, but do not have love, I am only a resounding gong or a clanging cymbal," she softly read aloud the familiar verses. "If I have the gift of prophecy and can fathom all mysteries and all knowledge, and if I have a faith that can move mountains, but do not have love, I am nothing. If I give all I possess to the poor and give over my body to hardship that I may boast, but do not have love, I gain nothing. Love is patient, love is kind. It does not envy, it does not boast, it is not proud. It does not dishonor others, it is not self-seeking, it is not easily angered, it keeps no record of wrongs. Love does not delight in evil but rejoices with the truth. It always protects, always trusts, always hopes, always perseveres. Love never fails."

She closed the Bible and held it for a moment, contemplating the scripture. Then she set the Bible aside and resumed her translation of Goethe. She would leave a note for the minister with her books, ask him to send them to Mutti Clara.

The day passed, and night descended.

At twilight, a silver-haired man the guards called the shoemaker was let into Mildred's cell. His expression impassive, he searched her mouth for gold fillings, found none, and cut her hair short to bare her neck for the blade. She shivered, unused to the cold air on her scalp and neck. The shoemaker departed and a guard brought her a pair of wooden clogs and a coarse, sleeveless, open-necked smock. He ordered her to put them on; she obeyed, though her hands shook so badly she struggled to pull the smock over her head.

Another guard arrived, handcuffed her wrists behind her back, and grasped her bony elbow to steer her from her cell. Flanking her, the two guards led her down the corridor to the exit, then outside and across the courtyard to the execution shed.

Her throat constricted; her mouth went dry. She stumbled on a cobblestone but a guard seized her by the upper arm and kept her on her feet. This was where Arvid died, she realized as they ushered her into the execution chamber. Reverend Poelchau stood just inside the doorway; he held her gaze and nodded to remind her that he was there for her, not for the Reich. She swallowed hard and nodded back, hardly able to bear so much compassion and pity after months of cold indifference.

Her gaze darted around the room, heart thudding in her chest. Half of the chamber was concealed by a black curtain. Several officials sat at a table to her right. One stood and read aloud from a paper, but her ears rang and she could not quite make out his words. She grasped that the men at the table were confirming her identity and acting as witnesses as her death sentence was read aloud.

Somehow even then she could not quite believe that this was how her life would end.

The official set down his paper and turned to a man clad in a long black coat, white gloves, and tall black hat. "Executioner," he intoned, "do your duty."

The black curtain was pulled aside to reveal a stark white chamber. There were two arched windows on the far wall covered with blackout curtains. In front of them, an iron beam with eight sharp meat hooks was fixed into the ceiling; a wave of grief washed over her, for she knew Arvid had been hanged from one of them.

On the right stood the guillotine, all gleaming brass and polished wood.

She turned to the minister, wistful, heartbroken. "*Und ich habe Deutschland so geliebt!*"

And I have loved Germany so much.

The guards led her to the guillotine and forced her to kneel. Her thoughts flew to Arvid. With her last breath, she too would pray to the power of love. Everything she had done to bring her to that moment had been done out of love—for Arvid, for the Germany that once had been, for her friends, for the many innocents who suffered.

It could not all have been in vain.

A man spoke, and the blade fell.

CHAPTER SIXTY-TWO

1943–1946

Greta

Winter reluctantly gave way to spring, but Greta caught only glimpses of the changing seasons during her brief walks around the paved courtyard of the Alexanderplatz prison. The piles of dirty snow in the corners between buildings melted. Soft breezes defied the high walls to caress the wan faces of the prisoners, evoking memories of cherished gardens with the scent of distant flowers and overturned earth. Slender shoots of grass grew up between cobblestones; anywhere else they might have been trodden underfoot, but here the prisoners took care to avoid them. Let something thrive in that dismal place, the women seemed to say as they stepped over a patch of green here and another one there. Greta savored the glimpses of color as much as she did the fresh air and warm sunshine on her face. As springtime dragged on in tedium and dull fear, she expected each day to be her last, and she doubted she would see the summer.

On the last day of March, a guard banged on a metal door for attention. "Kuckhoff, Buch, Terviel, Brockdorff, Van Beek, Berkowitz!" he called out as he passed along the corridor unlocking cell doors. "Collect your things and report at once!"

Seized by dread, Greta swiftly gathered her few possessions and stepped out into the corridor, where several of her comrades stood clutching their small bundles and glancing around with trepidation. Like Greta they were all *Todeskandidaten*, death candidates, and she saw in their eyes her own terrified certainty that they were about to be transported to Plötzensee and the guillotine. Then the guard called out the names of Elfriede Paul, Lotte Schleiff, and others sentenced to prison terms, and Greta's certainty faltered.

As they were led from the processing office to the exit, Erika paused before the commissioner, whom she knew from the preliminary investigation. "Excuse me," she said, with her usual confidence, "where are we being taken?"

He scowled, annoyed by her boldness. "You'll find out when you get there."

The guard ordered the prisoners to proceed outside. They obeyed, but as Greta passed the criminal secretary, he murmured, "You're going to a place where you'll have it much better."

After she and her companions were loaded into the green police van, Greta repeated the secretary's comment, but they regarded it as skeptically as she did. The secretary could have meant it cynically, in that death would be more merciful than their wretched lives. They tried to discern their route from turns and sounds, and from glimpses of pavement visible through a crack in the wheel well, but it was impossible. Only after the van halted and the doors were flung open did they discover that they had been transferred to the women's prison on Kantstrasse in Charlottenburg.

Greta's heart raced as they were led inside and processed. She looked about surreptitiously, risking a beating for her curiosity, but desperate for a glimpse of her dearest friend, whom she knew had been held there before and might be there yet. As she was being led off to her cell, something in the matron's firm but rational manner compelled her to blurt, "Please, Frau Oberin, is Mildred Harnack here?"

Something that might have been sympathy passed over the woman's expression. "Frau Harnack was executed at Plötzensee in February."

Greta heard gasps from the other prisoners and a low moan of anguish, but she could scarcely breathe, torn apart by shock and grief. Dazed, she stumbled along in the line of prisoners to her cell, where she sank upon her bunk and wept for her lost friend.

One April morning, moans of pain echoing down the corridor woke her a few hours before dawn. Later that morning, she heard through the prison grapevine that Liane Berkowitz had gone into labor. A frisson of excitement and anticipation circulated throughout the cellblock all day and into the evening. Bets were placed, prayers offered. One of the more lenient guards divulged that Liane was in the prison infirmary and she seemed to be progressing well. Flooded with memories of cradling sweet newborn Ule in her arms, Greta had to bite the inside of her mouth to keep from weeping.

Then, during exercise three days later, she spotted Liane shuffling around the courtyard, leaning heavily upon her cellmate's arm. Greta maneuvered through the ragged circuit of women until she reached the teenager's side. "I had a baby girl," Liane told her, her eyes glowing with joy in a pale, wan face. "I named her Irena. She's beautiful, so beautiful." Suddenly she grasped Greta's thin sleeve. "They took her away from me. Do you think she'll be all right?"

"I'm sure she'll be fine," said Greta, although she knew nothing of the sort.

"Maybe they'll let my mother take her." Liane shook her head, frowning thoughtfully. "No, they wouldn't do that. Maybe they'll give her to a nice family to adopt. I could find her after the war."

"I'm sure she'll be well looked after," her cellmate soothed. "After the war, or sooner if we're released, I'll help you search for her."

"So will I," said Greta, thinking of Ule, cherished and protected at her parents' home, as safe as any child could be in wartime.

Every day after that, she looked for Liane in the corridors and the courtyard, but a week passed without another glimpse of her. Uneasy, Greta asked around and was told that she had been transferred to the Berliner Frauengefängnis Barnimstrasse, a prison that provided slave laborers for the munitions industry. Greta hoped Liane would be given light duties until she had fully recovered from childbirth.

In May, Greta too was given new work—making paper butterflies to be used as decorations at Nazi rallies. She had to choke back laughter at the absurdity of it. Dozens of her friends had been killed, her husband was awaiting execution, and she herself lived in daily expectation of losing her head to the guillotine, and yet there she sat from morning through night, day after day, folding and cutting and pasting colored pieces of paper into the shape of pretty insects. It was surreal. She could not think of anything more poorly suited for one of Hitler's ugly, hateful speeches than a kaleidoscope of paper butterflies. She was tempted to write to Göring and urge him to stick to the usual black eagle with oak wreath, although anything menacing and cruel would do.

She was adding fuzzy black antennae to a gold-and-black butterfly when a guard entered the workroom and called out her name. Her heart thudded and she stood, keeping her eyes downcast in the usual posture of deference. "Come with me," the guard ordered. She had no choice but to obey, and as she followed him through corridors and down stairs, with every step she became more afraid and more certain that he was escorting her to Oberin Weider's office, who would inform her that she was being transferred to Plötzensee for her execution.

But suddenly the guard halted in front of another door, unlocked it, and gestured for her to enter. "You have twenty minutes." When she merely stood there, bewildered, he gestured again impatiently. Quickly she entered the sparsely furnished chamber, much longer than it was wide, with four high, barred windows on the long wall casting light upon a few scattered tables and chairs. A man and a woman seated beneath the farthest window rose stiffly from one of the tables, and when the faint sunlight shone on the man's silver hair, recognition struck her with almost physical force.

"Papa?" she said, voice breaking. "Mutti?"

A moment later they were in one another's arms.

Twenty minutes was too brief a reunion for all they had to say, but a fortnight later Greta's parents were permitted to visit her again, and at the end of June they returned, bringing Ule with them. Greta wept as she embraced her son, anxious that he might have forgotten her but reassured by his shy, delighted smile that he knew her on sight. How her parents had managed to get permission for these family visits, she did not know; when she asked, they made evasive replies about a favor from a friend, and she knew not to pursue it. Whoever was responsible, however it had come about, she was profoundly grateful.

Her parents promised her they would come whenever they could, but she saw them only once in July and not again until early August, and on both occasions, Ule was not permitted to come. One day at the end of the month, she was reading in her cell when she heard a key in the lock, and her heart leapt with anticipation. She quickly rose, hoping she was being summoned to the visiting room, but whereas the guards always opened the door quickly with a sharp clang of metal, this time the door opened slowly. When the prison chaplain entered, her heart went into her throat and she sank back into her chair.

"Now they are all dead," the priest said hollowly. "Your husband and the girls. All of them."

She stared at him in silence for a long moment. "When?"

"August fifth." The priest paused to clear his throat and mop his forehead with a handkerchief. "Your husband was hanged at a few minutes past five o'clock. Marie Terweil, Hilde Coppi, Cato Bontjes van Beek, and Liane Berkowitz soon followed."

She felt something inside her chest crumple, like a sere brown autumn leaf crushed in a fist. "Do you know what will become of their children?" she asked, her voice sounding strangely distant over the roaring in her ears.

He did not know, but he offered to make inquiries. Nodding her thanks, she forced herself to rise and stumble to her bunk, where she lay down as gingerly as if she were broken and bruised and might shatter on impact.

Adam was gone. Mildred was gone. Arvid, Libertas, Harro, Elizabeth, Cato, Liane—they were all gone. Dead. Surely she would be next. But when? Why was she still among the living?

What a cruel punishment it was to be the last of her friends alive, knowing her own death was imminent.

A few weeks later, she was called to Oberin Weider's office and handed a summons to return to court on September 27 for a new trial. Full of dread, suspecting a trap, Greta would have torn the notice into tiny shreds if the matron had not been observing her so closely.

"We need a sympathetic librarian here," Oberin Weider remarked, an odd non sequitur, or so Greta thought. "Maybe also a medical assistant. Work like that would make the time pass more swiftly. See if you can stay in Charlottenburg. We—that is, all of us, including the sergeants—hope that your new sentence will not be more than three years, in which case we can keep you here."

Greta nodded respectfully, hiding her confusion. The matron spoke as if Greta could choose her verdict and where she served her time. And when in the history of Nazi justice had a death sentence been overturned in favor of a three-year prison term? Perhaps Oberin Weider was trying to soothe her so she would be easier to manage, but babbling nonsense at her was not the way.

Greta had no choice but to report to the Reichskriegsgericht. This time, however, she had no fear, only anger and defiance. What more could they do to hurt her? They had already separated her from her son, killed her husband, murdered her friends, sentenced her to death. They had captured and executed everyone in the resistance that she could possibly betray, so torture would be pointless. What could be worse than the death sentence she had already received? They could not chop off her head twice.

When she was brought before the judges, she met their gazes steadily, determined not to let them see any nervousness or intimidation. The prosecutor, Dr. Linz, began by addressing the court, noting for the record the reason for the new trial. After the first trial had concluded, one of the lead defense attorneys, Dr. Rudolf Behse, had so strongly objected to the verdict that he had submitted an official protest. The court chairman had been sufficiently impressed with his argument to pass on the recommendation to the legal inspector, who had called for a new trial, a new sentence.

Then, as Dr. Linz continued speaking, he mentioned something else that sent an electric jolt through Greta's body. She stared at him, stark incredulity overtaking every other emotion.

Her death sentence had been revoked in May.

Although no one had informed her, the Reichskriegsgericht had canceled her execution four months before.

She struggled to compose herself as her new trial commenced, her thoughts in a tangle of confusion and indignation. Much to her relief, Manfred Roeder, the original prosecutor, had been transferred and would not be involved in these proceedings, and her first impression was that Dr. Linz was nothing like Hitler's Bloodhound. She was astounded when he announced that he intended to pursue a sentence of a maximum of five years in prison, without loss of honor but not including time served. But just as she felt a faint kindling of hope, the other judges sternly assured her that they intended to do everything in their power to disregard his recommendation.

The judges interrogated her vigorously for four hours, throwing statements from the original trial in her face, as if it were her fault that they could no longer extract incriminating testimony from the dead. They turned and twisted every word that she spoke, until finally, overcome with lethargy, she fell silent. They would believe what they wanted and do as they wished. Finally the judges withdrew to deliberate, and when they returned, they announced that she was sentenced to ten years in prison and ten years' loss of civil rights for assisting in the preparation of a treasonous undertaking and aiding and abetting the enemy.

When court was adjourned, Greta stood as ordered, wondering what had just happened. She was taken from the courtroom to the police van to the prison to her cell, too bewildered and mistrustful to allow herself even a fleeting moment of joy or relief. They had vowed to execute her once. They could easily change their minds. She would trust that her death sentence had been commuted when she walked out of prison a free woman, and not one hour before.

Her wariness seemed prescient a few days later, on October 5, when she was informed that she must return to the Reichskriegsgericht to meet with the judicial inspector. Immediately skeptical, Greta found herself thinking of Harro and the sham courier mission to the Russian front that had culminated in his arrest. She was tempted to remind the warden that no pretense was required in her case. She was already their captive. If they intended to take her to Plötzensee and the guillotine, she could not stop them.

Outside, the sky was cloudless blue, the air cool and crisp, a perfect autumn day. Her escort handed her off to another guard waiting outside by the police van. "Are you Frau Kuckhoff?" he asked, eyeing her curiously.

"I am."

He nodded, opened the back of the van, and offered his arm to help her inside. She raised her eyebrows at his strange show of courtesy, but she accepted his assistance. He must be new, she decided. He would change. Absolute power over helpless prisoners would corrupt him the same as it did everyone else.

Until the guard halted the van and opened the door, she did not know whether he had driven her to the Reichskriegsgericht or to Plötzensee. Never before had she felt such relief upon seeing the imposing courthouse. Inside, she was taken before the judicial inspector, who brusquely led her through some official formalities before signing off on her new sentence. Then, unexpectedly, he removed his glasses and sat back in his chair with a sigh. "I regret that the other defendants who were tried with you have already perished at Plötzensee," he said. "Better to be still alive, albeit with a long prison sentence."

"Yes, sir," Greta murmured, looking down at her hands in her lap to conceal a surge of anger. How dare he feign sympathy. Her husband was dead, her friends were dead, and *he* felt regret? Poor him. She hoped remorse ate him up from the inside out.

"It vexes me that my proposal concerning your sentence was not accepted," he continued, oblivious. "However, any judgment handed down by this court will stand until the end of the war—may that not be too long in coming."

Greta looked up sharply. No doubt his version of victory included Nazis marching along Downing Street and Pennsylvania Avenue. How strange it was that they could both yearn for peace and yet envision it so differently.

The same guard was waiting outside the chamber door to escort her out to the van and back to prison. Suddenly, a few meters away, he halted and regarded her squarely. "It's a beautiful day, and we're often urged to conserve petrol. We'll walk back to the prison instead."

Greta looked at him askance, immediately wary, but he jerked his head in the direction of the pedestrian gate and started off, and since she had nowhere else to go except back into the loathed courthouse, she followed after him. As soon as they had turned the corner a block away, he said, "Who would you like to share your good news with first? Do you have any friends who live nearby?"

Suspicious, she hesitated. She longed to speak with her family, but she dared not implicate them. Then she thought of Hans Hartenstein. The court already knew he was her friend, and that she had given him legal guardianship of Ule earlier that summer, when she realized that she must appoint someone to be responsible for him if her parents passed away before he reached adulthood. Hans had been one of the witnesses at her wedding, and she had known him since her student days. He had been a prominent official at the Ministry of Economics until he had resigned his post in 1937 rather than join the Nazi Party. Although he had supported their resistance network in secret, acquaintances in the Reich hierarchy believed him to be apolitical, and he still had many friends in positions of influence.

For the first time, it occurred to her that Hans was probably responsible for obtaining permission for her parents and Ule to visit her in prison.

"I have a good friend in Nikolassee," Greta said, studying the guard skeptically. "I'd like to tell him first. He can spread the word."

"Ah, Nikolassee." The guard grimaced. "That's too far. I have so little time, no more than three hours."

"Of course," she said, stung, a bit breathless from trying to match his strides. Another taunt, another cruel joke. She should have known.

"Listen," he said. "I had to take your husband and some of your friends to Plötzensee, and it was very difficult for me."

Not half as difficult as it was for them, she thought bitterly, but she said nothing.

"I don't understand how Germany has come to this." He shook his head. "I'll never understand people. I'll escort you somewhere, yes, but not to Plötzensee." Suddenly he halted and faced her. "Come with me to a pub. I know one nearby. It's quiet, and you can talk on the phone."

Again he gestured for her to follow him, and, compelled by curiosity and a lack of options, she did. To her astonishment, he led her to a quiet pub with a public phone in the back, gave her his wallet, and told her to order some food and call whomever she wanted. She hesitated only a moment before snatching his wallet from his hand and going to the bar to order a plate of *Knackwurst* and *Spätzle* and a beer. After she had eaten, she eyed the guard warily as he sat eating a few breakfast steaks and an apple, apparently unconcerned about what punishment he might face if they were caught.

Slipping into the phone booth, she called Hans. "Are you free?" he asked, incredulous. He listened solemnly as she told him of her sudden change of fortune. "Oh, Greta. Your life has been spared, but the years ahead will be hard."

"I know," she said, tears springing to her eyes. "If only Adam's execution had been delayed another month, he could be with me right now."

"I'll do everything I can for you, you know that."

"All I ask is that you watch over Ule. Help my parents however you can."

"On my life, I swear I will," he said, impassioned. "Greta, my friend, your grief will be easier to bear once the war is over. Do everything you can to keep yourself healthy until then."

Voice breaking, she promised to try. She asked him to speak with her parents, and then, reluctantly, she hung up, wiped her eyes, and returned to the guard. He escorted her around the bombed-out neighborhoods to Charlottenburg, and as she passed through the prison gates, she considered the length of her new sentence and realized that Oberin Weider would have to find someone else to be her librarian or medical assistant.

Two days later, she was loaded into a police van and transferred to the Royal Central Prison in Cottbus, about 130 kilometers southeast of Berlin, 25 kilometers west of the Polish border. On the morning after her arrival, she was put to work with the other inmates on the prison assembly line making gas masks for German troops.

There were no more visits from her family, no packages, few letters. The days were long and difficult, wretched and tedious. Every morning she woke, remembered where she was, and thought: Ten years. Ten years, but she would live, if she refused to let this bleak existence kill her.

She fiercely believed the Allies would prevail. She only had to outlast the war.

As the long months passed, Greta sustained herself with memories of Adam, thoughts of Ule, and vivid, vengeful daydreams of how she would relentlessly pursue Manfred Roeder until he was brought to justice. She had been at Cottbus for more than a year when she and several dozen other political prisoners were transferred to Schloss Waldheim in Saxony. Within the castle's ancient and cold stone walls, they were crammed into cells until there was scarcely room to breathe, several prisoners to a bunk, arms and legs and elbows in one another's way. They were skin-and-bone wraiths of their former selves, heads shaved, clad in rags, tormented by hunger, illness, vermin. Their futures had been whittled down to two possibilities—liberation or death. The question haunting each of them was which would come for them first.

They received almost no news of the world beyond the cellblock and the factory assembly line where they toiled from dawn until dusk. Greta listened carefully for details the prison staff accidentally let fall, and it was in this way she learned that the Allies had landed at Normandy, that Allied troops assisted by the French Resistance had liberated Paris, that the Wehrmacht had launched Operation Watch on the Rhine, a massive campaign on the western front. As 1945 commenced with heavy snows and punishing cold, Greta and a few daring companions tried to gauge the progress of the war by taking turns stealing glimpses through the windows while others stood watch, or by listening intently to the roar of aircraft overhead. As spring came to Schloss Waldheim, the rumble of artillery more frequently penetrated the thick stone walls of the prison, first distant, but every day coming inexorably nearer.

One morning in early May, Greta woke to the sound of a strange, mechanical cacophony somewhere outside, followed soon thereafter by a commotion somewhere in the building. Heart pounding, she joined two other women at the cell door, straining and stretching in an attempt to peer down the corridor, but the angle made it impossible. They heard the banging of metal and men's voices raised in shouts and rough laughter steadily approaching.

"They're speaking Russian," Greta exclaimed, just as the heavy door at the end of the corridor opened with a crash. Then, suddenly, a trio of Russian soldiers appeared, the one in the lead with the guard's heavy key ring in hand. The young men spoke to them cheerfully in Russian as they unlocked the door.

The door swung open and the prisoners spilled out, merging into a flow of other ragged, filthy, emaciated women. The Russian soldiers were going from floor to floor, cell to cell, unlocking doors, freeing everyone. Running, staggering, shuffling from the cellblock, by some wild instinct the women found the prison commissary and began devouring the bread and jam and milk the guards had left behind. Greta spared a fleeting thought for them—had they fled ahead of the Russian tanks or had they been taken captive?—as she ate her fill, almost weeping from relief and euphoria. She was free. Liberation had come before death after all.

She was free.

In the days that followed, Soviet officers interviewed the former prisoners, made sure they were fed, had the ill and injured attended to by their medics. Some of the women were terrified of them; after Operation Barbarossa began, the Nazi propaganda machine had filled their heads with harrowing stories of women and girls viciously raped by invading Russian soldiers. But the troops who liberated Schloss Waldheim harmed none of the inmates. Whether this was because these particular soldiers were exceptionally well disciplined, or because they considered political prisoners their comrades, or because nothing about the frail, wretched figures they beheld inspired either violence or lust, Greta could only wonder.

When the commanding officers discovered who Greta was, they accorded her great respect and admiration, and offered their deepest sympathies for the loss of her husband and friends. They asked her to help them manage the prisoners, many of whom wanted nothing more than to return home to their families, many of whom had no homes to return to. Greta agreed, but as the days passed and she steadily recovered her strength, she was overcome by an urgency to reunite with Ule and her parents. The Soviet troops could not linger; their orders were to push on deeper into Germany toward the capital. They asked Greta to stay, to remain in charge until another division arrived from the rear to take over, but she respectfully declined. "I have been separated from my son too long already," she said. "I will not delay any longer than absolutely necessary."

"Where has your son been all this time?" the officer asked.

"Living with my parents in Frankfurt an der Oder. That's where I intend to go, as soon as I can."

He shook his head, his expression grim. "Comrade Kuckhoff, you won't find your family there. The citizens fled before the advancing Red Army, and the empty town was burned to the ground."

For a moment Greta could not breathe. "Then I'll go to Nikolassee," she said, voice trembling. "My son's legal guardian lives there. My parents and Ule probably sought refuge with him, but if not, he will know where they are."

She found some forgotten uniforms in a storeroom and swiftly pieced together a dress, cutting it narrow, for she had lost more than twenty pounds since her arrest. When it was complete, she made her farewells to the commanding officer, thanking him profusely for her freedom. Before she departed, he gave her a special pass verifying her identity and authorizing any Soviet soldier to help her however she required. Even then, he warned, she should try not to be caught out alone if she could help it.

She packed a bundle of food and set off on foot for Nikolassee. Sometimes she fell in step with other refugees, women, children, the elderly, all walking away from horror or toward a distant loved one or some imagined place of safety. Greta scarcely recognized the war-ravaged landscape. Roads were pockmarked by bomb craters. Railroad lines had been reduced to scorched, twisted heaps of metal. Bridges were gone, with only traces of stone rubble left behind, forcing her to alter her route again and again.

She walked for days, finding shelter for the night in abandoned cottages or dilapidated barns. Once she hitched a ride with an old farmer, his wrinkled, age-spotted hand gripping the halter of an old nag hauling a load of firewood or straw. Sometimes she passed farms that had miraculously escaped destruction, and the aromas of ersatz coffee or baking bread or frying potatoes would drift to her through the open windows, making her stomach rumble. She did not stop and beg for their hospitality. She was just as likely to be shot as to be offered kindness.

Hungry, exhausted, aching from exertion after so many years of confinement, she persisted, one foot after another, driven by one thought—to find her son.

At long last she came to Nikolassee, and with her waning strength she knocked on Hans Hartenstein's front door. His wife, wan and timorous, answered, but at first she did not recognize her visitor. Then, with a cry of wonder, she brought Greta inside, sat her down, brought her food and drink, but even as Greta gratefully accepted all of it, she repeatedly asked for Ule.

It was then that she learned that only a month after their last phone call, Hans had died on an operating table after his bunker had received a direct hit during an air raid. The Reich had taken custody of Ule and had placed him with a German family living in occupied Poland.

After all she had gone through to get to him—

Greta's vision went gray and she fainted.

Hans's wife looked after her until she felt strong enough to continue on to Berlin. The city was a devastated ruin, a field of rubble where a few surviving structures stood like mute, hollow-eyed witnesses to immeasurable violence and death and misery. Miraculously, her old apartment building was scarcely touched. When she knocked on her landlord's office door, he gaped at her as if she were a ghost.

"I no longer have a key," she told him. "Do you have a spare?"

Still wide-eyed, he nodded and scurried to his desk to search for it. To her surprise, he returned with not only a key, but also a bundle of mail. "I saved these for you," he said gruffly. "Sorry about your husband. I always liked him."

"Thank you," she murmured, her gaze fixed on the stack of letters, neatly tied with twine. "I can't believe you kept these. We've been gone years."

He shrugged and scratched at the white fringe of hair on the back of his head. "I didn't know where to forward them, and it didn't seem right to throw them away, seeing as some of them came so far."

Puzzled, Greta leafed through the envelopes, glancing at the postmarks. Dispersed among the letters from German acquaintances were two from her friend Anna Klug in London, several from Wilhelm von Riechmann in Geneva, and many from Sara Weitz from all over the world—Geneva, Edinburgh, Stockholm, New York. Her hands trembled as she studied a postcard, a watercolor portrait of Bascom Hall with a white banner printed in red with the slogan "University of Wisconsin—Madison, Wis." On the back Sara had written, "Wish you were here!"

Greta choked out a laugh, or a sob, as she traced the words with a fingertip. Sara had sent the postcard in October 1944, when she could not have known whether Greta was even still alive to read it. Such astonishing optimism. Greta wished she could take hold of some of it for herself. She would need it.

Haunted by memories, she climbed the stairs to the apartment she had once shared with Adam and Ule and countless secrets. In parting, the landlord had told her that the Gestapo family who had occupied their apartment after their arrest had fled months before, and he personally had rid the place of any sign of them.

It was surreal, walking through her own front door again after so much time away.

There was new wallpaper in the kitchen, the bookshelves had been drastically depleted, but most of her and Adam's furniture and some of their belongings remained. She drifted slowly from room to room, touching a bureau here, straightening a picture frame there. Adam's map of the Soviet Union was gone, as was the curtain he had used to conceal it.

Adam was gone, but she remained, and Ule was out there somewhere.

She would bring him home.

The Soviet administrators she met with were considerate and helpful once she showed them her pass and they realized who she was. Soon after their first meeting, they informed her that they knew the names of Ule's foster family and that they had been evacuated from Poland to Germany.

For the first time since the Russian troops had liberated Schloss Waldheim, Greta felt a stirring of hope. "Then my son is alive?"

As far as they knew, yes, he was, alive and somewhere in Germany. They would continue to search.

In the meantime, Greta resolved to find the orphaned children of the other resistance women, to see for herself that they were alive and well, to do for them whatever she could.

She was too late to help Liane Berkowitz's daughter, Irena. At first the baby girl had lived with Liane's grandmother, but at some point— the sources were unclear—Reich authorities had taken Irena away. Two months after her mother was executed, she died under unexplained circumstances in a hospital that already had become infamous for Nazi euthanasia operations.

Shortly before Christmas 1945, Greta located young Hans Coppi, born at the women's prison in Charlottenburg ten months before his mother was executed at Plötzensee. At three years old, the little boy already had his father's inquisitive gaze and his mother's lovely features. He was living with his grandmother, and had no memory of his brave parents or, mercifully, of his own brief time behind prison walls.

A week later, Greta reunited with eight-year-old Saskia von Brock-dorff, her former neighbor. The little girl had a sweet face and long blond braids, but her father would not allow anyone in the family to talk about the resistance, and Saskia did not understand what had happened and was angry at her mother for abandoning her.

That will be remedied, Greta silently vowed. If she accomplished nothing else in life, she would make sure that when her friends' children were old enough, they would understand what their parents had done, and why they had done it. They would understand that their courageous mothers and fathers had sacrificed their lives for a noble cause—for freedom, for an end to oppression, to fight for those who could not fight for themselves.

She would watch over all of them for the rest of her life, for their sake and that of the lost resistance women who could no longer embrace their beloved children.

For too long Greta's own arms were empty. She persisted in her search for her son, meeting with Soviet authorities, American authorities, imprisoned Nazi bureaucrats who sullenly gave information in exchange for small rewards. She befriended American soldiers, feeling a special affinity for the Jews among them, who had confronted unimaginable horrors as they had liberated the Nazi death camps on the march across Germany. They were friendly and generous and brave, and they cheerfully took her and her friends' children on jeep rides, and gave them chocolate, and promised they would pester Army intelligence to track down Ule's foster family.

And then, early in the New Year of 1946, Greta received a telegram from an American army nurse. Ule had been found. They were bringing him home.

All that day she watched from her window, and when the American officers' staff car halted in front of her building, she flew downstairs, heart racing, breathless, and outside to the pavement, where she found her son standing between two officers, gazing up at their apartment building with a curious frown, as if he almost remembered it but not quite.

"Ule," Greta cried, kneeling, holding out her arms to him.

He turned at the sound of his name. Their eyes met, and a slow smile spread over his face. Then he was running toward her, and then he was in her arms, and then she swept him up and held him close as if she would never let him go.

Author's Note

True to her word, Greta Kuckhoff became a watchful, supportive guardian to the children of the Rote Kapelle, encouraging them in their educations and careers for the rest of her life. The orphans described her as a woman of compassion, dignity, and integrity who provided them with encouragement and support, but sternly disapproved of any wrongdoing. Their parents had sacrificed too much for them not to live exemplary lives.

In 1946, Greta, Günther Weisenborn, Adolf Grimme, and Falk Harnack submitted a brief to the International Military Tribunal at Nuremberg accusing Manfred Roeder of crimes against humanity based upon his use of torture in interrogations and relentlessly cruel methods in prosecutions. However, although Nuremberg prosecutors concluded that Roeder should be tried for war crimes, he convinced U.S. Army intelligence that he was uniquely qualified to help them track down Soviet spies. They took custody of him, moving him beyond the court's reach while he spun tales of his own innocence and former resistance fighters' ongoing ties to the Soviet Union. By the time the Nuremberg officials turned Roeder's case over to the German courts in October 1948, the Americans had already released him and he had settled comfortably in northern Germany. Despite pressure from Greta and other survivors, the lackluster investigation into Roeder's war crimes was suspended entirely in 1951. He became involved in radical right politics and continued to accuse the Rote Kapelle of wartime treason until his death in 1971.

Reunited with her son and mother, Greta settled her family in the eastern half of the divided capital and began working as a social worker for the municipality of Berlin. In August 1961 the Berlin Wall went up, separating her from the West.

In East Germany, where the Rote Kapelle were respected and hailed as heroes, Greta was honored for her wartime resistance activities, but she emphasized that she was not interested in receiving accolades for following her conscience. She did, however, wonder what everyone else had been doing while she and her friends were risking their lives. It should be made clear, she wrote in 1947, that others too "ought to have taken part in the struggle—there would have been fewer victims. . . . [E]very citizen must be challenged, so that he will finally see clearly it wasn't a question of the victims, but a matter of clever, well-thought-out deeds. A little less fear, a little more love of life in a few hundred thousand and the war wouldn't have been possible or would have been over sooner."

In addition to writing a memoir and preserving her husband's literary legacy, Greta succeeded in business and politics, becoming president of the East German national bank and vice president of the German Council of Peace. She died in Wandlitz in Brandenburg on November 11, 1981, at the age of seventy-nine.

Even after Mildred and Arvid were arrested, other members of their extended family continued their resistance work. Arvid's cousin Dietrich Bonhoeffer had returned to Germany, where his brother-in-law Hans von Dohnányi—organizer of the thwarted 1938 conspiracy to oust Hitler—arranged for him to work for military intelligence. Under the cover of assignments and travel abroad for the Abwehr, Bonhoeffer worked as a courier for the resistance, and with Dohnányi arranged for many German Jews to escape to Switzerland. He was arrested in April 1943 and held in military prisons, Buchenwald, and Flossenbürg concentration camp until his execution in April 1945, two weeks before the camp was liberated by United States infantry troops and one month before Germany surrendered. Dohnányi, arrested on the same day as Bonhoeffer, was held in Sachsenhausen until his execution in early April 1945.

Arvid's brother Falk Harnack, a member of the White Rose resistance group based in Munich, was arrested and tried along with other members of the cell in April 1943. Astonishingly, he was found not guilty and was released, unaware that the Gestapo intended to observe him in hopes that he would unwittingly lead them to additional members of the Rote Kapelle. Still an active-duty soldier, in August 1943 he was sent to the Greek front, but in December Himmler, frustrated and angry that he had betrayed no one, ordered his arrest. Alerted by a sympathetic superior officer, Falk fled, joined the Greek partisans, and fought the Nazis until the end of the war, when he returned to Berlin and joined Greta's efforts to see Manfred Roeder prosecuted for war crimes. He became a director and screenwriter, one of the most important in postwar Germany. He died in Berlin in September 1991.

Sara Weitz is a fictional character inspired by the young Jewish women of the Rote Kapelle. I would have preferred to include a historical figure, but I needed my four narrators to interact with one another, and I was unable to find the perfect person who also would have known Greta, Mildred, and Martha. Since it was absolutely essential to me to include this important perspective, I created Sara, drawing upon the experiences of young women whose wartime activities were similar to those depicted in the novel.

Although Sara and her family are fictional, their friends the Panofskys were very real, and they did safely escape to Great Britain. In 1944, Hans Panofsky—the boy Mildred and Martha had observed playing with his sister, Ruth, in the garden of Tiergartenstrasse 27a in 1933—enlisted in the British army and fought the Nazis. After the war, he studied at the London School of Economics, and in 1948, Hans, his father, sister, and stepmother emigrated to New York, where Hans earned a BS in sociology and a master of library science degree from Columbia University. After earning other advanced degrees from Cornell and the New York State School of Industrial and Labor Relations, he became a professor in the new Program of African Studies at Northwestern University. Hans enjoyed a long, distinguished career, and he and his wife, Gianna, were involved with civil rights organizations including Amnesty International and the Chicago chapter of the NAACP. After his beloved wife's death, Hans moved to Madison, Wisconsin, to be closer to family. I often wonder if he walked the same paths along Lake Mendota and through the University of Wisconsin Arboretum that Mildred and Arvid had loved so dearly.

After leaving Berlin and Boris Vinogradov in 1937, Martha Dodd Stern remained intrigued by communism and stayed in contact with Soviet intelligence from a distance. As she contemplated working with them in an official capacity, she continued to pursue her literary goals. In 1942, she published her second book, *Ambassador Dodd's Diary*, a collection of her father's letters and journal entries, edited with her brother. In 1945, she fulfilled a longtime dream by publishing a novel, *Sowing the Wind*, the story of a once kindhearted World War I flying ace corrupted by Nazism. That same year, she and her husband, Alfred, adopted an infant son. In 1953, Martha and Alfred's interest in communism and leftist causes brought them to the attention of the House Committee on Un-American Activities. When they were subpoenaed to testify, they took their son and moved to Mexico City. Four years later, after an American counterspy testified that Martha and Alfred were part of a Soviet spy network, they were indicted on espionage charges; in response, they fled to Prague. As the years passed and Martha witnessed communism in practice rather than in theory, she became disillusioned with the system, and its lingering appeal vanished entirely during the Prague Spring of 1968 when the Soviet Union invaded Czechoslovakia. In 1979, a U.S. federal court reluctantly cleared her and her husband of all charges of espionage due to the lack of evidence and the death of witnesses, but as much as she longed to return to the United States, age and infirmity had made travel too arduous. She died in Prague on August 10, 1990, at the age of eighty-two, four years after the death of her husband. To the last she staunchly believed that helping the Soviet Union against the Reich had been the morally responsible thing to do, at a time when most of the world stood idly by, reluctant to intervene as Europe hurtled toward disaster.

Mildred Fish Harnack's family back in the United States did not learn about her unhappy fate until months after her execution. The first indication that something dreadful had happened surfaced on May 16, 1943, when a concerned neighbor showed Mildred's sister Marion an article from the *Milwaukee Journal* reporting that the husband of Mrs. Harnack, "a former Milwaukeean," had been executed for treason and that all of her property had been confiscated by the German Reich. "The official announcement did not make clear whether Mrs. Harnack, wife of an official in the German ministry for economy, also was implicated in a sensational conspiracy which still awaits clarification," the reporter ominously noted. Mildred's eldest sister, Harriette, appealed to the Vatican for their help in getting in touch with Mildred, but in September 1943 the family received a reply from the Apostolic Nunciature of Berlin informing them that "Mrs. Harnack died in the beginning of this year."

In the first few decades after the war, despite the University of Wisconsin's efforts to honor their courageous alumna, Cold War tensions compelled the United States government to bury her story because they considered Mildred and Arvid to be Communist sympathizers— due in no small part to Manfred Roeder's self-serving falsehoods. Only in more recent decades, with the destruction of the Berlin Wall and the release of the Harnacks' KGB and FBI files, have their contributions and those of all the members of the Rote Kapelle resistance circle become better known. Since 1986, Mildred's birthday, September 16, has been designated Mildred Harnack Day in Wisconsin public schools, and she is honored for her bravery, persistence, and willingness to make the ultimate sacrifice in the fight against totalitarianism.

In more than a dozen separate trials between December 1942 and July 1943, the Reichskriegsgericht convicted seventy-seven members of the Rote Kapelle. According to Gestapo records, at a time when the Reich vigorously strove to limit women's roles in society to *Kinder, Kirche, Küche*, nearly half of the Rote Kapelle were women. Although most of the strategic decisions were made by the group's male leaders, Arvid Harnack and Harro Schulze-Boysen, the women assumed responsibility for recruiting members, organizing meetings, collecting intelligence, acting as couriers, translating, copying, distributing leaflets, concealing radios and other illicit equipment, sheltering fugitives, and many other activities that put their lives at risk, often to a greater extent than their male counterparts. Of the forty-five members of the Rote Kapelle who were sentenced to die, nineteen were women— courageous women from all walks of life, not trained spies or armed soldiers, but ordinary and extraordinary women who committed all that they had and all that they were in the struggle against fascism so that evil would not triumph over the earth.

Acknowledgments

I am deeply grateful to Maria Massie, Rachel Kahan, Alivia Lopez, Leah Carlson-Stanisic, Elsie Lyons, Carolyn Bodkin, Juliette Shapland, and Tavia Kowalchuk for their contributions to *Resistance Women* and their ongoing support of my work. Geraldine Neidenbach, Heather Neidenbach, and Marty Chiaverini were my first readers, and their comments and questions about several early drafts of this novel proved invaluable, as always. Nic Neidenbach generously shared his computer expertise to help me in crucial moments.

I am indebted to the Wisconsin Historical Society and their librarians and staff for maintaining the excellent archives on the University of Wisconsin campus in Madison that I relied upon for my research. Many thanks to David Null, University Archivist, for directing me to the Mildred Harnack Project archives at UW. Additional sources that informed this book include:

Shareen Blair Brysac, *Resisting Hitler: Mildred Harnack and the Red Orchestra* (New York: Oxford University Press, 2000).

Martha Dodd, *Through Embassy Eyes* (New York: Harcourt, Brace, and Company, 1939).

William E. Dodd Jr. and Martha Dodd, eds. *Ambassador Dodd's Diary 1933–1938* (New York: Harcourt, Brace, and Company, 1941).

Greta Kuckhoff, *Vom Rosenkranz zur Roten Kapelle: Ein Lebensbericht* (Berlin, Verlag Neues Leben, 1972).

Eric Larson, *In the Garden of Beasts: Love, Terror, and an American Family in Hitler's Berlin* (New York: Random House, 2011).

Roger Moorhouse, *Berlin at War* (New York: Basic Books, 2010).

Anne Nelson, *Red Orchestra* (New York: Random House, 2009).

William L. Shirer, *Berlin Diary: The Journal of a Foreign Correspondent, 1934–1941* (New York: Alfred A. Knopf, 1941).

I also consulted several excellent online resources while researching and writing *Resistance Women*, including the archives of digitized historic newspapers at the Library of Congress (http://chroniclingamerica .loc.gov), Genealogybank.com (http://genealogybank.com), and Newspapers.com (http://www.newspapers.com); the website of the United States Holocaust Memorial Museum (http://www.ushmm .org); the University of Wisconsin Libraries Campus History Project "Honoring Mildred Fish Harnack" (https://www.library.wisc .edu/archives/exhibits/campus-history-projects/honoring-mildred-fish-harnack/), and Wisconsin Public Television's *Wisconsin's Nazi Resistance: The Mildred Fish-Harnack Story* (https://wpt.org/nazi-resistance/main).

Most of all, I thank my husband, Martin Chiaverini, and our sons, Nicholas and Michael, for their enduring love and tireless support. I love you a million billion. I love you infinity.

Insights,
Interviews
& More . . .

Meet Jennifer Chiaverini

Michael Chiaverini

JENNIFER CHIAVERINI is the *New York Times* bestselling author of numerous acclaimed historical novels, including *Mrs. Lincoln's Dressmaker*, and the beloved Elm Creek Quilts series. A graduate of the University of Notre Dame and the University of Chicago, she lives with her family in Madison, Wisconsin. ❧

Behind the Book

A few years ago, in early autumn,
I came across a post on social media
from the Wisconsin Humanities
Council, a black-and-white photo of
a smiling blonde woman bundled up in
a warm coat before a stand of evergreens.
"September 16 is Mildred Harnack Day,"
the caption read, "the day Wisconsin
remembers the Milwaukee woman
who holds the tragic claim as the only
American woman executed on direct
orders of Adolf Hitler."

The contrast between the grim
words and the woman's gentle smile
immediately captured my imagination.
The post linked to a lengthier article
about Mildred, which in turn led
me to a Wisconsin Public Television
documentary about her; her husband,
Arvid; their fellow University of
Wisconsin alum Greta Lorke; and
the rest of the circle of American and
German resistance fighters the Gestapo
called the Rote Kapelle (German for
"Red Orchestra") for the treasonous
"music"—crucial military and economic
intelligence—they broadcast to enemies
of the Reich.

As I delved more deeply into Mildred's
life story, I became inspired not only
by her courage, but also by her ties to
my hometown. Within the pages of
letters and memoirs I discovered that ▶

Behind the Book *(continued)*

Mildred and Arvid had spent some of their happiest years in Madison in the 1920s. Many of their most cherished memories were set at some of my own favorite places—the University of Wisconsin campus, State Street, the UW Arboretum, Picnic Point, and the wooded path along the shore of Lake Mendota.

In 1929, Mildred followed her beloved husband to his German homeland, where they struggled to pursue academic careers despite the obstacles of a global economic depression and the rising menace of fascism. As I researched these crucial years in Mildred's life—a time when she found herself shocked and dismayed by a surge of malevolent populism that threatened to destroy everything she loved most dearly about her adopted country—the parallels to our own time were harrowingly evident.

By 1937, Arvid had risen to a senior position within the Reich Ministry of Economics. After much thought and moral anguish, he joined the Nazi Party as a cover for his clandestine efforts to warn officials in the United States about Hitler's secret preparations for war. Working with a carefully selected network of trusted allies, Mildred and Arvid gathered intelligence and passed it on to Mildred's contacts within the United States government. These included the American ambassador, William Dodd, and his vivacious, impulsive, and flirtatious daughter, Martha.

By the autumn of 1940, the Harnack resistance circle had discovered the secrets of Operation Barbarossa, Hitler's plan to invade the Soviet Union, and had warned the Soviets about Hitler's impending betrayal. As the Nazis' Final Solution intensified, the Harnacks' resistance circle helped imperiled Jews flee the country. They collected invaluable information from an ally on the staff of the Luftwaffe and forged a strong network with other resistance groups. They collected evidence of Nazi war crimes, and fomented opposition by distributing illegal posters, pamphlets, and transcripts of President Roosevelt's speeches.

What I found most remarkable about Mildred's resistance circle was that at a time when the Reich vigorously strove to limit women's roles in society to Kinder, Kirche, Küche, nearly half of the Rote Kapelle were women. Although most of the strategic decisions were made by the group's male leaders, Arvid Harnack and Harro Schulze-Boysen, the women assumed responsibility for recruiting members; organizing meetings; collecting intelligence; acting as couriers; translating, copying, distributing leaflets; concealing radios and other illicit equipment; sheltering fugitives; and many other activities that put their lives at risk, often to a greater extent than their male counterparts. Of the forty-five members of the Rote Kapelle who received death sentences in Nazi courts, nineteen were women—courageous women from all walks of life, not trained spies or armed soldiers, but ordinary and extraordinary women who risked everything to fight injustice and defend the persecuted.

After World War II, although the University of Wisconsin honored their courageous alumna with articles and memorials, the United States government deliberately buried Mildred's story, compelled by Cold War tensions and suspicions that she and Arvid were Communist sympathizers. Only after the destruction of the Berlin Wall and, more recently, the release of the Harnacks' KGB and FBI files has the significant role of the Rote Kapelle come to light.

I hope that *Resistance Women* will illuminate this nearly forgotten story of Mildred Harnack, Greta Lorke Kuckhoff, and their brave friends, and that readers will be inspired by their bravery, persistence, and willingness to make the ultimate sacrifice in the fight against totalitarianism. ∾

Reading Group Guide

1. Had you heard of Mildred Fish Harnack or the Red Orchestra before reading *Resistance Women*? What role do novels have in our understanding of history? Did *Resistance Women* change your perception of World War II or Nazi Germany?

2. From Mildred's and Greta's humble beginnings to Sara's and Martha's more privileged upbringings, *Resistance Women* tells the story of women from very different backgrounds. Discuss how their unique personalities contributed to the resistance fight. Which woman's story resonated with you the most?

3. In response to Mildred saying that she is no longer surprised by the fighting between the Communist Reds and the Nazi Browns, Arvid responds, "Darling, you must never become accustomed to the extraordinary and outrageous. If you do, little by little, you'll learn to accept anything." Do you agree? In what ways does Mildred take his advice to heart? What examples of this accepting of the outrageous have you seen in your own life?

4. Kinder, Küche, Kirche (children, kitchen, church)— the traditional vision of women as purely domestic— is mentioned more than once by Mildred and her comrades. The slogan dates from the eighteenth century but reappeared in Hitler's Germany. Why do you think the Nazis chose to glorify homemaking and childrearing in their vision of the Reich? How did that idealized vision of housewives contrast with what women were actually doing in Germany during the war years?

5. When forced to decide whether to help translate Hitler's manifesto into English, Greta ultimately decides to work on the translation. Was that the right decision? What was her motivation for doing the work?

6. Despite having a young child, Greta and Adam still chose to take part in the Red Orchestra. Would you have done the same?

7. What did you make of Sarah's relationship with Dieter? What do you think her life would have been like had she chosen to stay with him and get married?

8. Mildred goes home to the US at one point, but chooses to return to Germany, to Arvid and the work of resistance. Was that a foolish decision? A brave one? What would you have done?

9. "Perhaps Germany will serve as a warning," Arvid says. "May they learn from us to snuff out fascism in America when the first sparks arise and not delay until democracy goes up in flames all around them." Has America learned that lesson? What factors might cause fascism to rise in America as it did in Nazi Germany? How would Americans combat it? ᗡᘺ

An Excerpt from
Mrs. Lincoln's Sisters

Chapter One

May 1875

ELIZABETH

A whimsical breeze rustled the paper beneath Elizabeth's pen as she wrote in the garden, but she held the sheet firmly against the table with her left hand and it was not carried aloft. She lifted her pen and waited for the gust to subside rather than risk smearing the ink, and in that momentary pause a light shower of blossoms from the plum tree fell upon her, the table, and the head of her sixteen-year-old grandson Lewis, sprawled in a chaise lounge nearby, so thoroughly engrossed in Jules Verne's *Around the World in Eighty Days* that he did not notice the petals newly adorning his light brown hair. She smiled, tempted to rise and brush the blossoms softly to the ground with her fingertips, but he looked so charming that she decided to leave them be.

It was to Lewis's mother she was writing—Julia, her eldest child and only daughter. Julia's husband, Edward

Lewis Baker Sr., had been appointed United States consul to Argentina the previous year, and when the couple moved to Buenos Aires, Lewis came to stay with his grandparents. Ninian and Elizabeth's gracious home on Aristocracy Hill in Springfield had more than enough room for one much adored grandson, and they were delighted to take him while he finished his education, or indeed for as long as he wished.

The breeze subsided, leaving the delicate fragrance of hyacinth and narcissus in its wake, but before Elizabeth could again put pen to paper, the dull, chronic ache in her abdomen suddenly sharpened. She must have gasped aloud, for Lewis glanced up from his book. "Are you all right?" he asked, brow furrowing.

She managed a smile. "Perfectly fine, dear. I'm merely . . ." She inhaled deeply, ignoring the stab of pain, and forced a sigh of contentment. "Enjoying the lovely spring air."

He peered at her inquisitively, unconvinced. "Are you sure? Would you like me to have Mrs. Henderson or Carrie fix you a cup of tea?"

"I have one," she replied, gesturing to the cup on the table. A pale lavender petal floated upon the surface of the amber liquid, which was not proper tea but a tincture of ginger, willowbark, and raspberry leaf prepared for her by an elderly woman of color respected throughout the city for her knowledge of herb lore. No one but Elizabeth and her loyal housekeeper knew that she partook of the remedy almost every day, sometimes twice, morning and night. Although the brew temporarily relieved her symptoms and evidently did her no harm, she knew that Ninian and her sister Frances would chide her for wasting money on flavored water when her doctor had assured her that the aches and pains were all in her head.

At the time, knowing that a sharp rebuke would merely confirm for the doctor the accuracy of his diagnosis, Elizabeth had managed, with great effort, to nod politely and thank him. Although she had agreed to avoid strenuous activity, she had declined the laudanum he recommended. Only later, when she ▶

and Frances were alone, had she said what she truly thought. "And the droplets of blood on my undergarments, are they all in my head too?" she had demanded indignantly, albeit in an undertone, lest anyone overhear and be shocked by her impolite language.

Frances herself had looked somewhat shocked, but her late husband had been a doctor as well as a storekeeper, and she had probably heard far worse. She had assured Elizabeth that her pains and aches and blood were merely symptoms of the change of life, something all women must endure, and in time they would subside. Elizabeth hoped her sister was right, but feared she was not. At sixty-two, Elizabeth had passed through the change several years before, or so she had thought. This felt like something else, but if her doctor, her husband, and her closest sister said it was nothing, who was she to question them?

The pain faded back to a faint, dull ache. Setting down the pen and taking up her spoon, Elizabeth fished the plum petal from her teacup, set it on the saucer, and sipped the herb woman's brew. Even if unusually flavored, it was rather tasty, and made all the better with a spoonful of honey stirred in. The concoction did her no harm, she reminded herself, so no one else need know of it. If ever the time came when it failed to ease her pains, she would insist upon seeing another doctor.

As she set down her cup, the back door opened and Carrie emerged, small and fair in her gray dress and white apron and cap. "Mrs. Edwards, ma'am," she said, bobbing a curtsey, "there's a gentleman at the door who says he must speak with you most urgently."

Elizabeth was not expecting any callers. "Did he give you his card?"

"No card, but his name is Mr. Smith. Not *your* Mr. Smith," the maid added quickly, referring to another of Elizabeth's brothers-in-law, her sister Ann's husband. "I would have shown him in."

"Of course." Puzzled, Elizabeth rose. "I can't think of any

urgent business I have with any Mr. Smith, or with any gentleman, for that matter."

"Do you want me to see to it?" Lewis swung his coltishly long legs over the edge of the chaise lounge and prepared to stand. "I can direct him to Grandfather's office or send him on his way, whatever seems best."

Elizabeth smiled indulgently, gestured for him to stay seated, and gave in to the impulse to brush the flower petals from his hair. "Thank you, dear, but I believe I can manage."

She accompanied Carrie back inside and through the house to the front entrance, where she found a slim fellow perhaps a decade older than her grandson standing on the doorstep, clutching his hat, and surreptitiously trying to peer through the front windows. Dismissing Carrie, she smoothed her skirts and opened the door. He brightened at the sight of her, and in the customary exchange of pleasantries that followed, he identified himself as Mr. Philip Smith of Elkhart. The unfamiliar name revealed absolutely nothing about his purpose in wanting to speak to her—and that, coupled with his keen gaze and palpable eagerness, made her instinctively wary.

"I regret that I cannot invite you in," she said. "Mr. Edwards is not at home presently, and I assume your business is with him. Perhaps if you leave your card—"

"Oh, no, I'm here to see you," the man interrupted, nodding for emphasis. "I must say, madam, I'm pleased to see you looking so well under the circumstances."

Her heart thudded. "Circumstances?" Her thoughts flew to Julia and Edward in far-off South America, to her beloved Ninian a few blocks away. "I don't understand."

"Surely you do." His gaze turned disbelieving, impudent. "You *are* Mrs. Lincoln's sister, aren't you?"

Of course. Why else would a stranger turn up uninvited at her door if not for Mary? Morbid curiosity-seekers did not plague the family as frequently as they once had, ten years after her brother-in-law's horrific assassination, but every so often a ▶

snake slithered out from beneath a rock. "I am one of her sisters," Elizabeth acknowledged, bristling. "I beg your pardon, but I was not expecting callers, and I must—"

"I won't need more than a moment of your time." He stepped forward as if he meant to block the door with his foot before she could close it. "Would you care to make a statement about Mrs. Lincoln's sad misfortune?"

"A statement?" Which misfortune? There were so many from which to choose, not that Elizabeth would know of any recent mishaps, not that she would ever confide in a random stranger who appeared on her doorstep without so much as a—

Then she understood. "You're with the press," she said, drawing herself up and fixing him with a withering look.

"Yes, as I said, Philip Smith, *Elkhart Gazette.*"

"You most certainly did *not* say." Grasping the doorknob, she said, "You have no honor, sir, but if you leave now, I won't summon the police and have you charged with harassment and trespassing. Good day."

She shut the door firmly and slid the bolt in place, heart pounding, mouth dry. Mr. Smith rang the bell and called her name as she shrank back into the foyer, bewildered and upset. Her family had been tormented by vile stories in the papers through the years, but rarely had a reporter violated the sanctity of their home or sought out Elizabeth in particular. How dare a reporter approach her now? She was a private citizen, not a politician who had deliberately chosen a public life. How could anyone think her so devoid of compassion and loyalty that she would conspire to dredge up ugly incidents from Mary's past? An estranged sister was a sister yet.

Unless—

Perhaps Mr. Smith was not looking into Mary's past but her present.

Elizabeth forced herself to take a deep breath, to think clearly, to remember precisely what he had said. He wanted a statement, not Elizabeth's reflections upon her sister's history but her reaction to some new incident. She pressed a hand to her forehead. Oh, Mary. What new scandal had she become entangled in, to the embarrassment and mortification of her family?

Whatever had compelled that reporter to visit Springfield, it was something so dreadful that he had expected to find Elizabeth in distress, and so significant that he assumed she already knew of it. And yet he had found her utterly unaware. How could this be? How had Mr. Smith outpaced the telegraph?

Unsettled, she went to the dining room in search of the morning newspapers, which her husband always read over breakfast. Elizabeth had slept poorly the night before, owing to the ache in her abdomen, and by the time she had risen and dressed, Ninian had already left for work. She did not remember seeing the papers folded on the table in front of his empty chair, and they were not there now. She went next to his study, but the papers were not on his broad mahogany desk. Nor were they in the library, where the tall bookshelves were neatly filled with law books and works of history and natural science, as well as a few popular novels and volumes of poetry. Nary a scrap of newsprint caught her eye.

She went to the parlor and rang for Mrs. Henderson, who had just returned from the market. The housekeeper confirmed that the papers had been delivered that morning as usual, and that she herself had glimpsed Mr. Edwards reading them at the breakfast table. She was as mystified as Elizabeth regarding their apparent disappearance, but she offered to search for them. In the meantime, Elizabeth returned to the garden to ask Lewis if he had any idea what had become of the papers. He had not seen them that morning either, nor had he spoken to his grandfather except to exchange hasty greetings as Ninian departed the house in a rush.

"Has something happened?" asked Lewis, setting his book aside and rising.

Before Elizabeth could reply, Mrs. Henderson emerged from the house steering a reluctant Carrie along by the elbow. ▶

Bringing the maid to a halt before them, she fixed the girl with a stern look. "Tell the missus what you told me."

Eyes downcast, the maid meekly said, "Mr. Edwards told me to burn the papers."

"What?" exclaimed Elizabeth. "And yet you watched me search the house for them and said nothing?"

"I'm sorry, ma'am. Mr. Edwards said to keep mum about it."

"Oh, for heaven's sake." Elizabeth felt a pang of distress. "Did he say why he wanted you to burn the papers?"

The young maid pressed her lips together and shook her head, but the only explanation was that there was something in the papers Ninian did not want her to see.

As Mrs. Henderson warned Carrie that they would have a serious discussion later about the consequences of keeping secrets from the missus, Elizabeth sent Lewis out to buy replacement papers. She paced in the garden as she waited, torn between annoyance with Ninian and apprehension for the dreadful news he had tried to conceal from her.

When Lewis returned, she knew from his stricken expression that he had paused to scan the front pages on the way home. "What is it?" she asked, a tremor in her voice. "What has my sister done?"

Lewis said nothing, but merely shook his head and held out the stack of papers. She took the *Chicago Tribune* from the top, unfolded it—and froze, breathless, when the familiar name leapt out at her in bold headlines.

CLOUDED REASON.

Trial of Mrs. Abraham Lincoln for Insanity.
Why Her Relatives and Friends Were Driven to This Painful Course.
Testimony of Physicians as to Her Mental Unsoundness.
Hearing Strange Voices—Fears of Murder—Sickness of Her Son.

14

What was Seen by the Employees of the Hotel.
Tradesmen Testify Concerning Her Purchases of Goods.
She Is Found Insane, and Will Be Sent to Batavia.
Scenes in Court.

Head spinning, Elizabeth sank down at the table where
her letter to Julia lay forgotten, weighed down by her teacup.
She could scarcely breathe as she read of how Mary had become
so feeble of mind and so eccentric in her habits that a council
of eminent physicians and concerned friends had gathered
to determine what should be done to protect her from harm.
A judge had ordered a warrant for her arrest, and on Saturday
last, she had been brought unwillingly into court, "pallid, her
eye watery and excited," accompanied by several unnamed
friends. Also present, his eyes, too, "suffused with tears," was
Robert Lincoln, her eldest and only surviving son, at whose
behest the hearing had been called. Word of the insanity trail
had spread swiftly through the city, and the courtroom had
been densely packed with curious citizens and members of
the press. One by one, witnesses had been called to the stand,
where they had testified in lurid detail about Mrs. Lincoln's
nervous derangement, her frenzied shopping sprees, her
inexplicable terrors and strange imaginings that her son
was deathly ill or that she herself was being stalked by sinister
black-cloaked men determined to murder her. The witnesses
had agreed that the poor, afflicted widow was not of sound
mind, and that for her own safety she must be committed to
an asylum.

The jury had adjourned, and in the interim Robert had
approached his mother, attempting to comfort her, but she
had rebuffed him with the tearful exclamation, "Oh, Robert,
to think that my son would ever have done this!"

Only a few minutes later, the jury had returned with their
verdict: Mary Lincoln was insane and must be consigned to the
State Hospital for the Insane. The judge had quickly conferred ▶

with her son and her friends, who had agreed that she would instead be admitted to Bellevue Place in Batavia.

"Oh, my poor sister," murmured Elizabeth, pressing her fingertips to her lips, heart aching. And poor Robert, to have watched in helpless horror as his mother's condition had become so desperate that he had felt obliged to pursue this heartbreaking course. But had it indeed been necessary? Mary was troubled, her behavior erratic, but was she insane? Surely not. Surely all she needed to ease a mind troubled by years of unmitigated grief was compassion and sympathetic companionship, nothing more.

But who would provide her with such spiritual comforts? Not the unnamed friends who had accompanied Mary to her trial; obviously they had not held her back from her precipitous fall and could not save her now. Nor could Elizabeth, even if she wanted to, for Mary had not spoken or written to her in years. Frances was kind-hearted and dutiful enough to shoulder the burden, but Mary was estranged from her too, just as she was from her longtime rival Ann and even from dear Emilie, everyone's favorite. Of all their siblings and half-siblings still living, Elizabeth could not think of any who had not offended Mary, or been offended by her, and remained in her good graces. Perhaps a cousin or niece or childhood friend could be prevailed upon—

But no. It was too late for a loving friend to volunteer to soothe Mary's mental wounds with gentle ministrations and kindnesses. She had been committed to an asylum at the instigation of her own son. Elizabeth knew Robert well, and she was certain that her nephew never would have resorted to such drastic measures if he had believed any other treatment would suffice. All she could do now was pray for God's healing grace and hope that Dr. Patterson's sterling reputation was well deserved.

What else was there for a sister to do?

Anguished, she turned to the other papers in hopes of finding a more optimistic account of the trial, but each report confirmed

16

the first one she had read. Lewis read silently beside her, taking up the pages as she discarded them, his youthful features clouded by concern. "Is there anything we can do?" he finally asked, raking a hand through his tousled brown hair.

"I don't know, dear," she said. "I need time to think."

"Shall I fetch Grandfather home at least?"

"No," she replied, her voice harder than she intended. "I'll see him soon enough."

Later that afternoon, when Ninian returned home from work, she met him in the foyer, wordlessly beckoned him to follow her into his study, and closed the door behind them. She had arranged the replacement newspapers on his desk, but he did not even need to glance at them to know that she had discovered what he had tried to conceal. "I had hoped to spare you grief," he said, without preamble, before she could properly accuse him. "It was a vain hope, I know that now. I knew it as soon as Carrie put the papers on the fire."

"Did you honestly believe that you could keep this from me indefinitely?"

"I hoped to delay the inevitable, to give you a few more hours' peace. I know you haven't been well."

"Indeed? I thought that you agreed with the doctor that my pain is only in my head—" Abruptly Elizabeth's words were choked off. The doctor's words took on an entirely new, foreboding meaning in the shadow of Mary's confirmed madness.

Ninian must have seen the frantic worry in her eyes. "You are not your sister," he said firmly, taking her in his arms and kissing her on the forehead. "You are not mad. You simply need a more qualified doctor and a better diagnosis."

"Oh, Ninian." Relieved, she closed her eyes and clung to him. "I'm glad you believe me, but . . . perhaps we should believe Mary too."

"You think the verdict is wrong, that she isn't insane?" He gestured to the newspapers on his desk. "I assume you ▶

read about her delusions of an Indian pulling bones from her face and wires from her eyes? That she hears raps on a table predicting the date and hour of her death? That she was wandering the hotel clad only in her nightdress? That she spied smoke coming from the chimney of a nearby building and became frantic that the city was burning down? That she accused a man of stealing her pocketbook, which turned up in her own bureau drawer?"

She held up a hand to interrupt him. "Yes, yes, I read the testimony. Every lurid detail is seared into my mind. I'm not disputing that Mary is deeply troubled, but I'm not certain that confining her to an asylum is the best way to help her."

"Several esteemed physicians were on that jury," Ninian reminded her. "We should trust their expertise. From everything I've learned—and I spent a good portion of my day investigating this very subject—Bellevue is no grim institution with scowling guards and bars on the windows, but a quiet, healthful resort in the countryside supervised by skilled doctors and devoted nurses. Mary will be well looked after there, and whatever her affliction may be, she will benefit from fresh air and rest. If your sister truly isn't mad but is merely exhausted, the truth will come out in time."

"I suppose—" Elizabeth inhaled shakily. "I suppose that's true. I hope it is."

Ninian looked as if he might say more, but he hesitated and took her hand. "Darling, whatever your sister's prognosis may be, the days ahead are going to be difficult. The press is certain to exploit Mary's misfortune for profit, and as her family, we may all find our names paraded before the public soon."

"Soon?" She offered a mirthless laugh. "I'm afraid the parade has already begun. While you were at the office, a reporter turned up on our doorstep and asked me for a statement. Thanks to your misguided attempt to protect me, I had no idea why he had come and made no comment at all. I can only imagine how he'll portray my confusion in his article: 'Mrs. Lincoln's Sister Utterly Indifferent to Her Plight.'"

"He wouldn't dare," said Ninian. "Even if you had known what he was after, a dignified silence still would have been the only appropriate response."

"Even so," said Elizabeth, "where news of my family is concerned, I'll thank you to protect me a little less vigilantly."

To her disappointment, he promised no more than to consider her words. She knew that meant he would rely upon his own judgment when deciding what to reveal to her, as he always had. Well, then. No more lying abed for her, regardless of poor sleep or discomfort the night before, if being informed meant racing him to the morning papers.

She slept no better that night, but nonetheless she woke with the sun, washed and dressed, and descended the stairs only a step or two behind her husband, who had risen later but needed less time to attend to his clothes and hair. The newspapers were folded neatly beside Ninian's plate, and after they were seated, Elizabeth raised her eyebrows at her husband, who sighed, kept the *Illinois State Journal* for himself, and passed her the *Chicago Tribune*.

She had prepared herself for the worst, and yet the article that immediately caught her eye rendered her stunned and breathless.

MRS. LINCOLN ATTEMPTS SUICIDE.

Chicago.—Between 2 and 8 o'clock yesterday afternoon Mrs. Lincoln attempted to commit suicide by poisoning. After being removed from the court room where she was adjudged insane earlier that day, her lunatic symptoms became quite violent, and she was put under the strictest surveillance, it being feared that she might do injury to herself. To-day she escaped from her room and hurried to the drug store of Frank Squair, under the Grand Pacific Hotel; she ordered a compound of camphor and laudanum, ostensibly for neuralgia. Knowing her mental condition, Mr. Squair pretended that he had none ready, ▸

and that it would take half an hour to put it up. She said she would call in again for it, and then walked out into the street, whereupon she took a carriage and drove to two other drug stores. Mr. Squair, guessing her intentions, had followed her, and in each case was able to warn the druggist not to provide her with the compound. Then, seeing that she intended to return to his own store, he hurried back and prepared a tincture of burnt sugar and water with a few drops of camphor. Supposing this harmless mixture to be what she had ordered, she left the store and immediately drank the entire bottle. She returned to her hotel, but upon discovering soon thereafter that the mixture had no effect, she tried to leave her room again to obtain a stronger dose, but was prevented. She will be removedto the private hospital at Batavia, Illinois, this afternoon, where she will have every attention.

"Ninian," Elizabeth gasped, "my sister—"

"Yes, I know." He set the *Journal* aside and reached across the table to clasp her cold and trembling hand. "It's terrible, but she's safe, unharmed. No doubt she's being watched very closely so that she won't be able to repeat the attempt."

"She was being watched very closely before, and yet she evaded her guards." Elizabeth shook her head, fumbled for her water glass with both hands, raised it to her lips, and carefully drank, wishing it was the herb woman's elixir. "How could a woman of her age and infirmity slip past her guards in broad daylight? How do we know she won't manage it again?"

"We both know how clever she is. Her guards underestimated her yesterday, but surely now they will be more vigilant." Shaking his head, Ninian took up Elizabeth's newspaper and scanned its version of events. "Your sister insists that she is sane, but this desperate act proves she is not. Thank God she was stopped before she harmed herself."

"Thank God," Elizabeth echoed. Sick at heart, she fervently hoped that those entrusted with Mary's safety would take their jobs far more seriously than they apparently had thus far.

Mary's suicide attempt confirmed the jury's verdict, or so Ninian believed. Elizabeth could not dispute the reasonableness of his conclusion, and yet she felt a stirring of doubt.

Was her sister's attempt to take her own life truly the impulse of a deranged mind, or was it the desperate act of a sane woman horrified to be confined to an insane asylum against her will?

How had Mary come to this?

Once they had been the Todd sisters, the belles of Lexington and Springfield. In the years that had unfolded since those bright seasons full of promise, they had all endured tragedy. Some of the sisters had lost homes, others fortunes, or husbands, or children. None but Mary had tried to take her own life.

But none of the Todd sisters had risen higher or endured more tragedy than Mary.

Could she be saved by the bonds of sisterhood, worn thin yet still enduring? ▸

Chapter Two

July 1825

FRANCES

Frances had not expected to spend the Fourth of July in her family's own garden, disconsolate, watching over her little sister Ann while she dozed on a quilt spread on the soft grass. Nearby, Elizabeth and Mary played Graces, tossing a hoop back and forth from a stick held in one hand, their laughter and playful teasing sounding forced, even from Mary, who reveled in merriment and fun. Like their brother Levi, who had gone off somewhere on his own after their plans were canceled, the sisters had expected to spend the warm, sunny day at the glorious Independence Day celebration now well under way at Fowler's Garden on the outskirts of Lexington. Nearly everyone planned to turn out for it, including all of Frances's school friends, wearing their prettiest summer frocks and hats, with their hair neatly brushed and curled or braided and adorned with ribbons of red, white, and blue. Roast pig and great haunches of beef would be sizzling on spits over a fire, and there would be pies bursting with fruit, sweet lemonade for the children, and whiskey by the keg for the grown-ups. There would be speeches and music, games and gossip, flags and bunting and fireworks. Best of all, Frances would have been free to run off with her girlfriends for the entire day, putting as much distance between herself and her little sisters as possible without leaving the fairgrounds.

She felt a pang of guilt for the disloyal thought. Little Ann wasn't so bad; it wasn't her fault she was still toddling around in diapers, a responsibility rather than a playmate. Six-and-a-half-year-old Mary, on the other hand, was insufferable. Pretty and charming, with a dimpled smile, clear, wide-set blue eyes framed by dark lashes, an abundance of cleverness and funny jokes, and an easy grace and daintiness that eluded Frances, she won the admiration of nearly everyone, from Mama and Papa and Grandma Parker to their neighbors and teachers. Even Frances's own best friends didn't mind if Mary tagged along after them, though she was three years younger. Mary made them laugh and invented the most amusing games, entertaining her friends until Frances felt quite forgotten.

It was exactly the same at home. Mary enchanted everyone so completely that they seemed not to mind, or even to notice, her determination to have everything her own way exactly when she wanted it. If Mammy Sally was braiding Frances's hair, Mary would dart over with her brush and wheedle and beg until Sally hastily finished with Frances so she could devote herself to Mary's long, silky locks of rich chestnut brown with flecks of gold. If Mama was reading Frances a story, Mary would squeeze in between them on the sofa and ask her to start over from the beginning, and of course Mama would smile and comply. If Auntie Chaney asked the children if they would prefer cornbread or beaten biscuits for breakfast, Mary would quickly call out her own choice and plead for it so sweetly that the temperamental but exceptionally talented cook would nod and get to work as if no one else had spoken. If Frances was confiding quietly in Elizabeth, their much-admired eldest sister, Mary would dart over to shoehorn herself into the conversation, even if Frances was in the middle of sharing a very private secret, which Mary would soon blab all over the neighborhood. Later she would feign surprise when Frances, furious and embarrassed, reproached her. "She didn't mean to hurt you," Elizabeth would say, excusing her when Mary grew tearful and begged forgiveness, as if Frances were the one at fault.

Frances struggled to forgive Mary when her younger sister wronged her, to be as tolerant and patient as Mama and Elizabeth, but Mammy Sally wasn't fooled. "You best snuff out that jealousy before it make you sour and mean," she warned Frances once, ▸

An Excerpt from *Mrs. Lincoln's Sisters* (*continued*)

an amused glint in her eye. "You was the center of attention when you was the baby sister. Now it's Miss Mary's turn."

All Frances could do was nod and promise to try, but honestly, how was that admonition supposed to make her feel any better? What good did it do her now to know that she had once been the center of attention if she didn't remember how lovely it had been?

Anyway, Mary wasn't the baby sister anymore; Ann was, and newborn brother George Rogers Clark Todd was younger still. Sometimes Frances guiltily hoped that Mary too would soon find herself overlooked and forgotten as attention shifted to her younger siblings. Recently, as if sensing that possibility, Mary had taken to pretending that Ann did not exist—except when the younger girl wailed, impossible to ignore. Then Mary would grimace and stuff her fingers in her ears.

Frances smiled smugly to herself whenever she observed signs that Mary was becoming anxious about her place in the family, but almost immediately she would feel ashamed of herself. Mary was oblivious to her ugly thoughts, but even so, Frances would try to make up for them by inviting her to play dolls together or offering to read her a favorite story. Mary was unimpressed by Frances's generosity. "You hate dolls," she would reply, or, "I can read it myself." The rebuffs were insulting, but they made Frances feel vindicated for her unsisterly thoughts, so it wasn't all bad.

Still, no matter how much Mary provoked her, Frances knew it was a sin to take pleasure in a sibling's unhappiness. Brothers and sisters were precious. Accidents or illnesses could snatch away any of them at any moment, just as a fever had taken baby brother Robert three years before. Mama had been terribly sad for a very long time, until Frances had almost forgotten the sound of her merry laugh, once as clear and light as a silver bell. Blessedly, Ann had come along about two years later, and their cheerful, smiling Mama had returned to them from wherever she had gone, no longer lost to them. Surely, Frances and Elizabeth privately agreed, the new baby's arrival would drive any lingering sadness from the household.

So it had seemed, until that deceptively lovely July Fourth day as Frances sat on the quilt beside slumbering Ann, her gaze fixed on the house, on the window of the bedchamber where her mother burned with fever.

Just two days before, the reassuringly calm midwife— Mrs. Leuba, the watchmaker's wife from down the street— had arrived with her bag of instruments and poultices. She had smiled at the children and climbed the stairs to Mama's room, alone. Behind the closed door, Elizabeth whispered to Frances, their mother lay in bed with the windows shut and the curtains drawn, the air still and stifling. The precautions kept out harmful drafts but did little to muffle their mother's moans, which sent a shiver down the back of Frances's neck and made her faintly ill from worry.

She did not overhear her mother's ordeal for long, for soon after the midwife's arrival Papa told Mammy Sally to take the children up the hill to Grandmother Parker's house, where they were to remain until Mama had been safely delivered of her child. There Elizabeth dutifully helped their grandmother look after Mary and Ann, and Levi helped the servants with the outside chores, but Frances spent the hours pacing on the front porch and gazing intently down at her own home, built on the lower half of Grandmother Parker's lot. She tried in vain to glimpse signs of movement through the drawn curtains of her house, cringing whenever the wind carried a particularly sharp cry of pain to her ears. Grandmother Parker eventually called her inside for supper, but Frances returned to her post as soon as the table was cleared.

At dusk, she begged, "May I please run down to the house and find out what's taking so long?"

"Sometimes a woman's travail can last a day or more," Grandmother Parker replied, but she agreed to send her maid to inquire, since Papa had expressly asked her to keep the children away. The maid returned with the welcome news that everything was going as expected. Papa sent his love and told them not to worry, but how could Frances not? ▶

The next morning she picked at her breakfast and halfheartedly agreed to mind Ann so her grandmother could finish sewing some garments for the baby's layette. It seemed ages until Papa finally strode up the hill—light brown hair tousled, cheeks ruddy, blue eyes shining with pride, tall and strong and handsome—to announce that the children had a new baby brother.

Levi, who had fervently prayed for another boy, cheered and punched his fist in the air, while Elizabeth, Frances, and Mary laughed with delight and hugged one another. Ann looked on, confused, thumb in her mouth, until Papa laughed and swept her up in his arms. "If you promise to be quiet and not tire your mother," he said, looking around at the older children, eyebrows raised for emphasis, "you may come see her now and meet your new brother."

They promised to be good, so Papa led them home and upstairs to Mama's bedchamber. They found her sitting up in bed supported by thick down pillows, her face pale but eyes shining, a tiny swaddled bundle in her arms. One by one she called the children forward and introduced them to little George, wrinkled and red-faced, his eyes squeezed shut. When it was Frances's turn to meet him, he gave a start and a tiny fist burst free from the swaddling blanket. "He's waving hello to you," Mama said, soft laughter in her voice.

Frances smiled, thrilled. Little George had not shown such favor to anyone else.

After Frances ceded her place beside Mama to Elizabeth, she watched Papa quietly confer with Mrs. Leuba as she packed her black bag. They smiled and nodded as they spoke, so although Frances couldn't make out their words, she knew all was well. Mrs. Leuba left soon thereafter, promising to return in the morning to check on mother and baby.

Eventually Mammy Sally shooed the children out of the room while Grandmother Parker settled down in the chair at Mama's bedside. Papa, who had stayed up all night, dragged himself off to Levi's bedroom, flung himself down on the bed, and quickly sank into a deep sleep. Frances and her sisters tiptoed off to the parlor, but although they thought they were playing quietly, Mammy Sally soon ordered them outside. Joyful and relieved, they ran and played on the shady hill between their house and their grandmother's, Ann alternately balanced on Elizabeth's hip or Frances's. Whenever they asked Mary to take a turn carrying her, she would recoil, shaking her head and protesting that Ann was too heavy for her.

"Just hold her by the hand then," said Frances irritably. "You should take a turn minding her."

"I minded you when I was your age," Elizabeth said, offering Mary an encouraging smile, as if it was worry rather than disinterest that kept Mary from eagerly volunteering. "You and Levi both."

Mary sighed and grudgingly let Ann cling to her hand as she unsteadily followed Elizabeth and Frances around the yard. Mary hated to be restrained from skipping along the stone paths or dancing over the lawn, free and unencumbered, and as soon as she could persuade Elizabeth to take over for her, she pried her fingers free of Ann's grasp and darted away.

Mama was too weary to join them for supper, but she was feeling so well that, as Papa assured the children, he could keep his promise to take them to the Independence Day celebration the next day. Mama would stay home and rest, with Grandmother Parker, Auntie Chaney, and Mammy Sally there to tend to her and the baby.

But the next morning, Frances discovered, Mama had come down with a fever in the night. Responding swiftly to Papa's summons, Mrs. Leuba had administered draughts and applied poultices, but when she left shortly after dawn, lips pressed together and strain evident in the lines around her eyes, Mama was no better.

The children were still at breakfast, pretending to be cheerful for little Ann's sake and murmuring worriedly ▶

among themselves, when Papa returned from fetching his friend
Dr. Warfield, a professor at Lexington's Transylvania Medical
School. "Papa?" Mary called, bolting from her chair, but the two
men hurried past the kitchen and up the stairs without a word.
Elizabeth lay a hand on Mary's shoulder, gently pushed her back
into her seat, and encouraged her siblings to finish eating, but
none of them were hungry anymore.

A faint tremor in her voice, Auntie Chaney scolded them for
not cleaning their plates and sent them out to play. Neither she
nor Mammy Sally nor Papa had mentioned the Independence
Day celebration. Indeed, their agitated father had scarcely spoken
a word to any of them as he raced in and out of the house on
errands, and as they left through the back door, the silent looks
they exchanged conveyed that they all knew their mother was
very ill—much too ill for Papa to leave the house except to fetch
another doctor.

As the day passed that was exactly what he did. After
Dr. Warfield left, Papa summoned Dr. Dudley, a professor of
anatomy and surgery at the university who was well liked by
all and known for his cheerful manner. But he wasn't smiling
when Frances glimpsed him approaching their front door with
his black leather bag, then scarcely pausing to remove his hat as
Papa grasped his arm and led him upstairs to Mama.

Auntie Chaney remembered to feed them lunch, but she made
them eat outside on the veranda. They preferred eating on the
veranda in the summer, but that day it seemed like a punishment,
a means to keep them away from Mama. They picked at their
food, but only Ann, unaware of the tension that gripped the rest
of them, ate more than a mouthful.

"Do you think—" Frances hesitated, then rephrased the
question she was afraid to ask. "Do you think Mama will get
better?"

She had directed her question to Elizabeth, but Mary blurted
"Of course she's going to get better! What a stupid thing to say.
She's just tired from having a baby."

Stung, Frances was about to retort when Levi said somberly, "Mama isn't just tired. Papa wouldn't call Mrs. Leuba and two doctors if she was only tired. He would just let her sleep."

"She has a fever," said Frances, knotting her fingers together in her lap. "I heard Mrs. Leuba tell Mammy Sally. A fever took baby Robert—"

"That's different," said Mary. "That was a baby sickness. Mothers don't get baby sicknesses."

"Sometimes they do," countered Frances. "Anyway, I'm not saying Mama has what took Robert, just that a high fever is very bad—"

"Let's not talk about it," Elizabeth interrupted, giving Frances a pointed look and tilting her head toward Ann, and then ever so slightly toward Mary, who had risen from her chair, face flushed, chin trembling, glaring at Frances as if daring her to speak another horrid word.

Resigned, Frances said nothing more about the terrible, cold, sinking fear in her stomach that seemed to spread throughout her chest and into her limbs as the day passed. By midafternoon, as she sat on the blanket minding Ann while Elizabeth distracted Mary with games and Levi wandered off to find some mischief, a third doctor had replaced the second—Dr. Richardson, a standoffish fellow less popular in Lexington than Dr. Warfield and Dr. Dudley, but a specialist in midwifery and women's ailments.

At least that was what Grandmother Parker told them when she arrived to look after them while their mother was subjected to complicated medical treatments they were too young to know about. But Frances knew something of this forbidden knowledge, for she had surreptitiously read a book Mrs. Leuba had left for Mama when she entered her confinement. She wondered if they had given Mama calomel for purging, or laudanum to reduce cramping, or if they would perhaps try bloodletting. The descriptions hadn't bothered Frances when she had read the words on the page, but when she imagined the treatments ▶

An Excerpt from *Mrs. Lincoln's Sisters* (continued)

being inflicted upon her mother, she felt sick and wanted to sob. She couldn't seek comfort from anyone, however, because she wasn't supposed to have read that book and it was her own fault for doing it on the sly.

Grandmother Parker sent them to bed early, even Elizabeth, who crept from her own bed into Mary's when the younger girl began weeping into her pillow. Eventually Elizabeth was able to calm her, and to the sound of her younger sister's sniffling, Frances drifted off to sleep.

In the morning she woke to an unsettling silence. As she sat up in bed, Elizabeth stirred, one arm still around Mary's shoulders as she slept. Their eyes met, and they both knew that something was terribly wrong.

Slowly they washed and dressed, delaying the blow to come, then crept quietly from their room rather than wake their sisters. The door to their parents' bedchamber was closed, and from behind it came the sound of low, muffled weeping. Papa? Frances had heard him weep only once before, when baby Robert—

A chill swept over her, so cold she could scarcely breathe. She felt Elizabeth take her hand. "We must be brave for the little ones," her elder sister choked out in a whisper.

Frances's first contrary instinct was to think that maybe they wouldn't have to, maybe it wasn't what they feared. Her next thought was, *Who will be brave for me?*

They descended to the kitchen, where they found Auntie Chaney fighting back tears as she sliced and buttered bread for their breakfast as if it were an ordinary day and not the worst of all their lives. She and Mammy Sally abruptly broke off their hushed conversation when the children entered. "Poor little lambs," Mammy Sally said and held out her arms. They ran to her embrace, but Frances couldn't hear her words of comfort over the roaring in her ears. She didn't want to hear them. Until she did, she could cling to the hope that everyone was sad only because Mama was very ill, nothing worse than that, and in time she would get better and no one would need to be sad anymore.

But Grandmother Parker entered then, ashen-faced and trembling, George in his swaddling blanket in the crook of one arm. She grasped the back of a chair for support, inhaled deeply, and told them that their mother had passed away in the night.

Frances stumbled through the hours that followed in a daze, numbly looking on as Levi and then Mary joined them in the kitchen and absorbed the terrible news. Before long Ann's plaintive cry drifted downstairs to them, and since Elizabeth was holding Mary, tears streaming down her own face as she tried to soothe her younger sister, Frances was sent upstairs to get Ann. "Mama is gone," Frances told her as she changed her diaper and washed her face and hands, but Ann only blinked at her, uncomprehending. Lucky Ann, Frances thought, but immediately realized how wrong she was. Ann would have no memories of their beloved mother in the years to come. Even sad memories were better than none.

Frances carried Ann downstairs and fed her some bread and butter. Soon thereafter Papa appeared, eyes bloodshot, face pale and haggard, and told them in a husky, unfamiliar voice that they must all come upstairs and say good-bye to their mother. For a moment Frances felt a rush of hope: they could not say good-bye if Mama had already left them. But when her father and grandmother took them upstairs and arranged them around the bed and she saw her mother lying in repose on the pillows, her laughing eyes closed forever, her graceful hands folded upon her chest, Frances understood, and she felt a terrible surge of rage toward her father for unwittingly deceiving her.

The children said their hesitant good-byes, all save Ann, who frowned and repeated, "Mama? Mama?" as she looked from the still, silent figure on the bed to the faces of her father and siblings, uncomprehending. She dutifully kissed their mother's cheek when Frances held her near, but then her brow furrowed and she began to cry because everyone else was crying.

Papa's voice broke as he handed baby George to Mammy Sally and told her to take the children away. As soon as she led them ▶

from the room, Levi bolted down the stairs and out the back door, while the sisters went to the parlor, waiting for whatever would happen next, dreading it.

Sick at heart, Frances longed to rest her head on Elizabeth's shoulder and find comfort in her soothing words and gentle embrace, but Mary had gotten there first, scrambling onto Elizabeth's lap the moment she sat down, wailing and shrieking with grief so that Frances could barely hear herself think. There was nothing for Frances to do but find herself a place on the sofa opposite and cuddle Ann on her lap, since she absolutely refused to be put down. Frances glowered at Mary as she waited for her sister to calm herself and take a breath so that she could have her turn in Elizabeth's arms, but Mary would not be consoled. That was the moment when Frances knew that Mary would always— *always*—need Elizabeth more than she did, and that Elizabeth would always be there for her, trusting that Frances would be fine on her own.

She would have to be, Frances realized, hugging Ann a little tighter as she burned with grief and resentment. Mary would always come first. ❧